# At Peace

Discover other titles by Kristen Ashley at:
www.kristenashley.net

Commune with Kristen at:
www.facebook.com/kristenashleybooks
Twitter: KristenAshley68

# At Peace

Kristen Ashley

First ebook edition: May 2, 2011
First print edition: January, 2015

ISBN: 0692352856
ISBN-13: 9780692352854

*This book is dedicated to my nieces, Jill Caroline Wynne and Karen Christine Wynne.*
*The sweetest, kindest, funniest, most beautiful and precious girls ever born.*
*And I'm not prejudiced.*

# One

## My Neighbor

I stared at the dark ceiling and listened to Axl Rose demanding to be taken to Paradise City.

The song was sweet, as was the AC/DC, Poison, Whitesnake and Ratt that had preceded it, but it wasn't sweet at…

I turned to look at my alarm clock on the nightstand…

Three thirty-three in the morning.

The party had started at twelve twenty-two. I was okay with that, seeing as it was a Friday. I figured in this neighborhood they'd cool it at one thirty, maybe two. I also figured, if it went beyond that, Colt would go and have a word.

Alec Colton was my neighbor. He lived across the street and one house down. He and his girlfriend, February Owens, had a new baby and he was a cop. I couldn't imagine he'd put up with a trip down memory lane, '80 s hard rock style, until nearly four in the morning. Not with a new baby and all that entailed to your sleep schedule (or lack thereof).

But the music hadn't stopped.

My neighborhood was quiet, or, at least, it had been for the four months Kate, Keira and I had been living in it. It was February. Who had loud, late parties in a quiet neighborhood in February?

At least Kate and Keira were at sleepovers. If they'd been home, I would have lost it way before now.

But, I lost it…

I looked at the clock…

At three thirty-four in the morning.

I threw back the covers and went to the bathroom, snatching Tim's old, plaid flannel robe off the hook on the back of the door. His mom bought him that robe. He'd had it before we'd been married. Now it was soft as plush, worn in but not worn-out, and it was still super warm.

Shrugging on the robe, I stomped out of my room, through the open plan study into the living room that fed into the dining area that fed into the kitchen. Then I went to the side door in the kitchen where a tangle of footwear littered the floor.

Both Kate and Keira were early bloomers. They were now both my height, even Keira, though she was only fourteen, and we all wore the same shoe size. I yanked out Keira's hot-pink wellingtons with the big daisies on them and pulled them over the thick socks I had on to ward off the night chill. I jacked the thermostat way down at night, saved on heating, saved on utility bills. Money wasn't exactly flowing and raising two teenage girls, money was an important thing to have. Then again, it was even without two teenage girls. Though I hadn't really known a time in my life when there weren't kids in it.

One day I was a kid, the next I was a wife and mother.

Never regretted it, not a single day, not until one year, three months, three weeks and two days ago. Then I didn't really regret it. But life sure as hell changed.

I disabled the alarm, unlocked the side door, stomped into the night and stopped dead.

I had no idea where the music was coming from, but I wouldn't have expected it to be coming from my next door neighbor. This was because whoever that was, they were never home. In the four months we'd lived there, I'd seen a shiny black, new model Ford pickup truck in the drive a few times, maybe two, three. I'd seen the lights on in the house once. Other than that, no one home.

But now, it was lit up like a beacon, the music way louder standing outside. So loud, it was a wonder the windows didn't bow out with the sound.

But there was no shiny black, new model Ford pickup truck in the drive. Instead, clear as day because of the lights blazing from the house, I saw a shiny, red new model Porsche.

This all struck me as a surprise. No word, no sound, no nothing from that house in four months and now it was lit up, loud music blaring and there was a non-American car in the drive. As far as I knew the only neighbor on the block who didn't own American was February. She owned a convertible Beetle. Everyone else, including me, had American-made.

And no one on this block could afford a Porsche, not in their lifetimes.

Even living there for such a short time, I knew my neighbors because this was a small, Indiana town. We'd lived there a week and we'd met all our neighbors. They'd come over with cakes, cookies and casseroles. We'd been invited to Christmas parties. We waved and called hellos, or good-byes, or even walked over to have a gab if we were out shoveling the walks or getting in our cars to go somewhere or we were coming back. We chatted when we ran into each other at the grocery store, post office, Frank's restaurant or a high school basketball game. Kate, Keira and I had lived there four months and it felt like we'd been there fourteen years.

But I didn't know my neighbor with the shiny Ford pickup who lived next door and I didn't know them because they were never home.

Now, whoever they were, I was going to meet them.

I stomped through the snow, hearing it crunching underfoot even with the music. The top of the snow had refrozen with the frigid night but I didn't feel a thing. I was too angry. I had to work tomorrow, be at the garden shop at eight, which was only a few hours away. I'd been woken up with AC/DC's "Hell's Bells" and had been tossing, turning and fuming ever since. Now my blood was boiling and I was going to have to take care not to lose control. I had a temper, unfortunately. I didn't blow often but when I blew, I *blew*.

And one of the reasons I was angry was because if Tim was here he'd be doing this. He'd have done it three hours ago, approximately halfway through "Hell's Bells."

Tim liked his sleep but it wasn't that. He didn't tolerate anything that might bother his girls. If it woke me up, it would wake him up and he would know I'd been disturbed. That would tip it for him and he'd be out the door like a shot. He'd take his gun and he'd take his badge and he'd take his pissed-off, big man, hotshot cop attitude and he'd put a stop to it, make no mistake.

Fuck, but I missed him.

I made it to my neighbor's front door and didn't delay. I lay on the doorbell and knocked on the door, knowing they'd never hear one or the other and even with both it would be a miracle to be heard over that sound.

It was now Van Halen. David Lee Roth was singing "Panama," another of my favorites. It was a memory song. Good times were had when that song was played, good times being ruined by that song being used to piss me right the fuck off.

I knocked louder and kept my finger pressed to the buzzer.

"Hello!" I shouted to the door.

It was thrown open. The blazing lights from inside blinding me for a second, I focused, my blood cooled about a hundred degrees and I stared in complete shock.

"Who are you?" she asked on a shout over the music.

Holy shit, it was Kenzie Elise. Kenzie *Elise. Kenzie freaking Elise.*

I'd seen nearly all of her movies (except when she started to branch out and do those crappy art house films, which made little sense to me or the critics, even though she was doing them trying to become known as an *actor* rather than a rom com sweetheart and she kind of failed at this endeavor).

I loved her movies, especially the rom coms (the thrillers were pretty good too). I loved her. She was awesome.

But now, with her standing in a crackerbox house, in a crackerbox neighborhood, in a small town in Indiana, I was staring at her in shock.

Kenzie Elise couldn't be my *neighbor*. That was impossible.

But there she stood, tall because she was really tall anyway, but she was also a step up and she was wearing sky-high platform, stripper shoes with straps that wound up her skinny calves.

And skinny they were. She was ripped—every muscle in her body could be seen. As could her breastbone, prominent and, I had to admit, immensely unattractive. I could see all this because she was wearing an emerald-green lace teddy, deep-cut down her non-existent cleavage, high-cut up her bony hips. She had to be ten, fifteen, maybe even twenty pounds underweight. So skinny, it was a little scary.

But she had that trademark mane of wild, long, strawberry-blonde hair, cornflower-blue eyes and cute-as-a-button face.

And she was standing in the doorway of the house next door, the blue eyes in her big head on her stick-figure body staring down at me.

"Who are you?" she repeated, and I jumped, coming out of my trance.

"Um…your neighbor," I replied. "Could you turn the music down?"

"What?" she shouted, but when I was going to respond, her blue eyes left me and looked over my head.

I saw lights flash on the house and I turned around to look too.

A shiny black, new model Ford pickup truck was turning into the drive.

Shit!

I turned back to see she was smiling, really pleased about something. Her face had gone soft and knowing, in an intimate way that made me feel highly uncomfortable.

From the look of her, daddy was definitely home. I was big time third wheel of this particular party and I needed to get out of there.

"Listen, can you turn the music down?" I asked on a shout, but she ignored me, her eyes riveted over my shoulder.

I'd seen the lights go out and now I heard a door slam.

"Excuse me!" I yelled over the music, getting a bit desperate. "I live next door," I lifted my left arm to point at my house, "and your music is really loud. Can you turn it down?"

"Hi, lover," she purred and how she purred over that music, I couldn't imagine, but she did it.

I turned around and froze.

Standing behind me was a man, a big man, big in every way. He was tall, taller even than Tim and Tim had been six foot two. He was also broad. His shoulders in his black leather jacket were wide and unmistakably powerful.

And he'd been beautiful, once. It was plain to see, under what he was now, that his features had once been perfect, high cheekbones, an appealingly sharp slant to his square jaw, a strong brow. Now there were lines coming in arrays from his eyes and more around the sides of his frowning, full lips.

And there were also scars down his left cheek, two from about a quarter of an inch under his eye that curved over his high cheekbone coming closer together and ending where, if he had a dimple, his dimple would be. These scars were not puckered or disfiguring outside of the actual marks. They just marred the faultless male beauty that had once been his face, making it, with the addition of the lines, rugged and interesting and more than a little scary.

All of this, with his dark, unruly, way overlong hair, was enough to make him look sinister in a compelling, magnetic way.

And then there were his eyes. Sky-blue eyes. *Sky*. Fucking. *Blue.*

Kate and Keira had their father's gray-blue eyes, striking as they were framed with Tim's long, dark lashes. I'd never seen eyes as beautiful, as striking, as breathtaking as Tim, Kate and Keira's.

Until now.

He was using those eyes and that rugged face to glower at a point beyond me. Actually *glower*. And he was doing this in a way that I felt a chill glide down my spine. He scared me so deeply, being so dark, so scarred, so huge, so obviously furious that I was rooted to the spot. I couldn't move even though I really wanted to.

Then he moved. He strode forward right by me and automatically, as if compelled to do so by the sheer force of his aura, I turned as he walked past. I watched as he planted a big hand in Kenzie Elise's emaciated breastbone and he pushed her off.

My mouth dropped open as she flew back on her platform stripper shoes, her arms flying out to the sides to find purchase as she wheeled backwards. There was nothing to grab onto and she tripped gracelessly off the side of her shoe but righted herself before going down.

I stared, unable to do anything else. It was like watching a hideous accident caught on film and aired on television. You didn't want to see, but you had no choice but to watch because, no matter how your brain screamed at you to do it, you couldn't tear your eyes away.

Without stopping, he stalked into the house and disappeared. Then the music abruptly stopped.

"Cal—" Kenzie Elise started, her hands lifted, placating.

"Shut the fuck up," I heard his growl, his voice low, deep, rumbling and as sinister as his appearance. I heard it, but I didn't see him and Kenzie's back was turned to me. He was still out of eyesight but, wherever he was, she was watching him.

All of a sudden I realized my goal had been attained. The music had stopped. Therefore it was time to go home and let this domestic situation play out without an audience.

I turned to leave but heard his voice again.

"You."

Stupidly, I looked into the house to see his eyes on me.

"I—" I began to make my explanations that I was going to go home, but he came at me and I stared as he did. His powerful body was moving in my direction and I was caught, seeing the danger but somehow my limbs were useless even though my brain screamed at them to *move*.

Faster than it seemed possible, he was right in my space, his big hand was wrapped around my upper arm and he pulled me into the house. This didn't hurt, not his hand on me or him dragging me into the house. It probably didn't because I didn't struggle and I didn't struggle because I knew this man could break me like a twig.

So I found myself standing in my next door neighbor's house, me in hot-pink daisy wellingtons, a nightie and Tim's robe. My neighbor in faded jeans, black motorcycle boots, a black t-shirt and a black leather jacket. And Hollywood movie star Kenzie Elise in a barely-there, emerald-green, lace teddy and platform stripper shoes.

How did *this* happen?

It was like a dream. A weird, bad dream that you woke up from and felt strange and unsettled and it left you thinking, *What the fuck?*

But, it was happening. I was there, breathing, conscious, and all I could think was, *God, I miss Tim.*

"Stay," my neighbor commanded to me in his deep, scary voice.

I tipped my head back to look into his clear blue eyes and I could do nothing but nod.

Then he let my arm go and stalked into the depths of the house.

"Cal, darling, I just wanted—" Kenzie Elise started, but he disappeared from sight so she stopped speaking.

I wondered why she didn't go after him instead of standing there with me in the room, the front door open, wearing nothing but that teddy that left little if anything to the imagination.

Then again, in his frame of mind, I probably wouldn't follow him either.

It was at this point I wondered why she didn't run to her Porsche and get gone.

I didn't run because he'd told me to stay and I didn't think it was a good idea to defy him. He didn't seem mad at me, not at that juncture, and I wasn't fired up to make him that way.

She didn't look at me and I eventually pried my eyes away from her, but I was able to do this because he returned, carrying in his arms a bundle of clothes. He walked right by her, right by me and right to the door where he threw the clothes into the snow.

My mouth dropped open again.

"Cal!" she shouted. Rushing on her stripper shoes to the door, she peered out at her clothes then whirled back around again to look at him, her eyes never once hitting me. She was avoiding me or ignoring me. I didn't know which, but I thought both were good ways to play it.

He had her purse in his hand and he was sauntering back into the room. He yanked out a set of keys as she turned back to him.

"*You threw my clothes in the snow!*" she shrieked then jumped to the side as he tossed her purse at her. It was open and stuff flew out everywhere as it sailed through the air and more stuff flew out when it landed on the floor.

"*Cal!*" she screeched, bending, bony knees to her chest, ass to the ground and scrambling to get her things.

I started to bend too, to help her but stopped when his voice sounded.

"Don't."

My head snapped back to look at him and his eyes were pinning me to the spot. He was so angry, visibly livid, and so frightening, I forgot how to breathe.

I slowly straightened, forcing air into my lungs as Kenzie scrambled on the floor, now on her hands and knees in her teddy and stripper shoes, shoving stuff into her purse.

"This is *insane*," she snapped, and she was definitely right.

He was taking a key off her keychain and had this task accomplished by the time she made it to her feet with her purse again intact, which was lucky for her because he tossed her keys to her without hesitating to make sure she was prepared. She lunged to grab them, bobbled them but kept them in hand.

"Out," he ordered tersely.

"Cal—" she started.

"Get the fuck out."

"This scene is ridiculous," she hissed, leaning toward him, which, I thought, was not a very good idea.

"You're right," he agreed.

She changed strategies so fast I wasn't keeping up.

Her voice was a purr again when she began, "Darling, I thought—"

"What, Kenzie?" he asked, his eyes moving the length of her, his lip curled in disgust. "You thought what? Fuck, woman, I had better head in junior high. You think I'd come back for more from *your* mouth? Sloppy. So sloppy, I was fuckin' embarrassed for you."

At his words I'd drawn in breath, but Kenzie's face had gone paler than her signature flawlessly-pale-skinned pale.

When Kenzie stood still as a statue and didn't speak, he noted. "You're still here."

"I—" she started.

"Need to get a fuckin' clue," he finished for her. "Christ, how many times do we need to do this? It was a mistake, biggest fuckin' mistake I've made in years. When I was doin' you, *I* faked it. I had to jack off in the shower to get off after I was done with you."

I swallowed, wanting really badly to be anywhere else, *anywhere* but there.

"You faked it?" she whispered, sounding horrified and beaten, her voice like a little girl who, way too early in her young life, just found out there was no Santa Claus.

"Yeah, and if your head wasn't so far up your ass, you woulda noticed. Instead, you keep playin' out this fuckin' drama, and swear to Christ, it happens again, it's not gonna make me fuckin' happy."

He seemed to be pretty unhappy currently, but I'd just met him, maybe he could get *more* unhappy, which meant I never wanted to be near him again.

"Cal, I—" she started again, but he leaned forward and her mouth slammed shut.

"Not gonna say it again. Get. *The fuck*. Out."

Thankfully, she'd had enough. She turned, avoiding my eyes, and walked in her teddy and stripper shoes out the open front door into the snow and bitter cold.

I stood unmoving as he stalked to the door, slammed it, and to my extreme discomfort, locked it.

I swallowed again.

Then I said softly, "I'd like to go home now."

He turned to face me and his eyes leveled on mine.

I pressed my lips together and my stomach clenched.

He didn't speak and I didn't know what to do.

Finally, his eyes dropped and I watched as they slid slowly from my face down my body to my feet and, just as slowly, starting back up to my face.

During this journey I realized that my robe had fallen open and he could see my nightie. Pale lavender satin, short, hitting me at the upper thighs but there was a three-inch hem of smoky-gray lace below that. The same lace was at the bodice over the cups of material covering my breasts. The nightie fit close at my chest and midriff but there was room to move around my hips and thighs. It was nowhere near as risqué as Kenzie's teddy. It left something to the imagination, and that was good, unless you had an imagination.

Carefully, I pulled the edges of my robe together, his eyes speeded up to hit mine and I knew the instant they did, without any doubt, he had an imagination.

My mouth went dry.

"I'm Joe Callahan," he stated.

"Hello, Joe," I said quietly.

"Cal," he corrected me and I nodded but remained silent.

When this stretched the length of the Porsche firing up and reversing out of the drive, Joe Callahan prompted, "You are?"

"Your neighbor."

His heavy, dark brows went up. "Does my neighbor have a name?"

I shook my head and his heavy, dark brows drew together.

"You don't have a name?" he asked.

"I think I want to leave," I told him.

His face got hard but his voice got soft when he said, "Listen, buddy—"

"No, please, Joe, I want to leave."

"Cal."

"Whatever. I'd like to leave," I repeated.

He started toward me and I backed up, lifting a shaking hand and he stopped, his eyes dropping to my hand before cutting back to my face.

"I live next door, that's it," I said softly. "I wanted the music to stop. It's stopped. Now I'd like to leave."

His eyes held mine and something was happening in them, I just didn't know what and, after witnessing that scene, listening to the way he spoke to her, what he said, how he said it and the utter humiliation he inflicted, I didn't care. Then his gaze dropped to my body again, he closed his eyes and stepped to the side.

I wasted not even a second. I ran to the door, unlocked it, threw it open, ran out and across the snow to my house. I threw myself through the side door, closed it, locked it, threw the chain and armed the alarm.

Then, quaking head to foot, I slid off the wellies, made my shaky way to my bedroom and got in bed with Tim's robe on, pulling up the covers to my neck.

I turned my head to the frame sitting on my nightstand. I could barely see it in the dark, but I didn't need to see it. I had the picture it held memorized. Tim and me, close up. He was behind me, both his arms around my shoulders, wrapped across my upper chest, his jaw pressed to the side of my head, my head slightly turned into him. He was looking at the camera. I had my eyes closed.

We were both laughing.

"Miss you, baby," I whispered to the frame, my voice shaking as hard as my body still was.

The frame had no reply.

It fucking never did.

The next morning, Joe Callahan's house was quiet and the shiny black, new model Ford pickup was gone.

It wouldn't come back for three weeks.

It was four o'clock in the afternoon, I'd been at the garden shop all day and during the day it had snowed.

I was sick of snow and I wished I'd picked Florida or Arizona or somewhere that didn't have snow when I'd packed up my girls and fled Chicago.

Furthermore, Kate was driving now. She'd turned sixteen and she got her license and I bought her a car. Tim would have been pissed I bought her a car. Then again, he'd have been pissed I bought myself a Mustang. As a cop, he'd seen too many accidents so he was all for staid, sturdy cars that were built so tough you could drive them through a building and only have to buff out a few scratches. He might have driven like a lunatic (which he did), but he wasn't a big fan of me doing it (which I didn't unless I was in, say, a Mustang). And he wasn't a big fan of spoiling the girls.

Then again, with a dead dad, spoiling them had become something of a habit.

And anyway, I didn't have Tim anymore to help me take them places and pick them up. I also didn't live in a household with two cars unless I bought one for Kate.

So I did.

She was a good driver, responsible, my Kate.

Keira, now, Keira would probably be picked up joyriding when she had her learner's permit with *me* in the car. Keira was a magnet for trouble. Kate would rather die a thousand bloody, painful deaths than break a rule or get into trouble. Keira would make a deal with the devil for a killer pair of shoes and not even blink.

Even if Kate was responsible and a good driver, I still hated it when she drove in snow.

This was what I was thinking as I drove home from the Bobbie's Garden Shoppe, my now full-time job. I found out that morning that I was now full-time since Sabrina had her twins a week ago. She'd called Bobbie the night before and told Bobbie that her maternity leave was indefinite.

"Thank God, the bitch could moan," Bobbie had said this morning when she gave me the news and asked me to go from part-time to full-time. "Saves me from firing her ass, 'cause, when she wasn't moanin', she was jackin' around even *before* she was luggin' them twins around. Yeesh, two babies in that belly of hers, looked like seven."

Bobbie was not wrong about that, *any* of it.

But I was too busy thanking God for the full-time job. Tim's life insurance policy had been used up on my Mustang, Kate's car and taking a whack off the mortgage because of the down payment I put on the house. It had also gone out the door with the move. I had his pension, which helped, but not much.

I'd put the money I made on selling Tim and my house into savings for the girls' college. Tim'd had to pay off student loans forever and he wanted the girls to have their college paid for. We'd been saving, but we didn't have near enough for the two of them. I thought Tim would have wanted that, the house we'd bought together, fixed up together and lived in together as a family being sold and the money paying for the girls' future. Using that money from our house was like him and me giving it to them. I liked that idea and figured Tim would too.

Even with a low mortgage and no car payments, I still had a teenager driving and insurance was a bitch. Utilities, groceries for three people and we were living in a small town but it was part-farmers, part-blue collar and part-affluent. The affluent part meant all the kids tried to keep up with the Joneses with designer gear, jeans, purses, shoes, the right makeup, the important accessories like MP3 players and cell phones. Hell, Keira's cell phone bill, considering she texted seventeen thousand times a day, nearly broke the monthly bank even though I told her time and again not to do it.

Bobbie paid pretty well considering, and she had full benefits for full-time, which was more important. Her garden center was enormous, the biggest in three counties and everyone went there. She sold it all, lawn furniture, craft and hobby stuff, pet supplies, not just plants.

But I worked the plants. I was good at it, always was and spring was coming. Even with the snow, it was getting close to gardening season and things, always steady, were definitely picking up for Bobbie.

I turned on my street, deep in my inspection of the roads, which, I noted with some relief, had been mostly cleared. The spring snow was wet and sloshy, not icy, thank God. Kate would get home okay.

I took in a relieved breath and it caught in my throat when I saw the shiny black, new model Ford pickup in Joe Callahan's driveway.

"Shit," I whispered on my exhale.

I drove past it, turned into my drive and parked under the awning that came out from my two-car garage. The previous owners had torn down the one-car garage and put in a two-car one with a double awning at the front. This worked since the garage door opener didn't work and I didn't have the money to replace it. I further didn't enjoy cleaning snow off my car.

The previous owners had also built an extension all along the back of the house. This meant we had an extra bedroom with full master bath and an open plan study that ran off the living room/dining room area.

Most of the other houses on the block had extensions too. And two-car garages or the garages had added awnings. They also had built-on back decks (our place did too, again along the back of the house) or above ground pools or playsets. You name it, it was there.

It was a family neighborhood, established, middle-middle income folks or old-timers who'd been there for ages and stayed there because their mortgage was paid off. Families just starting out or couples who liked where they lived so, when they needed more room, they just built on. Yards were huge, there was plenty of room and anything they did, they did it house proud so it only upped the standard for the entire neighborhood.

The only house that had no add-on, except a back deck, was Joe Callahan's. It was still a two-bedroom crackerbox, kitchen, dining room/living room and two bedrooms with a full bath.

I'd been lucky to find a place on that street.

Lucky, except for Joe Callahan.

I went into the house, dumped my purse and headed back out.

I needed to shovel. Part of living in that neighborhood was taking care of it. You shoveled. Joe Callahan's neighbors on his other side, Jeremy and Melinda, cleared Joe's front sidewalk part of the time, the other part I did it. It wouldn't do for anyone to let down the 'hood, and since Joe wasn't there, someone had to do it.

No way I'd do it that day, though. No way in hell. He could shovel his own damned walk.

I went out to the garage and grabbed my leather work gloves and the snow shovel.

You could say I pretty much missed Tim a lot. When I was in a fight with Keira, which was too often and Tim used to be able to handle her better than me, definitely daddy's little girl. Then again they both were. When Kate would get wound up by an assignment, an assignment that was something she could do no sweat, but she wanted to do it perfectly, better than any kid in the history of kids could do and Tim could settle her down too. When I was in bed at night, alone and wanting more than my vibrator to take care of business, wanting Tim's hands, his mouth, his cock and, maybe more than all those, the sweet nothings he would whisper in my ear.

And when I had to shovel the freaking snow.

I started at the front stoop and made my way down the walk that led to the drive, the snow heavy and wet, but at least it was easily removed. I was shoveling a line down our drive, which would take for-freaking-ever to clear, thinking of the price of Bobbie's snow blowers and how much my discount would be and if she'd put them on an end-of-season sale when Colt's GMC pulled into his drive.

Feb Owens and Alec Colton were pretty famous. I'd known them before I moved in and I'd known what happened in that town before I'd moved there. It was sick what happened to them, that serial killer obsessing on Feb and Colt and killing people that Feb knew. Everyone knew about it. It made national news and she was so gorgeous, and Alec Colton so hot, that made the story bigger news.

But I found shortly after moving in that they were cool. They were also happy. It was like that whole deal didn't touch them. At the time I moved in, she was at the end stages of pregnant and they'd been high school sweethearts, separated by something I didn't know and finally back together.

I'd married my high school sweetheart so I got that, totally, their happiness. Then again, Tim got me pregnant at seventeen so I kind of didn't have a choice.

Still, I wouldn't have chosen anything else. Not then, not ten years later, not until someone shot him and even then I would have still chosen Tim. I would have just chosen Tim having a less dangerous job. And I definitely would have chosen not to get served what I got served after.

I shoveled and watched Colt swing down from his truck.

Then I stopped shoveling when he turned my way and called, "Hey, Cal."

My body turned to stone.

"Yo," a deep voice said from right behind me.

Stiffly, I turned and stared at Joe Callahan standing right there, *this close* behind me. I hadn't heard his approach. He was wearing jeans, a black thermal and his black leather jacket. In the daylight, as gray as that daylight was, he was different. The sinister was gone. The only thing left was the rugged and interesting.

"Hey, Violet," Colt called, and I stiffly turned back.

"Hey, Colt," I called to him and watched February, carrying their little boy, Jack, coming out of their house and her head was turned to see who Colt was talking to.

"Wow!" she yelled. "Hey, Cal!"

"Feb," Joe Callahan's voice rumbled.

"You in town awhile?" Colt asked, taking Jack from Feb and expertly planting the baby in the crook of his arm while his other arm slid along Feb's shoulders.

"Nope, leave tomorrow," Joe Callahan answered.

"Got time for a beer at J&J's?" Colt asked.

"Yep," Joe Callahan answered.

"Vi? What about you?" Feb asked me.

I'd been to Feb's bar, J&J's Saloon, a half a dozen times. Her family ran it, which meant I met them too. It was a nice place. It had been around awhile so it was worn in, the kind of joint you liked to stay and drink a few. Everyone in town hung there and Feb's family made you feel welcome.

I liked having a drink there, shooting the shit with Feb, who was nice, and her brother Morrie, sister-in-law Dee, and mom and dad, Jackie and Jack, who were all just as nice as her.

Still, there was no way I was going when Joe Callahan was going.

"Thanks, I have something on," I answered.

"Another time," Feb called.

I nodded. They both lifted a hand in farewell and headed toward their house.

"Later, Cal," Colt called.

"Yeah," Joe Callahan called back.

I went back to shoveling, deciding I'd pretend he wasn't there.

This effort failed when his big hand curled around the handle of the shovel.

I stayed bent to my task but tipped my head back to look at him.

"How you doin', buddy?" his voice rumbled. It was a soft rumble, and not pissed-off or post-drama that involved a Hollywood movie star, it was a lot different, and my stomach, for some strange reason, pitched.

"Can you let go of my shovel?" I asked.

His answer was to pull the shovel out of my hands.

My stomach pitched again, this time for a different reason, slightly afraid. I straightened and turned to him.

"Can I help you with something?" I asked.

"Your name's Violet," he told me.

"Yes."

"Violet," he repeated quietly.

"Yes," I repeated too, not liking him saying my name quietly because I kinda *did* like his rumbly deep voice saying my name quietly.

He took a step into me and I stood my ground. He couldn't exactly cause a scene in my driveway, not with Colt home across the street. Joe Callahan might be big, and he might even be bigger than Alec Colton, but I figured no one messed with Colt. It might get ugly but it'd be a fair fight.

Joe Callahan's neck bent so he could look down at me and he started speaking as if we'd been having a long conversation, I'd been asleep the first part and woke up during the middle. "She makes six million dollars a movie, two movies a year, four times that in foreign endorsements for everything you can imagine. Hair shit, ice cream, you name it, they pay her enough, she sells it."

He was talking about Kenzie Elise.

I had absolutely no interest in this and started to tell him this fact. "Joe—"

He cut me off. "Anywhere she goes, people ask for her autograph, take photos of her, grovel and do shit you wouldn't believe just to get her attention. Because of all that, she's so far up her own ass it's a wonder she can see. Problem is, she's got a lot of company up there."

"I don't care about this," I told him.

He continued talking like I didn't even speak. "I don't shit where I live, normally. She played me. I had no fuckin' idea she was what she was until I got played then I wanted no part in that."

"I think I got that," I reminded him of the fact I was there while he made that point to her.

"It happened once, once was enough. The sex was shit, buddy."

"I got that too." And that was an understatement. I *definitely* got that.

"She gets no for an answer never. It doesn't happen to her. She gets what she wants when she wants it, always. She wanted me. She'd been playin' games like that to get my attention for six months. It was affecting my work, which I was not thrilled about, but I could deal. That night, she invaded my home. Stole my keys, had one made, found out where I lived and came in uninvited, playin' her games. Uncool."

I had to admit, he wasn't exactly wrong, this was uncool. I knew this. I knew this better than he could understand. I knew *exactly* how uncool this was.

That didn't change the fact that he humiliated her to the point of making her scramble around on the floor in a teddy to pick up her stuff and walk into the cold night to gather her clothes from the snow. That kind of humiliation was extreme and uncalled for.

Before I had the chance to explain this to Joe Callahan, I heard cars approaching. I looked up to see Kate's little, white Ford Fiesta followed by a bright yellow pickup coming down the street.

Joe and I stepped off the drive into the snow of the yard as the two cars pulled into the drive. Kate and Keira got out of the Fiesta, but I was staring at the strapping, tall boy-man who folded out of the pickup.

Keira skipped through the snow to me and she did this quickly.

"Hey," she said, and I tore my eyes from the strapping, tall boy-man to see my last born staring up at Joe Callahan looking like she was gazing at whoever was her current boy band heartthrob (and I didn't know who that was, Keira went through crushes like she did clothes, which was to say swiftly and at random).

"Hey," Joe said back.

"I'm Keira," Keira announced.

"Cal."

"Cool," Keira breathed and looked at me then blinked, leaned in and whispered, "Kate's got a *boyfriend*."

Oh shit.

My eyes sliced to the strapping, tall boy-man who had walked to Kate, slung an arm around her shoulders and they were now walking to us.

Their eyes were on Joe.

"You're Joe Callahan," the boy-man said, staring at Joe like he, too, was seeing his current hero, be that football star, baseball star or the like.

"Yep," Joe answered.

"Awesome," the boy-man whispered.

Kate tore her eyes from Joe and looked at me. "Mom, this is Dane. He's here to study. Is it cool with you if we do it in my room?"

My body locked and I stared at my first born.

It was fair to say that it was *not* cool with me that she and this strapping, tall boy-man who thought Joe Callahan was awesome studied with my sixteen year old daughter *in her room*. It was fair to say that if Tim was standing beside me, and not Joe Callahan, his head would freaking explode at such a question. It was fair to say Tim's head would explode because, when he and I were supposed to be studying in my room, we were, instead, making Kate.

*Fuck!*

Now what did I do?

I couldn't say no in front of *Dane*. He'd think I was the un-awesome, uptight mom and Kate would be embarrassed. No way Kate should ask me this question in front of *Dane* and make me look like the un-awesome, uptight mom and force me to make the choice of doing what would give me peace of mind. Therefore asking them to study, say, in the study or embarrassing her in front of her new possible boyfriend who was strapping, tall and also good-looking therefore likely very popular. Which would be important to any girl but especially important to my girl who had just been forced to leave the school she loved where she left behind a million of her friends she'd known forever to move to a school four hours away, in a small town in Indiana where she knew *no one.*

*Fuck!*

"Sure," I said through clenched teeth.

Kate beamed. I tried not to groan and Kate, *Dane* and Keira headed toward the house.

"But Kate," I called after her, "I want your door open."

Keira giggled. *Dane* grinned. Kate looked at me, her eyes skidded to Joe then back to me and her cheeks got pink.

"Okay," she called back.

Thank God.

The front door closed behind them and Joe advised, "You should give her condoms."

My eyes flew to his and I blinked.

"What?" I asked.

"Condoms, buddy, you of all people should know you should give her condoms."

"What's that supposed to mean?"

"She yours?"

"Yeah."

"She's drivin', which means you had her, what, when you were fifteen, sixteen?"

"Eighteen." By the time of her birth, of course. Her conception was another matter, but I didn't share this with Joe.

He just looked at me then again he didn't really need to say more, his point was made.

"Can I have my shovel back?" I asked.

He didn't give me my shovel back.

Instead he said, "Come to J&J's tonight, I'll buy you a drink."

This wasn't really a question but I decided to treat it like one. "Thanks, but…no." Then I repeated, "Can I have my shovel back?"

He turned fully to me and again stepped into my space. It took a lot but I held my ground and tipped my head back to look at him. I had to tip it back far. He was that close and he was that tall.

"I'm tryin' to be neighborly," he said quietly.

"Neighborly would have been not draggin' me into your house and treatin' me to that scene."

"I needed a witness and you were the only one available."

"A witness?"

"Yeah."

"Why?"

"Because Kenzie's a pain in the ass. If she can make trouble, she will and the bitch can make trouble for me. I got a witness as to the way things went down, and I'm guessin' she's not hot to share that scene with anyone, she'll keep her mouth shut. I don't, she can share whatever she wants to share, make the whole thing up. I was right, she's keepin' her mouth shut. She doesn't then I produce you who says it like it was."

"Produce me?"

"It's not gonna happen. She's not gonna say shit."

"Produce me to who?"

"What?"

"Who would you produce me to?"

His head cocked slightly to the side and his brows drew together. "Clients."

"What clients?"

"Potential clients who might be swayed into not hirin' me if they hear some bullshit Kenzie cooked up."

"What kind of clients?"

He got closer and I really wanted to edge back, but I didn't when he asked, "Buddy, you serious?"

"Yes."

"I'm in security."

"Security?" He nodded and I went on. "What kind of security?"

"Kenzie Elise security."

I stared at him, feeling my lips part and my eyes get wide.

I had Security to the Stars living next door.

Wasn't that just the shit of it? There I was, in my predicament and I had Security to the fucking *Stars* living next door and I hated him because he was a huge jerk. I couldn't have made him a plate of cookies when I saw the shiny black, new model Ford pickup in the drive and charmed him with my rapier wit. *No.* I had to get embroiled in a situation when he was scraping off a movie star who had fallen in lust with her mysterious, rugged and interesting-looking bodyguard at the same time finding out myself during said situation that he was a huge jerk and falling in instant hate with him.

"So, seeing as you do what you do, and considering Dane's reaction to you, I guess you're pretty famous around here?" I asked and he shook his head.

"Not famous, people just know what I do and sometimes who I do it for. They're famous, not me."

"That stuff rubs off."

"Not really."

"Dane looked pretty impressed."

"He's seventeen. That ain't hard to do with a seventeen year old."

"Still I'd guess, around here, you don't often hear no either."

"I'm not 'round here often."

God, he had an answer for everything.

"Even so, *no* on the drink, okay Joe?" I said. "Now, can I have my shovel back?"

Just like he'd done that night, he studied me for a while, something happening behind those blue eyes, something I didn't get.

Then he gave me my shovel, turned and walked away.

I gave up on the drive. It would take forever and there was a tall, strapping boy-man in my daughter's bedroom. Therefore, I shoveled the sidewalk at the front of the house, went inside where I did all sorts of things loudly. Such as make dinner or call questions to Keira even when she was right in the living room, so Kate and *Dane* couldn't forget I was close.

When *Dane* left after he ate dinner at our house and I found out I kind of liked him, I watched out the window as Kate walked him to his pickup.

Then I forced myself not to watch because firstly, I didn't want to see and secondly, I was not an un-awesome, uptight mom who would watch her daughter and her new boyfriend out the window.

But as I was turning away, my head whipped back and my eyes narrowed on the drive.

Except for under my car, Kate's car and Dane's pickup, the drive had been shoveled clean of snow.

I stopped looking out the front window to look left, out the window at the side over my kitchen sink facing Joe's house.

The house was dark and there was no shiny black, new model Ford pickup in the drive.

There wasn't one the next morning either.

Or the next.

Or the two weeks after that.

# Two

## Hunger

I drove home from the garden shop thinking a variety of things.

First, I was thinking that full-time paychecks didn't mean much of a change to part-time ones, especially when taxes and insurance were deducted.

Second, I was thinking that I spent an awful lot of time while Kate and Keira were growing up wishing I could do things. Things like go to a movie whenever I wanted. Things like take a long, hot bubble bath when the spirit moved me. Things like reading a book without the word "mom" shouted over and over again (as in, "Mom, where's my backpack?" and "Mom, Keira's bothering me," and "Mom, I'm hungry").

Now, with Kate out with Dane all the time (or in with him at our house, which I preferred seeing as I could keep an eye on them, however I still didn't see much of Kate during these times) and Keira, who seemed to be attempting to make an art form out of socializing, they were never home. I could go see a movie, have a bubble bath and read a whole book if I wanted to. But, of course, since life mostly sucked and not a whole helluva lot worked out for me, I didn't want any of that anymore.

All I wanted was my girls to be home.

I could have probably handled this better if Tim was at home. Or I knew he was coming home. Instead of knowing I was going to an empty house, a one-woman dinner and nothing but aloneness until weeknight curfew hit (eight o'clock) or weekend curfew hit (ten o'clock for Keira, eleven for Kate). Unfortunately, this wasn't an option.

I turned down the street and my mind left these thoughts as I saw the lights on and the black pickup in the drive at Joe's house.

"Great," I muttered under my breath.

It bothered me that he was home. Why, I couldn't imagine. He'd be gone tomorrow and I didn't care about him anyway. I doubted he'd come over and ask me to have a drink with him at J&J's or that I'd even see him at all. And there was no snow to shovel, making me think he might be a decent guy even though I knew he was not.

And I knew he shoveled my snow, I knew this because I asked Colt if he'd done it and he'd said no and I'd asked Jeremy if he'd done it and he'd said no. Since my other close neighbors were either too old (Myrtle, the widow who lived across from Joe, and Pearl, the spinster who lived across from me) or bitches (Tina, who lived next to me on the other side), it had to be Joe.

But him being home, seeing his truck in his drive, for whatever reason bothered me, I couldn't deny it.

I turned into my drive and parked under the awning. The days were staying lighter longer. But night was edging in, it was getting late. Bobbie had asked me to do a bit of overtime and I did it. I needed the money for one. For another, why not? There was no reason to go home when Kate and Keira were both out.

I grabbed my purse, exited the Mustang and I stopped when I heard a woman's laughter.

I looked right to see Joe in his black leather jacket and jeans, sauntering to his truck.

Behind him was a woman in a skintight, black mini-skirt and a jean jacket. She had loads of long, wavy blonde hair and she was petite but wearing a pair of high-heeled, black boots.

She was trotting after him on a half-run with such grace it was like she'd been born in high-heeled, black boots. She was still laughing and I stood in my open door, one arm on the roof of my Mustang, watching as she caught his hand and skidded on her heels, pulling his hand to her. He turned. She tipped her head back and she must have said something, something I didn't hear, something she thought was funny for she laughed again.

But I could swear, even with the distance, I saw the white flash of Joe's grin. I didn't know him very well but, if asked, I would have said it wasn't physically possible for Joe *to* grin.

Then he folded her in his arms, enveloping her with his large body and his head came down, hers tilted back, and they started making out.

A sharp pain gripped my heart.

It hurt to watch. It hurt a lot and yet I couldn't tear my eyes away.

There was something about his big body in his dark clothes, his powerful arms around her, holding her close to his long frame, enfolding her in a way that was about sex (or leading up to it, probably) but looked like more. Maybe safety, protection, his dark head bent to her blonde one, all of this, for some reason, cutting me clean to the bone.

I wanted that for me. I missed that. God, did I miss it, and I wanted it back. And it felt, in that moment, I'd never have it again.

And that fucking hurt.

I tore my eyes away, and as silently as I could so Joe wouldn't hear, I closed the door to my car and walked to the side kitchen door. I was about to insert my key when the door was thrown open from the inside. The light switched on, Keira and Kate stood in the frame and they shouted, "Surprise!" at the same time I felt a strong arm curl around my belly from behind. I was lifted clean off my feet and whirled in the air.

I screamed, loud and piercing, my knees going up, my fingers curling around the arm at my waist as I was whirled yet again by whoever had me. Kate and Keira ran out of the house and jumped around us in dual teenage girl excited tizzies as we twirled.

We stopped moving and my feet were planted on the ground when I heard my brother Sam say softly in my ear. "How's my big sister?"

When I heard his voice, I screamed again, this time loud and joyous, turning in his arm and throwing my arms around his neck. I held on, kissing his cheek, his jaw, his neck, jumping up and down while I did this as Kate and Keira, their arms around both of us, jumped up and down too, also screaming loud, ear-splitting, teenage girl squeals of delight.

Sam stopped hugging me so he could wrap all of us in his arms and his head tipped back so he could shout, "These are my girls!"

I looked up at my brother, his beautiful face, his warm, brown eyes, his light-brown hair (that needed a cut, I noted) and my hands slid from his neck to wrap around his waist. I planted my face in his chest and held on tight.

"Most beautiful girls in the world!" Sam kept shouting. "That's right! Drink it in! Sheer gorgeousness!"

I tilted my head back because he seemed to be talking to someone instead of shouting at no one and I saw his head turned to the left, toward Joe's house.

My head turned that way too.

Joe and his woman, not locked in a make-out session but instead simply standing close to each other, were looking our way.

"No female on earth prettier than this pack!" Sam declared. "You hear what I'm sayin'?"

I looked toward Sam. "Honey—"

He ignored me, still addressing Joe and his companion who were still watching Sam's show. She was smiling, I could tell. Joe was not.

"You're fine, must admit," Sam tipped his head to Joe's female friend. "But nothin's finer than my girls!"

Keira giggled. Kate got up on her toes to kiss his cheek. I started pressing my huddle toward the kitchen door. My brother Sam was also tall and he was no slouch. He could probably hold his own with, say, Morrie, Feb's brother. I doubted he could last a round with Security to the Stars and he might buy a round if he talked about Joe's woman like that.

"Let's go inside," I coaxed.

Sam wasn't done with Joe and his friend though. I knew this because he felt the need to announce to them, "Havin' dinner with my family. All *fuckin'* right!"

"Sam!" I snapped, finally forgetting Joe and his partner. "Hello? The f-bomb is off-limits around teenage girls."

"Mom!" Keira cried. "They say it at school all the time."

"Maybe so, but they don't say it in my driveway or," I looked at Sam, "in my house."

"Relax, shit," Sam smiled, dropping his arms but turning and throwing one around my shoulders as he used his other hand to guide both Kate and Keira into the house in front of us like he herded teenage females for a living.

"Shit's off-limits too," I told Sam and he looked over his shoulder toward Joe's house.

"Violet's uptight! I'm here five minutes and she's lecturing me," he shouted, and I shoved him through the door, turned toward Joe's and started shouting myself.

"Sorry, really sorry! Show's over!"

"No probs!" the woman shouted back good-naturedly.

Joe seemed to be staring at me and he didn't say a word.

I scooted inside and closed the door.

"He texted me!" Kate told me practically before the door closed. "At school, said he was coming to town and wanted to surprise you."

"Took a long time gettin' home, Vi-oh-my, waited frickin' forever," Sam noted. "What, you live at that garden center?"

"I was doing overtime," I answered as I shrugged off my corduroy coat. I turned to put it on a hook by the door, an action that served double duty of allowing me to avoid the look Sam gave me.

"Uncle Sam made his world-famous spaghetti carbonara," Keira announced. "I was lookout. We shut off the lights when I saw your car on the street."

I turned again to look at the kitchen and saw that my brother did make spaghetti carbonara. He also made the mess that came with it.

Kate rushed up to me and grabbed my forearm, pulling down on it, informing me, "He's staying a couple of days. He's gonna meet *Dane*."

Lucky Sam. He was going to meet the awesome *Dane*.

"If that's cool with you, Vi," Sam said.

Like he had to ask.

It was cool with me. It was cool he stayed a couple of days or a couple of years. That wasn't loneliness speaking. That was how much I loved my little brother.

"That's cool."

"*Excellent!*" Keira shouted.

"I'll get the stuff for the pull out," Kate offered then ran from the room.

"Keira, honey, set the table," I told my other daughter.

"Sure," she agreed, moving to the cupboard and Sam got close to me.

"We'll talk about overtime after dinner," he said quietly.

My eyes shifted to the side, up and caught his. I nodded and walked into my house.

~

We ate spaghetti carbonara at the dining-room table and I only felt a twinge of hurt when Sam sat in Tim's chair instead of beside Keira where he usually sat one of the million times he was around for dinner when we lived close to him in Chicago. I wondered if my girls felt this same twinge, but watching them through dinner, I figured they were too excited by Sam's visit to notice.

Sam made garlic bread and a big Caesar salad to go with the spaghetti. The whole thing was delicious, not only because it wasn't dinner for one or I didn't have to cook it, but because Sam's spaghetti carbonara could be world-famous if the world was lucky enough to get a taste.

I was sipping my wine as the girls were finishing up eating. Both had been talking about their new school, their new friends, and Kate, of course, shared a great deal about the fabulous *Dane*. Therefore they weren't paying a lot of attention to their food.

I watched as Sam got up and walked to his bag, which was on the floor by the couch in the living room. Bending at the waist to paw through it, he came back to the table with something in his hand as Kate popped the last piece of bread in her mouth and Keira finished her last bite of spaghetti.

Sam moved to stand beside Kate, slapped something on table and said, "One for you." He slapped something else down and went on, "Another for you." He moved around the table as Kate picked the somethings up, inspected them, her eyes got huge and her mouth dropped open. Standing beside Keira, he repeated this process using the same words. "And one for you, another for you."

"Oh my *God*," Kate finally breathed, the cards held close to her face as if she could not believe her eyes and needed close proximity to the wonders she was viewing for them to be real. Her eyes were huge.

Sam came to me, put something by my plate and finished. "And for you."

I looked down at the gift cards next to my plate as Keira shouted, "Five hundred dollars at Lucky!"

"And two hundred at MAC!" Kate put in on a yell, waving her two cards around.

I looked down at my gift cards. One was for five hundred dollars on a disposable credit card. The other was two hundred dollars at MAC.

In shock, I looked up at Sam, but the girls had sprung from their seats and were jumping up and down again with their arms wrapped around him, jostling their uncle as they jumped.

"You gotta earn 'em, babies," Sam said, holding them close in his arms and kissing the tops of their heads. I watched him give them a squeeze before he ordered, "Clear the table and do the dishes, yeah?"

Kate didn't mind chores. The minute she was asked to do something, she did it. Didn't procrastinate, she got it out of the way and moved on.

Keira hated them and would procrastinate as long as humanly possible then bitch the entire time she was doing it. But for seven hundred dollar gift cards to her two favorite stores, she'd do the dishes. Hell, who wouldn't?

Therefore, they both agreed on shouts, "Yeah!"

Then they raced around the table, grabbing plates and Sam grabbed me. He took my arm and lifted me out of my seat, nabbing the bottle of wine from the table as he did. I snagged my glass and Sam's hand slid down my arm to curl around my fingers. He picked up his glass with practiced ease, carrying it and the bottle as he guided me to the study.

I'd put Tim's old desk in there with our old computer and the girls sometimes studied in there at their dad's desk. I'd also put the two recliners Tim had in his man cave at home in there at angles in the corner and that's where Sam took me. I curled into a recliner, my feet in the seat, knees to the armrest and Sam topped up my glass then his own and sat in the other recliner.

"Sam, the gift cards—" I began, knowing he didn't have that kind of money.

Sam cut me off, saying, "Dad."

I felt my mouth go tight.

"Vi, don't," Sam warned. "Just take it and use it for somethin' stupid. You know that'd piss Mom off most."

It certainly would. Mom hated anything frivolous, most especially frivolous spending, and trendy clothes and makeup, for that matter.

"She know Dad gave you the money to buy those cards?" I asked.

"She will when she balances the checkbook."

"Dad'll catch it."

"Dad doesn't care."

I looked Sam in the eye. "And I don't care either. Too little, too late."

"Vi—"

I shook my head. "Too little, too late, Sam."

I looked toward the kitchen, watching the girls tidying up, their thick, healthy, long, dark hair gleaming under the overhead kitchen lights. Their flawless, youthful skin glowing. Their thin, coltish but blooming teenage girl bodies moving with unconscious grace. I took in my girls as they moved around. Girls who had very little to do with their grandparents after my parents disowned me when I got pregnant at seventeen, announced I was keeping the baby and marrying the father, something they disapproved of immensely. Or at least Mom did.

Then I asked Sam quietly, "Dad want them to know it's from him?"

"That's your call."

I sighed, thinking I'd tell the girls. It was only fair. But I wouldn't like it.

"Vi," Sam called and I looked at him. "Why you workin' overtime?"

This made me sigh again.

Then I answered, "Because Kate's got Dane. She's wrapped up tight in him, even though they've only been dating a few weeks. And Keira's made friends with the entirety of the eighth grade class. They're not home much and I'd rather make some extra cash putzing around a garden center than come home to an empty house."

I watched my brother's eyes go soft and looked away.

Sam read me and changed the subject but he chose one that was no less uncomfortable even if it was not nearly as sad. "You hear from him?"

"Nope," I answered instantly.

"Nothin'?" Sam sounded surprised.

"Nothin'."

I felt Sam lean into me, so I looked at him as I took a sip of my wine.

"I been snoopin'—"

I felt my body grow tight, fear clutching my insides and I leaned into my brother.

"Sam—"

He shook his head. "Someone's gotta do somethin'. He's not done with you."

"That someone doesn't have to be you."

"Vi, someone's gotta do somethin'."

"Let the police deal with it."

I watched Sam clench his teeth, seeing his jaws flex out at the sides, and it was his turn to look away.

"Sam, promise me you'll let it go," I said softly.

"Can't."

"Sam—"

His eyes locked on mine and he repeated, "Can't."

"You don't know what you're doing."

"I'm bein' careful."

I leaned in further and hissed, "You don't mess with this guy." Sam didn't answer and I put my hand to the armrest and got even closer to my brother. "You know, you *know* what happened to Tim, and he was doing his *job*...you know you do *not* mess with this guy."

"So I let him mess with my sister?"

"He'll forget about me."

"Yeah?"

"Yeah."

"Bullshit."

"Sam—"

"Bullshit, Vi."

"Think about Melissa."

"She agrees with me somethin's gotta be done."

My brother had been with his girlfriend Melissa for ten years. They lived together for nine of those ten years but never married. They talked about it all the time, but they were always enjoying their lives too much to get around to doing anything about it. Mel and Sam had both been close to Tim, adored him. Sam felt like Tim was his brother. Tim had felt the same. We were all tight. When Tim died, they took it hard, nearly as hard as me and the girls. And Mel had attitude, just like Sam. I knew that Sam spoke the truth when he said Mel agreed something had to be done. Not only because they'd loved Tim but because they loved me and the girls.

"Talk to Barry," I suggested.

"I'm talkin' to him."

"What's he say?"

"He understands a brother's gotta do what he's gotta do."

Yes, Barry would understand that. Barry was as crazy as Tim *and* Sam.

"Sam, Barry's a cop and he said he won't rest—"

"And he isn't."

"Then let Barry do his work."

"That doesn't mean he doesn't need help."

"Not from you."

"Just leave it, Vi."

I looked into my brother's hard face for a few seconds then I turned away, swallowing and thinking maybe it wasn't good we were so close. Maybe it wasn't good I loved him like crazy and he felt the same way. Maybe it wasn't good Melissa thought the world of me and my girls.

I pulled in a breath, let it out and took another sip of wine.

Then I let it go. I had no choice and I knew it. Sam was stubborn, always had been, so I whispered, "Tell Mel to come down with you next time, yeah?"

"Will do," Sam whispered back then changed the subject again. "Who's the big guy next door?"

My eyes moved to my brother. "What?"

"Big guy next door with the blonde chick? She your neighbor, is he, or both?"

"He is. Joe Callahan."

"Good neighbor to have," Sam remarked.

I felt my eyebrows inch together. "Why?"

"Looks like he could crush a rock with his fist."

"Why does that make him a good neighbor?"

"Also looks like someone you do not want to mess with."

Sam wasn't wrong about that.

"Again, why does that make him a good neighbor?" I asked.

"People don't let shit happen in their 'hoods that shouldn't happen. He's your neighbor, that asshole thinks to mess with you down here, I figure this Joe guy'd wade in."

The thought of Joe Callahan getting involved in my troubles sent a chill up my spine. "Let's just hope that asshole doesn't think to mess with me down here."

"He does, you should have a word with this Joe."

That was not going to happen.

"Sam—"

"Maybe I'll have a word, explain things, ask him to keep an eye out."

I leaned forward again and snapped, "Don't do that."

"Why not?"

"Just don't, okay? Seriously."

My brother watched me then asked, "You got a problem with this guy?"

"No," I lied quickly. "He's just not around very often and I came down here to escape that whole mess. I don't want everyone in my business."

"Vi—"

"I don't, Sam. If something happens then I'll talk to Colt. He's a cop, lives across the street. He's a good guy, a good cop. It'll be fine."

"The dude who had that serial killer after him?"

"Yeah."

Sam shook his head. "Christ, he'll just love it if that asshole bleeds into his town after that mess went down."

Sam wasn't wrong about that either.

"Can we just enjoy your visit and not talk about this shit?" I suggested.

"We can after you answer one question."

I sighed again then asked, "What?"

"You need money?"

Sometimes it was irritating how well my brother knew me.

I did need money. Things were tight, not to the point where food wasn't on the table, but to the point where it was a constant, nagging worry at the back of my head because I could give my girls what they needed but not a whole helluva lot of what they wanted and that sucked.

"I'm good."

"Yeah?"

My voice got soft when I lied, "Yeah, Sam. I'm good."

"Okay, then you use that two grand I set on your nightstand to make yourself a pretty garden."

I felt my eyes get wide and my mouth drop open, but I didn't speak.

"And you can't refuse it," Sam continued. "It's from Mel and me and Mel'll go ballistic, I come back with that money."

"Sam, I can't take that."

"You don't, I'm up shit's creek with Mel."

"Sam—"

He leaned forward again. "How many times you and Tim bail me out, hunh? How many?"

"But—"

"More than two grand's worth, a fuckuva lot more."

"I can't—"

"Payback, babe."

"Sam—"

His hand came out, hooked me around the neck and pulled me across the space between the kitty-corner chairs so my face was in his face.

"Payback," he whispered.

I pressed my lips together to fight the sting of tears in my eyes. Before Melissa, Sam had been a wild one, always doing stupid shit, always coming to Tim and me to bail him out and we always did. Even though it had been years and we never expected anything in return, Sam would feel that weight pressing on him. It would live with him, right under his skin. He needed to do this, I knew it, so he could work that weight out from under his skin and I needed to let him.

I pulled in breath through my nose, nodded, and I watched my brother smile.

The next morning, Joe's truck was still in his drive, but his house was quiet.

The morning after that, the morning Sam left, Joe's truck was gone.

"Shit, Vi, sorry, I got a callout," Colt said after he flipped his phone shut and shoved it in his back jeans' pocket. He was seated at the barstool next to me at J&J's Saloon.

I looked down at my mostly finished cranberry juice and vodka. It was my third. Morrie was currently making my fourth. I hadn't moved from my stool for a while so I didn't know the extent of my drunkenness but I figured, since I didn't drink much, I was closing in on pretty smashed.

"That's okay," I told Colt who was my designated driver seeing as I came to the bar with him and Feb after she caught me getting my mail from the mailbox after coming home from work. We'd called our hellos then she'd suggested I go in with her and Colt to J&J's for a night out.

I'd said yes because it was Friday and on Fridays normal people went out to have a drink, socialize, unwind.

I'd also said yes because Kate was out with Dane and she'd asked for an hour extension on her curfew because there was some party she just *had* to attend. All the other kids had later curfews and she explained she'd look like a dork if she had to be home by eleven.

I'd allowed this because I was a moron. I knew this party wasn't about kids sedately drinking punch and discussing possible college applications they wished to submit. I just hoped my responsible first born would act responsible. I also hoped her boyfriend, *Dane*, who seemed more into Kate than she was into him (if that was possible), would take care of my daughter.

I'd also said yes to J&J's because Keira was at a sleepover, which meant Kate and Keira being out, the house would be empty and I'd rather be at J&J's having a drink sitting by Colt, who was a nice guy (and proved to be a fun guy, in a lighthearted, teasing, big brother kind of way) and not home by myself yet again.

"You want me to drop you home now?" Colt asked.

Morrie slid my drink in front of me and I smiled at him then looked at Colt and, still smiling, shook my head. Colt looked at my drink then at me and he smiled back.

He turned to Morrie. "Can you get Darryl to take Violet home?"

"I'll get a taxi," I said quickly because I might have been heading straight toward smashed but it was Friday night and the bar was packed so I knew Morrie couldn't afford to let his employee, Darryl, take a trip out to play driver to me.

"That's cool, Vi. Darryl can take you or I will," Morrie stated, smiling at me.

Man, he was *so* nice. They *all* were.

"Really, I'll get a taxi," I smiled back.

"I got her," a deep, rumbly voice said from behind me.

I twisted on my stool, looked up, up, *up* and saw, standing behind me, Joe Callahan, his hair longer and more unruly, wearing his black leather jacket, a black t-shirt stretched across his wide chest, faded jeans and black motorcycle boots.

"Yo Cal," Morrie greeted as I stared at Joe.

"Yo," Joe greeted back.

"Great, Cal, thanks," Colt muttered. I looked from Joe to Colt and watched Colt call to the back of the bar, "Feb, baby, got a callout."

"All right, honey," she called back. "See you later?"

"Yeah," Colt replied, grinning at her then he slid off his stool and lifted a hand to squeeze the back of my neck. He nodded to Joe and Morrie then he took off.

Through this I sat there thinking firstly, that Joe freaked me out a bit considering he could come up behind me and I never heard him coming, and secondly, that I didn't want him taking me home.

I put my elbow to the bar, my head in my hand and I aimed my mouth at my straw. Capturing it, I sucked up cranberry juice and vodka and considered this dilemma.

"Beer?" Morrie asked Joe before I came to any conclusions about my dilemma.

"Yeah," Joe replied and slid in between me and the empty stool beside me, which meant he came in close to me as well as cut me off from the bar as Colt and I were sitting on the last two stools by the wall.

He didn't sit though. He stood there even after Morrie opened a bottle of beer, set it on the bar top and walked away. Then he still didn't sit, just took a pull on his beer, his body mostly facing me but his torso was twisted to the bar.

Then his torso twisted to me and he looked down into my eyes.

"You talk to her about condoms?"

Again, it seemed he was starting a conversation in the middle, but, even mostly drunk, I knew what he was asking.

"No."

He didn't respond, just looked at me, and I also knew what his silence meant.

"Kate's responsible," I explained though it was none of his business, and even though my daughter *was* responsible, I was declaring this mostly hopefully.

"Were you responsible?" he asked.

"No," I answered truthfully and pointing out the obvious.

He kept looking at me then he took a pull at his beer.

I aimed my mouth at my straw, captured it and sucked up some more drink.

I released my straw and asked, "Did you shovel my snow?"

His blue eyes leveled on mine. "What?"

"That day, when it snowed, did you shovel my drive?"

He didn't answer at first, then he said, "Yeah."

When this knowledge was confirmed, I pulled in breath not knowing what to say because this was a nice thing to do and he didn't seem like a nice guy.

Then I settled on, "Thanks."

He didn't reply.

I was sucking up more vodka and juice, my head still in my hand, my elbow still at the bar when he spoke again.

"Your man gone?"

My chest got tight and my eyes lifted to his.

"What?"

"Your man. Came home last week. He gone?"

I blinked at him thinking about Tim coming home and how impossible that would be, and how beautiful, then I realized what he meant.

"That wasn't my man. That was my brother, Sam."

He nodded and took a pull of beer. I stared at him.

Then for some stupid reason I asked, "What about your woman?"

His eyes came back to mine but he didn't reply.

"The one you were with that night Sam came," I prompted.

"Nadia?" he asked like I'd know her name.

"The blonde."

"Nadia," he stated.

"She around?" I asked, not knowing why, but also thinking that I wanted to know the answer and not knowing why about that either.

"Nope," Joe replied.

"Oh," I whispered and aimed my mouth at my drink.

We were silent a good, long while, me halfheartedly sipping at my drink, Joe standing and taking intermittent sips at his beer. This was not comfortable for me. I felt the need to fill the silence but found I had nothing to say. However, watching Joe, he seemed comfortable in some kind of zone where he, his beer and the bar were one and he was content with that.

Finally I figured out what to say. "You don't have to take me home. I can get a taxi."

His eyes again came to me and he noted, "You live next door."

"Well…yeah."

"Buddy, I can take you home."

"What if you want to go home and I want to stay?"

"I'll wait."

"What if I want to go home and you want to stay?"

"I'll come back."

Yeesh, he had an answer for everything.

"That's silly."

"Why?"

"Because it is."

This was lame but with that much vodka in me, and considering I didn't drink much, it was all I had.

I figured he thought it was lame too because he didn't bother to respond.

I captured my straw with my mouth and took another drink.

We lapsed back into silence, Joe turning back to the bar and leaning two elbows on it, cradling his beer in both his hands until I found another topic of conversation.

"So, I'm guessin' Kenzie's keepin' her mouth shut."

Joe's head turned and he looked at me. "Yeah."

"Everything cool with your clients?"

"Yeah."

"You're home a lot more than normal," I remarked stupidly since I didn't want him to notice that I noticed. But at the same time I was bizarrely worried that Kenzie Elise was costing him clients and that was why he was home more than normal.

"Yeah," he said then said no more and I'd run out of steam on that particular conversational gambit.

When I fell silent, Joe turned his head away and, keeping one elbow to the bar, with his other hand he lifted his beer to his lips and arched his neck back to take a pull. This fascinated me for some drunken reason. He had a muscular throat and I could see it as it arched and worked with his swallow. Furthermore, his jaw was on display. I noted how attractive it was and that was fascinating for some drunken reason too.

I tore my eyes away from his throat and jaw and caught on the little tray of fruit Feb, Morrie and Darryl used in the drinks. Wedges of lemon and lime, cocktail onions, olives and maraschino cherries.

"You know," I started to inform Joe and just his head turned to me again, "back in the day, you could impress a guy just by tying the stem of a cherry in a knot with your tongue."

Why I said this, I had no idea. I just couldn't sit there, silent and sipping my vodka and cranberry juice while he did the same with his beer. It was just too weird. I couldn't hack it. I had to talk about something.

"Yeah?" he asked.

"Yeah," I answered.

"You do that often?" he asked.

"Not really," I answered since I was with Tim and only Tim, back in the day and then forever. But it had impressed Tim. "Seems strange to me, why that'd impress a guy."

Joe made no attempt to enlighten me.

"It's good you all grow out of that," I noted sensibly.

"Give you fifty dollars right now, you do it."

I blinked. "What?"

He straightened, pulled his wallet out of his back pocket, flipped it open and pulled out a bill. Then he placed it on the bar between us and I saw it was a fifty dollar bill. I looked up from the money to him when he spoke.

"That's yours, you do it," Joe said as he shoved the wallet back in his pocket.

"Are you serious?" I whispered.

Joe didn't respond verbally. He just reached out and nabbed a cherry by the stem, turned and held it out to me.

I stared at the cherry. He was serious.

"Fifty dollars to knot the stem with my tongue?" I checked, just to make sure.

"You can't do it."

"I can do it. I'm just…" I paused. Coming off my elbow I reached out and took the cherry from him. "Out of practice."

Joe didn't say anything and I wondered how I got myself into this. I was going to be sitting there moving my mouth around like an idiot while Joe watched and probably in the end not knotting the dumb cherry stem.

But I couldn't back out now. It wasn't about the fifty dollars. It was about my pride.

I plucked the cherry off the stem with my teeth, looked anywhere but at Joe as I chewed and swallowed, took a sip of my vodka and cranberry juice to clear my mouth in preparation for my endeavor then popped the stem in.

Within seconds, I'd done it. It wasn't hard at all. I guessed it was like riding a bike.

I slid the stem from between my lips, showed him the result and set it on my cocktail napkin.

His clear blue eyes were on the stem when I asked, "You impressed?"

His head tipped to my glass. "That your last?"

I stared at him a second not following before I asked, "Last drink?"

"Yeah."

"Um…" I tried to gauge if he was trying to say he was ready to go home since he was my ride. It would be rude to make him stay longer when he wanted to leave, so I answered on a question just in case he was ready to hang out awhile since I wanted to hang out awhile. "Yes?"

"Drink up, buddy."

I guess he wasn't ready to hang out awhile.

I was weirdly deflated the cherry stem knotting thing hadn't impressed him. Tim thought it was the shit.

I lifted my drink and put the straw to my lips, sucking back the rest of my vodka at the same time Joe's fingers wrapped around my upper arm. He slid me off the stool as I kept the glass in my hand, straw to my mouth and sucked. I also kept sucking on my straw as Joe grabbed my purse from the bar and handed it to me then slid the fifty from the bar and shoved it in my front jeans pocket.

I looked up at him when he called, "Morrie, Violet paid or is she on a tab?"

"Tab," Morrie answered.

I was realizing that I might be drunker than I expected seeing as I was standing, which everyone knew made you drunker after you sat for a good while and imbibed. Therefore, since I was assessing the level of my drunkenness, I didn't intervene when Joe dug his wallet out of his pocket, pulled out some bills and tossed them on the bar.

"That doesn't cover it, I'll catch you later," Joe told Morrie.

"You got it, dude," Morrie replied.

Joe shoved his wallet back in his pocket and pulled the drink out of my hand even though I was still sucking the dregs out through the straw (making that slurping noise). He put it on the bar, grabbed my hand and dragged me to the door.

He was parked on the street several car lengths down from the bar. He bleeped the locks as we approached and when we got there, he pulled open the passenger side door.

For some reason his truck seemed significant to me and my first ride in it even more significant. So I just stood in the door, staring at the seat I should be planting my ass in and not moving because I was both unbelievably scared and utterly thrilled. Neither feeling made a lick of sense but I had them both all the same. It was like, if I got in his truck and the door closed on me, my life was going to change radically.

"Buddy, climb up," Joe sounded impatient when I just stood there staring in his truck and he used my hand to push me closer to the seat.

I tipped my head way back and looked at him. "You have a nice truck," I informed him mostly in an effort to stall.

Joe ignored my compliment and ordered, "Climb up."

"Maybe I should walk home," I suggested.

Joe stared down at me a second then he let go of my hand, bent at the waist, slid an arm behind my knees and one around my waist and, within half a second, my ass was in the seat. Another half a second, the door was closed.

Joe Callahan just lifted me bodily into his truck.

I took in a deep breath and closed my eyes.

"What's the matter with me?" I whispered into the cab and opened my eyes to see Joe had rounded the hood. He opened his door, swung his big body behind the wheel and slammed his door.

We were both in and that feeling of fear assailed me, along with the thrill, but the thrill was edging out the fear. I was in the passenger seat of a car. It wasn't me driving. It wasn't me responsible. It was me who got to sit back and relax and be taken home.

And I was in that truck with Joe Callahan. Joe Callahan who was scary and thrilling all in himself. He was more man than I'd ever known and I spent most my adult life around cops. His maleness filled the cab, dangerous, assertive, assaulting my senses. I didn't like him. I was pretty sure of that fact, but I admitted, drunk and sitting in his truck, that he fascinated me and not because he was Security to the Stars. Because he was Joe Callahan.

"You wanna buckle up?" Joe asked, and I turned to see he was facing me, forearm on the steering wheel. The truck was running and Joe was looking as impatient as he sounded.

He wanted to get home.

I wanted to know where he got those scars on his cheek.

"Sorry," I mumbled and buckled up.

Joe put the truck in gear and pulled into the street.

"This is nice of you," I said as he drove.

Joe didn't answer.

I realized Joe wasn't much of a conversationalist at about the same time I realized the truck was nice. It was clearly top of the line with all the bells and whistles and he took care of it. It wasn't just shiny on the outside, but the inside was clean and looked brand new. The ride was quiet and smooth and Joe drove the big truck like he was born behind the wheel of a pickup.

As he drove silently, I was again reminded how nice it was just to sit back and let someone drive me home. There was no particular reason I was having this feeling since, not but a few hours earlier, Colt and Feb took me to J&J's. And Tim always drove. I couldn't remember a time when we went somewhere when he wasn't at the wheel. This never bothered me. I didn't care if he drove. It only bothered me when he wasn't around to do it anymore, but, after nearly a year and a half, I'd gotten used to it. Now I realized I missed it.

I was so deep in these thoughts I didn't notice that we were on our street until Joe turned into his drive and something new hit me. Like being in the truck with him, the sensation was strong, it was scary and it was thrilling. After seeing this truck in his drive on and off for months, even before knowing Joe, but definitely after, and now sitting *in* his truck, *in* his drive, staring at his house through the windshield, a vantage point I never thought I'd have, I felt something I didn't understand. There was something profound about it. Something I couldn't put my finger on. But for some weird reason, it felt life-altering.

I jumped when Joe's door slammed and I found myself nervous. I turned and fumbled with my buckle, getting it released only when Joe pulled open my door. I hitched my purse up my shoulder and hopped out of the truck. Joe had his hand on the door so I moved out of the way. He threw it to and I looked at him to give him my thanks again for the ride, but he was moving.

I stood there for several beats as I watched his big body walk across the yard toward my house.

Even though I lived next door, in Joe Callahan style, he was going to walk me safely home.

I didn't know what to feel about this but had no time to figure it out and no choice but to follow him, pulling my purse from my arm and digging through it to get my keys as I walked.

I had my keys in hand, the correct one between my fingers, and Joe was standing in the light I'd turned on by the side door when I arrived. I stopped. Joe took the keys from my hand and he slid the key into the lock, turned it, slid it out and opened the door.

I swallowed nervously as the beeps went for the alarm. Moving just beyond him, I twisted my torso into the house, punched in the code and the beeping stopped. I took a deep breath, pulled my torso out of the house, turned and tipped my head back to look at him.

In the outside light, the night shrouding us, he looked sinister again just as much as he looked rugged and interesting and something new assailed me. It was that fear, that thrill, but there was something else. Something insistent, needy, like a hunger I didn't quite understand, and my mouth went dry at the power of it.

"Thanks for the ride," I whispered, unable to speak any louder.

Joe didn't respond nor did he move.

I didn't know what to do. I had thought he was eager to get home, but he had his opportunity to escape and he was just standing there, staring at me in that way of his, something working behind his eyes.

Then I realized that I was being rude.

"Would you like to come in…?" I hesitated then finished, "For a drink or something?"

At first, Joe didn't reply.

Then he said softly, his tone strange, like he was talking to himself even though I was right there, "You already think I'm a dick."

I felt my heart beat faster and I whispered, "Joe—"

Joe cut me off. "So, don't matter tomorrow morning you still think I'm a dick. 'Cause now, even though you're drunk, I'm gonna take you inside and fuck you 'til you ache."

My heart stopped beating and my breath stopped coming which was bad, considering Joe grabbed my hand and pulled me into my house. He stopped to close and lock the door then he tossed my keys on the counter, pulled my purse off my arm and tossed that on the counter too. He dragged me through the kitchen, the dining area, the open study and straight to my bedroom.

I didn't struggle. I didn't do anything even when he stopped in my room, let my hand go and shrugged off his leather jacket, letting it drop to the floor. Then his hands came to my little corduroy jacket and he pulled it down my arms.

"Uh..." I mumbled, lifting my hands belatedly as he moved closer. "Joe—"

But my hands hit his hard chest then my arms were squashed between our bodies when one of Joe's arms sliced low around my hips and he yanked me to him, his other hand fisted in my hair, twisting tight. I felt an illicit pain against my scalp that I shouldn't have liked, but I did. I liked it a lot. So much I felt it not only in my scalp but throughout my body. His fist in my hair positioned my head, tugging it back but tilting it to the side so when his mouth came down on mine hard, I was right where he wanted me.

And I wanted to be there. There was no other thought, not to protest, to push away, to fight. I just wanted to be there, pressed against him, his arm around me, his hand in my hair and his mouth on mine.

I opened my mouth, his tongue spiked in, I liked the taste of him, the feel of his tongue and my body liquefied in his arms. My hands forced their way from between our bodies so my fingers could slide into his thick, over-long hair and I pressed deep into his big body. I gave no thought to what I was doing and who I was doing it with. I gave no thought to anything. I just felt and what I felt was unbelievably good.

His kiss wasn't gentle. It was greedy, demanding, and I liked it. So much I mewed in protest when he took his mouth away but didn't protest when his hands went to my t-shirt and yanked it over my head, pulling it free and tossing it away. He moved into me, turning me, guiding me to the bed and I went down on it. Joe towered over me, pulling up a calf to yank off my boot then my sock then he went after the other one and did the same. Without delay, he leaned in, his hands went to my buckle and he'd undone it and my jeans and had them down my legs before I could take two breaths.

And I was breathing hard, already turned on. I came up to sitting, which meant I collided with Joe when he came down on me.

That's when it really started.

I yanked his shirt out of jeans and pulled it over his head, his arms lifting to help me. I tugged it free and threw it to the floor then his hands came back to me and his mouth, his tongue, his teeth. I wanted them and all they were doing to my mouth, my neck, my ears. It was brilliant, my body was alive, vibrating, like I'd woken up from a seven hundred year sleep but what woke me was an electric shock. At the same time I wanted what he was doing to me back from him. I used my hands, my nails, my mouth and tongue everywhere I could touch, every inch I could taste.

It was wild, almost a struggle. I couldn't get enough of him, take enough from him. No matter what I got, I wanted more, like a craving that hollowed out my insides, needing to be filled.

Joe was the same but he was stronger, keeping me on my back no matter how I tried to roll him. Along the line he disposed of my panties then he got my bra cup down and drew my nipple into his mouth sharply. My back arched, my fingers fisted in his hair as his tongue jabbed at my nipple then sucked it in fiercely and I fucking *loved* it.

"Yes," I breathed, and he moved to the other side, scraping my bra cup down again and repeating what he did to the first. His fingers having replaced his mouth at my other nipple, they pinched and twisted. It was rough but it felt brilliant and my hips rose in a reflexive demand.

"Joe," I whispered, suddenly needing him inside me. My hand moved from his hair and slid down the sleek skin of his back, to his side, his waist, but his crotch was too far away.

He came back over me and his mouth took mine in another hard, bruising kiss and my hand found him, palming his groin, finding him hard. I moaned into his mouth and bucked my hips.

"Fuck me," I pleaded, rubbing my hand against him, opening my legs.

He didn't hesitate. His hand pushed mine aside and he undid his jeans.

"You on the Pill?" he asked, his voice gruff.

"No," I answered and felt the tip of his cock pressing against me. I wanted it inside me so badly it was an ache. My hand slid into his jeans, curling around his tight ass in an insistent demand.

"Fuck it," he groaned and drove in deep.

I gasped then held my breath as he filled me. He was huge. So big, it was a shock to be that full.

Then I had to start breathing when he started moving, driving deep, filling me full again and again, rough, hard, almost brutal, his big hands going to my hips and lifting me to plant himself deeper. Then I wasn't breathing, I was panting.

My nails dug into his back, my hips rising, helping him to go deeper. I wrapped a calf around his waist, digging my heel into his back to leverage my hips, my other leg wrapping around his thigh.

"You're so big," I whispered.

"You like it," he pointed out the obvious. I made no response. I couldn't. That's how much I liked it.

"Harder," I gasped, wanting it harder, wanting the pounding never to stop. But even demanding it, still thinking he couldn't fuck me harder. There was no way he could fuck me harder. But I was wrong, he could and he did.

It built fast. It had been a long time, I felt it coming and I wanted it. I reached for it, the nails of one hand scraping his back, the other hand fisted in his hair, begging, "Fuck me harder, Joe."

His mouth was at mine, his breath ragged when he murmured, "You like it rough."

"Yes," I breathed.

"Good," he muttered, kissed me deep and fucked me harder.

It was happening. I could feel it and when it started, I tore my mouth from his, arched my neck, my back, and announced on a throaty, breathy moan, "Joe, I'm coming."

"Christ," Joe bit off as it hit me. It was so huge, my body shook with it and I tightened my limbs around him, pulling him close.

I felt him thrusting as I came, suspended in the glorious moment, beautiful.

I was coming down when his thrusts became even more powerful. Then his hand left my hip, his fingers sunk into my hair, fisting and twisting again. His mouth slammed down on mine and he groaned, his hips driving into mine once, twice, three times then, on the fourth, he planted himself to the root and stopped.

His lips slid from mine, down my cheek, my neck, where he buried his face and he stayed fixed deep. I lay under him, bearing his heavy weight, feeling full of his cock, immune to anything but his body, his heat, his weight, his prick. There was nothing in the world but me and Joe Callahan and I liked it like that.

Suddenly he slid out and his weight was gone. His heat, his body, all vanished and it was just me in the bed.

I blinked at the suddenness of it and closed my legs, rolling to my side, curling up, my eyes moving to him in the dark. He was standing at the foot of the bed doing up his jeans. Nothing entered my mind. I could still feel him between my legs, my brain fuzzy with drink and sex, my body sated. He bent to the floor then straightened, pulling on his t-shirt.

Mindlessly, I watched as his hand went to his back pocket. He yanked out his wallet, flipped it open, pulled something out, he returned his wallet to his pocket. My brain still not having kicked into gear, I didn't move as he bent over the bed, putting a hand in it by my belly, the fingers of his other hand sliding up the inside of my forearm, which was lying on the bed. When he reached my open palm, I felt the edges of a card against my skin as he curled my fingers around it.

Then he trailed his fingertips down my hip and outer thigh as he said, "Call me, buddy, anytime you need a ride home."

My body locked at his insinuation, but I had no chance to ask a question or make a retort. He disappeared and, seconds later, I heard the outer door closing.

I laid there a long time, curled mostly naked on my bed, the air in my room chill as the knowledge seeped into me that I just let me next door neighbor, Joe Callahan, a man I disliked, fuck me so hard I ached. I'd even begged him to do it.

And it seeped into me that, after thirty-five years, I'd just taken my second lover and I'd done this like a slutty, drunken barfly, letting a guy I barely knew and didn't even like pick me up, take me home and fuck me so hard I ached. Hell, he didn't even need to work at it. He just dragged me out of the bar, I followed him to my house and then he dragged me to my room.

And it seeped into me that this guy, Joe Callahan, thought he could do that to me whenever it struck my fancy to let him, calling him to service me and then he'd pull out, leave me mostly naked and alone and not even kiss me before he left. And I couldn't fucking blame him.

And this knowledge seeped into my bones, bitter and humiliating.

I heard the front door open and I froze.

Kate was home.

I whirled into motion. Jumping off the bed, pawing through my clothes on the floor, I found and yanked on my underwear. Then I ran to the bathroom, pulled Tim's robe off the hook on the door and shrugged it on, feeling for the first time the soft, warm flannel against my skin like a burn.

I tied the belt tight and walked into the living room, pulling my hair out of my face, hoping to God my daughter couldn't read the heinous deed I'd done in my expression or the line of my body. I looked to the DVD clock under the TV in the living room and saw it was two after midnight. My responsible Kate was home on time and her boyfriend, who I didn't want to like or trust, had brought her home by curfew.

I headed to her room, the light coming through the door which was opened a crack.

I stopped at the door and knocked softly.

"Yeah, Mom," she called, and I pushed the door open and stood in its frame, my arms wrapped around my belly.

"Hey, baby, have a good time?"

She was texting someone and I knew it was Dane even though he'd just dropped her off. Her head came up from her phone and she grinned at me.

"Yeah," she said softly, her face just as soft.

Oh fuck.

"Dane have fun?" I asked.

She nodded and looked back down at her phone. She hit send, slid it shut and tossed it on her nightstand.

"I like him, Kate. He's a good kid," I told her.

Her head twisted to me and she studied me a second before she dealt a blow she didn't know she was dealing. And, if she did, it would cut her to the quick. Kate felt. She felt everything, but she felt other people's pain far more than her own, one of the few things she got from me.

"You think Dad would have liked him?"

I hid my flinch at her question and I did it by thinking about her question.

I'd made a pact with Tim early on that we'd always be open and honest with our girls. A pact that he regularly broke as they grew older and he found he had trouble with the facts of life and relaying them to his daughters, seeing as they were female. A pact, since I was female, I was able to keep.

"No," I told her. Her face fell and I went on. "But only because you're his little girl and you always will be. He wouldn't like him, not now, but he'd come around because Dane's a good kid."

Her face brightened, just slightly, and she asked, "You think?"

I walked in, got close to her, wrapped my hand around her head and pulled her temple to my mouth.

"I know," I whispered and kissed her before finishing. "Get some sleep, honey."

Her body had leaned into mine with my embrace, but she pulled away when she replied, "All right, Mom."

"Sleep tight."

"You too."

I walked to the side kitchen door, locked it, armed the alarm and then moved back to my room. I got in bed wearing Tim's robe, thinking that sleeping tight was an impossibility with what happened that night.

I was right.

"Home for dinner!" I shouted my order to my girls from my room as I heard them preparing to go to the mall and I finished preparing to go into work.

It was late morning after the Joe Incident. Bobbie had called and asked me to put in a few hours. She might have gotten a good full-time worker when Sabrina quit but that still meant she was down a part-time worker and hadn't found anyone she liked to replace me. Since Bobbie didn't like many people that would probably take a while. Overtime was beginning to be a regular thing, but I wasn't complaining.

"When are you done?" Keira shouted back.

"I'll be home after five," I answered, again on a shout.

"Cool! Later, Momalicious," Keira shouted.

"Bye, Mawdy!" Kate yelled.

"Be careful!" I yelled back, flicking the covers over my bed and a small, white business card flew up into the air.

I stilled and stared at the card as I heard the door slam in the other room.

The card had settled back on my bed. I saw the print on it and it was blurry because I was not focusing as I stared at it. I was feeling the bitterness and humiliation that leached into my bones last night, bitterness and humiliation I'd made a huge effort to ignore all morning, start burning.

My breath started coming fast and shame bled into the acid that had taken root in my marrow.

Last night I wasn't so drunk I didn't know what I was doing. I wasn't so drunk I had a hangover. I wasn't so fucking drunk I shouldn't have stopped it.

But I didn't. I not only let it happen, I participated and I'd *begged.*

Not thinking (I never did when I got angry), I snatched up the card and then went to my jeans which were still on the floor. I pulled the fifty out of the pocket then I dropped the jeans on the bed and marched out of my room. Then I marched through the house out the side door.

Joe's truck was in the drive.

I had no intention of facing him but I had every intention of making a point.

I was heading toward his mailbox when I heard the music and I switched directions, walking up his yard to his drive, instantly changing my mind about facing him. I saw the garage door open, the music coming from there. Black Sabbath, not Kenzie Elise loud, just loud enough to hear.

There was a car in the garage, the hood up. I couldn't see what kind of car it was, all I could see was Joe bent over it, working on the engine.

I walked right up to him and when I got close, his head turned to me but his torso stayed bent over the engine. When it did, before he could say a word, not that he was going to, I stopped and tossed the card and fifty in his direction. They fluttered through the air, but I didn't wait to see his reaction, didn't say a word, didn't watch where the card and bill landed. I turned and walked away.

I didn't get very far. A firm hand curled around my upper arm and I was yanked back.

"What—?" I snapped, not finishing because he whirled me around and pulled me into the garage. "Let me go!" I demanded as he reached up, and with a violent wrench, he pulled on a cord causing the apparently well-oiled garage door to rumble on its rails and crash down.

There we were, alone in his dark garage with his car and Black Sabbath.

Me and my stupid temper.

"Take your hand off me!" I bit out, twisting my arm and he did. He let me go.

He took his hand off me but only to lift it and, as he did the night before, exactly the same, his fingers fisted in my hair and his other arm wound around my hips, pulling me into his body.

"What are you—?" I started, but his mouth came down on mine in a punishing kiss that surprised me, scared me and excited me, the last one far, far more than the first two.

I didn't want it to happen, didn't expect it would happen, not in a million years. In fact, looking back at it later, which I did a lot, too much, I didn't know how it *did* happen.

But one second he was kissing me, the next second he was shuffling me to his car. He yanked the rod out that was holding the hood up and it came crashing down. The sound jolted me, but not with fear or surprise, with excitement as Joe pulled my jeans skirt up to my waist, yanked my panties down and they fell to his garage floor. Then, his hands at my ass, he lifted me. I wrapped my legs around his hips and he planted me on the hood of the car, his hand between us, working his fly, my hands in his t-shirt, roaming his skin.

Then he was inside me, fucking me on the hood of his car. Fucking me like the night before, hard, deep, rough, violent, and I loved it. I lifted my hips to greet it. My hands curled on his ass to encourage it. My tongue tangled with his in my mouth to build it.

Then I came, not as hard as the night before but different, sharper, shorter, not better but just as fucking good.

His hips bucked into mine long after I came. He was still kissing me and I locked him tight in my limbs as I took his thrusts until he buried himself to the hilt, growled in my mouth and the taste of that growl nearly made me climax again.

He stayed planted inside me as it hit me I'd done it again, on his car, in his garage no less. I turned my head away but he didn't seem to mind.

He just used this opportunity to glide his tongue along my neck, which, it killed me to admit, felt so fucking good it made me shiver.

Then he pulled out and yanked me to my feet.

I was looking to the side and down at the floor, but I wobbled, my knees weak from my orgasm, and his big hands spanned my hips to steady me.

There was something about this, something tender, something so un-Joe that I couldn't hack it. I yanked free, stepping away, pulling my hair out of my face, beyond humiliated. So far beyond it, I didn't know what that was. At the same time I felt fucking great, I felt electrified, alive and I hated myself for that, but I hated him more.

I leaned down and snatched my panties from the floor, clearing my mind, thinking of nothing but getting the fuck out of there. I yanked them on, shimmied my skirt down, and without looking at him, walked swiftly to the side door.

I didn't make it. His arm hooked at my belly, his other one wrapped around my chest and he yanked me back into his body.

His lips at my ear, he murmured, "I want you in my bed tonight, buddy."

I shook my head once, a terse, angry shake even as his words slid through me like a different kind of burn, hardening my nipples, tickling between my legs, bringing back that feeling I had last night. That hollow feeling. That hunger. Even though I'd just had him not five minutes before.

I pulled out of his arms, reached out, yanked open the door and ran straight to my house.

I lay on my side, curled into a ball, which was my seven hundred and fifty-fifth position of the night.

The room was dark. It was the dead of night and even though I barely slept the night before, I was wide awake.

Not comfortable, I turned and looked at the clock.

One forty-seven in the morning.

I closed my eyes and whispered, "Fuck."

Joe was next door in his bed, maybe waiting for me.

This was all I could think of from ten o'clock, when I slid into bed with a book I couldn't focus on, to now.

I shouldn't go, *couldn't* go. I shouldn't even *want* to go.

Even knowing this, I threw back the covers and went to my closet. I pulled out a long cardigan, my brain battling itself as I shrugged on the sweater and walked out of the room.

I headed to Keira's room first. She was a heavy sleeper, like me. Nothing woke her and nothing used to wake me, at least when Tim was in the house. Now I woke at the barest sound.

I pushed open her door and whispered, "Keira?"

I looked at her bed, no movement.

I walked in. She had the room at the front of the house, Kate's room sandwiched between the hall and mine. Keira's room was girlie, not frilly, but full of pinks, purples, daisies and posters of boy bands and teenage vampires. Her clothes were strewn on the floor, her desk a mess. Her curtains were drawn, but I could see the darkness of her hair against her pillow. Tim's hair. Both of them got Tim's hair, Tim's eyes, Tim's lean frame. They'd lucked out.

I stifled the urge to touch her hair, kiss her cheek, left the room and crossed the hall to Kate's room.

Kate was like Tim. She slept light. She was a worrier, like Tim and now, like me.

When Tim was alive, I didn't worry, not ever. I felt, if we were all together, nothing could harm us. We'd take our knocks, but we'd survive them. This feeling had a lot to do with Tim taking care of most everything. This feeling was now gone because he was gone, not taking care of most everything and because we'd never be all together again.

I pushed open her door. Kate's room couldn't have been more different than her sister's. Champagne colored walls, black accents, sophisticated except for the posters on the walls. They were for bands I'd never heard of, but whoever they were, they actually wrote their own music and played their own instruments. Her floor was clear, her stuff organized.

I only whispered her name when I was close to her bed.

"Kate."

I saw her dark hair on her pillow and she didn't move either.

I wanted her to move, to roll to her back and say, "Mom, stop acting like a slut."

She didn't. She slept and I left her to it.

I walked to the side kitchen door and slid on some Crocs. Then I unarmed the alarm. With my hand to the door handle, the sane, good mom, good person part of my brain won out. I dropped the handle and walked toward my room, but my feet took me right by my bedroom door to the sliding glass door at the back of the study. My fingers unlocked it, slid it to the side and I stepped out into the chill night air. I closed the door and walked to the steps of the deck, down them and into the grass.

I turned to Joe's house.

Through the dark, I hurried to his house knowing this was wrong. It was stupid. He was probably asleep by now anyway.

But my feet kept moving.

His deck was deeper than mine, jutting out further, but it didn't travel the length of his house like mine did. Mine was rectangular, his was square. The steps on mine were at the front, his at the side and I ran up them, counting them as I went. Four steps. Then I found myself standing at his sliding glass door.

There was no light on. If he was waiting for me, wouldn't he turn on the light?

He would, anyone would. No one who shoveled a woman's snow from her drive would make her meet him for a clandestine sexual assignation at his unlit dark deck. In fact, his whole house was dark.

It was clandestine but he wouldn't want me to sprain my ankle, would he?

No, he was sleeping. Time to go.

I turned and headed toward the stairs and my heart skipped when I heard the sliding door open but my feet kept moving toward escape. I was almost at the stairs when I was caught with an arm around my waist and pulled back into the heat of his long, hard body.

His rumbly voice sounded in my ear. "Where you goin', buddy?"

"Joe," I whispered, my voice trembling and I could say no more.

He let my waist go but grabbed my hand and yanked me into the house. Sliding the door to, he turned to me and bent. Lifting me at the knees and waist, he carried me through his living room, down the hall and turned right. Then he carried me to his bed and threw me on it. I bounced only once because, if there was going to be a second time, this was thwarted when his body came down on mine.

His hand was in my cardigan at the shoulder, pulling it down.

"I—" I began.

"Shut up," he cut me off.

"Okay," I whispered.

Then his mouth came down on mine.

I was on my knees, Joe underneath me, his hands at my hips, pulling them down to his face.

I had been bent over him, using my mouth and hand on his beautiful shaft at the same time his mouth was on me. But what he was doing between my legs with his mouth took my full concentration. So I'd given up, and when I did, Joe had turned me around and settled me back down.

Now I arched my back as the orgasm washed through me. He tugged my hips, his mouth kept working me, voracious, prolonging the climax exquisitely.

Even when I was done, Joe lapped at me and that felt so good, I had to lean forward and clutch the headboard or I would topple over.

Then he moved me, pushing me off but not letting me go, sliding me down his body so I was on top of him, my forehead in his neck, his hands moving on my skin.

He wasn't done, which was so shocking it could even be record-breaking. I could feel him hard against me and that was impossible. Since I walked in (or, more aptly, been pulled in, carried in, then thrown on his bed), we'd gone at each other like teenagers. I'd had four orgasms, Joe, three. I'd lost count of the positions, lost track of the sensations. Each time we finished, his hands and mouth kept at me, that hollow feeling would come back and I'd need it sated. I'd need to feed the hunger that overwhelmed me, a hunger for him. I'd do anything to satisfy it and I did.

I felt no embarrassment once it started. I didn't feel like a slut, a bad mother, a terrible person. I didn't worry about my nudity or if he liked what I was doing. This shit was natural, like I was born to be in Joe Callahan's bed and it was natural to him too, like Joe Callahan was born to be in me.

When his hand slid up my side and in, curling around my breast, I lifted my head to kiss him but caught sight of his alarm clock.

"Shit," I whispered, maybe the first word I said since he caught me outside other than "Joe," "Faster," "Harder," "Yes," and "More."

Joe hadn't said much at all. Then again, he was using his mouth for far better things.

Now his neck twisted and he looked at the clock then at me.

"What?"

"I've gotta get home."

"Why?"

"I have two girls."

"They awake at six o'clock?"

I smiled at him and, weirdly, his big, warm body stilled under mine and his eyes dropped to my mouth when I did.

"Okay, no, there's no way they're awake," I answered. "But we also have nosy neighbors."

His eyes slid up to mine and his hand slid from my breast, around my side, up my back and into my hair as he asked, "So?"

"So, Tina Blackstone is a bitch. She sees me coming from your house in the morning wearing a nightie and a cardigan, she'd talk."

He didn't respond but he didn't need to, his face said it all.

Therefore I answered his unspoken repeat of, *So?*

"I know *you* don't care but, like I said, I've got two girls. It wouldn't be good if Tina Blackstone talked." I pulled myself further up his body and touched my lips to his then said softly, "I've got to go."

His hand fisted in my hair and the pads of his fingers dug into my hip, just for a second, then his arms went loose.

But that second counted.

It counted a whole helluva lot.

I slid off him and scrambled beside the bed, feeling suddenly conscious of my nudity. I gave him my back as I pulled my undies up then slipped my nightie over my head. I shrugged on my cardigan at the same time I twisted my feet, toeing my Crocs to right them and sliding them on.

"Buddy," Joe called, and I turned to see him lying on his side, his elbow in the bed, his head in his hand not, obviously, conscious of his nudity, or at least not self-conscious about it.

I didn't blame him.

His body was far more beautiful out of clothes than in them. Like his face, its perfection not marred by the scars but instead made more appealing, his long, lean, muscled body was not spoiled by the long, jagged white gash that sliced diagonally across his tight abs and the creased, darkened circle of skin halfway between his right pectoral and his shoulder.

"Come here," he growled softly.

My feet took me to him. I put a knee to the bed and leaned in and Joe did the rest. His hand, lying on the bed, came up, hooked me behind the head and he pulled me closer. So close, my mouth was on his.

"I want you back tonight," he ordered.

He wanted me back.

I smiled against his mouth.

When I did, his eyes grew intense then his head slanted. I lost sight of his eyes when mine closed because he kissed me hard, open-mouthed and so long, he came up from the bed, his other arm curved around me and he pulled me to him. When I landed on him, he twisted me so my back was to the bed and kept kissing me.

His kisses were so good, I forgot I was supposed to be leaving until his lips disengaged from mine and his face disappeared in my neck.

"Don't we have nosy neighbors?" he asked my neck.

"Shit!" I cried, rolled him to his back and tore out of his arms.

I was nearly on my feet by the side of the bed before I stopped, put a hand back in the mattress, one at his scarred cheek, leaned in and gave him a quick kiss.

Then I gained my feet and, not looking back, I ran from the room, down the hall, through his living room, out the sliding glass door and to my house.

I was feeling so fucking great, instead of running, I could have skipped.

The day passed like it was coated with molasses.

I'd thought to get a nap, but once I got home from Joe's, even though I'd had virtually no sleep for two nights, I found I was incredibly energized.

I stripped my bed. I put in laundry. I made a grocery list. I paid bills. I took a shower and did myself up like I always did, even after Tim died.

Tim liked my hair smoothed out with the hair dryer. He liked it when I put on makeup even if he preferred it light. Tim liked it when I made an effort with clothes. Tim said I was the sexiest cop's wife in history and he said it in a way where I knew he believed it completely and was proud of that fact. He liked it when I'd come into the station. He got off on the fact that the other guys found me attractive (or, at least, he told me they did). I was his, he told me, and he had something beautiful, he told me that too. Never, not once, not even when I was heavy with Kate and Keira, did he make me feel anything but beautiful.

It was something that I forced myself to do after he died, keeping up my appearance. It was for him but it was also for me. A way of not giving up when I wanted to do nothing but that, give up, give in, stay down, beaten.

Though that morning, I made a bit of an extra effort.

The girls got up and I made them pancakes. They did their chores, cleaning their rooms and I went to the grocery store. I was going to make my breaded pork chops and spiced rice, Tim and Keira's favorite. It took forever to make but it would be a treat because Kate loved it too. Though Kate's favorite was my seafood risotto, my favorite as well. They'd started as recipes from a magazine, but after years of experimentation, I made them both even better, therefore I considered them all mine.

This was my thing, something else Tim would brag about. Our garden was the most beautiful one on our block (even I had to admit that) and Tim thought my cooking was the bomb and he bragged about both freely. He liked to have people over and we did all the time, but he said it was so he could show me off.

The seafood would be too expensive, unfortunately, so it was going to have to be pork chops.

When I went to the grocery store, Joe's truck was there. When I came back, it was gone. This made my stomach clutch with fear and it made me act like an idiot. As I put away groceries, vacuumed, folded clothes, loaded and unloaded the washer and dryer and did ironing, I found reasons to go to the kitchen window and look out to his drive, checking to make sure he came home.

But he had to come home, for me. I might have only ever had Tim but I wasn't stupid. A man like Joe Callahan didn't wait up for a woman until two o'clock in the morning. He didn't throw her on his bed and have sex with her for four straight hours. He didn't react that way, reflexively, especially when she told him she had to leave. And he didn't want her to come back.

Unless he wanted *her*.

Which, I told myself, all meant he wanted me. Not for a convenient fuck, there was more going on here and I knew it.

That bitterness and humiliation had washed away and something else replaced it. Something I didn't expect, not from Joe. Hell, not from anyone. But it was something that I liked.

Tim and I had great sex our whole married life. I was not his first, he had a girl before me, but I was his last. We'd taught each other everything we knew. We were open, honest, even adventurous, and it was regular and often. Not like clockwork, but spontaneous, fun, sexy. We both had healthy appetites, Tim especially, and he loved it that I met his appetite (though, he didn't brag about that, or at least not that I knew about).

But he'd never fucked me on the hood of a car, one second working on an engine, the next going at it with me like it was necessary for his existence. He'd never fucked me for four hours straight like he was just as hungry for it as I was. Like he had to get his fill for fear the beauty of it would be torn away, never to be had again.

And I understood that now. God, did I.

I didn't take anything for granted, not anymore.

I was going to get my fill.

When I went to the kitchen to start the pork chops, I saw Joe's truck in the drive and instead of that settling inside me, my body electrified. I felt the specter of his mouth, his hands, his shaft driving inside me and it was so strong, I had to lean into the counter to hold myself up when my knees went weak.

Shit, he was like a drug and I realized I'd been jonesing for him all day.

I also realized, dumping the breadcrumbs and spices into the Ziploc bag, preparing the breading for the chops, that I liked him.

He shoveled my snow. He saw me outside shoveling my snow. He knew I'd given up the chore to see to Kate and Dane and he'd finished it for me, making it safe for me and my girls to pull out of our drive.

And he remembered the conversation about the condoms. And, even though I was guessing it was well out of character, he'd tried to explain his behavior with Kenzie and he'd had a good reason to be angry, even though he took it too far in my opinion. But he was an aggressively masculine man, she had to know that and she'd played with it. She should have known better. She should have seen that coming.

And he'd waited up for me, until late, and he didn't want me to go.

I liked that he didn't talk much and I liked that he let his face speak for him. I liked how big he was and that he could carry me around and he did, that he could pick me up and plant me in his truck and he did. I liked that he was rough with me. No, I loved that. I wasn't the mother of his children. I was a woman, a woman he wanted and he made that abundantly clear and I liked that too.

And I liked that sometimes he looked at me and there was something working in his eyes, something I didn't quite get but whatever it was, it was about me.

And it was good.

I just knew it.

Joe Callahan couldn't be more different than Tim Winters, and to my shock I was okay with that. I wasn't stupid enough to think after the last two crazy days that Joe was going to be the next love of my life. But I wanted this. I wanted him. I wanted to explore what was happening and I wanted it a lot.

And I couldn't wait to get back to his house, his bed, *him.*

Dane came over for pork chops, and after he helped Kate do the dishes (another checkmark on the good column for Dane). Then he and Kate settled in the recliners in the study to do their homework. I sat with Keira on the couch in the living room and read at the same time Keira was watching TV and I watched Dane and Kate.

They were cute together. Dane was a handsome kid and he complemented my pretty daughter. And he was gentle with Kate. I liked the way he looked at her when she was talking like there was nothing else he wanted to do but hear what she had to say. But I especially liked it when she didn't know he was looking at her like he thought she was the most beautiful thing he'd ever seen and he couldn't believe his luck.

So, okay, I liked my daughter's boyfriend. I smiled to myself, tilted my head to my book, didn't read a word and felt that hollowing out of my belly.

Just a little longer to wait.

I pulled on my violet underwear that was liberally dosed with black lace. In fact, the ass of the panties was all lace; there was only a lace-edged triangle at the front. The demi-bra had such a deep edge of lace you could see my nipples through it. The bottom of the cup and the straps were violet satin, however.

Over these I pulled on my black satin nightie, no lace or other adornment. It was just low cut so you could see the bra and had slits to my hips on the sides so you could see the panties if I moved.

I'd bought these for Tim about two weeks before he was murdered and never worn them. I was holding on to them for a special occasion like, say, when the girls were spending the night at his parents' house. He'd liked my sexy undies and nighties and I'd made it a habit to wear only them for him.

After he died, I'd meant to throw the lingerie out.

Now I was glad I didn't.

I yanked on the black satin robe that went with the nightie, not wanting to wear Tim's robe to Joe's. Tim's robe could stay on the door when I was with Joe. It might be chill outside but Joe wasn't that far away.

Before I left my dark room, I bit my lip and put my fingers to my wedding rings. I hadn't taken them off, never considered it, but I wondered if I should now.

My eyes went to the picture on my nightstand and I felt something move in me then settle. It wasn't painful. I'd already had the pain, nearly a year and a half of it.

It was life.

"You know I'll always love you," I whispered to the picture.

The picture didn't reply but I knew Tim knew. I'd want this for him too if it was me who was gone and him who remained, though it would totally suck. I wouldn't want him to be alone though. I'd want him to be excited, to feel alive, to live his life and find happiness.

But I left my wedding rings on. I wasn't ready for that.

I walked through the dark house. It was far earlier, just eleven thirty, but the girls were out, I'd already checked. I disarmed the alarm and looked at the tangle of shoes by the door. None of them would complement my outfit so I decided against shoes.

I hustled to the back sliding glass door, opened it, slid through it, closed it and then hopped down the steps, running slowly across the yard, the spring dew cold on my bare feet.

His house was dark again, no light on outside, but I didn't pause. I skipped up Joe's deck steps and before I hit the top, his sliding glass door was opened.

He stood in it, bare-chested, wearing jeans, the top button undone. My breath caught and my step slowed as I walked to him.

He didn't move from the door when I stopped in front of him and I watched, holding my breath, as his eyes travel the length of me.

Then his arm shot out and hooked around my waist. He pulled me inside and slid the door to.

His fingers glided into the hair at the side of my head and his chin dipped down so his face was close to mine.

"Baby," he whispered. "You aren't wearing any shoes."

He called me "baby."

And he was worried my feet were cold.

Yes, something was happening here.

I melted into him and put my hands on his neck.

"I couldn't find any that went with my outfit," I explained quietly.

His hand tightened against my scalp and I watched in sheer fascination as he grinned. I'd never seen it but from afar and that close, it was un-fucking-believable.

My stomach dipped, but I didn't get to enjoy the view for very long because his fingers pressed in, pulling my head up. I went to my toes and he kissed me.

The lingerie was pretty much a wasted effort. Joe liked it, I knew, because he growled when he saw it, but he didn't take much time to enjoy it before he took it off.

He was just as energetic as last night and as insatiable and I decided he probably got a nap.

I had not, so after round two, I wanted more but I couldn't hack it. I made this point by sliding off his body, snuggling into his side, wrapping my arm around his belly and resting my head on his shoulder.

His fingers gripped my hip.

"Buddy?" he called.

"Sleepy," I mumbled.

His fingers gripped my hip harder then he turned into me, my head slid from his shoulder to his pillow and his other arm stole around me.

"Violet."

"Yeah?" I whispered.

He didn't speak but his body seemed weirdly tense.

I tilted my head back and looked at him.

"Joe?"

"No one calls me Joe."

"Isn't that your name?"

"Yeah."

"Do you not like it?"

He didn't respond.

"I like the name Joe," I told him, moving in closer.

His arms got tight.

I kissed the base of his throat then my head settled back into the pillow and I fell asleep.

# Three

## Done

Joe Callahan woke with Violet in his arms.

This didn't happen, ever. Even if he took a woman to his home, which was rare, she didn't spend the night. On the more frequent occasion when he was in their bed, he left after he was done no matter how creative they got with asking him to stay.

He fucked them; he didn't sleep with them, no exceptions.

He dipped his chin while opening his eyes and heard her hair move on the pillow. When he caught sight of her face, she was looking up at him.

Good fucking Christ, she was beautiful.

"Hi," she whispered, her voice as sleepy as her fucking gorgeous face and he felt that one, single, quiet word in his gut and in his dick.

He didn't respond and she didn't seem to mind. She snuggled into him, tucking her face in his throat but her hand slid up his chest, her fingers moving to run gently along his jaw.

He felt her touch in his gut and dick too.

This was a mistake. A huge, fucking, mammoth mistake. Just like Kenzie but far worse.

He knew it.

He knew it the minute he kicked Kenzie out of his house, turned to Violet, saw her in those fucking ridiculous boots, sexy-as-hell nightgown and ratty robe and realized who she was, what she was and that he wanted her.

He knew it when he walked across his yard while she was shoveling the snow and he explained himself, something he never fucking did.

He knew it when he told Colt he'd take her home, knowing when he did he was going to fuck her and standing at her side in the bar, waiting for his opening, which she gave him again and again, looking so fucking cute, sucking on her straw and then, Jesus, knotting a cherry stem with her goddamned tongue.

He knew it when she went hot for him the minute he kissed her then she begged for it rough.

He knew it when he fucked her on his 'Stang, no control, his brain in his dick.

He knew it when she crossed her yard for him that first night he had her in his bed.

He knew it the first time she took him in her mouth, not sloppy, fucking Christ, the woman could use her mouth.

He knew it when she came on his face, no inhibitions, shit, but she was unbelievable and she was his. His. All of her, his.

But, most of all, he knew it the first time she smiled at him.

He knew this was a mistake.

"I need to go," she mumbled into his throat and tilted her head back, pushing up a bit to come face to face, her hand cupping his jaw.

She did need to go, he needed her to get the fuck out of there but he still didn't loosen his arms.

Then she tipped it.

"Do you want to come over for dinner tonight?"

There it was.

"I'm done," he said and watched her blink.

"What?"

"Done," he repeated, and her head pressed into the pillow as she tilted it to the side in confusion.

"Sorry, I don't—"

"With this. It was good, buddy, but I'm done."

He felt her body lock in his arms as the softness of sleep and sex faded from her face and shock and pain replaced it.

His arms, not taking direction from his brain, tightened.

"Done?" she whispered and that shock and pain was heavy in that word.

"Buddy—" he started, but she moved.

She tore out of his arms and crawled over him so fast, even if he tried, he couldn't grab her.

But he didn't try.

She pulled her robe on, didn't bother with her underwear and nightgown, didn't even pick them up from the floor. She left them where they were.

"Violet," he called, but she belted her robe and he watched her run, the robe billowing out behind her as she went.

He rolled to his back and put his hands to his face, swiping them hard against his skin as he listened to the sliding glass door open then shut.

It cost him to stay still, on his back, in his bed and not go after her. It carved through his gut, the pain acute. The only way to get rid of it was to fucking move, to follow her, to go and get her, to drag her right back.

But he took the pain and stayed put.

Then he rolled to the side and he could smell the scent of her fucking hair on his pillow.

# Four

## The Mall

Cal barely got the door to his truck shut when he heard his name.

His eyes went to the sidewalk and he saw Colt, dripping with sweat and coming back from a run, slowing to a walk as he turned up Cal's drive.

Colt was breathing heavy but not hard. The man was in shape, even six years older than Cal, who was thirty-nine. Colt was built tough and stayed that way.

"Yo," Cal greeted.

"Can we talk?"

Cal examined Colt's face and he nodded at what he saw and led the way to his house, not looking toward Violet's. It had been two weeks since that morning. He'd left the next day and hadn't been back.

He let them in and Cal went to the fridge in the kitchen. He took out a bottle of water and tossed it to Colt who caught it. Then he took out a beer for himself and twisted off the cap, flicking it into the open trash bin.

"We got a problem," Colt announced after he sucked back some water.

"Yeah?" Cal asked and he took a pull of his beer.

"In the neighborhood," Colt went on, and Cal wasn't surprised.

Tina Blackstone had hooked up with Cory Jones, a match made in hell. They'd been together on and off for a while at the same time Cory kept going back to his on and off wife. It wasn't pretty and it could get loud, though he wasn't around much to hear it. Cal wasn't surprised it had escalated into what Colt described as a problem. Tina was a bitch and Cory was a fuckwad.

"What's up?" Cal asked.

"It's Violet," Colt answered, and Cal felt that sharp pain carve through his gut.

"Violet?"

Colt leaned a hip against the counter, nodded and took another slug from his water, his face set at one emotion—unhappy.

Dropping his hand, he explained, "Got a call from a Detective Barry Pryor, Chicago PD."

Fuck.

He didn't want to know but he asked all the same, "About Violet?"

"Yeah," Colt nodded. "Pryor was her husband's partner."

*Fuck!*

Past tense, that was not fucking good.

"Was?" Cal asked.

"Her husband was murdered, a hit. He was investigating a local big man, got too close. They whacked him about a year and a half ago."

Cal clenched his teeth and looked out his front windows. He couldn't see her house from his vantage point but that was where his eyes aimed.

Cop husband. Murdered. A hit. Now she was alone, shoveling her own goddamned snow and raising two teenage girls.

Jesus fucking Christ.

"It isn't over," Colt told him and Cal's eyes went to his friend.

"Come again?"

"Pryor says that Violet caught this guy's eye."

Cal's whole body went tight.

She could do that, Violet could. She could catch anyone's eye. He knew this because she caught his.

"Caught his eye?" Cal asked in a low voice.

"Yeah. Bad news, this guy. Thinks he's untouchable. Apparently, while Vi's husband was investigating him, he was investigating her husband. Found out about her, liked what he saw, took to her. Pryor thinks that could even be why this guy moved on her husband."

"You are fuckin' shittin' me."

Colt shook his head. "No," he said. "Got in her business after the hit, if you can believe that shit, made it clear he was interested after he ordered the hit that killed her fuckin' husband. Made it so clear, it got unhealthy and she packed up her girls and moved away."

Cal didn't take his eyes from Colt as he took another pull of beer and he suspected he now looked unhappy too. Not unhappy like Colt, a lot more fucking unhappy.

When he dropped his hand, he asked, "He been to town?"

"Nope, but Pryor is close to her, her family. She told her brother a cop lived across the street, her brother talked to Pryor, told him to call us and give us a heads up so we could keep an eye out. Says she hasn't had a visit here, but the brother and Pryor think he's not done with her."

Cal ran his tongue along his lower lip and then clenched his teeth again.

Colt kept talking. "We need to keep an eye out, Cal. You should go over, talk to her. I know she's got an alarm but it was installed before she moved in. You should give it a once over."

"That's not gonna happen," Cal replied and Colt stared at him.

"What?"

"She's not gonna let me look at her system."

"Cal, she's cool. She'll probably be grateful."

"She's not my biggest fan."

Colt's eyes narrowed with surprise. "Why not?"

Cal didn't answer and he didn't take his eyes from Colt.

He watched Colt's body go on alert. "Christ, you fucked her?"

Cal still didn't answer.

"You fucked a cop's widow?" Colt sounded disbelieving and pissed. Then again, he was a cop. He'd feel that like no one else.

"Didn't know she was a cop's widow."

"Fuck, Cal, loss is written all over her," Colt clipped, definitely pissed.

"Not in your business, Colt, don't see that shit like you do."

"Bullshit."

It was. It was bullshit. He'd seen it in Violet's eyes, her face, the way she held her body, the dead in her voice when she spoke, and, just like fucking Bonnie, he'd wanted to fix it. Bonnie's shit was different, life started bad for her but in the end Bonnie's shit was of her own making. Not a tragedy forced on her, one she created. He couldn't fix Bonnie. He'd tried, he'd failed. He wasn't going to go there again.

"Get her out," Cal told Colt. "You and Feb ask her and her girls over, let me know when she's gone. I'll recon her house and report to you. You can work something out for her with Chip."

Colt didn't answer this time, just stared at him.

"And I'll keep an eye out," Cal finished.

Colt returned to their earlier subject. "It's done with her?"

"What?"

"You done with her? You finished it?" Colt pushed.

"Yeah."

Colt stared at him again then shook his head and took a drink of water.

Then he looked back at Cal. "Not my business, but, man, are you fuckin' crazy?"

Cal's body got tight again.

"Yeah, it's not your business, Colt."

"Known you awhile, Cal."

"Still, not your business."

"She's sweet. She can be funny when she forgets to be sad. She's good to her girls, a great mom and fuckin' gorgeous. Her ass is nearly as fine as Feb's."

He was wrong about that. Violet's ass was far superior to Feb's. Feb had a sweet ass but Violet's entire body was built to make a man want to fuck her, want it so much, made it hard to think of anything else.

No, it wasn't only that, it was built to make a man want to fuck her and it was built to be fucked. Her tits, her ass, her cunt, pure fuckin' heaven.

"Noticed that," Cal remarked.

"And still, you fucked her and moved on?"

Cal was getting angry. "Like I said, not your business."

It was then Colt made a mistake.

"She's not Bonnie."

Cal straightened and his body got even tighter.

"We're not talkin' about this."

Colt disagreed. "Bonnie was a long fuckin' time ago."

"Colt, stand down. This isn't your goddamned business," Cal warned, his control slipping.

Colt stared at him, his mouth tight, his eyes angry. Then he shook his head in a way that made the point he thought Cal was an asshole and an idiot. This pissed Cal off but he let it alone. He liked Colt, respected him, lived across from him a long time, knew him before Colt moved across the street. Colt had even been there during Cal's nightmare. Cal had always liked and respected him.

"I'll let you know when you can slip in and I'd appreciate it, you stay alert," Colt was letting it alone too.

Cal nodded.

Colt nodded back, lifted the water in a gesture of gratitude and said, "Later."

Then he left.

Cal put his beer to the counter and walked to his second bedroom. It was practically empty. His dad's old medical bed was in there from when his dad was sick, not much else.

He opened the curtains and looked out the window at Violet's house.

Her Mustang wasn't there, her daughter's Fiesta was. It was four thirty. Violet was probably at work but her daughters were home from school, likely alone and he hoped to Christ her alarm was programmed for doors and windows and her girls armed it when they got home.

As he stared at her house, thoughts crowded his head.

Violet had a dead husband, an asshole obsessing about her and a neighbor who fucked her over.

Christ, but he was a dick. He should never have touched her.

He walked back through his house, opened the side kitchen door nabbing the key off the hook as he went. He opened the garage door and moved behind his 'Stang to the back and started digging through his boxes of equipment. It was all shit, that was why it was back there and not in use somewhere.

He went back to the house, locked the kitchen door and went out the front door, locking that.

He walked to his truck, swung in and headed to Indianapolis.

It was the next day and Cal was standing in Colt's yard by Colt's GMC, talking to Colt.

"You bought the shit?" Colt asked, his eyebrows up.

"New system, Chip can pick it up, put it in," Cal answered. "Coupla things on order but they'll be in soon."

"You haven't reconned the house."

"Been in that house before, Colt, a fuckin' million times when the Williamses lived there. I know what she needs."

Colt stared at him a second before he nodded and asked, "Is Chip gonna be able to install your system?"

This was a good question. Cal knew Chip, only boy in town who installed security and his work was good. But Cal had bought some serious equipment for Violet's house, the like your normal suburban folk couldn't afford and didn't even know existed. But the people who paid for his services not only knew it existed, they demanded it and they needed it with the sick fucks who invaded their lives. Chip might not be able to work with it.

"I'll go through it with him. What he doesn't know, you get Violet out and I'll install it."

"She isn't Kenzie Elise, Cal, you got her top of the line, it's doubtful she'll be able to pay for it," Colt pointed out.

"I'll work that out with Chip."

In other words, words he wasn't going to give Colt, she wasn't paying shit.

Colt studied him and Cal let him then Colt nodded again.

"I'll talk to Vi, then I'll talk to Chip," Colt said.

"Let me know," Cal replied. "I've got a job I can't postpone means I'll be outta town again in a few days. He needs to put her top of his list and come and get the equipment. If I need to go in, it needs to be soon."

"Got it," Colt opened the door to his GMC and explained, "Gotta get to the station."

"Yeah."

"Later."

Cal lifted his chin and turned while Colt climbed into his truck. He walked across Colt's yard but his eyes were on Violet's house. This was because her daughter was standing in the drive, her butt to the door of the Mustang which was parked behind the Fiesta, her eyes were on him.

Fucking great.

He crossed the street, walked past Tina's house and was halfway past Violet's when her daughter skipped to the end of the drive and called, "Hey, Mr. Callahan."

Jesus. She called him Mr. Callahan.

He lifted his chin.

"We're goin' to the mall," she informed him, and since she was speaking to him and she was Violet's kid, instead of walking right by her like he would normally do, he stopped.

Even though he didn't respond, she took his continued presence as indication she should keep talking. "Then we're goin' to dinner and then a movie. Mom's gonna spend Uncle Sam's money that he gave her when he was here."

Cal had no response to this and he wanted to be the fuck out of there by the time Violet got out of the house.

He looked to her place to gauge how much time he had and saw the older girl walking out, which he thought was a healthy signal to get a move on, but he didn't. Finding himself curious, he looked between Violet's girls.

Neither of them looked like Violet. They were pretty but they didn't get their mother's rich, thick, dark hair with that auburn tint to it, they didn't get her curves and they didn't get her green eyes. Their hair was nice; it was also thick and long. They had nice eyes and decent bodies, but they were too thin in a way that, even though they were young, he knew they wouldn't fill out. They must look like their dad.

Sucked for them. They were pretty and they'd get prettier but they'd never be knockouts like their mother.

"We already spent Uncle Sam's gift cards," the younger one kept speaking and Cal's eyes went back to her. "Kate and me. I got these shorts and a bunch of other stuff." She pointed to her shorts but Cal's eyes didn't go to her shorts, they went to the drive.

Violet was there and she was wearing that cute, little jeans skirt that fit tight at her ass and hips and hit her a couple inches above her knees. It was the one he'd fucked her in.

Christ.

She had stopped dead, keys in her hand, purse suspended at her forearm, her hand had stilled in the act of draping it over her shoulder. She was staring at him, her lips parted, her face pale, her eyes wide and he felt that look, her stillness. It locked in his chest, it didn't feel good and he detested the feeling.

She was wearing purple, she was always in purple. This time it was a light purple blouse with little, short, poofy sleeves. The shirt fit tight at her ribs and showed a hint of cleavage because it fit tight at her tits too. Her hair was down. It was long, not as long as her girls, she wore it to just above her bra strap. It was gleaming and sleek but flipped at the layers. He knew how thick it was, how soft, and his hand itched to fist in it.

Taking his mind off that, his eyes traveled the length of her and stopped at her shoes, which were purple too, much darker than her top, two thin straps, one at the toes, one around her ankle and a strap that connected the two. It went up the middle of her foot and it had a bunch of flowers on it. The shoes were low, not heeled, and they looked fucking great on her. He liked his women in heels but he liked those purple shoes on Violet better than any heels he'd seen in his whole fucking life.

"Hey!" her younger girl shouted, his eyes sliced to her and he saw she was watching him closely. He also saw that her excited, teenage girl act was just that, an act. She'd seen him checking out her mother and what she said next confirmed it just as it confirmed she was a little schemer. "You wanna come?"

"Keira!" both the older one and Violet cried, the older daughter loud, Violet on a snap.

"What?" the younger girl asked, trying to look innocent as she twisted her head to her mother and sister. "He'll have fun." She looked back at him and grinned. "We Winters girls, we're *loads* of fun."

"I'm sure Mr. Callahan has better things to do than go to the mall," Violet stated and walked to the Mustang, hitching her purse on her shoulder.

"Do you have better things to do, Mr. Callahan?" the girl asked.

Cal just stared at her.

"Malls are a blast," she told him.

He didn't reply mainly because he didn't agree, not even a little bit.

"And we're goin' to The Cheesecake Factory for dinner and it's great there."

"Keira, seriously, leave Mr. Callahan alone," Violet ordered. "Get in the car."

She was standing in her opened door, the keys in her hand, her eyes on her daughter. The other girl was standing in the other door without the keys but her stance and her gaze were an exact replica of her mother's.

"And we're going to see the new Nicole Bolton movie. It's supposed to be *awesome*," the younger girl went on, completely ignoring her mother.

"Keira!" Violet called sharply, and her voice jolted Cal to action.

He moved and when he moved, he moved toward Violet. He didn't know why but he did and as he did, he watched her body get tight and watching it made his jaw get tight.

He made it to her. She tipped her head back to look at him, her gorgeous face filled with panic which he took advantage of when he tugged her keys out of her fingers.

"I'm drivin'."

"Yippee!" the younger girl screeched.

"What?" Violet whispered.

"Move outta the door, buddy." She blinked, the panic gone, confusion in her expression and she stayed put so he told her. "Can't drive, you on my lap."

Her body jerked and the confusion cleared, her face shifting straight to angry. He'd seen that look on her face before when she'd thrown his business card and the fifty at him. She wouldn't like to know it but her display of attitude was hot, then and now.

"Why is Mr. Callahan driving?" the older girl asked and Cal looked to his right to see she'd moved out of the way and the younger one was pushing into the backseat.

"Mr. Callahan is—" Violet started to speak to her daughter but Cal cut her off.

"Cal," he turned to the girl and repeated, "Cal."

"My girls don't call their elders by their Christian names," Violet told him, her voice ice, and when Cal turned back to her, her face was ice too.

"We could call him Uncle Cal," the younger girl suggested, her head and shoulders shoved over the driver seat so she could look at them.

Christ. Uncle Cal was worse than Mr. Callahan.

"Can we go? If we don't, we'll miss the movie or we'll have to cut the shopping short," the older girl asked, resignation in her tone and impatience. Then she shoved into the backseat and pulled the passenger seat back into place.

"Yeah, or we'll miss the chance to have cheesecake at The Cheesecake Factory," the younger one said, her eyes were on him as she finished, "Obviously, that's the best part."

Cal looked at Violet.

"Get in, buddy."

"But—"

He leaned into her, she reared back into the door but he ignored that even though he felt that in his chest too, and repeated, "Violet, get in."

She glared at him then slid by him, careful not to touch him as she did so. Then he watched her stomp around the hood of the Mustang and get in, slamming her door.

Cal folded himself into her car and had to adjust the seat, the wheel was practically in his crotch. Violet was tall, like her girls and unlike any woman he'd ever had, but she wasn't nearly as tall as him.

He closed the door and settled in. The new Mustangs were sweet, not as sweet as his '68 GT but still sweet. Violet, he found, had as good taste in cars as she had in clothes, shoes, underwear and nightgowns.

He slid the key in the ignition and fired up the car. It roared to life, he threw it in reverse and pulled out of her drive.

"Hey, Cal, do you know any of the Buckley Boys?" the younger girl, Keira, asked from behind him.

"Just because he does what he does, Keira, doesn't mean he knows everyone who's famous," the older girl, Kate, informed her sister.

"I know 'em," Cal said and heard both girls pull in their breath.

He did know them. They were all little shits. A boy band of five brothers, thought the sun shone out of their asses. They'd paid huge and he'd taken a special job, leading a detail of bodyguards again, covering them for an event. They were individually and collectively such a fuckin' pain he turned down the next job their manager offered him.

"Really?" Keira breathed.

"Yep," Cal replied.

"What're they like?" Keira asked.

"You don't wanna know," Cal answered.

"No, really, I do. I *do* wanna know," she told him, and she sounded like she did really want to know.

He tried to find a way to explain it without using the words "assholes," "fuckwads" or "dickheads."

"You met 'em, you wouldn't think much of 'em." This was met with silence, so, since he was stopped at a stop sign, Cal asked, "I might need to know where I'm goin'."

"Keystone at the Crossing," Kate answered, and Cal looked to his right to see Violet had her purse in her lap, her fingers clutching it so tightly he could see white at her knuckles and her head was turned to look out the side window.

She didn't like him there, in her car, with her girls, with her. He knew it just as he knew he shouldn't be there.

But he was, even though he had no fucking clue why he was.

Except for the fact that some asshole was out there, some asshole who had killed her husband but wanted her, and Cal didn't like the idea of Violet and her kids going to the mall, to dinner, to a movie, without protection.

So he was there.

"Right," he muttered, put the car in gear and turned toward Keystone at the Crossing.

"Mawdy, you goin' to Lucky?" Kate asked her mother.

"No, baby," Violet answered softly, and Cal felt her two words in his chest too *and* his gut. This wasn't unpleasant. It was nostalgic and it was so strong, his hand tightened on the wheel.

He remembered his mother using a voice like that with him a long time ago. Her girls were lucky they had that, Violet's soft voice, her calling them "baby."

The fuck of it was, however their dad talked to them, they didn't have.

"Why not?" Keira asked.

"Not my thing," Violet replied.

"You'd look hot in Lucky clothes," Keira announced and then asked, "Don't you think, Cal?"

He had no idea what she was talking about.

But he didn't have to answer, Violet spoke. "It's Mr. Callahan."

"They can call me Cal," Cal stated.

"They're not gonna call you Cal," Violet returned.

He looked at her to see she'd turned her head to him then he looked back at the road.

"Why not?"

"They need to respect their elders."

"I don't like Mr. Callahan," Cal told her.

"Then we'll call you Uncle Cal," Keira put in.

"Keira—" Violet started.

"Cal'll do," Cal cut Violet off, not about to be called Uncle Cal either.

"Joe, they're not gonna call you Cal," Violet repeated.

There it was. Joe.

He didn't feel that in his chest or his gut, he felt her calling him Joe in his dick.

His dad's name was Joe too. So, since birth, everyone had called him Cal. According to his dad, his mother had come up with the nickname.

But Bonnie'd called him Joe. She was the only one who did. It irritated him the first couple of times that Violet called him that. Then he started to like it, mainly because she was moaning it when his cock was inside her, her nipple was in his mouth or his tongue was at her clit. And he still liked it because it reminded him of those times.

"You call him Joe?" Kate asked, entering the conversation. "I thought everyone called him Cal."

Kate, obviously, had been hearing about him at school, something that Cal didn't care much about. It wasn't new.

Violet didn't reply. She'd looked out the side window again.

"Can we call you Joe?" Keira asked.

"No," Violet responded.

"Sure," Cal said over her and for the life of him, again, he had no clue why he did.

"Cool! Then it's Joe," Keira decided.

"I like Joe. Joe's a cool name," Kate muttered.

Violet sighed. This meant she was giving in and it also meant she was a pushover with her girls. He wondered if this was the way it always was or if this was in response to their father being dead. He reckoned it was the last.

For the rest of the drive Keira carried on the conversation with Kate interjecting occasionally, but Cal and Violet contributed absolutely nothing. Then again, Keira didn't even need Kate's input. The girl was a talker.

They made it to the mall. Cal parked and got out, pulling the seat up for Keira who scrambled out with that enthusiastic grace only teenage girls seemed to have. As he slammed the door behind her, he looked across the roof and saw Violet and Kate were also out. He beeped the locks when Violet closed the door and Keira ran to her sister, linking arms with her and they hustled to the mall. Obviously shopping was a favorite pastime. It was like the girls were made of metal and the mall was a high-powered magnet pulling them in.

Violet didn't look at him and she walked more calmly toward the building.

Cal fell in step beside her.

"Buddy—"

Suddenly, she stopped and tipped her head back to look at him.

"I saw you talking to Colt."

Her voice was quiet but not soft. It was an accusation.

Before he could say anything, she kept speaking.

"I know you know."

"I know," he confirmed.

She stifled a flinch and went on. "It isn't your job to look after us."

"Violet—"

"It isn't your job."

She was right. It wasn't. But that didn't mean dick because he was going to do it. He didn't tell her that, he just kept looking at her.

"You're here because Keira's making it her mission to befriend everyone within a twenty mile radius. She misses home, she had tons of friends and family at home and she's social. She's trying to recreate that," Violet informed him, though she was wrong. He was invited by Keira because her daughter loved her and knew Violet missed her husband and Keira was looking for a replacement to take away her mother's pain. He'd done the same thing with his dad after his mother died. It didn't work but he'd done it.

Cal didn't tell her that either.

"We'll get through this…" her hand lifted and she gestured at the mall, "and we'll go home and you'll disappear like when we first moved in. You'll be a shiny Ford pickup in your drive and that's it. Yeah?"

"No."

He watched her upper body jerk and she stared at him.

Then she repeated, "No?"

"What Colt tells me, your situation is extreme."

"It's none of your business."

"You live next door."

"It's still none of your business."

"You got two girls."

He watched her swallow as something crossed her face before she hid it.

Fear.

Cal felt that lock in his chest too.

"This is my business, buddy, people pay me a lotta cake to keep them safe," he told her.

"It might be your business, Joe, but *this* is not your business."

He leaned into her and she held her ground, glaring up at him.

Quietly, he reminded her, "I've had my dick in you." He watched the color hit her cheeks, she opened her mouth to speak but he kept going. "That makes it my business."

"That's ridiculous," she hissed.

"No, it sure as fuck isn't."

"I don't want your help."

"Too bad."

"Joe—"

"Too bad."

"Dammit, Joe—"

She stopped speaking because he grabbed her hand and started walking, hauling her along with him.

Her girls were standing inside the mall doors looking out at them, and when they hit the sidewalk, Violet twisted her hand out of his.

Cal allowed this. He was there looking out for her and her girls. He wasn't there to give them any ideas or start anything up again with their mother.

They walked into the mall, and even though Violet said she wasn't going to Lucky, that was the first place she directed them.

She stopped just inside the store, looked at her daughters and stated, "You both have one hundred and fifty dollars to spend in here."

Cal thought this would be met with shrieks of joy but it was not. Both girls looked at their mother and didn't move nor speak. Keira even turned her ankle to the side with sudden discomfort.

"Hello?" Violet called. "Did you hear me?"

"That money's for you," Kate said to her mother.

"Yes, and I'm giving it to you," Violet returned.

"Granddad gave that money to Uncle Sam for you to use," Keira put in.

"He gave it to me to do with what I wanted and I'm doing that," Violet told her daughter.

"We already spent our money," Kate replied firmly.

"So now, spend more," Violet responded even more firmly.

Neither girl responded nor did they move.

They all looked at each other, locked in silent mother-daughter combat. Cal wondered who'd win, but if he had to put money on it, his money would be on Kate and Keira.

As he watched the silent showdown, he decided he liked Violet's girls.

"I know!" Keira suddenly exclaimed, breaking the tense silence. "I'll be your personal shopper!" She jumped forward, grabbed her mom's arm, yanking on it, turning to Cal and Kate. "You guys, go get coffees. I'm gonna find Momalicious some *kick butt* Lucky!"

"Keira—" Violet began, but Cal turned to Kate.

"Let's go," he said, jerking his head to the doors of the store and he waited while she glanced at him then headed out.

Cal followed her then walked beside her as she headed to the coffee place, making a bee-line straight to it. She knew this mall like the back of her hand and she obviously drank coffee.

She didn't speak and acted like she was uncomfortable though she wasn't awkward. Cal was wrong that they didn't get anything from their mother. They had a hint of her attitude and they had her natural grace.

When they got to the front of the line, Kate ordered three complicated drinks and then glanced hesitantly up at him.

"Coffee," he said.

"Americano?" the clerk asked.

"Whatever, just coffee."

This seemed to confuse the kid then he rallied and asked, "Room for cream?"

Cal just stared at him. He grew flustered, bent his head to the cash register and started pressing buttons. Then he grabbed a paper cup and wrote something on it and set it by the big coffee machine with the other three cups.

He heard Kate laugh softly and he looked at her, seeing he was wrong again. Violet's daughters weren't just pretty. With Kate's face relaxed and smiling, she was more than pretty. She wasn't a knockout, but she was something else and it was all good.

Kate went for her purse but Cal murmured, "No."

She looked up at him and pulled her lips between her teeth as he paid.

They walked to the other end of the counter, waited for their coffees and nabbed them when they arrived.

Quietly and politely, Kate told him, "Cream and sugar are over there."

"I take it black."

"Oh," she whispered, nodded then turned and led him back the way they came.

Halfway there, shyly she said, "I'm going out with Dane Gordon."

He knew she was. He knew the Gordon kid too. Good-looking boy, kickass tight end. Rumor had it that colleges were already scouting him even though he was a junior. Kate had scored with him. Then again, Gordon probably felt the opposite and he wouldn't be wrong.

"Yeah?" Cal prompted when she didn't go on.

"He, well…he thinks you're the bomb."

Cal didn't reply. He knew the kids in town thought this and they thought it because he knew a lot of famous people, but his job was far from glamorous.

She went on. "He says he wants to do what you do…after school."

"Someone gives him a full ride, he should go to college."

She nodded. "He's thinkin' he'll do that too, but, um…maybe do what you do after."

"Smart."

Her head jerked around and up. She smiled at him and he found he was wrong again. She got her mother's smile and that locked in his chest too, also not in a bad way.

"Pays good, girl, I'm not complainin'. But the folks I look after, they're a pain in the ass," he told her truthfully.

"Would you talk to him?" she asked. She was back to shy but she pulled up the courage to ask because she liked this guy.

This was where he reckoned this was heading and he shouldn't do what he was going to do. Violet would be pissed and he didn't even *want* to do it, but he did it anyway.

"You see my truck in the drive and he's around, come over."

This bought him another smile and she whispered, "Thanks."

The minute they hit the store, Keira ambushed them, her arms filled with clothes.

"I'm gonna be *your* personal shopper too!" she told him, her eyes bright and happy. "I found a bunch of clothes that would look *killer* on you." She looked down at the pile in her arms and muttered, "I hope I got the sizes right." Her head tilted back to him again. "The dudes at the counter saw you and guessed."

Jesus. He was not going to try on clothes. Everything he owned he bought at the Levi's store, except his leather jacket which Bonnie bought for him. He went in, got it, didn't try it on and got the fuck out. He went shopping probably once every three years.

"Keira, I'm not sure Joe's into shopping," Kate wisely shared with her sister.

"But these clothes are *awesome*. Some of the shirts will go with his eyes," Keira replied.

Cal looked down at the pile of clothes then at Keira.

"Girl, I wear black and I wear Levi's."

Unlike any other human being on earth who heard the way he spoke, Keira was not deterred. "But Lucky jeans are *the best*."

"I wear Levi's."

"But you haven't even tried Lucky."

"Keira, he said he wears Levi's," Kate put in.

"What's going on?" Violet asked and they all looked to the side.

He was wrong again, this time about the clothes. Violet was standing there wearing a skintight, purple, low-cut tank top and a pair of jeans that were so fucking sweet on her, his hands itched again to touch her in order to peel those jeans off her.

"Oh my *God*, Momalicious!" Keira screeched. "We have to get you that tank in every color."

She was not wrong.

"Those jeans are hot, Mawdy," Kate noted on a happy smile.

She was not wrong either.

Violet twisted and looked at a tag then back at them. "I could buy a car for the price of these jeans."

"They last *forever*," Keira informed her mother.

"Maybe so, honey, but—" Violet started.

"You don't buy that outfit, buddy, I'm buyin' it for you," Cal entered the conversation.

All three females turned to stare at him. Violet with color in her cheeks. Keira with a huge smile on her face (also her mother's, though Cal had never seen Violet smile that big). And Kate with shock.

Violet shook off her response first. "Joe—"

He cut her off. "It looks good."

"But—"

"Get it."

"I don't think—"

He leaned into her and dropped his voice. "Seriously, buddy, fuckin' get it. It looks good."

He watched as she closed her eyes, and the look on her face, he wished he'd kept his fucking mouth shut.

When she opened them again, her eyes were blank.

Her voice was soft when she asked, "Can you try not to say the f-word in front of my daughters?"

Before he could reply, Kate spoke.

"It's okay, Joe. Kids at school drop the f-bomb all the time," Kate assured him, and before Violet could say anything, she turned to her mother. "Mom, Joe's right. You should get that. It looks really great on you."

Violet drew in breath and nodded. "All right, baby, I'll get it."

"I'm gonna go get more of those tanks," Keira said, dumping the clothes she picked for Cal in her sister's arms even though the girl was holding two cups of coffee. "Wardrobe staples. Perfect, you can wear them all the time, in the summer, in the winter under tops and cardigans…" Her voice trailed off as she took off on her mission to find more tanks.

"You want me to put these away, Joe?" Kate asked him quietly, and he nodded to her.

Then in an afterthought, he murmured, "Thanks, girl."

"No problem," Kate whispered and took off.

Violet looked up at him.

"This is yours," he told her, handing her a cup.

She looked down at it, seeming confused for a second. She took the cup from him and muttered, "I'm gonna go change."

Then she took off.

Cal watched her move through the store.

Then Cal wondered if her husband used to shop with her and his kids. He wondered if the man stood in some store with a coffee waiting for his girls to do what they did. If he got impatient with it because it wasn't a whole helluva lot of fun, except when Violet walked out of a dressing room, looking so fucking sweet she made the whole thing worthwhile.

Then Cal wondered if someone told him that he'd eventually be whacked if her husband would ever get impatient waiting for his girls to do what they did. Cal figured, unless her husband was an asshole, he wouldn't. He'd take his girls shopping, to dinner and to the movies every fucking night.

Cal walked to the counter and leaned into it to wait for Violet and her daughters. The kids manning it scattered, something that happened a lot with Cal because he was big and because he was how he was. This didn't bother him. It was a bonus with his profession.

He took a sip of coffee and he tagged where both girls were in the store and Violet's feet under the dressing room door. He kept them tagged, though mostly with his ears, listening for their voices, pinpointing the sounds they made as he scanned the store and the mall beyond.

No threat, he would feel it. He'd had a lot of practice.

Then he found them with his eyes again and waited impatiently, because it wasn't a whole helluva lot of fun, for them to do what they did.

Cal pulled Violet's Mustang into her drive.

It was after she'd bought her jeans, another short skirt Keira made her try on (and it was sweet too, though nowhere near as good as the jeans) and four of the same tank tops in different colors.

It was after her daughters dragged them to a shoe shop, which was torture compared to the jeans store considering Violet tried on at least twelve pairs of shoes. She eventually bought a pair of high-heeled sandals she swore she'd never wear but both her daughters declared she had to have. Again, her daughters weren't wrong. They were sexy as all hell.

It was after dinner, which was the only glitch they had after his conversation with Violet in the parking lot, considering he paid and she made it clear she didn't want him to. She made this clear by having what could only be described as a quiet tantrum right in front of her daughters and the waiter.

Keira, who should pursue a career as a diplomat, waded in and suggested her mom pay for Cal's movie and popcorn to even things out. Violet gave in and Cal allowed this but only because he had no intention of eating popcorn.

And it was after a fucking boring romantic comedy that both girls declared was *the best movie they'd ever seen.* This was mostly because they liked Nicole Bolton's clothes and they thought the actor who played her love interest was *gorgeous.* Cal and Violet had both stayed silent on the subject. Then again, they didn't need to speak. Even Kate went on about it so there were no openings to get a word in.

Cal parked, switched off the ignition, opened his door, unfolded his body from the Mustang and pulled the seat forward for Keira.

"Thanks, Joe!" she hopped out and tipped her head back to look at him. "And thanks for dinner."

Cal didn't reply verbally, just dipped his chin.

She leaned into him and whispered conspiratorially, "Told you it would be fun."

Cal couldn't say it was fun, but he could say it was far from boring, except the movie.

Keira didn't wait for him to respond. She turned and bolted to the side door.

Kate followed her, carrying her mother's shopping bags and calling, "Thanks for dinner, Joe."

Cal lifted his chin to her. She waved then jogged to the side door and disappeared through it behind her sister.

Violet came to stand in front of him.

She lifted her hand, palm up. "My keys."

Cal didn't give them to her.

Instead, he looked her in the eyes and told her, "What I'm gonna say is gonna piss you off."

He watched her press her lips together as she braced her body and she asked, "What?"

He didn't delay. "Colt's gonna talk to you about your security system. Man named Chip, good guy, is gonna update it. Chip can't do what I designed for your system, I'm gonna do it."

Her lips parted and she stared at him.

Then she leaned forward and hissed, "You are *not*."

"Buddy, I am."

"No, you are *not*."

"You can stand there and snap at me all you want. It's gonna happen."

"I can't afford a new security system."

"No one said you're payin' for it."

Her mouth clamped shut and she took a step back on her foot like he'd shoved her.

Then she came back in close, tilting her head way back, her eyes narrow. She was, as he suspected, seriously pissed.

"You're not payin' for a new system for me."

"I am."

"It isn't gonna happen."

"It is." She opened her mouth to speak but Cal angled his head so his face was in hers and he got there first. "Be pissed at me 'cause I fucked you over. That's cool, you got a right, I fucked you over and it was a shit thing to do. But you got two girls to look after and neighbors who're willin' to wade in to help. It's not that you'd be a fool not to take the help. It's that you'd be a shit mom if you didn't do all you could to keep yourself, and them, safe. What happened with us happened. It's over. Now I'm bein' neighborly. Colt and me are willin' to help keep you and those girls safe, and, buddy, you got no choice but to accept that and you know it."

She stood there, not moving, not blinking, just staring straight into his eyes.

Then she whispered, "What happened with us happened?"

"Violet—"

"You're right," she said quickly and softly. "You're security to the stars and if you're willin' to help, I should take it. But I'm gonna tell you even though I figure you know, I think you're an asshole. I don't only not like you, I *hate* you. I *hate* how you played me. I *hate* that I was so fucking stupid, I let myself get played. I *hate* that you know about this because I *hate* that *you* know *anything* about *me*. And I *hate* that I have to accept help from you." After she dealt her lethal succession of blows, she finished with, "But I'll do it…for my girls."

And before he could speak, she reached in, yanked her keys out of his hand, turned on her sandal and walked swiftly away.

Cal watched her go, listened to her side door slam and dropped his head to study his boots.

Then he walked to his house, let himself in and went directly to the fridge to get a beer. He twisted off the cap, flicked it into the trash bin, lifted the bottle to his lips and took a healthy pull.

He held the bottle in front of him, studying the label without seeing it.

Then he threw the bottle through the doorway of the kitchen. It flew into the living room and smashed against the wall.

# Five

## Daniel Hart

I was running late and that *sucked.*

Chip hadn't been able to install the full system that Joe had designed and Joe hadn't been able to get to it before he had to leave. So now that it was a week later and Joe was back, he was coming over to see to it.

Feb and Colt were having a barbeque and I'd promised Feb I'd go over and help before everyone showed up. I was supposed to be over there fifteen minutes ago, which was fifteen minutes before Joe was supposed to show.

The girls were off as usual. Keira was coming back with her friend Heather to go to the barbeque. Kate was at work at Fulsham's Frozen Custard Stand. Dane who, regardless of the fact that Kate had a car, took her to work and picked her up, was going to go and get her and they both were also coming to the barbeque later. I'd told Colt to tell Joe I'd leave the side door open for him and Colt had obviously done this because now I heard the side door open.

I ignored this and finished gunking up my hair with the goo that made it look so good and then rinsed my hands. Then I walked from my bathroom into the bedroom to put on my jewelry, stacking on the silver bangles, putting in my silver hoop earrings, clasping on my silver watch. I spritzed with perfume and turned to the bedroom door.

Joe was leaning in the frame watching me.

At the sight of him, my stomach tied into an instant knot.

I had no idea why he was standing there watching me. I felt all that needed to be said was said, so I glanced into his eyes briefly and headed his way expecting, since I said all that needed to be said and I was pretty honest about it, he'd move out of mine.

He didn't.

I stopped and looked up at him.

His rumbly voice was low when he said, "We should talk, buddy."

I didn't want to talk, so I replied, "Please move."

"Violet—"

"Move."

"We live next door to each other, woman," he pointed out.

"Yes and you get this done, that's all there is," I returned.

He straightened from the frame but stayed in my way and his voice was soft when he said, "It was good."

I felt my mouth fill with saliva and my sinuses tingle with tears and I swallowed them both down.

"Get out of my way, Joe."

"We both know we couldn't take it there."

I didn't know that. I didn't know anything about him. It was only him that knew that.

I didn't tell him that, I said, "Out of my way."

"Shit, Violet, it doesn't have to be like this."

I felt my head jerk but my eyes stayed pinned to his.

"No? You don't think so? Well, that's where you're wrong." I leaned into him slightly and went on. "Not man wrong, men think they can fuck anything that moves and just carry on. Let me educate you, Joe, even though you had that scene with Kenzie then weeks later you went through Nadia and God knows who else then moved on to me, so you should know. But, just in case you haven't figured it out, women aren't built that way."

"That's your world, buddy. Lotsa women are built that way. Nadia for one."

I didn't believe that for a second.

Therefore, I said sarcastically, "Right."

"Right," he replied.

"You think that, but trust me, you're done with her, she goes home and cries into her Oreos."

He shook his head. "You don't know her."

"Okay, well, I know Kenzie wanted more."

"Kenzie wanted what Kenzie wanted and she thinks she'll get it, no matter what it is and she acts out when she doesn't. Christ, the bitch is thirty-two years old and she's been married four times."

This was true. I'd read all about it in magazines.

"Listen," I told him, deciding it was time to end this conversation and move on, "I was supposed to be at Feb's twenty minutes ago."

Joe wasn't done with the conversation. "It was sex. It's always sex. Just sex. With you, it wasn't that. I didn't know you lost your husband. I didn't know the shit that was goin' down with you."

He was making it worse, telling me it was just sex. I knew he thought that, of course, I just didn't really need it confirmed.

"Now you know, so get out of my way."

His hand came up, his fingers curling around my neck and he leaned his face into mine.

"Woman, in this life, you have to have learned, you need all the friends you can get. That's what I'm offerin', okay?"

God, now he wanted to be my *friend.* It was like he was reading this shit out of a book, how to be the most insulting you can be without even trying.

I yanked my neck from his hold.

"Fuck off, Joe."

He shook his head, still didn't move out of the way and I noticed he looked like he was getting a little angry.

"Joe—"

"You know where I live. The offer's on the table when you wanna grow up and put it behind you."

I let these words bounce around in my head for several seconds.

Then, instead of letting those words make my head explode, I decided to let them go.

Though, I decided not to let it go graciously. "Don't hold your breath waiting for that to happen. Now could you get out of my way?"

He watched me, that something, whatever the hell it was (and I told myself I didn't care what it was), working behind his eyes. Then he stepped out of my way.

It took a lot out of me, and I struggled to keep it together, but I managed to walk by him, through the study, into the kitchen to grab my keys and the plate of cupcakes I'd made for the barbeque and out the door without running.

I was pretty proud of myself.

"Okay, so, *that*, I'll come out of man hibernation for," Cheryl announced.

I looked at Cheryl and followed her eyes to see that Joe had joined the barbeque.

Shit.

Cheryl and I were sitting in the grass in the sun in Feb and Colt's backyard. My legs were out in front of me and I was wearing my little army green skirt and my violet tank top I bought at Lucky with Joe and the girls.

I'd helped Feb for a few hours before people showed, making macaroni salad, whipping up devilled eggs, cutting up tomatoes and onions, forming hamburger patties, dumping chips into bowls and then carting it outside to sit on a table under a sideless tent that Colt set up. We did all of this while looking after Feb's beautiful baby boy, Jack, as her cat Wilson alternately raced around the house or meowed for the treats Feb refused to give him. Also while trying not to tread on the adorable German shepherd puppy Feb bought Colt for his birthday.

This was their once-a-year barbeque, marking the coming of summer where they closed down the bar and had a good day with family and friends. All their employees were invited including Darryl who was a bartender, his wife Phylenda and their kids. Ruthie, a waitress. Fritzi, who cleaned the bar in the mornings. And Cheryl who worked behind the bar sometimes but was also a waitress and Cheryl brought her seven year old son, Ethan.

Also there were Feb's brother, Morrie, his wife Dee, their kids Bonham and Tuesday and Feb's parents, Jack and Jackie. Our neighbors, Jeremy and Melinda, Myrtle and Pearl were invited too (Tina and Cory were not but, according to Feb, Cory was on the outs with Tina, on the ins with his wife Bethany, and Tina was nursing her snit, not to mention Feb hated Tina because she was a bitch). Feb's best friends Jessie (and her husband Jimbo) and Mimi (and her husband Al and their kids) and Colt's partner Sully (and his wife Lorraine) were also there.

And now, so was Joe.

I watched him walk up to Colt who was manning the burgers, dogs and brats at the barbeque, baby Jack held to Colt's hip. They did man nods and then Joe leaned down to the cooler by the grill and nabbed himself a cold one.

I guessed he was done with my super-sophisticated alarm system. He must be good. It didn't take long. He had only been working at it a few hours.

I sipped my margarita, glared at him and told Cheryl, "Don't go there."

"Hunh?" Cheryl asked.

I didn't know her. I'd seen her at J&J's a couple of times, she'd made me a drink or two. However, we'd been sitting out in the sun together drinking margaritas for at least thirty minutes. In some circles of American females, this meant you were automatic BFFs.

Therefore, I repeated, "Don't go there. Player."

"And you know this…?" Cheryl let that hang.

I turned my head and just gave her a look.

Her eyes got wide then she noted, "I didn't peg you as the type."

"What type?"

"The type to get played."

I shook my head. "Seein' as I've had two men in my bed, my husband, who took my virginity when I was seventeen, and him," I tilted my head toward Joe, "I'm not."

At this news, Cheryl's eyes got even wider. "No joke?"

I shook my head again. "No joke."

"Wow," she whispered.

"Wow is right," I returned.

"What happened to your husband? Divorce?"

"He was shot in the head by a gangster."

Her mouth dropped open, her face went pale and I felt like a shit, telling her like that. I'd never told anyone like that. Hell, I didn't think I ever told anyone. Barry, Tim's partner, and Pam, Barry's wife, had made all the calls.

"It was a while ago," I explained, my voice gentler. "He was a cop."

The surprise slid out of her face, her hand came out and she gave my knee a quick squeeze before it moved away.

"Rough," she murmured, and I nodded to that understatement. "How long ago?"

"Year and a half."

"Then not *that* long ago."

I looked at my feet. "Nope."

"You wanna talk?"

I looked at her and repeated quietly, "Nope."

"You do…"

Seriously, the folks in this 'burg were *so* nice.

It was my turn to squeeze her knee so I did and muttered, "Thanks."

She turned her head and her gaze went to Joe. My gaze went to anywhere but Joe.

"Was he good?" she asked curiously.

Good wasn't the word for it. In fact, there were no words for it.

I decided not to tell her that. Instead I said, "Yeah."

Her head turned back to me, and softly, she said, "Be fun to play, hon, been a while for me and let's just say I've had a few more boys in my bed than you. But only…" She paused, "You done with him?"

I wasn't done with him; he was done with me, which totally made me done with him.

"Oh yeah, I'm done."

"You mind?" she asked.

"Have at it," I invited, though I had to admit it hurt, thinking of Joe moving on even though I knew it shouldn't and I didn't even know why it did.

It was sex, just sex, he told me so his damned self. I was an adult, I knew the score. My girlfriends who hadn't found the man they adored at fifteen years old had been telling me stories like this for ages. Apparently, since Tim was dead, it was my turn to get fucked over by an asshole.

However, since I liked Cheryl, I added, "But check your heart at the door."

Her brows went up. "You didn't?"

"What?"

"Check your heart at the door."

I shook my head again. "I didn't fall for him but I thought there was something there. I was an idiot. It had been…losing Tim…" I licked my lips and Cheryl waited silently while I pulled it together, took a deep breath and finished. "Let's just say, he made me feel like a moron because there wasn't anything there. Nothing. Just sex. He was done with me fast. It lasted only a coupla days and he's my next-door neighbor."

Cheryl was staring at me when she said, "Jesus."

"Yep."

She looked back at Joe, mumbling, "Maybe I'll steer clear."

"That'd be my advice."

"Still, he's hot." Cheryl was still mumbling and I forgot about Joe and me and looked at her.

She was very pretty. A lot of blonde hair cut to hit her shoulders, fake boobs, long legs, attractive meat at her hips. She dressed kind of slutty but she worked it and it looked good on her. Her black skirt was super short, her white tank was super tight. She had on a black bra you could see through the tank and she was wearing high-heeled silver slut sandals even though we were at a backyard barbeque.

But the look she was giving Joe after what I told her made me think she might not be so good at picking men.

This was confirmed when she asked curiously, still checking out Joe, "You know how he got those scars?"

"Nope. Don't know much about him. We didn't talk."

She looked at me and grinned. "Action man?"

More like Superman, but I didn't tell her that, I just said, "Yeah."

She leaned into me. "My advice, though you didn't ask for it, I'm still givin' it to you, enjoy it for what it was. It was obviously good and a girl needs to get her some. Nothin' wrong with that." Her eyes went back to Joe then came to me. "He reopens that door, Vi, walk through it and take what you want. You find another man who's good to you and wants more, you can walk away. But *that* was my booty call and he lived next door?" She paused, her head having jerked toward Joe and she grinned again. "I wouldn't waste that opportunity."

This idea was so preposterous, I laughed out loud.

She laughed with me and when we were done laughing, she lifted her margarita glass.

"I'm dry, babe, you want another?"

I handed her my glass. "That'd be cool, thanks."

Her eyes slid across the yard to the grill again and she went on. "I'm thinkin' I want a brat." She looked back to me and her look was wicked when she suggested, "Maybe you wanna come with?"

I shook my head.

"You look hot in that tank," she encouraged.

"Joe's seen the tank. He was at my house this morning and he was with me when I bought it."

Her head tilted to the side in confusion. "He was at your house this morning?"

"He's installing a security system at my house, not by my choice." I sighed when she looked even more confused and explained, "It's complicated."

"I thought you said it was a couple night thing. He took you shopping?"

"Shopping was after he was done with me, before the security system." When she just stared at me, I finished. "It's a long story, also complicated."

She nodded and got up, saying, "I'll get our margs and my brat then come back and you can tell me."

"It's not interesting," I warned.

She looked down at me on the grass from her slut shoes, high-heeled height and remarked, "Known a lot of men, mostly assholes and players, so got some experience, so much you could pretty much say I'm an expert. Don't know a single player who takes a woman shoppin' and installs a security system in her house after he's done with her." She leaned down a bit and smiled, saying, "So, babe, gotta say, this complicated business sounds all kinds of interesting."

Before I could reply, she walked away, somehow managing to walk through grass in high, spiked heels without looking like a fool, and I decided Cheryl was very cool.

"Momalicious!" I heard shouted from beside me and I turned to see Keira running into the yard, her arms wheeling, her hair flying, her face in a full-on smile.

She threw herself at me and I caught her because I had no choice and went down on my back. She slid off my side and got up on a hand to look down at me.

"Get *this*!" she shouted.

"Hello, my darling Keira," I cut her off and my eyes went up to see Heather, Keira's friend (who, incidentally, looked exactly like a Heather, petite, tons of curly-to-frizzy red hair and about seven million freckles all over her body). I came up on both elbows and said, "Hey, Heather."

"Hi, Miz Winters." Heather smiled at me.

"Mom!" Keira called my attention to her. "Guess what?"

"What, baby?"

"Heather's dog had *puppies*!" she shrieked.

Oh fuck.

Keira had always wanted a dog, always. She'd been at Tim and me since the minute she knew dogs existed and she could speak intelligent English. Tim had wanted a dog too. It was me who held back because I loved dogs and my dad got me one when I was nine. She'd been run over when I was fifteen and that had been the worst day of my life, losing my dog (until two years later, when I found out I was pregnant and Mom and Dad had thrown me out of their house).

I didn't want that for my daughter (or Tim, for that matter), the inevitable day when your beloved family pet would go away. I wanted to shield Keira—whose heart, like mine and her sister's, was too big for her own good—from that hurt.

Now it seemed ridiculous. She'd lost something far more precious than the family pet.

"They're all white and so fluffy and cuddly and Heather's dad said they'll give us one for only two hundred dollars!" Keira went on.

I stared at her.

Two hundred dollars?

The money situation had settled, mainly because Bobbie still hadn't found anyone part-time and she didn't seem to mind paying me overtime.

It was high season for her (outside of Christmas—Bobbie put on a whale of a Christmas at her shop, her displays were extravagant and you could buy anything Christmas there, she was known for it, people came from neighboring states just to shop at Bobbie's for Christmas crap or simply to wander around). I was getting five to ten hours a week on time and a half which helped loads.

But she could find someone and things would change. I didn't need an extra mouth to feed, even a canine one and *especially* a canine one that cost two hundred dollars.

"That's a lot of money for a dog," I told Keira.

"They sell them for a lot more than that. He's gonna give us a deal," Keira replied.

I was acutely aware of Heather standing there so I said to my daughter, "Let's talk about this later, honey."

"I know what you're thinking," she told me. "But we can't have the puppy for a couple of weeks and I thought I could save my allowance until then and talk to Kate. She and I can go halves."

There was no way in hell Keira was going to save her allowance for however many weeks it took to wean a puppy.

Kate saved her money and spent it frugally. She got the job at the Custard Stand for the summer for extra cash and because it was the cool place to work. It was a coup she got it. Everyone who worked there did it because most of the kids hung out there, so she was essentially making cones and sundaes during a summer-long party. But with Dane carting her everywhere, her Fiesta barely ever left the drive, she was depositing her money in her account and not even paying for gas.

Keira, on the other hand, went through money like water. With my overtime and Kate's work, Keira's household chores had increased. She'd complained but she did it because I upped her weekly allowance from ten dollars to twenty. But it was a wonder, with the way Keira was with money, that her allowance didn't go up in a puff of smoke the minute I handed it to her.

"We'll talk about it later," I repeated.

"Mom—"

I lifted up a hand and put my fingers to her lips, saying quietly, "Later, baby."

She emitted a heavy sigh and said against my fingers, "All right."

I moved my fingers from her mouth to slide into her hair and I pulled her forehead to my lips and kissed her there. When I let her go, I knew there were no hard feelings because she lifted up and kissed me back the same way.

God, I loved my daughter.

Her head turned, her eyes caught on something, her face went bright and she shouted, "Joe!"

I looked across the yard and saw Joe, Cheryl holding a brat in a bun standing next to him, watching us.

My stomach again tied in knots.

Keira scrambled up, jumped over my body and grabbed Heather's hand. Then she dragged Heather across the yard straight to Joe.

Okay, so I loved my daughter but she was a nut and I hoped she didn't have some kind of teenage-girl crush on Joe. That would suck, for Keira and for me.

"I have *got* to take a load off." I heard Feb say from my side.

I tore my eyes away from Keira skidding to a halt in front of Joe, bringing Heather up beside her, tipping her head back and saying something to him. Mostly, I had to admit, I tore my eyes away from Joe dipping his chin to stare down at my daughter, his face going soft when he did.

I looked up at Feb, who had a Diet Coke in one hand and baby Jack at her hip. I sat up and lifted my arms.

"Give him to me."

She handed Jack over to me, mumbled, "Thanks," and collapsed into the grass beside me.

I settled Jack into my lap or, more aptly, I let Jack squirm and play in my lap. The kid was active. Feb pulled her hair out of her face and lay back on an elbow.

"How're the wedding plans goin'?" I asked her and her eyes came to me.

"Something I've learned," she said. "When a man tells a woman he wants the wedding *big*, the *biggest*, the woman should tell him he has two choices. Either he plans it or she'll buy the tickets to Vegas on the Internet."

I smiled at her. "Hard work?"

Her eyes went to baby Jack doing baby squats in my lap while holding onto my hands then they moved to Colt who was smiling at Morrie while Morrie told a story. Finally they came back to me and she grinned.

"Not really."

I looked at Feb then I looked at her yard which was filled with food and drink and sunshine and people she cared about. She and Colt had been through the ringer, even made national news, and here she was with her baby and her man and her family and friends, living a good life.

Hope. There was always hope. Losing Tim, I'd lost sight of that. I'd thought I'd found it, stupidly, but then I'd been played by Joe and made too much of it. My daughters were healthy and happy and moving on to boyfriends and dogs. Tim was gone, but there were still sun and friends and life.

"You need any help," I said to Feb. "I'm right across the street."

"Thanks but with Mimi, Dee and Jessie in the mix, I got all the help I need," Feb replied, baby Jack lurched forward and grabbed onto my hair, yanking hard. "God, sorry, Vi. He's strong like his dad."

I extricated his baby fingers from my hair and smiled at her. "Not a problem at all, forgot how this was." I looked down at Jack. "Sounds stupid but, remembering, it feels good."

"Only a mom would say that. He pulls Jessie's hair, she freaks."

I kept smiling at her and as I did so, I watched her face change.

"Gonna say this quick, Vi, don't wanna fuck up the day. But you know I know how it feels to have some creepy psycho messin' with your life. You need to talk, you need anything from Colt or me, we're here. Anytime. We know how it is and we don't like that you're across the street with your girls, alone. It's messin' with Colt's head, thinkin' this guy could come anytime, fuck with you and he might not be around. So he messes with you or you get freaked or you just want company, don't think about it, you just call. It'd make Colt feel better, you do. He prefers doin' somethin' rather than hangin' around worrying. Yeah?"

I didn't know whether to feel bad, considering that my situation was messing with their heads, or to feel good that I lucked out and moved across the street from such good people.

I decided to feel good.

"Thanks, Feb. That's sweet."

"Don't tell me it's sweet, honey, tell me you'll call."

I nodded and pulled her son close to my chest, wrapping my arms around him to give him a squeeze. Then I dropped my head and kissed the top of his dark-haired, soft, fuzzy baby one.

"I'll call," I mumbled against Jack's baby head.

"Good," Feb said softly.

I took in a breath, nuzzled Jack's baby head and he squirmed, not thrilled about his captivity. So I let him go and took his hands, allowing him to bounce in my lap again when Feb muttered, "Matchmaker."

I looked up to see Keira, Heather and Joe under the sideless tent. Keira had my plate of cupcakes in her hand and she was shoving them at Joe.

Shit.

"She's social," I told Feb and watched as Keira pointed at me, pointed at the cupcakes and then rolled her eyes and let her head fall back in a *Mom's cupcakes are to die for* gesture.

Shitshit*shit*!

My cupcakes were good, even I had to admit that. Another recipe I'd fiddled with, yellow cake with crushed up bars of gourmet dark chocolate baked in them and vanilla bean frosting that was simply orgasmic. So much so it was a wonder any made it to the cupcakes since I ate most of it while icing.

But it wasn't that Keira wanted to share the bounty of my cupcakes. It also wasn't that my daughter had a crush on Joe.

It was that she wanted him for me.

Shit!

This annoyed me and surprised me. Tim had been gone awhile it was true, but not *that* long.

Then again, life had changed, *I* had changed and I didn't hide my pain when Tim died. The girls were also in pain and I didn't want them to think they had to hide it either. I didn't want them to bury that only to have it eat at them later and, weirdly, I wanted us to give that to Tim. I wanted my girls and anyone to know I was inside out with losing Tim. I wanted people to see it because they'd know who Tim was and what he meant to me and that he was the kind of man whose death would cause that kind of pain. Because he was.

But my daughter loved her mother; Keira would want to take away that pain.

Shit!

"Keira's a nut," I told Feb, and I looked from my daughter and Joe, who had taken a cupcake and was in the process of taking a huge bite, to Feb.

"And Cal's a good guy," she said back. I felt my body jolt at the look on her face and I knew that she knew about Joe and me. How she knew, I didn't know. But she knew.

"I—"

"We'll have drinks, you and me, one day soon. I'll explain and maybe, when I do, you'll give him a break and a second chance."

A break? A second chance? What was she talking about?

First of all, he didn't deserve a break. Secondly, he didn't want a second chance.

"Feb—" I started.

"Feb!" Colt yelled. "Baby, we got any more Bud?"

"I feel like I'm at work," she muttered then shouted across the yard, "Yeah, it's in the fridge in the garage."

Colt looked at his woman. Feb looked at her man. I knew where this was going. Even though he mowed the lawn, erected a tent and stood at the grill for the last two hours and she'd probably been planning this for weeks and preparing for days, doing the grocery shopping, cooking and running around, they were locked in a standoff as to who was going to replenish the drink coolers. She was sitting in the grass, taking a break. He was manning the grill, which he considered work even though it was mostly just standing there. Therefore, Feb was going to lose.

"Shit," she muttered, losing, and looked at me, getting up. "Can you take care of Jack? I gotta go get more beer."

I smiled at her. "Absolutely."

"Momalicious!" Keira called as Feb walked away. "Joe *loves* your cupcakes!"

Everyone turned to Keira, Heather and Joe, but I only saw Joe's eyes on me. I doubted he told Keira that he "loved" my cupcakes (though, he'd be a freak of nature if he didn't at least like them, they were delicious). I further doubted he was thrilled that Keira announced it to everyone.

But, whatever.

I avoided Joe's eyes and shouted back, "I can die happy."

Then I looked down at Jack and cooed at him softly while smiling. He smiled back and did a baby giggle. I snatched him in my hands, shoving him into the air while he emitted another baby giggle then bringing his belly down to my face to give him a nuzzle so I could get another giggle.

Baby Jack didn't disappoint.

"Nice cupcakes, buddy." I heard from behind me half an hour later, and I saw in front of me, Feb, who I was talking to, lift her gaze to some high point over my shoulder.

Joe obviously was there.

It sucked that he could sneak up on me.

"Crap, Scout got hold of my shoe," Feb muttered. "Be back."

I watched as Feb rushed across the yard to the puppy, who looked really pissed at one of her flip-flops. The dog was jerking his head back and forth, flip-flop between his teeth then putting a paw to the shoe and tugging at the strap with his mouth.

"Violet."

My eyes went from the dog to Joe.

"Yeah?"

"We need to talk about your system."

I didn't say anything but I also didn't move away. I just looked at him and waited.

"Chip fucked up the wiring. Not a big deal but it's gonna take some more time."

"Whatever," I muttered, looking away.

"I'll do it in the morning."

"Fine."

There was a pause then a terse, "See you haven't decided to grow up."

My eyes went back to him and I opened my mouth to speak but I heard a shouted, "*Mom!*"

It was Kate's shout, it was high-pitched and the sound turned my blood to ice.

I felt Joe tense at my side and he and I both turned to look along the side yard of Colt and Feb's house toward my house. Dane's yellow pickup was in the drive beside my Mustang but Kate was running fast across the street toward me, Dane coming after her.

I started running to Kate and met her in Colt and Feb's front yard. As I moved, I felt Joe moving behind me.

My hands went to her shoulders and I got close.

"Honey, what's goin' on?"

"The porch," was all she said.

Dane stopped behind her but I looked beyond him to my porch.

Then my heart stopped.

There was a huge, flamboyant bouquet of purple flowers—roses mixed with dainty violets—on my welcome mat. So huge and wide, I could see them from across the street. They came halfway up the door and spread wide across it.

Daniel Hart's calling card.

He knew where I was.

And Kate knew what those flowers were. Since Tim died I got a delivery, exactly like that, like clockwork every Saturday morning for months. I'd called the florists and told them to stop, which they did. But then a new florist would send them. Eventually Barry or one of Tim's other cop buddies would sit in our drive on Saturday morning and take them away before the girls could see them, but until I sold the house and moved, they never stopped coming.

I looked at Kate and saw she was trembling. "It's okay, honey."

"But, he knows where we live."

"It's okay," I lied to and for my daughter.

I felt movement and looked to my left to see Joe was stalking toward my house. Then I felt more movement and I saw Colt and his partner Sully following Joe.

I looked at Kate. "Go and get yourself and Dane a burger, okay?"

"But—"

I gave her a smile and hoped it wasn't as shaky as it felt. "Dane's a football star, honey, he needs his grub."

"Mom—"

I moved my face close to her face and squeezed her shoulders. "Go, look after your sister. Yeah?"

That would get her, giving her something to do, something responsible, something that made her feel she was helping out her mom. Kate's mind would be turned from panic to duty by that.

"Okay," she whispered.

I let her go, nodded to Dane who looked worried (therefore, I knew Kate had shared the situation with him) and he followed Kate as she walked to the backyard.

I turned and watched only to see Keira standing in the yard, Feb's squirming puppy in her arms, her eyes locked on our house. Feb and Cheryl were standing on either side of her.

"Feb," I called, her eyes went from my house to me and I tipped my head to Keira.

Feb nodded, put her arm around Keira's shoulders, moved Keira's stiff body around and she led her to the back of the house, Cheryl, Kate and Dane following.

I watched until I lost sight of them then I ran to my house.

Joe, Colt and Sully were standing at my front door. Joe had a little white card between his fingers but he looked from it to me when I hit the yard and he watched me run until I stopped at their huddle.

"Talk us through this," he ordered the minute I arrived, his head jerking to the flowers.

"It's Saturday," I explained stupidly.

"And?"

"He sends me flowers every Saturday."

Joe's mouth got tight and even in the bright sunshine of the day he shifted straight to sinister.

"You been gettin' flowers?" Joe asked, and I shook my head.

"This is the first here," I answered.

His eyes went to Colt.

"Moratorium," he growled, and I blinked in confusion at his strange word.

"We'll call the florists in town," Sully said quickly and I got it then.

"That won't work, I tried that," I informed them, Joe's eyes came to me and it took a lot for me not to shrink from him, he looked so pissed.

"We'll be thorough," Joe told me and I couldn't do anything but nod because, the way he said that, I didn't doubt for a second they would.

"What comes after this?" Colt asked, and I looked at him.

"Gifts," I answered. "Then visits."

"What kind of gifts?" Colt asked.

"It could be anything, it started small. Like he sent caviar, which was weird. Then he sent fancy champagne and gift certificates to nice restaurants for me and the girls. Then he started to send jewelry."

"Expensive?" Colt asked, and I nodded.

"Visits come after the jewelry?" Joe asked, and I nodded to him too. "What'd you do with the shit?"

"Gave it to Barry, Tim's partner. He's got it all still, at the station."

"How much time we got?" Joe went on.

"I don't know, it went on for months and then he started to come 'round."

"Don't suspect we got months," Sully muttered and I suspected he was right. It had been months, me being away. I figured Daniel Hart would speed things up a bit.

"You talk to him?" Joe asked.

"He just showed, sat outside in his car. Then his man would come to the door, knock on it. Then he would. I didn't go out in the beginning, didn't answer the door. Barry talked to him at first and it didn't work so then Barry talked to him officially and that didn't work either. In the end, I talked to him a couple of times, thought he'd get it. That didn't work either. Barry helped me get a restraining order so, after that, he'd sit in his car just outside of order range and just watch."

"You don't talk to him now," Joe commanded. "Colt or me talk to him. We aren't here, you stay in the house and call the police. We're here, you stay in the house and call one of us then you call the police, got me?"

I nodded.

"He come when the girls were with you?" Joe asked.

"Yeah."

I watched Joe's face go hard as granite before he continued. "He come when the girls were home alone?"

I nodded and repeated, "Yeah, in the end, that's when I decided to move."

"Fuck," Colt muttered.

"All right, buddy, listen to me," Joe stated. "You stay in the fuckin' house, you keep the alarm armed at all times, you keep the doors locked. Even when you're home, alarm on, doors locked. You only work in your yard if you know Colt or me are here. You go to your car with your keys in your hand, ready to roll. You lock your doors in your car the minute your ass is in the seat and the door is closed, at home, comin' from work, at the store. You tell Kate the same. You stay in the fuckin' house if he shows. That's your job, that's all you do. You leave the rest to me, Colt and the cops. Got me?"

"Got you."

"You get anything, flowers, gifts, calls, hang ups, you think someone's followin' you in your car, you think someone's watchin' you, you even get a bad fuckin' feelin', you report it to Colt or me. Yeah?"

I nodded again and whispered, "Yeah."

Joe's eyes moved over my face and he declared, "He's gonna go away."

I licked my lips and didn't say anything.

"Buddy, he's gonna go away."

"He found me." I was still whispering and I had started trembling.

Joe's voice was a lot less tight and scary when he said, "Yeah, he's found you. His problem is, you moved to the right fuckin' place. Okay?"

"Okay," I said, but I didn't believe him, not for a minute.

Joe read that and got closer. "He's through dickin' with you, Violet."

"He's pretty powerful," I whispered, tipping my head back to look at him.

"He's a man, just a man."

"A powerful man."

"Lotsa different kinds of power, buddy."

I stared at him, tall, broad, strong, sinister Joe Callahan and the look on his face made his words penetrate.

I swallowed and said, a lot more convinced this time (but not thoroughly convinced, it must be noted), "Okay."

Joe held the card up between us. "What's this mean, 'DH?'"

I looked at the card then in Joe's eyes. "It's his initials. Daniel Hart."

Joe's torso shifted back, his eyes cut to Colt and his face wasn't granite. It was carved from ice, as were his eyes.

"You didn't tell me it was Hart," he said to Colt.

"You know him?" Colt asked, and I stared at Joe in shock as his one word answer seemed to come from somewhere ugly in him.

"Yeah."

"How do you know him?" I asked, but Joe didn't look at me, he kept his eyes on Colt.

"We gotta talk."

"Joe—"

"We'll talk now," Colt said over me.

I butted in. "Hang on a second, Joe—"

"No. Now I'm gonna fix Vi's wiring, we'll talk later," Joe told Colt, ignoring me.

"But—"

"Gotcha," Colt said.

Joe looked at Sully. "You deal with the flowers." Then to Colt, "Get her outta here."

"Hang on!" I snapped, but Joe was moving away, Sully was moving toward the flowers and Colt had hold of my arm.

"Party time, Vi," Colt said softly to me, and I looked up at him as he pulled me gently away. "Time to forget this shit."

"But, I wanna know—"

Colt's hand gave me a squeeze then it dropped to take my hand and he did this all without stopping as he walked me across my yard.

"Time where you deal with this is over. Hart brought this to my town, now it's my problem. We clear on that?"

I looked at him and saw he looked weirdly both relieved and angry. I suspected the relieved was because now he had the excuse to get in my business and sort this, seeing as he was a cop. I knew that look, that feeling, Tim had it too. Tim wouldn't let his neighbor be harassed by a crazy crime lord either. On the other hand, I suspected Colt was angry because he knew how this felt, having some creepy psycho sending flowers.

"We're clear," I whispered and said a short prayer of thanks to God that He steered me in the right direction and let this house in this town be on the market when I was looking for refuge.

"We get to my house, I'll give you my numbers and Cal's. You program them into all your phones and Kate and Keira's. Okay?" Colt told me.

"Okay."

We hit the street and he dropped my hand but his arm went around my shoulders and he quit talking.

So I called, "Colt?"

He looked down at me as we stepped up on the sidewalk on his side of the street. "Yeah?"

"Thanks."

He didn't reply except to give my shoulders a squeeze.

I looked to my feet thinking Tim would like him. And I thought Colt should know that.

"My husband Tim, he would have liked you."

Colt looked back down at me. "'Spect I'd like him too, seein' as he had good taste."

That was nice so I smiled.

He stopped me in his yard, looked back at my house and then back down at me.

"You're safe here, Vi."

I hoped he was right.

"Thanks for that too." It wasn't much but it was all I had.

Even so, Colt gave me a look that said he understood I wanted it to say more and he understood what I wanted it to say.

He squeezed my shoulders and led me into his house where we stood in his kitchen and he wrote out a bunch of numbers.

The first thing I did when I got home was program the numbers into all our phones.

Even Joe's.

# Six

## Booty Call

"You're quick," Joe said to Kate and Keira, sounding impressed and surprised.

Kate looked at her toes. Keira beamed at Joe.

We were standing in our living room and Joe was giving us a lesson on the intricacies of our security system, and apparently the girls had picked it up quickly.

It wasn't rocket science but it also wasn't pressing four numbers into a keypad either. We all had remotes that controlled the system that we could use in the house and others that we kept in our cars. We also had more than sensors at the windows and doors, we had electric eyes pointing at all sorts of angles all over the house. And there were camera feeds that fed into the computer on the desk in the study where, if we thought someone was out there, we could flip through a bunch of cameras that were pointed in a variety of directions outside the house so we could see all the sides of our house. We could even switch these cameras to night vision if it was dark. Last, we had panic buttons on the remotes, new keypads by all the doors, in each of our rooms by our beds and little ones to carry in our purses that did double duty since they had GPS, so Joe or Colt could lock in on us (or our purses) everywhere we went.

No joke.

Electric eyes, night vision, panic buttons and GPS tracking.

My crackerbox house had a system that I was sure rivaled Buckingham Palace and my girls and I had security that would make the Queen feel comfy. I figured her guards were no slouches, but she'd take one look at Colt and Joe and say, "You're hired."

Therefore, for the first time in a very long time, I felt somewhat safe.

"Mom, you should make Joe your pork chops to say thanks," Keira told me, and my mind went from the Queen of England and my novel feeling of being safe to my nutty daughter who was looking at Joe and telling him, "Mom's pork chops are the *bomb. Way* better than her cupcakes."

"Keirry, Mom's chocolate chunk cupcakes are *so* better than her pork chops," Kate put forward her opinion and looked at Joe. "It's the frosting."

Joe looked at me on the word "frosting" and my stomach hollowed out, which made me miss it when it tied into a knot. That hollow feeling was much worse. I'd had it since he ended things. It came usually at night when my mind turned to Joe and all he'd done to me, all I'd done to him, how much I liked it, and therefore my mind didn't turn away. In the end, I'd have to reach for my vibrator, which was so not as good as Joe it was not funny.

I didn't like that hollow feeling when I was alone in my bed in the dark. I sure as hell didn't need it standing in my living room with my girls *and* Joe.

"You only say that because you like her seafood risotto," Keira said to Kate and then to Joe she said, "The risotto is all right but the pork chops *rock*."

"Joe should pick," Kate decided.

"How about we let Joe go home and rest?" I suggested. "He's been workin' on the house a long time. He probably could use putting his feet up."

"Yeah, you can come tomorrow," Keira told Joe. "Mom usually makes her good stuff on Sunday. The garden center closes early on Sundays so she's got time."

"Can Dane come too?" Kate put in, and I sighed, wondering if I should call Dane's parents and ask for partial child support since he was over eating our food so much and, while doing it, eating so freaking much of our food. My girls were healthy eaters but the way Dane ate I was glad I didn't have boys.

"Dane can come," I said to Kate, she smiled big and turned toward her room.

"I'll call him now," she announced while moving, desperate to talk to him even though Dane had left only twenty minutes ago. Waving at Joe, she called, "Thanks Joe," then she disappeared down the hall.

Keira looked from Joe to me to Joe and I knew that little, devious head of hers was working. I also knew I was going to have to do something about it, I just had no clue what.

"I'm gonna go listen to music, *not*," she assured Joe, "The Buckley Boys. I'm over them."

"Good call," Joe said to her and my eyes narrowed on his mouth because I could swear it was twitching.

Keira leaned in and patted Joe's arm and I felt my eyes un-narrow because they rolled. Only Keira would have the guts to pat scary, sinister, rugged, huge Joe Callahan on the arm. Marine drill sergeants probably cowered when he walked into a room. Not Keira, no. She patted him on the arm like he was her puppy.

"You're cool, Joe," she told him, her voice weighty, as if she was bestowing a grave honor on him even though a blind person could sense his utter coolness.

Joe didn't answer but Keira didn't seem to mind. She turned and disappeared down the hall. Seconds later we heard music, another crap boy band whose music, if there was any justice in the world, would be outlawed.

"Your girl's got shit taste in music, buddy," Joe noted and my eyes went to him.

"She'll grow out of it," I said this hopefully rather than confidently because Kate had been into boy bands until she was around twelve then she'd switched to real bands. But Keira was holding on and the bloom didn't seem to be going off the rose.

Joe seemed okay with standing in my living room, which I was *not* okay with, so I suggested, "Don't you have to go put your feet up?"

Then he made a mistake.

His mistake was asking, "Am I invited to dinner tomorrow night?"

Seeing as the last time I asked him to dinner I was naked in his bed thinking that we were starting something good and he told me he was done with me, I decided that invitation wouldn't be voiced twice. My girls could do it then I could renege on it. This was my right since he fucked me over. He might have put in a killer security system, but I didn't ask for it so I didn't owe him shit.

Therefore I answered, "No."

His eyes never left my face when he muttered, "I didn't think so."

"You wanna be involved in this shit, your call," I told him quietly so the girls wouldn't hear. "Anytime you wanna back out, that's your call too." Joe didn't reply, he just kept looking at me. So I decided to finish it. "And I'd appreciate it, you didn't make friends with my girls, it isn't cool."

"Not me makin' friends with them," Joe pointed out.

"Then it'll be you who discourages them from doin' it."

"Not gonna be an asshole to your daughters."

"You had no problem bein' an asshole to their mom," I reminded him.

I watched him go from annoyed to angry. He got close, both his body to mine and his face in mine, and his voice went low.

"Gotta admit, I regretted it. Your mouth is sweet, other parts of you sweeter," he told me. "The way you behaved since, buddy, figure I saved myself a world of hassle. You can be a bitch."

I felt my body get tight but I inched my face closer to his and spoke as low as he did. "Thank you for your service, Joe, you can go now."

"There it is," Joe muttered. "The bitch."

"I can't believe you," I hissed. "You're in my living room callin' me a bitch."

"That's 'cause you're actin' like one."

"Then I suggest you save yourself the hassle and leave."

He didn't move. He stayed in my face and his voice was even lower when he said in that way where he sounded like he was talking to himself, "Wonder if it'd be worth it."

"What?"

"Breakin' you."

I blinked then I repeated, "What?"

He didn't hesitate handing me his utterly unbelievable response. "Turnin' you over my knee, spankin' that ass of yours until you break and let go of the bitch."

I felt my breath catch as my stomach both hollowed out and twisted into a knot.

"*What?*" I hissed.

"Might not be worth it, but it'd be fun doin' it."

I clenched my teeth and said through them, "Get out."

He didn't get out. His big hand came up and curled over my hair at the back of my neck and he brought my face even closer, to within an inch of his. It was so close I could feel his breath on my lips, but all I could see was his clear blue eyes which were staring right into mine.

"Make you beg me to stop," he muttered. "Make you do anything to make me stop, promise to let go of the bitch and be nothin' but sweet to me."

"Take your hand off me," I whispered because, even though his words were pissing me off, for some insane reason I really wanted to kiss him. I wanted this so much my mouth was dry and my body hurt from holding it away from the heat of his.

"Play with you while I do it, make you squirm at the same time I make you beg."

My stomach unknotted, I felt wetness rush between my legs and it took everything I had not to move into him.

"Joe—"

The minute I said his name, his hand tightened on my neck almost like a reflex action.

"Yeah," he whispered and I held my breath, not understanding what his "yeah" meant but the way he said it made it sound like it meant something important. Then he muttered his own name, "Joe."

My eyes dropped to his mouth and I started to lean into him because I couldn't hold back anymore. I had to kiss him, put my hands on him or that hollow feeling was going to start eating out my insides.

But he let me go. I went forward on a foot and righted myself in time to see him disappear through my front door.

"I *hate* you," I whispered to the door and I meant it, even though my body—nipples hard, tingles between my legs, every inch of skin electrified—felt something else.

It wasn't until much later, when I was in bed, the girls were asleep and I'd put aside my vibrator after a lackluster orgasm that I realized I'd never asked Joe how he knew Daniel Hart.

The screeching woke me.

Cory was home.

This happened a lot, Tina screeching at Cory. It was usually during daytime hours but it wasn't unusual for it to happen at night.

I turned my head to my alarm clock and felt my temper flare because it might not be unusual for it to happen at night, even late at night, say eleven-ish, but it *was* unusual for it to happen at one fifty-three in the freaking morning.

"You *dick*!" Tina shouted. "Did you fuck her before comin' to me? Hunh? Did you?"

God, it sounded like they were right outside my bedroom door.

And if it sounded like that to me, it might sound like that to Kate and Keira.

I threw back the covers, ran to get Tim's robe, shrugged it on and nabbed Joe's remote from my nightstand as I walked quickly to the back door.

"*Fuck that! Fuck you! And fuck her!*" Tina shrieked.

I hit the remote to disable the alarm as Joe taught us to do, slid the door open and stepped out on my deck. I looked to my left to see that Tina and Cory were, for some unknown and ungodly reason, playing out their latest drama on her deck.

"You have *got* to be *shittin'* me!" Tina screamed to whatever Cory mumbled (I never heard Cory during the screeching, only Tina, then again they probably heard Tina in Bangladesh, she was that loud). "You *dick*!"

I ran down the steps into my yard and across to Tina's.

I was at the foot of her side deck steps when I spoke. "Hey, could you keep it down?"

Tina's eyes came to me, and Cory, whose back was to me, turned.

Cory was a decent looking guy, nothing to write home about but he wasn't ugly. What made him unattractive was that I got the sense he was clueless and pretty much didn't care what kind of shit he had to take, just as long as he got laid as often as he could.

Tina, on the other hand, was very pretty, dark curly hair, blue eyes, great skin. She had a bit of extra weight on her but she carried it well and used it to her advantage. Therefore it looked good but, unfortunately, she knew it.

She liked to get herself some, as Cheryl would say, and she liked to control what she got, which made Cory perfect for her, in a way. Cory loved his wife, though, which kind of sucked for Tina. She'd bitten off more than she could chew with him and I always wondered why she didn't spit him out.

All of this I didn't know for certain. I wasn't close to Tina. She was the only neighbor who was not friendly (at all). I'd gotten most of it from Feb, Myrtle and Pearl.

Tina's eyes focused on me through the dark and she snapped, "Fuck you too."

I opened my mouth to speak but I didn't when I saw Tina's body straighten with a jolt. She looked over my shoulder and her face paled, I saw it even in the dark.

Then I heard Joe rumble from behind me, "Speak to her again like that, Tina, I'll wring your goddamned neck."

Slowly, I turned to see he was, indeed, behind me, very close behind me wearing jeans, a tee and, like me, he had bare feet.

Oh, and he looked pretty ticked.

"Cal—" Tina started.

"Shut it," Joe growled. "Vi's got two girls who don't need to hear your filthy mouth. I hear this shit again, it's gonna piss me off and you don't wanna piss me off."

"I—" Tina started again, but Joe's eyes cut to Cory.

"Pick one or lose both, but be a fuckin' man, for Christ's sakes. You let her get outta hand again, I'll hold you responsible."

"All right, Cal," Cory said quickly, his hands coming up. "We'll be cool."

Joe didn't respond. He didn't need to. I suspected even Tina wouldn't wake the sleeping giant that was Joe Callahan again.

Then Joe, obviously done with Tina and Cory, grabbed my arm and turned us both toward my yard. He didn't let my arm go as he marched me through my backyard, up my deck stairs and to the sliding glass door. He slid my door shut, yanked the remote out of my hand and pressed some buttons. Then he marched me to the steps and down them again.

We were almost in his yard before it registered on me that we were heading to his house.

"Joe, where are we going?"

"You shut it too," Joe growled at me and I felt my chest squeeze because he was still pissed but now it seemed he was pissed at me.

"Joe—" I began, but he pulled me up his steps, through his opened sliding glass door and he threw it closed.

Then he backed me up against the wall by the door, his body got in my space and he got in my face.

"What'd you think?" He was still growling and I was breathing hard, not knowing what was happening.

It was the dead of night. How was it that one minute I was sleeping, the next minute I was listening to Tina shrieking, the next minute I was listening to Joe be threatening and the next minute I was in his house, he was in my face and he was pissed at me?

He was right, I'd been a bitch to him but not recently. It had been hours ago.

"Joe, I wanna go home," I said quietly.

He ignored my request. "Tell me what you thought."

What I thought at that moment was maybe I should answer his demand. Perhaps that might help. Though I didn't understand his demand, which was a problem.

Therefore, tentatively, I asked, "Thought about what?"

"About us."

"What?" I whispered.

"I make a promise to you in my sleep or something?" Joe clipped.

I was again whispering when I said, "No."

"I fucked you when you were drunk, not that drunk, buddy, but I'll admit, you were drunk. And I fucked you on the hood of my car. But *you* walked across your yard to get to *me* twice. How does any of that translate into a promise from me?"

"You didn't promise me anything, Joe," I told him and realized then he didn't.

"So what's your fuckin' problem?"

"I don't have one." Or at least I didn't anymore.

I had read something into it just because of some reflex action he had when I told him I had to go, when he'd called me baby and when he made some mention about me not wearing shoes. That was it and there was nothing there except what I was so sad and lonely I had twisted into something I wanted to see. He'd given no indication that it was anything more than what he said it was.

Just sex.

"Yeah you do," Joe clipped.

I shook my head. "No, really, I don't."

"Bullshit."

"I don't."

"I'm not gonna be a dick to your daughters because you tell me to and I'm not gonna put up with your shit because you read somethin' into what happened."

"Okay," I agreed quickly.

"I don't need to walk out of my house and run into your wall of attitude."

"You won't," I promised.

"You're standin' there tremblin', scared outta your fuckin' skull even though I'd never fuckin' hurt you, tellin' me what I wanna hear. How do I believe you?"

"Um…" I treaded cautiously but pointed out, "You did kind of drag me to your house in the middle of the night."

"We need to work this shit out," he stated in a way that made it clear that he thought dragging me to his house was a perfectly natural thing to do.

"We could have maybe done it over coffee or something," I carefully suggested an alternative.

"Yeah? Last four times I spoke to you, you acted like a bitch, told me to fuck off, told me you hated me, you gonna have coffee with me now?"

"I make pancakes every Sunday morning, you're welcome to come over," I offered.

I didn't actually want him to come over. I wanted him to let my arm go and I wanted to get the fuck out of there.

"Don't be scared of me, Violet," he warned.

"That's kind of hard when you're bein' scary, Joe," I explained.

When I told him this, instantly he let me go and stepped back.

Then he growled, "Go home."

I just stood there, staring at him in the dark.

Then hesitantly, sounding stupid, I asked, "Are you coming over for pancakes?"

"Yeah, buddy, I'll be over to your house for fuckin' pancakes," he clipped, his voice dripping with sarcasm. "I'm sure you can't wait."

"Joe—"

"Go home."

"Joe—"

"Go home, Violet."

"I kind of need my remote," I whispered.

He didn't move so I did, taking a cautious step toward him, my hand lifted, palm up. He didn't put the remote in my hand. Instead, he tossed it into a chair and then I was in his arms and his mouth had slammed down on mine.

I shouldn't have let it happen, I knew that, but I did.

And I did because firstly, I was fucking *thrilled* he wanted to kiss me. Secondly, because this time I knew the rules to his game. And lastly, and most importantly, I loved him kissing me. I'd been hungry for it for weeks and having it back, I was going to take it.

The first time we had sex, it was a battle which he won.

This time, it was war.

I didn't know if it was the last time I'd have him. The times before, he let me take a little but most of the time Joe took what he wanted from me.

Now I was going to get what I wanted.

We didn't even make it to the bedroom. We were too busy with our hands and mouths, both colliding as they touched, tasted, explored and pulled off clothes. It was going fast and Joe was losing because I was determined. Therefore Joe took advantage, hooked an arm around my waist, shoved my lower body to the side and tagged me with a calf behind my knees which immediately buckled. I went down but he controlled my fall so I didn't crash to the floor. Then his body covered mine and I lost the advantage.

"My turn," I panted into his ear, my hand wrapped around his hard cock as his hand curled around my breast. "I want you on your back."

"Next go," Joe growled back and his finger and thumb rolled my nipple.

My back arched as that shot straight through me but I didn't give up.

"Joe, my turn."

He pinched my nipple and that felt so fucking good, my entire body bucked.

"Baby, you can have me next go."

"Joe—"

"I'm gonna fuck you in a minute. We don't have time for you to play."

That sounded good to me, so I whispered, "Okay."

His mouth came to mine and he ground his cock into my hand. I liked the feel of him, hard and big. I missed it and having him pressed into my hand made me squeeze him, the nails of my other hand dug into the muscles of his back and I mewed low.

"So hungry," he muttered, his tone rough but approving.

"Starving," I whispered my admission.

"Then let's fill you up."

That sounded even better.

His hand left my breast, slid down my side and his fingers hooked into my panties, the only piece of clothing either of us was wearing, and he did all this as he kissed me deep. I lifted my legs, curling my ass off the floor as he pulled down my panties, and I kicked them off when he got them to my ankles. I didn't delay in dropping my legs and spreading them for him. He rolled between and I barely got them wrapped around his hips before he had me full.

My mouth tore from his as my neck arched and my fingers curled into his ass.

"Joe," I breathed.

His hand fisted in my hair and he positioned my head so he could again take my mouth.

"You say my name, buddy, you say it in my mouth," he ordered.

"Whatever you want," I agreed as he pounded inside me.

"Whatever I want?"

"Whatever you want."

"Careful what you promise me, buddy, even in your state."

"Just fuck me, Joe."

I could swear, through his thrusts, I felt his grin against my mouth.

Then he muttered softly, "You got it, baby."

Then he fucked me, harder and harder, until I came and when I did, I moaned his name in his mouth.

Surprisingly, the next "go," after he carried me to his bed, Joe let me "play."

It was brilliant.

Then he played, and I had to admit, that was even better.

After a double orgasm that was so fucking splendid, if I could write, I would have written pages of poetry about it, I passed out.

I woke up and looked at the clock.

It was five seventeen.

I hadn't been asleep long and wanted to sleep more but I needed to get home.

I looked at Joe who was on his back, one of his arms under me but curled up around me. I was pressed into his side and he appeared to be asleep.

I kind of wanted to watch him sleeping but I didn't think that was allowed during a booty call. That was something I did with Tim, on occasion, because I loved him so much and he looked so cute when he was asleep.

Joe didn't look cute. He looked a little scary and a lot delicious.

But watching someone sleep was something lovers did. We weren't lovers. This was something else entirely, something that didn't involve intimacies like watching someone sleep. I reckoned the intimacies shared during a booty call had pretty stringent boundaries and I'd read that situation wrong once, I wasn't about to do it again.

I moved and his arm tightened, his eyes opened and his chin started to dip.

I didn't catch his eye, just pushed against his tight arm, trying to roll away.

This didn't work.

"Buddy," he called softly, his voice gruff.

"I gotta get back to the girls," I mumbled.

"After," Joe muttered.

"I have to go."

His arm loosened. I rolled to my other side, but then his other arm wound around me and he yanked me into his front.

"I said, after," he growled into my hair, pressed his hard cock against my ass and my resisting body stopped resisting.

He pushed into me, rolling me to my belly. Then his hand went between my legs and he cupped my pubic bone, gently pulling me to my knees as my torso stayed in the bed and my head stayed in the pillow.

And I retained this position for a while, first while Joe's mouth worked me then while he was on his knees behind me and his shaft worked me.

After, when I was done and he was done, his hips pressed into mine, taking me off my knees and back to my belly. His body covered mine for only a second before he rolled us to our sides, his fingers drifting from between my legs, up my belly to glide along the curve under one breast.

He lifted up and kissed my shoulder then at my ear he said, "Now, you can go home."

Released from my booty call, I started to move away but his fingers at the underside of my breast suddenly moved up and curled around.

"You understand what this is?" he asked, and instantly I nodded.

I knew what it was. Sex. Just sex. A booty call. A really fucking good one.

"My truck's in the drive, buddy, you're welcome in my bed."

"Okay," I whispered into the pillow, my eyes closed, unsure what to make of this but deciding I'd think of it when Joe hadn't just given me an orgasm and I didn't have his body pressed to mine, his hand curled around my breast, his mouth at my ear.

He moved, his whiskered chin scraping my skin as it pulled the hair away from my neck and he kissed me there.

Then he let me go.

Without looking at him (mostly because I was naked but also because I was uncertain about how I felt about the state of affairs, primarily me being naked, thoroughly fucked by a man I went from not liking, to hating, but kept screwing, and I'd never left a man in his bed, in his house, to run home in the shortest walk of shame in the history of womanhood, except, of course, the times I did this with Joe), I escaped his room, threw on my nightie, underwear and robe as fast as I could in his living room and I got the hell out of there.

Stupidly, for the next several hours, my eyes went to any window they were near and I peered out.

I wasn't on the lookout for Daniel Hart's delivery men, his car, his driver or him.

I was wondering if Joe would come over for pancakes.

Kate and Keira got up, I made pancakes and Joe never showed.

So there it was. Booty call.

I took a shower and got ready to work the afternoon shift at the garden center.

Cheryl had told me there was nothing wrong with a girl getting some. And getting it from Joe was good. So he wasn't going to be the next love of my life. At least I wouldn't be totally alone anymore, not if his truck was in the drive. And I doubted it would be hard to call it off if, someday, some guy who did want to "take it there" walked into my life.

It wasn't great. It wasn't perfect. It was kind of sad after what I had with Tim.

But it was better than where I was without him.

I figured I could live with that.

Even so, I was on tenterhooks on the run up to dinner, thinking, since the girls asked him, he'd come over. I didn't make pork chops or risotto because, with having to work, I didn't have time to make it to the grocery store. I just made meatloaf.

But it didn't matter.

Joe didn't come for dinner.

# Seven

## Visit from Bonnie

Cal lay in bed, his window open, listening.

He'd been gone a week and a half, had to leave the day after things smoothed out with Violet to see to some work.

He'd told her he was going before she slipped out of his bed the second night they were together, telling him she had to go home to her girls. She hadn't slept with him that night, just told him she needed to go after they'd finished their second round. It wasn't even midnight.

Her car hadn't been in the drive when he got home that day, but the boyfriend's yellow pickup and Kate's Fiesta were there. From his driveway he could see the girls through the kitchen window, laughing and looking like they were making dinner. Dane was sitting on the counter facing the windows, laughing with them. If they were laughing, things were good. Colt had called while he was gone, reporting there were no more flowers and Vi hadn't received any further gifts.

He knew Daniel Hart though. He knew the man wouldn't be done until he had what he wanted, something else caught his eye or someone made him done.

Cal just hoped something else caught his eye.

How life could make it that Hart's current obsession moved in right next to him, the wife of a man Hart murdered, when Hart had also murdered Cal's cousin Vinnie, Cal had no clue.

He had been struggling with the decision of whether or not to make the call to Vinnie Senior, his uncle, since Cal found out about Violet and Hart. But after talking with Colt, he decided to wait to see if Hart lost interest before he talked to Vinnie. A call to Uncle Vinnie about Daniel Hart would mean a call to Sal and then there'd be war. Sal was itching for it. Then again, so was Uncle Vinnie.

He heard the sliding glass door to Vi's house open and he shook his head in the dark, grinning.

Then he threw the covers back, knifed out of bed, grabbed his jeans, yanked them on and went to his back door.

He had it open before she hit the steps and he met her on the deck.

She tipped her head back to look at him.

"Hi," she whispered as if they were in her bedroom and she didn't want her girls to hear.

"Buddy, get inside," he ordered, pulling the remote from her hand. He walked past her, down the steps, across their yards, up her steps, and pressing the buttons on the remote without looking at it, he disarmed the alarm before he got close to the door and tripped the sensors. Then he went through her sliding glass door, closed it, locked it and walked through her house. Unlocking the side kitchen door, he nabbed the key he'd seen on a hook on the wall behind the door and he walked out, locking the door and hitting the buttons on the remote that would arm the alarm.

She was perched on the arm of his father's chair when he came back. She had her black satin robe on but he could see the lace of another of her sexy nighties hugging her cleavage through the opening of her robe.

"Where'd you go?" she asked as he was sliding his door shut.

He turned to her and tossed the remote on the couch.

"You're in the wrong room."

"Where'd you go?" she repeated.

"Your system is tight, Vi, but you can't leave a door unlocked. I locked it, went out your side door." He lifted his hand, the keys to her kitchen door jingled from his fingers then he palmed them and pushed them in the pocket of his jeans. "Now, like I said, you're in the wrong room."

She stood and whispered, "Thanks for thinkin' of that, Joe."

Christ, why did his dick twitch every time she said his name?

He decided he was definitely done talking in the living room.

Therefore, he growled, "Get in my bed."

"Joe—"

There it was again.

Fuck, she undid him and she did it just saying his name.

"Bed."

She hesitated then she whispered, "Okay."

He watched her turn and walk down his hall like she had all the time in the fucking world.

He gave it a second to get himself under control so he didn't go into his room, rip her nightgown off and scare the shit out of her when he did her.

Then he followed her.

"I have to go," she said against his neck.

She was on top of him, his cock still inside her, he was still hard, he'd come not a minute before (she'd come earlier but she still rode him hard until he found it) and now she was talking about going.

He had an arm draped around her waist, the other hand in her hair and he tightened both to make his point.

But he made it verbally too. "Not done with you, buddy."

"Really, Joe, I should go."

He looked to his clock, it was nearing midnight.

"You tired?" he asked.

"Yeah," she answered.

His arms got tighter. "Then sleep."

"Joe—"

He pulled her off his dick and rolled them to their sides, shoving his knee between her legs, forcing her to wrap her thigh around his hip and he did this to make another nonverbal point.

She got his point and whispered into his throat, "My girls are alone."

"Anyone gets near your doors or windows, your alarm will go off. I'll hear it, so will Colt, and we'll move on it."

"But—"

"Not to mention it's wired straight into dispatch and Colt's told them, they get the signal, they go in hot."

"But, I—"

Cal tipped his chin down to look at her and tugged on her hair to force her to tilt her head back.

When his eyes caught hers, he spoke, "I thought for a second they were unsafe, I'd be in your bed."

"Are you sure?" she whispered.

What he was sure of was that he was relieved that she wasn't slipping out of his bed to make some bitchy point or that she was using him to get off and leaving him to go home and sleep. Why he was relieved, he had no fucking clue. Any other woman did any of that shit, he wouldn't care less, and some of it he'd encourage.

Vi, it'd piss him off.

He was also sure nothing would happen to her girls. Daniel Hart might have money and power, but he didn't have anyone on his payroll who could slip through Cal's system.

"I'm sure."

Her body relaxed, settling into his. He loosened his hand in her hair and she tucked her face back in his throat.

"It's weird," she said softly and after she spoke her body got tense again.

He waited for her to say more but she fell silent.

"What's weird?" Cal prompted.

"Nothin'," she replied quickly.

"Buddy."

She changed the subject, not that she introduced the subject in the first place. Still, she changed it.

"I'm just gonna doze before I go home."

"Vi, what's weird?"

"Really, it was nothin'. I was just thinkin'."

"About what?"

"It's not a big deal."

His hand slid from her waist to her ass. He cupped it and he squeezed his warning while verbalizing it. "Not gonna ask again."

She was silent a second before she sighed.

Then she asked his throat, "How do you play bodyguard and be home all the time?"

"What?"

She tilted her head back so he again dipped his chin.

"You're security to the stars, how do you guard them if you're here so much?"

"Don't do the bodyguard thing much anymore, buddy," he told her. "Special gigs if the pay is good. Mostly do their systems."

"Systems?"

"Kinda like I did for you."

"Really?"

"Yeah, means I have to deal with their shit for a week, not for fuckin' ever."

"So you just install their systems?"

"Nope, stopped doin' most of the installs a while ago too. Just design 'em, contract out to guys I trust to install the hardware and I come in to do the wiring."

"Really?" she repeated as if this was surprising.

"Yeah. That surprise you?"

"Um…I guess not."

Cal rolled into her, taking her to her back and got up on a cocked arm, elbow in the bed, his head in his hand, and he looked down at her shadowed face as he ran his fingers in random patterns across the skin at her ribs.

"They call me in, I recon their houses, tell 'em what they need, do the design, hand it over to firms who do the installs, maintenance and watch. Wiring is my signature. My systems are sound, but my wiring is impenetrable. No one can do what I do. My designs are comprehensive, seamless, but my wiring is what they pay for. "

"But you used to be a bodyguard?"

"Natural progression."

"Oh," she whispered, but he knew there was more.

"What?" Cal asked. She didn't respond so his hand flattened on her ribs and he pressed in lightly before he repeated, "What?"

"If you only do, um…recon and design, how'd you get mixed up with Kenzie?"

It was then Cal understood her hesitation.

He blew out a sigh, rolled to his back and she rolled with him, coming up on an elbow with her head in her hand like he'd been moments before.

"Sorry, was that…?"

Cal cut her off. "Kenzie had a situation. Stalker. Bad shit. The guy was fucked up. He broke into her house while she was out, did shit you don't wanna know. They upped her security. He slipped through it, did his shit again. They called me to look into her systems. I made some modifications. She was there when I did the walkthrough. I have a reputation. She'd heard about it, she talked to her people, wanted me close, and I didn't blame her. This guy was whacked. She has three houses, I designed new systems for all of them in the meantime, until they caught this guy. I took her back at her request and she paid big for it. She took an interest while I was doin' that. You know the rest."

"Did you stop having her back after you two—?"

"Yeah."

"So you were, um…having her back when you were gone so much before?"

"I don't hang in Indiana in the winter, buddy. Got a place in Florida. I hang there. Come home to check on things every once in a while. Kenzie got a message to me, I knew she was at my house. That's why I was home that night. I came home to deal with her."

"Oh."

She fell silent and he could see even in the dark that her eyes were resting on the bed beside his shoulder. She was naked beside him after he'd fucked her, they were talking, another thing he never did with a woman, and she wasn't touching him.

And Cal found he didn't fucking like that.

He reached out and wrapped his fingers around her forearm, sliding them down to her hand which he brought up to his chest and pressed it flat.

When he did this, her eyes came to his face.

"Did they catch him?" she asked quietly.

"Who?"

"Kenzie's stalker."

"Yeah, a coupla weeks after I quit her. It was in the news, buddy."

"I must have missed that," she whispered then asked, "Do you see a lot of stalker stuff with those people?"

"Yeah."

"Do you help?"

"Yeah."

"So you know a lot about it."

He left her hand at his chest and curled his fingers under her hair where her head met her neck.

"Yeah, baby."

Her body relaxed into his again. "Do they catch them a lot?"

"Always."

"Always?"

"Yeah," he told her, not telling her that the folks who got that obsessed sometimes crossed over the line, doing stupid but seriously sick shit and exposing themselves, but usually terrifying the person they were stalking in the meantime.

"How do you know Daniel Hart?"

Cal didn't hesitate in answering. "He killed my cousin in Chicago."

Her body jerked at his words and she whispered, "What?"

"He killed my cousin. My mother was Italian, she was from Chicago. My cousin fell in with a family and the family he was in with is a rival of Hart's. There was a skirmish for territory. Vinnie was whacked during the skirmish."

"Who got the territory?"

"Hart."

The syllable was loaded when she muttered, "Oh."

"Mafia's not big on givin' up territory," Cal told her.

"So um…"

"So, Vinnie hasn't been forgotten."

"How long ago was it?"

"'Bout seven years."

The syllable was still loaded when she repeated it but it was a different weight this time when she murmured, "Oh."

He put pressure on her neck, her elbow slid out from under her and he pulled her cheek to his shoulder. Her hand glided down his chest then to his side so her arm could wrap around his stomach.

"Sorry about your cousin," she whispered into his skin.

Cal didn't reply.

"Were you close?"

Cal replied to that but his reply was an understatement. He practically grew up with Vinnie Junior. Vinnie was like a brother.

"Yeah."

"Sorry."

"Thought you were tired."

"I am."

"Then why you talkin' not sleepin'?"

"Sorry," she mumbled.

"It was a question, buddy. Somethin' on your mind?"

She hesitated then said, "Tomorrow's Friday."

She didn't go on so Cal prompted, "And?"

He could barely hear her when she whispered, "That makes the next day Saturday."

The fingers of his hand still resting at her neck tensed into her scalp.

"Flowers aren't gonna come."

"What if *he* comes?"

"He does, Colt or I'll deal with it."

She pressed her face into his shoulder and her arm gave him a squeeze but she didn't let go and he knew why when she whispered, "Joe, he freaks out my girls."

"We'll deal with it, buddy."

She went on like he didn't speak. "I could handle it if it was just me, but he freaks out my girls." She took in a breath, let it out and her head and arm relaxed again. "They act like they're cool but those flowers scared them."

"You'll be okay and they'll be okay."

"How can you be sure?"

"Because there's no alternative."

She gave a sharp, surprised laugh and her head came up to look at him. "You know, you're right."

He did know he was right so he didn't reply.

She dropped her head, her arm left his stomach and both suddenly stilled. She seemed suspended for a minute before her cheek went back to his shoulder and her arm draped around his stomach again.

She was going to touch him somehow, do something like she did before, running her fingers along his jaw. But she didn't. She was holding back and Cal felt the loss of that and the emptiness it left locked in his chest.

"I'll shut up now," she muttered but then asked, "Should we set your alarm?"

"You'll be okay."

"Maybe we should set your alarm."

"I'll get you home on time."

"Sure?"

"Go to sleep."

She hesitated then she whispered, "Okay."

He knew she didn't sleep for a while but she didn't say another word.

Cal stared at the ceiling and ran the tips of his fingers along the skin of her hip and ass until he felt the weight of her body settle into him.

Then he stared at the ceiling and wondered why the fuck he was lying in bed talking to Violet and after, running the tips of his fuckin' fingers along the skin of her hip and ass so she'd relax and go to sleep.

Coming up with no answers, he fell asleep.

Cal heard it, a car on the street, bumping the curb violently and his body jolted awake.

He opened his eyes. The room was dark and Vi was a dead weight against his side, her leg curled over his thigh, arm heavy on his gut, forehead pressed against the side of his neck.

He listened, the window still open in his room, and heard a car door slam.

It wouldn't be Hart. Hart liked to make statements so Hart wouldn't do his business in the dark when there was no one around to notice. And Hart wouldn't send someone who would be loud and therefore sloppy.

It had been a long time, years, but Cal knew what it was, knew it was coming and he knew it because he felt the acid injected straight into a vein.

Then the banging came at his door.

"Fuck," he whispered as Violet woke with a start at his side, her head coming up, her hand lifting to pull her hair out of her face.

The banging didn't stop.

"Joe," she breathed, fear in his name.

His hand went to her jaw, forcing her to look at him, and his head came up from the pillow.

He put his mouth to hers and said, "It's not that, baby. It's okay. Don't worry. Just stay here, I'll take care of it."

He kissed her lightly then slid out from under her, grabbed his jeans, yanked them on and buttoned them as he walked out of his room.

He didn't need this shit, not ever but mostly not with Vi in the house. He didn't want her to see or hear what was about to happen. Cal couldn't be sure how the scenario would play out and in what order. But it always played out the same scenes, it always had a theme and it was never pretty. It used to happen frequently, but it had been so long since the last one, he thought it was over.

Unfortunately, he was wrong.

He turned on a lamp in his living room, went to his door and looked out the peephole.

There she was, still banging on the door.

Bonnie.

He unlocked and threw open the door and Bonnie lurched forward drunkenly, her arm flying out to grab on to the doorframe to steady herself.

Her head tipped back and he looked down at her, not shocked at what he saw even though she'd deteriorated significantly since the last time he saw her. However he was surprised that the familiar pain he always used to have when he saw her didn't slash through his gut.

"Hey, Joe," she slurred as if she'd seen him only yesterday, twisting her face into a travesty of a come on and he winced when he heard her say his name.

He didn't reply and looked beyond her to see an old, beaten up, faded Nissan Sentra parked on the street in front of his house. The front wheel was up and over the curb in the grass between the sidewalk and the road.

Christ, in her state, she'd driven there.

She put her hand on his bare chest.

"Arn choo gonna lemme in, da'lin'?" she garbled, and Cal looked back at her and fought back another wince.

He stepped away from her touch but grabbed her upper arm and pulled her in. He positioned her outside the swing of the door and closed it. This wasn't easy. She was small, even smaller now that the drink and drugs had emaciated her body, but she was out of it. Cal had a lot of practice dealing with fucked up people, earning it in his days as a bouncer. But Bonnie was so far gone she was like a standing ragdoll.

He pulled her into the kitchen, flipping the switch and the overhead lights came on.

"Damn," Bonnie complained, her hand flitting up to cover her eyes, "thas bright."

Cal positioned her by the counter and let her go, reaching to the top of the fridge to nab his phonebook.

She leaned into the counter then used it to hold her up as she slid into him, her hands coming back to his body at his sides.

"Lez hava drink," she suggested.

"You don't need a drink," Cal told her, stepping away from her hands, putting the phonebook on the counter and flipping through it to get to the listings for taxis.

"Always needa drink," Bonnie mumbled and that was the God's honest fucking truth. She always needed a fucking drink.

He found the number for a local taxi company and pulled the phone off its charger.

"Whatcha doin'?" she asked, leaning further into him, taking a drunken step forward when her lean pulled her off her feet.

"You're goin' home."

"Aww, Joe. I'm 'ere for you, baby." She fell forward further, her face aiming at his chest, her wet mouth slid along his skin and he fought the sick the touch of her mouth churned in his gut. "Give you wha' choo need," she murmured.

His stomach curled and he wrapped his fingers around her arm again, pulling her away, setting her at arm's length. She leaned heavily against the counter and he took another step away, out of shot.

She tipped her head back to look at him, her haggard face sadly confused like she had no idea where she was or how she got there. Then he watched her work at it and finally focus on him.

"Joe," she whispered.

He heard Bonnie say his name and then, in his head, he heard Violet saying it. Not just when they were fucking, when they were talking or even when she was pissed at him. No matter when Vi said it, it hit him—in his dick, his gut, his chest—and it wasn't in a bad way.

He'd thought, until that moment, that it reminded him of Bonnie. But looking at his ex-wife, it wasn't that. Whatever it was, it wasn't about Bonnie. It was all about Vi.

He stared at Bonnie and saw her hair was long and partially ratted. The natural blonde had been dyed lighter and the dye job was bad. So bad it had a weird tint of green in places. It'd been a while though, the roots were showing, lots of them. Her natural color came through but there was gray in it, like she was far older than she was and she was only thirty-eight.

He tried to call up what she used to look like, the girl he'd fallen for. But staring down at her, her freakishly thin body. Her gaunt face. The purple-blue under her eyes. The yellowish tinge under her skin. The lines around her mouth from smoking too much. And her clothes that were wrinkled, cheap, maybe even secondhand and far from clean. Taking all that in, he couldn't call up the Bonnie who used to be.

All he could see, and in that moment, staring at Bonnie, he could even feel her against his hands, his body, was Vi.

Bonnie was short, five foot five. Vi had to be five eight maybe pushing five nine. Bonnie had always been thin, but she'd had great tits. Now they were sad and sagging under her worn and faded camisole that showed way too much of her unhealthy skin. Vi, Cal knew from what she told him about when she got pregnant with Kate, was a few years younger than Bonnie, but she'd had two kids and still her body was fucking unbelievable, ample ass and tits, tight skin, slightly rounded stomach. Even losing her husband, she hadn't lost any vibrancy.

Vi was a fucking firework compared to the washed out woman he'd married twenty years ago that was standing in his kitchen.

Cal looked at her wondering again, even after years of giving that shit his headspace, after what happened, what she did, he wondered what drew him to her in the first place. What made him ignore all the signs and think he could work his ass off to turn a shit life good for her, for him.

As usual, he came up blank.

Violet, right now naked in his bed, had lost her husband and had some dickhead making her life a misery and she was shoveling her walks, calling her daughters "baby," taking them to the mall and making them pork chops. Her life had turned to shit but she was cushioning her girls from that. She was giving them a nice home in a town where neighbors threw barbeques and her daughters could catch the eye of the local football hero and listen to crap boy bands in their bedrooms like normal kids never touched by tragedy.

She wasn't drinking, smoking cigarettes and weed, snorting coke, scoring crack and falling to pieces.

This knowledge hitting him, as usual, he wanted to get shot of Bonnie. But this time it was because he wanted to get back to Vi.

"Where do you live?" he asked her.

"Wha'?" she asked, back to confused.

"Bonnie, I'm callin' a taxi to take you home. Where do you live?"

She stared at him, swaying a bit then she said, "Doan wanna go home."

"You're goin' home."

She blinked then slid along the counter to him, stopping when he took another step back.

"Joe."

"Where do you live?"

"Baby."

"Fuck, woman, tell me where you live."

He watched as her face worked. She was struggling, she knew the finale already. It was the same every fucking time. Why she played out this scene, he had no clue and he detested it. But he knew she'd go for it, even knowing how it would play out. He knew what was coming.

"Bonnie—"

"Twen'y for a blowjob."

There it was.

Cal closed his eyes.

"Come on, da'lin'," she whispered, and he opened his eyes to see she was sliding along the counter again, her chin low, looking at him from under her lashes, a total fucking farce.

"You need to get home."

"You can do me up the ass for two hun'red."

His lip curled and he wondered how many times she said that to how many guys, strangers, anyone who was willing to pay to get off with her. Looking at her he doubted she did good business.

Then he felt it and looked to his left to see Violet standing in the hall, wearing his t-shirt, her dark hair a tumbled mess around her face and shoulders. His tee fell long on her, over her hips but he could see most of her long legs. The whole of her, even in the middle of the night, looked vital, alive and sexy as all hell, polar opposite to the sad case in his kitchen.

But she was leaned against the doorway into the living room, her eyes on Bonnie, her face pale.

She'd heard.

Cal clenched his teeth and looked back at his ex-wife.

"You got a choice, you can let me put you in a taxi, I'll pay, or I'm takin' you to Indy and droppin' you off at the first place I can stop."

"Got a car, Joe."

"You aren't drivin' in your state."

"Doan wanna go home."

"That's not one of your choices."

Her body jerked and she looked to her right, belatedly feeling Vi's presence.

"Hey," Bonnie called, smiling drunkenly at Violet. "We 'avin' a pardee?"

"Can I help, Joe?" Vi asked softly, walking into the living room, and Cal looked at her.

It was useless. She was there, she'd heard. He could no longer shield her from this scene but still he tried as he spoke softly back to her. "No, buddy, go back to bed."

"You wanna drink?" Bonnie asked Vi.

"No, thanks," Vi replied, not going back to bed, moving into the kitchen, her eyes glued to Bonnie as she moved.

Bonnie jerked a thumb to herself. "I'm Bonnie."

"Violet," Vi whispered, her tone uncertain.

Bonnie looked to Cal. "Shiz preddie, Joe."

Cal wondered what Violet would do but he didn't have to wonder long.

Though if he'd have guessed he wouldn't in a million years have guessed she would do what she did.

She walked to his side and shoved into it with her shoulder pushing back his arm. She then plastered her front to his side, sliding her hands along his body, one at his stomach, one across his back and she wrapped him tight. He didn't know what she was saying with her action, whether it was a claiming, telling Bonnie her thoughts on the state of play with Cal, a show of support for Cal, or both. At that moment either way worked for him, but both was better.

Other than pushing her away, he had no choice but to drape his arm around her shoulders, which was what he did.

Bonnie's upper body swayed back as she took them in.

Then her eyes drifted up to Cal's and her face was disbelieving when she asked, "She yours?"

Bonnie's tone was now not only drunken but surprised, her face twisted with hurt and uncertainty. Even after all these years, this was a blow to her. Cal saw to his pissed-off amazement that somewhere in that fucked up head of hers, she still laid claim to him, even after what she'd done.

She'd never been to Cal's when he'd had a woman there. But even Bonnie couldn't be so far gone as to see all that was Vi in his tee pressed possessively against his side and not make the comparison. Not see that this time, it wasn't just going to be a no because she had wasted her life away, and her body, but mostly because of their fucked up history. Instead it was because she'd obviously been replaced by a far superior model. Even wasted, she couldn't twist that messed up head of hers into thinking she could talk him into a trip down memory lane, if he paid for it, of course. She had to know he'd never want her mouth on him, his dick in her, when he had Violet.

Cal didn't answer. He was too angry and he wanted this done. Instead, he looked back down to the phonebook to find the number on the ad and he curled Vi closer.

His head came up when Bonnie suddenly declared, "Thiz iz mah house!"

Her eyes were narrowed on Vi and she'd swayed forward.

He knew this drill too, when she got pissed. He'd been living with that a long time, even before she let what happened happen. He was reminded of the vicious, out of control way Bonnie could get pissed every time he looked in the mirror.

Cal gave Violet a squeeze and murmured, "Go back to bed, buddy."

Before Vi could move, Bonnie lurched forward, shouting, "Mah house!"

Then she lost her footing and dropped gracelessly down to her hands and knees on the kitchen floor.

Violet's body jolted at his side and she stepped back, swinging Cal's torso with her in what seemed to be an effort to move him to safety. But only his torso went because his feet stayed planted. He'd seen this all before.

"Fuck," he muttered, his eyes on Bonnie.

"Joe—" Violet whispered, and he knew she was watching Bonnie too.

"*Mah house!*" Bonnie screeched, her head snapping back, her lank hair drifting. "Mah man!"

Cal hit the buttons on the phone to call the taxi.

Bonnie crawled toward them and lifted a hand when she got close. Cal moved Violet behind him, dropping his arm and stepped into Bonnie as she took a clumsy swipe at their legs and missed.

He put the phone to his ear.

"Shouldn't we get her up?" Violet whispered, her hands on his lower back, fingers curling into the waistband of his jeans. She was so close he could feel her tits in his tee brushing against his skin.

"Yeah, I need a taxi, one one eight Elm. Pre-paid, it's goin' to Indy," Cal said into the phone after the dispatcher answered.

"Joe—" Violet whispered, pressing closer.

Bonnie lifted up to her knees, still swaying, her eyes slits and they were on Vi. "You thin' your shid doan stink."

"Soon's you can get here," Cal said into the phone.

"We should help her," Violet said at his back.

"Id stinks jus' like mine!" Bonnie declared.

"Give me a second," Cal told the dispatcher and turned to Violet. "Go get my wallet on the nightstand. I need my credit card."

She looked up at him and opened her mouth to speak.

"Do it, buddy," he ordered gently.

She closed her mouth, nodded, glanced down at Bonnie and then rushed out of the room.

"Id stinks!" Bonnie shouted after her, reeling to the side and down on a hand.

"Christ, Bonnie, shut it," Cal clipped.

Bonnie turned to glare at him and came back up to her knees, throwing out a hand to grab onto the counter and pull herself up.

While she did this, she asked, "Whas she doin' in mah house?"

Cal didn't reply.

With a fair amount of effort, Bonnie got to her feet and repeated louder, "Whas she doin' in mah house?"

Violet rushed back. She had his wallet in her hand and he took it from her then he used his arm to sweep her behind him again. She moved back into position, close to his back, fingers curled into his jeans.

Bonnie glared over his shoulder at Violet as Cal read out his credit card number, confirmed the address then hit the button to turn off the phone.

The second he threw it on the counter, Bonnie snapped at him, "Ahy come home, shiz in mah house."

Cal was losing it. Even if Vi went to the bedroom she could still hear, the walls were thin and she'd already seen the worst of it just catching sight of his ex-wife, much less Bonnie crashing drunkenly to the floor. He was done with her shit, totally over it. He had been for nearly two decades.

Therefore, he didn't guard his response from Violet when he reminded Bonnie, "Woman, this hasn't been your house for seventeen years."

"Mah house!" Bonnie declared, her eyes shifting drunkenly to Violet and focusing. "Joe's mah man."

"Maybe we should get her some coffee," Violet whispered her suggestion in his ear.

"Doan whan coffee. Whan you *out*!" Bonnie yelled.

"You don't get to say who stays and who goes in this house," Cal told Bonnie, and her torso pitched as she focused on him. She blinked, confusion hitting her face then her torso pitched again and she got down to the matter at hand, the reason she was there, the only reason she ever came.

"You gonna gimme money or wha'?"

"Do I ever give you money?" Cal asked and the answer was no, he never did, not once, not even in the beginning. No, especially not in the beginning.

"Need money," Bonnie answered.

"Yeah, I know. Know why you need it too. Don't work hard so I can piss my money away on that shit."

"Need money," she mumbled.

"Find it somewhere else, woman, this is the last time I open the door for you. Next time you show, I'm callin' the cops and they can deal with you."

Her torso swung back and her hand came up, her head shaking.

"Joe, cops, no."

"I'm not jokin'."

She leaned in and had to put her hand flat on the counter to hold herself up. "Wanna come home."

"Don't know where that is but I know it isn't here."

She blinked slowly and her head drifted to the side, her face going slack then filling with something else Cal was familiar with and he knew they were moving to the next part of the scene. The part he hated the most.

She whispered to the counter, "Was only 'appy 'ere wid you."

Cal was again surprised when that pain didn't come like it always did every time she got to this.

He'd never in the past responded. This time, he did.

"Then you shouldn't have fucked it up."

Her eyes came back to him. "You know 'ow id was, Joe."

"Far's I can see it's still that way, Bonnie."

"I need you to keep me straight."

"You don't wanna get straight."

"Ged straight for you, promise."

Now *that*, also familiar, made the pain slash through his gut and he felt his body get tight fighting it.

She'd promised that so many times, it was a fucking joke. He'd bust his balls guiding her off that dark path, and the first chance she got she'd veer right back there. In the end she'd had more reason than just Cal to stay clean, all the reason in the world. She didn't get that.

Then she killed it.

He felt Violet close in on his back, her hands coming out of his jeans to slide up and her fingers curled around his ribcage at the sides as she pressed herself into his back and held on.

At the feel of her softness pressed to him, the heat of her, suddenly Bonnie vanished, the scene in front of him melted clean away, and his mind went completely blank.

She was so close he could smell her hair, a hint of her perfume, could feel her knees brushing his legs. Everything that was Vi was pressed deep into him, soft and strong, like she wanted him to absorb both those things from her so he could deal.

He'd never had that, not in his life with his mom dying when he was eight, his dad losing it then finding Bonnie and taking on her shit. He'd never had anyone give anything like that to him. He didn't know what to do with it. Until Violet gave it to him, he'd forgotten he'd had it from his mother, forgotten it even existed.

"Joe, da'lin'—"

His name coming from Bonnie brought him back into the room.

He cut her off. "I know you're hammered and probably high but you got any healthy cells in that twisted, fuckin' brain of yours, you need to fire 'em up because what I'm gonna say to you needs to sink in. Do not come back. You come back, I call the cops and then I'll sell this fuckin' place and disappear."

"Joe—"

"I do not exist for you. In your world, I stopped existing seventeen years ago."

"We were made for each other, ev'ryone zed we were," Bonnie whined.

"They said that in high school, for Christ's sakes, then you showed them different."

She winced and Cal ignored it, twisting his neck to look at Violet who, when she felt his movement, tore her gaze from Bonnie and caught his eyes.

"Let me go, baby, I gotta get her outside."

She nodded, her fingers giving him a squeeze, her body pressing deeper for a second then she stepped away.

"We were made for each other," Bonnie told him as he advanced on her, grabbed her arm and dragged her to the front door.

When he hit the door, his eyes went to Violet. "I'll be back soon's I get her in the taxi."

"I'll be here," Violet replied.

He opened the door and hauled Bonnie out of it. Then he hauled her down the drive to the sidewalk.

He pulled her to a stop and looked down at her. "Your car isn't gone by noon tomorrow, I'm havin' it towed."

"Can't pay to ged id back."

"Not my problem."

She blinked at him then she did it again. Finally, he watched the drunkenness clear as something profound and ugly sunk in, bringing with it momentary clarity, and she whispered, "You hate me."

"Yeah," Cal told her the truth without hesitation, not fucking believing she didn't already know it to the depth of her bones. "I do. I've hated you every fuckin' day for seventeen fuckin' years. The memory of you is like acid in my fuckin' veins."

He watched her face shift, begin to collapse, her lip trembling. "You loved me once."

"I don't now."

"Joe—" she started, but he didn't let her finish.

"You give a shit about me at all, after all I did for you and all you did to fuck up my life, you give the barest, little, inkling of a shit, you won't come back. You won't remind me. You won't set that acid to workin' in my veins."

She stared up at him, her once pretty blue eyes clear in her moment of lucidity. Then she nodded and awkwardly pulled her arm from his hold. She moved to stand a foot away from him, staring at the street, biting her lips, her body gently swaying like a fucking willow branch caught in a light wind.

Five of the longest fucking minutes in his fucking life slid by before the taxi came. He shoved Bonnie in the backseat, slammed the door, pulled out his wallet, leaned in through the passenger side window and yanked a fifty out, handing it to the driver.

"Take her home. She doesn't know where home is, take her somewhere safe, a shelter if you know where one is," Cal ordered.

"Gotcha," the driver nodded.

Cal stepped back and the taxi pulled away.

He watched the street long after the car had gone from sight. That acid was still in his veins, he could feel it. It had started pumping the minute he woke up and knew she was back and the only time he didn't feel it eating at him was when Violet was pressed to his back.

He stood outside a long time, apparently too long because Violet slid into him again. This time pressing up to his front and wrapping her arms all the way around him.

He dipped his chin to see she was gazing up at him.

"Come inside, baby," she whispered.

It was her calling him "baby" like she did her daughters, sweet, gentle, tender, that one word getting under his skin, making Cal give it to her straight and he didn't delay. But he also didn't share it all with her, not even half of it.

"That was my ex-wife."

Violet pressed closer. "I figured something like that."

Cal noted the sudden absence of the toxin searing through his system just as he noted that Violet's face was soft, her eyes searching his through the dark. She wasn't casting judgment. Nothing was working behind her eyes, wondering about him, about Bonnie, about how he could have been with Bonnie, about the scene she'd just witnessed. She was focused solely on him, and he suspected, even though she didn't know it was there, she had to know something was, so she was focused on taking away the burning sting of the poison a visit from Bonnie always left him with.

He'd never had that either, but having it then from Vi made him lift his hand and cup her jaw, tilting her head back further so he could bend his neck and touch his mouth to hers. He'd done that twice tonight, kissed her lightly, and he couldn't remember if he'd ever done that to a woman in his life.

When he did, she unwrapped one of her arms from his waist and her hand came up, her finger slid down his hairline then all of her fingers glided into his hair.

She lifted up on her toes, and against his mouth, she urged, "Come inside, Joe."

She moved away but grabbed his hand and he allowed her to lead him into his house.

"Fuck," Cal whispered, his hands in Vi's hair, his palms at the sides of her head, his fingers curled around the back.

She was on her knees in front of him. He was standing, her hands were at his hips, over his jeans, she'd only pulled his dick free before she started working him.

Now, if he didn't stop it, he was going to come in her mouth.

He pulled out, leaned down and yanked her up with his hands in her pits. He twisted her, throwing her on the bed, and he covered her.

"Joe, I wanted to—"

His hands found her hips. She was wearing underwear so he wrenched it. Her hips jerked and she gasped to silence as the material tore free and he tossed it aside.

He wrapped his hand around his cock, guided the tip inside and surged in.

So slick, so tight, he hadn't even touched her, didn't kiss her. She just led him to the side of the bed, dropped to her knees, unbuttoned his jeans, wrapped her hand around his dick and pulled him free then she went down on him. He loved it that she so obviously got off on giving him head.

"Joe," she breathed when she was full of him.

She liked his dick. Christ, she fucking loved it and didn't mind him knowing it.

His hand fisted in her hair and he brought her mouth to his, fucking her hard as he kissed her. She kissed him back, lifted her cocked legs and pressed them to his sides so he could ride her harder and drive even deeper.

"Yes, baby," she moaned into his mouth, rocking her hips to meet his thrusts.

She'd worked miracles with her mouth. If she didn't hurry, he was going to come before her.

"Buddy, hurry, I want you to come with me."

"Harder, Joe."

"Split you in two, I fuck you harder."

Her arm tightened around his back and her fingers slid into his hair.

"I can take it."

He drove into her harder, deeper, so much her breath hitched with each stroke.

"Baby?" he called.

"Love that, Joe," she whispered.

He couldn't believe it but she proved it by kissing him.

He felt it start for her, her cunt spasmed, sucking him deeper and that felt so fucking good, he had no choice but to let go. So he did and he experienced, for the first time, sharing an orgasm simultaneously with a partner.

It was *outstanding.*

When he was done, he gave her his full weight and only shifted to a forearm when he heard her breath go heavy.

"Joe—"

Before he thought about what he was doing, his head came up and his eyes locked on hers in the dark.

"You even think of tellin' me you're goin home, I swear to Christ—"

Her fingers came to his lips just like he saw her do to Keira at Colt and Feb's barbeque.

"Baby, relax," she whispered. "I was just gonna tease you about tearing my underwear."

He felt something contract in the left side of his chest, something he didn't get. It wasn't exactly painful, but it was strong enough that it made itself known. His fingers curled around her wrist and he pulled her hand away.

"I'll buy you another pair."

"I don't need another pair." Her thighs, still at his sides, pressed deeper. "Anyway, it's worth the loss to have that memory. Big, bad, scary

Joe Callahan, security to the stars, losing control and ripping away my underwear."

He pushed his hips into her and he heard her suck in breath.

"Not a big fan of bein' teased, buddy."

Her arms tightened around him and she whispered, "Then whoever did it to you wasn't doin' it right."

Cal didn't reply and she gave him another squeeze of her arms.

"We got about an hour, Joe, I need to sleep."

He again didn't reply but he pulled out and righted her in the bed. He tugged off his jeans, pulled her key out of the pocket, putting it on the nightstand and tossed the jeans aside. Then he stretched out beside her and yanked the covers over them. She settled into him, wrapping a leg around his thigh, her arm around his gut and setting her cheek to his shoulder.

He stared at the dark ceiling and moved his fingers on her hip and ass until he felt her relax into him.

He thought she was asleep when she mumbled, "You okay, honey?"

She meant Bonnie.

He closed his eyes and his hand palmed her ass.

"Go to sleep, Vi."

"All right," she whispered on a weak squeeze of her arm.

He felt sleep claim her and he knew he needed to be shot of her. He needed this done. He shouldn't have started it up again. Even with her getting the way it was, he should never have fucking started it again.

But he did, and even knowing he should end it, he had no intention of doing that.

None whatsoever.

She slid away from him and his eyes opened as he felt her body leave his bed.

He looked at the clock. It was six forty-seven.

Fuck. They should have set the alarm, they'd overslept.

She was hurrying, standing at the side of the bed, her hands on his tee, ready to pull it off.

"Leave it," he growled, her body jolted and she twisted to look over her shoulder at him.

"What?"

"Wear my tee home," he ordered.

"Wear it home?" she asked, sounding confused and turning to face him.

"Yeah."

"But—"

"I wasn't askin'," he told her. "Wear it home."

"I—" she started, stopped, he watched her face get soft, then she whispered, "Okay."

She bent down and grabbed her robe and nightgown and turned to leave.

"Buddy."

She turned back.

"Get over here."

"Joe, I slept late," she told him.

"Come here."

She hesitated then walked the three steps to the bed. He reached out, grabbed her hand and yanked hard so she came off her feet, her hand and a knee landing in the bed. As she came down, he dropped her hand and hooked his fingers around her neck, pulling her mouth to his.

He kissed her, her tongue tangling with his in that way he liked, like they were locked in some kind of hot, sexy battle for supremacy, winner takes all. After some time, he let her mouth go but not her neck.

"You kiss me before you leave my house."

She was breathing heavy and she whispered, "Okay."

He touched his mouth to hers for the third fucking time in less than a fucking day.

Then he said, "Go home."

"'Bye, Joe."

"Later, buddy."

He watched as she turned and walked across his room before he called her name.

"Vi."

She whirled. "Yeah, Joe?"

He reached to his nightstand and hooked her key ring on a finger then held it out to her.

She rushed back, snatched the key from his hand, leaned down, fingers to his cheek and brushed her lips against his. Then she pulled back, grinned at him, he felt that contraction in his left chest again before she straightened, turned and disappeared.

He fell to his back and his hands went to his face, rubbing his skin.

And again he decided he should end it.

His life was good. He didn't need anything to derail it. He'd worked hard. He kept going the way he was, he could retire to a good life by the time he was fifty.

He traveled a lot, was never home, hated the fucking winters in Indiana, the cold seeped into your bones. He had no idea why he kept the house there except that it reminded him of his dad, some vague memories of his mom, and then there was the six months when Nicky was there.

His beach house in Florida was in the middle of nowhere, two bedrooms, tiny, a twenty minute drive through the bush just to get to a grocery store. Perfect.

Vi'd hate it. He'd taken a woman there once, didn't remember her name, blocked it out because the bitch whined for two full days and he eventually drove her and her suitcase out, dropped her at the airport and left her there.

He had his job, his place in Florida, his plan for his life. He didn't need Violet's shit, her problems, her baggage, her kids. He didn't need to compete against a dead man, a cop, probably a good man. A man he couldn't win against. Not only win Violet, but her daughters.

Then there was the time when she found out the whole story of Bonnie, his dad, Nicky. How sick that all was, how crazy sick it was. He remembered, like it was yesterday, the looks on people's faces when they saw him after it happened. Their shock, disgust.

No, he needed to end it with Violet. He definitely needed to be done with her.

He knew it and, taking his hands from his face and rolling to his side, smelling her hair on his pillow, he still knew it.

He just had no intention of doing it.

# Eight

## Come to Jesus

I opened the kitchen door to see, over the bar opening into the dining area, Kate and Dane going out the front door.

"We're goin' to Joe's, Mom," Kate called on a wave, Dane waved too, and then they were out the door.

I stood where I was and stared at the door, wondering why Kate and Dane were going to Joe's. I also wondered why my daughter casually informed me of that fact like she went to Joe's every evening before dinner.

"Yo, Momalicious, what's for dinner?" Keira asked, wandering down the hall and pulling me out of my stupor.

I closed the door behind me, entered my house and put my purse on the counter, I did this deciding to wonder, for the fifty thousandth time since I lifted the ban on Dane coming to the house when I wasn't there, if I should have lifted the ban on Dane coming to the house when I wasn't there. This was something Kate had difficulty with now that it was summer and she didn't see him at school every day. So I'd given in, but only after I'd given her an honest sex talk which left us both uncomfortable. Hopefully Kate more so, or at least enough for her to just say no.

Then I remembered that Keira asked me a question, so I answered her. "I don't know, baby. What do you want?"

"Fried chicken," she answered.

"That takes marinating," I informed her of something she already knew.

"No, I mean *Kentucky* Fried Chicken, not Momalicious Fried Chicken." She grinned and leaned a hip on the counter. "After a hard day at the garden center, I wouldn't make my fabulous mother cook fried chicken."

Oh shit, she wanted something.

I crossed my arms on my chest and looked at my daughter.

"All right, gorgeous, what do you want?"

She put her hand to her chest. "Moi?"

"Spill."

"Just fried chicken," she told me then smiled wickedly. "And a cut-rate American Husky doggie that's cute, white and super fluffy."

The dog. The damned dog. Since the barbeque all she could talk about was the two hundred dollar dog.

"We'll talk about the dog later."

"Mom!" She leaned into me. "The weeks are sliding by. They only have five puppies and they've already sold three."

"Give me more time to think."

"I can't!"

"You can."

"Mom—"

"Keira."

We locked eyes and I knew I'd win, I always did. Keira had the patience of a gnat. In no time, she huffed and stomped a foot then started out of the kitchen.

"Hey," I called after her as the phone started ringing. "Why's Kate goin' to Joe's?"

"Dunno!" Keira called back and I grabbed the phone.

"Hello?"

"Hey, babe, get your ass down to J&J's tonight," Cheryl said in my ear. "I'm off and since your hot-as-shit, bad boy, player, next door neighbor is off-limits and I'm feelin' a hankerin' for some man company, I need someone to go on the prowl with me."

Since the barbeque, Cheryl had started to call me daily. I knew why. One, she was a nice person. Two, she liked me. Three, she knew it sucked my husband died and thought I needed a friend. Four, she knew it sucked that Joe had played me and thought I needed a friend. Five, she knew it sucked that Daniel Hart was messing with my head and thought I needed a friend. And last, she didn't have a lot of friends and even I knew I was a good one, she obviously guessed I was, so she wanted me to be her friend.

Feb had told me the day after the barbeque that Cheryl had asked for my number and Feb asked if it was okay if she gave it to her. I said yes, and since then every day she'd called.

"Cheryl—"

"Not that you'd be my first choice seein' as you're hot too, so you might cut into my action. But Colt's workin' so Feb's home with the kid. Jessie's a fuckin' loon and she scares me a little. Mimi's got kids and Al's out with his buds tonight so she's in. Dee's workin' so she's out. And I got a night off and a babysitter so it has to be you and it has to be tonight."

"Cheryl, there's something I haven't told you," I said, grabbing a soda from the fridge and heading to my bedroom, opening it with a pop and fizz.

"What?" Cheryl asked.

"Hang on, I need to get to my room," I said quietly, even though there was music coming from Keira's room, another boy band playing, so she probably couldn't hear me. But you couldn't be too careful.

"Ooo, juicy if the girls can't hear," Cheryl said into my ear.

I closed the door to my room, took a drink from my pop and sat on my bed.

"It's about Joe."

"Your hot-as-shit, bad boy, player, next door neighbor?"

I grinned at the phone. "Yeah, him."

"What about him?"

"Well..." I hesitated. "It's back on."

"*What?*" Cheryl yelled.

"Um..."

"How long?"

"What?"

"How long's it been back on?" Cheryl was getting crotchety with impatience.

"Since the night of the barbeque."

She was quiet a moment then slowly, she said, "You. Are. Shittin'. Me."

"No."

There was a pause then a shrieked, "*Why haven't you told me?*"

"I was, um…he went out of town and I wasn't sure that, um…when he got back that we'd still…"

"Is he back?"

"He got back yesterday."

"Are you still—?"

"Yeah."

"I knew it."

"You did?"

"Girl, a man does not get like he got when those flowers were delivered when it's nothin' but a convenient next door booty call."

"It's still a booty call."

"Bullshit."

"No, he made that clear. It's just sex."

I heard a "poof" sound of expelled breath over the phone then, "Yeah, right."

"Colt got intense when the flowers were delivered too," I reminded her.

"Yeah, Colt also had the asshole of all assholes doing sick fuck crazy-ass shit to him and Feb for twenty freakin' years so he knows your pain like no other."

Cheryl did too. She was involved in that mess as well. Not for twenty years but also not in a good way. Not that there was a good way in that mess, except maybe the fact that the crazy guy ended up being riddled with bullets. She'd told me all about it a couple of nights ago. I'd been astonished that she'd pulled it together so fast. It had been over a year ago, but still, she was right. It was "sick fuck crazy-ass shit" and she made it to the other side.

Then again, Cheryl had shared other stuff in her life so I got the firm impression she was a fighter.

"Your hot-as-shit, bad boy, player, next door neighbor doesn't know your pain," Cheryl went on in my ear. "He's just goin' all alpha male when someone fucks with his woman."

My heart lurched and I whispered, "I'm not Joe's woman."

"Babe, seriously? Wake *up*."

"I'm not."

"All right," she said. "Tell me, how are you not?"

"Well, he hasn't asked me out on a date," I started.

"He fuck you?"

"Um…yeah."

"That's a date to a guy," she declared. "Next."

I started giggling. "Cheryl, really, he's made no promises."

"They never do."

"Tim did."

"Tim was eighteen, a decent kid and got his bitch pregnant. Only the not-decent guys, like Ethan's fuckhead father, bolt when that shit hits. You lucked out."

I knew that. Boy, did I know that.

"Anyway, what else?" Cheryl pushed.

"You met him. I don't know how he was with you but he's pretty straight and he made it clear. His truck is in the drive, I'm welcome in his bed. Other than that, no go. I've asked him over for dinner, pancakes, even the girls asked him over for dinner. He never showed."

"He took you to the mall."

"He got shanghai'ed by Keira."

"Girl, you been off the market way too long. You marry a man, he's lawfully bound to drag his ass to the mall with you. Your girl is cute and she's sweet and she's funny but there is no fuckin' man on this fuckin' earth who goes to a fuckin' mall unless there's someone he wants to be with while he's there or there's some shit-hot sale on TVs. A sweet, cute, funny teenage girl asks him or not. And that's the God's *honest* truth."

I licked my lips and thought about last night. I thought about how Joe met me on the deck like he was waiting for me to come over, as anxious to see me after a week and a half as I was to see him. I thought about how Joe walked back to my house to make it safer for my girls. I thought about that whole sad, crazy, ugly drama with his sad, scary, drunk-and-high ex-wife and how he was and how he let me be with him after. I thought about how he wanted me to walk home in his t-shirt. If that didn't make a statement, him giving me his clothes, even demanding I wear them, nothing did. And I thought about what Cheryl was saying.

And I could not go there again.

"Cheryl," I said softly, "I can't go there again."

"Babe—"

"No, I just can't. Okay? This is what it is, all it is, and I'm cool with that now that I know what it is. I live my life and I'm not alone some of the time and the sex is fantastic. I can take only that. Something else comes along then it comes along. Joe'll deal."

"Something else comes along, Joe's fuckin' head will explode."

I wasn't sure that was true. I wasn't sure that Joe wouldn't shrug, say, "Enjoy your life, buddy," and walk away. I wasn't sure of that at all.

So I needed to stay right where I was and not go there again.

"Can we stop talking about this?"

Cheryl was silent then she asked, "You comin' out with me tonight?"

I couldn't go over to Joe's until the girls were asleep anyway, so I said, "Yeah, sure, sounds fun."

"It'll be a blast. Meet you there at, say, eight thirty?"

"Great."

"Cool, see you then and...dress down, babe. I don't need the competition."

"Shut up, you're gorgeous."

"I'm a dick magnet."

"We'll find you a good one."

"Well, hopefully you can spot 'em because I can't," she told me then finished, "Later."

"'Bye."

She hung up and I got up from my bed. Taking another sip from my soda, I crossed the room, opened the door and yelled, "Keira! You comin' with me to KFC?"

"Yeah!" Keira yelled back.

I put the phone on its charger in the kitchen and grabbed my purse. Keira hit the kitchen and I hustled my daughter out the door. I managed not to look at Joe's house at all as I got in my Mustang, pulled out and drove away.

I looked in the bathroom mirror and hoped Cheryl wouldn't be pissed at me.

I decided not to dress down but to make an effort. I didn't know why, just that after KFC (with Dane eating the vast majority of the bucket, which I knew he would and also why I bought an entire bucket), I got the urge to make an effort. I hadn't done anything since before Tim died (except dress for his funeral) where I could make myself up, wear something a bit nicer and feel good about myself for a while. So I did it.

However if Cheryl wore spike-heeled slut sandals to a backyard barbeque, I figured my effort would pale in comparison.

I finished my lip gloss and walked to my bureau, selecting jewelry and putting it on. Then I looked down at my phone.

Since I started my preparations, I'd looked to my phone about two dozen times, struggling with whether or not to make the call.

Then I snatched it up, thinking, *fuck it.*

I went to the phonebook, scrolled down, found the number Colt had given me and I'd programmed in as "Joe's Cell" and I hit go.

It rang three times.

Then it was answered with Joe's rumbly voice saying, "Yo."

"Joe?"

Silence then, "Vi."

"Hey."

"What's up, buddy?"

"Um…"

I wanted to know. Why I didn't ask my daughter and her boyfriend I didn't know, but I mostly didn't because she didn't offer the information and I was careful not to be too nosy with my teenage daughter. But I still wanted to know.

"Vi," Joe called in my ear.

"Why did Kate and Dane come over today?"

Joe didn't hesitate in answering. "Dane wanted to know about what I do."

"What?"

"Kate talked to me at the mall, said Dane was interested in my business. He's a senior next year. He's considerin' his future."

"Oh," I muttered, thinking again that Dane was a good kid, taking time to consider his future and being smart enough to talk to an expert about it. Then I looked to the clock, saw it was already eight twenty-five and that I needed to get out of there, so I muttered, "Well, thanks."

"Violet."

"Yeah?"

"Is that it?"

"Yeah."

"Everything else cool?"

"Um…" I decided on a different ring then the one I put on, took the one I had on off and slid the other one on and said, "Yeah, sure, why?"

"You seem distracted."

"I'm a mom. We're always distracted."

"Know some times you aren't distracted, buddy."

I stopped moving and I felt a rush of heat between my legs, remembering those same times.

"Joe," I whispered.

"What's on your mind?"

Did booty call partners care what was on their booty call's mind?

"Um…"

"Vi." His rumbly voice was a warning. He was, I found, not fond of asking twice.

"Keira wants a dog." I blurted.

"Come again?"

"Keira wants a dog. She's always wanted a dog. Her friend Heather's dog had puppies, they're some kind of breed that costs a lot of money and Keira wants one."

"So get her a dog."

"They cost two hundred dollars, they're an extra mouth to feed and I need vet bills like I need a hole in the head."

This was met with total silence. Silence so total, it scared me and I stopped randomly pawing through my jewelry box and listened to the sheer totalness of the silence.

Then softly, Joe said, "It's dog food, buddy."

"I know."

"That's not an extra mouth to feed."

"Um…"

"You hurtin'?"

"Hurtin' for what?"

"Money."

I swallowed, thinking this was definitely not booty call territory.

"We're good."

Again that utter silence.

Then he muttered, "Bullshit."

"No, we're fine."

"We'll talk when you get over here tonight."

We would?

"Joe—"

His voice dropped low when he ordered, "Wear my shirt over, baby."

My stomach flipped, not pleasantly, and I whispered, "You want it back?"

"No, wanna fuck you in it again."

My stomach flipped again, this time pleasantly, and I whispered, "Okay."

"Better than your nightgowns."

"You've never fucked me in one of my nightgowns," I reminded him. "You always take them off."

"Skin feels better than lace, buddy."

"Oh."

"Those things are sweet, but you look better naked."

"Oh."

Wow.

He thought I looked better naked than in my nightgowns?

*Wow.*

"Anything else distractin' you?" he asked.

It seemed to me, he wanted to talk. It seemed to me, he wanted to take the constant mom load off my mind. A load I used to be able to share with Tim. A load I'd borne alone for too long.

That's what it seemed like to me.

Then again, that was probably what I wanted it to seem like.

"Well, except for the fact that I lifted the ban off Dane bein' here when I'm not and wondering if that was the right thing to do, no."

"Looked in your house last night when I got home. The kids were all in the kitchen, makin' dinner and laughin'. You were good, least last night."

"Really?"

"Yep."

I liked the thought of Joe looking in my house and seeing the kids laughing. That felt good.

It felt good until Joe continued. "Still, he's a teenage boy so every other minute he's thinkin' about gettin' in her pants."

That felt bad.

"Joe!"

"Bein real, buddy. You should know that and you should talk to her about condoms."

"I've already talked to her about abstinence."

Joe burst out laughing and I froze, listening to the richness of it. I'd never heard him laugh. I wasn't even certain he *could* laugh. He was my hot-as-shit, bad boy, player, next door, security to the stars booty call. He was a serious, scary, rugged, sinister, alpha male. Men like that didn't *laugh*.

When his laughter died down, I could still hear its timbre in his question. "Your folks talk to you about abstinence?"

"My mother is asexual. I think my father kidnapped Sam and me."

"Everyone's mother is asexual."

"Not like my mother. She's a robot programmed to one emotion, disapproval."

"See you're close with your ma."

"She doesn't even send me a Christmas card."

Again, there was silence, this time it was strangely weighty, then he asked, "No shit?"

"No shit. She has nothing to do with me or my girls."

"That's fucked."

"Yep."

"You send her one?"

"Every year, but only because I semi-kinda like my dad because he buys gifts for the girls on the Internet that he can hide from my mom amongst other purchases."

"Your family sounds kind of fucked up, buddy."

"I'm American, it's the American way."

"Got that right," he muttered.

I wanted to ask about his family. I knew his mother was Italian and from Chicago but there were a lot of Italians in Chicago, that's why they made the best pizza in the world there (outside of Italy, I was guessing, since I'd never been to Italy). When he spoke of her, he said "was" which made me think she wasn't around anymore. He also had a murdered cousin named Vinnie that he was close to who happened to be in the mafia, pre-murder. This was kind of scary information to have and I was trying to ignore it, especially since Daniel Hart was involved. That's all I knew.

But I didn't think it was my place to ask and I had to get to Cheryl. I was now, officially, late.

"Joe, I gotta go."

"All right, Vi." I started to say good-bye but he went on. "I see Dane again, we'll have a talk."

I blinked then asked, "About what?"

"About respect."

"Respect?"

"Respect for his woman. Takin' care of her."

I froze again.

Then I whispered, "Joe—"

"Figure you don't regret what happened to you, you got Kate, but that shit goes down for them, it could play out differently. They should be clued in. Yeah?"

Why was he being so nice?

And laughing?

And interested in everything?

I didn't come up with any answers because Joe kept talking. "Speakin' of that, Vi, you said you weren't on the Pill and we haven't—"

"I, uh…went back on after the first time, we, uh…" God, how embarrassing. "Anyway, no worries. It's all good."

How fun, telling my booty call I'd been having regular periods.

He cut into my embarrassment with a quiet, "Good news, baby."

And why was he calling me "baby" more often?

I wasn't complaining, but did booty calls use sweet nothings?

I needed to ask Cheryl so I repeated, "Joe, I have to go."

"Use your side door tonight, lock it."

"Okay."

"Later."

"'Bye."

I slid my phone closed and stared at it.

He kept moving the goalposts for this booty call business. How could he say no to dinner but then talk to my daughter's boyfriend about condoms and respect for his "woman?"

It didn't make sense and I didn't have the time or experience to stand in my bedroom pondering it. I needed to get to J&J's.

And anyway, Cheryl would have the answers.

I wandered back to the bar from the bathroom, seeing Cheryl sitting at the bar, a fresh drink in front of her, a fresh drink in front of my empty stool and an extremely attractive, tall, dark blond man standing behind her. She was twisted in her stool, looking up at him and chatting.

I was not wrong about her outfit. She definitely made me pale in comparison. No man was looking at me considering the amount of cleavage and leg she was displaying. I'd actually seen two guys walk into tables because they were mesmerized by her flesh display.

I slid by a couple of people, having to get close to the blond guy Cheryl was talking to to get to my seat. He looked down at me as I squeezed by and I saw he had nice, dark brown eyes and was more than a little attractive up close as I slid onto my stool.

"Hey," he said, and I heard he also had a nice, deep voice.

"Hi," I replied.

He kept looking at me and I smiled at him, waiting for Cheryl to introduce us. When she didn't, I looked at her to see she was looking down to

Colt's end of the bar (which was the way I thought of it since Colt always sat at the last stool of the bar, closest to the wall, the office behind him). She was smiling a little, sneaky smile and I was about to look over my shoulder to see what she was smiling at when the man spoke.

"I'm Mike."

I looked up at him and said, "Violet."

"I know. Cheryl mentioned she was out with you tonight."

"Ah," I said because there was no real response to that.

I picked up my cranberry juice and vodka and sucked on the straw.

He kept talking. "You should also know I know you because I work with Colt."

I put down my drink and asked, "What?"

"I'm a cop. Lieutenant Mike Haines."

"Uh…"

"It's okay, Violet. I just didn't want you to find out later that I knew your deal. Would suck, we had a conversation, I didn't mention it and then you found out I knew all about it. You'd think I was a dick. So thought it best to lay it out there."

That was nice, so I smiled and said, "Thanks."

He smiled back and said, "Hope it's not weird. Can't imagine how weird it'd feel, someone knowin' you before you know them. Don't know how Feb handles it when the serial killer tourists hit the bar."

Feb had mentioned this to me at the Christmas party at Myrtle's house. She told me how the people who heard about her bad business and read about it in the book that was published came to the bar. It was quieting down, but at first it was constant and she, nor Colt, nor anyone in town, liked it much.

"Unfortunately, I think she's used to it," I told him.

He smiled again, and this time, I noticed he had a nice smile. In fact it was a really nice smile. "Yeah."

"Anyway, thanks for bein' honest."

"Colt doesn't talk. He just briefed us in case shit went down," Mike assured me.

I smiled again too and said, "Well, glad you're briefed."

"Has shit gone down?"

I shook my head. "Since the flowers? No."

Cheryl, who had been silent during our conversation, suddenly stood up.

"I'm gonna go visit the powder room. You two talk." She looked up at Mike and said, "You can take my stool. I'm gonna cruise the room before I get back. Just in case Colt didn't give you the full brief, she works at the garden center and has two daughters. They're gorgeous, good kids. And she's nice, so, you fuck her over, you're on my shit list." Then she looked at me and said, straight out, "He's got a son and a daughter and he's single. His divorce was finalized two months ago. Don't know what's up with the divorce. I quizzed Colt, he was locked up tight, Feb too. Joint custody. Haven't met his kids so I can't vouch for them, they could be hooligans. Beware." Then, after sharing those tidbits, she clapped me on the shoulder, Mike on the arm and ordered, "Commence flirting." Then she walked away.

I watched her move and I did it with my mouth hanging open. I knew it was hanging open but I couldn't find it in me to close it.

Mike took her stool and leaned into me so I swung my eyes to him.

"Relax, Violet." He put his hand to my knee, gave it a squeeze then took his hand away. "I'm all for flirtin', if you're up for that, but we can also just talk."

"I've no clue how to flirt," I blurted. "I married my high school boyfriend."

He grinned and I noted he had a nice grin too. More than nice, it was devilish. Then he asked, "Wanna learn?"

I laughed at the concept of Lieutenant Mike Haines, one son, one daughter, joint custody, teaching me how to flirt in J&J's Saloon and said, "Sure, sock it to me. How do you flirt?"

"You want the hardcore stuff or the subtle stuff?" he asked.

I picked up my glass and rested the straw on my lip, looking at him the whole time, and decided to be adventurous. "Hardcore."

Then I used the tip of my tongue to nab my straw, sucked back some drink and saw his eyes watch my mouth do this.

Then his eyes came back to mine and he muttered, "You're full of it."

I swung my drink away and asked, "What?"

"The straw ploy," he dipped his head to my drink, "advanced flirting." I looked at my drink then at him when he finished approvingly, "The tongue, nice touch."

I was feeling suddenly strange and I put my straw back to my lips, mumbling, "Um…" then I covered the fact I didn't know what to say by sucking up another sip.

Mike went on. "Next thing you'll do is tie the stem of a cherry in a knot with your tongue."

I choked on my cranberry juice and vodka.

Mike put a hand to my back, which was easy to do considering I was leaned nearly double trying to take in deep breaths while still choking.

"Hey, you okay?"

I lifted up, placed my glass on the bar and patted my chest. "Just…went down the wrong tube," I gasped.

"Take another sip, it'll help," Mike advised. I took his advice and he was right.

I put the glass back on the bar, looked at him and said hesitantly, "So, um…flirting question."

"Shoot."

"Do you mind if I ask how old you are?"

"Nope," he smiled.

I smiled back when he didn't answer and asked, "How old are you?"

"Forty."

"Okay, I'm thirty-five."

He was still smiling when he said on a prompt, "Right."

I carried on. "And you're saying, at our ages, the knotting the cherry stem flirting trick still works?"

"Sweetheart, I'll be a hundred and two and that'll work like Viagra."

*Shit!*

"Why?" he asked, watching me closely.

"Just that, I thought you boys got over that at, say, nineteen, maybe twenty."

"Nope."

I couldn't believe it. I'd flirted with Joe the *entire time* we were at J&J's together. No wonder he thought he could take me home and fuck me.

"Violet, you okay?"

"No," I told Mike. "Not too long ago, a guy told me he'd pay me fifty bucks to tie a cherry stem with my tongue. I thought he was jokin' around."

Mike grinned and said, "Sorry, darlin', he wasn't."

"Shit," I whispered.

"You do it?"

"Yeah," I told him. "He didn't seem impressed."

"Oh, he was impressed," Mike assured me.

I guessed he was since he dragged me out of the bar not five minutes after, took me home and fucked me.

God, I was an idiot.

"You get the fifty?"

"Kind of…we had somewhat of a fight the next day and I threw it in his face."

Mike burst out laughing.

"What?" I asked when I thought he could hear me over his laughter.

He leaned in. "The next day?" He shook his head as I realized what I gave away, or what he thought I gave away, which was, essentially, what I gave away and then he whispered, "Darlin'."

"I'm an idiot, aren't I?"

"God's honest truth?" he asked.

"Hit me," I told him.

"You squeezed by me, I thought you were the most beautiful woman I've seen in this town since Feb came home. Now I think you're cute as all hell but still beautiful. What I don't think is that you're an idiot."

I bit my lip then I whispered, "Thanks."

"Won't pay you fifty bucks, but I'll take you to dinner tomorrow night, you tie a cherry stem in a knot with your tongue," he offered and I felt my body still. "Though, you should know, you don't, I'll still take you to dinner tomorrow night."

"Are you asking me out on a date?" I asked moronically.

"Yeah," he answered quietly, not making me feel like a moron.

I didn't know what to do. I liked him but Joe had been acting differently, and considering Cheryl and I hadn't been there but for a drink that led into two when Mike showed and she knew everyone in the bar and introduced me to all of them so I hadn't had the time to ask her about Joe, I didn't know what to think of Joe.

However Joe had been clear what I should think of Joe. And seeing as Joe was pretty clear about most everything, I figured Joe would be clear if I should think differently about Joe.

And Mike was handsome, nice, funny. He had a great smile and a devilish grin and he thought I was beautiful.

Therefore I said, "Okay."

"Remind me," he said, and I blinked.

"Remind you?"

"Remind me, tomorrow night, you let me kiss you when I take you home, to thank Colt for takin' that case that hit my desk so he's workin' tonight and I'm here with you."

I was wrong. Mike was handsome, funny, he thought I was beautiful and he was really, freaking nice.

"Are your kids hooligans?" I asked, and he smiled.

"Yeah, terrors. It's good they're growin' up and out of the house with their friends most of the time, now they can terrorize other people. Your girls?"

"Kate's okay, except she's wrapped up in a boy so she pretty much doesn't exist unless his essence is inserted in the atmosphere. Keira's a pain in the ass but at least she's funny while bein' a pain in the ass."

"Sounds like teenagers."

"You should be warned, Keira also listens to boy bands." I watched him flinch and couldn't help but laugh.

"My son Jonas is *in* a band. Drums," he informed me.

"Ouch."

He nodded and added, "Loud."

"Ouch again."

I grabbed my glass and took another sip.

His eyes dropped to it and he asked, "Do you want another?"

I shook my head and said, "I drove here." Then I leaned into him and shared conspiratorially, "See, rumor has it, cops hang in this bar. Wouldn't be good for a girl to get tipsy and then slide behind the wheel of a car."

He leaned in closer too and grinned before saying, "Yeah, I heard that rumor too, and cops really don't like that shit. But, if I buy you a drink, you'll promise to get you and Cheryl a taxi?"

I nodded as I sucked on my straw.

He watched my mouth then shook his head, muttering, "Flirting lessons, fuck me."

"I'm not flirting," I told him.

"Then sweetheart, you're a natural."

I didn't respond because I watched as his eyes went behind the bar. He gave a jerk of his chin then tipped his head to me, which I suspected was his nonverbal, man ordering of another drink for me. His eyes came back to me but then they jerked over my shoulder and he straightened a bit. He focused on something then looked at me.

"Violet, there a reason Joe Callahan is lookin' at me like he wants to rip my head off?"

I felt my body tense, my chest expand, and I whispered, "What?"

His eyes went back over my shoulder and I watched his frame relax as he muttered, "Must be seein' things."

I looked over my shoulder to see Colt's stool empty, so was the one next to it. A bunch of people I didn't know were huddled at the end of the bar. No Joe.

"I know Cal's helpin' out with your thing, he's your neighbor," Mike said, and I looked back to him. "Coulda sworn he was just there, lookin' pissed as all hell."

"He wasn't there?"

"He was there, now he's gone. Man's fast, always was."

At the thought of Joe being there, I licked my lips then bit them and Mike's gaze grew more intense. "There a reason he might be lookin' at me that way?"

I stared into his eyes and remembered he was honest with me right off the bat. He deserved the same thing.

"Joe and I are complicated."

"You call him Joe?"

"Yeah."

"No one calls him Joe."

I shrugged.

"How complicated?" he pressed.

"I don't really know. But I think, in the end, not very."

"What does that mean?"

"Honestly?" I asked and he nodded. "I wish I knew. I don't. All I know is, he's being cool about the security thing, he's helping to keep my girls safe and he and I are not very well defined."

"Not very well defined?"

"Not at all."

"Sounds like Cal," he muttered and a chill slid across my skin, so cold I shivered. "You cool with that?" Mike went on.

"Not really."

"You want defined?"

"I had clearly defined for seventeen years. It wasn't perfect but it was pretty damned good. So, yeah, I want defined."

"Not fuckin' with you, Violet, swear to God, but Cal's not about defined."

I knew that but it sucked having it confirmed.

"He's given me that impression," I told Mike.

Mike's jaw got hard and he looked at the bar as my drink was placed there by Darryl. He pulled out his wallet, slid a bill on the bar, gave Darryl a curt nod and I took the final sip of my last drink before I placed the empty by my new one.

"Mike?" I called and his eyes cut to me.

"Yeah?"

I took in a deep breath and asked, "How are you with defined?"

"I liked defined. My wife liked designer handbags that I couldn't get her on a cop's salary, our credit card bills were out the roof, month after month, no matter how much I talked to her about it. The house, not big enough. The car, not sporty enough. She married a cop, don't know what she thought she'd get, 'specially when she also didn't think she needed to work. So her definition of defined wasn't mine. But yeah, in the end, defined is a fuckuva lot better than not defined, as long as both people get where they're goin'."

"I like designer handbags," I told him.

"Great," he muttered.

"I work though."

He looked at me.

"And, well, obviously, I like my daughters to eat and maybe, if I can swing it, my youngest to have the dog she's always wanted and that's more important than a handbag."

He kept looking at me then said softly, "Yeah."

"And, by the way, all women like designer handbags," I told him, grabbed my drink and took a sip, then finished, "Just to warn you. If you're lookin' for a woman who doesn't like them, well…you're kinda screwed."

He grinned and asked, "They all need one a month?"

I choked on my drink again, luckily not to the point I had to lean over and deep breathe, then asked, "She bought one a month?"

"I won't get into the shoes."

"Sure, I'd like one a month, if I was Ivana Trump."

"I ain't Donald."

"They're divorced too."

He burst out laughing and I laughed with him. This laughing felt good. I hadn't laughed like that in a while or smiled that much. The laughing was especially good since his face was even more handsome when he was laughing.

We talked awhile then Cheryl came back, coming up empty on her cruise. She started to relay the information about how all the men in the bar were losers and Mike wisely decided it was time to move on. He got my address, my phone number and told me he'd be at my house the next night to pick me up at seven thirty.

He also leaned in, his hand curled around my neck and he touched my mouth with his then his lips went to my ear and he whispered, "It'll be better tomorrow night, sweetheart, promise."

Before I could say a word, which I didn't get it together to do since I was concentrating on a little flutter in my stomach, he let me go and left.

"I'm livin' in this town a year, I got nothin'. You're here a few months, you got two hot guys all over you," Cheryl bitched while sitting down then she shouted, "Dee, I'm dry!"

"Cheryl, I'm screwed," I told her. "Joe was here."

Her eyes came to me and she said, "Sure thing, babe, saw him. Why you think I tagged Mike? Mike comes in all the time, totally knew you were his type. That works out I should sell my services as a matchmaker."

I was still letting the first part of what she said sink in. "You saw Joe?"

"Yeah, he came in while you were in the bathroom."

"Why didn't you say anything?"

"And miss my chance at forcin' the come to Jesus? No way!"

Dee put Cheryl's drink in front of her and moved away. Cheryl put the straw to her lips and sucked up a huge sip.

"A come to Jesus?" I asked through her sip.

She put her drink on the bar and turned to me. "Yeah, he sees you gettin' flirted with by a hot guy, he either moves to protect his property or he steps aside. Either way, you know where you stand and you know what you gotta do. Come to Jesus."

"So, you orchestrated that?"

"Am I your friend?"

"I don't know. It depends on if Joe's head explodes."

"Don't you want it to?"

"Cheryl, you haven't been around him when he's pissed. He's kinda scary."

"He get physical?"

"Not really, unless you mean sexually physical, then the answer is yes, a lot. But that's the good part."

She grinned. "I hope it does. If it doesn't, Mike's cool. He's also nice. He's also hot and hopefully sex with him is the good part too. So you win either way."

She wasn't wrong about that, but somehow, it felt like she was.

I sucked back more of my drink, looked where Mike looked when he saw Joe and I saw someone I didn't know sitting on the stool next to Colt's. I thought about Joe and going over in his t-shirt that night and I thought about Mike and our date.

And I thought about how my life was a lot less complicated before Daniel Hart blew it to pieces by ordering a hit on the man I loved who was the father of my children.

Then I sighed and sucked back more drink.

Even though we were both only slightly tipsy, being good citizens (and imbibing in a bar that did indeed get frequented by cops), Cheryl and I took a taxi home. I got dropped off first.

I pulled my remote out of my purse, disarmed the alarm, went in the side door, locked it and armed the alarm again. I checked on Keira, who was sleeping, then Kate, who was also sleeping.

As I was heading to my room, my cell in my purse started ringing.

I walked to it on the kitchen counter, pulled it out, saw the display said "Joe's Cell" and my breath caught in my throat.

Then I slid the phone open, put it to my ear and forced out, "Hello."

"Get your ass over here."

"Joe—"

"Now, buddy."

Then I heard nothing, he'd disconnected. I stood frozen in the dark of my kitchen with a dead phone to my ear and I was thinking maybe Cheryl's come to Jesus idea wasn't such a good thing.

I was also thinking maybe I should hole myself up in my bedroom. But Joe not only knew where I lived, he lived next door and he'd installed my alarm system and most likely had the knowledge of how to bypass it. So I was pretty much screwed.

And what was I worried about anyway? These were *his* rules. I'd asked him to dinner, he'd told me he was done with me. What? I couldn't go to dinner when someone asked me because Joe, apparently, wasn't done with me?

I hit the buttons on the remote to disarm the alarm, grabbed my keys, unlocked the door, exited my house, locked the door and armed the alarm. I walked between my house and my garage and turned right toward Joe's deck.

I got into his yard and nearly tripped.

He was standing in the dark on his deck, his hip against the railing, his foot crossed at the ankle, his arms crossed on his huge chest, waiting for me. He was wearing what appeared to be a black t-shirt (he didn't seem to have anything else), jeans (he also didn't seem to have anything other than jeans) and boots (probably his motorcycle boots, which was all I'd ever seen him wear).

I walked up two of the four steps before he moved, leaning down to grab my hand. Then he dragged me up the two remaining steps so fast I almost tripped again. He swung me into his house and let me go, turning to slide the glass door shut and turning back to me.

"Joe—"

"You play that game often, buddy?"

"What?"

"On your stool, drunk and cute, suckin' on your straw?"

"You have the wrong idea."

"Yeah? You played me the same, exact, fuckin' way."

I felt some of my fear sliding away as anger replaced it.

"*I* played *you*?"

"Felt like I was watchin' a movie after a rewind."

I leaned forward and hissed, "You *dick*!"

He moved and Mike was right. He was fast. I was backed up against a wall before I knew what was happening.

My anger died an early death and I was back to scared.

"Joe—"

His hands were sliding around my back and down to my ass as he said, "I play you tonight."

"No!" I cried. "Joe, listen to me, I've never flirted."

"Baby, you're the best fuckin' flirt I've ever met."

"Yeah, I know. I found out tonight," I told him, putting my hands to his chest and getting up on my toes. "Listen, Mike told me about the cherry thing and the straw thing. With you, I was just drunk. With him, I was just sipping my drink."

"You did the cherry thing with him?" he growled.

"No!" I cried again. "He just told me about it, that, um...men even at a hundred and two, would...um, like that."

"You know men like that."

"I've been with the same guy since I was fifteen. Tim liked it. I just thought he never grew out of it since he'd been with me since he was sixteen. I mean, it's not hard, doing that with a cherry stem. It isn't like pole dancing or something."

Joe was silent.

"Anyway, I've never had to flirt," I continued. "Tim asked me out in the lunch line in the cafeteria in high school. I was buying bad pizza and chocolate milk. Do you get what I'm tellin' you?"

Joe remained silent.

"Joe," I whispered, my hands sliding up to his neck, "I didn't play you. I don't know how to play anyone."

"He ask you out?"

Oh shit.

I closed my eyes.

"He asked you out," Joe said softly.

I opened my eyes and whispered, "Joe—"

"And you're goin'."

"Joe—"

"When?"

"Tomorrow night."

"I leave Sunday."

"For how long?"

"A week, maybe two, meetings are pilin' up."

"Oh."

His hands slid down my ass to my thighs as he bent slightly. Then I was going up, he pulled my legs apart and I wrapped them around his hips as his hands slid back to my ass and my arms went around his shoulders. Carrying me, he started walking down the hall.

"I'm not leavin' for two weeks not gettin' my fill of you."

"Joe—"

"You come to me after he's done with you."

Oh God, why was this so fucked up?

"Joe, I don't—"

He put a knee to his bed and then my back was to it and he was on me.

"You come to me or I come to you. Buddy, you want me fuckin' you with your girls in the house, then you stay home. You don't, I hear your feet on the steps of my deck."

His hand pulled my blouse from my jeans as I asked, "You're not askin' are you?"

His fingers pulled down the cup of my bra when he answered, "Nope."

"Joe—" I whispered when his thumb swept over my nipple and I felt only that and forgot what we were talking about.

"Vi," he called, and I realized I'd closed my eyes, so I opened them and focused on him. "There's five hundred dollars on my nightstand. When you go home in the mornin', you take it."

My body stilled under his.

"What?"

"It's for Keira's dog and food."

"The dog only costs two hundred dollars."

"Then you can buy a lot of food."

"Joe, you can't do that."

"You don't buy her the dog, I talk to her tomorrow, find out where the dog is, I buy it and the food."

"You can't do that."

His thumb did another swipe and I bit my lip.

"She wants a dog," he stated.

"But—"

"Baby, she lost her dad. She should get a fuckin' dog."

I swallowed and my body relaxed under his.

"I know," I whispered and I did know. I'd known since the minute she brought it up.

"So take the money, buy her the fuckin' dog."

I put my hand to his scarred cheek and ran my thumb along his cheekbone.

"I'll pay you back," I promised.

"That's for Keira. There's no payback for Keira. You need somethin' from me, we'll discuss payback."

"Joe—"

His mouth came to mine. "Done talkin' now."

"Joe—"

"Might be gone two weeks, we need to fuck."

"Joe, please."

"What?"

I dropped my head and slid my nose along his jaw until my mouth was at his ear and I whispered, "Thanks for the dog."

With my mouth at his ear, his mouth was at mine when he whispered back, "Shut up, buddy."

Then his finger met his thumb and he pinched my nipple and my mind went blank again.

# Nine

## Visitor

I lay on my back on my bed staring at the ceiling and hearing the TV in the other room. Kate, Dane and Keira were watching a movie that, from what I could tell, had a lot of explosions.

My cell phone was on my stomach, my hand curled around it and I had two choices. Either I *needed* to make the call to end things with Joe or I *wanted* to make the call just to talk to Joe.

I closed my eyes.

Things couldn't get weirder or more messed up.

It was now Thursday.

On Saturday, during the day, I'd had to have the talk with the girls, telling them I was going out on a date. I couldn't just trip out the door with an unknown man and call, "See you later!" as much as I wanted to. I had to do what I could to make this transition from Mom and Dad, to Mom no Dad, to Mom dating as smooth as possible even though that was *im*possible.

I still had to try.

So I stood at the kitchen counter while they both sat on stools at the bar opposite me and I told them I met a man named Lieutenant Mike Haines and we were going out on a date.

I expected they'd both be pissed. They loved their dad and I couldn't imagine that, the time having come when I was moving on with life, dragging them with me, they'd be thrilled to bits.

What I didn't expect was Kate to say, "That's great, Mawdy."

But I kinda expected Keira to snap, "What about Joe?"

Which was what she did.

I closed my eyes but opened them when Kate asked Keira, "What *about* Joe?"

"Joe's a hottie," Keira replied to Kate.

"Yeah, he's a hottie, so? Mom likes the clean-cut guys," Kate returned and this was true. Tim was a clean-cut guy and Tim had been the only guy who I'd liked. Then again, it was kinda untrue, Joe was anything but clean-cut.

"Joe bought us dinner, told Mom she looked great in her Lucky's and gave us electric eyes," Keira retorted, and when Kate opened her mouth to speak, Keira finished, "And he likes her cupcakes."

"Maybe this Mike guy'll like her cupcakes too," Kate suggested.

At this point, I was feeling weird about my girls talking about the men in my life liking my cupcakes so I waded in. "Girls—"

Keira looked at me and declared, "I like you with Joe."

Kate leaned into Keira and declared, "She's not *with* Joe."

Keira's head twisted around to Kate and she returned, "She *could* be. He likes her, I can tell."

"All right," I cut in, "enough. This is a date, just a date, with Mike. Joe, Keira baby," I looked at my youngest, "let's just let that lie for now."

"He likes you," Keira stated stubbornly.

"I like him too," I agreed and it was the truth, surprisingly. "He's been good to us. But I'm kinda takin' this one day at a time and I need you girls to let me do that." I leaned both forearms on the counter and finished, my voice quieter. "I'll do my best to make good choices, for you and for me, but I also need you to trust me to do that. Can you trust me to do that?"

"Yeah, Mawdy," Kate said instantly but she would say that instantly. She trusted me, like she trusted her dad. She trusted us both implicitly.

Keira glared at me. "I like Joe."

"Can you give it up with Joe?" Kate cried, and Keira transferred her glare to her sister and then she said something that hit me like a punch in the gut.

"He needs Mom and us more than we need him. He needs a family. He's over there, all by himself, he has nobody. We have each other." She looked at me and stated, "He needs somebody. I can tell."

"Baby," I whispered, feeling the sting of tears in my eyes.

She threw up a hand as she hopped off her stool. "Go off with your Mike guy, I'm cool with that." She looked at me but her body was turned away. "But I still like Joe."

Then she walked down the hall to her room and I heard her close her door.

I looked at Kate who was staring after her sister, her face thoughtful.

"Katy honey?" I called and she turned to me. "Are you really cool with me goin' out with Mike? I mean, you girls and your dad—"

Kate cut me off. "Can't say I don't wish you were goin' on a date night with Dad to Rico's and we were in our old house and Grams and Gramps were just down the street but…" She shook her head and looked away but I saw the tears glistening in her eyes before she finished, "Whatever."

"Katy."

She slid off her stool not looking at me and muttered, "Gotta get ready for work."

"Kate—"

She stopped and turned to me. "Can Dane come over while you're out with Mike?"

"Sure, baby."

I mean, what else could I say?

"Thanks," she mumbled and then headed down the hall.

I dropped my head and looked at my midriff through my arms thinking that could have gone better.

I was also thinking about what Keira said about Joe.

Then the phone rang. I straightened, happy to have something to take my mind from my thoughts, walked to it, picked it up and put it to my ear.

The minute I said "Hello," whoever was on the other end hung up.

Mike called while I was at the garden center and told me that he got reservations at Costa's and I should dress nice.

This was a miracle. I'd heard about Costa's, a lot about it, and everyone said it was great (Feb especially loved it, she'd mentioned it more than once, but then I noticed Feb liked her food). But it wasn't easy getting a table there, especially at short notice.

This was also nice, Mike thinking to call and tell me to dress up. He'd obviously had a wife and knew the drill (this was something I suspected that Joe didn't know, considering Bonnie was his ex and they'd been over for at least seventeen years, if I read it right, though he could have five ex-wives as far as I knew). I was already panicking about my double decker night starting with Mike and ending with Joe. I didn't need to worry about my outfit.

And it felt good, going home, getting gussied up to go out on a date. I'd never actually done that as an adult. It was kind of exciting and scary at the same time. I wore my clingy lavender dress that Tim thought was hot and my new high-heeled sandals that hadn't, until then, made it out of the box. I liked having a reason to wear them. It felt good.

Even so, I'd kind of been hoping that the date would suck, which would make my life easier since I could call things off with Mike if it didn't work out.

But the date didn't suck. Mike picked me up and I noticed yet again he was very good-looking but this time I also noticed that he dressed well (blazer, shirt and jeans, casual for what was supposed to be a dressy night, but he pulled it off because he had a good body, broad shoulders, lean hips, long legs—he wasn't as tall as Joe but he was taller than me, even in my sandals and that was saying something).

And the date was good because Mike was like he was at the bar, easy to talk to. He smiled a lot. He teased. He flirted. He laughed and he made me laugh. He was into me and made no bones about it, which felt better than having a reason to wear high-heeled sandals.

And the food was amazing.

As easy as Mike was to be with at the restaurant was as anxious as I got on the drive home, which was to say by the time I got home I was a wreck. First, he told me he would kiss me, which meant second, I had kids at home who I didn't want to see me kissing someone and last, I had a booty call next door who I also didn't want to see me kissing someone.

But Mike had an answer for that too. He got out of the car and came to my side as I got out then he took my hand and he didn't lead me to the door. He led me to the open stretch between my house and garage, out of sight of anyone but someone who really wanted to look.

Then he took me in his arms and he kissed me.

At first I was disappointed.

Not long after, I realized that Mike didn't kiss like Joe, hard and demanding right off the bat. He also didn't kiss like Tim, hot but sweet and familiar.

Mike was a stealth kisser. It started slow and soft and he built the heat. Before I knew it, his hand was at my ass, pulling me into his hips, his other arm was wrapped around my shoulders and I was plastered against him, feeling his hard body, his kiss, his arm and hand and what his tongue was doing in my mouth and I was feeling it *everywhere.*

He pulled away and I noticed my hands were in his hair, both of them, behind his ears and I didn't realize I'd put them there to hold him to me.

"Not gonna thank Colt," he muttered. "After that, gonna buy him a bottle of bourbon."

"Mike—"

"Wanna see you again, sweetheart."

For some reason I replied instantly, "Okay."

He smiled and he had a *great* smile, even greater close up.

"When?" he asked.

"What?"

"When can I see you?"

"Um…when do you want to see me?"

"You're comin' to my house, Wednesday night. I'm makin' you dinner."

"Okay," I said again, and again I said it instantly even though it was beyond crazy talk to say okay to dinner at his house after a first date and with Joe on the hook.

Then I stopped thinking of all this when he kissed me again. The second time, the fire only banked, he was able to build the heat a lot faster. And he did.

Then he walked me to my door, came in long enough to meet Kate (who tried to be nice and succeeded), Dane (who thought Mike being a cop was "*way* cool, dude") and Keira (who studied him like he was a specimen under glass and not a very interesting one).

I showed him the door, apologized for Keira being a pain in the ass and he grinned, cupped my jaw and whispered, "Wednesday."

I nodded, my knees a little shaky, and he left.

I told the kids not to stay up too late and went to my room.

When I'd closed my door, thrown my purse on the bed and sat down to take off my sandals, my cell in my purse rang. I pulled it out and the display said "Joe's Cell."

I closed my eyes, sucked in breath and felt like a slut. This was mainly because I was acting like one.

I slid my phone open, put it to my ear and said, "Hello."

"Wear those shoes over here."

"Joe—"

"The dress too."

My stomach dipped.

"No," Joe ordered. "Lose the dress, just the shoes."

"Joe—"

"Later, buddy."

I didn't know what to think about Joe watching me go out on a date with Mike. I also worried that maybe he saw us making out. I *did* know what to think about me making out with one guy and barely sitting down before the next one called and told me what footwear to wear to his booty call.

Nevertheless, I wore the shoes.

And, being a slut, I was glad I did with the way Joe fucked me while I was wearing them.

The next morning before I had to go home and before Joe was leaving town, something new happened.

He woke me earlier than I had to get up to be home well before the girls would know I was gone and he woke me with his hands and his mouth. He used them like he'd never used them before—not hard, not demanding, not greedy, but gentle, tender, generous, taking his time and he let me do the same.

And after we both climaxed, when all four of my limbs were wrapped around him and he was kissing me softly while gliding in and out of me, I realized that Joe Callahan just made love to me. For the first time, he didn't fuck me, he made love to me.

Honestly, I couldn't say which was better, they were both fantastic, but it was a beautiful and welcome, albeit confusing change.

I didn't think he had it in him and it made matters far, far worse knowing he did.

"I've gotta get home," I whispered against his mouth.

"I know," he whispered back.

I ran a hand through his hair and down his scarred cheek, my fingers halting there but my thumb gliding along his lower lip.

"You're scary beautiful," I told him, unable to stop myself, and his eyes went intense but he shook his head.

Then he said, "You're just beautiful, buddy."

Oh God.

My hand tensed against his face and I breathed, "Joe."

"Go home, Vi."

"Joe—"

He kissed me quiet then muttered, "Get to your girls."

I had no choice, so I said, "Okay."

He pulled out of me, rolled off and I rolled out of bed.

I yanked on my underwear, pulled on his tee from the night before (I was stealing that too—he wouldn't miss it, he had a million of them), grabbed my dress, my shoes, went back to the bed, leaned in and kissed him.

"Come home safe," I whispered.

"Later," he replied.

Then I forced myself to walk calmly out of his room.

Mike had called every day since our date. He didn't say much, he was either busy at work and couldn't talk long or he had his kids with him.

But what he said was nice.

Wednesday late afternoon, he called to say he had to cancel because he had to work. He didn't seem happy about it.

I didn't know what to feel.

Relieved, a little. Disappointed, definitely. Confused, absolutely.

Joe didn't call at all.

But the person who hung up did.

They called every day then hung up.

It was when they called and Keira answered then they hung up that I got worried because Keira told me that wasn't the first time and because Kate told me she'd had several hang ups too.

So I called Colt and told him about the hang ups and he said he'd look into it.

Daniel Hart had never called and hung up. He didn't seem the type. And, for that reason, this scared me. There was no logic in being scared. It could be some kid from Kate and Keira's school. Maybe Keira had an admirer who didn't have the courage to say hello. Or maybe it was some idiot kid who thought it was funny.

But I got a bad feeling about it.

So I didn't need to be freaked out by what Daniel Hart would do next and hang up calls from psychos or maybe stupid kids.

And I didn't need to be dating a nice, handsome guy who made me laugh and laughed with me and who was good kisser, like Mike, while being Joe's booty call.

I was a mother. I needed to set an example. And I needed to get my shit together.

Therefore, Joe being gone and not around to get under my skin, I decided Joe had to go.

It was brilliant and I loved it. Even fighting with him, I loved it, as crazy as that made me. He scared me but he also made me feel alive. I'd never met anyone like him, and even with Tim, I'd never felt that alive.

Tim was about contentment and happiness. We had our ups and downs, we fought, but mostly life was even and good. I believed in him, our life, our family and he believed in all that too and he never gave me any reason to doubt that he did. The girls and me, we were his world and he let us know it.

It was steady, strong and beautiful. It wasn't the wicked ride on a roller coaster that was Joe.

But those roller coasters were always the best ride in the park.

Even so, I knew it wasn't right for me and it wasn't right for my daughters.

So he had to go.

I lay in bed with my hand curled around my phone and decided I needed to make the call to end things with Joe.

I lifted the phone, slid it open and scrolled down to "Joe's Cell," took a deep breath that hitched in the middle, closed my eyes tight, opened them and hit go.

I put the phone to my ear.

It rang twice then Joe said, "Yo."

"Hey."

"Buddy."

I closed my eyes tight again.

I really liked it when he called me "buddy," maybe even better than when he called me "baby."

"What's up?" he asked.

"Um…" I could say no more. I wanted to…no, I didn't want to, I *needed* to…but I couldn't.

There was a hesitation then, softly, "Baby."

Nope, I was wrong. I liked "baby" more.

"Somethin' happen?" he asked, voice still soft.

"What?"

"He get to you?"

"Who?"

"Hart."

Damn, he was worried about me.

"I don't know," I told him. "We're getting hang ups."

"Shit," he muttered. "You tell Colt?"

"Yeah."

"He didn't tell me."

"Oh."

"I'll call him," Joe said then he asked, "What'd Colt say?"

"He said he'd look into it."

"That all?"

"He didn't go into specifics of what lookin' into it would mean."

"I'll get specifics," Joe stated firmly.

Yes, he was worried about me.

Okay, yeah, I liked him. Shit.

"The girls gettin' the calls?" Joe asked.

"Yeah."

"Shit," he clipped, sounding pissed now. "They freaked?"

"I think they're a bit worried. This is new, it's never happened before."

"Not Hart's style."

"That's what makes it weird and scary."

There was a pause then he said quietly, "You'll be all right, buddy."

"No alternative."

He laughed shortly before saying, "Right."

I didn't reply.

Surprisingly, Joe did. "That why you called?"

No, it wasn't.

"Yeah," I lied because I chickened out. I'd do it later, in a note I'd put in his mailbox before Kate, Keira and I went on vacation (not that

I had money for us to go on vacation but maybe I could sell a kidney or something). "You're probably busy, I should let you go."

"Vi, I'm drivin' in LA. I don't have a cell glued to my ear, they might arrest me."

I didn't think. If I did I would have quashed it. So, not thinking, the giggle slid right out of me.

Joe Callahan, rugged, tough guy, alpha male cracked a joke.

And it was a funny one.

When I stopped giggling, I told him, "I wouldn't want you to get arrested."

"Me either, been there, it sucks."

This surprised me.

"You've been arrested?"

"Hard knock life, buddy. You saw my ex-wife crawlin' drunk and whacked out of her mind on the floor."

I blinked at the ceiling.

First he cracks a joke then he's sharing. Before that, before he left to be away from me for two weeks, he made love to me, slow and sweet.

What did I do with this?

"I grew up, she didn't," he went on sharing.

"So you were arrested when you were a kid?"

"Juvie was my second home."

"Wow."

"Wasn't home sweet home, buddy. Like I said, it sucked."

"I'm sorry," I said softly.

"I'm not, taught me a lesson. That's life, you learn or you die."

God, now he was being a sage and he was good at that too.

"Keira get her dog?" Joe asked.

"Next week," I told him. "They aren't totally weaned yet but we gave them the money and she picked the one she wanted. She's over the moon, she can't wait. She so can't wait, we also have a dog food bowl, a dog water bowl, a dog bed in Keira's room and four enormous bags of puppy chow in the garage."

"Sounds set."

"That dog is so set, it isn't funny. The thing is tiny. It'll take him a year to get through that puppy chow. I just hope he doesn't eat any of my shoes. Feb's puppy eats all her shoes."

I heard his soft laughter, something else I'd never heard from him and something else I liked, before he said, "Hang on a second, gotta give the keys to the valet."

"Valet?"

"Yeah, at the hotel."

"Oh."

The thought of Joe at a hotel with a valet surprised me. He seemed more like a motel on a deserted highway type of guy, somewhere to crash where your car was outside your front door, ready for a quick getaway.

I waited, listening to what were sounds of Joe giving his keys to a valet then Joe said, "Back."

I liked him being back. I also liked that he wanted to keep me on the line, so when I said, "Hi," I said it softly.

"Jesus," he muttered.

"What?"

"We'll get to what when I get to my room," he told me mysteriously then continued. "Speakin' of your garage, you need to start parkin' your Mustang in there."

"What?"

"Your 'Stang, buddy, sweet ride. You should take care of it. You need to park it out of the elements."

"I can't."

"Your garage is full, you should clear it."

"No, I mean, the door won't open, it's jammed shut. Something wrong with the garage door opener."

He said nothing for a second then he said, "I'll look at it when I get home."

I felt my breath leave me and I stared at the ceiling.

He bought my daughter a dog.

He made love to me.

I'd heard him laugh and crack a joke.

He was going to look at my garage door and he listened and advised when I talked about the girls.

And he wanted me on the line.

And, again, he bought my daughter a dog. And he did it because she lost her dad.

"Violet?"

"What?" I whispered.

"You okay?"

"Yeah," I lied but I wasn't. I wanted to believe in him, I really did, and he was giving me a lot to believe in.

"Where are you?"

"Home."

"Yeah, baby, but where are you?"

"In my bedroom."

"Where?"

"Where in my bedroom?"

"Yeah."

"On my bed."

"The door closed?"

"Um..." I looked at the door I'd closed to mute the explosions from the movie the kids were watching then I replied, somewhat confused, "Yeah."

"You wearin' jeans or one of your sweet skirts?"

Oh Lord, I wasn't confused anymore.

"Joe—"

"Baby, answer me."

"A skirt," I whispered.

"Pull it up."

"Joe—"

"Vi, pull it up."

"Are you in your room?"

"Yeah."

"Joe, I've never—"

His voice was sexy low when he said, "I'll talk you through it, baby. Now I want you to pull your skirt up for me."

I bit my lip and tucked the phone in the crook of my shoulder then I shimmied my skirt up.

"Okay," I whispered.

"It up?"

"Yes."

"At your hips?"

"Yeah, Joe."

"All right, buddy, slide your hand in your panties."

Oh God, I was going to come and I hadn't even touched myself.

"Violet?" he called.

I slid my hand in my panties.

"Joe," I whispered when my finger hit my clit and the feel of it slid through me.

"Christ," he muttered, his voice gruff.

"Are you—?"

"No, wanna listen to you."

"You want me to do it alone?"

"I'm here, baby."

I rolled my finger, my neck arched and a mew came out of my throat.

"That's it," he murmured. "Think of my mouth there."

I kept rolling my finger, thinking of his mouth there and moaned, "Joe."

"Jesus, buddy, you already sound close."

I was. This was hot. I'd never done anything like this.

And anyway, thinking of his mouth there, hearing his voice on the phone, it worked.

"I like your voice," I whispered then my hips bucked and I moaned again before I breathed, "I wish you were here."

"Not as much as me. Sounds so good, baby, this I'd like to see."

I didn't reply, just pressed and rolled my finger and ground my hips into it.

"Next time you're in my bed, you do this for me," he told me.

"I don't think—"

He cut me off to order, "Slide your finger inside."

"I like what I'm doin'."

"Do what I say, Violet, slide your finger inside."

I stopped rolling and slid my finger inside. It wasn't the first time I'd done it but it had been a long time and it felt nice.

"How wet are you?" Joe asked.

"Very."

"Christ, I miss that cunt of yours," he growled.

"Joe," I breathed, feeling myself spasm at his growl.

"Make yourself come, baby."

"Okay," I whispered.

He talked me through it and I came, not loud, quiet, but it felt good and he heard.

After, I slid my hand out of my panties, pulled my skirt down and rolled to my side, curling my legs up and feeling strangely that this was one of the most intimate things that had passed between us and he was most of a continent away.

"When're you comin' home?" I asked softly.

"Soon, doublin' up on meetings. I should be home by Saturday."

"Good," I whispered.

"How're you feelin'?"

I smiled into my pillow and answered quietly, "Nice."

"Right now, I'd like to lick your fingers clean." Another mew slid from my throat and when it did he growled again, this time unintelligibly.

"*Mom!*" I heard Keira screech, my body jerked on the bed and I sat upright.

"What the fuck?" Joe asked in my ear.

"*Mom!*" Keira screeched again, this time closer.

"Oh my *God*!" Kate yelled.

"Oh God, Joe." I threw my legs off the bed and started running to the door.

"Call Colt," Joe ordered urgently.

"Okay."

"Now, buddy, right now."

"Okay," I slid my phone shut and threw open my door.

Keira was outside the door, her hand lifted toward the knob.

"*Mom!*" she shrieked in my face.

"What, baby, what?"

"The door…she's at the door."

She?

I looked into the living room to see both Kate and Dane at the window staring out.

Kate looked at me and breathed, "Oh my God."

I couldn't hear her, I just read her lips.

"Come away from the window," I ordered as I rushed to it, but they didn't move so I got in front of Kate and looked out.

Then I breathed, "Oh my God."

Kenzie Elise was standing at the door. She was wearing a drapey, ripped up, sleeveless t-shirt that looked like it cost more than my couch, skinny jeans and high-heeled platform, shiny taupe pumps. Her long mane of strawberry blonde hair was out to *there* and she had more makeup on than I wore on my date with Mike.

"Do you think she's got the wrong house and is lookin' for Mr. Callahan?" Dane suggested.

She didn't have the wrong house but that didn't mean she wasn't looking for Joe.

I watched her lift her hand and press the buzzer and I guessed, by the irate way she did it, it wasn't the first time. In a perfect world, I would be in the position to ask Joe to install a doorbell that was louder, say, one you could hear while you were having phone sex.

She turned and her eyes fell on us at the window and she didn't look happy when she'd turned and she looked less happy when she spied us.

I jumped away from the window and went to the door.

"If she's lookin' for Joe, tell her he joined the Peace Corps," Keira advised quickly. She'd surmised the situation and clearly wanted to run interference on Kenzie's bid for Joe, making certain I had a clean go.

I gave my daughter a look, hit the necessary buttons on the alarm panel and opened the door.

When I did, Kenzie looked down her nose at me. She actually tilted her eyes, not her head, to stare down her nose at me from her towering height in her platform heels.

"Hey there," I said, like she or any other famous movie star came to my door every day and like the last time I saw her she wasn't practically naked and crawling around on the floor.

"Is Cal here?" she asked.

Damn. I knew she was looking for Joe.

"No, he's in LA," I told her.

"How do you know where Joe is?" Keira asked, and I looked behind me to see Keira, Kate *and* Dane had all gathered close to my back. Keira was staring at me. Kate and Dane were staring at Kenzie.

"He told me," I said to Keira.

"When?" Keira asked.

I would have paid money at that moment to have a less astute daughter.

"She calls him Joe?" Kenzie interrupted us with her question and I looked back at her because she sounded kind of pissed and when I looked at her she was glaring at Keira.

"Yeah, we all call him Joe," Keira shared. "Or, at least, Mom, Kate and me do. Dane calls him Mr. Callahan."

Kenzie's eyes came to me and I was right, she was pissed.

"He doesn't let anyone call him Joe."

I opened my mouth to speak but Keira got there before I could.

"He lets us call him Joe. He likes it."

I wracked my brain for a way to intervene and stupidly offered, "Would you like to come in, have a pop or a beer?"

She stared daggers at me and announced, "We need to talk."

I didn't know what she wanted to talk about, though I did know, whatever it was, *I* didn't want to talk about it. But I couldn't exactly shut the door in her face in front of the kids because they didn't know anything about anything and I didn't want them to.

Therefore, I invited, "Okay, come in," then I stepped out of the way.

Her eyes swept Kate, Dane and Keira then they came back to me.

"Alone."

I looked into my house. There wasn't much alone space in my house unless I took her to a bedroom which I wasn't going to do.

Then I saw the sliding glass door to the deck. It was a nice night, not muggy, fresh and warm. The deck was perfect.

"We'll go sit on the deck," I told her and swung my arm out, showing the way. She sashayed in, all leg (or, more aptly, bony leg) and swaying hips and she walked through my house as if prolonged exposure to the air the girls and I breathed would contaminate her.

I walked behind her and ordered the kids, "Go back to your movie."

"Mom—" Keira started.

"Come on, Keirry, let's finish the movie," Kate urged, her eyes on me. She grabbed her sister and started pulling her to the couch.

I threw my eldest a smile, saying a silent prayer to God in thanks He gave me one sane daughter and hustled behind Kenzie.

She pulled the door open herself and walked out, her pumps sounding on the wood of my deck as she headed straight to the wrought iron furniture Tim had bought me at an end of season sale three years ago. The furniture was fantastic, a circular table, wide, comfy chairs that rocked and a big umbrella. There were also two loungers. All of these had elegant, tailored gray pads on them.

She dumped her big, slouchy, designer handbag on the table without looking at me or my garden and started digging through it.

I closed the sliding glass door and approached her, stopping out of distance of her nails.

She pulled out a gold case, selected a cigarette, dropped the case back in her purse and put the cigarette to her lips, lighting it with an elegant, slim, gold lighter.

Then she let out a plume of smoke and stared out at my lawn.

Without anything to say to her, I looked around my deck.

If I wasn't at the garden center, at the grocery store, doing laundry, ironing, cooking, cleaning house, buying expensive dog food and water bowls, sleeping with Joe or just plain sleeping, I was in my yard.

My boss Bobbie gave great employee discounts and I took advantage as much as I could on our tight budget. I'd used some of the money my brother gave me to augment this but most of that I tucked away for a rainy day. But, even if I said so myself, I didn't do half bad with my yard.

The front of the house had window boxes on all of the windows stuffed full of flowers bursting out and greenery trailing down. I had sections of split rail fence at one side of my drive and another where the drive met the front walk that ran from the drive parallel to the house. I'd planted lush, tall grasses around the fences with low to the ground flowers that had filled in beautifully in the Indiana soil. I had a burgeoning hanging basket by the front door and the front walk was lined with vibrant, healthy bedding plants. It looked great.

The back was better. The lawn was just lawn but I'd fertilized it and put weed killer on it and it looked brilliant, rich green, thick and lush. But it was the deck that was the show stopper with its posh furniture. I'd bought bunches of terracotta pots in every size and they were everywhere, stuffed full of flowers of all colors and varieties. It appeared random but I spent ages fiddling with them until I liked what I saw.

And it looked beautiful. I had a way with flowers, always did. I had a part-time job in a florist shop before Tim died because I loved flowers. And Bobbie let me do the displays at the garden center and everyone was talking about them. I even had a customer come up to me the week before and offer to pay me to have a look at her garden, said she was hopeless and needed garden direction. I was going to her house on my day off next week.

"You fucking Cal?"

I started and my eyes jerked to Kenzie when she spoke.

I didn't know what to say. Her question was nosy and rude and more than a little psycho, considering Joe had made it perfectly clear in a way that couldn't possibly be ignored that this kind of information was none of her business.

And why was she there, considering Joe had made it perfectly clear in a way that couldn't possibly be ignored that her infiltration into his life was not welcome?

And anyway, I had kids in the house. Was she nuts?

I looked back at the house and through the sliding glass doors. The kids didn't have their faces pressed to the glass which was good and I hoped they couldn't hear.

"You're fucking him," Kenzie went on, and I looked at her again.

"Would you mind telling me why you're here?" I asked.

She had one arm crossed at her ribs, her other elbow resting on her wrist and her cigarette hand in the air. She swung her hand to her face, took a drag then swung her hand out as she exhaled the smoke.

Then she looked me top to toe.

"What's his deal?" she asked, though I didn't think she was asking me even if I was the only one there. I found I was right when she went on. "You're fat."

I felt my body go solid.

I was not fat. Okay, so, I wasn't thin nor was I rail thin and emaciated like her, but I couldn't be described as fat.

"I'm not fat," I stated.

She sneered and took another drag off her cigarette.

I'd had enough. In fact, I should have slammed the door in her face.

"Listen, if I can't help you with something, maybe you'd like to—"

"Vi?"

I twisted around and saw Colt standing at the end of my deck looking at us.

"Hey, Colt," I called.

His eyes moved to Kenzie. I saw his face register recognition, but that was it then his eyes came straight back to me.

"You okay?" he asked, walking down the deck toward the steps and I saw he had his badge on the belt of his jeans.

"I'm fine," I told him as he jogged up the steps. "I just—"

"Hi there," Kenzie breathed, and I swung my head around to look at her to see she was gazing at Colt like he was a hot fudge sundae with tons of whipped cream, nuts and a cherry.

"Hey," he replied, barely glancing at her and his eyes came to me. "Cal called, said the girls were screamin'?"

Joe had called Colt for me.

My stomach did a little flip.

"Um…they were a little excited about a movie star bein' at the door."

Colt's eyes sliced through Kenzie again then they came back to me.

"You better call Cal. He's worried it was somethin' to do with your thing," Colt told me.

He was worried about me.

My stomach did another little flip.

"I'm Kenzie Elise," Kenzie butted in, and I looked at her again.

"I know who you are, found out about ten minutes ago you keep callin' Vi's house," Colt said to her. My mouth dropped open at this news and I stared at Kenzie realizing she *was* nuts. "Gonna have to ask you to stop doin' that," Colt went on.

"You have my number?" I asked, but she ignored me, her eyes glued to Colt.

"I'm looking for Cal," Kenzie told Colt.

"How did you get my number?" I asked, but she didn't answer because Colt spoke.

"You want to talk to him, you call his girl. You don't call Vi's house and hang up."

His girl? What girl? Joe had a girl?

I forgot about finding out how Kenzie got my number, the more pressing matter at hand was Joe having a "girl."

"Lindy won't give him my messages," Kenzie said to Colt.

"I'll let Cal know his secretary is fallin' down on the job."

Joe had a secretary?

Joe stayed in hotels with valet parking and had a secretary?

"Now, unless you have some business with Violet, might be a good idea you move along," Colt ordered but did it in a way that sounded like a suggestion except it was a suggestion you couldn't exactly deny.

Kenzie denied it. "It's important I speak to him."

Colt stared at her for several long seconds like he didn't know what to make of her but what he was coming up with wasn't much. Then he reached into his back jeans pocket, pulled out his phone, flipped it open and hit some buttons.

He put it to his ear, his eyes on the deck while it rang then he said, "Yeah, Cal, Colt. Everything's cool except Kenzie Elise is standing on Vi's deck. She wants to talk to you." A second passed, Colt grinned at the deck and said, "Yeah, I'll put her on."

He offered Kenzie his phone.

Kenzie didn't look at either of us before she took the phone and put it to her ear.

"You let her call you *Joe*?" she snapped into it without saying hello, which, personally, I thought was a mistake.

I watched as she paused, listened, her face grew even paler than her normal pale (there it was, proof her snapping at Joe was a mistake) then it twisted before she said, "I have another situation and only you can help me out." Again she paused then, "I don't want him, I want you."

I thought this also was a mistake. Joe didn't like it much that Kenzie thought she could get what she wanted when she wanted it.

I watched as she was silent for another moment then she said, "No." Another pause then a hissed, "I can't believe you won't help me!" Yet another pause while her eyes came to me and she snapped, "I don't think so!" She listened for about two seconds then she took the phone from her ear, jerked it toward me and bit out, "He wants to talk to you."

I took Colt's phone. Glancing at her then at Colt, I put it to my ear and announced, "She called me fat."

"Buddy—"

"I have my own stalker, Joe. I don't want to have to deal with *yours*."

He burst out laughing and I didn't think anything was funny.

"I have your movie star stalker standin' on my deck, calling me fat and she's callin' my house and hangin' up. This is *not* funny."

Joe's laughter vanished. He was silent then he said in a soft but scary voice, "What?"

"Your movie star stalker is the one doing the hang ups."

There was no silence before Joe demanded, "Put Colt on the phone."

"What?"

"Give the fuckin' phone to Colt," he clipped.

I decided to give the phone to Colt seeing as Joe sounded pretty freaking pissed so I sure didn't want to talk to him anymore.

Colt put it to his ear and said, "Yeah?" He listened for a while and said, "Gotcha. Later." He flipped his phone shut, shoved it in his jeans and looked at Kenzie. "Cal says you aren't off Vi's property in five minutes, he calls some guy named Marco. He says you'd know what that means."

I looked at Kenzie and I could tell straight off she knew what that meant. Her face had bleached completely of color, her eyes had gone wide, her lips had parted and she looked scared.

Quickly she flicked her cigarette butt in my yard, snatched up her purse and stomped to the stairs.

"Ms. Elise," Colt called and she turned, foot on the step, hand on the rail and looked at him. "Do I have your assurance that you won't be callin' Vi anymore and there won't be any more visits?"

"Yeah, whatever," she mumbled and kept going.

"Ms. Elise," Colt called again, turning fully toward her and Kenzie, now standing in my grass, stopped and looked up at him. "Not whatever. No more calls, no more visits. Yeah?"

"Yeah. Right. Fine," she said and looked at me. "Fine, tell him I won't bother him anymore, or you. Okay?"

When it appeared she actually wanted an answer from me, I said, "Okay."

"Just make sure he doesn't call Marco," she said to me.

This seemed important to her so I nodded.

She started away but turned back and looked at me and when she did, she'd changed. Everything about her changed. She didn't look scared anymore. She looked lost and afraid. A different kind of afraid. A worse kind.

"He made me feel safe," she said quietly. I blinked at her honest, open admission and she kept talking. "I don't feel safe very much. Ever, really. Cal made me feel safe."

When she seemed again to be waiting for an answer, I answered, "He has that way about him."

"He belonged to me, I'd always feel safe."

At that moment, I realized I knew exactly what she meant.

I walked to the railing, looked down at her and said, "I'm not sure Joe's the kind of guy who could belong to anyone, Kenzie."

She stared at me a second and the way she did it I actually felt sorry for her.

"You call him Joe, he belongs to you," she whispered, and before I could say anything or have a reaction to her words other than that feeling of being punched in the stomach, she turned and gracefully ran on the toes of her fancy, shiny platform pumps across my lawn and around the house.

I watched the space where she used to be for a few seconds before I felt Colt's arm come around my shoulders. I turned my head to look up at him.

"That was kinda sad," I told him.

He looked to the side of the house then down at me. "Woman who has everything but really has nothin'."

I sighed then I nodded. Colt dropped his arm, jogged down the steps and walked out into my yard to pick up the cigarette butt.

He looked at me. "Shame this mars your yard, babe. You do good flowers."

I smiled at him. "Thanks."

"I'll toss this out," he said, lifting the butt. "You good now?"

"I'm good, Colt. Thanks for comin' over."

"Anytime, Vi," he said and turned to leave. "Later."

"'Bye, Colt. Tell Feb I said hi and tickle Jack for me."

"Will do," he called as he turned the corner of the house.

I stared after him for a while too. Then I went into the house and all the kids watched me walk to the kitchen.

"She gone?" Kate asked.

"Yep," I answered, pulling a bottle of cheap white wine out of the fridge feeling this was the time that cheap white wine was created for.

"What'd she want?" Keira asked.

"Joe," I answered.

"And?" Keira prompted.

I found the corkscrew and looked at Keira through the bar opening. "Joe doesn't want her."

"*Killer!*" Keira hissed, pumping her fisted hand in the kind of gesture you'd use on a trucker to get him to honk his horn.

I looked at Kate. "You think it's something in the water or is she just touched?"

"She's just touched," Kate said, Dane laughed, and they hit the play button to restart the movie.

I poured myself a glass of wine and went back out to my deck with my phone in my hand.

I barely had my ass to the seat when it rang. I looked at the display and it was Joe.

I slid it open and put it to my ear. "Hi."

"She gone?"

"Yeah, drama over." He didn't reply so I asked, "Who's Marco?"

"Her manager," Joe answered.

"She seems pretty scared of him," I remarked.

"Reason to be."

"What reason?"

"She's where she is 'cause of him. Her problem is, she made a deal with the devil."

"A deal with the devil?"

"Marco's bad news," Joe told me.

"Bad news how?" I asked.

"Bad news, she steps outta line, he yanks her back and he isn't nice about it."

That didn't sound good. That sounded face pale, lips parted, eyes wide not good.

"What?" I whispered.

"He can get physical, buddy."

"Physical, as in, he *beats* her?"

"Yeah," Joe answered. "She's his cash cow. He skims off the top of everything she does, lives a good life. She does shit that might rock that boat, he doesn't like it and makes that known however he has to."

"That's awful."

"Yeah, but it isn't your problem and it isn't mine. It's the deal she made."

A thought occurred to me so I asked, "Why didn't you call Marco before when you were having problems with her?"

"It was just me, I could deal with it and I didn't want to be responsible for him gettin' in her face. Fuckin' with you and the girls, she wasn't makin' it about me. She was draggin' you into it. I thought I could make my point, fuck, I thought I *did*. But I didn't. She fucks with you and the girls, she needs to know I'm serious. Now she knows."

I took a sip of my wine thinking that my world, not too long ago, even when Tim would come home and talk about some of the shit he'd seen, was a little bubble of goodness. Now the stuff that kept pricking it without Tim to keep that bubble strong and resilient was scary crazy.

"Buddy?"

"Yeah?"

"You all right? She say anything else to you?"

Yes, she did. She told me Joe belonged to me.

But I wasn't going to tell him that.

"No, just flicked her cigarette butt in my yard and left."

"Fuck, what a bitch," he muttered.

"That's okay, Colt got it."

He sighed then said, "Good man."

"Joe?"

"Yeah, buddy?"

"Would you have called Marco?"

He didn't hesitate before he answered, "Yeah."

This shocked me and it also disappointed me. "Really?"

"Really."

"But—"

"Baby, she was callin' you and the girls were pickin' up, gettin' freaked out. It had to be stopped, that was my last option. She forced my hand."

"Joe—"

"She forced my hand, Vi. She did it to herself with this crazy shit. You back a man in a corner, you gotta bear the consequences when he does what he has to do to fight his way out."

He was being a sage again.

And it hit me then that she didn't back Joe into a corner. She tossed the girls and me there. Joe hadn't threatened that Marco business when she was doing her thing to catch his attention. He thought he could deal with it and he didn't want to scare her like he just did. But he pulled out the big guns for me and the girls.

I didn't want to make this into a big thing. I didn't want to make the same mistake and start to believe. But he was giving me no choice.

I took another sip of my wine then changed the subject because this kind of subject you didn't talk about over the phone.

"Well, thanks for dealing with it all the way from LA."

"Don't thank me, I'm the reason she was there."

"She was here because she has the hots for you. It isn't your fault you're hot."

I heard his soft laughter again, I decided I liked it again, then he said, "Baby, you're killin' me."

"How am I killin' you?"

"You can be sweet and hilarious when I'm close enough to give payback."

My stomach dipped and I pulled in breath to control my fluttering heart.

"What's payback?" I whispered.

"Be sweet and hilarious in my bed, I'll show you."

"Joe—"

He cut me off. "What're you doin' now?"

"Drinking cheap white wine on my deck. What are you doing?"

"I gotta go get food."

"Oh, okay. I'll let you go."

"All right, buddy."

"You're back on Saturday?"

"Yeah."

"See you then."

"Absolutely."

I sighed and it was a happy sigh because I would see him, he wanted me to, and Saturday was only one-ish day away.

"'Bye, Joe," I said softly.

"Later, buddy," he replied back softly.

I slid my phone closed and then tapped my forehead with it.

I had, of course, called him to end things but instead we talked, we had phone sex and he gave me about a dozen reasons to believe in him. Then, through various other phone calls, he gave me more reasons to believe.

I put the phone on the table and took another sip of wine.

I needed to call Cheryl or I needed to talk to Feb or I needed to call one of my friends in Chicago.

But it was late and it was rude to call late, especially when the conversation I needed to have would likely take hours.

So I put my feet up in the chair, looked at my gorgeous grass and my pretty flower pots, and as I sipped my wine, I decided to see what Saturday might bring.

# Ten

## Talks

Cal turned his truck into his drive but he'd seen Vi as he drove down the street.

She was working in her front yard wearing a pair of very short shorts that showed off her tanned legs, a dark purple tank top that showed more tan skin and her hair was in a ponytail at the back of her head. He'd have been pissed she was working in her yard without him at home next door, but he also saw Colt mowing his lawn, so he knew she was safe.

After he pulled into his drive, he turned his head to her and saw she'd straightened from whatever she was doing and looked his way. She swiped the back of her arm against her forehead, she had something in her hand and she was wearing garden gloves.

He grabbed his bag and got out of the truck. After he slammed the door, his eyes went back to her and she was walking toward him. She'd made it across her drive, was in his yard and she'd lost the garden tool and the gloves.

He headed to his front door and waited for her to arrive.

She did, stopping not a foot away and tipping her head back to look up at him, her hand up to shield her eyes from the sun.

"Hi," she said softly.

"Where're the girls?" Cal asked.

"At the mall," Vi answered.

Cal didn't respond. He turned to his door, unlocked it, opened it, stepped in and tossed his bag to the floor. Then he reached back through the door and yanked her in, slamming the door behind her and backing her against it, his head already coming down to take her mouth, his arms moving around to crush her to him.

She met him, their mouths and bodies colliding, as hungry for it as he was. He moved her from the door and shuffled her across the room to the couch, his hands on her shorts, her hands on the fly of his jeans. Their mouths still going at it, Vi didn't waste time, pulled him free, her hand wrapped around his hard cock and she was stroking.

He yanked down her shorts and underwear, she stepped out of them and he shoved her back onto the couch, following her down.

In order to distract him while she tried to roll him, she used her tongue on his neck and her nails down his back. But he slid a hand from her ass, down the back of her thigh to her knee, gripped it, pulled her leg out and wrapped it around his hip.

"I want the top," she said into his ear, her voice was a demand which turned into a moan because his hand went from her leg to between them so he could press his finger to her clit. When he did, with a moan, she slid her other leg out from under him and hooked it around his thigh.

"I'm ridin' you, buddy."

"No fair, you always get the top."

"Not always."

"Most of the time."

"You can have the top tonight."

"Promise?"

"Yeah."

Her mouth came to his, her eyes smiling then he kissed her and feeling her wet, as usual with Vi, his control slipped and he replaced his finger at her clit with his dick in her cunt.

"Joe," she breathed against his mouth, her breathing his name against his lips forcing him to drive into her harder and she whispered, "I'm glad you're home."

Yeah, he was home and it felt fucking great.

He rode her hard and she lifted her hips to meet him, her legs tight around his hips, her fingernails digging into his back and he rode her until she came, and longer, until he did.

He stayed buried inside her, his face in her neck, her arms and legs wrapped around him and he listened as her breath steadied.

Eventually, since Vi didn't seem to be able to be quiet very long, she asked, "How was your flight?"

"Early," Cal said into her neck and went on, "Long."

"I've never been to LA."

"Not missin' much, buddy."

"I heard it's fun."

His head came up and he looked down at her, her ponytail spread on his couch, her mouth swollen. Christ, she was beautiful.

He pressed his hips into hers, got off on watching her lips part and her eyelids lower, and then he told her, "Never been there for fun."

She smiled at him and her arm left his back so she could curl her fingers around his neck.

"You should try it."

"Don't do much for fun."

"You should try that too," she said softly, her fingers coming up to stroke his jaw.

He didn't reply, just let the tone of her words and her touch settle in.

Yeah, he was home.

He never thought about it, it never entered his mind. He lived his life and went where he needed to be.

But Vi on his couch, he realized for the first time he could remember, it was good being home.

"Is most of your work out there?" she asked.

"Yeah."

"Why didn't you move out there?"

"'Cause LA is insanity, filled with fruits and nuts. Indiana is sanity, meat and potatoes. I'm a meat and potatoes man."

She'd watched his mouth while he talked then her eyes came to his when she said, "Yeah, fruits and nuts are good on occasion, but you need meat and potatoes."

He smiled at her. She smiled back then she lifted up her head to kiss him gently, which was good, saved him the trouble of bending his head to do the same.

Then a phone rang and her head went back to the couch but twisted to the side.

"That's my cell," she told him.

Cal reached out an arm, grabbed her shorts and dragged them across the floor. He pulled her cell out, looked at it and the display said "Sam's cell."

"Sam," he told her.

Her eyes got big, she snatched the phone out of his hand, slid it open and put it to her ear.

"Sam!" she cried loudly. "What's up, baby brother?"

The brother. The brother she obviously cared about because she was still lying under him, his dick inside her, and she seemed to have forgotten.

He slid out. Her chin dipped, her face grew soft and her lips parted and he grinned at her because all of that told him he'd reminded her and she liked him where he was.

"What?" she said into the phone distractedly. "Sorry, yeah, I'm here."

Cal moved down her body, pulling her tank up under her tits and then he put his mouth to her ribs.

Her fingers slid into his hair.

"What?" she asked again. His mouth moved down further and she said, "Yeah, things are good. You?" He circled her navel with his tongue. She sucked in her stomach and her breath and she said, her voice sounding choked, "Can you hang on a second?" She tugged at his hair and he lifted his head to see she had her hand curled over the phone and it was away from her face. "Stop it, Joe."

"You taste good, buddy."

Her eyes got wide then they narrowed and she hissed, "Stop."

He slid down further, to between her legs. She scrambled up to get away and he caught her hips, yanking her under him while surging up and covering her with his body.

He put his mouth to hers and he whispered, "All right, baby, I'll stop."

"Thank you," she snapped, her eyes still narrow.

He grinned at her again and she put the phone back to her ear.

"I'm back," she said and looked at him. "No, it's nothing, just an annoying neighbor." Cal laughed softly and shoved his face in her neck so he could run his mouth along her skin. "What?" she asked. "No joke!" she cried. "Yes, definitely, *absolutely*." She was silent a second then asked, "Mel too? Oh, Sam, the girls'll be thrilled to bits." Another pause and then, "How long?" His head came up, he shifted a bit to the side, settling on an elbow in the couch to watch her talk while he righted his jeans and she said, "That's all?" Her eyes came to him and she went on. "Well, we'll take it, even if it's only a weekend." Another pause then, "Yes." Another pause. "You got it. I'll definitely make it. Kate'll be beside herself, she hasn't had my seafood risotto in ages. Anything else you want?" She listened, her face changed, her eyes went unfocused and a look settled on her features, affection, plain as day. She loved her brother, it was obvious, she didn't try to hide it, and she said, "Yeah, we can do family time, you bet."

Cal found his hand moving toward her face then it cupped her jaw, his thumb moving out to stroke her cheekbone, and he watched her eyes shift to him, that love still shining there and that contraction hit him in the left of his chest again. This time stronger than before, nearly painful. She focused on him but that look didn't move from her face.

"Yeah, we'll see you then," she whispered, her eyes still on Cal. "Can't wait, Sam." She paused to listen then said, "Me too, love you…my love to Mel. 'Bye."

She slid the phone shut and Cal asked, "Let me guess, your brother's comin' to town?"

A smile split her face and she nodded. "Him and his girlfriend, Mel. Next weekend."

"Good news, buddy."

"Definitely."

She reached down, nabbed her panties from the floor and he slid to the side as she lifted her legs then her hips as she yanked them on. The minute her legs settled back to the couch, he rolled his lower body over hers again and her eyes came to his face.

"He close to your folks?" Cal found himself asking and then watched as she burst out laughing. His question was so hilarious, she rolled into him, sliding her arms around him, holding on as her body shook with laughter at the same time she shoved her face in his chest.

"Vi," he called.

She pulled her face away and tipped her head back.

"That was funny."

"I could tell."

She grinned at him. "The answer is no, Sam is *not* close to my parents. Neither of us are. Me because I got pregnant at seventeen and married the baby's father after which they disowned me. I think it was less me getting pregnant and more me getting pregnant by Tim. Tim was not my mother's idea of a perfect match. Tim's dad was a fireman, his mom a nursing assistant. My dad was an officer at a bank and my mom was, and still is, a lady who lunched."

This surprised him. There was nothing about her that hinted she came from money.

"Sam was a hellion," she went on. "He started rebelling when he was about five and didn't stop until a few years after he met Mel and she had enough time to calm him down. Still, my transgression was apparently worse than Sam's gazillion fuck ups so, after I screwed up so royally according to Mom and she turned her back on me, she made it her mission to stay in Sam's life. He puts up with it, mostly because he gets on with Dad. She does it, I reckon, because she's not stupid and she knows when she's slobbering in her Jell-O she'll need someone to come and visit her so she'll have someone to bitch to."

Cal looked down at her and found his mind moving to her at seventeen, pregnant and probably scared out of her fucking mind and her mother turning her back on her.

Then his mind moved to the woman lying on his couch who dressed like she dressed, worked like she worked, made a house like she did and created and raised two girls like hers, now carrying on alone. He couldn't believe any mother wouldn't be proud of all of that.

"Musta been hard, buddy," he said softly and her head tilted to the side.

"What?"

"Makin' a life at seventeen."

She shook her head, her eyes drifted and her face grew soft when she said, "Tim's folks weren't like my folks." She looked back at him and continued. "They loved him, they loved me. They thought we did the right thing, just too soon. They took me in when my parents kicked me out. We got married in their backyard, sweetest wedding you've ever seen." Her voice got quiet when she said, "His mom did that."

Her face was still soft with the memories as she went on.

"We moved into their garage while Tim went to college. They'd done it up as a TV room and changed it to a bedroom so we could move in, helped me, helped Tim, took care of Kate, the whole shebang. A couple years later, they even built on a big addition at the back where they had their own bedroom, bathroom and living room and pretty much gave us the rest of the house. We didn't move out until a couple of years after Keira was born. Tim had finished school, was in uniform and, by then, we had a down payment for a house. We moved in down the block from them. They were pretty much in our lives almost daily since I found out I was pregnant."

Although Cal was relieved she hadn't had it rough after her parents kicked her out, he didn't want to talk about this, about her husband, about her life and memories that made her voice go quiet and her face get soft.

Even not wanting it, he still asked, "You still close to them?"

She swallowed and sadness swept the softness from her face. She looked like she looked when he first met her. A look he hadn't seen in a while. A look he didn't like. She missed them being down the street, but mostly, she missed her old life.

"They call, the girls especially, a couple of times a week," she answered. "I talked to them a lot when we first moved, but not so often now that I'm working full-time. So, no, we're not close anymore. I'm not fired up to go to Chicago and they aren't big on traveling, so they've visited only twice."

"Chicago's only four hours away," Cal pointed out.

"Chicago is where Daniel Hart lives."

"I wasn't talkin' 'bout you goin' there, buddy."

She shook her head. "They go to Florida once a year, Joe. Two weeks. In January. They stopped by on their way there and back. That's all they do. They're both still working, both full-time and they're just not like that. They stick to their 'hood, what they know. They were relieved when Tim and I moved down the block instead of further away. Even fifteen minutes would be out of their comfort zone unless Tim went to go get them. It's not so much his dad, it's his mom. She's quiet, really shy. She likes what she knows, the rest I think scares her."

This, Cal did not get. He couldn't say he knew much about families since his had died with his mother, but he spent enough time with Uncle Vinnie, Aunt Theresa and their kids Vinnie Junior, Carmela, Benny and Manny to know they were loud and in your business even if your business was six states away. Carmela had moved with her husband to California and Vinnie Senior and Aunt Theresa used every excuse they could to visit her. When Carm's first kid lost his first tooth, they got on a fucking plane.

And they'd taken him on when his mother died. Even before that, they were down from Chicago visiting. Vinnie Senior was close to his sister, he didn't like to be away from her long. But when Cal's mom died and they cottoned on to the state of his dad, their visits were more frequent and, eventually, they'd come, get him and take him to Chicago. Vinnie Senior, with Vinnie Junior in the car, driving down on a Friday to pick him up for the weekend, bringing him back on a Sunday so he'd be home before he had to go back to school.

"Is, um…" she hesitated. He focused on her, she bit her lip and asked, "Your family close?"

"Mom and Dad are dead," he told her and he listened to her suck in a soft breath.

"Really?"

"Yep."

"Joe," she whispered.

He couldn't handle that, hearing the sadness in her voice when she said his name. He couldn't handle it because he didn't fucking like it.

He sat up suddenly, taking her with him and planting her astride him then he slid his hands over her ass and changed the subject.

"Not gonna get your garage door fixed hangin' on my couch."

She put her hands to his neck and studied his face. Then her thumb came out and stroked the underside of his jaw.

"Yeah," she said softly, letting it go and he decided he liked that, Vi reading his face and knowing she should let it go. Then she asked, "But could I ask you a favor?"

"Shoot."

"Will you talk to Sam?"

He felt his body get tight and his hands flexed into the flesh of her ass.

He did not want to talk to her brother.

She was working her way under his skin. Every day, she got in deeper, even when she wasn't with him. He'd be working a job, sitting in a meeting, and he'd wonder what she was doing, if she was working, what she was wearing, where her kids were, if they were safe. He wondered if Dane was keeping his fucking teenage kid's hands off Kate and thinking he'd break his neck if he wasn't. He wondered if Keira was friendly to everyone like she was friendly to him and hoping to Christ she didn't strike up a conversation with some sick fuck pedophile whose neck he'd also have to break if he fucked with Keira.

These were not Cal's usual trains of thought.

And it was worse at night. Trying to get to sleep, he thought of Vi in other ways, her hands, her mouth, her smell. Christ, some nights, she was so real in his thoughts, he could smell her hair on his pillow, feel her ass in his hands like it was right then, hear her saying his name, feel her body heavy in sleep against his side.

When he heard Keira's far away scream and Kate's yell and the fear in Vi's voice, he'd nearly come out of his skin being so far away and powerless to step in if something was going down. And he couldn't remember the last time he was as pissed as when he heard it was Kenzie doing the hang ups, shit in his life affecting hers. And, again, he was so far away, on the fucking phone and she was dealing with it with Colt.

He didn't like this, any of this.

His life was steady before Vi. He liked that.

"Joe," she called when he didn't answer and he focused on her. "Forget I said anything. You don't have to."

He didn't want to but he knew he was going to.

And that was the fuck of it.

"What do you want me to talk to him about?"

"It's just that…" She started to move from him and muttered, "Forget it. It's no big thing."

His hands went from her ass, lifted, crossed and slid around so he could lock her in his arms.

"What do you want?"

"I…" she started then stopped, looking away and biting her lip.

"Baby, for fuck's sake—"

Her eyes snapped back to his and she said, "He's snoopin' around Hart."

Cal's arms convulsed as a very bad feeling soured his gut.

"What?"

"Sam. He's snoopin' around Hart. I don't know what he's doing but he was close to Tim and he's close to me and what happened to Tim and after to me hit him hard. He's—"

Cal cut her off. "That's whacked."

Her body jerked then she said, "I know, but—"

"It's not only whacked, it's stupid."

This time her body tightened in his arms and her eyes narrowed.

"He's not stupid. He's my brother and he's—"

"Stickin' his nose in shit he shouldn't. Jesus, Vi, Hart'll chew him up and spit him out."

He fucked up. He knew it the second her face twisted with pain and her body wrenched, her hands going from his neck to his chest to push away.

He let her go but twisted so she landed on her back and he landed on her.

"Buddy—"

"I know that, Joe," she interrupted on a whisper. "I know *exactly* what Hart will do."

"I know you do," Cal whispered back.

"That's why I want you to talk to Sam. That's the favor. I want you to tell him to stop, explain things to him. Get him to let the cops deal with it."

"He's here, you set up the meet. I'll have a word," Cal said immediately.

Her chin jerked then she blinked.

"What?"

"When he's here, you set it up, I'll have a word."

She stared at him a second as if she'd never seen him before.

Then she breathed, "Really?"

"Yeah."

He felt her body relax under him and her arm slid around him, her other hand gliding up his neck and into his hair as her leg moved from under him to wrap around his thigh.

"Thanks, Joe."

He knew it the minute she spoke. He knew that was all he needed, those two soft words with her limbs wrapped around him and, God help him, he'd do anything for her.

Jesus, he was fucked.

"Need to see to your garage," he told her.

He was leaving her arms after he fucked her on his couch and listened to her sharing her life with him so he could fix her garage door opener.

Yes, fucked.

"Okay," she whispered.

He lifted up, pulling her up with him. He waited until she yanked up her shorts and retied her ponytail and together they walked over to her house, Vi going to her yard, Cal going to her garage.

Twenty minutes later, he was in his truck heading to the hardware store, buying her a new garage door opener.

Cal watched the Fiesta pull into the drive.

Kate had barely come to a stop when Keira was out the door and running at him, her hair flying, her arms wheeling like she'd run to her mother at Colt and Feb's barbeque.

"*Joe!*" she screeched.

He was on a ladder in Vi's garage, installing the new garage door opener. He looked down at Vi's daughter who'd come to a halt by the ladder and was smiling up at him. Doing this, he was thinking the only sound better than hearing Vi say his name was hearing Keira say it.

"Hey, girl."

"I'm gettin' a dog!" she announced.

Cal dropped his arms and asked, "What kind?"

"American husky."

"Good breed," Cal said even though he had no clue whether that was true or not.

"I know!" she yelled as if he wasn't right there in front of him. "I've been looking them up on the Internet." She got up on her toes and whispered loudly, "Though, it says they bark a lot. I haven't told Mom that part yet."

"Hey, Joe," Kate said, joining their party.

"Kate."

Her eyes were on the opening to the garage then they came to him and she remarked, "You got the door open."

Cal didn't respond as the door was open so he didn't think she needed an answer.

"When we moved here, Mom spent, like, forever tryin' to get that door open," Kate told him.

"Yeah?" Cal asked, lifting his arms, tipping his head back and going back to the opener.

"What're you doin'?" Keira asked and Cal looked through his arms to Keira.

"Installin' a new garage door opener."

Keira and Kate looked at each other. Keira grinned big. Kate's eyes came back to him and she looked thoughtful.

"That's cool, Joe," she said softly, her eyes going to the ceiling. Then she looked at him and finished, "Thanks."

"Please tell me you left enough clothes and shoes at the mall for the rest of the population of Indianapolis to buy so people aren't walkin' around in tatty, non-designer clothes they got at Goodwill," Vi joked, walking up to them and Cal dropped his arms again.

"We're doin' our part to help out the economy," Keira said to her mother.

Vi came to a stop and looked at her daughter. "What'd you buy?"

"A pair of shorts you will just *love* and a new pair of flip-flops that are *awesome* and there was a buy two get one free at that accessories place so I bought four and got two free, a bunch of bracelets and necklaces. They're sah-*weet.* You can borrow them," Keira answered.

Vi stared at her youngest a moment then looked to her oldest. "What'd you buy?"

"Nothin'," Kate grinned. "I'm gonna borrow Keira's stuff."

"You are not," Keira snapped. "Mom can borrow it but *you* can't."

Vi's eyes went to Cal and she shook her head then they went back to Keira. "You two fightin'?"

"No," Keira said.

"Yes," Kate said.

Vi knew instantly who was lying and who wasn't. So she looked at the one who'd be honest with her and asked Kate, "Why?"

"She and Heather want to go to that party at Jody's house with me and Dane," Kate answered.

Vi's gaze went to Keira. "I thought we talked about that."

"Mom," Keira whined.

"You aren't goin'. That's for juniors and seniors."

"Kate's a sophomore," Keira returned.

"Kate's a junior now, school's over," Vi retorted.

"I'm old for my age," Keira shot back.

"Honey, you're fourteen goin' on twelve. You'll be forty-five goin' on twelve. You're locked in girldom. You'll be livin' in a house with daisies on the walls and wearing pink wellingtons when you're married and have six kids," Vi replied.

"I'm not havin' six kids," Keira snapped, not stupid enough to deny she was all girl and would be until the day she died.

"And you're not goin' to that party," Vi said softly but firmly, using a voice that, from the look on Keira's face, she knew that was the end of the discussion. But Vi wasn't going to leave it bad, so she told them both, "Guess who's comin' to town next weekend?"

"Uncle Sam!" Keira shouted, guessing immediately and also immediately losing her attitude.

Vi smiled. "And Melissa."

"That's *awesome*!" Kate yelled.

Vi turned to Kate. "Baby, can you bunk with Keira on her futon so Sam and Mel can have your room?"

"Sure," Kate agreed instantly, her face bright, her mouth smiling, obviously loving her uncle like her mother loved her brother if she'd give up her space.

"This is *so cool*!" Keira announced.

Vi slid an arm along Keira's waist and gave her a squeeze before letting her go and saying, "It certainly is, honey. Now go get your bags, take 'em into the house and leave Joe alone, yeah?"

"Yeah," Keira grinned at her mom then at him and said, "Later, Joe."

"Later," Cal replied.

Keira took off and Kate moved toward the house but she was looking at Cal. "You want a Coke or somethin', Joe?" she asked.

"Sounds good," Cal answered, ignoring the fact that his brain was trying to decide if he liked quiet Kate calling him Joe better than loud Keira.

"I'll get it," Kate muttered and walked away.

Cal looked from Kate to Vi and she was staring at the ceiling.

"How much did that cost?" she asked the garage door opener.

"You, tonight in my bed with your hand between your legs," Cal answered quietly and her eyes shot to his.

"What?" she whispered.

"You heard me."

She looked to the drive to see Keira down at the end carrying her bags and waving across the street at Feb who had Jack at her hip and was talking to Myrtle in her front yard. Then Vi looked at him and got close to the ladder.

"You want sexual favors for a garage door opener?" she asked, sounding slightly pissed but more disbelieving.

Cal turned his attention to the opener. "I do the work, I decide the payback."

"I'm your booty call, Joe, not your prostitute."

At her words, unexpected words, words that pissed him right the fuck off, Cal turned his attention back to Vi.

"My booty call?" he asked quietly.

"Yeah."

"Booty call?" he repeated.

"Yeah," she repeated too and he saw she was pissed as well but he reckoned she wasn't as pissed as he was.

He put the screwdriver he had in his hand on the top of the ladder, climbed down and got close to her. She didn't retreat. Then again she never did, either because her attitude made her stupid or because she had a backbone. He figured it was both.

"Booty call?" he asked again, hoping she'd cotton on to the tone of his voice.

She didn't.

"Yeah," she repeated yet again.

He studied her then, he had no idea why, but just to piss her off further, he stated, "You aren't pissed that's what I want. You're pissed you want it so bad you can't wait to give it to me."

He succeeded in his effort at pissing her off more. Her eyes narrowed, she leaned closer to him and hissed, "I can't believe you."

"You been thinkin' about it since I said it on the phone."

Her eyes got wide then he watched her clench her teeth as she fought for control, but he was too angry to give her the time.

Instead, he bent at the waist to get into her face and informed her, "Buddy, what we got is what it is. It might not be what you want, but you gotta admit, what it is is good. What it isn't is a booty call and it pisses me off you'd say that. And it pisses me off you'd think I'm on a fuckin' ladder in your goddamned garage, installin' a fuckin' door opener so I could buy a fuckin' session with you."

"That's what you said," she accused.

"And that's what I want as payback, I told you, straight out. I also told you, I do somethin' for you, we talk payback. I'm doin' somethin' for you so that's what I did. You didn't like that idea, it made you uncomfortable, all you gotta do is say."

"So every time you do something for me, it'll require payback?"

"Buddy, that's life. You always work to balance the scales. You don't wanna owe someone something, even if it's only in your head that you owe 'em and they don't give a shit. It'll fuck with you. So you give back to balance the scales."

He knew he had her with the way her face changed, not that she nodded in understanding. Instead she looked more irritated because he was right.

"That said," he went on, "I'd buy this and install it for nothin'. You need to take care of your car and Kate doesn't need to be scrapin' ice off hers either. I thought you'd let me do that and know those scales stayed balanced, I wouldn't have said shit. But you wouldn't let me do that. I know because you asked how much the fuckin' thing cost."

She glared at him, even more irritated because he was again right.

Then she changed the subject and he knew she was trying to piss him off further too.

"If I'm not a booty call, what am I?"

He looked over her shoulder to see Keira skipping across the yard, swinging her bags, going to the front door of the house.

Then he looked at Vi and muttered, "Jesus, Vi."

"No, I wanna know. What is it that we've got?"

"What it isn't is a booty call."

"You said that already."

Cal glared at her and she took it, waiting, silently demanding an answer.

So he answered, "I enjoy you, you enjoy me, for as long as it's good."

"That's it?" she asked, her face carefully controlled, her body tense, fighting to hide her reaction to his words and, in doing so, not succeeding in hiding the fact that he'd gotten under her skin too.

Shit.

He should have never fucking started this again.

He forced his voice to soft when he replied, "I thought we had an understanding, buddy."

She held his eyes a moment before she stepped away, murmuring, "Yeah, we did."

The side door opened and Kate called out, "Here's your Coke, Joe."

Cal looked from Vi to Kate and saw Kate also got her mother's walk, cool, calm, unconsciously moving her hips, swaying her ass, in possession of her body in a way that no teenage girl should be. Dane probably saw her walking down the hall and knew he'd go for it.

Or he'd seen her smile.

First chance he got, he was having a conversation with Dane.

She made it to him and handed him the Coke.

"Thanks girl," Cal muttered.

"You want a sandwich?" she asked. "We got turkey and roast beef."

Vi's kids were polite. Cal wasn't surprised.

"I'm good."

"You want one, just call," she said, looked at her mom, gave her a small smile and then she walked away.

"I've got shit to do," Vi mumbled, but Cal reached out a hand and grabbed her arm.

When she turned back to him, he said, "We're not done, buddy."

She looked at him and replied, "I don't think I'm comin' over tonight, Joe. I got things to think about."

He knew what she'd be thinking about. She'd be thinking about ending it. He also knew she should and, she didn't, he knew he should.

But he wasn't ready.

"Vi."

Carefully, she pulled her arm from his hand and asked, "You gonna be in town awhile?"

"Yeah."

"We'll talk later," she said quietly and moved away.

He let her. He let her because Colt was now with Feb and Myrtle across the street and he'd taken Jack from Feb. He had the baby held close to his front, both arms wrapped around the boy but his eyes were on Cal. So were Feb's. Myrtle didn't notice, she was busy gabbing.

Cal opened the Coke, took a drink and set it aside.

Then he went back to the ladder.

Fifteen minutes later, he was standing in front of the garage door testing the remotes when a dark blue Chevrolet Equinox pulled up to the curb and Mike Haines jumped down.

Cal watched him, his mouth getting tight, seeing Mike's eyes on him as he walked up Vi's drive and noting Mike's mouth was set tight too.

"Cal," Mike greeted.

"Mike."

Vi came out the side door, her eyes jumping between them, uncomfortable and unprepared for this scene.

Mike turned to Vi, watched her walk up to them and said softly, "Hey, sweetheart."

"Hi," she replied, and Cal felt his gut get tight.

"Got plans tonight?" Mike asked Vi, and Cal watched Vi's eyes remain glued to Mike.

"No, why?" she asked back.

"Thought we'd reschedule dinner for tonight," Mike answered, and Cal knew the asshole was making a point, doing this with him standing right… fucking…there.

"Um…"

"My place, six o'clock," Mike said firmly, not waiting for her to reply. "You still got my address?"

"Yeah."

"Good," Mike said, again talking soft. He lifted a hand to her jaw. "You have troubles findin' it, you give me a call, yeah?"

She nodded. He leaned in and touched his mouth to hers.

Cal locked his body to steel against the heat burning in his chest.

When Mike's head came up, Vi's eyes slid to Cal, she pressed her lips together and looked back to Mike. "Um…Mike—"

"Six o'clock."

"Um—"

He dropped his hand and cut her off. "See you then." He turned, nodded to Cal, Cal nodded back and Mike moved to his SUV.

Vi watched Cal.

Cal went back to testing the remotes and the door slid up.

Then he heard her shout, "Mike!"

Cal looked at Vi then at Mike who was standing at the back of his car.

"Yeah?" Mike called back.

"Do you need me to bring anything?" Vi asked, making her point too and that burning in his chest grew hotter as Mike smiled.

"Just you, sweetheart."

"Okay, see you later."

"Later."

Mike got in his SUV and drove away.

Vi watched the street.

Cal closed the garage door.

Then Cal said to her, "Buddy, your remotes."

She looked up at him and asked, straight out, "You don't even care, do you?"

Oh he cared, too fucking much.

"We're not that," he reminded her.

She stared at him and he saw it in the backs of her eyes. Disappointment, even pain, and he nearly lifted his hand to touch her but he didn't have the time.

She stepped back and whispered, "Right."

He was a dick. Christ he was a dick, he should cut her loose.

For the life of him, he just fucking couldn't.

She started to turn but he called to her, "Vi." Her eyes lifted to his and he held out the remotes. "Door's workin'. These're your remotes, one for you, one for Kate."

She stared down at the remotes in his hand as if she had no idea what they were but whatever they were scared the shit out of her.

Then, taking the remotes, her voice flat, she whispered, "Thanks."

"Buddy—"

"See you later," she said quickly.

"Vi."

He could say no more. She walked away, cool, calm, her hips moving, her ass swaying and he watched her until her side door closed.

He looked at her garage door.

Then he walked to his house.

Cal was sitting outside on his deck at dusk, his feet up on the railing, knees cocked, looking at his yard without seeing it, his second beer in hand.

Vi's Mustang was gone, she was at Mike's.

He took a pull from his beer then looked to the side hearing it and waited, finally seeing Colt round the house.

"Hey," Colt called.

"Yo," Cal replied.

"Mind company?" Colt asked, coming up the steps.

Cal did. He didn't want company. He also didn't want to talk about whatever Colt was over to talk about. But he didn't want to be alone with his thoughts. Thoughts of Vi at Mike's. Thoughts of Mike's mouth on Vi, his hands. Thoughts that were fucking with Cal's head.

"Nope," he said to Colt. "Beer's in the fridge," he offered. "Bring me one."

"Gotcha," Colt muttered, sliding the door open and stepping inside.

Cal looked at his yard then he looked at Vi's.

He paid a service to mow his in the summer, that was it. It was green because this was Indiana and they'd been having regular night rains and random day thunderstorms, but it was nowhere near as healthy as Vi's.

Vi couldn't afford to pay a service. But you could see in the small ditch that delineated their property where her lawn stopped and his started. Hers was greener, no weeds, thick. Her deck had fancy garden furniture with an umbrella, not white plastic chairs like his. She had little and big pots of flowers all around, bright colors, vibrant, alive.

The Williamses who'd lived there for as long as Cal could remember were house proud. They took care of their place, built on the extension in the back, put in the deck, updated the bathroom and kitchen, installed the alarm. When old Dec Williams died, his wife Martha moved to Bloomington to be close to her kids and grandkids, selling the house she'd lived in for fifty years to Vi.

Even as well as Dec and Martha took care of their house, Vi did it better.

Colt came back, scraped another plastic chair next to Cal's and handed Cal his beer. Cal took it, downed the dregs of the last one and set the bottle on the deck as Colt sat down and put his feet up on the railing, knees cocked like Cal's.

"Weather's good," Colt remarked.

Cal didn't answer. It was a warm evening but no humidity. The day had been sunny, no clouds, a fair breeze. There was no need to answer.

"You comin' to the wedding?" Colt asked.

"Yeah," Cal replied though he wanted to go to a wedding like he wanted someone to drill a hole in his head. He liked Colt and Feb enough to go, though. They wanted him there, he'd be there.

"I'll tell Feb. She's livin' and breathin' this wedding, you show without RSVPing, her head might explode."

Feb, as far as Cal could tell, was pretty laid-back. He showed and didn't let her know he was coming, she wouldn't have cared less.

"You know Audrey?" Colt asked, and in the middle of taking a pull off his beer, Cal's eyes went to his friend.

He swallowed and lowered the beer.

"Who?"

"Audrey Haines."

There it was. Fuck.

"Nope," Cal answered.

"Total bitch," Colt noted. "Lazy bitch. Mike ran himself ragged for years, used to do side work, security for a while then he made detective and started doin' without, even havin' to make his kids do without so she could sit on her ass in a designer track suit and watch soaps in that huge fuckin' house. He gave up. Divorce was final two months ago. The whole department celebrated. Good man like that doesn't need to go home to that shit."

Cal didn't reply.

"He's into Vi," Colt went on.

Cal took a pull of his beer. That didn't need a response either. Cal knew Mike was into Vi, he knew why. Not to mention, Mike had made a point of making that fact clear to Cal.

Colt fell silent and contemplated Cal's yard while they both drank beer.

Eventually Colt continued. "You knew Melanie."

Cal did. He'd lived across the street from her since Colt and she moved in.

Colt's ex-wife Melanie was pretty, shy, sweet, but shit scared of life. Cal never knew why they broke it off, didn't ask, but he figured it was because it'd get old, dealing with that shit, no matter how pretty she was.

"Yep. How's she doin'?" Cal asked, since Melanie had been caught up in that scene with Feb and Colt, Denny Lowe kidnapping Melanie and holding her, Feb and Susie Shepherd hostage.

It didn't say much for him but Cal was glad Susie'd been caught up in it. He'd fucked her. They had one night, she was good, but he was done and she'd almost acted like Kenzie when he didn't want seconds. Difference was, Susie wasn't annoying when she wanted something. She was a total bitch. How she thought she'd get what she wanted acting like that, he had no idea. Likely because her daddy spoiled the bitch rotten. He thought that maybe she'd take a look at her life when some psycho serial killer shot her. Susie didn't. She was still a bitch, therefore, as far as he knew, she was still alone.

"Don't know," Colt answered his question. "Took a while but she pulled her shit together, though I haven't heard from her for months. Don't think I will, what with Jack bein' born and the wedding comin' up."

Cal didn't disagree. Melanie didn't seem the type to hang on. Cal wished his ex was the same.

"You know why we split?" Colt asked. Cal looked at him, lifted his brows and Colt carried on. "Couldn't fix her."

Cal pulled in breath through his nose and looked away, muttering, "Colt."

"Tried, man, years, fuckin' years I tried. She wanted a kid so fuckin' bad, Christ, obsessed with it. And she hated it when Feb would come into town. Pissed me off, she'd get so tense when Feb was here. Melanie thought I'd stray."

Feb and Colt had been an item in high school and after it. When they broke it off everyone, even Cal who was young back then, maybe sixteen, had been surprised. They seemed solid, more solid than anyone he knew. And Feb was gorgeous.

On the one hand, he didn't blame Melanie with Feb being Colt's ex, having their history. On the other hand, Colt was Colt and that kind of shit was not Colt's gig and everyone knew that too, the person who should have known it most was Melanie.

"Sucks," Cal muttered.

"Nope," Colt muttered back, his eyes on the yard. He took a pull from his beer, then continued. "She didn't take off, I'd have a lifetime of that crap and I wouldn't have Feb."

Surprised, Cal glanced at Colt. That was cold, Colt wasn't like that.

Colt didn't take his eyes off Cal's yard as he kept talking. "Had years of that shit, tryin' to fix her, bustin' my ass to figure out what was in that fuckin' head of hers, wonderin' where I was goin' wrong," Colt's eyes slid to Cal. "Then I got a woman doesn't need fixin', not anymore, and now life's sweet."

"Colt—" Cal started.

"Mike's into her, Cal, but Vi's into you."

"You think she don't need fixin', you're wrong," Cal told him.

"Patchwork, man, not major fuckin' repairs. Been there too. The job doesn't last long and it's worth the effort."

Cal looked at the yard and took another pull of his beer.

"We do our own thing," Colt continued. "The day starts with Feb in my bed then we go our own way and, Cal, man, you wouldn't believe how sweet it is knowin' at the end of the day she'll crawl right back into my bed."

Cal was pleased Colt had that. Good man like him deserved it. Good woman like Feb deserved it too.

But after what went down with Bonnie, Cal quit thinkin' about what he wanted, his mind focused entirely on the end game. Retire early, kick back, do his own thing in his own company. He'd take his fill of women along the way and after he got where he wanted to be. But all he'd ever wanted growing up was a family, and what Bonnie did, he wasn't going to go back there. He'd given too much the first around. He was empty.

There was no way he was telling Colt this so Cal stayed silent.

Colt didn't take his hint.

"You fixed her garage door opener."

"Yep."

"It back on?"

It was none of his business but Cal repeated, "Yep."

"Cut her loose, Cal."

Cal looked at Colt and with the way he did most men would cringe.

Colt just held his gaze.

Cal stayed silent.

"You should cut her loose," Colt reiterated quietly.

"Not your business, Colt."

"It works out with Mike, it'll be good for them both."

Cal knew that. He knew Haines, not well, but he knew him. Haines was a good man. Haines would shovel her snow. His wife was that big of a bitch, Haines would appreciate what he had in Vi and he'd let her know it.

Cal looked away and stared at his yard.

"In a minute, we'll sit and drink beer. Now I'm tellin' you, you're all kinds of crazy, havin' her next door, into you and not makin' some effort to see where it'd lead. You'd be good for her, but better, she'd be good for you. You don't wanna make that effort, your call. But you should stop fuckin' with her head and let her get on with her life and find someone who's willin' to put in the effort."

When Colt stopped speaking, Cal continued contemplating his yard.

After a while, he asked, "You done?"

"Yeah," Colt answered.

Cal didn't do anything, not even nod. He just looked at his yard and took another pull of his beer.

Colt did the same.

I walked up to Mike's townhouse, a new build but not that new. The trees had filled in a bit, it'd been around a few years—with a discerning eye I decided maybe five, maybe a couple more.

It was a development, a few detached or duplex ones but mostly rows of townhouses, party walls. In Mike's row, Mike was in the middle. There was a narrow two car garage at the front, most of the house on top of the garage but there were rooms to the side.

I knocked on the door and didn't wait long for Mike to answer.

"Hey, honey," he said, stepping aside, letting me in.

"Hi," I replied, walking by him.

He closed the door. I looked up at him at the same time his arm hooked me at the waist, pulling me to his body and his head came down.

He obviously saved the stealth kisses for the first date or maybe special occasions. He didn't give me a stealth kiss, patiently building the heat. His mouth opened over mine, his tongue slid inside, and essentially, he threw a kiss Molotov cocktail and I ignited.

When he lifted his head, I'd plastered myself to his front and again had both my hands in his hair.

"Wow," I breathed.

He smiled. I gave him more of my weight—that's how much I liked his smile—and he took it, his smile getting wider.

Then I thought, I was *such* a freaking slut.

"Sorry about Wednesday," he said.

"I was a cop's wife for fifteen years, I know the drill," I told him.

"Your man stand you up a lot?" Mike asked.

I shook my head. "No, but he liked his job, he only ever wanted to be a cop and it was important to him. Since it was important to him and he didn't make too much of a habit of it, I didn't throw a hissy fit when he had to work. You learn to deal, and with two kids, it wasn't like there wasn't always something to do."

His arm got tight but he didn't reply. Then he let me go but took my purse, threw it on a chair in the little foyer and led me to the left into a kitchen.

It wasn't the greatest kitchen in the world. Mine wasn't huge but it was long and had a lot of counter space. His was newer, better appliances, was in a u-shape, small and had shit counter space, but whoever designed it did the best they could do with the space they had. There were tons of cupboards. A five burner stove set in the counter. Wall oven built into a unit, a microwave over it, cupboard over and under the appliances. A huge double door fridge that would hold enough food for a battalion. And there was a small table sitting in the bay window facing the front of the house.

"You eat meat?" he asked.

"Yep."

"Good." He went to a bottle of wine on the counter. "You drink red?"

I grinned at him. "Yep."

He grinned back. "Good."

He opened the wine while I asked, "How long you been here?"

"Bought it with my half of sellin' the house. Audrey and I sold before the divorce. She didn't want me to have it and she couldn't afford it. Been here about nine months."

"You like it?"

"Would prefer livin' closer to work but need three bedrooms and this has that. Couldn't find anything in town that'd work for me and the kids."

"Where does...um...Audrey live?"

"Apartment in town. Two bedrooms. Kids hate it, they have to share. Jonas is fourteen, Clarisse twelve, they're way too old to share…" He trailed off and handed me a glass of wine before he finished. "She went through her take from the house in about a month. She drives a brand new Merc but lives in a two bedroom dump, can you believe that shit?"

I shook my head, not able to believe that shit, thinking unhappy thoughts for him and his kids, taking a sip of my wine and noting instantly it wasn't cheap.

"Sweetheart," he called and I focused on him. "You should know I'm goin' for full custody. Talked to my lawyer two weeks ago."

He said this like a warning, like he'd expect me to think this was a bad thing.

"Good," I told him.

His eyes moved over my face, something working in them. I didn't know for certain what but it wasn't like Joe studied me. I could see plain as day whatever he saw he thought was good.

I felt my stomach flutter.

When his eyes caught mine, he said, "We'll eat in a while. You wanna see the house?"

"Okay."

He took my hand and led me out of the kitchen. "Got an HOA, they take care of the greenspace, doesn't look like yours," he said, drawing me down a hall off his foyer and looking back to me. "They should hire you, though."

It was a quiet compliment, not effusive but effective.

"Thanks," I whispered, my belly fluttering again.

He showed me the living room at the back. It ran the length of the house and it was huge.

There was a dining room table to one side set to seat four but you could see it took leaves to make it bigger, two more chairs at the wall.

The rest was family furniture, big sectional couch, a couple of recliners, comfortable, sturdy but attractive. Stuff you lounged on with your kids and watched TV. There were pictures of the kids and Mike and other photos of other people, his parents (I could tell) and others, maybe his sisters, brothers, their families, friends and they were all over the place. There were shelves with books, DVDs, music, games and a large, flat screen TV, tables everywhere to put drinks on, a nice stereo.

Two bay windows, one by the dining table, the other in the living room area, French doors in the middle with tall, slim windows at their sides that opened on a deck.

I could see a huge, electric grill and decent furniture on the deck, not a bad-sized yard, which a dog was lying in. A golden retriever, staring at the doors, tongue lolling, knowing there was company, waiting to be let in so she could give her greeting.

Looking around, I saw that Mike had made an effort. This wasn't a bachelor pad townhouse he brought his kids to when they came for their time with him. This was their home. A place they could lounge. A place they'd be comfortable and feel safe. I didn't know a man could do something like that and I didn't know, in knowing it, that something like that could be so attractive. But it was.

"You have a dog?" I asked.

"Got custody of Layla in the divorce."

"Layla?"

"Clapton. Great song," he looked out the windows, "great dog."

He was right, it was a great song. He had good taste in music.

I looked out the windows to see Layla was now at the door, her tongue still lolling, her body shaking because her tail was wagging so hard.

"She do something to be put into doggie prison?" I asked.

Mike looked at me and asked back, "Pardon?"

"She's in the yard, there's a guest. She's obviously being punished."

He grinned at me and shook his head. "She's excitable. I didn't want her jumpin' on you." His head tilted to the side and he finished, "Least, not 'til I got my chance to jump on you."

There it was, that flutter again.

"You should let her in before she explodes," I suggested.

"You like dogs?"

"Love 'em. Keira's gettin' her first next week. An American husky."

"You should go golden," he advised, walking to the door, and Layla was watching him and pacing, her tail still wagging, her tongue still lolling.

"Keira has her heart set," I replied.

He opened the door and Layla burst in. Completely uninterested in her daddy, she ran straight to me and jumped up the minute she got to me, butting me with her nose, her hind legs bouncing, her front legs pawing at my chest.

"Layla, down," Mike ordered, his deep voice commanding.

She instantly obeyed but she still butted my legs with her head, her body shaking and moving, even though I was bent over her, giving her head a rubdown while trying not to spill my wine on Mike's nice carpet.

"She'll calm down as soon as she gets used to your scent," Mike said, coming back to me.

"She's okay," I assured him.

He took my hand and I straightened as he guided me away from Layla and out of the living room, back down the hall to the foyer that I now saw had a door leading to the garage, another to a half bath and a set of stairs. Layla followed, or I should say, she eventually led the procession, knocking me into Mike as she forged ahead of us on the stairs. She then stood at the top, waiting for our arrival, her tongue still out, her face set in the doggie question of, "What's taking you guys so long?"

We made it to the top and Mike showed me Jonas's room, Layla sweeping in and running through it like she was an enthusiastic tour guide.

I saw his boy was obviously into music. There was a drum kit set up and a guitar on a stand and the walls could not be seen for all the band posters on them. The bed was unmade and the drawers were open with clothes spilling out.

"He's not big on pickin' up his room," Mike told me.

"I would guess that's in the Teenage Boy's Handbook seeing as it's also in the Adult Man's Handbook. Gotta train 'em early."

Mike chuckled and showed me Clarisse's room, Layla again running through it even over the bed, which was made. His daughter's room looked almost identical to Keira's except not pinks and purples. Instead blues and yellows and instead of daisies, there were butterflies and there was not a mixture of boy band and teenage vampire posters, there were only teenage vampires.

I looked up at Mike. "You load your gun with silver bullets?"

"Clarisse tells me that only works on werewolves."

I burst out laughing and Mike smiled at me before he threw an arm around my shoulders and then he showed me a smaller room with more shelves and a high-backed, black leather swivel chair in front of a large desk with built-in storage and a computer on it. There was a comfortable looking armchair in the corner with a table and a standing lamp beside it. A study for him, for the kids, a private place to be, to do your homework or read. It was nice.

Then he led me out of there and took me down the hall, showing me his room.

That was nicer. It had more French doors, a small, private deck leading off. The room was huge, so was his bed, and his bed was cool as all hell. A dark wood, heavy sleigh bed with a taupe, tan and chocolate paisley comforter. Layla didn't play tour guide here. She got to Mike's room, she ran straight up and jumped on the bed, settling on her belly, her head on her paws.

I ignored the dog's invitation to join her on Mike's bed and Mike told me there was walk-in closet and showed me the master bath with double basin, separate bath and shower. The bath was bigger than most, oval, sitting in a platform with a step up. The bathroom was enough for me to buy this house. It was awesome, a woman's dream.

He led me out and I was feeling weird about taking a tour of his bedroom. I hadn't been on a second date since I was in high school but I was thinking this was unusual.

I felt so weird, I didn't think before I remarked, "That's quite a bed."

"Audrey paid six thousand dollars for that bed," Mike replied.

I stopped dead and stared up at him.

"What?"

"Yep, six thousand fuckin' dollars. She loved that bed. Won't say much for me, honey, but, seein' as I actually paid for it and I knew she loved it and no way we could sell it and make that cake back, I made certain I got it in the divorce. Our divorce wasn't pretty. She fought me on everything, had no ground to stand on, lost huge." He smiled. "Lost her fuckin' bed."

Since he did pay for it and he should get it and it was a great bed, I smiled back at him.

"Anyway, Clarisse and I got a thing, Scary Movie Friday Night. She's with me on a Friday, we watch horror movies, bowls of popcorn, tubs of ice cream." His head tipped to the wall where there was a flat screen TV installed. "Jonas even stoops to join us every once in a while. Bed's perfect for Scary Movie Friday Night."

I thought of Mike with his unknown daughter having a Scary Movie Friday Night, a twelve year old girl watching horror flicks, cuddled up to her big, tall, strong, handsome dad and I didn't have a belly flutter. My eyes filled with tears and I looked away.

"Hey," Mike called.

I took a sip of wine and stared at the wall.

His hand came to my jaw and he repeated, "Hey," as he forced me to look at him.

"Can I use your bathroom?" I asked, staring at his nose.

"You can, you look at me and tell me why you got tears in your eyes."

I blinked back the tears, swallowed then looked at him and whispered, "Sorry."

"About what?"

"It doesn't happen much anymore, but when it does it throws me, always." I shut my eyes tight, opened them and repeated, "Always."

His hand with his wine glass curled around to the small of my back, pulling me closer, and he asked softly, "What doesn't happen much anymore?"

I shook my head, putting my free hand on his shoulder, my hand with the glass to his waist. He didn't seem at all hesitant about sharing about his kids, his ex, and being totally honest about it.

I didn't find it that easy.

But since he gave it to me, I figured I should give it back and when I figured that, I was reminded of Joe telling me about the scales.

Balancing them out.

Shit, Joe was too wise for my good and it pissed me off when he was right.

"Just that…" I trailed off, not knowing how to explain it. "Getting reminded of things. You know, like my girls'll never cuddle up to their dad again, watch a movie."

His face changed, grew gentle, his hand tensed at my jaw and he whispered, "Sweetheart."

I shook my head again. "It's okay, it's cool. Sorry. It isn't cool. Just that I should say, it's good that you have that with Clarisse."

"Yeah," he replied, his eyes never leaving mine. "'Cept, next time, it'll mean a helluva lot more than normal."

I bit my lip thinking I was standing mostly in the arms of a really good guy.

Mike read that I needed a subject change pronto and asked, "You wanna see why I bought this place?"

"Sure."

He let me go, took my hand and led me to the French doors and out onto the white-painted, wooden balcony.

There were a couple of Adirondack chairs there, also painted white, no pads. His yard below had a high fence all around to shield his business from the neighbors.

But I knew why he brought me to his bedroom when I saw, beyond his fenced yard, there was also a view of straight, flat cornfield, the corn growing, knee-height now. Beyond that were some dense woods.

Smack in the middle of it, there was a yellow farmhouse with white woodwork, a wraparound porch and a red barn with green lawn all around, some graveled drives, a white gazebo with wisteria growing from it, a grape arbor heavy with vines.

Something about the view stunned me. I'd seen many farmhouses but this one, from our elevated view, seemed picture perfect. There was intricate, lacy woodwork in the corners of the posts holding up the porch roof. The lawn looked like mine, green and healthy. And the pristine rows filled with the wide leaves of the growing corn, both spiky and bowed—all of it exquisitely cared for and cultivated showed these farmers loved their home, their farm, the pride went deep and it was amazing to behold.

Not a lot of people would think this was picturesque or at least not beautiful. It wasn't a beach or a view of the mountains, but I thought it was gorgeous. I could totally see buying this house if I could sit in an Adirondack chair, drink wine and stare at that view.

"Grew up in this 'burg and my high school girlfriend grew up on that farm," Mike told me and I looked up at him to see his eyes on the farmhouse. "She got married to some guy she met at Notre Dame, moved to DC. Her brother runs that farm now." He looked down at me. "I always loved that farm."

"Did you wanna be a farmer?" I asked.

"Fuck no." He grinned. "Still, liked her farm. Her folks were great too. And she had this sister…" he stopped talking and I waited for him to say more. His face had grown thoughtful in a faraway way and since he didn't seem to mind sharing, and he wasn't sharing, I figured he didn't want to, so I changed the subject.

"How'd you meet Audrey?" I asked, leaning against the railing and he came back to the conversation and leaned with me.

"Blind date."

"Really?"

"Yeah." He grinned again. "Friend of mine was dating a friend of hers. Thought we'd get on."

"Obviously, you did."

He didn't answer. He looked out to the farmhouse again, taking a sip of his wine. His face grew pensive again and I thought I read what this meant.

"You really liked her," I said softly, not wanting to push.

Mike's eyes came to me. "Audrey?"

"No, your high school girlfriend."

He burst out laughing.

"What?" I asked when he was mostly done laughing.

"Debbie was sweet, but she was career minded. Hated livin' here, couldn't wait to get out, doesn't come back often. She didn't want kids, wanted to be a lawyer and she became one. Her brother tells me she's a shark. Makes a mint, works eighty hour weeks, lives and breathes her work. Saw her at Christmas a few years ago, she was with her mom in the grocery store and she had her Blackberry in her hand, e-mailin' people while she was at home for the holidays, out with her mom, buyin' egg nog. Seriously, sweetheart, that is not my thing."

"And Audrey was your thing?"

The humor moved out of his face and he said, "You don't wanna know about that shit."

"I do, unless you don't want to tell me."

"Violet—"

"Mike, honey, I just nearly burst into tears in your bedroom. You can feel free to tell me about your ex-wife."

He smiled, took another sip of wine, then slid an arm around my waist, inching me closer. When he had me where he wanted me, he left his arm there.

"I won't lie, lookin' back, she gave me signals, lots of 'em. But she could be funny, fuckin' hell, she could be funny. Never laughed so hard as I did with Audrey in the beginning, thought that'd be my life, laughter. She was gorgeous and she made me laugh and I kept my focus on that and ignored the signals. It started six months in, after we got back from our honeymoon, which, by the way, she demanded was at an all-inclusive that cost a fuckin' fortune. I was twenty-four. My parents had to help me pay for it."

He paused to allow me to let this information sink in, I nodded for him to continue and he did.

"We'd moved into our apartment but she wanted another one, bigger, more exclusive in a development with a pool. I couldn't afford it but I loved her, so the minute the lease ran out, I moved her into her new apartment. Two months later, she found a house she wanted to buy and it kept goin' from there. She never hid it from me. I just wanted to think eventually she'd have what she needed or she'd be happy with what she had, or at least, she'd be happy just to have me. She never was."

I placed my hand on his chest thinking Audrey Haines was all kinds of fool. His arm gave me a squeeze and he went on talking.

"I should have ended it before we got down to kids, but if I did," he shrugged, "I wouldn't have my kids."

"Worth it then," I murmured.

"Definitely," he smiled.

Layla, done with giving her hint that camping out on the bed meant we should join her there, came out and started to head butt our legs.

"I should start cooking," Mike said, letting me go to pet his dog who, remembering he existed, appeared in throes of ecstasy to have his big, strong hand scratching behind her ears.

"Can I help?" I asked and he stayed bent to Layla but twisted his torso to look up at me.

"You always cook for your girls?"

"Mostly, yeah."

"Then no."

There it went, the belly flutter again.

"You always cook when your kids are here?" I asked.

"Yeah."

"Then I'll help."

He gave Layla a playful push and came to me, his hand curling at my neck, pulling my upper body close to his as his neck bent so his face could get close to mine.

When he was close, he whispered, "I like you, Violet."

"I like you too, Mike," I whispered back.

He grinned, touched his forehead to mine a second then touched his lips to mine a second then he said, "Let's go cook."

Being a good dad, Mike knew how to cook. The au gratin potatoes were already cooking in the oven and he made London broil and green beans and he had fresh bakery rolls to go with.

We ate at his kitchen table with Layla lying mostly on Mike's feet then we did the dishes together. After the dishes, Mike made ice cream sundaes with lashings of caramel and chocolate syrup on gourmet vanilla bean ice cream, whipped cream on top, sprinkled with pralines. I took note of this, since they were simple but absolutely delicious. My girls would love them.

We ate these on the couch with Layla sitting by my side, her head on the seat by me, staring at me while blinking, telling me she needed ice cream or she'd die.

Mike noticed and called her off. She gave in with an irritable groan and lay down by my feet.

Conversation through dinner and dessert wasn't heavy. We didn't share life stories and I didn't tear up again. We talked (mostly about our kids), we laughed (mostly about our kids) and he proved again he was easygoing and easy to be around.

Then he took my bowl, ordering me to fill up our wine glasses, and he left the room. I did as he ordered and was taking a sip when he got back. He sat down beside me, took my glass out of my hand, set it on the coffee table, put his hands to my pits, dragged my ass across his lap and over until I was on my back and he was on top of me.

Then we were making out on his couch.

I wasn't certain how I managed to get myself into these situations, fucking Joe on his couch that morning, making out with Mike on his that evening. But I was certain I wasn't doing a lot to avoid them. I figured, partially, it was because both, in their own way, were pretty freaking magnificent. The other part was that I liked being with both men. I liked it in entirely different ways. But I still liked it.

His mouth moved from mine and his face disappeared into my neck. I felt his tongue trail from the back of my ear down the line of my neck where he stopped, and while I shivered, he asked, "Where're your girls tonight?"

"At home, hopefully not throwing a wild party with boys and kegs."

His head came up and he was grinning when he looked at me. "That something they would do?"

"Kate, no. Keira, yes, once she figures out kegs exist. Kate would be running through the house trying to get people out or cleaning up and fretting the whole time that someone would break a glass or knock over the TV. Keira would be in the kitchen, not a care in the world, shot-gunning beers."

He was still grinning when he asked, "Yeah?"

I grinned back and shook my head. "No, they're both good kids. They're probably watching a movie while Kate texts Dane, who's out with his friends tonight, and Keira texts everyone in three counties. But I know Keira. There'll come a day when my house will look like the day after in a 80's Brat Pack movie."

"*Weird Science,*" he said on a smile.

"*Sixteen Candles,*" I one-upped him.

"You need to get home?" he asked, and I looked at the clock on his shelves.

It was eight thirty. I didn't need to get home. And even though it made me a terrible person, being on the couch with Mike, who I liked too much in a way that was so confusing I couldn't unravel it in a million years, I wanted to be home late, just in case Joe was watching for me.

"No," I replied when I looked back at him.

"Good," he muttered and his head came back down.

We made out more and it got heavy, mainly because we both liked it, but the progression was slow, natural, strangely like we'd fooled around on his couch hundreds of times before and when we did it, we always knew we had all the time in the world. This was a change from Joe, a nice one but one that reminded me of Tim, who also took his time, and I'd liked that too.

Eventually Mike's hand curled around my breast and his thumb slid over the fabric of my blouse at my nipple.

I sucked in breath against his lips and arched my back to press into his hand.

"Sweetheart," Mike called, and I realized my eyes were closed so I opened them.

"Yeah?" I whispered, his eyes got soft, his lids lowered and his mouth touched mine as his thumb slid back across my nipple and I inhaled again.

"I wanna fuck you, honey," he said quietly, and I held my breath, wanting him to and not wanting him to, both at the same maximum strength.

He went on. "Right here or I take you to my bed. But before I do that, we gotta talk."

"Okay," I whispered, unsure about this talk because I was pretty sure what this talk was going to be about.

His hand left my breast and he fell to his side. Rolling me to mine with his arm around me, he got up on an elbow, head in hand and looked down at me while he tangled his long legs with mine. I decided to get up on my elbow too and I rested my other hand on his chest.

"You ready for this?" he asked softly, and I closed my eyes, drew breath into my nostrils and remembered he was a really good guy.

I opened my eyes and replied, "I don't know."

"We can go fast, we can go slow. I'm good with both. What I'm not good with is us goin' fast when you wanna go slow but you not sayin' anything, yeah?"

I nodded.

He spoke again and my entire body went solid because what he said introduced the part I knew he wanted to say.

"I'm also not big on sharing."

"What?" I asked, even though I knew exactly what he meant.

"Cal was at your house today."

Shitshit*shit*!

I tried to be casual. It wasn't like it was 1890 and I had to make sure no one saw my ankles. These days, women played the field just like men.

Right?

"Yeah, he was," I affirmed, even though he was there, Joe was there and I was there when Mike asked me over for dinner.

"What was he doin' there?"

"Fixing my garage door opener."

"He do a lot a shit around your house?"

"Um…just the alarm system and the garage."

"Things still complicated?"

The answer to that question was: more than ever.

Except, after that afternoon when Mike asked me to his house right in front of Joe and Joe didn't blink, he didn't freaking care, not even a little bit, maybe they weren't.

I just didn't want to admit it yet. Even though I knew. At the back of my mind and at the bottom of my heart, I knew.

I also knew, when I uncomplicated things, it would hurt a lot more than it should and more than I could take right then.

"He's wound you up," Mike said on a sigh.

"What?"

"Cal, he's wound you up. Women get like that with him."

"They do?"

"Yeah, the whole history…women love that shit."

"What whole history?"

Mike stared at me then he asked, "You don't know?"

"Don't know about what?"

"About Cal, his wife, his dad and his kid."

I felt my body twitch and I whispered, "His kid?"

Mike stared at me a second then muttered, "Fuck."

"Fuck what?"

Mike didn't answer.

I got up on a hand and looked down at him. "Fuck what, Mike?"

Mike pushed up too. Then, with his arm around me, he pulled me further up the couch to the armrest. He leaned back against the couch and pulled me to him, into his arms, my chest pressed to his, his hand in my hair.

Then he said in a way I knew he didn't want to say it, "The story is 'burg lore so someone's gonna tell you, might as well be me."

I waited.

Mike spoke again. "You know Feb and Colt's story? How they were the big item in high school, even before, everyone said they were born to be together?"

I nodded.

"Well, Cal and his ex-wife, Bonnie, they were that way too."

I blinked, not believing that, not for a minute. Not about the emaciated, lank-dirty-haired, filthy-slutty-clothed Bonnie who crashed to the floor after offering the tall, huge, strong, amazingly beautiful Joe the opportunity to take her up the ass if he paid for it.

"That can't be true. I've met Bonnie. She's—"

I stopped talking when I saw Mike's face register out-and-out shock. "You met Bonnie?"

"Yeah."

"Cal's Bonnie?"

I didn't like to think of her that way but I still answered, "Yeah."

"Jesus, how'd you meet her?"

"I was over at his house, she came over."

"You have got to be shittin' me."

I shook my head and said, "No."

"You sure it was Bonnie?"

I nodded my head and said, "Yes."

Mike looked away and he muttered, "Jesus Christ."

I was confused and I explained why. "It wasn't pleasant, but I got the impression it happens a lot. She was asking for money."

Mike looked back at me and he looked pissed. I'd never seen him look pissed and it was kind of scary. Not Joe-pissed-scary, but still, pretty freaking scary.

"She came to Cal's house and asked *Cal* for money?"

"She was wasted, and high, a total mess."

"She wanted money for drugs," Mike surmised.

"Or booze."

"No, Violet, she wanted money for drugs," Mike stated firmly, and I stared at him.

"Okay," I replied slowly.

"She's a junkie," Mike informed me.

That wasn't surprising. She definitely looked and dressed the part, not to mention acted it.

"I guess so."

"No, she *is*. Look up junkie in the encyclopedia, sweetheart, Bonnie Wainwright's picture is right there. The bitch has been a mess for years."

It seemed out of character for Mike to refer to anyone casually as a bitch so I started to get scared.

"Maybe you should tell me the story," I suggested.

"Nab our wine, honey, we're gonna need it," Mike ordered. I didn't take that as a good sign but I twisted out of his arms, nabbed our wine off the coffee table and came back, giving him his and taking a sip from mine.

Mike shifted a leg under me so he had one foot to the floor, his thigh angled on the seat, me mostly in his lap, partly between his legs, his other leg the length of the couch, still tangled with both mine.

This was a comfortable position, one of safety, togetherness.

It didn't register on me as I braced for Mike's story.

"Like I said," he started, "Bonnie and Cal were an item, like Feb and Colt. But Bonnie's dad was an asshole. Big wig at the church, holier than thou, but not so holy he didn't go home and beat the shit outta his wife and kid."

I closed my eyes and dropped my head.

"Yeah, sucks normally, but this was bad and I mean *bad*. Asshole didn't try to hide it. Both of 'em on a regular basis walked around with their eyes blackened, lips split and swollen, arms in slings, limpin', holdin' themselves funny. Christ, I was a kid, one year ahead of Cal at school, we went to the same church and I saw 'em all the time and even I knew what they caught at home."

I opened my eyes and looked at him.

Mike kept talking.

"Everyone knew but those two were so cowed, they never called the cops. No one could do shit about it if they didn't report it and they didn't. She was pretty back then, Bonnie was. God, beautiful. All the boys thought so, even young, in junior high. But she only had eyes for Cal and he only had eyes for her. They started it when they were young, twelve, thirteen, somewhere 'round there. Never apart. Always together, Cal and Bonnie. After they hooked up, I never remember seein' one without the other."

Mike paused and I didn't say anything mainly because I couldn't say anything so he went on.

"Cal was helpless to save her from her dad, drove him crazy. He acted out, got trashed, did shit, got into trouble, lots of it. She wasn't with him, he was carousin'. But Bonnie was somethin' else. Minute she hit high school, she went wild. Partying, out all the time, missin' school, drinkin', smokin' pot, doin' anything she could do to forget home. Started with that, got worse, acid, coke, crack, whatever she could get her hands on. Cal was her boyfriend and he turned into her bodyguard. He cleaned up his act, drove her where she wanted to go, looked after her while she had the time of her life, got her home safely. It was like he knew she needed that escape, her rebellion, and he was gonna give it to her but make sure she was safe while doin' it. The minute they graduated, they got married. They got married the same fuckin' day. Drove straight down to Tennessee and did it. Came back, moved in with Cal's dad. She never went back home, far's I knew. Even if she wanted to, Cal wouldn't let her. Everything he was was about protectin' her from that shit and gettin' her clean. He acted like it was the only reason for him to breathe."

My mouth was dry and I needed to blink but I couldn't. I was frozen, staring at Mike.

But he wasn't done. Not even halfway.

"Cal's dad was a wreck, lost his wife when Cal was a kid. When she was gone, he lost his will to live. He held down a job by some miracle since he was drunk most the time. Loved her, though, people still talk about it, especially with what happened with Cal and Bonnie. How ole Joe and Cal are cut from the same cloth, one-women men. Joe lost Angela and his world caved in, he didn't have the strength to dig his way out. Cal lost everything and he dug himself out, walked away but he's never goin' back."

"Lost everything?" I whispered.

Mike nodded. "Yeah. Cal moved Bonnie into his dad's house, by this time his dad was sick. Cancer. Been smokin' two packs a day for years. Cal worked two jobs, maybe three. He was a bouncer, security at the mall, anything he could do. Especially when Bonnie seemed to clean herself up and she got pregnant, had Nicky."

"Nicky?"

"Their son. Would have been good, except ole Joe bein' at home sick, Cal workin' his ass off for Bonnie and Nicky and because his dad's insurance was shit. Joe was dyin' in that house with Bonnie in it and the kid. Bonnie fell off the wagon, Cal'd drag her back on. She'd fall off again, Cal dragged her back on. It was relentless, but he never gave up."

"He did, they're divorced," I stated, though divorced or not, Joe never mentioned a child, his son, and fear had hold of my soul that *she* had him. That wreck of a woman was raising Joe's boy.

"Yeah," Mike clipped. "He got shot of her. He got shot of her when he came home and found the cops all over his house. She was out of it, took the dad's drugs. Don't even know what he was on, pain killers probably. Got smashed, for some reason decided to give her baby a bath, and then she forgot he was in the tub—"

Pain shot through me, agonizing pain, infiltrating every cell in my body. I knew where this was going and I couldn't stop it before I cried, "*Don't!*"

Mike's arm was around me and it got tight as his voice got quiet.

"Yeah, sweetheart, Nicky drowned in the bathtub. Ole Joe found him, saw the state of Bonnie, called the police, but it was such a bad scene, he was so far gone health-wise, he had a heart attack. He was dead before the cops got to the house. Cal showed up, his kid dead, his dad dead and his wife arrested for involuntary manslaughter."

I was shaking my head but Mike kept talking.

"Colt got the callout. He was the first on the scene."

"Please, Mike," I whispered, turning away, setting my glass on the coffee table and Mike leaned into me, setting his glass beside mine and his arms pulled me to him again.

His arms were strong, this was a better position of safety and togetherness. But after hearing that about Joe, Bonnie, his son, his dad, it *totally* didn't register on me. I was trembling in a way it felt like I'd never be able to stop.

"It was fucked up. Totally," Mike's voice was almost a whisper. "She did time, not much, criminally negligent. Cal divorced her while she was inside. I thought it was over, least for him. I had no idea she ever came back. I can't imagine why the fuck she would. Her comin' back, askin' for money, that's not only fucked up, it's plain cruel. His dad was dyin' but not dead, she essentially killed him. Her kid, shit. Her kid. Cal's boy. Totally fucked."

I stared at him and whispered the God's honest truth, "Women don't love that shit, Mike."

He gave me another squeeze of his arms and replied, "No, sweetheart, that wasn't what I meant. They love the broken man, the heart that bleeds, think they can fix it."

"I had no idea."

"Now you do, you wanna fix it?"

My eyes slid over Mike's shoulder and I looked out his window.

That nightmare had obviously happened seventeen years ago. I hated it that Joe experienced that. It felt like acid in my veins, I hated it so much.

But I knew, the way Joe was, the way he looked, the way he acted, there were likely a lot of women before me who knew all about it and tried to fix him.

Joe just couldn't be fixed.

A one-woman man, like his dad, Mike said. Did everything for her. Kept her safe, tried to keep her straight and was good enough to put her in a taxi instead of slam the door in her face when she'd killed his baby and essentially killed his father.

A one-woman man, he'd just picked the wrong woman, the *really* wrong one.

Joe was never going to be fixed. He didn't want to be, and therefore, he never would.

"Violet," Mike called and I looked at him.

"No," I replied. "I don't want to fix Joe."

That was a lie. I did. I really wanted to. I wanted to so badly I could taste it in my mouth, feel it hollowing out my belly, like that hunger I had for him.

I just knew I couldn't.

Mike's hand came to my face, his fingers curving around my jaw, his thumb at my cheek, using it to bring it close so his mouth could touch mine then he gently pushed me away an inch but his hand didn't leave my face.

"Thinkin' I killed the mood," he muttered.

I gave him a weak smile and agreed, "Yeah."

"Not a bad thing, sweetheart, 'cause I'm also thinkin' you need time."

My weak smile died and I agreed again, "Yeah."

"You want me around while you take that time?"

I closed my eyes and dropped my forehead to his shoulder.

Then selfishly and stupidly, I whispered, "Yeah, Mike, I do. If you wanna be around."

I felt his body relax against mine and he murmured, "Good, 'cause I wanna be around."

I lifted my head, needing the mood to shift again, not back to before but to something normal, sane, that didn't include drowned babies or Joe's broken heart.

Therefore I asked, "You mind if we watch a movie?"

"I'll only mind if you don't cuddle up to me while we're doin' it."

My smile was less weak when I said, "I think I can do that."

"Then go pick what you wanna watch."

I kept smiling at him and started to pull away but went back to him.

"Mike?" I called when his eyes caught mine.

"You're practically in my lap, honey," he answered on a grin.

"Thanks for puttin' up with my shit," I whispered.

His face got soft and his hand came back to curve around my jaw. "I'm a slow learner, sad but true, but one thing I learned. There're women whose shit is worth puttin' up with and women whose it isn't. I'm guessin' you're the first category."

"I don't know, I've got a bad temper," I told him honestly.

"Then I'll try not to piss you off."

"That would be advised."

He grinned, kissed me lightly again, dropped his hand from my face and said, "Go pick a movie."

"Okay," I replied, got up and picked a movie. Mike put it in and we cuddled on the couch while we watched it.

The movie was good, and since Mike owned it, he obviously liked it.

The best part was being tucked, my back to his front on the couch, my head on his bicep, his arm tight at my waist, our legs entwined, doing a bit of nothing, watching a movie, in a family room, in a family house, with a dog stretched at the side of the couch.

That was the best part.

And I loved it. I even had to admit I loved doing it with Mike, just as I admitted that I'd prefer doing it with Joe.

But Joe didn't cuddle and watch movies or make dinner or have a dog.

And Joe never would.

Cal was still on his deck when night had fallen and he heard Violet's Mustang in her drive.

As if she was doing it to piss him off, she didn't use the garage.

He stayed on the deck taking another swig of beer, which one he had no clue, he'd lost count, as he heard her side door open and close.

He stayed where he was, staring into the dark, knowing she wasn't going to come to him that night, the first night he was home in a long time she wasn't in his bed.

It was a while later, he was considering getting another beer or going for the bourbon, when he heard her side door open then her keys jingle to lock it.

He waited then looked to the side when he heard her feet hit the steps to his deck.

She walked up to him and stopped by the chair Colt had vacated hours ago.

"Don't say it," she warned.

He had no idea what she didn't want him to say but he replied, "Buddy, I didn't say a word."

She hesitated then sat down next to him, cocking her legs and putting her feet up on the railing.

She was in her clothes, a jeans skirt, tighter than the other one. In fact, it was tight all the way down the sides of her thighs, a slit up the front. She had on a little purple blouse, the neckline was wide, showed her chest, not her cleavage, and it was loose but cinched at her waist. She was barefoot.

He didn't have to ask if she had a good night, not that he would have. She left at a quarter to six. It had to be close to midnight, maybe after. Plenty of time to eat and do all sorts of shit if you were having a good time. He knew what he'd be doing if Vi was at his house that long, exactly what he *did* do when Vi was at his house that long. He reckoned Haines wouldn't be far off that mark. What he knew was, if Vi had let him fuck her, she wouldn't be sitting beside him right now.

Cal didn't want to feel relieved but that didn't mean he fucking wasn't.

For once she seemed happy to be silent, but Cal was not.

He downed the last of the beer and dropped his hand.

"Should give Haines a clean run."

He felt rather than saw her head turn in his direction but she didn't speak.

"Not gonna do that, buddy," he told his dark yard. "You might not like what we got, but I do."

"Joe," she said softly, and when she did, he wondered why they were sitting on his deck rather than in his bed.

He turned to her. "You don't like it, you're the one's gonna have to end it."

She didn't say anything, not for a while, then she said quietly, "I'm tired, Joe."

He turned back to face his yard.

"Then go to bed."

She hesitated then moved. But he didn't hear her feet padding down his steps. He heard his sliding glass door open then close.

He sat where he was, staring at his yard and he did this for a long time. Then he reached down, grabbed the two beer bottles that had collected by his chair when he stopped bothering to take them in when he went to get another. He went into his house, to his kitchen, dumped the bottles in his trash and he went to his room.

Violet was in his bed. She didn't move when he came in, didn't move when he took off his clothes. But she made a noise low in her throat and shifted when he got in bed. Then he settled on his back. She was curled with her back to him and she again didn't move.

He listened to her steady breathing.

Fuck, she was asleep in his bed, not waiting for him, not about to turn around and have a conversation, suck his cock or ride him. She was asleep.

*You wouldn't believe how sweet it is, knowin' at the end of the day, she'll crawl right back into my bed,* Colt had said.

Cal closed his eyes then rolled into Vi, curling an arm around her stomach and pulling her into his body, noting she was wearing one of his tees.

He smelled her hair as he bent his neck and the bridge of his nose rested against her crown.

"Joe?" she called. He'd woken her but she still sounded half-asleep.

"Go back to sleep, baby."

"Okay," she whispered and her body settled into his.

He didn't know why she was there, didn't know why she kept coming back, didn't know, she could have a good man like Haines, why she left Haines's house and ended her night in Cal's bed.

And he didn't care.

She was there.

Cal pressed into her, and within minutes, he was asleep.

# Eleven

## Big Purple Bow

I woke up, opened my eyes, lifted my head and looked up at Joe.

When I did, he dipped his chin and his beautiful, clear, sky blue eyes locked with mine.

He was wide awake.

I was pressed to his side, my thigh thrown over his, and his arm was curled around my waist. His other arm was cocked, his head resting on his hand.

"Hi," I whispered.

He looked at the clock then at me.

"I'm on my back, buddy."

I closed my eyes and dropped my head, planting my face in his chest.

What the hell was I doing?

I didn't know but I knew what I was going to be doing.

I moved my face so my mouth was on him. Then I moved my body so it was straddling his. I slid down, enjoying what I was doing more and more, got close to my goal but he pulled me up so I was face to face with him.

"You gonna wrap your mouth around me?" he asked.

"Yeah," I answered.

His hands tugged at the tee I was wearing.

"You suck my dick, baby, you do it naked."

I shifted, excitement gathering tight between my legs at his words. Then I sat up, still straddling him, and pulled off his tee while he watched. I slid to the side, pulling down and kicking off my panties then I straddled him again, looking down.

"Happy?" I asked.

His hands spanned my ribs and he grinned.

"Yeah."

"Do you mind if I carry on?" I asked.

"Have at it," Joe invited.

I shook my head.

Then I had at him with my mouth, and when I knew he was close because his hands holding back my hair so he could watch became fists, I released him and positioned myself over him. Wrapping my hand around his cock, I guided it inside and I rode him, one hand in the bed for leverage, one at his chest for contact. Both of his hands were at my hips, coaxing, encouraging.

"You don't hurry, Vi, I'm takin' over," he warned, his deep voice hoarse.

"No you aren't, this is my turn."

"Your turn's gonna come with my fingers or my mouth, not my cock, you don't hurry."

I wanted it from his cock so I rode him harder and he groaned.

"Christ, buddy, that ain't helpin'."

I leaned down and kissed him, still moving. Joe slid a hand between us, pressed a finger hard against my clit and that finger rolled.

I came instantly, moaning his name into his mouth.

"Thank Christ," he groaned back, his hips surged up and he came too.

I collapsed on top of him and both his arms wrapped around me, one going to my hair, pulling it away from my face then tangling in it and staying there.

"You gotta go home, baby," he told me but he kept me locked in his arms.

"In a minute."

"Vi, the girls."

"They sleep late in the summer. Sometimes Keira sleeps until eleven."

His arms gave me a squeeze. "Honey, the neighbors."

I blinked and my eyes, with a view to his neck, saw nothing.

He'd never called me "honey."

I pulled myself together and whispered, "Joe, baby, in a minute."

His arms gave me another squeeze and he muttered, "Not me who gives a shit."

I couldn't help it, I grinned.

Then I thought I was lying with Joe in his bed in the house where his son died, his father died and his ex-junkie-wife had committed criminally negligent involuntary manslaughter.

How he could be here, I didn't know, I couldn't imagine.

But I hated him there. He should sell that house. Why he didn't and then never came back, I had no clue.

Then I wondered what *I* was doing there.

But I knew. Stupid me, coming home last night after a great night with Mike, great, the *best*, dumping my purse, going to my room, slipping off my shoes and lying on top of my covers, staring at the ceiling and thinking of Mike. My mind shifted against my will and I started thinking of Joe over here, in this house, this goddamned house, filled with memories of tragedy, and he was all alone.

I couldn't fix him, I knew it, but here I was trying to do it.

Joe's hand sifted through my hair then his fingertips came to my hairline and did it again, holding it back as he twisted his neck so his mouth could get to my ear.

"You're stayin', buddy, got a mind to eat you," he murmured.

I shivered.

He never quit, but I didn't mind. Not at all. I was freaking addicted to it.

I lifted my head but Joe's hand didn't leave my hair.

"I should go back," I said, not moving.

"Yeah," Joe replied. "You should."

I still didn't move. Neither did Joe.

"Vi," he called.

"What?" I asked.

Slowly, he smiled.

Then he rolled me to my back.

After a while, I didn't know why I was always whining to be on top.

Being on my back was just fine.

I slid out of Joe's bed and pulled on his tee.

"Buddy, you keep stealin' my tees, I won't have any left."

I nabbed my undies and stepped into them, my head up looking at him as I did.

"You gave me the first," I reminded him.

"You stole the next two," he returned.

"I only stole one."

"You're wearin' number two."

I couldn't believe he was keeping track.

"I'll send Keira and Kate to the mall to buy you new ones."

"Christ, don't do that. Fuck knows what they'll come back with."

I gathered my clothes, tucked them in my arm and looked at him in bed, scarred belly and pectoral on display, but then so was his chest. It was nice, all of it. Very nice. Even though the sheet was pulled up to his waist. If it wasn't then the view would have been nicer.

"They take direction," I told him.

"When I was at the mall with you, Keira picked a bunch of shit for me. One of the shirts had fuckin' flowers on it."

A little giggle escaped me at the idea of Joe wearing a shirt with flowers on it.

"And it was pink," Joe finished and a much bigger, louder giggle burst out of me.

"You'd look good in pink," I told him when I stopped giggling.

"Lucky you're outta arm's reach, buddy, or I'd smack your ass."

I grinned at him then I blurted, "It's Sunday."

"So?"

"Sunday's pancake day."

His face closed down and he muttered, "Buddy."

"Offer's on the table, Joe. That's all I'm sayin'," I told him quickly, got close, put a hand in the bed and touched my mouth to his, but when I pulled slightly away, I finished, "And I make fucking good pancakes."

Then, fast as I could, I straightened and moved out of the room.

There it was again, me acting stupid, trying to fix Joe.

I tried not to look at his house as I moved through it. But even though I tried, I saw that it was likely he hadn't changed a thing. It was tidy, even clean. Though the thought of Joe cleaning was worthy of another giggle, it was true. But it was dated and drab, much more dated than seventeen years ago. I figured the house hadn't changed since Joe's mom died, whenever that was, but by the looks of things it was a long time ago.

I went to his sliding glass door and out, hustling across the deck, down the steps, but I caught movement. I looked across Joe's yard, my yard, and I saw Tina Blackstone in her yard, wearing a nightie and a robe, watering the flowers in her big, half-barrel, wooden tubs on her deck.

She was watering her flowers but her eyes weren't on her flowers. They were on me and even a yard away, I saw her mouth hanging open.

Shit!

I waved casually to her, rethinking way too late wearing Joe's tee seeing as, if I was in my clothes, she wouldn't know that I was over at Joe's house, having sex with Joe, but now she couldn't help but know. She couldn't miss it.

But who would have thought Tina would be out in her yard on a Sunday morning before eight o'clock watering her flowers?

Her flowers were nice, which was surprising. She didn't seem the type to have a green thumb or even give a shit. They weren't as nice as mine but they were nice. Still, it was Sunday. Even I, before Joe, wasn't out on a Sunday before eight o'clock watering my flowers.

I headed to my side door, fumbling with my jeans skirt to pull out the key and remote, hitting the remote so my sensors would go off and then struggling with my key. Seeing Tina had weirded me out and right then I was certain everyone would see me.

I got into the house, rearmed the alarm and shot to my room.

I took a shower and got ready for my day. I had the afternoon shift at the garden center and I needed to talk to Bobbie about changing the schedule so I could have next weekend off for Sam and Melissa.

After a load of laundry went in and I'd checked my e-mail, Kate and Keira got up. They were still in their pjs on the stools at the bar. Kate was wearing a big t-shirt and a pair of slouchy pajama bottoms. Keira was wearing a camisole and a pair of slouchy pajama bottoms. Kate's hair was down and partly tangled from sleep. Keira's hair was in a messy ponytail at the very top of her head. I was at the stove, flipping the first batch of pancakes when Keira made a strange gurgling noise.

Thinking she was choking on orange juice, I turned to her, but she had an alarm remote in her hand and her eyes on the side kitchen door.

She jumped off her stool, hit some buttons on the remote and screeched, "*Joe!*"

I whirled to the door and stood staring at it, spatula in hand as Keira unlocked it, yanked the door open and Joe was standing there. I'd seen him through the window of the door but seeing him standing there, full body, my breath—already stopped—escaped me.

"I don't know why you're here but you *have* to have some of Mom's pancakes. They're better than her cupcakes," Keira announced.

"That good?" Joe asked, his eyes on me.

Keira grabbed his hand and tugged him in, lying, "Yeah, definitely."

"Hey, Joe," Kate greeted.

"Hey, girl," Joe greeted back.

"You can sit on my stool," Keira offered.

"We should sit at the table, seein' as there's so many of us. I'll get the plates," Kate decided.

"Girl—" Joe started, but Kate was on the move and Keira had dropped his hand and was charging into the kitchen to help Kate.

I was still staring at Joe.

The girls exited the room balancing plates, cutlery, napkins, butter and maple syrup as Joe came to me.

"Can your girls take over pancakes?" he asked, his face serious, and seeing it, something ugly slid through me.

I nodded.

"Kate," he called, looking into the dining area. "Take over here, yeah?"

She looked through the opening of the bar at Joe then at me then she nodded to Joe.

Joe took the spatula out of my hand, put it on the counter, took my hand and dragged me to my bedroom.

He closed the door and looked down at me.

Then he lifted his hands, both of them, and settled them where my shoulders met my neck.

"I'm not here for pancakes," he told me.

I nodded, staring up at him.

"But I'm stayin' for pancakes."

I nodded again, still staring.

"Went out, looked to your house, you had a box at the steps to your front door."

Damn. I knew it.

"White?" I asked. "Big purple bow?"

I watched as his face went hard then he nodded. "Big bow, big box."

"Did you get it gone?"

"Yeah, it's in my house. Called Colt."

I nodded again.

"That his thing?" Joe asked.

"Yeah."

"It's Sunday," he told me.

"Yeah."

"He ever do his thing on Sunday?"

"No." His hands gave me a squeeze and I asked, "What's that mean?"

"Don't know." He was watching me closely then he asked, "How solid are you right now?"

"Not very."

He hesitated, nodded and said, "All right."

"Why?"

"Later."

"No, I need it to hit me all at once so I can deal with it and move on, not spread it out. Spreading it out is bad. So, even though I'm freaked, I want to know."

"Sure?"

I nodded.

His hands at my neck slid up to my jaws and he pulled me close, dipping his chin so he was close too.

"Box was just out of sensor range," Joe told me.

"What?" I asked.

"Box was out of sensor range. I got sensors set so even if someone approaches the door, you know in the house, a preliminary alarm goes off so you're aware. Remember, I told you that."

I nodded. I remembered.

"You set the alarms for sleep, which I'm guessing you did when you came to me last night..." He let that hang and I nodded again.

He had bunches of settings for the sensors, including one for when we were awake but in the house so, say, the postman came, or perhaps Kenzie Elise, we didn't jump out of our skins because the preliminary alarm went off. But, in the middle of the night, no one should be lurking at our doors. So we had what he called a sleep setting too. It set off an alarm that we could hear, and Joe and Colt could too so they could investigate (and the bad guy could get the hint and go away), but only sent a message to dispatch if the doors and windows were breached or one of us didn't turn the alarm off before the timer ran down on the message being sent to dispatch.

Joe went on. "Anyone got close, the sensors would trip. Whoever put that box out there knows how the sensors are set."

"But you can see them," I reminded him.

"Box was just out of sensor range," he repeated.

"You said that."

"You can see them, buddy, but you can't see the range."

I sucked in breath, realizing what this meant.

"It's a message, Vi," Joe whispered, like whispering would soften the blow. "He's tellin' you he knows my system."

In other words, Daniel Hart was telling me he could get to me.

"Joe," I whispered.

"He can't bypass it," Joe stated.

"He knows it then he can bypass it."

"He can't."

"But, Joe, he knows—"

"Vi, he'd have to shut down the electrical grid for the entire fuckin' county to bypass my system."

I blinked at him and asked, "Really?"

"Yeah. That wirin' Chip fucked up?" he asked back, and I nodded yet again. "There you go," he finished secretively, not enlightening me any further to the method to his madness that made him Security to the Stars.

"Why has he not done anything for weeks and now a box?" I asked.

"Don't know," Joe answered.

"Should I tell my girls?"

"Don't know."

He was full of it. He might not know but he had an opinion.

"You never know what's right with kids, you just wing it so what do you think? Should I tell the girls?" I pressed.

He sighed and his hands slid from my jaw to my neck and down my back so he was holding me loosely in his arms.

"They're smart, they're aware of the situation, they love you. Think they'd be pissed, buddy, you didn't clue them in."

I nodded. He was right, even though I wasn't certain I'd do it seeing as I was a mom and didn't want to freak them out more than they already were.

"What was in the box?" I asked.

"Didn't open it. Colt's comin' to get it. You got a restraining order against him; he shouldn't be sendin' you gifts. You got the RO in Illinois, I need to check with Colt to see if the RO is in effect in the State of Indiana, likely is. We'll be havin' a conversation about that later and they're gonna go over the box. Maybe they can lift a print, lean on him for breaking the RO."

"Hart wouldn't make that mistake with the prints."

Joe sighed, his arms gave me a gentle squeeze, and he said, "I know."

I stood in his arms, feeling both pissed that this had started again and it just never seemed to *freaking* go away and feeling scared because this was back, it was here, in this safe little town and it just never seemed to *freaking* go away.

"I'll be over for your seafood, buddy," he said.

I focused on Joe and blinked.

"What?"

"Your brother and his woman, you're making your seafood shit, I'll be here."

Was he inviting himself over for a family dinner?

"Um…" I mumbled.

"I get to know him at dinner, we have a nice night, move it to J&J's. I ask him to play a game of pool, have a word."

Oh. He wasn't wanting to be part of the family dinner. He was thinking about doing the favor I asked him to do.

This was both nice and disappointing.

"Okay, we'll be doing that Saturday."

"I'll be here."

I nodded again and told him, "Tina Blackstone saw me coming out of your house this morning."

He stared at me a second then he muttered, "Great."

I tilted my head to the side and asked, "Thought you didn't care?"

His eyes locked with mine and he said, "Don't. But you do and that means I gotta walk over to that bitch's house and lay it out for her. Don't like her, don't wanna walk over there and lay it out for her."

"Lay it out for her?"

"Tell her she keeps her mouth shut or it'll piss me off. Lay it out for her," he explained.

I stared at him, feeling his hard, warm chest under his tee where my hands were resting thinking that it was a miracle how he could be so detached and so involved at the same time. Protecting me and the girls in a variety of ways, taking care of us in other ways and yet, at the same time, in a weird way, holding himself apart and not really being there.

Suddenly he asked, "Your walls thin?"

"What?" I asked back, confused at his strange question.

He tipped his head to the wall that connected my room to the rest of the house. "At my place, buddy, the walls are paper thin. Same here?"

I looked over my shoulder at the wall.

My room had been built as an extension so the side wall used to be the back wall of the house. The rest of the house the walls were paper thin. If I was in the kitchen or living room, I could hear the girls in their rooms.

If I was in my room, nothing, as evidenced when Kenzie Elise rang the doorbell.

"This is an extension," I told him.

"Know that, Vi," he told me.

"That wall is pretty solid."

He looked at the wall then back at me and nodded.

"Why?"

"Don't want your girls to hear me comin' in. *Really* don't want them to hear me fuckin' you."

I felt my breath catch.

Then I whispered, "What?"

"He's playin' his games with you, first, you aren't gonna wanna leave your girls here alone. Second, I don't want them here alone. So, I gotta come to you."

And there it was again, detached but involved.

A miracle.

"Joe—"

"What time do they go to sleep?"

"Joe—"

His loose arms tightened. "What time, buddy?"

He wasn't going to let it go, so I answered, "Ten, but they aren't out until eleven. I mean, Keira is. She likes her sleep and drops off immediately. Kate texts Dane for a while and listens to music, but she's usually out by eleven."

"I'll wait until after eleven."

"Joe—"

"You want me to stay away?" he asked, and I didn't. I knew I didn't, which was totally fucked up.

"No."

"You got a key to the sliding glass door?"

"I did but I've lost it."

"Find it," he ordered.

"Okay," I whispered, throwing my bid for Mother of the Year in the garbage.

"I'll come in, they won't hear me. I'll be gone before they get up. They'll never know I'm here," Joe assured me.

I figured that was true. Even when I was awake, Joe could sneak up on me.

"Okay."

His voice got low and tight, like he was forcing out what he was saying and I knew why when he admitted, "Don't like that shit, Vi. Us next door sleepin', some fuckwad comin' to your house while the girls are here, droppin' off gifts."

Shit, that was a lot more involved than it was detached.

Why did he constantly give me mixed signals? It was driving me up the freaking wall.

"I don't either," I agreed.

"So, we do our thing here."

"Okay."

He looked at the door. "How you gonna play it with the girls?"

I took in a deep breath and let it out. "Don't know yet. I need to think about it."

He nodded, telling me he'd keep it quiet then he said, "Pancakes."

"Yeah."

He let me go, took my hand and walked me out of my room.

I sat in my car, doors locked like Joe ordered me to keep them, and I stared at Bobbie's Garden Center.

I was early for work and I had a lot on my mind, a lot I needed to get sorted before I clocked in.

Earlier, Joe and I had left my room only to smell bacon cooking.

The smell hit me. It was an emotional hit, instant and hard.

Since Tim died, the girls and I had pancakes, not bacon, the pancakes enough to fill us up.

On pancake Sunday when Tim was alive, we had bacon because Tim liked bacon and pancakes weren't enough to fill him up.

The girls had made bacon for Joe.

Me having a conversation with Joe in my bedroom was not normal. In fact, it'd never happened. But the girls didn't comment. They didn't ask questions. They just threw us looks, waiting for me or Joe to share. We didn't, and surprisingly, they let it go.

Like when Sam was there, Joe took Tim's seat and this hit me hard too. Minutes later, it hit me harder because the girls again didn't seem to mind. They acted like Joe sat there all the time. They didn't act like this was strange or uncomfortable. They were animated, talkative, not desperately so, naturally, even Kate.

And as we settled in to eating, I found I liked this, like I liked it when Tim was alive and we had pancake Sunday. Family sitting around the table, eating, talking about the week they had, the week to come.

Joe also seemed at ease. Not talkative, Joe wasn't talkative but, in his mostly non-verbal way, he encouraged the girls to do it.

Keira I knew had designs on Joe for me because she liked him and she wanted him to know she liked him. Therefore she chatted enthusiastically with Joe about every subject under the sun. None of these subjects Joe had even a hint of interest in, he couldn't, it was teenage girl stuff, but he never let on that he didn't.

It was Kate who surprised me.

When she got to talking about some of the bands she liked, Joe told her he knew their music. He hadn't met them like The Buckley Boys, but he listened to the bands she liked. I could tell he liked Kate's taste and I could tell Kate liked this music, more than I expected. She was really into it and she enjoyed sharing that with Joe since he liked their music too.

But it was more. She seemed to take his approval of her taste as praise and she blossomed under it. I saw her do it right over pancakes.

Joe left, we did the dishes, and as the girls got ready for their day, I searched for the key to the sliding glass door. I found it in the junk drawer in the kitchen, having no clue how it got there since keys went on the hook by the side door, but I suspected Keira was the culprit mostly because she always was.

Before I went to work, I took it over to Joe's.

I knocked on his front door, wanting to give the impression, should anyone be watching, that this was a friendly neighborly visit, rather than getting caught by someone while I snuck around the back which would indicate a *very* friendly neighborly visit.

When Joe opened the door he was wearing nothing but loose athletic shorts and expensive-looking running shoes and he was sweating a lot. He destroyed my neighborly visit ploy by grabbing my hand, yanking me into the house and slamming the door.

I saw a bunch of weights in the living room I hadn't noticed before, a weight bench pulled into the center of the room. He was working out.

Um…*yum.*

I looked from the bench to him and, holding the key up between us, I said, "Key."

His hand closed on the key, his other hand nabbed me around the back of my neck, his head came down and he kissed me, hard and long.

I was breathing heavily, my hands on his sweat slicked chest when his head came up.

"Great pancakes, buddy," he murmured then let me go, turned away and walked to the kitchen like he hadn't just laid a huge kiss on me, one that made my knees weak and my breath heavy.

I tried to get my head together and my body under control as I heard the key hit his kitchen counter. He went back to the weight bench and grabbed a bottle of water. He tipped his head back to take a long swallow and I walked to his kitchen, washed his sweat from my hands and then walked to the front door.

"'Bye, Joe," I called, my hand at the door and his eyes hit me.

"Tonight, buddy," was his farewell.

I nodded and walked to my car.

I was getting in deep and I knew it. I liked him and I liked him more every time I was with him. Now I liked that my girls obviously liked him.

But that wasn't where it could go, not for Joe who was happy with me sleeping in his bed after I'd been out on a date with another guy, something I wasn't happy with, something that hurt.

And I knew it would never go there unless I fixed him and I had no idea how to fix him. But I had the strong suspicion that trying would be even more heartbreaking because I suspected, no matter what I tried, I'd fail. It might even be devastating when I failed, not only for me, but for my girls who'd said a lot when they cooked Joe bacon.

I looked at my purse, reached out and pulled out my cell.

Then I continued on my path of doing stupid, crazy, selfish shit that made me a bad person.

I slid it open, scrolled down to "Mike's cell," a number I'd programmed into my phone after he called me the first time.

I hit go.

It rang once, only once, when Mike answered.

"You all right?" he asked as a greeting.

He knew about the box.

"You know about the box," I said just to confirm.

"Colt called. I'm at the station now. They're goin' over it for prints."

Shit. He'd gone into the station on his day off because he heard about my box.

"They find anything?" I asked.

"They've lifted a few, gotta put them in the system."

"Okay."

"You all right?" Mike repeated.

"No."

His voice was gentle when he said, "Sweetheart."

I sighed into the phone.

"Where are you now?" he asked.

"What?" I asked back.

"I'll come get you. We'll go get lunch or a coffee at Mimi's or somethin'."

He didn't want me to be alone and freaked, more clear-cut evidence he was a nice guy, a good guy, maybe a great guy. More clear-cut evidence that I was a terrible person, keeping him on a string instead of cutting him loose until I figured out where my head was at and could give him what Joe called "a clear run."

"I'm at the garden center. I have an afternoon shift," I told him.

"I'll come over tonight," he told me.

I closed my eyes and sighed again.

I didn't need Joe at the breakfast table and Mike at the dinner table. Further, my girls didn't need that.

"As far's I know, both girls are home tonight, Mike, and I'm not sure they're ready for that," I said softly.

"Your call, sweetheart, but you want company or need to talk, you know how to find me."

"Thanks, um…actually, that's why I'm calling."

"Yeah?"

"Well," I started, "see, I haven't told the girls about the box and I don't know if I should. They saw the flowers but they don't know about the box. They acted okay after the initial freak out of the flowers, but I know it bothered them. Nothing's happened in a while and back home in Chicago, the flowers, gifts and visits were regular. They might think it's tailing off and, well…" I closed my eyes tight again then opened them and finished, "I'm a mom, Mike. I don't want them to have to worry about this but I don't want them to forget to be vigilant or to be angry with me that I kept this from them. They're not adults but they're not young anymore. I don't know what to do."

"Don't tell them," Mike advised immediately, and I blinked at this advice, which was contradictory to Joe's.

"You think?"

"This shit was goin' down with Audrey, I'd tell Jonas, but no way in hell I'd tell Clarisse."

"Why not?"

"Know you're strong, figure you got strong girls, you've all been through a lot. But girls are girls, boys are boys. Jonas would want to do his bit, even if it couldn't be much, to take care of his mom. He's gotta learn to be a man, and you're unlucky enough that shit like this comes up, that's the way you learn. Clarisse needs her head filled with thoughts about butterflies and teenage vampires for as long as she can think about butterflies and teenage vampires."

Like Kate and Keira were to Tim, Clarisse was Daddy's Little Girl.

I felt my stomach flutter.

But I said, "That's kinda sexist, Mike."

He didn't take offense, mainly because he didn't agree with me and he thought he was right.

I knew this because he said firmly, "That's the way it is, honey."

I didn't reply as it hit me. I'd asked him because he was Mike, he was a parent, but I also asked him because his opinion would likely be the same as what Tim's opinion would be if he'd been alive. He might not know my girls like Joe did, but it was important to me to know what Tim would do and Mike just told me. It was good to know, except now I was more confused than ever at what to do with the girls because, even knowing, I wasn't certain I agreed. It wasn't like I agreed with everything Tim thought either.

Mike went on. "But, I don't know your girls. You gotta do whatever you think is right, and Vi?" he called my name and stopped talking.

"Yeah?"

"Whatever you do will be right, sweetheart."

I felt tears fill my eyes because this, just this, was exactly what I needed to hear, and I whispered, "Thanks, honey."

"I wanna see you, make sure you're all right. I'll stop by Bobbie's sometime today."

"Okay," I agreed immediately, selfishly and stupidly.

"Got the kids this week, but they're all over the place all the time so I could take you to Frank's one night this week."

"I don't know my schedule. My brother and his girlfriend are coming into town next weekend and I've gotta ask Bobbie for a change."

"Find out, you can tell me when I stop by."

"Okay," I agreed, again immediately, selfishly and stupidly then I said, "I have to get to work."

"All right, I'll let you go," he replied then said softly, "Hang in there, honey."

"I'll try."

"Later, sweetheart."

"Later, Mike."

I slid my phone shut and tapped it on my forehead.

Then I dropped it in my purse, unlocked my doors and hurried into work.

After work, I walked into J&J's.

My girls were out for the evening, Kate with Dane, Keira with a pack of friends who'd scheduled a last minute movie that one of her friends' dad's was crazy enough to take a pack of girls to. I had my visit from Mike at the Garden Center and we'd set dinner for Tuesday. Bobbie cleared me for the weekend. I had Sunday off anyway and she knew she'd been leaning on me a lot. I never asked for anything so she rearranged the schedule and gave me the time I needed.

Now with a clear night, I decided I needed girlfriend advice.

I'd thought to go home, pour a glass of wine and call one of my friends in Chicago. I was closer to them, obviously, though our communication via e-mail, texts and phone calls had trailed off as well when my job went full-time, not to mention overtime. But they knew me, most of them for ages, and they'd give good advice.

But they all also knew Tim and loved him and I wasn't certain how they'd feel about me moving on, especially how I was doing that. They were my friends, they'd want to help, I knew that, but I couldn't do it. I couldn't share this, what was happening, how I was behaving and I was worried how they'd react and what they'd think of me.

And they didn't know Joe.

Feb, her sister-in-law Dee and Cheryl were all working, as was Darryl, and I was relieved that both Feb and Cheryl were there. Perfect.

"How's tricks, babe?" Cheryl called as I walked down to Colt's end of the bar and sat on the stool next to his empty one.

"In-freaking-sane," I told her honestly. Her eyes got big, Dee and Feb were also both looking at me and the minute I said this they moved as a pack to my end of the bar.

It was Sunday at J&J's, a Sunday in the summer. There were a few people in, not many, regulars who couldn't care less if it was summer and sunny. They were, as usual, camped out for the long haul.

"You want a drink?" Dee asked me when she hit my end of the bar.

"Diet Coke," I answered.

"Girl, your face says shot of tequila," Cheryl noted, staring at me closely.

"That bad?" I asked.

Feb leaned her elbows on the bar and looked into my eyes. "What's up, Vi? Is it the box?"

Colt had told Feb about the box too. I wasn't surprised. Tim had told me everything about work. I didn't know if this was allowed and I never asked because I didn't want him to think he needed to stop, but I never breathed a word to anyone about anything he said. The shit he saw, the shit people did, he had to let it go and I was that sponge that could soak it out of him, find a way to wring myself dry but let him go back to work feeling clean.

"No, not really. It's…" I looked at the three of them. I didn't know Dee all that well but I couldn't exactly ask her to take a hike. This was her bar.

But I couldn't stay locked in my head anymore.

I needed to unlock the door and choose my path, but before I did that, I needed direction.

So the minute Dee placed my Diet Coke on the bar, I started talking and I told them everything, in somewhat explicit detail, about Joe and me. Mike and me. Joe and the girls. Mike and his house, dog and being a good guy. Joe's terrible history and our fucked up status. Mike's not-as-terrible but still-not-great history and our confusing status.

By the time I was done talking, all three were leaning toward me, their forearms on the bar.

"Lose the neighbor," Cheryl advised the minute I stopped speaking.

Feb's head turned to her, Cheryl sandwiched shoulder to shoulder in the middle of her and Dee, and her eyebrows shot up when she asked, "What?"

"Not worth it," Cheryl decreed. "Been there, done that, got the fuckin' t-shirt and it didn't fit, so I threw the motherfucker out."

"Cal's a good guy," Feb stated.

"Yeah, he is and he's provin' that. Still, he's fucked up and a man stays fucked up for seventeen years, even Wonder Woman couldn't fix his shit," Cheryl replied.

"I've heard that story and, Cheryl, girl, you gotta admit, there's a reason that kind of thing would fuck him up for seventeen years," Dee put in.

"Yeah, not sayin' that. Story breaks my heart and I barely know the guy. But Vi's got other priorities and I orchestrated a come to Jesus, not to mention, Mike asked her out right in front of him. He had no reaction, he's happy for her to play the field, a man like that?" Cheryl flipped her hand out. "He's stayin' stuck in his hole and he ain't goin' *nowhere*," she asserted.

Feb's eyes came to me. "A good woman puts in the effort, knowin' Cal, she might get a helluva reward."

"She might get her heart busted too," Cheryl returned and Feb looked at her.

"I think, what he did with this Bonnie, if he's got a good woman, that kind of energy he gave to Bonnie turned to her and her kids and it was for good things, not somethin' like keepin' a junkie clean, Cheryl, can you imagine?" Feb asked.

"Yeah, I can and I have and it isn't imagination, Feb. Trust me, babe, it's fantasy land," Cheryl shot back.

"Morrie likes Cal," Dee said. "So does Jack. Jack thinks he's the shit. I heard him say once that, even when Cal was a kid he was sharp as a tack, damn near a genius. Said it was a waste, kid that intelligent was bein' raised by a drunk. Said Cal had it better growin' up, he'd be in a different place right now."

This both surprised me and didn't. I had an inkling that Joe was more than Joe let on he was because he was very wise, had a secretary, casually valet parked his car, owned a place in Florida and everyone knew the kind of clientele he had. People like that didn't call on any average guy to set up their systems for them. They called on the best because they could afford to pay for the best.

"What's that got to do with anything?" Cheryl asked. "Morrie and Jack like Mike too."

"Just pointing out the facts," Dee replied.

"Fact is, he's hot. Fact is, he's got a thing for Vi that runs deep enough for him to do what he'll allow himself to do to take care of her and her girls. And the fact is, what he'll allow himself to do is not what she needs," Cheryl retorted to Dee and looked at me. "You got one life and the minute you popped out those babies, you gave yourself one priority in that life. You take care of *you*. If you take care of you then the rest will slot into place for those girls. They'll learn, watchin' you, that they gotta put themselves first, do what's right for their peace of mind, find out what they need and settle for nothin' less. Trust me on this, Vi, 'cause I've lived the nightmare. You can't live your life for someone else, you can't go out there fixin' all the men whose hearts are broken. That's livin' for someone else when you gotta be livin' for *you*." She leaned further into me and said softly, "You came in here knowin' the answer to your question, babe, and you know it. He's sexy as all hell, he makes you feel good and he gives it to you regular. You like it but that's all you're gonna get and you had everything once, you know how that feels and you also know you won't settle for less."

I just stared at her, silent. Not that I was participating in the conversation but I had nothing to say.

Because I knew she was right.

She kept talking. "You play with him as long as you want. Your gut will tell you when the time is up. And you're doin' right, keepin' Mike on that string. He's hot too and gorgeous and you don't want him to move on while you're sorting your head out. You want him right where he needs to be when you're ready to reel him in."

"That's selfish," I whispered.

"That's lookin' out for *you*. Not one fuckin' thing selfish about that, and you been honest, he knows the score and he told you flat out he's willin' to hang around. And he's willin' 'cause he ain't stupid. He knows what kind of woman you are and he knows in the end, you're gonna be with him and his dog in that big, ole, six thousand dollar bed and he's happy to wait. When your sexy neighbor doesn't flinch at a man askin' you out right in front of him, what's that tell you about Mike?" Cheryl ended on a question.

I licked my lips, dropped my head and stared at my Diet Coke because I knew what that told me about Mike. Cheryl was right. I knew all of this before walking into the bar.

"Yeah," Cheryl said gently, her hand covering mine which was resting on the bar. She gave it a squeeze and said, "You're probably drivin' but I'm callin' Reggie, gettin' us a pizza. You fill your belly with pizza, you can also add a bit of vodka to the mix and you need vodka. Cheryl's orders."

After she delivered that line, she walked away, heading toward the phone.

I looked at Feb who was watching me, but Dee spoke.

"Sorry about all this Vi. On the face of it, lotsa women would think this was a great problem to have. But I can tell it's eatin' you."

That was an understatement. It was more than eating me.

To communicate that, I nodded and said, "Yeah."

"You need to talk, get my number from Feb. Anytime, hon, yeah?" I nodded again and she leaned in. "I mean that, okay? Not fun, bein' new in town and not havin' your girls around you. So you need girls and I'm happy to be one of them. Cool?"

I smiled at her because this felt good and she was right, I did need girls and I said, "Cool."

She smiled back, threw Feb a look and walked around the bar, lifting up the section that was hinged so she could go and collect empties.

"Vi," Feb called and I looked from Dee to her and she leaned in too, her voice quiet, almost a whisper as she said, "I needed fixing."

I swallowed and her hand came out, covered mine and held on tight.

"If Colt gave up, thought I wasn't worth the effort…" She shook her head. "God, don't know what I'd do."

"Feb," I whispered back.

"My life was shit, Vi, absolute shit. I was breathin' but I wasn't livin'. I felt nothin', just moved through life, empty. Colt filled me up. He didn't give up on me until I was full. Now, honey, life is so full, every day I wake up next to him and I feel like I'm bursting." Her hand squeezed mine and she whispered, "It's beautiful."

"I'm so glad for you." I was also still whispering.

"You got it in you to give that to Cal, don't give up on him. Man's empty, he needs someone to fill him up."

I licked my lips and fought back the tears that sprung to my eyes.

Her hand released mine and she said, "Mike's a good guy too. Don't get me wrong. Whatever you decide, you decide, and I'm right there with you, yeah?"

I nodded even though I knew, without a doubt, she liked Mike but she wanted me with Joe.

Great. Just what I needed, more contradictory advice.

"What do you like on your pizza?" Feb asked. "If it isn't olives and sausage, we'll have to order another one. That's all Cheryl'll order, she never asks anyone what they want."

"That sounds good. I'm not picky," I told her.

"Great," she replied. "Girls' night at J&J's on a Sunday, perfect. Best day of the week and one of the best things you can do, hangin' with your girls."

She wasn't wrong so I nodded at her and smiled.

"Be back in a sec," she told me and moved away.

I took a sip of Diet Coke.

I was glad I came to J&J's, it was better than going to an empty house and eating dinner for one. It was lots better, especially since it turned into girls' night.

The problem was, I came to get their help to get my head straight and I was more torn than ever.

I heard the sliding glass door open and I rolled to look at the clock.

Eleven twenty-three.

I rolled to my back, wishing I wasn't awake and waiting for Joe. Wishing I hadn't, a half an hour ago, done a new kind of walk of shame, checking on the girls to make sure they were asleep. Wishing I had magic because I'd been lying in bed the last hour and a half, thinking of that scene with Bonnie, how Joe had been after it, knowing now that he was empty, like Feb said. Because he wouldn't be able to survive that scene without getting torn up inside unless there was nothing to tear up. And I wanted the magic to be able to fill him up like Feb was. Make him laugh and smile regularly like she did. Give him that look she had, where you knew life for her was good but she didn't take it for granted because she knew how it felt when life could be bad and she appreciated what she had.

I left my door open for him and Joe closed it then I watched his shadow walk to the bed. I saw him bend, his boots hitting the carpet, heard his clothes rustle as he moved and heard them fall to the ground. Then he reached in and my bedside light was on.

I blinked and felt the covers being swept back and was able to focus when the wall of his body hit me.

"Joe—"

I stopped speaking because his lips were on mine, his tongue spiking in my mouth, his hands going up the tee, his tee that I wore to bed.

He kissed me breathless then lifted his head, his hands still moving on my skin along my sides, hips, over my ass.

"Talked to Tina," he told me in that way of his where he started a conversation in the middle like we'd been talking for a while not making out after him just getting to my bed.

"Yeah?" I whispered, because I still hadn't gotten over his kiss and it wasn't helping that his hands kept moving, lazy and light, on my skin.

"Yeah. Think she got the message."

"What'd you say?" I asked, my hands drifting on his back, his sides, over his ass.

"Told her she didn't see what she thought she saw. I hear it from anyone that she told someone she saw what she thought she saw, shit would go down where she might not be able to see anything, since her eyes would be swollen shut."

My hands stopped moving and my eyes got wide. "You threatened her?"

"She's Tina."

"Yeah, but you threatened her?"

"Buddy, I already lived here when she moved in with her husband and I watched her take her time, fuckin' years, cuttin' off his balls. It was painful to watch. She's a bitch. I know you know that but I don't think you know how big a bitch she is."

"She's already scared of you," I informed him.

"Good, then she'll keep her trap shut."

"Joe, you shouldn't threaten women."

"She isn't 'women,' she's Tina."

I couldn't help it, even though I was horrified that he did what he did, my body started shaking with laughter because he was right.

"Anyway, wouldn't actually do it but I know she doesn't know what to make of me because she doesn't know what to make of a man she can't lead around by his dick. So she doesn't know I wouldn't do it. So I'm guessin' our secret is safe."

My hands started moving again. "Well, thanks, I guess."

He grinned down at me. "You're welcome, I guess."

My hands both slid over his ass and stopped, my fingers gripped and I lifted up to touch my mouth to his. "Turn out the light."

"Nope," he replied and my head settled back on the pillows.

"Nope?"

"Nope."

"Joe—"

"Got shit we gotta get outta the way before we play."

My hands flexed into his ass again but not for fun this time.

"What?"

"Talked to Dane," he announced.

"What?" I whispered.

"Caught him before he went into the house to pick up Kate. Asked him over. We had words, or I gave him some words. Don't think you'll be buyin' any baby shit anytime soon."

My hands went from his ass to his waist and I held on.

"Please, Joe, tell me you didn't threaten a seventeen year old kid."

"Fuck no, Vi. Jesus."

"What'd you say?"

"Let's just say, he gets where I'm comin' from," Joe unusually evaded.

"Where are you coming from?"

"Kate's off-limits."

My stomach did a somersault.

"Joe—"

"He understands respect. I reckon he understood it before, but I reminded him."

"Was he cool when he left?"

"He's into her, got the impression he was glad I was lookin' out for her. He's a good kid."

I didn't know what to do with this. This was bigger than the rest. This was Joe out-and-out taking care of Kate, not for me, for Kate.

"Joe—" I started again.

"Still, gave him condoms."

My body went solid underneath him but my fingers dug into his waist.

"What!" I snapped.

Joe shrugged. "Shit happens."

I turned my head on the pillow, looked at the bed and breathed, "Oh my God."

His hand came to my face and he forced me to look at him. "Baby, it's bein' smart."

"It's giving him ideas."

Joe smiled. "Buddy, he's already got those ideas."

I knew this but I didn't need to be reminded of it so I glared at Joe and his smile got bigger as his head lowered and he kissed me.

I tried to be pissed off. But when his kiss grew deeper and his hands up my tee got greedier, I forgot to be pissed off.

"Turn off the light," I repeated, not knowing why he turned it on in the first place. When we were at his house, we never turned on the light.

"No, baby," he said softly against my mouth, his hand leaving the tee, going to my arm, trailing down it as he slid off my body to the side.

"Joe, why—"

I stopped speaking because I knew why when his hand guided mine to my panties and then it guided it in.

"Joe—"

His finger pressed my finger against my clit and he murmured, his voice thick, "Gonna watch."

"Joe—"

"When you're done, you're gonna watch me."

My hips bucked up and I felt my lips part in wonder.

I liked this idea.

"That made you wet," he muttered, his finger guiding mine down and then both his and mine slid in and I moaned as he finished, "Or wetter."

"God, Joe," I breathed, grinding down on our fingers.

He slid them out and took them back to their original position.

"Make yourself come, baby."

"Okay," I whispered, and he left his finger where it was so he could feel it as I did as he asked.

This wasn't hard because his head came down and his mouth went to my ear and he encouraged me by whispering stuff to me that turned me on so much I was squirming. His head came up and his eyes moved to my legs and I watched him, his face openly hungry and I knew, in the moment right before I came, he felt that hollow feeling, that hungriness for me that I felt for him.

The moan tore from my throat and his mouth slammed down on mine, swallowing it, drowning it out so the girls couldn't hear.

He cupped his hand over mine around my sex and kissed me until I came down. Then he pulled our hands free, rolled to his back, positioning me at his side and he guided my hand over his at his cock as his other hand forced my head close, my mouth on his.

"Hold on, baby," he muttered, and I wrapped my hand around his on his shaft and held on.

I alternately kissed him and watched him, liking both but liking watching him better.

I returned the favor when he came, swallowing his growl.

His hand moved away but I stroked him while he came down. Then he lifted his head and kissed my shoulder, left the bed and went to the bathroom. He came back, turned out the light and settled in on his back, again positioning me beside him.

His hand sifted through my hair and he whispered, "You like that, baby?"

"I like everything with you, Joe," I whispered back and twisted my neck to kiss his chest.

At my words, his hand fisted in my hair then he used it to pull up my head and hold it steady for his mouth to take mine in a deep, heady kiss.

He settled us back to where we were and I stared at his shadowed chest in the dark.

Then I took a chance.

"I know it isn't why you're here but I don't care," I said to Joe in the dark, my arm moving around his waist, closing in, going tight. "I'm glad you're here because I like what we just did and because I like you in my bed and because I feel safe and I feel my girls are safe. I don't want you to go all Joe on me and remind me that isn't what we are. I don't care it isn't. You should know that's how I feel and I haven't felt safe for a year and a half and you cannot know how much that sucks. So," I twisted my neck and kissed his chest again then murmured into his skin, "thanks for makin' us safe."

I settled back, cheek to his shoulder and gave him a squeeze.

His body had gone still while I talked, still and tense. I felt it but I ignored it and decided to go for the gusto.

"And, by the way, I liked having you at my table and the girls did too. I know that isn't what we are but you're welcome there anytime you get hungry and I'm cookin'."

"Vi—"

"Shut up, Joe."

"Buddy—"

"I said, shut up."

Surprisingly, he shut up.

And he didn't do what I worried he'd do, retreat, not in any way. He turned into me, slid his knee between my legs, forcing my thigh to hook on his waist and he gathered me close in his arms as mine went around him.

He didn't say anything, not a word. He was silent.

I fell asleep before him. I knew I did because his weight didn't settle but his arms kept me locked tight.

But I fell asleep hoping that maybe I just gave him a little something that would make him feel less empty.

And I was hoping hard.

# Twelve

## The End

Cal left Nadia and went to his truck.

He didn't fuck her. She wanted it but he wasn't in the mood and he had to get home.

It was going to end with Vi tonight.

He knew it because when Nadia got dropped at his place, Vi, Kate and Keira were saying good-bye to Sam and Melissa in their front drive.

The timing couldn't have been better. Tina was also getting in her car and Colt, Feb and Jack were just getting back from somewhere. They all saw Cal greet Nadia in his drive with a kiss, they saw him put her in his truck and they saw him drive away.

He'd looked through them. Tina looked smug; he could see it two yards away, the fucking bitch. Colt looked pissed, Feb worried. Sam and Melissa looked confused.

But it was Vi, Kate and Keira that hit him, straight in the left chest, a twist and squeeze so brutal it was a wonder he didn't drop to his knees.

Kate looked shocked but in that way someone looks when they just got hit with a surprise attack, not expecting it and then, all of a sudden, they get socked in the gut, the wind knocked clean out of them.

Keira looked betrayed. It was plain on her face, betrayal and pain.

But Vi looked like he'd inflicted a mortal wound, face pale like he'd shoved a knife in her and twisted it, letting her blood leak out.

He just got in his truck and drove Nadia to her place.

⁓

The last week with Vi and the girls had been good.

He'd stayed home. After the gift had come, he'd had Lindy rearrange his appointments, telling his clients he had an emergency.

The gift had been an enormous, expensive vase. No card, no prints that came up in the system, just some random message from a dickhead who liked fucking with people's minds.

Cal checked Vi's front steps before joining her in bed at night and he checked them after he got up and went home in the morning. Nothing more.

But Vi had changed. After that night she found him on his deck drinking beer, she'd changed. She wasn't unconsciously getting under his skin just by being Vi. Now, she was digging her way in.

And he was letting her.

He knew she went to dinner with Mike because she let him know.

But when he hit her bed, every single night for a week, she was all about him, all about finding that opening, tearing it wider, forcing more of herself in.

Fucking her had always been great, but it got better. She didn't lie when he'd made her make herself come and she watched while he did the same, she liked everything they did together. He thought he had her, she was all his when they were fucking, but she proved differently. When he was in her bed, she opened something up in herself and there was so much of it flooding out, if he wasn't careful, he'd get washed away.

And she talked to him in whispers either before he fucked her or after or in between. She talked about work, about the side job she got doing up someone's yard, about maybe starting her own business next summer if that worked out. She talked about Keira's new dog who was creating havoc in the house. She talked about the girls, their friends, the crazy shit they did and said, laughing softly against the skin of his shoulder, by his ear, her face pressed into his neck.

He laughed with her because the crazy shit they did and said was funny. And he liked the idea of her setting up her own business designing people's gardens. By the look of hers, she'd be good at it. He liked hearing the hint of excitement in her voice, as if that was something she never thought of but something she really wanted to do, a dream that snuck up on her. He liked listening to her share pieces of nothing, scraps of life that somehow measured up to a full meal.

And he also liked that both Keira and Kate had taken to popping by his house when their mom was at work, just to say hi or ask him to dinner or tell him they were going to a movie and seeing if he wanted to come (he never went, but then again, they didn't figure he would—they were just using it as an excuse to talk to him).

He liked it because, when they did he knew they were okay, just being kids having a good time over the summer and not touched by Daniel Hart's madness. He liked it because, each time, they grew more comfortable with him, less hesitant, more sure of themselves, and they stayed longer and longer. They were opening themselves to him too, giving just by talking, letting him know they liked having him around.

He didn't eat at Vi's table, not after the pancakes, so no more family time that felt too good but was pretend. He was a stand in, not who they wanted to see in that chair, so it sure as fuck was not something he needed.

Except when he went over to have dinner when Sam and Melissa were there last night.

That's when he knew he had to do something.

Because the girls acted like he was over all the time (which he was, they just didn't know that). They acted like he wasn't a stand in. They acted like he was a welcome staple in their lives and they'd welcome it if he became more of a staple. Keira teased him. Kate even grabbed his hand and clutched it when she laughed at something he said. Like their mother, they were sucking him in, using him to plug that hole their father left and their combined power was almost unbeatable.

But it was also because he liked Sam and Melissa. Sam acted toward Vi like Cal remembered Uncle Vinnie acting toward his mom. He didn't hide his affection for Vi and her kids. He loved him. The world shone in his eyes when he looked at them and he let them know it.

He was fucking hilarious too and an easy man to like. His woman was the same, funny and easy-going, a straight-talker and she felt like her man did about his family. It wasn't like she'd been in their lives since she met Sam. It was like she'd been in their lives the length of it. They were a unit, bonded tight and unbreakable. A family that was blood but their bond ran deeper than blood.

What Cal had always wanted.

And Vi behaved just like her girls. She wasn't demonstrative with Cal but she found her times to give him looks, touch him, promise things with her eyes that needed no words.

They'd gone to J&J's after dinner and Sam and Melissa proved they were what they were, funny and able to have a seriously fucking good time. Vi let herself loose with them, laughing more than he'd ever seen her laugh, her face relaxed, happy, and even more beautiful than normal because of it.

If he let himself go, he would have enjoyed it. Instead, he had his word with Sam and got the fuck out of there.

His word with Sam didn't go as easy as his words with Tina and Dane did. Sam wasn't going to stop and told Cal this flat out then he took the time to explain. Cal understood his reasoning, even admired it, but he gave it back to Sam straight that he was playing with fire and, he got burned, so would Melissa and Vi.

"This is your business because…?" Sam asked.

"Because Vi asked me to have a word," Cal replied.

"And because you're fuckin' my sister," Sam returned.

Cal stared at him and didn't respond. He wasn't surprised Sam had figured this out. Vi might have found her times but that didn't mean no one was paying attention.

"She talks about you, so do the girls. They like you. I'm cool with that," Sam told him. "She needs good shit in her life and the minute I saw you, brother, you struck me as good people. I'm happy for her. But you installed a security system that rivals the Pentagon's to help keep her safe, so I'm guessin' you know where I'm comin' from."

He did. He just didn't agree with it.

"I'm tellin' you, you need to stand down," Cal repeated.

"And I'll tell Vi-oh-my you did what you could. But I'm not standin' down."

Cal again didn't respond.

Sam held his stare for a while and finally asked, "We good?"

They weren't anything, or they wouldn't be.

"Yeah," Cal replied.

"Fantastic. When we come back and Vi makes her risotto again, I'd hate to see you sittin' there glarin' at me while I'm eatin' it. Shit's fuckin' ambrosia and, brother, you're kinda scary. Would ruin the risotto."

Nothing would ruin Vi's risotto. That shit was the best thing he'd ever tasted in his whole fucking life.

Cal wanted to laugh. He didn't because he knew, Sam came back, he wouldn't be sitting at Vi's table eating anything.

He finished their pool game, said his good-byes to a surprised Melissa and a shocked Vi and he got out of there.

He went home, called Nadia and set it up for the next day.

It needed to be done.

It didn't matter Cal didn't open the door. The three of them were charging through. Vi, Kate and Keira, female battering rams who were relentless.

And he needed to close it down, cut her loose, cut all of them loose so he could close himself off and open the way for them to move on to a good life.

But Vi had to end it. It had to be her decision this time so there was no going back.

So he was forcing her hand.

He was sitting in the dark, in his living room, in his father's chair with a bottle of bourbon, a glass half full in his hand when he heard the sliding glass door open.

He'd been home an hour. It took longer than he expected for her to come over.

She slid the door closed and stood at it, her back against the glass, a shadow silhouetted by the moonlight. He didn't know how she knew he was sitting there. He'd never been sitting in his living room when she came over. Then again he usually met her at the door. But she knew.

"Did you fuck her?" she whispered.

"None of your business, buddy," Cal forced himself to say.

"You don't use protection with me, Cal, so yeah it is. Did you fuck her?"

He didn't hear any words after she called him Cal. His body had frozen, his mind had blanked.

"I asked you a question," she prompted, still whispering.

"You want this scene then yeah, I fucked her, Vi," he lied.

She was silent.

He knew she'd hate it when he reminded her softly, "You don't get to do this, buddy. This isn't what we have."

"I know about Nicky."

It took everything he had not to surge to his feet.

"Come again?" he asked only after he unclenched his teeth.

"I know about your son, Nicky. Your dad. I know about Bonnie. I know everything."

Cal swallowed the acid taste burning his tongue then he said, "Everyone knows. It isn't a secret, Vi."

"You're empty."

He stared at her silhouette. How she knew that, he had no fucking clue, but she wasn't wrong.

"Yeah," he agreed.

"Nothing can fill you up," she stated.

"Nope," he agreed again.

"You won't let it."

"Barrel's got a hole in the bottom, buddy, everything leaks out no matter how much you pour in."

She was silent a moment then she whispered, "Right."

She turned to the door and his hand gripped his bourbon so hard he had to focus everything on loosening his grip or the glass would shatter.

Before she opened it, she turned back. "You don't know, Cal, you have no idea. You've shut yourself up for so long in this fucking house with your tragic memories, you have no idea what's about to walk out your door. Kate, Keira and me, we could have plugged that hole. We could have filled you so full, you'd be bursting. We would have loved that chance. We'd have given it everything we had, no matter the time that slid by, graduations, weddings, grandbabies. You'd have been a part of us and we'd have given everything we had to keep you so full, you'd be bursting."

Cal didn't reply.

"Joe," she whispered. "You let me walk out this door, you'll lose your chance."

Cal didn't move.

Vi waited.

Cal stayed seated.

Vi slid open the door, walked through and slid it to. He didn't hear her calmly walking across his deck to the steps. He heard her running.

When he heard that, the glass shattered in his hand.

# *Thirteen*

## The Beginning

It was bad timing. Then again, it was never good timing for shit like that.

Never.

*Ever.*

But this was different. This was the worst.

Because Cal was home.

He had been home once in the last two and a half months. Once, for a night, gone the next day. I hated myself, but I'd looked. I always looked to his drive, even through the windows, a million times a day at first. I was getting better, bucking the habit. Now I only looked when I drove home, or drove away, or got in or out of the car.

Progress.

Though I wore his t-shirts to bed every night, I knew I shouldn't. I kicked myself every time I pulled one over my head. I just couldn't stop.

The gifts had been coming, Colt and Mike had been dealing with them. Cal wasn't around to care. Not that he would have cared if he was around, but he wasn't around.

It wasn't regular or steady but the girls knew about the gifts now. Keira had found the next one to come which was two days after the end of Cal and me. A Tuesday, another first. I didn't know what was in them and Mike and Colt didn't share. They told me they were keeping in close contact with

Tim's partner Barry in Chicago and they also told me they'd ordered cruisers to cruise our street randomly, which they did. It wasn't the same safety I felt when Cal was in my house, in my bed or even next door, but it made me feel a little better.

I didn't care much either. Let him send gifts. Whatever. I had a life to lead. That was hard enough. Fuck Daniel Hart.

The girls had taken Cal's exit from our lives as I knew they would and I kicked myself—hourly at first then daily—for wrapping them up in that shit.

Just so I could have good sex, just so I could get off. A booty call. I'd hurt my girls for a booty call. Cal said it wasn't that, but it was. It was exactly that.

They didn't know the extent of it and I tried to act normal and hide from them how it cut me to the quick, not as bad as I suspected, no, even worse, far worse, him being gone. But they were my girls. They felt deep. They sensed things. They knew me and I knew they knew something big had happened and it involved Cal.

At their accurate assessment of the situation, they rallied around their mother.

Keira had done an about face. Cal didn't come up hardly at all. In fact, in the house he ceased to exist. Even Dane had obviously been handed the edict that he didn't talk about Cal. But when Tina mentioned Cal at that barbeque, Keira called him Mr. Callahan like he was a shadow in our lives, nothing more.

Kate refused to talk about him, switching the subject when he came up at the barbeque and it seemed almost that she hurt even more than her sister. Keira had always been Cal's champion but they'd formed a bond somehow, Kate and Cal. Maybe over music preferences and pancakes, I didn't know. What I did know was that Kate was cut to the quick, just like her mom.

And Cal came up only when Tina brought him up at the neighborhood barbeque Jeremy and Melinda had a month ago and she'd brought him up three times in front of me and my girls, the stupid bitch.

Not taking Cheryl's advice, I didn't reel Mike in. I kept him on the line, but I'd put my hand way too close to the fire and got burned. I was trigger-shy.

With patience, he stayed as close as I would let him. We dated. He even came over for dinner with the girls who were both very nice to him. I made him my pork chops and he'd said he'd loved them and ate them like this was true, something Keira approved of greatly and let this fact be known to Mike effusively. We made out and it was as good as ever. I'd even spent the night at his place when both of the girls were at a sleepover and his kids were with Audrey. We'd watched a movie in his room, fooled around in his bed, but we hadn't had sex. It was just that it had gotten late so he'd invited me to stay. I'd slept in his big bed, in one of his t-shirts and in his strong arms and I liked it. It felt healthy. It felt safe. It felt sweet.

But it didn't make me vibrate. It didn't electrify me. It didn't make me feel alive.

I didn't need that shit. Healthy and safe I needed, sweet was a bonus. I didn't need to vibrate and feel alive because, when it was gone, it led to feeling dead and that was no fun at all.

Mike didn't push it. I suspected that he'd sensed things had changed with Cal. And he knew I needed it slow. He knew this because I told him. So we took it slow.

He didn't introduce me to his kids. He wasn't certain which way I'd lean and he knew they didn't need that shit in their lives. If I leaned the wrong way, they shouldn't be caught up in that. He was a good dad. A better dad than I was a mom, I knew that for certain.

So it was bad timing that Cal was home when I was dusting in the living room and I saw the Jag turn into my drive. I knew who was in that Jag and I knew why they were turning in my drive. There was only one reason they'd come all the way down here to turn in my drive and I knew that reason.

Just seeing the Jag I knew it.

I knew it, knew it, *knew it.*

And it burned a hole in me.

I walked to the door, Keira's new puppy, Mooch, following on my heels, yapping his puppy yaps. I disarmed the alarm and opened the door, dustrag still in my hand and Mooch ran out into the yard, but I didn't really notice.

The situation was worse. I saw the minute I walked out.

Feb was kissing Colt good-bye by his GMC, Jack in the crook of her arm.

Myrtle was trimming her rose bushes.

Tina was sunbathing in her front fucking yard when there was no need to do this, considering she had sun loungers on her back deck, and I knew why.

She was in a bikini in her front yard because Cal was washing his truck in his drive.

All of them were looking at the shiny, burgundy Jaguar in my drive. I knew this because I swung my head around to take them all in.

Then I looked at my dad who was walking across the yard toward me, his face sharing the news before he said a word. My mom, slower, unfolded out of the car, her eyes on my house, her face not communicating hideous loss like my dad's, but registering dislike.

"Sweetie…" Dad said when he got close and it burst out of me.

It was loud, shrill, high, so much of all of those, it was a wonder all the windows didn't explode in every house in the block.

"*No!*"

Then I turned, ran through my door and slammed it, locked it and stood with my back to it, looking around my living room.

I dropped the dustrag and, mindless, I ran to the shelves, picked up the photo of Tim, the girls, Sam, Mel and I that Tim and Sam took for-*fucking*-ever to set up on that stupid *fucking* tripod, and then another *fucking* age to program the stupid *fucking* timer to take a picture of us all that Christmas day. Mel and the girls and I had laughed at them, laughed and laughed at their antics. How long it took. Teasing Tim and Sam. Giving them stick.

Good times.

The best.

I threw the frame across the room and the frame cracked, the glass shattered.

I grabbed the next one, me in my hospital bed, a newborn Keira in my arms, Tim on one side, his arm around me. He was holding a squirming Kate. Sam on my other side, his arm around me too. Both of them had one leg on the floor, one leg on the bed. All of us scrunched up in that damn hospital bed. I looked tired but we were all smiling (except Kate, who was squirming). Sam had sat with Kate and Tim's parents in the waiting room the whole time Tim was in with me and Keira in delivery. The whole time, he never left. Not for a second. He didn't tell me that. Tim's parents didn't. I just knew.

I threw that too and the glass shattered.

"Violet!" I heard my father shout, pounding at the door. "Honey, let me in."

I grabbed the next frame, Sam wasn't in that one at all, and still, I threw it.

More pounding at the door, more of my dad's shouts, pleading to let him in.

Then I threw anything I could get my hands on, stupid knickknacks, more frames. I didn't even see what they were. I just grabbed them and threw them, trying to force out the feeling that had my heart and gut and mind in its grip, so tight…God, it was going to kill me.

Suddenly, the door popped open and Cal was in my house. He'd forced the door open with his shoulder.

I stared at him in his black t-shirt, his motorcycle boots, his jeans. But he didn't stare at me. He came at me.

I ran.

I ran over some glass, feeling it cut open my bare foot but I didn't cry out. There was no pain. I felt it, but it wasn't pain. The pain was in my heart, my gut, my head. There was no room for any other kind of pain.

Before I could take another step, I was swung up, finding myself in Cal's arms and instantly I fought him. Out of control kicking, punching, bucking, if I could get my mouth on him, I would have bit him.

"Vi, baby, calm down," he muttered, struggling to hold me and control my flailing limbs.

I didn't speak, just grunted through my thrashing.

He sat in a recliner in the study, easily subduing my struggles with a big hand wrapped around both my wrists. He locked a strong arm around my waist and he yanked me to his chest, my hands held fast between us.

I snapped my head back and glared into his sky blue eyes.

"Fuck off, Cal!" I shouted in his face and watched him flinch.

I kicked out with my feet but I felt my ankles get caught in a firm grip and I looked that way.

Colt had hold of my ankles. He was in a squat, looking at my foot then he looked at Cal.

"She's bleedin'."

"The glass," Cal muttered.

Colt looked to his right. "Baby?" he called, not letting go of my ankles.

"Gotcha." I heard Feb say but I didn't look her way.

"Violet, honey," my dad's voice drifted to me.

I kept my eyes glued to Colt, not looking at Cal.

"Get him out of here," I ordered Colt. "Get them both *fucking out of here*!"

Colt's expression registered surprise, he looked to his right again, then to Cal.

"That your dad?" Cal asked me but I didn't look at him so his hand tightened on my wrists. "Look at me, buddy."

I looked at him and demanded, "Let me go."

"That your dad?" he repeated.

"Yes," I spit out.

"What's the deal here?" Cal asked.

"Sam's dead," I announced, and I watched Cal close his eyes. I watched it and it was slow. So slow, it felt like it took a year for his eyes to close.

"They found him yesterday," my dad said softly. Cal's eyes opened and he looked over my shoulder but I didn't see any more. My dad confirming with words what I knew in my soul went straight through me, so devastating, its wake was immeasurable. It made my eyes close and my body went slack on Cal's.

"We told Melissa we'd tell you. We drove down last night, didn't want to do it on the phone. We got here late. Stayed at the hotel by the highway. We thought—"

"She's good, Colt, get him outta the house, get his story," Cal said to Colt, cutting off my dad.

Colt dropped my ankles and I dropped my head. I couldn't hold it up anymore and I could feel it coming. I needed my energy because it was going to rip me to shreds.

Cal let go of my hands and both his arms went around me, my forehead hit his shoulder and he pulled me close so my face was in his neck.

Then they came. They were silent but my tears shook my whole body in great, fucking quakes.

"Clean her up, call Dane." I heard Cal order. "He's probably with Kate. If he isn't, he'll know where she is. Tell him to get her, they get Keira, and tell him to get them home."

"Okay," Feb whispered. I felt wetness on my foot and I heard glass being swept up but I had moved my hands to Cal's shoulders, my fingers digging in, holding on, pressing in, my body to his, my face in his neck, as the tears kept shaking me, making it hard for me to breath.

I sucked in breath and even to me the effort sounded painful. Cal's arms tightened and Feb worked on my foot.

I lost time, having no idea how much slid by and not caring as I cried.

Sam was dead, my beautiful brother was gone. Tim had been doing his job but Sam had been doing what he was doing for me.

"He was doing it for me," I whispered into Cal's throat.

"Quiet, buddy," Cal whispered into my hair.

"He was trying to make me safe."

"Stop it, Vi."

"Mel," I breathed, thinking of her for the first time, fresh pain sliced through me. My body jerked with it and Cal's arms gave me a squeeze.

"The girls'll be here soon, baby, you gotta get your shit together," Cal said gently.

My mind was running away with me. "I don't even know this man."

"Focus, baby."

"Why does he want me to suffer so much?"

"Baby, focus."

"Why can't he leave me alone?"

"Shit," Cal muttered and he did it in a way that my head came up to look at him and he was staring across the room at the front door.

"Mom?" I heard Kate call.

I looked where Cal was looking and saw Keira, Kate and Dane standing just inside the door.

Myrtle had my vacuum cleaner out. I didn't even know she was there. I could see through the window that Colt was standing on the front porch, Jack to his hip, his phone to his ear, his head turned, his eyes on the girls.

Before I could move, Cal stood, me in his arms, and he carried me halfway across the study. Carefully, he let my legs go but his arm at my waist held me close to his body. So close, I was suspended, my feet barely touching the floor.

The girls watched this without moving a muscle.

"Girls, come to your mother," he ordered and both looked at him then they moved hesitantly into the room.

I tried to push away but he held me firm and when they got close they only had eyes for me.

I put my hands on both of their necks and I pulled them closer to Cal and me.

Then I bent my head to them, pulling them in further so we were in a little huddle.

"Something's happened to Uncle Sam," I whispered.

I clutched at their necks but they knew, they knew, just like me.

Kate tore free, taking two steps back, her face colorless, her eyes wide with pain.

Keira fell to the floor.

Cal let me go and went after Kate.

I dropped to the floor and gathered Keira to me.

"*No!*" I heard Kate screech. "Nononono*no*!"

I looked to her to see her beating Cal's chest, his arms around her, letting her do it.

Keira just shoved in close, burrowing into me and cried in my arms.

"Oh baby, my baby, my sweet baby," I cooed, gathering her as close as I could and rocking her.

"Hush, girl," Cal murmured. My head came up again and I saw Kate clutching Cal, her arms wrapped around his waist, her hands bunching his t-shirt, her face buried in his chest and he had his arms locked around her too, holding her close.

I watched as it overwhelmed her and her legs buckled. Cal caught her. Bending, he shifted her into his arms and carried her into my room.

I had no idea why, but I got up, pulling Keira with me. She didn't struggle but she was hard to control, her tears still coming, violent, unrestrained. I guided us into my bedroom and Cal was in my bed, his back to the headboard, Kate curled into him full body, her face again shoved into his chest, her arm tight around him, her legs curved and tangled with his.

I moved Keira to the other side and instantly she crawled in, moving straight to Cal, to Kate. She burrowed into his other side and locked her arm around Cal and Kate, her head to Cal's belly.

I slid in behind Keira, holding her close. Having nowhere to put it, I rested my head on his shoulder and did my best to wrap both my girls in my arms.

Cal's one arm was around Kate's waist, his other arm slid around my shoulders. I couldn't help but hope that he was holding Kate as tight as he held me. It felt steady, strong, safe, when life had just knocked us right back down to our knees.

"Should I call Doc?" I heard Feb ask.

"Her foot that bad?" Cal asked back.

"It's deep. I wrapped it up but I can see it's still bleeding," Feb answered.

"Call him."

"Okay."

Feb closed the door but I heard, in the living room, Myrtle turning on my vacuum.

I bent and kissed Keira's head then reached to kiss Kate's.

"We'll see this through, babies, we will. Promise," I whispered.

Keira's body bucked with the next wave of tears that my words caused and Kate's breath hitched so hard, it made me wince.

"Hang on tight, babies, we'll see this through." I kept whispering then my tears came back and I forced my face into Cal's neck and his arm curled me closer.

"We'll see this through," I mumbled and then my breath snagged as I felt Cal's lips on my forehead.

I should have pushed him away, forced him out of my bed, kept my girls to myself. He had no business being there.

But I couldn't. He was warm and strong and solid and big enough to surround us with all of that and we all needed it. We needed something to hold onto.

He could go away later.

And anyway, he would.

Keira fell asleep first, Kate next, Vi last.

All their weight was heavy on him, Keira's head still at his gut, her arm tight around his hip. Kate's head at his chest, her legs still tangled with his, her body dead weight against his side. Vi's face in his neck, her arm around Keira.

Cal's back was still to the headboard, his head tipped back and resting against it, his eyes on the ceiling. He was fucking uncomfortable but he didn't move a muscle.

He heard the door open and he righted his head.

Colt was leaning, shoulder against the doorjamb.

"Doc's here," Colt whispered.

"Tell him to come back," Cal whispered back.

Colt nodded, his eyes did a sweep of Cal under a pile of exhausted, grief-stricken, sleeping females in Vi's bed.

Then he looked at Cal, shook his head, grinned and walked away.

Crazy fuck.

Keira made a noise in her sleep and pushed closer.

Cal closed his eyes, trying to blot out the feeling.

But he couldn't blot it out. It was insistent, not to be ignored.

It hit him the minute he saw Vi standing, shoeless, carrying a dustrag, wearing shorts and a tank, the first time he'd seen her in two and a half months and she was shrieking. Fuck, the sound of her shrieking the word "no." He'd never forget it, not in his life. That word, the way she said it, seared a path straight through him.

And it kept coming when he ran to her house after the crashing sounds came from it, the dad pounding on the door.

And more of it came when he forced his way in and he saw her, that loss claiming her expression, fresh this time. So difficult to witness he felt it settling on his fucking soul.

And more of it came when she pressed into him, giving him her grief.

And more, when Kate beat at him, and more when she collapsed into him under the weight of her sorrow.

And more when they all curled into him, one by one.

And now, that feeling in the left side of his chest wasn't nagging
It was constant, but it wasn't pain.
He felt full.
Christ, the way it felt, he was full to bursting.

# Fourteen

## Vinnie's Pizzeria

"Mom!" Keira yelled, and I sighed.

"I'll be out in a minute," I yelled back and looked in the full-length mirror on the back of my bathroom door.

I was tired, so fucking tired, and I looked it. I hadn't slept deeply since Cal disengaged himself from us so Doc could take a look at my foot, give me a couple of stitches and then proclaim in a heavy way that held more than one meaning, "You'll be just fine."

I'd looked into the old man's eyes and I couldn't help but believe him. I'd never met him but he seemed a man who knew what he was talking about.

This didn't last very long, believing Doc that everything would be fine, but at least it helped for a while.

By the time Doc left, Cal had disappeared. Colt had already called some guy who was fixing the door and Mike had come over and he'd stayed over. He spent the night, sleeping on the couch in deference to the girls. He didn't give me a choice about this, he just did it and I was glad he did. It was good knowing he was there.

He made us scrambled eggs, bacon and toast the next morning. While doing it, and while we were eating it, Mike was demonstrative to me, firmly demonstrative in a way the girls hadn't seen him be before and in a way it felt like he was fed up with the waiting game and staking his claim.

I let him. I was too overwhelmed to fight it and his demonstrations of affection felt so good, I didn't want to fight it. In fact, I needed it. The girls were in a fog of grief anyway. They barely noticed.

I slid through the day in a fog too, talking to Mel, who sounded like I felt, taking a few calls from friends from home, Feb, Cheryl and Dee coming over, spending time. Myrtle popped by with a casserole. Pearl brought homemade brownies with walnuts.

I noticed Cal's truck didn't leave his drive and I noticed this when, surprisingly, a bigger truck backed into it and two men loaded it with Cal's furniture—what appeared to be all of it.

This was a surprise but I didn't care. It wasn't my business. He'd been cool the day before, and as much as it hurt when it ended, *he* didn't hurt me. I'd done it to myself. He'd been honest with me, he'd told me the way it was. It was me who had again taken it further than he ever intended to go. Why he was sitting on his couch the night it ended, drinking something I couldn't see, just could see it wasn't beer, I didn't know. But that made no never mind. He was. It ended. That was it.

I was grateful he'd been around for all of us when we got the news about Sam. I'd thank Cal one day, when I felt stronger and if he wasn't currently moving house in order to get away from the crazy Winters women whose business kept butting into his lonely, fucked-up life.

"Mom!" Keira shouted again, this time with heavy impatience and unmistakable irritation.

"I'm coming!" I shouted back, giving one last look at my outfit in the mirror.

I'd never spent more money on an outfit in my life and didn't suspect I'd ever be in a position to do it again. A dark gray, light wool dress and a little matching jacket. The dress was tight everywhere, scooped neck, short sleeves, a thin, fabric-covered belt at the empire waist. The little jacket that went with it was tailored beautifully and fit like it was made for me with a double row of classy ruffles at the bottom back.

I'd bought it for Tim's funeral knowing I'd never wear it again, not ever, and still spending a fortune on it. I was on such a mission to find the perfect outfit I went to so many stores all over Chicago that I'd lost count. I was obsessed with it, almost frantic. I wanted to give Tim that, to go to his service, his funeral and the gathering afterward being what I was to him—his pretty, sexy wife who made an effort.

It was good I did. Someone got a photo of me in my outfit and it was in the paper. The public got off on grief like that, the fallen cop doing his job for the citizenry, losing his life protecting the people, and the grieving wife he left behind.

Now, fuck me, I was wearing it again.

For Sam.

My beautiful Sam.

I closed my mind from that, limped from the bathroom into the bedroom and grabbed my purse from the bed, not looking forward to driving four hours there and four hours back. I was so damned tired, not sleeping, my mind filled with garbage. And my foot hurt. I couldn't imagine it being pressed on the accelerator for eight hours. I'd have asked Kate to drive, at least part of it, but she looked more worn out than me.

So it was me who had to drive.

Mike asked if he could take us, but I'd said no. He'd never met Sam and he'd have to take a day's vacation from work. Those days should be for fun, not funerals.

He was not happy about this, not even a little bit, and he let me know that fact. This was not easygoing Mike behavior. He was definitely staking his claim and I wondered if he'd heard about Cal. If I had it in me, which I didn't at the time, I would have told him he had nothing to worry about, not anymore, not ever again.

In the end, I'd gentled my refusal and told him to take a day off when he and I could have fun. He didn't like this either, but he didn't fight me on it likely because he was a good guy and he didn't want to have our first fight the day after I found out my only, and beloved, sibling had been murdered just like my husband, *exactly* like Tim (Colt had told Mike this, Dad having told Colt, and Mike told me).

I snatched up my pumps from the bed and headed to the door. I was wearing flip-flops until I had to force on the pumps. I was not looking forward to that, but then again, there was pretty much nothing I was looking forward to that day.

I walked out of my room and Keira was standing just outside my door.

"Mom!" she snapped, even though I was standing right there.

"What, baby? I'm right here," I replied.

Then I felt him. I looked to my right and my mouth dropped open.

Cal was standing there wearing a black suit and a dark gray shirt that matched my dress almost perfectly. A shiny tie the same color as his shirt was dangling loose around his neck, his shirt was open at the throat.

I'd never seen him in anything but t-shirts and jeans, except when he was naked, of course. He looked really good in a suit and his suit was amazing. He might not spend a lot of money on his usual wardrobe, but even I could see that suit cost some cake.

"We have to get going," his deep voice rumbled at me.

"What?" I asked, confused by his suit, his presence and his words.

"Joe's taking us. I called and asked him yesterday," Kate, who was standing close to Cal, explained to me.

In silent shock, my eyes went to her and when they did she slid closer to Cal. Then I felt my eyes grow wide as her hand reached for his and curled around it.

Cal didn't pull away. In fact, his fingers curled around hers too.

When they did, she leaned her shoulder into his arm.

Holy fuck, what the freaking *hell* was this?

"I—" I started.

Cal cut me off. "We gotta get on the road."

"But—"

"Let's go, buddy."

"Oh!" Kate cried suddenly, her head tipping back to look at Cal. "I need to make you a sandwich. We all have sandwiches because we're not gonna stop. I didn't know what to make you. Do you want ham and cheddar, turkey and Swiss, roast beef and Swiss, or all of the above?"

"I'll eat whatever you make, girl," Cal said, looking down at her.

"Okay," she replied, let go of his hand and ran gracefully on her high-heeled, black slingbacks to the kitchen.

"Mom!" Keira hissed, leaning toward me, eyes narrowed, clearly not pleased at this remarkable turn of events. Obviously Kate hadn't shared her plan with her sister.

"Um..." I said to Cal. "Can we talk a second in my room?"

"Nope," he replied and remained unmoving.

"Keira, get Joe a coffee for the road. He takes it black," Kate called from the kitchen.

Keira glared at me then glared at Cal and, obviously feeling the need for an unusual show of decorum in the face of the day's events, she decided against throwing a tantrum. But still, she stomped to the kitchen.

I limped to Cal and got close.

"What are you doing?" I whispered.

"Takin' you and the girls to Sam's funeral."

"But—"

His hand came to the side of my neck and squeezed so further words froze in my throat.

His head dipped down so his face was in mine. "You're dead on your feet, baby. You gotta get there safe, you gotta get home safe. I'm seein' to that," he said softly. "Now, get your ass in the car."

"Cal—"

His hand tightened on my neck. It felt reflexive but it was strong enough to make a point, so I again shut up.

His face got even closer when he ordered, "You call me Joe."

I stared up at him and I knew my mouth was hanging open but I'd lost the knowledge as to how to close it.

He let me go and turned away.

I stood there and didn't know what to do.

I looked into the kitchen and Kate was bustling around, wrapping up a sandwich so huge Dagwood Bumstead would be in throes of ecstasy, then grabbing an extra bag of chips, going to the fridge to get another pop and finally pulling out two more candy bars. Obviously my daughter thought Cal being a mountain of a man he'd have a mountain of an appetite. Then again, when he was over for breakfast, he ate six rashers of bacon with his four pancakes so she probably wasn't wrong. She shoved it all in the cooler as Keira jerked a travel mug at Cal, her other hand wrapped around mine.

"We ready?" Cal asked the Winters girls.

"I am," Kate announced, hefting up the cooler.

Cal carried his travel mug to Kate, took the cooler from her and walked out the side door.

Kate followed.

Keira glared at me then she followed.

I stood there a few seconds before I went to the door, armed the alarm, closed it, locked it and limped to the Mustang.

The girls were already in the cramped back, the cooler between them. Cal was bent double, adjusting the driver's seat. My door was open.

I limped to the car, got in and slammed my door.

Cal folded himself in beside me and slammed his.

Keira shoved my travel mug between the seats and snapped, "Here."

I took it, muttering, "Thanks, baby. You take Mooch over to Pearl's?"

"Yeah," she replied and sat back on a verbal huff.

Cal hit the ignition and the car roared to life.

His arm went around my seat as he backed out and I kept my eyes glued to the windshield as he did this.

He twisted the car into the road, took his arm from my seat, changed gears and we were on our way.

Well, one thing I could say about this, the *only* thing, was at least I didn't have to drive.

Violet fell asleep the minute they hit I-65 outside Lebanon.

The girls had their sandwiches just outside Merrilville, Kate unwrapping his in a way he could eat the massive creation without half of it falling in his lap. She handed him his Coke, she opened a bag of chips for him and she half unwrapped a candy bar to finish his enormous lunch (he'd had to refuse candy bar number two).

Keira, when he caught her eyes in the rearview mirror, glared at him, or when he didn't catch them, he saw she was staring out the window, her expression set to sad.

Both girls were quiet, maybe because they were deep in their thoughts but probably because their mother was sleeping.

As they hit the affluent area of Chicago where the service was being held, Kate gave Cal quiet directions.

He turned in, the lot already mostly full, mourners looking their way as they pulled in, eyes staying glued to the Mustang as he found a space.

Cal got out, pulled forward his seat and looked in the back.

"Both of you, out this side," he ordered quietly.

Kate scrambled out. Keira threw some attitude with her eyes then scrambled out after her sister.

Cal put the seat back and got in the car. Then he leaned into Vi and put a hand to her knee.

"Honey, wake up."

He squeezed her knee as her eyes fluttered then she came to with a start.

She straightened in her seat and looked around.

"We're already here?" she asked softly.

"Yeah, baby."

Her head slowly turned to him and she blinked. Then her chin tipped and she looked at his hand at her knee.

Cal gave it another squeeze but didn't move it.

"You want a sandwich before we go in or do you just wanna go in?"

Her confused eyes came back to him and she said, "I have to put on my shoes."

He looked at her feet in flip-flops and back to her.

"You have them on."

She shook her head, unbuckled her seatbelt, reached an arm to the floor and came up holding a pair of spike-heeled, sexy black pumps.

Cal's eyes went from the shoes to her face. "Buddy, you're not fuckin' wearin' those shoes."

"Yes I am."

"No, you're not."

"But, I am."

"You aren't."

She leaned toward him and whispered, "I can't wear flip-flops to Sam's funeral."

"You got stitches in your foot," Cal pointed out.

"So?"

"Vi."

"Cal."

He felt his mouth go tight as he squeezed her knee again.

They needed to have words, he knew that, not now, later, when she was herself again. When this shit didn't weigh heavy on her mind. When he could tell her the state of play had changed pretty fucking significantly. It had changed in a way that Haines's fucking SUV wouldn't stay parked in her drive all night. It had changed in a way that her ass would never be in that SUV again. It had changed in a way that she'd stop fucking calling him Cal and use his goddamned name like she used to.

But they'd have words later.

Now he needed to get her to her brother's service.

"Put 'em on," he gave in, taking his hand from her knee. "Let's go."

"I'll be out in a second," she replied.

"What?" Cal asked as he buttoned the collar of his shirt.

"I'll be out in a second."

"Vi, just get a move on."

"Cal, I said, I'll be out in a second."

Cal sighed and knifed out of the car. Then he threw the door to.

He made short work of knotting his tie, something he hated, preferring to have his fingernails torn out at the roots. Not that that had ever happened but he was sure he'd prefer it. The minute he was done, Kate moved into him and shoved a shoulder under his arm so he had no choice but to slide it around her shoulders.

Another thing that Kate did that she got from Violet.

Keira took a step back and looked away.

His brilliant idea with Nadia clearly didn't go down so well with Keira, exactly as he'd intended.

Jesus, he wasn't a dick, he was an asshole and he had some serious fucking work to do.

"She okay?" Kate whispered, peering into the window to look at her mom.

"No," Cal told her the truth.

Kate's arm around his waist flexed and he gave her shoulders a squeeze.

Then he saw through the window why Vi wanted him out.

She was sliding up a pair of black, lace-topped, thigh high stockings.

He tore his eyes away.

He'd had two and a half months without her, without any woman, and it felt like two hundred fucking years.

Minutes later, her door slammed and she limped around the car, going to Keira and putting her arm around her.

Cal studied her as she did this. Only Vi could go to a funeral looking like a classy sex kitten. The jacket was sweet, the tight dress sweeter and those fucking heels were unbelievably hot, even though it pissed him off she was wearing them.

Before he got his head sorted, Kate hustled Cal toward her mother and sister and she slid her arm around her mom's waist. This meant, while they walked up to the front doors with a number of people watching to the point they were staring, they did it in a row, arms around each other.

Score one for Cal and Kate.

In order to get through the door, Kate had to let her mother go, which she did.

Vi mumbled greetings as she went through the people, her arm was touched, she shook hands, had her cheek kissed. The girls were touched, gentle eyes falling on them as they moved through. Kate didn't let go of him as Vi let go of Keira when she entered the building. People were forced to move out of their way so they could both fit through the door together.

Once they made it inside, Cal was not surprised to see the place was packed and nearly every face was stricken. Sam was a well-liked man, he had a lot of friends and this was a shock to all of them.

Those friends closed in on Vi and the girls, sweeping him up with it as Kate held fast. There were tears, hugs, kisses, and a number of curious glances in his direction.

"Oh, Joe!" He heard a familiar voice cry and he and Kate turned to see Melissa, Sam's woman, moving quickly toward them.

When he met her he thought she was pretty, light brown hair she'd had streaked, blue eyes, good body, not tall, not short.

Now she was a mess.

Her hand fell on his arm and she squeezed. "I'm so glad you drove Vi and the kids up here. I was worried when she said she'd drive herself."

Without waiting for a response, she turned to Kate, pulled Kate into her arms and burst into tears.

Vi glanced at him as he stepped away so Keira could force herself into Melissa's embrace and finally Vi entered it.

Cal looked at the group who were now all crying then he looked over heads and scanned the room.

He found them standing up front by the closed casket.

Vi's parents.

The father, looking frail and ravaged and a million years old, the mother, looking cold and staring at Vi, Melissa and the girls as if she was watching something disgusting.

Cal leaned in, his mouth at Vi's ear, and he whispered, "I'll be back."

Her head came up and she nodded then she tucked her face into the huddle again.

Feeling the eyes following him, Cal walked straight to Violet's parents. They were standing next to an uncomfortable looking black man and woman, both about Cal's age.

He made it to her parents and glanced at the man.

"I need a word," he told him, noting he, like everyone else, was staring at Cal. But his gaze was sharper, shrewder. Cal smelled cop all over him.

Even though Cal thought he made his point, the man and woman didn't move away.

So be it.

Cal turned to Vi's parents. "I'm Joe Callahan. I'm with Violet."

Violet's father was staring up at him, his mouth open, surprise mingling with the pain etched in his face. They hadn't met, not officially and by the look of him, Cal's being with Violet came as a shock, though, Cal sensed, not an unwelcome one.

Her mother was staring at his scars, her eyes cold, the skin of her face indicating she'd had it lifted. Unlike her husband, it was clear she didn't think much of Cal.

"I'm Pete Riley, this is my wife, Madeline," Vi's father introduced himself and his wife.

Cal nodded and said, "I'm sorry for your loss."

"Thank you," Pete replied, but Madeline again didn't speak.

Trying his best to give it to them gently, Cal stated, "I know this day is difficult for you. It's also difficult for Vi and the girls. Don't make it more difficult for her or the girls by gettin' in their space unless they make it clear they want you there. Yeah?"

The black man and his woman made noises, the man's low, guttural, the woman's high, almost sounding like a strangled giggle, but Cal didn't take his eyes from Vi's parents.

"I…you…I don't believe—" Madeline started, her eyes going from cold to furious in a heartbeat.

Cal cut her off. "You turned your back on her, her man and then those girls seventeen years ago, you should believe."

Madeline's eyes turned to slits and she opened her mouth to speak but Pete got there before her.

"We'll steer clear," Pete announced quickly, still staring up at him.

"Peter!" Madeline hissed, and her husband leveled his eyes on her.

"We'll…steer…*clear*," Pete repeated in a firm, irritated voice.

Madeline's head jerked back in shock and Cal got the feeling the woman didn't often get spoken to like that.

It was too bad. Pete might have saved a lot of heartbreak if he'd brought her into line a long time ago.

"Appreciate it," Cal muttered, said not another word, turned and walked away.

"Callahan." He heard when he was five feet from Vi and the girls, and Cal turned back to see the black man and woman had followed him.

"I know you?" Cal asked the man, his eyes moving to the woman and back.

"Nope, but I know you. Alec Colton's told me about you," the man said.

"You know Colt?" Cal asked.

"Nope again. Talked to him on the phone." He stuck his hand out. "I'm Barry Pryor, Tim's partner."

Fucking great, the dead husband's partner.

Cal took the man's hand and shook it, Barry going for the gusto; Cal giving it back and Barry broke it off, suddenly grinning.

"This is my wife, Pam."

"I think I love you," was her totally bizarre greeting.

Cal didn't respond but took her offered hand and shook it too.

"Tim wanted to say that to them for…freakin'…*ever*," Pam told him then went on. "Well, not that, what he wanted to say would've had a whole lot of f-words, but that did the trick." She leaned into him. "If I didn't think I'd get stoned by all Sam's friends, I'd have laughed myself silly."

"They wouldn't stone you, baby. Sam would retch at this scene," Barry told his wife and then looked at Cal. "You told Sam he was gonna buy it, he'd tell you to cremate him, take his ashes to Rico's or Hoolihan's, pour a Guinness in it and dump it in Lake Michigan. That was, after everyone got blitzed out of their fuckin' brains."

Pam leaned to her husband and whispered, "Barry, don't say fuck in a house of God."

"Pam, this isn't a house of God, it's a fuckin' funeral parlor."

Pam gave Barry an irate look then rolled her eyes at Cal and Cal decided he liked Barry and Pam.

"Uncle Barry! Auntie Pam!" Keira cried loudly, rounded Cal and threw herself at Barry.

Barry's arms went around the girl and he bent his head so his lips were at her hair. "Hey, little donut."

"Auntie Pam," Kate came around his other side and walked into Pam's outstretched arms.

"Hey, shug-shug-sugar," Pam whispered in Kate's ear.

Violet, limping but trying to hide it, moved awkwardly to Cal's side and stopped several feet away, standing, favoring her foot and waiting her turn. She got it after Kate and Keira changed arms then Vi moved in for a big hug from Barry and a longer one with some swinging back and forth from Pam.

When she stepped back, Cal leaned in, caught her with a hand at her hip and pulled her into his side. Her head snapped up to look at him as her body pressed against his hand to get away, but he held her firm and he held her close and looked down at her.

"Take your weight off that foot," he ordered.

"Cal—"

"Weight off that foot."

"Cal—"

"Buddy, take your fuckin' weight off that foot before you tear the stitches."

Violet glared at him and he heard Barry speak.

"What stitches?"

"It's nothing," Vi answered.

"Vi got emotional when she heard about Sam, threw around some shit, glass broke, she cut her foot," Cal answered.

"Cal!" Violet snapped, and Cal looked down at her, brows raised.

"Stitches? Oh Vi, does it hurt? You need to sit down, baby," Pam advised.

"I'm fine," Vi lied.

"Take a load off then. Got a tall drink a' water beside you, girl, use it," Barry put in, nodding his head to Cal.

"Really, like I said, I'm fine," Vi repeated.

"Stubborn." Pam shook her head at Cal.

Cal didn't reply and didn't take his arm from Violet.

"Hey, guys," Melissa joined their group, sliding arms around both Keira and Kate. "They want to start. Let's get his stupid head trip of Madeline's over with so we can go to Hoolihan's."

"Mel, honey, I told you yesterday. We can't go to Hoolihan's with you, the girls can't come in," Violet told her.

"Oh yeah, right," Melissa whispered, looking startled for a second that this hadn't sunk in. Then she kissed the side of Kate's head then Keira's.

"I want you to come down soon, be with us for a weekend or for a while. Get away from here. Get away from—" Vi started, but Melissa interrupted her.

"Soon's I can, Vi-oh-my."

At Melissa using Sam's nickname for his sister, Violet finally gave him her weight. So much of it, her hand came around and she clutched his shirt at his stomach to remain standing. Part of this was good, her doing it. Part of it was bad because she didn't notice she was.

"Good," Vi whispered but her voice sounded choked.

Cal watched Melissa swallow and both Vi's girls pulled in their lips.

"This sucks, doesn't it?" Melissa whispered back to Vi.

"I still can't believe it," Vi whispered to Melissa.

"Wake up and reach for him—" Melissa stopped.

Kate dropped her head but Pam pulled her in her arms as Keira moved around and hugged Melissa front-to-front.

Barry cleared his throat.

"Callahan, let's get our girls to their seats," Barry suggested to Cal.

Cal nodded and they herded the women to the front row, opposite the aisle from where Pete and Madeline were sitting, the whole row to themselves. Sam's friends clearly weren't big fans of Pete and Madeline.

Kate maneuvered the seating arrangement so it was Keira, Melissa, Violet, Cal, Kate, Pam and Barry.

"I still can't believe they planned this ridiculous farce," Melissa hissed when they were seated, her eyes cutting to Madeline then back to Violet. "Shoulda married him, Vi, woulda had my say how the funeral would be."

"We'll get through this then the burial then you can get to Hoolihan's, honey," Vi returned.

"They even get near me, I'll rip their heads off," Melissa threatened, and Pam leaned forward and into Kate.

"No worry with that, Joe here warned them off," Pam informed Melissa.

Violet's body jerked and Keira, Melissa, Violet and Kate's eyes all jerked to Cal.

"What?" Vi asked Cal, but Pam answered.

"Told 'em not to get into your space, 'less you invited them. Sorry, Mel, but I swear, I nearly pee'd my pants laughing. Then when your mom got all," she whirled her hand in the air, "and said, all snooty, 'I can't believe…' Joe said he didn't know how she couldn't believe since she turned her back on you, Tim and the girls. I'm writin' that shit in my diary. Crap day, the worst, but always a little light shines through. That's my light today, seeing Madeline Riley's face when Joe was through with her."

Pam stopped talking but Keira, Melissa, Violet and Kate didn't stop staring at Cal.

"Did you really say that?" Melissa asked.

"Yep," Cal answered.

Tears filled her eyes. She drew in breath through her nose, swallowed and, after this struggle, finally whispered, "Somewhere, Sam and Tim are both smiling."

Kate, Cal noted, was smiling too. Keira, Cal saw, was now staring at her shoes. Vi was still staring at him.

Then she surprised him by saying, "Thank you. I don't know what I'd have done if Mom—"

While she was talking, he lifted an arm and draped it along the back of her chair, dipped his chin, got close to her face and cut her off.

"Shut up, buddy."

"Okay," she whispered.

The girls were there, her friends, her parents, and he didn't give a fuck. He dipped in closer and kissed her lightly on the lips. When he pulled away, those lips had parted and her eyes had grown wide.

Because she looked cute as hell, as well as totally lost, his arm curled from her chair to her shoulders and he pulled her into his body. Then he did the same to Kate on the other side. Kate curled into him and wrapped an arm around his stomach, resting her head on his shoulder.

Something had broken for Kate the day she found out about her uncle, it was clear. She'd lost two men in her life that meant everything to her. She was holding on with all she had to anyone who was left. Even Cal.

Vi looked at her daughter then she looked across Cal to Pam.

"Like him, girl," Pam whispered then winked at Vi. "Keeper."

Vi straightened and looked at the casket.

Cal grinned and felt Barry's eyes on him, so he turned his head.

Barry was looking at Kate then he looked at Cal. He sighed and gave Cal a nod.

Score another one for Cal and Kate, a big score. The dead husband's partner and his wife. Huge.

The minister took the podium and Cal turned to face front.

I stared out the window as Chicago slid by.

Cal had said we were going to dinner before hitting the road and I didn't argue. Sam's memorial (so *not* Sam and so *very* my mother) and his burial (ditto with it not being Sam, who wanted to be cremated but was buried because of my fucking mother) had taken it out of me. They were long, they were wordy and the pastor who spoke at both knew not one thing about Sam (nor did Mom arrange it so anyone else could say a freaking word). And I hadn't had anything but a couple of pieces of toast for breakfast. I was angry, hungry and exhausted and I hoped, after I ate, that I'd sleep all the way home.

I didn't know what Cal was up to and I didn't care, not now. I'd care tomorrow or the next day. But I was hoping his lunacy would be spent by then, he'd be on another trip, off on his job as Security to the Stars and I wouldn't have to bother.

He slid into a parking spot in the street that had two clear signs that read *NO PARKING* then he cut the ignition.

I stared at the signs then looked beyond them and around me, seeing that we were deep in the city. I hadn't been paying attention. Why Cal took us so far into the city, God only knew.

I looked back at the girls who were both leaned to peer out the side window.

Then I looked at Cal.

"Cal, you can't park here," I told him.

He ignored me and ordered, "Change your shoes, buddy."

Here we go again.

"I can't wear this outfit with flip-flops in public," I informed him.

He again ignored me and repeated, "Buddy, change your shoes."

I briefly considered how long it would take to explain to Joe Callahan why I could not wear flip-flops with a seven hundred and fifty dollar suit, knowing that even Tim would not get this concept. Hell, even Mike wouldn't get it and Mike seemed totally clued into these kinds of things considering how materialistic his ex had been. Therefore Cal definitely wouldn't and I decided it would be an impossible task, we'd end it in a verbal tussle and I was tired and hungry.

So I declared, "I'm not fighting about this and I am *not* changing my shoes."

His blue eyes locked with mine and I held his glare.

"Fuck," he muttered, giving in which was more lunacy. Cal didn't give in and now he'd done it *twice*.

"Language in front of the girls," I snapped.

"Baby, they hear it all the time," he returned, and I felt my eyes get wide in motherly affront.

Cal looked at my face then over the seat to the girls and asked, "You gonna say fuck because I say fuck?"

"No," Kate answered immediately.

"No, 'cause Mom doesn't like it," Keira replied waspishly.

Cal looked back at me and raised his brows.

I gave in this time, throwing my door open, getting out and pulling the seat up so Keira and Kate could get out safely on the street side.

Cal slammed his door, rounded the hood and walked to us, waiting as the girls got out. As Kate alighted and closed the door, I looked around Cal and saw a dark haired man in a nice, semi-shiny, dark blue polo-neck shirt and dark gray pants stalking toward Cal.

Getting close, the man shouted, "Yo! Can't park there."

Cal turned. The man skidded to a halt and stared up at him in wonder, as if he was seeing a ghost.

"Shit, fuck me, *Cal*?" the man whispered.

"Hey, Manny," Cal returned.

"Cal!" the man, apparently named Manny and apparently someone Cal knew, was now yelling.

I stared as he leaped forward and threw his arms around Cal, pounding him on the back in a way that sounded painful then he pulled back and looked at him.

"Holy fuck, man, Pop's gonna be frickin' beside himself, Ma too. They're both here. Holy fuck!"

"Manny," Cal said, moving toward me and pulling me to his side with an arm around my shoulders. "Vi gets pissy when you say fuck in front of her girls."

But Manny wasn't listening and I wasn't moving out of Cal's arm mainly because I was worried that Manny was having a heart attack and I'd have to jump in and attempt CPR (something I'd never done). His eyes had bugged out and he appeared to be fighting for breath as he looked at me, Kate and Keira.

Then he whispered, "Fuck me."

"Seriously, Man, the language," Cal warned, his voice going low.

Manny's body jolted then his face split into a huge smile and he jumped forward, arm extended to me. "Yo, hey, I'm Manny."

"Hi," I said back, taking his hand. He gripped mine hard, not shaking it, just holding on tight. "I'm Violet."

He nodded. "Violet, nice." Then he let me go and turned to Kate, hand to her. "Hey, pretty lady."

"Um…hi," Kate replied shyly, taking his hand. "Um…I'm Kate."

"Katy, like it," Manny told her, let her go and turned to Keira. "And you are, sweetheart?"

"Keira." She took his hand too, staring up at him, openly fascinated probably because, I belatedly noticed, he was a very good-looking, well-built Italian-American.

"Keira, pretty name. Excellent." Manny finished his round robin approval of our names then he let Keira go, moved quickly toward the door of the restaurant and announced, "Let's get you in, get your asses in a booth. I'll get Ma and Pop then we'll get you some Chianti and a big pie, yeah?"

Without much choice, we followed him; Cal's hand in the small of Kate's back, guiding her in front of us. I guided Keira with a hand at her waist. Cal's arm was still around my shoulders.

I looked up at the green neon sign over the door that said in slanting script *Vinnie's Pizzeria.*

Seeing it, it startled me as I'd heard of this place. Tim and I had always meant to find it and eat there. Rumor had it that it was a hidden gem, one of the best unknown restaurants in Chicago, especially for pizza or pasta, which, if that was true, was saying something, it being in Chicago. But it wasn't easy to find. We knew it was in Little Italy but Tim had looked and they didn't even have a phone listing. He'd always meant to use his cop resources to find the address but he never got around to it and, in the end, time ran out.

Manny went in first, holding the door and we all piled through. There were benches on either side of the door filled with people, more people standing around, obviously waiting for a table, and there was a bar, totally packed, again with people waiting for a table. They might not have a phone, evidenced by the fact that these people obviously didn't have a reservation, but they were far from unpopular.

Once we were in, Manny shoved by us and pushed through the people to the hostess station.

"Yo, Bella, next booth that's open, Cal and his girls sit there," Manny ordered a young girl who had to be no more than eighteen.

The minute he issued his order her face went straight to attitude and not the good kind.

"Man, you nuts? I got…" Her head tilted down and she (and I) looked at the sheet of paper that had scribbles on it, some at the top with a red mark through them, a whole load at the bottom that was just a very long list. Her head jerked up and she finished, "About a trillion freakin' people waitin'."

"This is family," Manny explained.

"Everyone's family," Bella shot back.

Manny got serious. I knew it by looking at him and listening to him, and if Cal's arm wasn't still heavy on my shoulders, I would have stepped back.

"Woman, shut down the attitude. This is my cousin Cal. Get him and his girls in a fuckin' booth."

His cousin?

Oh shit, this was *Vinnie's* Pizzeria, as in dead cousin Vinnie, murdered, like my brother and husband, by Daniel Hart.

I felt my body grow stiff but Bella's mouth had dropped open. She'd shut down the attitude and she was staring at Cal.

"You're Cal?" she breathed.

"Yep," Cal answered.

"*The* Cal?" she asked.

"Yep," Cal repeated.

"Holy shit," she whispered.

"Language, Bells, Jesus. There's fuckin' kids here," Manny admonished and Kate and Keira giggled.

Actually giggled.

On the day of their uncle's funeral.

If I wasn't freaked out, exhausted, hungry, dealing with Cal's lunacy, an unexpected visit to his family and it wasn't the day of my brother's funeral, I would have kissed Cal.

Cal heard the giggles. I knew this because his arm flexed on my shoulders, a reflexive action, but one that spoke to me.

Then again, I thought a lot of the shit Cal had done spoke to me and I'd been really, really *wrong*.

"What, we holdin' a conference? Why's everyone standin'…?" An annoyed female's voice came at us. Manny stepped out of the way, the voice stopped, and I saw a very round but also very attractive older Italian-American woman standing three feet away, still as a statue, staring at Cal.

Then she started chanting, doing that thing with her fingers to her forehead and shoulders. "Holy Mary, Mother of Jesus. Holy Mary, Mother of Jesus."

She rushed forward, lifted her hands and grabbed Cal on both sides of his head, yanking it down to her face.

Cal's arm fell from my shoulders and he muttered, "Hey, Aunt Theresa."

She pulled him closer and gave him a loud, smacking kiss on one cheek then the other then back to the other, jerking his head around while she did this and while I stared on in rapt shock that anyone would jerk Cal around this way.

She shoved his head away like she was pissed as hell, she lifted a finger in his face and shouted, "You never visit! What? We smell? The bed too lumpy last time you stayed? It's been two years!"

"Aunt Theresa."

She wagged her finger in his face. "No, none of that 'Aunt Theresa' business. Chicago isn't on the moon, Anthony Joseph Callahan, it's four hours away!"

Cal's arm went back around my shoulders, he pulled me to his side and he said, "Shut up so you can meet Vi."

She went statue still again then only her eyeballs came to me.

I didn't think she'd like Cal telling her to shut up, she seemed tightly wound, so I decided not to pull away from him or make any quick movements. She was already looking at me with her eyeballs, I didn't want too much of her attention.

"And these are Vi's girls, Ma, Katy and Keirry," Manny added, shoving Kate and Keira close in front of Cal and me, *way* too close to crazy Aunt Theresa, and Aunt Theresa's eyeballs moved between all of us, fast.

I wrapped my arm around Keira's belly and pulled her to the left side of my front, not a good enough distance from the frozen, but unpredictable Aunt Theresa, but at least she wasn't standing right in front of her anymore. Cal wrapped an arm around Kate's chest and pulled her to his front right.

When Cal did that to Kate, Aunt Theresa started moving again, doing that hand to the forehead and shoulders thing, calling loudly, "Oh, Holy Mary, Mother of God! Sweet Mary, Mother of God!"

"Jesus, Ma, you're freakin' them out," Manny muttered. She stopped calling out to Mary, turned and whacked him one, hand open, up the side of his head.

Good Lord, the woman was every Italian-American stereotype in the book.

"What in *the* fuck's goin' on?" A loud, booming man's voice shouted from behind Aunt Theresa.

She whirled and there stood a man, a good-looking one, older, a bit of a pot belly, definitely related to Manny (thus Cal).

"Vinnie!" Aunt Theresa yelled. "Cal's here, with *Vi* and her daughters *Katy* and *Keirry*."

But Vinnie's face, like his son's, had split into a huge grin. He took us all in, giving us that grin, and he walked by Aunt Theresa toward Cal, his arms wide.

Cal let me and Kate go and suffered another back pounding hug while Vinnie muttered a bunch of stuff in Italian. Vinnie ended the hug with his hands tight on Cal's neck.

"Cal," he whispered.

"Uncle Vinnie," Cal replied.

"Good to see you. Fuck, son, good to see you."

I stared at him seeing he meant this, it came from somewhere deep. In fact, he was nearly overwhelmed with emotion. If he burst into tears, I wouldn't have been surprised. He missed Cal and it was obviously good to see him.

Vinnie let Cal go and his eyes moved through us all. "Who do we have here? Honored guests? Why aren't their asses in a booth?"

"Table five's gettin' bussed, Vinnie," Bella put in.

"Well, help 'em bus it, girl. Family don't stand around at the freakin' hostess station," Vinnie replied.

"Right," Bella muttered then took off as it was clear Vinnie's word was law—as it would be at Vinnie's Pizzeria—and Vinnie turned to me.

"Vi?" he asked, hand out.

"Yes, Vi. Violet," I answered, taking his hand.

"Vi," he said firmly, his squeeze of my hand just as firm, his happy grin still in place.

"These are my daughters, Kate." I reached out and touched Kate's arm. "And Keira." I indicated Keira with my head, she was still in the curve of my other arm.

Vinnie shook Kate's hand then Keira's and looked at Cal.

"All beauties, Cal. You got an eye."

I looked up at Cal to see his response was to tip up his chin.

"We'll get you seated, soon's we can," Vinnie said, his eyes swept through us again, stopping at Cal, giving him a top to toe and then locking eyes with him. "What's with the getups?"

"Funeral," Cal murmured. "Vi's brother, Sam."

Vinnie's face froze, Aunt Theresa sucked in breath, and I felt Manny's eyes on us.

"*Cara,*" Vinnie whispered.

I swallowed, Keira pressed into my body, Kate shoved under Cal's arm so he slid it around her shoulders.

"Vi hasn't had anything to eat since breakfast, Uncle Vinnie. She needs some food," Cal ended the silence but he did it quietly.

Vinnie's body jerked then he clapped. "Right, table five. Food. A big pie. Specialty of the house. I'm makin' it myself."

He turned and we followed him through the heaving restaurant, every table and booth with people at it. The tables were covered with red and white checked tablecloths and the floors were wood, dark with age and use, but still shining. On the tables there were wicker-wrapped wine bottles with candles at the top and wax dripping down. The food on the tables I passed looked fantastic, and seeing it, I realized I wasn't hungry. I was starving.

Then my eyes caught on the walls. They were painted a warm, buttery yellow and covered in pictures, some small, some large, some medium-sized, looking thrown up randomly but I knew it was random like my terracotta pots on my deck were random. They'd been hung with care.

All were black and white. And, on closer inspection, they all had the same group of people in them. Some pictures of just one person, others one or two, others whole crowds. Most were candids, a very few were posed.

But they were all of family. I knew this just by looking at them.

They'd been taken over years. There were babies, toddlers, kids, young adults. A family growing up, its history covering the walls of Vinnie's Pizzeria.

I could see Theresa in them, Vinnie, Manny.

And I could see Cal, from little boy to full grown man.

Vinnie led us to the only empty booth in the place and ordered, "Pile in, we'll get you drinks."

He ordered it and Vinnie was the kind of man you listened to, but the photos had captured me, especially Cal in them, and I didn't move. I was staring at the eight by ten black and white picture that was hanging on the wall over the booth.

They were in the restaurant, standing by the hostess station. Two young boys, maybe thirteen, fourteen, around Keira's age, dark-haired, tall, already showing the promise of the handsomeness that would soon be theirs. They were standing side by side. One, his eyes lighter gray in the black and white photo, was staring straight into the camera, grinning huge but wicked. He had his arm slung around the shoulders of the other boy, who was partly bent forward and turned, his face in profile and the camera had caught him laughing.

Cal, the one grinning straight on and one of Vinnie's kids. Maybe the murdered cousin, Vinnie Junior.

If this was cousin Vinnie, it was true as Cal had said, they were definitely close. I knew this by the smile, the laughter, the casual, close, affectionate way Cal had the young man in his hold.

The thought of Cal as a kid was startling, seeing it even more so. But what was freaking me out was seeing his perfect, boyishly handsome face without the scars, carefree and absolutely happy.

I'd never seen it like that, never. Nothing even came close.

"Is that you, Joe?" Kate asked, and I tore my eyes from the photo to see both my daughters staring at it.

"Yeah, girl," Cal answered.

Kate's head swung around so she could smile up at him. "Wow, you were cute."

"Cute!" Theresa cried. "Every starry-eyed girl in a square mile radius had their eyes on my boys." Theresa looked at me and jerked her head to the picture. "That's my oldest son with Cal, Vinnie Junior."

Yep, like I thought, cousin Vinnie.

"I guessed that," I said softly, and at my tone, she flinched. It wasn't a big flinch but I caught it, I knew what it meant and I wondered if the pain ever went away.

Considering my back-to-back losses of Tim and Sam, it sucked to see Theresa's flinch and know, even after seven years, it didn't.

She held my gaze, hers getting soft as it swung to Cal then to me and I knew she knew Cal had told me about Vinnie. I also knew she read far more into this than was the truth because her face lost that hint of sadness and spread into a glamorous smile.

"Sit down, sit down," Uncle Vinnie urged and the girls scrambled in, both on one side as I slid into the other, Cal coming in beside me.

Vinnie turned and yelled across the restaurant, "Bella! We need breadsticks here and antipasto! On the double! Yeah?"

"Got it, Vinnie!" Bella yelled back.

"I'll get drinks," Theresa muttered and moved away without asking what we wanted.

"We'll get your belly full, Vi. You and your girls just relax," Vinnie promised, his eyes on me. I nodded, he nodded back and then he followed his wife.

I was happy to eat, more than happy, especially if the food tasted half as good as it looked.

But at that moment, I was in ecstasy to be off my foot. It was killing me.

Manny pushed into the booth beside Kate and both Kate and Keira stared at him, goggle-eyed.

"So, how long you stayin'?" Manny asked Cal.

"Leavin' after dinner," Cal answered, and Manny's brows went up.

"Shit, Cal, um…sorry, Vi, girls." He nodded at me then at the girls and looked back to Cal. "Shoot, Cal. Ma's gonna have a shit, I mean shoot hemorrhage you do a flyby for dinner and don't hang."

"Gotta get them home, Man," Cal told him.

"Could spend the night, leave early tomorrow. Let Ma at least make 'em breakfast," Manny urged.

"Not gonna happen," Cal told him.

"She's not gonna like it," Manny replied.

"Vi just lost her brother, Kate and Keira their uncle. She'll get that they want to sleep in their own beds tonight," Cal returned quietly, and when he did, what he said, how he said it, the fact that he knew that, I felt it hit me like it did when his mouth touched mine before the service after I found out he'd warned off Mom and Dad. That feeling in my stomach, going warm, getting soft.

"Well, I ain't tellin' her," Manny mumbled, and Keira giggled. So Manny flashed her a super-white smile, Keira's giggle died in her throat and her eyes grew dazzled.

I stopped watching my daughter's eyes grow dazzled when I felt Cal's fingers bunch my skirt in a fist and pull it up. My back went ramrod straight, my mind went blank and my hand went down to curl around his wrist.

Manny turned back to Cal and noted, "Sweet ride, Cal. The 'Stang. You get rid of the '68?"

"Ride's Vi's. I still got the '68," Cal answered casually as if he wasn't pulling up my skirt under the table and my hand wasn't tight on his wrist to fight him in this insane effort.

"Got good taste, babe," Manny grinned at me.

"Thanks," I replied but my word was tight.

Cal had my skirt up and he leaned a bit into me as his hand curled around the inside of my thigh and he pulled my leg up.

I couldn't do much but clutch his wrist since he was stronger than me. I couldn't exactly shout at him or wrestle him at the table, both of which I wanted to do.

Luckily, Kate drew Manny's attention by asking, "What's a '68?"

"Cal's Mustang, 1968 Mustang GT. The *Bullitt* car. Freakin' awesome," Manny answered, and as he did, Cal lifted my leg and I felt the side of his shoe against my ankle. Then I felt it slide down, taking my shoe with it.

The pump fell to the floor, and when the pressure released on my injured foot, the constant, nagging pain I'd had since putting the damn thing on subsided and my eyes rolled back into my head.

Heaven.

"What's a bullet car?" Keira asked Manny while I experienced heaven.

"Steve McQueen's ace ride in the movie *Bullitt.* The sweetest car ever built," Manny answered.

While this conversation went on, Cal lifted my leg further and hooked it over his knee, yanking it up his thigh so my skirt was hiked high, my calf and foot were dangling between his legs and then he leaned into me.

Whispering, he ordered, "You let Manny go get your other shoes or I carry you out. Your choice, buddy."

I pulled my head back and glared at him, at the same time I tried to jerk my leg away. But his hand was still at my inner thigh and it tightened so I got nowhere.

When I didn't answer, Cal asked, "What's it gonna be?"

I kept the pressure on his hand but he didn't let go.

"Vi?" he prompted.

"Shoes," I hissed.

Cal grinned and muttered, "Good choice." Then he turned his head to Manny, leaning back and reaching into his pocket. "Man, do me a favor. There's a pair of shoes on the floor of Vi's Mustang. Can you bring 'em in?"

Manny looked at Cal then me and said hesitantly, "Sure."

"Mom cut her foot. She's got stitches but she's still wearin' her pumps, which makes her limp more than she normally limps. Joe doesn't like that," Kate explained helpfully.

"Women are weird like that," Keira chimed in, defending my position even though Manny, being male, would never understand, but she was too young to know that. Though, I figured in about five, ten years, she'd learn. "We have to be wearing the right shoes," she finished.

Manny stopped looking confused and he grinned. "Then sure. We wouldn't want *Joe* to get pissed, would we?" Cal tossed him my keys. Manny caught them and slid out of the booth, saying, "Be back."

I again tried to tug my leg away. Cal's response was to slide his fingers into my stocking and push it down, so I froze.

"Would you show me your *Bullitt* car?" Kate asked Cal as he leaned forward and pushed the stocking further down my leg while lifting it to get to my calf and ankle (and I gritted my teeth).

"Take you for a ride, girl," Cal answered and I stopped gritting my teeth because my mouth dropped open.

"Really?" Kate breathed.

"Yeah."

"Can I drive it?" Kate asked.

Cal grinned, which took the sting out of his, "No."

"I like Mom's Mustang," Keira informed Cal.

"I do too," Cal replied, and Keira glared at Cal then at me as if Cal being a lunatic by being sweet and thoughtful and sharing and nice was *my* fault.

Cal leaned back and this was mainly because he had the stocking free of my foot.

He dropped it in my lap, settled my leg on his thigh and I gave him a look that should have at least set his hair on fire (but didn't), snatched the stocking up and tucked it into my purse.

"Drinks!" Aunt Theresa shouted as she made it to the table with a tray of drinks. "For the girls," she announced, setting two Shirley Temples in front of Kate and Keira, two girls that were beyond Shirley Temples. But then again, *I* would drink those Shirley Temples because the bottoms were filled with maraschino cherries, at least half a dozen of them, and they were more red than pink so I knew they were full of syrup. "Beer for Cal," she went on, plonking a bottle of beer in front of Cal. "And Chianti, for *cara mia*," she finished, putting a huge-bowled glass of red wine in front of me then plunking the bottle next to it.

"Thanks um…Theresa," I said.

"*Aunt* Theresa," she corrected on a smile. "Breadsticks are comin' outta the oven. Antipasto platter's up, Bella's gettin' it. Gotta check on my customers but I'll be back." Then she bustled off and we all watched her, even the girls turned in their seats.

Then the girls turned back.

"Your family's cool," Kate told Cal.

"Yeah, girl, they are," Cal told Kate and he meant this. I knew it by the way he said it, deep, weighty.

Kate knew it too because her eyes got soft as she looked at Cal then her soft eyes came to me.

I didn't need to know this about Cal. I didn't need to meet his family, see how he was with them, how they were with him, how nice it was, even beautiful. Furthermore, my daughters didn't need to see it.

But I didn't have any choice. Cal didn't give me one and that pissed me off.

I tried to yank my leg away again but Cal just kept hold as Bella swept through, dropping a basket of long, poofy breadsticks on the table, a little bowl of marinara sauce at the side and a huge antipasto platter full of salami, pancetta, olives, artichokes, mushrooms and slices of cheese.

I decided to ignore Cal and concentrate on breadsticks. I grabbed one and found it was warm. I dipped it into the marinara sauce and took a huge bite. It was coated with buttery garlic, the bread light but doughy, the marinara tangy and spicy, the whole thing utterly delicious.

It took effort but I managed not to roll my eyes in delight.

"These are *great*!" Kate said through a full mouth then shoved her breadstick back in the marinara, double dipping like Cal was Tim or Sam and this was allowed. Then she took another huge bite.

"They are," Keira stated, her mouth full too, but even so, I could tell she didn't want to admit this in front of Cal. But she couldn't help herself, that was just how good they were.

During my last bite, Cal's hand lifted my leg and he leaned into me, hooking it over my other leg so they were crossed. I looked at him to see he was looking at something across the restaurant, a small smile playing at his mouth and my eyes followed his.

That's when I saw a man, tall, not as tall as Cal, but taller than Manny and Vinnie. He was wearing a skintight white t-shirt, jeans and he had a long, white apron wrapped around his waist. The tee miraculously had no tomato sauce stains on it. The apron was covered with smears.

And he was movie star gorgeous. Beautiful body as evidenced by his t-shirt and even the apron at his narrow hips. Thick head of black, unruly hair. Roguish, dark brown eyes rimmed with thick lashes. Glamorous white smile, like his mother's.

He was looking at Cal, and as Cal slid out of the booth, his hand came up and his smile got wider, brilliant, breathtaking.

"Cal, *cugino*," he muttered as his hand took Cal's in a fierce grip even I could see.

Cal's hand gripped his fiercely too and muttered back, "Benny."

They leaned into each other and each gave the other a powerful blow to their backs before pulling away but not dropping their grip of hands.

I tore my eyes away from the two of them, both amazingly attractive in a way you didn't often see, or *ever* see. Maybe one, if you were lucky, but definitely not a double bill like these two. That was a miracle the like it proved there was a God.

Then I saw both Kate and Keira gazing up at them. Manny a memory, Benny, they'd never forget in their entire lives.

Then my eyes moved and I saw most of the women in the restaurant also looking, some openly, some glances, some even had mouths open, all of them in some way awed.

My eyes went back to the men as they detached. Cal came back to me, Benny, like Manny, scooted unceremoniously in beside Kate and Keira.

Kate emitted a sound that was half-strangled scream, half-moan. Keira just stared.

I looked back at the restaurant and saw that most of the women hadn't quit looking and it was a wonder, with the raw sexual magnetism being discharged at our table, how the lot of them didn't fly straight at us, sticking to Benny and Cal like flecks of steel to a powerful magnet.

"Hear you're Vi," I heard Benny say, and my eyes went to him.

"Yeah." I reached my arm across the table when he stretched his to me.

"Benny," he said after he took my hand in a warm grip. Not too firm, it was friendly firm. Then he let my hand go and looked at Kate and Keira.

Kate visibly stilled. Keira swallowed.

"Vi's girls, Ben, Kate and Keira," Cal told him.

"Heard about them too," Benny said, aiming his smile and hand at both in turn. Kate gulped as she took his hand. When Keira did, her eyes rolled back into her head.

I looked at Cal and he was grinning at them.

"Shoulda warned you, Benny's a lady-killer," Cal told the girls and both their eyes fluttered to him.

"I didn't think anyone could be hotter than you, Joe," Keira whispered, forgetting she hated Cal for a second. Forgetting everything in the presence of Benny.

"Ben, you're killin' me," Cal murmured, but there was a timbre of suppressed laughter in his voice. "Lost my position."

"Sucks, but you're used to it," Benny returned on a grin.

Cal shook his head and Benny looked at me.

"Dad's got your pie in the oven," he informed me then his eyes went to Cal. "Freakin' kitchen's crazed. He's got my kids in a tizzy. He's been retired from the kitchen a year and I just got them settled, it took that long. Now he's taken over, fifteen minutes back to drill sergeant and the place is pandemonium. Boys are droppin' shit, burnin' shit, nuts."

"Kick his ass out," Cal advised.

"*You* try to kick Vinnie's ass out when he's got an apron around his waist," Benny replied then looked at Keira and Kate and, for some reason, asked, "Your mom do somethin' good, somethin' better than anyone else you know?"

"Her garden," Keira chimed in instantly.

"Her seafood risotto," Kate told him the second Keira's last word was uttered.

"Her pork chops and spiced rice," Keira put in.

"Her chocolate chunk cupcakes with vanilla bean frosting," Kate added.

"When we were kids, she told the best bedtime stories," Keira went on. "All my friends wanted to stay over at my house because of Mom's bedtime stories. She was famous for them."

Benny's eyes slid to me and I felt Cal's on me too. I also felt my face get hot.

There was silence then Benny murmured, "All that sounds good."

"The best," Keira agreed, and I watched as Benny forced, with visible effort, his eyes back to the girls.

"Makes my point asinine. Was gonna tell you, she tries to teach you that stuff, you should run the other way." He looked back to me. "But, thinkin', that shit, you should let her," Benny told them, his eyes still on me, and I felt my face get hotter.

"I'm guessin' Uncle Vinnie shared the secret of his pies," Cal saved me by remarking.

Benny's dark brown eyes released me from their magnetic hold and he looked to his cousin. "Yeah. He taught me, said he wanted to retire from the kitchen. Now he's ordered a new sign, gets installed next week. Vinnie and Benny's Pizzeria. Screwed now, *cugino.* My name's gonna be on the building, I'm fuckin' stuck."

I couldn't tell if this was a complaint or considered an honor and Benny didn't let on which one it was.

"Mom doesn't like it when we hear the f-word," Keira butted in before I could figure it out or Cal could comment, then I watched her face get pink and she looked at the table.

"Good moms usually don't," Benny told her then leaned in and noted, "But bet you hear it all the time at school."

Keira looked at him and nodded.

"Bet you say it too," Benny teased, Keira bit her lip and avoided my eyes. In fact, she avoided everyone's eyes and she looked so hilariously guilty, Benny burst out laughing.

So did Cal.

And so did I.

On the day of my brother's funeral.

Then again, if Sam got a look at Keira's face, he would have laughed too.

"How'd you two meet?" Benny asked, sitting back, settling in, ready to stay awhile even though his kitchen was pandemonium. He stretched an arm along the back of the booth which stretched his tight tee across his chest and his ripped bicep, his arm spanning both girls, and both girls' eyes shot to me, their faces set to identical looks of joy.

"Violet's my neighbor," Cal answered, and Benny threw his head back and burst out laughing again.

When he finished, he shook his head, eyes on Cal. "Jesus. Only you could have the beautiful mother of two beautiful girls fuckin' move right next door. Shit." Benny looked to me again and said, "You got a sister, Vi, she's lookin' for a place, the one next door to me's for sale."

I smiled at him, feeling his compliment settle deep, but informed him, "I don't have a sister. Just a brother."

The humor faded from his face as the smile faded from mine, and like his dad, his eyes got soft, his expression turned gentle, and he murmured, "*Cara.*"

I bit my lip. He'd heard about that too.

Then I watched in fascination as his head turned and he looked at my girls. His hand curled and he slid the backs of his fingers along the now-reminded-of-her-grief Keira's jaw. After he did that, his arm curled around Kate and he pulled her into his side for an affectionate squeeze before his arm went back to settle on the booth.

Yes, Cal's family was cool.

In fact, they could be the coolest.

My mind was taken from this when I started to uncross my legs, and when I did, Cal's hand came back. It curled around my inner thigh and pulled my leg up and over his, where he dropped it on his thigh.

Vulnerable, tired and one breadstick not cutting through my hunger, I forgot myself. My head turned to him and I snapped, "Why do you keep doin' that?"

His head turned to me and his eyes leveled on mine. "You aren't puttin' your foot on the floor."

"Why not?"

"Buddy, can't believe I gotta remind you, but your foot is injured."

"You don't have to remind me."

"Then you don't need to ask why it shouldn't be on the floor."

"Yes, I do," I was still snapping.

His head dipped so his face was close to mine. "Aunt Theresa keeps a clean place. Still, not takin' any chances and I don't want your injured foot on what could be a dirty floor."

This was thoughtful and nice which pissed me off. Pissed me off enough to lose it and forget my vow to remember, forever and always, that Joe was gone. In fact, Joe never really existed. He was a figment of my imagination and it was Cal who remained.

I should have never forgotten.

But I did and therefore hissed, "It has a bandage on it, Joe."

The minute I uttered his name, his face changed. I watched stunned, spellbound, as his eyes got soft and his face turned tender. He'd never looked at me like that, not ever, and my stomach got soft again, and warm, my heart started beating harder and I couldn't help but lean closer, drawn by the power and beauty of that look aimed at me.

His hand came up, cupped my jaw, and I was so thrown, I didn't jerk my head away.

I still didn't when his mouth touched mine. He'd done that before, definitely, but never that way, never with that tenderness.

I felt my chest rising and falling because I found it difficult to breathe as his head bent, his mouth coming to my ear on the opposite side so Kate, Keira and Benny couldn't see or hear him.

"Your foot stays off the floor until Manny comes back with your flip-flops. Yeah?" he whispered in my ear.

"Okay," I replied instantly, whispering too.

His hand still at my jaw stayed at my jaw and he continued whispering. "A while ago, after I installed the system, when you were bein' a bitch, we were in your livin' room, you remember what I said?"

I remembered. I remembered like it happened yesterday. He'd said he was going to spank me and play with me until I begged and squirmed.

The memory made me squirm in the booth, but I nodded.

His hand at my jaw tensed then he threatened, "You call me anything but Joe again, honey, that's what you'll get."

I swallowed.

"Yeah?" he prompted.

"Okay," I whispered.

"Good."

He bent his head further, kissed my neck and his hand dropped from my jaw before he sat back.

Benny, Kate and Keira were all staring at us. Benny was smiling, *huge*. Kate was too. Keira looked slightly angry but more confused and I didn't blame her as I was feeling the exact same way.

"Well, *Joe*," Benny started, still smiling. "See you got your hands full."

"Yeah," Joe replied, giving my thigh a squeeze and sounding like he didn't mind at all. In fact, sounding like the idea of having his hands full was something he liked.

A lot.

"Glad to see it, *cugino*," Benny said, his smile smaller but his eyes had gone intense and he repeated, his voice low, heavy, even gruff and just as intense as the look he was aiming at his cousin. "Glad to see it."

I avoided his eyes, Kate's, Keira's, Joe's and I decided to let my leg over Joe's go. Manny would be back soon (I hoped).

Then I grabbed another breadstick.

# Fifteen

## Mike Wins

I woke up, belly to the bed, one knee cocked, but I kept my eyes closed, letting my senses test the bed, the room, listening for breathing, feeling for heat, hardness.

Nothing.

I opened my eyes and saw the bed beside me was empty.

Then I rolled to my back and saw the bed behind me was also empty (not Joe's side so this wasn't a surprise).

I stared at the ceiling and listened for noises in the bathroom.

Nothing.

Maybe I dreamed it.

I looked to the clock and it was after ten in the morning.

Late. Very late.

I sighed and looked at the ceiling again, all of it, the rest of last night and after we got home, tumbling into my head.

The breadsticks at Vinnie's Pizzeria were good. The antipasto platter yummy. The pie was the best pizza I'd ever had and I'd done copious pizza tasting research so it might be the best pizza ever made. The mascarpone cheesecake was sublime (the girls had big bowls of spumoni ice cream, homemade—I'd tasted it, and even with a gun to my head, I couldn't have told you if the ice cream or cheesecake was better). And the Chianti couldn't be beat. I'd never had better wine in my life.

This might have been why I drank the whole bottle.

Or, perhaps, it was because we were at the restaurant for hours.

The entire time we ate, and after, Vinnie, Theresa, Manny and Benny all came and went, sitting and chatting, standing and chatting.

Between pizza and dessert, Vinnie came and got the girls in order to give them a tour of the kitchen while Theresa sat on their side and chatted to Joe and me. Vinnie came back with the girls and Theresa took them on a tour of the front of the house while Vinnie sat with us and chatted. Then we had dessert.

Later, when most of the customers were gone (and all of my wine was gone), Theresa took me on a tour of the photos, most of which she told me she took herself. As she moved me around the restaurant, she shared stories of her kids, her brothers, sisters, Vinnie's sister (Cal's Mom), her aunts and uncles, Vinnie's aunts and uncles and all her kids' grandparents. There was love in her voice, and laughter, as she guided me around the room, smiling at her remaining customers, pointing at photos, sharing her life and her family through her words and her remarkable pictures.

I couldn't help but smile and laugh with her, even when she talked about Cal who sounded like a lovable hooligan (as told by her). He also definitely sounded like a member of the family, the unit, one of her kids, not a nephew, and I learned this was because, once his mom died and his dad lost it, Vinnie and Theresa had weekend and vacation adopted him. If he didn't have to go to school the next day or he wasn't in juvie, he was in Chicago at their house in the bunk bed over Vinnie Junior.

The girls joined me halfway through the photo tour, listening and appearing even more fascinated than me. Vinnie joined us at the end when we were at the front of the restaurant staring at a photo, place of honor, right when you hit the hostess station, the biggest one in the house.

It was taken at the front of the restaurant and it depicted Vinnie and a taller man, even more handsome than Vinnie (who was hot when he was younger). That man was Joe's father, Big Joe (Vinnie told me), and he and Vinnie were standing together in the middle of the grouping. Theresa was on Vinnie's right, Angela, Joe's mom, on her husband's left. A young Joe was standing in front of her, her hand on his shoulder, her husband's arm around Angela's shoulders, holding her snug to his side. Vinnie Junior with his sister Carmella in front of Theresa and Vinnie, Benny, a toddler, on her hip, Manny in Theresa's swollen belly. All of them were laughing, even the kids, even baby Benny had his head tipped back and was smiling up at his mother.

Cal was six in that photo. We knew this because Vinnie told us.

"Two days later, they found the tumor," he said softly and I heard Kate and Keira join me in pulling in breath. "Two years after that, almost to the day that picture was taken, Angela lost her fight."

At this news, Kate moved into me.

But my Keira, she moved into Vinnie.

He seemed startled for a second as she got close. His eyes had been staring at the picture, his mind elsewhere. Then he smiled a sad smile at Keira and slid his arm around her shoulders, his eyes coming to me.

"You never forget, *cara*," he whispered, knowing my pain. I felt the tears sting my eyes and Kate pressed in closer. "But, with time, you learn you don't want to."

I nodded, and silent as usual, Joe moved in behind me, his arm sliding around my stomach, pulling me and Kate into his front, another something I didn't fight because at that moment, I couldn't.

"Thanks, Vinnie," I whispered.

"You wanna talk, *cara*, have Cal give you my number," he offered.

I nodded.

"I mean that, Vi," he told me.

"Thank you." I was still whispering.

"We'll come down and visit soon, yes?" Theresa chimed in, and I looked at her, instantly forgetting my lovely moment with Vinnie and feeling panic.

"Yeah, Aunt Theresa, that'd be good," Joe replied, Theresa beamed and my stomach dropped. "Gotta get them home," Joe finished, moving us to the door.

"I'll get Mom's purse," Keira said then she started to move away, stopped, turned into Vinnie, gave him a hug around the middle with her cheek at his chest, tore free and started to run to our booth.

Vinnie's eyes watched her go then they went to Joe and the gentle and content look in them made my stomach drop more.

"Don't forget Mom's shoes, Keirry!" Kate called. "They're on the floor."

"Gotcha," Keira yelled back like they'd often been honored guests, family stopping for dinner at Uncle Vinnie's pizzeria and they could yell at each other and run through the restaurant.

We waited for her to get back and all of them, *sans* Benny who was sorting out his kitchen after Vinnie had let loose in it again, walked us out to the car. We got big hugs from Vinnie, Manny and Theresa then the girls piled into the car.

As Joe opened his side after getting another back pounding from Vinnie, Vinnie still with him, their hands in a grip, Vinnie close and talking about something that looked serious but I couldn't quite hear; Theresa caught my attention by catching my hand.

"Next time you're here," she started and my heart clenched because I knew there wasn't going to be a next time, "when it's a good time, a happy time, one you wanna remember, we'll get your photo. Put you and the girls on the wall with the rest of the family."

"Theresa—" I began, not knowing what to say and again pissed at Cal for putting me in that position at the same time confused why in the hell he would.

She squeezed my hand, cutting me off and whispering, "Bring him back to his family soon, yeah, *cara mia*?"

Shit.

"Yeah," I whispered back. I mean, what could I do?

"Thank you," she replied, kissed my cheek then stepped out of my door.

I turned to look at Joe, who was staring down at his uncle. I saw, somewhat astonished, that Joe's face was set tight. Vinnie's face was pale and—I gawked—*angry*.

What was that all about?

"You get what I'm sayin' to you?" I heard Joe ask quietly.

"I get it, son," Vinnie's voice was tense.

"Whatever it takes," Joe finished. I knew this was the finish for I saw Vinnie nod once, his hand jerked Joe's and then he clapped him on the shoulder, let his hand go and stepped away.

I thought I imagined the look on his face, his tense voice, when Vinnie looked at me and gave me a gentle smile.

"See you soon, Vi," he called.

"Yeah," I said again because there was nothing else to say.

I climbed in, Joe folded in, we slammed our doors and the girls and I waved at Vinnie, Theresa and Manny as Joe pulled away.

I thought, nursing my anger, there was no way I'd fall asleep.

But breadsticks, antipasto, great pizza, delicious cheesecake, a full bottle of wine and a weird and emotional day got the better of me and I passed out before we were out of Chicago.

I woke up with Joe's hand at my knee, his mouth at my ear.

"Wake up, baby."

My eyes fluttered open and I saw we were home and he was bent into my open door.

"The girls are out," he went on and I turned to see this was true. "Get out, buddy," he finished gently.

I exited the car and moved out of the way as Joe pushed the seat forward and bent in. Seconds later, he moved out again with Keira in his arms.

"I get her to bed, you can deal with her, yeah?" Joe asked but didn't wait for me to answer. He was striding to the door.

I fumbled with my purse, pulled out the remote, hitting the buttons then lamely hustled around him and unlocked it, pushing open the door as he walked through.

I tried not to let this affect me, Joe carrying Keira to bed. But it did, strong, hard, a sock to the gut, but a weirdly warm one, and even partly asleep and it being the middle of the night, it still pissed me off.

I hurried after them as best I could on my foot, catching up to them in Keira's room after Joe had put Keira on her bed and Joe walked by me as I walked into her room. His eyes caught mine but he kept going. I closed the door halfway and went to my daughter who always slept like a log. I took off her shoes and struggled with her dress, so much she half-woke. Helping her, we got on her pjs and I pulled back the covers.

"Where's Joe?" she mumbled sleepily as she settled in and I heard movement outside, footsteps, Joe and Kate.

"He's bringing Kate in."

Keira rolled to her side, her hands going under her cheek as she asked, mostly still asleep, "Do we have him back?"

That hit me too, a sock to the gut.

"No, baby," I answered honestly.

But she didn't hear me, she was asleep.

I pulled the covers over her, tucked them around, bent and kissed her hair.

Then I moved out, saw Kate's door closed and I went to it, knocking softly and going in at her call.

"Hey, Mawdy," she said. I'd caught her with her knee in the bed, she'd already changed. "Joe helped me in," she finished as she collapsed in bed and pulled up the covers.

I moved to her and tucked them tight all around.

Then I slid her hair away from her face. "That's good."

"I asked him to sleep on the couch, like Mike," she told me, and I felt my body freeze. I forced it to move, bent and kissed her hair.

"What did he say?" I asked her hair.

"He said, 'sure, girl,'" she muttered, her lips tipping up in a drowsy smile and she cuddled deeper into her pillows.

I was going to fucking *kill* him.

"All right, baby, go to sleep," I encouraged but it was a wasted effort, she was already asleep.

I turned out her light, left her room and closed her door.

Joe was dumping my purse on the kitchen counter, my pumps on the floor when I limped into the living room and through it, right to him.

I leaned in and hissed on a whisper, "You're not spending the night."

He took me in for a moment then replied, "Promised Kate."

"Then it'll suck, you needing to break your promise, because you're not spending the night."

"Yeah, Vi, I am."

"No, Joe, you're not."

"Baby—"

I leaned in further and demanded angrily, "Don't call me that."

His hand came to my neck and I was so furious, I jerked free. His hand stayed suspended in mid-air then both his hands moved quick, grasping my hips. They yanked me forward, my body slammed into his and his arms locked around me, one low at my waist, one high up my back. Caged.

"Let me go," I ordered, pushing against his shoulders.

"We gotta talk."

"Yeah, we do. Later, when I don't wanna rip your head off, we'll talk. There's a few things I wanna say to you. Now, you're gonna go."

"Nope."

"Joe!"

"Shut it, buddy."

I tried a different strategy. "The girls are both going with Dane and his parents to the lake early tomorrow. They'll be gone by eight. That's four hours away. I'm sure we'll be safe for four hours."

"I am too," he replied, and I knew what he meant.

"Joe—"

"Go to bed, Vi."

"Joe—"

His face came close and I stopped talking.

"You can go to bed or you can stay in my arms and argue. I'll tell you right now, baby, I'm tired and need sleep so I'm not arguin'. You stay in my arms, I'll be forced to find creative ways to stop that mouth of yours. You want that?"

He could just *not* be *believed*!

"We're over," I reminded him.

"I didn't agree to that decision," he shot back, and I felt my body turn to stone.

"What?" I whispered.

"Go to bed, Vi."

"But, Nadia…you said—"

He cut me off, threatening, "Should I get creative?"

I clamped my mouth shut and shook my head.

Joe held me awhile, staring at my face in the dark.

Finally, he leaned in and kissed my neck. Lifting slightly, he whispered in my ear, "Sleep."

Then he let me go.

I instantly turned and walked (okay, limped) as calmly as I could to my room.

I was trembling as I got ready for bed. My mind too full, too active, too *crazed*, I didn't even think when I pulled Joe's tee out from under my pillow, and after I took off my suit, brushed my teeth, washed my face, I slipped it on.

Then I got into bed.

My mind so active, so crazed, I thought I'd never sleep.

But I did.

And I did it soundly.

But I woke up when I heard the muted noises of the girls moving around and I felt him there, his shoulder against my cheek, his arm curled around my waist, my thigh thrown over his.

I didn't have a chance to react when he slid out from under me carefully then pulled the covers over me while I acted like a chicken and feigned being asleep. Nearly silent, he got dressed and left the room. But he left the door open partway and I heard the girls and Joe murmuring. Then I heard the doorbell, Dane's murmur mingled with theirs and finally the door closed.

Then silence.

I kept my eyes closed, waiting, but he didn't come back.

Somehow I fell back to sleep, telling myself that whole thing was a dream.

Now I was awake, hoping the same. But I knew he'd gotten into bed with me.

The bastard.

I stared at the ceiling wishing I hadn't encouraged the girls to go with Dane and his parents. They'd wanted to cancel and Dane had said it was okay, even that he'd stay and not go with his brother and parents to the lake, which they'd done every year since he could remember.

But a month ago, when they asked Kate to come along and to bring Keira, that was all either girl could talk about. I hadn't been able to give them a summer vacation and Dane's parents rented a cabin for four days, Thursday through Sunday. It was all water-skiing, tubing, lying out by the lake and getting a tan, fishing and barbeques every night. An end of the summer blast. A vacation, not a long one, but it sounded like a fun one. Something, not much, but it was something, and I wanted them to have as many somethings as they could get.

They didn't want to leave me and I didn't want them to, but I didn't want them to miss it either. I didn't want them to miss out on anything in life. I wanted them to live their lives while they had a chance and remember it could be a blast. Even now. Even so soon after Sam.

Especially so soon after Sam.

And Sam would want that too.

Now I realized my mistake. It was too soon, way, way too soon for me and, probably, for them.

I looked at the clock again.

They were probably already there or close. I'd call them after I had breakfast.

I got out of bed and padded to the bathroom. Using it, washing my face, brushing my teeth, I padded back out and into the kitchen. There was a note by the coffeemaker. I picked it up and read it.

*Hi Mawdy,*

*We left. We didn't wake you. Joe said to let you sleep. Call us, you need anything. Love you to pieces.*

*xoxoxoxox Kate*

*PS: Coffee's made, just flip the switch.*

*PPSS: Joe made it.*

I gritted my teeth.

Fucking *Joe.*

Under that:

*Hey Momalicious,*

*I'll keep my phone with me, even on the boat.*

*Love you.*

*xxooxxooxxoo Keirry*

*PS: Joe gave us each a hundred dollars! Isn't that cool?*

*PPSS: Don't forget to go get Mooch.*

Fucking, *fucking* Joe!

He was buying Keira, which would work in a flash and the bastard knew it.

I pulled in breath and instead of screaming, I sighed, dropped the note and flipped the switch on the coffeemaker.

Bobbie had given me until Monday off paid, which was nice. Being hourly, she didn't have to do that.

However she had also talked to me a couple of weeks ago about making me a manager. That salary would mean I'd get paid regularly what I got paid overtime, which would be good, having that kind of money steady. But it also came with a load of responsibility, which meant I'd still be working the overtime and have a bunch of headaches to go with it.

But she was through, she told me. She'd opened the garden center thirty years ago and she was plum tuckered out, (her words).

"Gotta take a break and you're the only one I ever hired I can trust with the place. So, now's my time. If you take the promotion, I get to have my time," she said, and I had to admit, since I liked her despite her being ornery (or because of it), I wanted her to have that time. Not to mention the steady pay.

But she still hadn't hired anyone to replace my part-time work. So if I became the manager, that meant I had to get trained to do what Bobbie did, none of which I knew how to do, and also find someone else and train them. Not to mention, there was a reason Bobbie didn't trust anyone else who worked there. Most of them were good, but it was just a job. They weren't like me, what they did was not something they loved. The others who worked there, they were pains in the asses, even for me and the rest of the crew, and I didn't have to supervise them and I didn't relish the idea of doing it.

And on top of that, Mrs. Cousin's yard that I'd redesigned and planted had gone over great. Mrs. Cousin loved it so much she showed it off and told all her friends all about me. Now I had two of her friends and her neighbor who all wanted me to work in their gardens, planting fall flowers and setting it up with bulbs for spring then coming back and sorting it out for the summer. Mrs. Cousin wanted me back too.

This meant I was working forty-five to fifty hour weeks and I had a shitload of other work. Money was coming in which was good and it didn't feel like work which was also good. But I could feel burnout coming. I knew it.

And, on top of that, what was next for me?

I thought through this as I slid the lever to turn the flow of coffee off. I got myself a cup and slid the lever back to let the rest of the coffee fill.

Mike was ready to take it to the next level. I knew it. I fucked that up, I'd lose him. I knew that too. He might be a nice guy but he also wasn't one you messed about and I didn't want to be the type of woman who messed a man about. He was going to lose patience and I sensed that was soon.

And, Sam was gone. Gone. There was nothing to be close for anymore, not even four hours away close.

And Daniel Hart was out there. He'd murdered my husband and my brother and he thought, even doing that, he could toy with me. He'd do it still, I knew it. I just didn't know what I'd do when he did. My choices were to unravel or go berserk, hunt him down and shoot him in the head. Neither were good for my girls (or for me, for that matter).

Joe was a wildcard and an infuriating one. I had no idea what was happening there, but I knew what *wasn't* going to happen. I also knew I needed to let him in on my feelings about that and I needed to do it soon.

At that thought, I took a sip of coffee, looked out the window toward his house and stared.

There was a dumpster in his front drive and a man was walking from the house to the dumpster carrying Joe's old carpet, rolled up and tossed over his shoulder. He got to the dumpster, did a hitch with his body and the carpet went into the dumpster, creating a cloud of dust.

What on earth?

I was so enthralled by watching this, I jumped as my phone rang and then I reached out to it, not taking my eyes from the window as I watched the man walk back into Joe's house.

"Hello?"

"Vi, honey?"

My eyes dropped to the sink.

"Bea," I whispered.

Tim's mom.

"Oh honey," Bea whispered back.

I put my coffee cup down and clutched the sink.

She heard my breath hitch.

"Oh honey," she whispered again then I sucked in another breath, this time without the hitch and she went on. "We wanted to go, Dad and me, but I couldn't face her. Dad said that Sam'd understand, knowin' how it was. But I felt so bad and I wanted to see you and the girls."

I understood this. My mother had been hideous to Bea and Dad, what I called Tim's father, Gary, because he refused to respond to me calling him anything else. My mom had been so hideous I remembered it like it was yesterday.

When it was all going down, when I found out I was pregnant and we had that awful family meeting where Bea and Gary were trying to talk my dad and mom into understanding and finding ways to help us out, my mother had been ice cold and downright ugly. Mom honed right in on Bea's frailties and the things Mom said, the way Bea was, Bea felt small, insignificant, worthless and she did because Mom wanted her too. Mom was such a bitch she was almost gleeful, making Bea feel that way.

Right in the middle of it, Gary had grabbed Bea's hand, pulled her off my parents' couch, tipped his head at Tim, who'd grabbed my hand, we all walked out and that was the last I saw of them for three years. They didn't come to my wedding. They didn't come to the hospital when Kate and Keira were born. They only came at Sam's urging to Kate's birthday party and that, too, had not been pretty (so we didn't see them again for another two years).

Bea had never forgotten. She was sensitive, but it was also that bad.

"I understand," I told her.

"I figured you'd be...you'd...everyone would want a piece of you. I wanted to wait until later so we could spend some time. Dad and I, we're gonna come down, stay the weekend, is that okay?"

My heart leaped then sank.

"Oh Bea, the girls are at the lake. I wanted them to have something fun and normal."

"Next weekend then," she said instantly.

I nodded. "Yes, I'd like that and the girls'll love it."

"Good," she replied softly then she hesitated and said, too casually, "Pam called."

Oh shit!

My head came up and my eyes saw the man walking out with more carpet.

"Bea—" I started.

She cut me off. "Says his name is Joe."

"Oh Bea, it isn't—"

"She liked him."

Fuck!

My mouth got tight. So tight I stayed silent. Then again, I didn't know what to say.

Bea went on. "Said he's real good with the girls, sweet to you. Big man, she said, a man you don't mess with."

"Bea, let me—"

Her whisper interrupted me. "I'm glad, honey." I closed my eyes and she continued. "Dad and me, we've been worried, you down there all alone. We know you wouldn't tell us, worry us, if it was still happening. What Pam said about this Joe, well, me and Dad, we're both glad."

I didn't speak because what could I say?

"Will we meet him when we're there?"

No they would *not.*

"He's out of town a lot," I told her, hoping he would be and willing to buy him a ticket to Timbuktu, drug him and put him on a plane if he wasn't.

"How does he look after you and the girls if he's out of town?" she asked, her voice rising a bit. She was getting scared.

"There's a guy across the street, a cop, a lot like Tim, good man. They take turns looking out for us," I assured her.

"That's good," she replied, her voice settling.

The man with the carpet had disappeared into Joe's house but I saw an SUV on the street. I focused on it and my breath caught in my throat.

Mike.

"Bea, I think I have to go," I said into the phone, not wanting to, wanting to talk to her. I hadn't had a good talk with my mother-in-law in ages and now, with Sam dying, it was the kind of time she was at her best. She might be timid and sensitive, but she was a great mother-in-law, a better mom, a stellar grandma and a good friend.

"That's okay," she told me. "We'll make a reservation in that hotel by the highway."

"You can stay here, have Kate's bed," I told her as I watched Mike pull into my drive. "She'll bunk with Keira."

"Oh, we couldn't."

"You did when you were here before."

She was silent while I watched Mike get out of his car, his eyes on my house and then I felt that sock in my gut when I saw he was angry. Very, *very* angry.

Then Bea said quietly in my ear, "That was before Joe."

I blinked, unable to keep track of Mike, Mike being inexplicably angry, Joe's carpet removal, Joe's truck in his drive and Bea.

"What?" I asked.

"He might not like—"

"You're stayin' here."

"We'll wait to meet Joe."

"It isn't like that."

"That's not what Pam says."

"But—"

Mike was walking to the front door and my heart was skipping a beat.

"I'll make him my chocolate cream pie, win him over," Bea decided.

Yeah, like chocolate cream pie could win Joe over. My cupcakes, pancakes and risotto hadn't made a dent in his armor. Bea's chocolate cream pie was the bomb but Joe Callahan was unwinnable.

"Bea—"

My doorbell rang and it sounded loud, louder than it ever sounded, too loud, and I jumped.

"You've gotta go," Bea told me.

"I—"

"See you soon, honey."

I was walking to the door as I said, "Bea—"

"Give my babies squeezes."

I sighed as I hit the alarm code in the panel by the door.

"Give Dad a squeeze."

"Of course, honey. 'Bye."

"'Bye."

I hit the button on the phone for off, unlocked the door and opened it to face my next drama.

And drama it was, for I'd forgotten I was wearing Joe's shirt.

This was bad. I knew it because Mike's eyes went from top to toe and his face went from angry to enraged.

"Mike—"

He cut me off too, by putting his hand in my belly, pushing me into the house, keeping his hand there even after he stepped in and closed the door.

He dropped his hand and stared down at me.

"Mike—"

I cut myself off when his hand came up, palm out and facing me, and I waited. He dropped his hand, looked away and a muscle in his jaw jerked.

Then he looked back at me.

"Been patient," he said softly. I opened my mouth to speak, he shook his head and I closed my mouth. "Please tell me, while you been draggin' me along, you didn't start fuckin' him again."

"I wasn't dragging you along," I whispered.

"Yeah, sweetheart, you were."

I always liked it when he called me sweetheart, but the way he did it then, I didn't like.

"No, Mike, I wasn't."

"Bullshit."

"I've been honest with you."

"You fuckin' him again?" he asked.

"Absolutely not," I answered.

"Why you wearin' his shirt?"

I considered lying, telling him it was Tim's. But Mike and I weren't about that and, I pulled this through, I didn't want to do it by making us about that.

"It's comfortable." At least this was true.

"He take you to the funeral?" Mike asked, and how he knew that I didn't know.

I nodded. "Only because Kate asked him to."

"You wouldn't let me do it, but you let him?"

"Mike, Kate asked him to."

"And I asked *you* to let me do it."

"Honestly," I whispered, beginning to lose it. Beginning to wonder why I cared. Beginning to wonder why I fucking got out of bed. At the same time throwing the phone on the couch. "I don't have the energy for this."

"I know life's shit for you now, Violet, but serious to God, this shit is fucked."

"What shit?" I asked.

"You bein' with me but him takin' you to the funeral and him leavin' your house the morning after."

"How do you know this?" I asked.

"Tina Blackstone stopped by the station, felt the boys needed donuts, even though the bitch has never done that before in her fuckin' life. Brought three dozen of them from Hilligoss, stayed while the boys ate, ran her mouth, enjoyed doin' it."

That bitch!

I stared at Mike a minute, allowing my blood pressure to drop.

Deciding to deal with Tina later, I affirmed, "He spent the night."

"But he didn't fuck you?"

"No, Mike," I told him, losing patience. It was slipping away and it was doing it fast. "He didn't fuck me. Kate's attached to him, she asked him to spend the night. She's feelin' a bit unsafe, seein' as her father and uncle have been murdered by the man who's stalking me. So we got home in the middle of the night and she wanted him to stay. He did. This morning he made sure the girls got off safe with Dane and his folks and he left. I didn't even get out of bed. I didn't even say good-bye to my babies."

My voice was choked when I finished speaking and Mike's face changed, the anger ebbed out, gentleness swept in and he took a step forward.

I took two back and he stopped.

"Sweetheart," he murmured.

*That's* how I liked him to call me "sweetheart."

But I shook my head and I told him, "It's over."

He blinked, slow, then asked, "What?"

"I'm sellin' the house. The girls and me are movin' to Arizona."

"Honey."

I was still shaking my head. "He'll fuck with me, Mike. He killed Tim, he killed Sam, and still, he'll fuck with me."

Mike moved forward, I moved back but he came at me faster and caught me in his arms. I forgot why I was retreating, put my hands to his chest and dropped my forehead between them.

"I can't do this anymore," I whispered. "You, Joe, Bea, Mel, Mom bein' a bitch, buryin' Sam, Vinnie, Theresa, Manny, Benny, Daniel Hart. It's all too much. I can't do this anymore."

Mike was quiet. He just held me in his arms as I fought back the tears.

When I won and did it on a sigh, he spoke. "Darlin', I don't even know who half those people are."

The way he said it, I laughed, turned my head and pressed my cheek to his chest.

Then I wrapped my arms around his waist and his arms got tighter.

"I was a dick," he said into my hair. "Comin' in here, givin' you that shit."

I let him off the hook. "You weren't. You were just a man."

"Well, yeah, I am that."

I pressed my cheek closer and gave him a squeeze. "Yeah."

"Girls aren't here, want you with me tonight."

I closed my eyes and didn't lift my head, nor loosen my arms when I said with all seriousness, "Mike, I wasn't joking. I need to let you go."

I felt his body grow still when he asked, "Why?"

I tipped my head back then, and said, "In case you hadn't noticed, men in my life end up with bullets in their heads."

"Sweetheart—"

"And I'm entirely fucked up."

"Vi."

I took an arm from his waist, placed my hand against his cheek and whispered, "And you deserve better than that."

"How 'bout you let me make that decision?" he whispered back.

"Mike, I repeat, I'm entirely fucked up."

"Sweetheart, I already know that." He grinned. "And, fuck me, but I kinda like it."

"Mike—"

"It's cute."

Finally, I gave him the truth. "And there's somethin' I need to work out with Joe and I don't want you feelin' on a string while I work it out."

His arms spasmed and that muscle leaped again in his jaw.

"What?" he whispered.

My hand at his cheek slid to his neck and I said, "Not that, not what you're thinking. But we gotta get something clear and, I know Joe, that'll take some doing."

"Violet."

"I got four days. The girls are gone, I got four days to do it. Can you give me that?"

"No."

"Mike—"

"Vi, you're in my bed tonight."

"Mike, listen to—"

His arms gave me a shut up squeeze so I did and he said, "No, Vi, you listen to me. You work it out with him. Talk. I don't give a fuck what it's about, don't wanna know. You come to my house tonight and you come prepared to spend the night."

Yep, he was getting impatient, staking his claim.

"Mike, I don't think—"

"And don't fuckin' bring one of his shirts. You sleep in tees, you wear one of mine."

"But—"

"And you take it home too."

Shit and damn. Joe was home a few days and my brother was fucking dead, I'd been semi-adopted by an Italian family in Chicago, my girls were back under his spell, and I was back in this unholy mess.

"I'm not ready for that."

"Yeah, you are and I am and he can have your days, you need to work shit out with him. But, while the girls are gone, I have your nights."

"What if we—"

"I want you safe. I wanna know you're safe and the only way I'll know that is you in my bed. He and Colt can keep watch durin' the day, but I'm tellin' you, Vi, I get the nights."

"Mike—"

He didn't let me finish again. This time he kissed me. Not his straight-to-fiery kiss, this one was a stealth one, light and sweet, building the fire.

I ended it with my arms wrapped around his neck.

"Six o'clock, sweetheart," he whispered. "Come on in, the door'll be open."

"Okay," I whispered back, because I was a total, complete idiot.

Then, just like Mike, he gave it to me honest.

"You don't get this, Vi, so I'll tell you. I'm fallin' for you." I closed my eyes. Mike kissed them in turn, and I opened them again. "I know you don't need that, sweetheart, but then again, you need it all the same."

This didn't make sense but it totally did.

I gave it back to him, just as honest.

"Mike, you deserve the best and I'm not sure that's me."

He just grinned, gave me a squeeze, kissed my forehead and repeated, "Six o'clock, door'll be open."

He let me go, turned and left.

I stared at the door.

Then I walked to it and armed the alarm.

Then I went to my cold cup of coffee, nuked it and stood in my kitchen, staring out my kitchen window, watching three men now carrying out to the dumpster what seemed to be Joe's entire freaking kitchen.

And while I did this I drank my coffee.

After I had a shower, I spritzed with my perfume, put on light makeup, my Lucky jeans and a blouse I always liked. The cotton looked almost tie-dyed, all in deep shades of grape, the split at the neckline was embroidered with green, lilac, lavender and blue flowers and there were braided strings hanging down from the top sides of the split, their weight holding it open. It fit loose but had an elastic waistband and elastic at the cap sleeves. It was kinda Heidi and kinda rock 'n' roll. I loved it. It made me feel good and I needed that in a big, honking way.

Then I picked up my phone, scrolled down to "Joe's cell" and hit go.

He picked up on ring two.

"Yo."

"It's Violet. We need to talk. Come over."

"Buddy, I'm in the middle of something."

"You come over here or I come over there and we do it in front of all the boys who're demolishing your house."

He was silent a moment before he sighed and said, "Give me ten."

"You got ten then I'm headin' over."

"All right, baby, cool it. I said I'd be over."

"Right," I said into the phone then slid it shut.

I had ten minutes and I knew what I'd do with them.

I limped out the front door, walked across my yard, cautiously jumped the split rail fence that separated the front of Tina and my yards, walked right up to her door and pounded on it.

She made me do this awhile before she opened it, her face a smirk. She knew this was coming and she wanted it, the bitch.

"Hey, Violet."

I didn't greet her. I said, "I hear you spread my business around again, we got problems."

She put her hand to her chest and said with totally fake innocence, "I don't know what you're talkin' about."

"Donuts for our boys in blue, tellin' Mike shit you have no idea what you're talkin' about, *that's* what I'm talkin' about," I unnecessarily reminded her.

The fake innocence melted away and her eyes narrowed. "Know you walked out Cal's back door wearin' his shirt. Know you're stringin' along a good man like Mike. Know that's fucked."

"You're standin' there throwin' stones when you regularly screw a married man," I fired back, watched her sneer even as she flinched and continued. "You don't know shit, Tina. But even if you did, it isn't your business, so keep your mouth shut."

"You gonna make me?" she asked, like we were eight and having a verbal tussle at recess during grade school.

"Yeah," I answered, not in the mood to be mature. "I got way too much fucked up crap happening in my life, I don't need to deal with you."

She leaned back and sneered, "What can *you* do to me?"

I decided to steal Joe's line. "Don't know, but you force it, I'll get creative."

"Bring it on," she snapped.

I shrugged and replied, "You got it."

Then I turned and limped away to see Joe standing in my yard, feet planted, arms crossed on his chest, his eyes aimed beyond me to Tina's house.

"What was that?" he asked when I'd jumped the fence again and got close.

"Nothin'," I replied, limped past him to my front door and I stepped through.

Joe followed me and closed the door.

"Vi, what was that?" he repeated.

"You and me, we're over," I announced *again.*

He crossed his arms on his chest, stared down at me and I forgot how scary he could look. He'd never done the arm crossing thing and that was super scary.

"I asked twice and I'll do it one last time, what the fuck was that with Tina?"

I noticed he ignored my announcement so I decided to answer him so we could get to what I wanted to get straight. Something that Joe wouldn't let me do if he was stuck on Tina.

"She saw you drive us away yesterday, she saw you leave the house this morning. She decided to bring donuts to the station and, while spreading her sugar cheer, share all that shit with the guys. Mike bein' one of them."

Joe's face got hard and far scarier and he turned his head in the direction of Tina's house to look at my wall.

"Mike and I are good, we're solid, she's tryin' to shake that up and I told her I'm not havin' that," I finished, bringing that subject to a close.

Joe's hard face swung back to me.

"You and Haines are solid?" he asked.

"Yes, which reminds me, you agree or not, we're over."

He shook his head.

I stared then asked, "Why are you shakin' your head?"

"Because we're not over."

"We are."

"We're not and you're not seeing him again," he declared.

My mouth dropped open.

Then I asked, "What?"

"You need to tell him it's done."

I felt my eyes get wide and I repeated, "What?"

"Do it today. He's a good man, you need to cut him loose."

I felt my body grow slowly solid but I leaned forward a bit while this was happening and asked, yet again, "What?"

"You're mine, the girls are mine. I'm stakin' my claim with you right now and, you force it, I'll do it with him too."

Did he…

Did he…

Did he just say *I* was his and *the girls* were his?

Did he just say he was *staking his claim*?

*Straight out?*

"Are you crazy?" I breathed.

"Nope."

That was when I lost it. It'd been building all day so it wasn't really a surprise.

"You have got to be fuckin' *kidding* me!" I shouted.

"Nope," he repeated calmly.

I took a step toward him and snapped, "You fucked someone else while you were fucking *me*."

"I lied. Never fucked Nadia," he replied, still cool as could be.

I sucked in breath at the same time my torso swung back.

"What?"

"I lied, buddy."

"Why would you do that?"

"Doesn't matter."

"Yes it does!" I shouted.

"The whole time I was with you, I wasn't with anyone else. Didn't even think about it."

I shook my head, taking a step back then two, his words pummeling me into retreat.

Then I stopped and rallied. "This doesn't matter, I don't care. We're over. I'm not goin' back there again."

"You're already back."

I stopped shaking my head and glared at him. "I am not."

"Buddy, you are. You never fuckin' left."

"How d'you figure that?" I asked sarcastically.

"You sleep in my shirt," he answered.

Oh fuck. Why was I such an idiot?

"It's comfortable," I snapped.

"And Kate told me, when Mike spent the night, he did it on the couch," Joe went on.

"He did that because he's being cool around the girls."

"I walked out of your room this morning, Vi, and neither of them fuckin' blinked."

I took those steps forward again (and then some), getting right into his space and stated, "Yeah, we need to talk about that too."

"Don't feed me some shit about you not wanting it. You were awake when I got up this mornin'. You didn't give me shit. You didn't say a fuckin' word. So don't try and bullshit me."

How did he know that? He was such a pain in the ass!

"I didn't want a scene in front of the girls."

"You wanted me to come back."

Yes, a total pain in the ass.

"I did not!" I yelled.

Then he moved fast and I retreated just as fast. I hit wall and he came in close, his hands at the wall by my head, fencing me in.

"Step back," I hissed.

"You're mine, Vi." he said and the way he said it, I focused on his face.

Very scary. Sinister. And definitely serious.

Joe Callahan was not a man to be fucked with, this I knew, and if I didn't, his voice and his face right then would have proved it.

"You let him touch you, it'll piss me off," he threatened.

"Mike and I are together," I whispered.

"Don't play that game with me or with him."

"Step back," I repeated.

"I'm warnin' you, buddy, don't play that game."

I shook my head and pleaded, "Joe, please, step back. I do not need this shit."

"Then don't force it."

"May I remind you, my brother just died!" I cried.

"Yeah, you lose this attitude, I can help you work that hurt out."

Who was this man? He held onto his tragedy for seventeen fucking years. How could he stand there and tell me he could help me work through mine?

"Really, Joe? Like you helped me work out my grief at losing Tim?" I asked sarcastically.

"That's not what I was offerin', buddy, but you want it like that, I'll give it to you."

"You're unbelievable," I snapped.

"I'm yours."

That socked me in the gut too, so hard it winded me and all I could do was stare up at him.

Taking advantage, his face dipped close and his hands curled around both sides of my head.

"First fuckin' time you smiled at me in my bed, that's when it happened," he murmured.

"Joe—"

"You're under my skin."

"Please—"

"I'm under yours."

I shook my head and his face got even closer. All I could see were his sky blue eyes. All I could feel were his lips a breath away from mine.

"I like you there, buddy, and you like me there too. Cut Mike loose."

"You can't belong to anyone. You're Joe Callahan, a one-woman man. The only one you ever belonged to was Bonnie and she's still got hold of you and always will no matter how fucked up, crazy sad that was."

His hands tightened on my head and he said, "Don't listen to 'burg lore. It's shit."

"You held on to it for seventeen years," I pointed out.

"She killed my son," he replied, and my heart lurched.

"I know," I whispered and my hands went to his waist, wanting to touch him, needing it, after he said those words, and doing it because I was crazy *insane.*

"You help me let that go, baby, I help you with Sam."

I shook my head but my hands clenched his tee at his sides. "I can't go back there again with you."

"Why not?"

"Because I don't know when you'll turn."

"Buddy—"

"You've done it to me twice."

"Vi—"

"And you've done it to the girls once."

I watched him close his eyes, knowing I'd scored a point and not feeling the least bit happy about it. But something was happening here and for me, and my girls, I had to do right this time.

So I pushed the knife in deeper. "Me, okay Joe. But not my girls."

He opened his eyes and locked them with mine.

"You feel it, I know you do. You know it isn't done."

"It has to be."

"It isn't. It won't ever be."

"It is, Joe."

He didn't respond, just stared into my eyes.

Then his mouth moved until it was touching mine.

Just with that touch, not even a kiss, my body went soft, my hands quit clenching his shirt and slid around to his back and a whimper glided out of my throat.

"Tell yourself that, baby. But, look at you," he murmured, his voice gentle not gloating, our eyes still locked. "You're mine."

Then his mouth went away but he bent his head, let mine go, kissed my neck and he walked away, out the door and I watched him through the window as he sauntered along my front walk to his house.

I stood there, pressed to the wall for a long time. It took a while but I realized I was breathing heavily.

Then I slid down the wall, knees to my chest. I wrapped my arms around my calves and hugged myself tight.

After some time, I pulled my phone out of my back pocket and I called my girls.

They told me they were there, in the cabin, unpacked and Dane and his dad had the boat in the water. The cabin was *way cool* and the lake was *phenomenal.* They were getting ready to go out on the boat and they sounded happy and excited.

I'd made the right decision, making them go. They had other things to think about, good things.

Sam would be glad.

When I was done talking, I slid my phone closed.

That's what I needed, exactly what I needed.

It wouldn't last long but it was something.

I got up off the floor and went to go get Mooch.

I sat wearing Mike's t-shirt in Mike's big bed, my ass to the mattress, my shoulders to the headboard, a tub of chocolate chip cookie dough ice cream melting in my hand.

Mike was stretched out beside me, on his side, head in hand, elbow in the pillow, eyes on me, wearing pajama bottoms and nothing else (he had a nice chest, unbelievable abs, the whole show leaner than Joe's, not as bulky, not scarred, but still amazing).

Layla was lying flat out on her side at the end of the bed, Mooch curled in her chest. Both of them were passed out due to the fact that they'd spent the last four hours pretty much destroying Mike's yard.

My cell was glued to my ear and Dane Gordon was whispering to me through it.

"She'd be mad, Miz Winters, me tellin' you this."

"That's okay, Dane, I won't tell her you called."

"Will you do it? Tomorrow morning? Let them both off the hook?"

"Yeah, Dane, I'll call."

"We'll come back Saturday, so we'll have another day and they won't feel they'll be screwin' up my vacation with my folks and Katy'll let me stay home so I can be around...um, for her, you know..."

Shit, but I liked this kid.

"Tell your folks I'll keep you fed. You want…" Damn, was I gonna do this? Yes, I was gonna do it. "You can tell them I'm lettin' you sleep on the couch."

Mike made a choking noise that sounded like swallowed laughter.

I glared at him.

"Yeah?" Dane asked in my ear, cut up because Kate was cut up about her uncle, not wanting to be far from his girl and the couch was as close as I wanted him to get.

"Yeah, Dane."

"Okay," he said and he sounded relieved. "Gotta go. Thanks Miz Winters."

"Yeah. 'Bye Dane."

"Later."

I slid my phone closed. Mike slid it out of my hand, threw it on his nightstand and turned back to me.

"Sweetheart, you are the biggest fuckin' pushover I've ever seen."

I slid my ass down his bed, pulling his shirt down as I did it so as not to expose my panties and begged him, "Please, shoot me."

"It's a six thousand dollar bed, darlin', I don't want a bullet hole in it."

I glared at him again then I threw my arm over my eyes.

He pulled the ice cream out of my hand. I felt him turn in the bed then he came back and pulled me into his arms.

I shifted so my hands were on his chest and I looked up at him.

"Talk to me," he ordered quietly.

"Well," I pressed closer, "Dane says that Kate and Keira are havin' loads of fun but it's all an act. He says they're sad, just coverin' it up. He says they want to be home, they're talkin' about me all the time. But he reckons they aren't askin' to go home because they think I want them to say. And he says I should call, say I want them to come home and that'll let them off the hook. But if I give them another day there, they do their duty to Dane and his folks but also get to come home to me. Dane drove down too so they'd have an extra car if the kids wanted to go out and do something, so he can drive them back."

"Good kid," Mike muttered.

"Yeah." I grinned at him. "Kate didn't inherit much from me but she got my taste in men."

Mike burst out laughing and rolled into me, his face going in my neck where he kissed me before his head came up.

"Kate's exactly like you."

I blinked at him. "What?"

"Kate. She's you. Totally."

"She looks like Tim."

"Yeah, but she acts like you, walks like you, smiles like you. Keira has your smile too."

"Really?"

"Yeah, honey. They're gorgeous but when they smile…" He let that hang as he grinned at me.

I moved my hand from his chest to his face and whispered, "Mike."

He turned his head and kissed my palm. Then he dipped his head, touched his mouth to mine and my arms wrapped around him.

"I like bein' here, with you," I said against his mouth.

His head came up and his eyes caught mine.

"I like it too, sweetheart."

Then, for some reason killing a great mood, I blurted, "I didn't get things sorted with Joe today."

His brows drew together and he asked, "You didn't talk to him?"

"I did, he kind of…didn't listen."

Mike rolled away to his back, but I kept hold and went with him as he muttered, "Fuck, Vi."

I got up on an elbow and looked down at him. "You can step back, honey, while I sort this out with him."

His eyes locked on mine. "You want me to do that?"

I did, to be fair to him.

And I didn't, to be totally selfish.

"Yes, to be fair to you," I said and felt his body tense. "No, to be totally selfish," I finished, voicing my thoughts aloud. Then I said, "But I know now where Joe's at and if I wasn't me, but your friend, I'd advise you to step back."

"I gotta worry about this shit?"

"No."

He studied my face then he asked, "You sure?"

"No."

He looked at the ceiling. I dropped down and pressed my forehead to his chest.

After a while, I felt his hand slide into my hair.

"This a 'may the best man win' situation, sweetheart?"

"I'm not a prize, Mike," I told his chest.

"Yeah you are, Vi. The best fuckin' prize there is."

My head came up and I looked at him. "We're talkin' hearts, here. You don't play games with hearts."

He got up on his elbows but didn't break eye contact as he declared, "You're wrong. Only games worth playin' are games of the heart."

"Someone loses," I whispered, and he grinned, did an ab curl and his arms wrapped around me.

He rolled me to my back, covered me with his body and put his mouth to mine before he whispered, "Tonight, I win."

Then he kissed me.

Then he set about winning me.

At least for the night.

And he did.

# Sixteen

## Gotta Remind You

The next morning late, I woke, Mike leaving me at his house in his bed after I gave him a drowsy kiss and went back to sleep as he went off to work.

I got up, took a shower, got ready for the day at Mike's house and went home.

I had Mooch in one arm, my bag dangling from my hand, my remote and key in my other hand and I let us in, dropping my bag and Mooch, who started instantly yapping his puppy yaps toward the kitchen.

As I closed the door, I turned that way and stared.

Joe was standing there, hand leaned into the counter, phone to his ear, eyes, or I should say *irate* eyes, pinning me to the spot.

"Yeah," he said into the phone, his eyes never leaving me as I stood frozen, staring at him. "You got it. Don't worry." He paused then he said, "Yeah, even when you get back." He paused again then said, "I'll tell her." Another pause then, "Yeah, later girl."

He flipped his phone shut and tossed it on the counter.

"What're you doing here?" I whispered.

Mooch somehow reading my tone shut up, sat down by my foot and stared with me at Joe.

"That was Kate," he replied, his eyes still skewering me.

"What?" I asked.

"She called yesterday, worried about you bein' alone. We made a deal."

This didn't sound good.

"You…" I hesitated, "made a deal with my daughter?"

"Yeah," he replied, not moving, staying leaned deceptively casually against the counter as he spoke. "She and Keira help me out with my house. I keep close and keep you safe."

"You made a deal with my daughters?" I repeated, though with a frightening nuance of change to one word.

"Works for me, seein' as I don't have a kitchen or bathroom or furniture. Now, stayin' with you, I do."

My chest seized tight.

"Staying with me?" I breathed.

"She called just now to check in."

I looked to his phone then to him, ruing the day that I programmed Joe's phone number into my girls' phones.

"I—"

Joe cut me off. "You spent the night with him."

I pulled myself together and stated, "That isn't any of your business."

"Thought I made myself clear yesterday, Vi."

"Yes, you did and I made myself pretty clear too."

"Yeah, baby, you did, fuckin' whimpering the minute my mouth got close."

Shit. Okay, he kind of had me there.

"Joe—"

"I told you not to play that game."

"Joe—"

"You played it."

I decided it was a good idea to start retreating so I did. Mooch started yapping. Joe stood there unmoving.

"I'd like you to leave," I told him.

"You forgot," he said, and I stopped moving backward.

"Forgot what?"

"Can't imagine you did. I didn't. I feel you at night, even fuckin' smell you, thought it was the same for you."

His words and all they meant washed over me and I stopped breathing.

"Gotta remind you," he murmured.

We locked eyes.

Then he moved.

I turned and ran.

Mooch followed me, thinking it was a game.

It was no game and I was way too slow. Joe caught me, swung me around, up over his shoulder and stalked into my bedroom.

"Joe! Put me down!" I demanded, pushing against his back.

He did. Bending at the waist, he threw me on the bed.

I turned and got up on all fours, scrambling.

He caught my ankles, yanked them, my knees came out from under me and he pulled me to him, twisted me to my back then he landed on top of me.

"Joe—" I tried, but his hand was in my hair. It fisted, he tilted my head and his mouth came down hard on mine.

Fucking hell, but that was it. It was insane but that was all he had to do.

He was wrong. I remembered. I remembered every second with him, even the ones when we weren't having sex, and I missed them. God, so much, I had to bury it, covering it with everything I had so it wouldn't break me.

But it all came back, the longing, the hurt, the hunger, everything we were, everything I wanted us to be and it was everything there was.

We tore at each other's clothes, yanking them off while we wrestled for supremacy, kissing, licking, biting, touching, scratching.

"Christ, baby," Joe growled as my hand wrapped tightly around his hard shaft.

"I missed you," I whispered my admission. Why, I didn't know. It just came out of me.

His face disappeared in my neck and his mouth at my ear, he ordered, "Spread your legs for me, buddy."

I did. He slid between, and without delay, he slammed inside, filling me.

My hands glided into his overlong hair and I moaned, "Baby."

"Wrap your legs around me, honey."

I did and used them. Heels digging into his back to lift my hips and he went in faster, harder, deeper.

"Good Christ, you feel good," he groaned in my ear.

It was debatable but I figured he felt better, though I wasn't going to argue the point just then. Instead I wrapped him tighter, his mouth came to mine and he kissed me.

Not long after, I was close, his mouth was on mine, but somehow he could feel it coming.

"Say my name."

"Joe."

He ground his cock in deep and demanded, "Who do you belong to?"

I closed my eyes and whispered, "You, Joe."

"That's it," he growled against my mouth, driving deep and I felt it as he urged, "Come for me, baby."

"Okay," I breathed and came, huge, hard, long, amazing, wrapping him tight, holding him close, pulling him deep as the orgasm he gave me had me in its grip, and it was so beautiful, I didn't want it ever to let me go.

It did. They always do, even the spectacular ones Joe gave me, and I came down in time to listen to and feel Joe's.

After, Joe stayed planted deep, his hand tangled in my hair, the other one at my ass, his weight heavy on me, his mouth moving at my neck and it was then I realized I really *was* a slut.

Mike and I hadn't had sex last night but we'd fooled around far more serious than ever before. Mike had given me an orgasm with his mouth and I'd returned the favor. I didn't know why he pulled back from the act; maybe he sensed I wasn't ready. But what we did was great, brilliant. He was a gentle lover (as far as I could tell), taking his time, like his stealth kisses, getting off on building the burn, patient, but in the end demanding.

I'd liked it a lot.

But not nearly as much as what I just had.

Two orgasms from two different men in less than twelve hours.

Yes, I was a slut.

When I came to this conclusion, Joe moved, pulling out and moving me with him, righting us in bed, pulling the covers down, sliding us between them, shoving the comforter back and then pulling the sheet up to our waists.

I didn't fight, struggle or say anything as he settled me into him. My mind was blank. No, not blank. Frozen in disgust at myself.

I came back into the room and saw that he'd slightly modified our usual position where I had my head to his shoulder, my body pressed to his side.

He'd pulled me partly over him, my cheek to his chest between his pecs, his fingers had wrapped around my wrist, positioning my arm around his hip, his knee had come up, hooking my leg with it so my calf fell between his legs and I was semi-straddling his thigh.

I could hear his heart beating, steady, strong. I'd never heard that before or never noticed it and its strength weirdly defined him. Strong, vital and alive.

He'd also yanked the sheet over us, to our waists. This was something I did with him in between times, unconsciously doing it, completely comfortable with our nudity while we were in the act but feeling vulnerable when we weren't. I'd pull the sheet up to our waists, not higher just there. Even after years with Tim, I'd done the same.

Tim had never pulled the sheet up. Joe noticed and he did.

And he remembered me, how I felt, even smelled. Like me, he remembered at night when we were apart.

I sucked in breath.

His fingers slid into my hair.

"It'll take two months to renovate the house," he said suddenly, and I blinked then realized he was starting the conversation in the middle again and my stomach got warm and soft at the memory of something Joe. Something I thought I'd never have back. I steeled myself against it but I knew this was a futile effort. "Took 'em a day to gut it but it'll take two months to renovate it," he finished.

I stayed silent because I didn't have anything to say, but also because my mind was not frozen and blank anymore. Now there was so much in my brain, I couldn't catch a thought.

"Girls're gonna pick carpet, paint, cupboards, shit like that. That's our deal," Joe went on.

God, Keira would freaking *love* that. Kate too.

I was screwed.

"In return, I'm in town, I stay with you."

My head came up with that. I looked at him and said, "Joe—"

I said no more because his hand was still in my hair. It slid to my neck and he yanked me up his body, lifting his thigh to assist him in this endeavor, its hardness pressed between my legs, an area still sensitive, which meant this felt good. When my face was close to his, his hand went back into my hair and pulled my mouth down to his to give me a bruising but short open-mouthed kiss.

"Love it when you say my name, baby," he muttered against my mouth when he was done. I felt my body soften, my jumbled head going blank again as I stared in his eyes and he went on. "Feel it in my dick every time."

My head gave a small jerk and I blurted, "You do?"

He grinned. "Yeah."

I liked it when he grinned. He didn't do it much so each time it felt like a gift.

But still, I said, "That's weird."

His grin became soft laughter and he rolled me to my back, mostly covering me with his body, his cocked thigh still pressed high between my legs.

"You don't hear it when you say it," he told me.

"I do hear it."

"No, you're not a guy so you hear it but you don't. The way you say 'Joe,' every man would wish that was their name."

"Okay," I replied because I really didn't have anything else to say to that statement and because I was busy trying to ignore the lovely squishy feeling that statement made me feel.

He bent his head and kissed my neck then his hands started roaming and his thigh moved an inch higher.

I bit my lip.

"Joe?"

"Yeah?" he asked my neck.

"You, um...can't stay here." His head came out of my neck, his hands stilled and he looked at me, so I forged ahead. "'Cause, um...Dane called and said the girls were fakin' it, havin' a good time. He and I made our own deal yesterday. I need to call them like, right now, and ask them to come home. They'll be back Saturday and I promised Dane and his parents he could sleep on the couch."

"So?" Joe asked.

"So, Dane'll be sleeping on the couch so you can't." This was one of the *two* reasons he couldn't, Mike being the other one. But I thought I'd start with Dane because mentioning Mike might make Joe mad and Joe naked and mad meant me acting again like a slut (or more like one, whatever that would be).

"Wasn't gonna sleep on your couch, buddy," he told me, and I blinked then I finally came to myself.

"You can't sleep with me."

"In your bed right now," he pointed out.

"Yes, but you carried me to it and *threw* me in it."

"You didn't struggle much then, Vi, and pointin' out the obvious, you aren't doin' it now."

He was right. So I pushed off and tried to slide away, but he gave me more of his weight which meant resistance was futile.

I glared up at him and demanded, "Get off."

He looked like he was trying not to laugh, a new look, a good one on him. "Too late."

"Off."

"You like me here."

"Off!" I shouted.

"You missed me. Told me so yourself, buddy."

God, I did do that, just blurted it right out.

I closed my eyes and turned my head away, but even doing this, I could hear his soft laughter and *feel* it against my body.

I didn't want to like it but I did.

Then something occurred to me and my body got tight and my head righted with a snap, my eyes opening.

"Shit," I whispered.

"What?" Joe asked.

"Do you hear that?"

Joe's face instantly got serious, his head cocked to listen then he looked at me and his voice was serious too when he asked, "What, buddy?"

"Nothing," I told him.

"Come again?"

"Nothing!" I cried. "Shit, hearing nothing means Mooch is getting into trouble."

If Keira wasn't around (and she was good with taking care of her dog) then it was me who had to deal with Mooch and Mooch, being a very active puppy, was a lot to deal with.

I couldn't do that with a big, naked man on me.

Suddenly that big, naked man wasn't on me. He was at the side of the bed and pulling on his jeans.

I stared as he walked out of the room.

Then I pulled the sheet up to my chest, sat up in the bed, bending my knees and watching the door, curious despite myself at what he was going to do. So curious, I didn't get out of bed, get my clothes on and run far, far away. Instead, I waited.

Not minutes later, Joe came back with a squirming dog under one arm and my purse in his other hand.

He dumped Mooch in the bed and my purse on the nightstand.

Mooch ran to me and jumped up, licking me with his puppy tongue and dousing me with his puppy breath.

"Need a new dog bed, Vi," Joe declared as I gave an active Mooch a rubdown and my eyes went to Joe.

"What?"

"Dog ate it," Joe told me, pulling my cell out of my purse.

"He ate it?" I breathed, wondering, if he had dog bed in his stomach, if that meant a vet bill in my future.

"Not all of it but he did a number on it."

"Shit," I whispered.

Joe tossed my phone on the bed then got in after he did that, grabbing the dog, stretching out on his back and pinning the puppy to his bare chest.

"Call your girls," Joe ordered as Mooch licked Joe's jaw.

I stared at Mooch licking Joe's jaw and the way Joe accepted this without looking angry or sinister or badass. Well, he still looked badass but not angry or sinister and I felt my belly go warm and soft again.

"Honey, the girls," Joe prompted when I didn't move.

He was calling me honey a lot lately, and stupid me, I liked that too.

He taught me a lesson (twice), a lesson that burned so deep I thought I'd never forget that night in his house with him in that chair, telling me he fucked someone else.

But here I was, right back where I began.

And I liked that too.

"Right," I whispered, snatched my phone from the bed and slid it open.

Joe moved the dog from his chest to the bed and Mooch started gnawing on his fingers. This Mooch did a lot and it didn't feel great. It started off okay, but if Mooch got into it, it hurt.

As my phone rang Kate's, I noticed Mooch was getting into it but Joe didn't push him off or even wince.

"Hi, Mom!" Kate called cheerfully into my ear and I heard instantly that Dane was right, she was faking it.

"Hey, baby," I replied.

"Everything okay?" Kate asked.

My eyes went from Mooch to Joe to see his head was to the pillows, one arm cocked, his hand behind his head and he was watching me.

"Not really," I said to Kate, moving my eyes from Joe's face to Joe's feet, which were crossed at the ankles and bare under the hems of his jeans.

Kate's voice grew concerned and she asked, "What's up?"

"Well…I don't want to, um…it's just that…do you think you and Keira could come home a bit early?"

"Are you okay?"

"Yes, I'm fine. I just kinda want you guys home with me. Do you think Dane's folks'll mind?"

"No," she said immediately. "They'll understand."

Yes, my girl wanted to come home.

It was now confirmed. Dane was a good kid and I was forced to like him, even love the guy.

Shit.

"Dane can um…" Damn! I looked back at Joe and widened my eyes at him but he just lifted his brows. Then I said, "If his parents'll let him, we'll look out for him. I know he's seventeen but he can stay with us, sleep on the couch and I'll keep him fed."

"Seriously?" Kate breathed.

I stopped looking at Joe, dropped my head to my knees and said, "Seriously."

"I think they'll be cool with that," she told me and she sounded genuinely happy now.

I turned my head, putting my temple to my knee and saw Joe was smiling at me.

There it was. I'd done the right thing.

"Good, honey, but enjoy today. Get your fill and then come home tomorrow." I told her. "But do it safe and slow, yeah?"

"Okay."

"Call me before you leave so I know when to expect you."

"Okay."

I decided to give her more to look forward to and shared, "Your Gram and Gramps are comin' down next weekend."

"Killer!" she cried, and I smiled, my eyes dropping to Mooch who was going to town on Joe's hand and, not thinking, Kate at my ear, I spoke to Joe.

"Joe, your hand is not a chew toy."

"Baby, he's fine."

"We don't let him chew on our hands like that."

"He's fine, Vi."

"Stop him."

"Honey, I said…he's fine."

The way he said this made me look at him and clamp my mouth shut. He was definitely done telling me Mooch was fine.

"Is Joe with you?" Kate asked, sounding beyond happy now. Sounding freaking thrilled.

I jerked my eyes from Joe and realized I was naked in bed with Joe and Mooch, talking to my daughter, who was thrilled Joe was with me.

God, total slut.

And also, totally screwed.

"Um…yeah."

"He's stayin' with us, you know, while his house is renovated. Did he tell you?"

"Yeah."

"Keira and I think it's great."

"Keira does?"

"Yeah."

"Really?"

"Yeah."

The hundred dollars.

"How much of Joe's money she have left?" I asked, and Kate laughed.

"We gave Dane's folks the money you gave us for food and stuff but we haven't had time to go shoppin' or anything, so all of it, I think."

"You get back, whatever you have left, you return it."

"What?" Kate asked.

"What?" Joe rumbled.

I ignored Joe and told Kate, "When you get back—"

I didn't finish because Joe sat up, reached in, pulled the phone out of my hand and put it to his ear.

"Money's yours, girl. Don't listen to Vi."

"Joe!" I snapped.

He nodded and said, "Yeah. Everything's good here. Tell Dane to remember the speed limit and that he's got precious cargo. No screwin' around."

My anger vanished, my body stilled and my mouth dropped open at listening to Joe sounding just like a dad.

"Right, see you tomorrow. Later." Then he slid my phone shut.

I stared at him then at my phone then my eyes went back to him. "I would have liked to say good-bye."

"Yeah, and you would have liked to say other shit," Joe said as he turned and tossed my phone on my purse.

"Like what?"

He turned back, his brows drew together and he got that sinister look when he asked, "Givin' my money back, Vi?"

"Two hundred dollars is a lot."

"No it isn't."

"Yes it is!"

"No, it fucking well isn't."

He was getting pissed but I figured I was getting more pissed.

I turned to him and declared, "Joe, you can't buy my girls."

His body went still and his face got hard and he didn't speak for long seconds. Seconds I didn't realize he was using to gain control.

Then, low and angry, he told me, "I'm not buyin' 'em, I'm takin' care of 'em."

"They're not yours to take care of," I snapped and immediately he moved. Mooch jumped away and I found myself plucked out of the bed and planted astride him, my knees in the bed, his arms locking me close.

"It was a shit time for you, the worst, but you were there and you saw 'em doin' it. They crawled into this same fuckin' bed with me, so did you, and when you did, you all became mine."

"That's insane," I informed him.

"That's the way it is," he shot back.

"Joe, we were beside ourselves with grief."

"Yeah, and when you are you don't lock tight to some guy you don't know or some asshole you hate. You lock tight to what's yours to remind yourself that it is and that you need it."

"That wasn't what was happening."

"Buddy, you're naked in my lap, your girls want me in the house, you're pissed at me, tellin' yourself it's over and all I gotta do is kiss you and you turn wild. This shit gonna sink in?"

"It did, twice," I reminded him. "And no matter the signals you gave me, Joe, it wasn't what I thought."

"Not givin' you signals this time, Vi. I'm tellin' you straight out and I'll tell you somethin' else. Always listen to your gut."

"Joe—"

"It told you you belonged to me. I'm tellin' you it was right."

I felt my heart start beating fast and that feeling in my belly again, the one I liked, so I whispered, "Stop it."

"And I'll tell you somethin' else. I'm fixin' up my house to sell it, we're movin' on from this, from Sam, from Hart, and we're doin' it together, you, me and the girls. And along the way, I want a kid, our kid."

I stilled and stared at him, his words another sock to the gut. But it was a gut that had already gone warm, it had gone soft, and even with the wind knocked out of me, I felt that gut flutter.

Then I asked in a whisper. "What?"

"You're not cool with that, I'll deal. The girls'll be all I need. But I'm not tellin' you what I need. I'm tellin' you what I want and I want a kid, with you."

"Oh my God," I whispered and his hand went to cup the back of my head and bend it to his.

"You got a lotta shit in your head, I know, but I'm layin' it out for you. There it is. That's what's goin' on here. Now, buddy, you need to cut Mike loose or I'll do it for you."

"Joe—"

"You want him to know you spent this mornin' with my cock inside you, you keep playin' this game. You wanna do it yourself, you end it with him."

"I keep trying to but he's like you. He won't listen."

"Then game on," Joe announced.

"Joe—"

"He shoulda listened."

"Why? You don't listen."

"You don't belong to him, you belong to me."

"That's insane too!"

"Baby, you told me so your fuckin' self."

"Sexual coercion."

He stared at me a second then burst out laughing, rolling me to my back and covering me with his body again.

"Joe, get off me!" I snapped, pushing ineffectually at his shoulders.

"Nope, feel like coercin' you again," he said in my neck.

"Joe, stop it."

"Keep sayin' Joe, baby, you're makin' me hard."

I growled, he grinned against my skin then, Lord help me, he lifted his head, his mouth came to mine and he coerced me.

Before I came I told him I belonged to him.

Twice.

Cal stood, back against his truck, arms crossed on his chest in the police station parking lot and he waited.

It took fifteen minutes before Haines came out, and when he did, he came out with Colt.

Fuck.

Both men looked to Cal, Haines's eyes narrowed, Colt's head dropped so he could study his boots and not give anything away.

Haines turned his head to Colt, said something, Colt nodded and they separated, Haines coming to Cal, Colt going to his GMC.

Cal's eyes remained on Haines as he walked to him but he knew Colt wasn't going far. This was confirmed when Haines arrived and Cal glanced Colt's way, saw his hips to the back of his GMC, his eyes on Cal and Haines.

"You got somethin' to say?" Haines asked, and Cal's eyes went back to him.

"Stand down," Cal told him.

His mouth got tight then he asked, "You shittin' me?"

"You're confusin' Vi," Cal explained.

"*I* am?" Haines asked then clipped, "Yeah, you're shittin' me."

"This isn't gonna end well for you," Cal went on.

"No, Vi makes a stupid decision, Callahan, it isn't gonna end well for her. I'm just positionin' myself to be there to pick up the pieces."

At his insinuation, Cal wanted to straighten from the truck, but he forced himself to stay relaxed against it. It wasn't like he hadn't earned a remark like that with his history with women and his history with Vi.

"You think I'll fuck her over."

"You're Joe Callahan's son."

This time it took everything for Cal to keep his back to the truck because his father sure as fuck hadn't earned that remark, but his voice vibrated when he asked, "What the fuck does that mean?"

"It means you're a one-woman man."

"Yeah, I am. Hasn't anyone clued in yet that that woman wasn't fuckin' Bonnie?"

He scored, direct hit. He watched it land as Haines's chin jerked to the side almost like Cal had clipped him.

"I thought she was," Cal forced his voice to steady, "but she wasn't."

"You sure?" Haines asked.

"Yeah, I'm sure," Cal answered.

"And how can you be sure?"

"'Cause no God is cruel enough to make the only woman you'll love be the one who kills your kid."

Another score, another direct hit. Haines's jaw went hard.

Haines changed tactics.

"You've torn through practically every fuckable woman in the county," Haines reminded him.

"Yeah, but none of them were Vi."

Another score, a muscle jerked in Haines's jaw. He knew Cal spoke the truth.

"She likes you," Cal informed him. "She wants what she had back."

"I'm not Tim."

"I'm not sayin' you are. I'm just sayin' you represent what she had."

"It isn't just that, we got somethin'."

Cal felt his own jaw tighten because he knew Haines spoke the truth.

Haines's voice also calmed. "And what we got, you can't give her."

"Same's true with me," Cal returned.

Haines's voice was actually soft when he asked, "What can you give her, Cal?"

"Everything," Cal answered, and he scored again. Haines blinked.

"She needs—" Haines started.

It was Cal's turn to soften his voice. "I know what she needs, Mike."

They stood staring at each other silently.

Cal broke the silence. "She's gonna come to you, break it off, cut you loose. This time, let her even if she tries to hold on at the same time."

Cal watched Haines's entire face go hard as the knowledge penetrated as to what Cal was saying and how much he knew of the game Vi was playing. It was a game she didn't know she was playing. She didn't have the experience. But she was running roughshod over Haines all the same.

"She was fifteen when Tim asked her out. She's got no idea what she's doin'," Cal defended Vi.

"I know that," Haines ground out.

"She's lost, with Sam gone, now more than ever," Cal went on.

"You aren't helpin' her get found, Cal."

"We're all lost, Mike. The best chance we got is to wander this life with the people who matter."

He'd scored again and he wasn't looking for it. Haines went from angry to watchful.

"You don't want her for her, you want her for you."

"Yeah," Cal replied instantly. "Isn't that what you want?"

"I want her because she's Vi."

"And I want her for the same, but because she is, she can give me what I need."

"And what's she get?"

"She gets to give me what I need."

"Nice," Haines bit out, back to pissed.

"That's who she is, man, haven't you figured that out? Isn't that what she does for you? Because if it isn't then you don't have her, nowhere near. That's what she is. That's what those girls are. That's who she made them to be. They exist to give you what you need. It isn't selfish, that's how they get off. Fuck, when I went to the mall with them, Keira tried to be my personal shopper."

Cal knew it cost him but Haines couldn't help but chuckle.

Then he asked, "No shit?"

"She picked a pink shirt," Cal told him then added, "With flowers on it."

Haines chuckled again.

Cal kept going. "She ever shove her shoulder in your pit, make you put your arm around her?"

The humor fled Haines's face but he didn't answer which was his answer.

"Katy do it?" Cal pushed.

"Kate did it?" Haines whispered.

"Vi did it when I needed her. Katy did it when she needed me."

Haines closed his eyes and looked away.

"Stand down," Cal repeated, his voice quiet.

Haines's eyes opened and he looked back at Cal, and when he did, Cal knew he'd won.

"You fuck her over—"

"I won't."

"You do…" He let that hang and Cal decided not to repeat himself. So Haines finished. "You don't give her everything, I'm back and I'll bust my ass to do it instead of you."

"I know that. She does too. So I reckon I better bust my ass so you don't have to."

"Wouldn't be work."

"Agreed."

They again stared at each other silently.

Haines broke the silence but he spoke quietly. "You gotta know you're killin' me, man."

Cal spoke quietly back, "I know, Mike."

And he did. He couldn't imagine standing down from Vi, not now. He'd pulled away twice thinking it was for his good and hers and neither time was the least pleasant. It was like tearing off a fucking limb.

Standing down for good would kill.

But if he knew Haines had with her what Cal had, he'd do it knowing he'd be doing it for her. Haines wasn't stupid. He knew she was tied in knots and a woman like Violet didn't get tied in knots for something that didn't matter.

Cal mattered to her.

Haines knew that.

So he was standing down.

"Fuck," Haines muttered.

Cal didn't reply. There was nothing to say.

Haines studied Cal then said, "Anyone else, I'd be fuckin' over the moon for you, Cal."

Cal remained silent but that didn't stop him from thinking that Mike Haines was a good man.

"Now, I'm not," Haines finished.

Cal lifted his chin.

The muscle jumped in his jaw again, Haines nodded then he moved to turn away.

For some fucking insane reason, before he did, Cal said, "She's out there."

Haines's eyes locked on his. "What?"

"Whoever she is for you, she's out there."

"Fuck me," Haines muttered.

"Mine moved in next door, man," Cal pointed out.

Haines turned fully to Cal and his mouth was twitching when he mumbled, "Joe Callahan, romantic."

Cal shrugged. Haines wanted to see it that way, fuck if Cal cared.

He pushed away from the truck, dropping his arms and turned to the door. He caught sight of Colt as he did it and Colt wasn't fast enough to hide his smile.

Crazy fuck.

Cal looked back at Haines as he pulled himself up into the cab.

Haines gave him a nod. Cal nodded back, slammed the door, buckled up, hit the ignition and pulled out of the station.

His phone rang as he drove down Grant. He yanked it out of his back pocket, looked at the screen, flipped it open and put it to his ear.

"Yo, buddy."

"Joe."

Hearing her say his name, he grinned at the windshield.

"That's who you called, baby."

"Where are you?"

"In the truck."

"Okay, but where?"

"On my way to your garden center to buy a dog bed."

He listened to silence.

This lasted a while.

Then he called, "Vi?"

"Yeah?"

"Honey, you called me, you actually gonna speak?"

"I, um…need you not to come home. I mean," she said the last two words quickly then kept talking fast, "to the house for a while."

"Why?"

"I'm having an impromptu girl's afternoon in."

He'd left her on her belly in bed after making her sit on his face until she came then fucking her until she came again. She didn't even twitch when he bent in, kissed her neck and whispered in her ear that he'd be back in a while.

He hadn't been gone an hour. Now she was having a girl's afternoon in.

This meant she was going to tell her friends everything which didn't make him happy because he didn't like anyone in his business. Then she was going to get shit advice. Then, maybe, she was going to do something stupid.

"Who's comin'?" he asked.

"Cheryl…" she answered.

Not good. That bitch was hard as nails.

"Feb…" she went on.

That was okay. Feb was cool.

"Dee…" she continued.

Wildcard. Dee Owens called 'em as she saw 'em and Cal had no clue how she'd see him.

"Jessie…"

Fuck, Jessie Rourke was a nut.

"Mimi…"

Christ, he'd fucked two of Mimi VanderWal's close friends.

"And Jackie."

Cal relaxed.

Jackie Owens was Feb's Mom, salt of the earth. Even with the rest of the hens in that coup, Jackie'd be the voice of reason and not many people were stupid enough not to listen to Jackie's reason, including Cheryl Sheckle and Jessie Rourke.

"Then, um…after, I'm goin' to Mike's," Vi said in his ear.

Cal didn't speak.

"Then, um…we need to talk," she finished.

"I'll go into the office after I get the dog bed. If I gotta stay gone, you need me to pick anything up?"

She didn't answer his question, she asked, "The office?"

"Yeah."

"What office?"

"My office."

"You have an office?"

Had he been closed that tight?

Christ, he had.

"Yeah, baby, I have an office in town. Got a girl named Lindy, schedules my meetings, my walkthroughs, sends invoices, does the books, arranges travel, orders the equipment if I do the install myself. Shit like that."

"In town? You mean, the 'burg?"

"Yeah."

"Lindy?"

"Yeah?"

"She live in town?"

"Avon."

"Oh."

"Take you to meet her," Cal offered.

"That's okay," Vi replied quickly.

Cal sighed then let it go and repeated, "You need me to pick anything up?"

She hesitated then repeated, "Pick anything up?"

"Coffee, milk, beer, pick anything up."

"*Groceries?*" she breathed, like the concept of groceries was foreign to her.

"Yeah, Vi, unless Armageddon hit while I was fuckin' you this morning and we missed it, I'm thinkin' grocery stores still exist and they're all still stocked."

He heard her soft giggle before she swallowed it.

His woman, Cal realized, was a nut.

"Vi?" he prompted.

"I don't drink beer."

"I do so we need it."

"Do you have some in your fridge?"

"Buddy, my fridge is at the dump."

"But wasn't it a perfectly good fridge?"

"Yeah, but my dad bought it at Sears thirty years ago so I don't think Katy and Keirry are gonna dig on it bein' in the kitchen they design."

"Oh," she said in a soft, sweet way he felt in his dick just like when she said his name.

He ignored it and asked, "So we need beer?"

"Um…yeah."

Christ, that was a long conversation to get down to needing beer.

"Okay, stick with me here, buddy, and concentrate. Do we need anything else?"

"I don't know, what do you eat?"

"Anything."

"We don't have Power Bars or Gatorade or anything like that."

"Vi, I'm not in training for the Super Bowl."

"Right," she whispered.

Cal started laughing.

"What's funny?" Vi asked over his laughter.

"You are, baby."

"How's that?"

"Gatorade?"

"Well, I saw you working out," she defended herself.

"So I'll buy water. You got eggs?"

"Yes."

"Bacon?"

"Yes."

"Oatmeal?"

"Yes."

"Then I'm set."

"Okay."

He pulled into the garden center parking lot and found a spot.

"I'm at the garden center."

She sounded distracted. "And Cheryl's just pulled into the drive."

Great, Cheryl got there first.

"Vi," he called.

"Yeah?"

Before Cheryl unleashed her claws, Cal decided now was the time to tell her.

"You know that hole?" he asked.

"What?" she asked back.

He didn't repeat himself, he said, "You were right. You and the girls plugged it."

He had her attention. He knew it because she was whispering when she repeated, "What?"

"I'm not empty anymore."

Silence then, "Joe—"

"Full to bursting, buddy."

A breathy, "Joe."

That made his dick twitch.

"Gotta go, baby."

"Joe—"

"Later."

He flipped his phone closed, jumped down from the truck and went into the garden center to buy a dog bed.

"And that's um…it," I finished my long story and looked around my living room.

I was sitting cross-legged on the floor. Feb was sitting by me, leaning back on her hands, her legs stretched out in front of her, baby Jack crawling all over her like she was a human jungle gym. Dee, Mimi and Jessie were on my couch. Jackie was in one armchair, Mooch, exhausted from eating dog beds and running around the yard with me in it for an hour, was flat out asleep on her lap. Cheryl was in the other armchair.

"Let me get this right, hon," Jessie said softly. "Your brother was killed, what? Three days ago?"

"Six," I answered. "They found him five days ago."

She nodded. "And since then Joe Callahan and Mike Haines have been goin' essentially head-to-head, no pun intended, to get at you?"

"Um…kind of, but not exactly," I told her.

"Babe, Cal's forcin' a meeting with all your loved ones by hornin' in on the funeral, not to mention you're meetin' his family in Chicago, and it's *the family*. And Mike's goin' for the gusto, makin' certain, if you pick him, that you don't forget about the family house, the six thousand dollar bed and the family pet, doin' it by givin' you the business in that bed *with* dog in attendance. They're definitely head-to-head," Cheryl informed me.

"Holy crap," Jessie whispered.

"Gotta say, livin' in this 'burg my whole life and knowin' Cal the length of it, there's a lotta gals, a number of them in a one mile radius of this house, who'd give their eyeteeth to eat pizza at Vinnie's Pizzeria and get a go at havin' their photo on the family wall," Mimi remarked.

"Gotta say, livin' in this 'burg my whole life and knowin' Mike the length of it, there's a lotta gals, some of them *next freaking door*, who would give their eyeteeth to have a shot at showin' Mike Haines that all women are not selfish, greedy, materialistic bitches like Audrey," Jessie noted.

"Same could be said for that girl next door wantin' Cal," Mimi told her.

"I think it can be taken as read that Tina Blackstone would just about jump anyone and it'd be difficult for that woman to prove anything against bein' selfish, greedy and materialistic," Jackie pointed out. "She's hardly a good example for debate."

"Cal," Feb spoke up, putting in her vote.

"Mike," Cheryl shot back.

"Cal's hot, but, seriously, he's a dawg," Mimi put in, looked at me and voted, "Mike."

"My guess is, Dawg Days are gone so my vote...Cal," Dee added.

"Put their names in a hat," Jessie suggested. "You can't go wrong."

"Jessie!" Feb hissed.

"What?" Jessie asked, looking around. "Am I wrong?"

"Joe Callahan," Jackie stated in a voice heavy with maternal authority and life experience and all eyes swung to her.

"Seriously, Jackie?" Cheryl asked.

"Seriously, Cher," Jackie replied, her voice no longer heavy but gentle. She looked at me and asked, "You wanna know why?"

I nodded.

"'Cause, when you talk about Mike, you look like a woman who's talkin' about a guy she likes. You talk about Cal, you look like a woman who's talkin' about the man she needs to breathe."

At her words, I stopped breathing.

"Jackie," Dee whispered.

"You do," Jackie told me. "Feb lost the man who helped her breathe, didn't take a full breath for twenty years until she got him back."

My eyes moved to Feb and she smiled at me then she pulled Jack off her legs and into her arms, making a nonverbal point that spoke such volumes, it was a wonder I wasn't swept away in its waves.

I looked back at Jackie and told her, "He's turned on me twice."

"Even tough men get scared," Jackie replied.

I felt my eyes get wide at the thought of Joe scared of anything and asked, "Scared of me?"

"Honey, the last woman he loved killed his child." I sucked in breath and she asked, "Wouldn't that scare you?"

"Yeah," I answered. "But he slept with someone else when he was with me."

"Told you he did," Jackie put in.

"Even if it was a lie, why would he lie, knowing how much that'd hurt?" I pressed.

"To make you hurt. Didn't have the strength in him to let you go, forced your hand so you'd do it," Jackie explained. "Man's strong so I reckon that's sayin' somethin' about what he feels about you."

"That's crazy," Cheryl muttered.

"You ever do anything totally irrational for self-protection?" Jackie shot her question in Cheryl's direction and she wasn't done. "Or for Ethan's?"

Cheryl bit her lip, which was her nonverbal answer.

Jackie's eyes came back to me. "He's a big guy, a scary one, fierce, tough, and because all that, while he's been puttin' you through the ringer, you had no idea you've been doin' the same damn thing to him."

"But—" I began but Jackie shook her head.

"You lost your man, your brother and honey, my heart's with you. That's awful. He lost his mom, dad and son. The last two because of the woman he chose, one he brought into his father's house, one he let bring his child into this world. That's a burden he's carried awhile and my guess is that burden is heavy. You two come with so much baggage, it's a wonder you don't get crushed. And that's the thing, neither of you did. And you found each other. It's time to unload that burden and find some joy," Jackie advised.

"What if I can't help him find his joy? What if I fail?" I whispered.

"Girl, you keep givin' up. The only way sure to fail is to give up," Jackie whispered back.

"He wants a baby with me," I told Jackie, and I heard some indrawn breaths at this piece of news (the only one) I had not shared.

"Give him one," Jackie returned as if it was simple as that (and, I had to admit, thinking about it made my belly flutter again).

But even so, I suggested, "Maybe he just wants me to have a baby."

"Oh crap, now she's makin' shit up," Jessie muttered.

"Babe, your shit's already confusin' enough, you don't need to make stuff up to make it more confusin'," Cheryl advised.

"This is true," Mimi said. "If Cal wanted a kid, he'd have about six dozen of them all over town."

"Unh-hunh," Jessie agreed on a nod.

"I'm not sure that's helpin'," Feb noted, watching me closely and she was right.

"Am I gonna be running into Joe's lovers everywhere I go?" I asked.

"Yep," Jessie answered and Mimi giggled.

"Great," I muttered.

"Happened to me with Colt," Feb told me. "Not everywhere I go but a few of his conquests come into the bar. I even spent time around him and Melanie when they were married." She leaned into me. "What doesn't kill us makes us stronger."

"I'm guessin' she's learned that," Cheryl mumbled.

"We all have," Jackie stated.

"I'm scared," I blurted.

"Of course you are," Feb said, folded her legs and leaned into me. "Remember you told me when you were worried about gettin' Keira that dog." She nodded to Mooch in her mom's lap. "How you had a dog and lost her and didn't want to put Keira through that?"

"Yeah," I answered.

"You're doin' it again, babe," Feb told me. "Protectin' yourself against hurt. You lost Tim and Cal hasn't made this easy on you, now you're gun-shy. But, honey, he's out buyin' a dog bed. Ask yourself, he's doin' that, why are you so scared?"

"It hurt when he turned," I whispered.

"He'll hurt you again. Men fuck up all the time. Tim golden the whole way through?" Feb asked.

"No," I answered honestly.

"You fight?"

"Of course."

"He piss you off?"

"Yeah."

"He hurt you by doin' stupid shit?"

"Not often but, yeah."

"Cal's a man, Violet. He's gonna fuck up. You are too. Honey, you know how that is, you lived with it with Tim. You also know, what you had with Tim, it's worth it and you gotta take the risk."

"Why?" I asked.

"You don't, what're you teachin' your daughters?" Cheryl, in an about face, joined our conversation. "To be scared, to wrap themselves in cotton, or to face life and fight for somethin' good?"

"I thought you didn't like Joe," I said to her.

She threw up her hand. "I forgot about the dog bed."

Jessie snorted but Dee and Mimi laughed straight out.

I reached out, put my hands to baby Jack and asked my question to Feb with my eyes. She answered by turning Jack to me. I took him and cuddled him close. He grabbed onto my blouse and hair and his face went to my neck, his wet, soft baby lips hitting me there, his tongue working at the chain of a necklace I was wearing.

"Like his dad," Feb mumbled, watching Jack. "He loves necklaces."

"Colt loves necklaces?" Mimi asked.

"This I gotta hear," Jessie leaned forward.

"Shit," Feb whispered.

"Are we done with Vi's thing?" Dee asked.

"I don't know, Vi, are we?" Jackie looked at me.

I bent my head and kissed Jack's shoulder.

We were done.

I knew. I knew even before they asked me. Joe was right. I knew when I crawled into my bed with him after the girls. Hell, I knew the first time he kissed me.

And now I knew because he was buying a dog bed for the dog he bought for my daughter.

And coming home with beer.

I whispered against little Jack, "Yeah."

"Good, so, what's this about Colt and your necklaces?" Jessie demanded to know, and I looked at her.

But Mimi spoke to me. "Feb doesn't kiss and tell. It sucks."

"I know. I told her about Jimbo and—" Jessie started.

"Don't repeat it!" Feb cried suddenly, hand up.

"What? It isn't weird," Jessie defended.

"Yes, Jessie, it is," Feb returned.

"It's just suckin' my toes. Does Cal suck your toes?" Jessie asked me.

I tried not to let my lip curl as I answered, "Um…no."

"Feels good," Jessie mumbled.

"Gross," Mimi was mumbling too.

"Do you have any beer?" Cheryl asked, standing up.

"No, Joe's picking some up on his way home."

Cheryl stared at me a second then she grinned and I realized what I said and how it sounded.

It sounded like it was.

Shit.

I rolled my eyes at her then said, "I have wine."

"Time for wine," Cheryl decreed, moving toward the kitchen.

"It isn't even four in the afternoon," Mimi told her.

"What? There're rules?" Cheryl asked.

"Yeah," Mimi answered.

"Fuck rules, I'm gettin' wine," Cheryl retorted. "Anyone want one?"

"Yeah," Jessie said.

"Sure," Dee called.

"Shit," Mimi mumbled. "All right."

"Small one for me," Feb told her.

"I'm in," Jackie said. I looked at her and she smiled at me. When she did I let that soft warmth invade my belly and for the first time didn't fight it.

Feb was lucky, not because of Colt (who was awesome) or Jack (who was adorable) but because she had a great mom.

I handed Jack off to Feb, got up and called to Cheryl, "I'll get the glasses." Then I announced to the women, "I got another problem."

"Seriously?" Dee asked.

I went to the kitchen, pulled open my cupboards with the wine glasses and looked over the bar into the living room to see they were all looking my way.

Then I said, "I need help exactin' retribution against Tina Blackstone."

Without even asking what she did, Feb stated, "I'm in."

"Me too," that was Jessie (not surprising).

"Absolutely," Dee added.

"This'll be fun!" Mimi clapped her hands.

"I'm all over that," Cheryl said from beside me.

"Oh shit," Jackie muttered, and I laughed.

My friends laughed with me.

I sat on Mike's stoop and watched the Chevy pull into the drive.

I didn't move as he parked in the drive, not the garage, got out and, eyes on me, he walked to me.

I didn't speak and he didn't either as he sat down on the stoop close to me, our hips pressed together as were the sides of our thighs. But his hands didn't come to me. He leaned forward with his elbows to his legs.

I leaned forward too.

I looked to my left and whispered, "Mike—"

"Cal visited me at the station."

I closed my eyes. His hand curled around the back of my neck and I still didn't open them.

"Sweetheart, it doesn't work, he jacks you around, you know where I live."

He'd made his decision, and as usual with Mike, it was the right one.

My eyes opened and looked into his.

"I jacked *you* around," I whispered.

"I knew what I was gettin' into."

"Mike—"

"Honey, a shot at you, it was worth it."

"Don't be nice."

"You want me to get pissed? Be a dick?"

"I think it'd be easier," I said truthfully.

"Can't do that, Vi." His hand gave me a squeeze and he let me go, leaning back into his legs but looking at me the entire time. "You were in deep with him, he was with you. Signals were all there and you told me as straight as you could. Before I even took you on our first date, I knew it by the way he looked at me the night I met you at J&J's. I still took my shot." He grinned. "Do it again, just for last night."

I shook my head and felt my mouth curve softly.

Then I felt my small smile die and I lifted my feet up to the step and bent into my legs, my cheek to my hand, my neck twisted to look at him.

"I liked bein' with you," I whispered and felt the tears hit my eyes.

His hand came back to me, pulling my hair from the side of my face and then staying wrapped around my head.

"I liked bein' with you," he returned.

The wetness fell. I felt it slide over the bridge of my nose, along my temple and I whispered, "I liked it a lot, Mike."

His hand tensed in my hair and he whispered back, "Sweetheart, you're killin' me."

"I wish—" I began.

"Don't, honey," he cut me off.

"Okay," I whispered.

He squeezed my head gently again then his hand went away. He got up and took my hand. I lifted up my torso and he pulled me off the step, walking me through his lawn to my Mustang. He stood with me at the door and his hands came to my jaws, pulling me up to my toes so he could touch his mouth to mine.

He kept his hands at my jaws when he told me, "He promised me, I stand down, he'd give you everything."

My heart flipped over.

"He did?"

"Yeah," Mike nodded then his hands tightened on my jaws. "He doesn't, Vi, you come to me and I'll give it to you."

I closed my eyes and nodded but I knew, that happened, someone would have Mike. He wouldn't be available for long. This was my only shot.

His thumb slid through the wetness on my cheek, the tears still sliding silently from my eyes.

"Sweetheart," Mike called and I opened my eyes. "You won't be comin' to me. Man I talked to today would move heaven and earth to give everything to you."

"Mike—"

"Didn't think that, no fuckin' way I'd stand down."

"Mike—"

His lips touched mine again and when his head lifted, he whispered, "Be happy, honey."

I nodded and whispered back, "You too, Mike."

He smiled and it was the first time he smiled at me in the hundreds he'd given me that it didn't reach his eyes.

"Yeah," he said and he let me go.

I got in my car, started it up and drove away.

Stupidly, I looked back in my rearview mirror.

He was pulling his car into his garage.

Life goes on.

Shit.

Cal was putting the beer in the fridge when he heard Violet turn in the drive.

He pulled one free of the cardboard, closed the fridge, twisted off the cap and turned to flick the cap in her trash but he saw her trash had a lid. He got close to it, his hand moving toward it, a sensor caught the movement and the lid lifted open. He stared at it then tossed his cap in. Sensing he was done, the trash bin closed.

"Fuck," he whispered, grinning.

Living with Vi was going to be an experience.

Then he realized she hadn't come in even though he'd heard her cut her engine.

He turned and looked out the window to see her standing in her open door, immobile, staring at his truck in her drive.

He decided to give her time. If she didn't come unstuck in twenty, thirty minutes, he'd go out and get her.

He moved to the counter opposite the sink, pulled himself up on it and took a drink of his beer, watching her staring at his truck.

She finally moved out of the car door, closed it and turned to the house. Mooch greeted her at the door. She dumped her purse on the counter with a glance at Cal, bent to pick up the dog and brought him up in her arms, close to her face so the dog licked her jaw as he squirmed in her arms and she tried to give him scratches.

She limped into the kitchen and asked, "You let him out?"

"Yeah."

"He do any business?"

"No."

"I'll let him out."

Then she limped out of the kitchen and to the back sliding glass door.

Cal sat on the counter and took another pull of beer. While he drank, he heard her shouting at Mooch mostly just teasing and playful then calling him encouragingly, which meant she wanted to come in. Finally, dog and woman came back into the house. The sliding glass door closed and Cal saw Mooch first because the dog came bouncing into the kitchen then tried to jump up Cal's legs.

Vi strolled in seconds later and walked straight to the fridge without looking at him, opened it and gazed inside.

"You have dinner?" she asked the fridge.

"Thought we'd go out."

Her body jolted and only her head turned to him.

"What?" she breathed.

"Out. To Frank's. Or get a pizza from Reggie's."

"Frank's," she said.

"You hungry?" he asked.

She nodded.

He jumped off the counter. "Let's go."

She closed the fridge, muttering, "I'll put Mooch in his box."

Cal dropped his beer hand after taking a pull and said, "Got 'im."

Then he put the beer on the counter, walked out of the kitchen, put the dog in the box and she was standing at the door with the alarm remote and her keys in her hands when he got back.

He took them both out of her hands, opened the door, put a hand to her hip, shoved her out the door, locked it and then guided her to his truck, arming the alarm with the remote as they moved.

They both got in and were on their way when he spoke.

"You talk to Mike?"

"Yes."

"It done?"

She was silent.

"Buddy?"

"It's done," she whispered.

Fuck.

It cut her up, doing that. Probably cut Haines up too.

He didn't touch her. He wanted to, but he didn't. She needed to break it off with a good, steady man to take a risk with another man who treated her like shit twice right after her brother was murdered like she needed someone to drill a hole in her head. But he didn't touch her because, Cal sensed from her mood, she didn't want that right now.

But he'd make it up to her, spend his life doing it, if it took that.

Though, knowing Vi, it wouldn't take that.

He parked on the street four doors down from Frank's, stopping to let her off at the door so she wouldn't have to walk it with her foot. She waited for him outside and she limped by his side to the door but she didn't touch him and he didn't touch her.

He opened the door for her and they walked in. Elaine, one of the waitresses, turned their way, smiled at Vi, her eyes went to Cal and her face froze.

Vi'd been there with Mike, from the look of Elaine more than once.

Violet took a step back and ran into him.

Cal touched her then. Sliding his arm around her waist, he moved to her side, pulled her to his and looked at Elaine.

"Got a booth, Elaine?" he asked.

Elaine looked at the wall of booths, two were open.

She looked back at Cal. "Take your pick, Cal." Her eyes dropped to Cal's hand curled around Vi's waist then up to Vi. "Hey, Violet."

"Hi, Elaine."

"What's shakin'?" Elaine asked as Cal moved Vi forward.

"World's upside down," Violet answered.

Elaine finally grinned. "I can see."

Cal didn't catch what Vi did, but whatever it was, Elaine's grin grew to a smile and Vi walked with him through the restaurant as eyes followed.

He let her go when they hit a booth, the last one against the back wall, more privacy.

She slid in. He slid in beside her.

She looked at him and asked, "Can you sit opposite?"

"No," he answered.

"Why?"

"I like you at my side."

Her expression gentled but she said, "I like my space."

"Say good-bye to that," Cal advised.

"What?" she whispered.

"Baby, I'm moved in, you got a new dog and, tomorrow, you got Dane sleepin' on your couch. You like space, you're fucked."

Her face ungentled and grew pale. "You're moved in?"

"I moved in this morning before you got home."

"Where?"

"Your room."

"How?" Her voice was rising.

"How?" Cal repeated.

"Yes, how?"

"Packed some shit, brought it over, unpacked it," Cal explained unnecessarily.

"Where'd you put it?"

"In your room."

"Yeah, but where?"

"Jeans and boots in the closet, dumped some tees in a drawer, razor in the bathroom. Done."

"Holy crap," she whispered then jumped when Elaine slapped two menus on the table.

"Should I have bothered with those?" she asked a pertinent question, tipping her head to menus no person who'd lived in that town longer than a month hadn't memorized.

"Not for me," Vi told her. "I want a Reuben."

"Burger," Cal said.

"Cheese?" Elaine asked Cal.

"Yep."

"Cheddar, Swiss, or jack?" Elaine went on.

"Surprise me," Cal told her and Elaine grinned again.

"Drinks?" Elaine continued.

"Diet Coke," Vi ordered.

"Beer," Cal said.

"Bud, Coors, Bud Light, Coors Light, Heineken—" Elaine listed.

Cal cut her off. "Bud."

"Onion rings, fries or both?" Elaine went on.

"Fries," Vi answered.

"Both," Cal told her.

"Gotcha." Elaine shoved her pencil behind her ear and slid the menus back off the table. She'd had her pad in her hand while they ordered but this was either for show or she held it by habit. She hadn't written a word before she walked away. The order would come to the table as they'd asked for it and the check would come with a total at the bottom, that was it, and it would be the right total. That was Elaine. That was Frank's.

"Joe," Violet called, and he turned to see she was out and out fretting. So he turned more fully to her and dipped his head close.

"Relax, buddy," he said softly.

"This is going really fast."

"I know."

"We need to talk."

"About what?"

"Nadia."

Cal pulled back. "What about her?"

"Who is she?" Vi asked.

Fuck.

He did not want to get into this shit, and what was more, she didn't.

"Vi—" Cal said low.

"No, I don't want to know. What I want to know is, honest, right here, did you sleep with her while you were sleepin' with me?"

Cal locked down his temper. "I already told you the answer to that."

"Okay, then, is she gone?"

Nadia was never gone. Nadia was always a phone call away.

He didn't share that.

"Yeah."

"Definitely?"

"Vi, not a big fan of askin' or answerin' twice."

"You lied to me."

"There was a reason."

"And that was?"

"To save you from me."

Her torso moved back and her eyes got big.

Cal wrapped a hand around the back of her neck, pulled her close and leaned into her.

"Thought I was savin' myself from you, but I was savin' you from me."

"I—" she started.

He cut her off. "You see these scars on my face?"

Her eyes went to his cheek then back to his. "Yes."

"Bonnie gave them to me. So high, her head was in the clouds, but it wasn't a good trip. She got pissed at somethin', I don't even know what, she came at me. Got me with her nails."

"Joe," she whispered, her fingers curling tight around his thigh.

"She got like that a lot. When she was pissed, she'd scream the fuckin' house down and it wasn't unusual she came after me. She only marked my face, and you probably don't know this, buddy, but you gotta come hard and dig deep to make marks like these with your nails."

"I…I don't know what to say," Vi muttered.

"Not tellin' you for you to say anything. I'm tellin' you because now it's happening. You're with me and you'll find this shit out about me. I look in the mirror every day and remember her marking me then I remember what else she did to me. Now you see it, right on my fuckin' face, you'll think about it too. Maybe it won't come to you every time you see it, but it'll come to you, and I know you, you'll feel it."

"Joe—"

His face got closer and he whispered, "That's what I was savin' you from, baby."

"It's you," she said incomprehensibly.

"What?" he asked.

"I didn't know she did it. Before you told me what you just told me, those scars were just you."

"Now you know."

"Those scars are still just you."

"Vi—"

"They are."

Fuck, was she serious?

"Vi—"

"Maybe you're right and I'll think about it sometimes. But most of the time, I don't even see them. They're just a part of you."

Cal had no response to that except the urge to kiss her.

So he did and he kept doing it until he heard the thud of a beer bottle hitting the table.

His mouth left Vi's and he turned to see Elaine putting Violet's drink in front of her.

"Bud, diet. Enjoy. Shout for a refill," Elaine said, her mouth curled up at the ends and then she walked away.

Cal turned to Violet who'd grabbed her drink and was sucking on the straw. It reminded him of her at J&J's, her elbow on the bar, her head in her hand, her straw between her lips, her eyes on him and half his concentration had been on her, the rest of it trying to stop his dick getting hard.

He hoped Frank hurried with their goddamned food.

Violet's eyes came to him. "We should probably not make out in Frank's restaurant."

"Why not?"

"'Cause it's mostly full."

"So?"

"Rumors fly."

"Buddy, my truck's in your drive and my tees are in your drawer."

Her eyes slid to the side then back to him. She put her straw to her mouth and muttered, "Right," then she sucked on her straw.

"It's a small town, we'll be the talk of it for about a week then someone else will."

"Okay," she whispered and put her glass down.

When she released her glass, he took her hand. Linking his fingers with hers, he brought their hands to his thigh.

"What else is in there?"

Her eyes lifted to his. "What?"

"In your head that we have to get sorted out?"

She laughed softly then replied, "You don't wanna know."

"Wouldn't ask, I didn't wanna know."

She leaned into him. "Joe, there's so much in my head, it'd take a year to get it sorted out."

"All right, break it down. What's priority?"

Her face set to confused. "Priority?"

Christ, she was cute.

"The most important, baby," he explained quietly.

"Um...all of it."

"First thing," he said.

"First thing?"

"Right now, first thing that comes to you, what is it?"

"Mel."

His brows drew together. "Mel?"

"She's...I know what she's feeling, Joe. I've been there and I'm worried about her."

His hand squeezed hers. "Buddy—"

"And she doesn't even have kids to make it easier."

"Then give them to her," Cal said and a surprised laugh came from her.

"I can't give her kids, Joe, it's anatomically impossible," she teased.

"You got two with phones and you got a car, honey."

Her face turned startled and she whispered, "You're right."

"Helps both ways. The girls and you call her regular, you get her regular. Go up to see her, get her to come down here."

"I don't think I can go up there, Joe, not by myself."

"Didn't say you're goin' by yourself. Wouldn't *let* you go by yourself."

Her hand spasmed in his and she whispered, "Joe—"

"What else you got?"

"Joe—"

He leaned in again. "What else's in your head, baby?"

She tugged her hand from his, lifted it and curled her fingers around his neck.

"Thank you," she whispered, and he saw tears trembling at the bottoms of her eyes.

"For what?" he asked softly, his eyes glued to her tears and her hand gave him a squeeze as he watched one slide down her face.

Before he could do a thing about it, her head came forward and veered to his left.

In his ear, she whispered, "For not wastin' time showin' me I made the right decision."

There it was. Vi didn't make him work at it long. It took less than thirty minutes.

Cal felt a twinge pierce the left side of his chest and he lifted his hand to her neck too. Sliding it back and up into her hair, he bent his neck in order to kiss hers and she turned her head and kissed the hinge of his jaw.

He'd never had a sweeter kiss. Not in his life.

His hand fisted in her hair and he lifted his head, positioning hers so he could kiss her.

"Burger!" Elaine announced, a plate crashed to the table and Vi jumped as Cal lifted his head. "Reuben!" she went on as Cal twisted his neck to look up at her, leaving his hand in Vi's hair. "You got cheddar. Surprise," she told Cal, smiled huge and walked away.

Vi giggled.

Cal let his woman go and turned to his food.

Vi squirted ketchup in a pile by her fries and noted, "One good thing about you movin' in..."

Cal left his burger suspended halfway to his mouth and looked at Violet, brows raised when she didn't finish.

"Don't think Dane'll have any ideas, you're in the house."

"He gets 'em, I break his neck," Cal muttered and took a bite of his burger then looked back at Vi to see now she had a fry loaded with ketchup suspended halfway to her mouth, her eyes wide, her face back to pale. He chewed, swallowed then assured her, "Relax, baby, I wouldn't actually do it."

"Don't threaten it either. You'll scare the shit out of him."

"Scare him enough not to get ideas?"

"Joe!" she snapped.

He grinned at her and repeated, "Relax."

"You can't go around threatening everyone."

"Sure I can."

"Joe!"

He put his burger down, turned to her and said seriously, "Baby, relax."

"Telling me to relax doesn't actually mean I'll relax, Joe."

"It should."

"Why?"

He turned and hooked a hand around her neck, pulled her to him and up to his face.

"Because the time when your head is filled with shit and you gotta worry about everything and everyone is over. The time when you can relax is now. So, I'll say it one last time, buddy, *relax*."

Her eyes moved over his face then he saw them change. In fact, her whole face changed. That look settled on her features that he'd seen once before when she was on his couch talking to Sam. Affection, plain as day, love shining in her eyes, all of it focused on him and he felt his left chest contract so powerfully, the feeling radiated throughout his frame and his hand tightened on her neck.

Before he could process this, she leaned up, touched her mouth to his, moved slightly back and whispered, "Eat, Joe."

Then she pulled away and turned to her plate.

Cal took his hand from her neck and turned to his.

He'd been ambivalent about the concept of God his young life, something that sent Aunt Theresa into a tizzy. But you lose your mom at a young age that shit's bound to happen.

He lost his ambivalence when he lost his dad who was a shit dad but Cal knew he'd once been a good one, a great husband and a decent man, and he lost his son the same day.

Now he reckoned, Vi moving in next door, maybe finally someone was looking out for him.

Or his luck had changed.

Whatever, he was grateful.

Sitting next to Violet in a booth in a damn fine greasy spoon, Joe Callahan lifted Frank's Indiana-wide famous burger to his mouth and took a bite.

"Joe," I breathed, my head arched back.

"In my mouth, buddy."

My head tipped forward, my hands went to his jaws and I rode him harder because I couldn't help it. His strong fingers were digging into my hips, pulling me up and pounding me down.

"Joe," I whispered into his mouth as I felt it coming.

His hand lifted to my hair, fisting, twisting and he growled, "Say it."

"I'm coming, baby," I whispered.

"Say it," he demanded.

My fingers went back and clenched in his hair. "I belong to you."

Then I came, slamming down, my back bowing, my moan escaping my mouth to be absorbed by his.

I was astride Joe but he was sitting up which made it easier for him, mid-orgasm, to flip me to my back and drive in harder. Something he did until he came right in the middle of giving me a deep, brutal kiss.

When he was done, his mouth left mine and slid to my neck, and as his cock glided in and out of me, my fingers moved through his hair.

We kept doing this awhile before his tongue ran the length of my jaw and he pulled out, rolled off, leaned down, yanked the covers over us and settled me into his side.

Joe was silent, as usual.

I couldn't be silent, as usual.

"School starts soon," I whispered.

Joe didn't respond.

"Back to school clothes," I went on.

The tips of Joe's fingers slid randomly around my hip and ass but he didn't speak.

"You goin' to the mall with us when we go shoppin'?"

Finally, Joe spoke.

"Hell no."

I smiled into his shoulder then my smile died.

"What should we tell them?" I whispered.

"The truth," he answered, knowing I meant the girls.

"That being?"

"I'm here now."

I gave his waist a squeeze and informed him, "It's not that easy."

"Only hard you make it hard."

"Joe—"

"Vi, I told you, I walked outta your room and the girls didn't blink."

"They were probably tired and they're emotional."

"They know the way it is between us."

His words shocked me so much I lifted my head and looked at him. "They have no clue."

"Buddy, Keira invited me to the mall and Kate brought me a Coke while I fixed our garage door opener and offered me a sandwich and that was before the scene when your dad and mom came callin'. They know."

"They don't."

"They aren't dumb."

"I know that."

"Okay, they don't know we're fuckin', but they know we mean something to each other."

He was right. They knew this. I knew they did with the way they acted the second time Joe turned.

Still, I stared at him and asked, "Do you think?"

He grinned at me. "Baby, clue in, the whole block knows."

"That's probably because of Tina's big mouth."

"It's because I installed your system at no charge, I fixed your garage and your daughters used to come over daily to talk to me. Been livin' here a long time, buddy, my whole life, and haven't done that kinda shit for anyone and no one came by to talk to me, 'specially not two teenage girls."

I stared then asked, "They came over daily?"

"Yeah, right before I fucked you over the second time."

I didn't know that Kate and Keira did that.

But I liked it.

"Oh," I whispered.

"So they get home, I take Dane out, you sit 'em down, tell 'em I'm here now. Ask 'em if they got questions, answer them. Done."

He thought it was that easy?

Obviously, he hadn't lived with the likes of Keira.

However, by all accounts (including my own experience with her) Bonnie was far more unpleasant.

"What if they don't like it?" I asked.

"We deal."

"How do we deal?" I pushed.

His hand flattened on my ass. "How 'bout we find out if they don't like it before we get wound up about it?" he suggested.

This sounded like good advice, simple, logical, but totally impossible.

If Joe thought that simple and logical was going to work, he was in for a world of hurt living for two months with three females.

I didn't share this with him, and since he was out of town most of the time, maybe he wouldn't notice.

I put my head to his shoulder and said, "Okay."

His fingertips went back to their random patterns and we were both quiet, me because I was in my head thinking about the million things there and Joe because he was Joe.

Suddenly he said, "Don't take the job."

I lifted my head again and looked at him. "What?"

"Manager at the garden center, don't take it."

I'd told him about Bobbie's promotion at dinner. Obviously he'd been thinking about it.

I pushed up to an elbow and looked down at him. "Why?"

"Money's the same as you're gettin' but it comes with headaches, headaches you don't have now. You won't be doin' what you like to do. You'll be doin' shit you don't like to do, workin' the same hours, gettin' the same pay. You want to advance, you ask her to make it worth your while. You like what you do, do what you do, fuck the promotion."

There it was again, simple, logical, and this time, doable.

I smiled at him. "You're right."

Joe didn't reply verbally. His other hand came up, slid into my hair at the side of my head, pulled my mouth down to his for a light kiss then he pressed down until I came off my elbow and my cheek was to his shoulder again. Then he reached an arm out and switched off the light.

But not before I saw the picture of Tim and me on my nightstand.

I pulled in breath through my nose. Joe's fingers came back to the side of my head to glide through my hair, pulling it back. He repeated this then his fingers slid behind my ear, down my jaw and his hand went away.

I exhaled.

"'Night, baby," I whispered into his shoulder.

His response was again nonverbal. His hand squeezed my ass then went back to its random patterns.

This felt nice and it was amazingly relaxing. So much so, I didn't realize that there weren't a million things tumbling around in my head.

Instead, I drifted right to sleep.

Cal woke when Vi's body jolted violently.

His eyes opened when he felt her go rock solid in his arms.

He waited as he listened to her breathing heavily and was about to call to her when she slid out of his arms and across the bed.

He watched her shadow move around the bed and rolled to his back as she walked to her dresser. She opened and closed drawers, doing it quietly. She thought he was asleep.

She closed a drawer and he watched her shadow again, this time she was pulling one of his tees over her head.

Maybe he should go to the mall with her and the girls when they went back to school shopping. He didn't, the way she was going, he'd run out of tees.

This thought made him smile.

She came to the bed, his side, and again he was about to call her name when she reached out a hand to the nightstand. Then he watched her shadow move out of the room into the study. She turned and disappeared.

She'd been carrying something.

The photo of her and her husband.

Cal closed his eyes and opened them again when he heard her back in the room. He watched her shadow walk to the dresser and she stood at it, her hands lifted in front of her. He couldn't see what she was doing but she was holding perfectly still.

She stood that way awhile before she moved, her hand went to the top of the dresser and he heard her drop something that made a soft clink.

Fuck.

Her wedding rings.

He'd noticed she still wore them. He'd seen them the first time he took her in fully in his living room when she was wearing those ridiculous boots and that sexy nightgown. Weeks after that, he'd thought Sam was her husband, a traveling man, the way she greeted him and he greeted her when he came to visit. He'd not thought much of her rings after their first time together, but he noticed them and he didn't like her wearing them. Never did. It might make him a dick, but he didn't.

Now he liked that she'd be with him in bed without them on, which also might make him a dick, but he didn't give a fuck.

Because now she really was all his.

She walked back to the bed and carefully slid in. Obviously still thinking he was asleep, she turned her back to him and curled up her legs.

Cal rolled back to his side, his arm moved out, hooked her around the stomach and he pulled her into his body, feeling hers was tight.

"I'm awake, buddy," he whispered into her hair.

"Sorry, did I wake you?"

"Yeah."

"I thought, while you were asleep, I'd—"

He cut her off, not about to make her say it. "I know, honey."

She was quiet.

Cal spoke. "You came awake hard, Vi."

She stayed quiet then said, "Nightmare."

"Sam?"

"Yeah," she whispered and her body started trembling.

Cal curled his arm tighter.

"Why is it harder in the dark?" Her voice was shaking like her body when she spoke.

"Demons in the dark," Joe replied.

"Yeah."

She was quiet again and Cal held her until the tremors subsided then she called, "Joe?"

"Yeah, buddy."

"I miss him."

His arm got tighter and he buried his face in her hair. "I know you do."

"Did you like him?" she asked.

"Yeah."

"He liked you," she whispered. Cal's arm tensed then he forced himself to relax and she said, "Wish you could have known him better."

"If I did, figure I woulda liked him better."

"Yeah, you would."

"Tell me about him, baby."

She was silent a moment before she asked, "Now?"

"It'll beat back the demons."

She again was quiet then she whispered, "You're right."

She nestled her ass in his groin, slid her arm along his and linked their fingers.

Then she talked about her brother, sometimes laughing soft, sometimes crying softer and she did this, and Cal listened to it, until she trailed off to sleep.

Cal held her tight even after she'd drifted off then his fingers slid from hers but curled around until his thumb found the naked base of her ring finger. It glided against her skin then he set her hand against her stomach and sighed into her hair, thinking, not for the first time, he really fucking liked the smell of Vi's hair.

Then he fell asleep.

# Seventeen

## I'm Yours

I stood at the mirror in my bathroom gunking up my hair.

I saw movement and turned to the right.

Joe was there and I watched him lean his shoulder against the doorjamb, his eyes at my hands in my hair.

For some reason known only to Joe, he'd gone with us to the mall back to school shopping. Because of this, he was wearing a shirt Kate and Keira had bought for him. It wasn't pink with flowers on it. It was black, tailored down his ribs, a straight hem and he wore it untucked, but you could still see his heavy belt buckle which had caught at the bottom flap under the buttons. It looked good on him, making his shoulders seem broader, his midriff leaner, his hips narrower.

My girls had an eye.

His eyes came to mine and he said softly, "They're here."

I pulled in both my lips.

"They're here!" We heard Keira shout.

"Oh shit," I whispered.

Joe grinned, pushed away from the jamb and came to me.

He positioned himself behind me and slid one arm along my belly, one across my chest. He pulled me to his body, dipped his head so his jaw was against my hair and he caught my eyes in the mirror.

"Relax," he said into my ear.

"Right," I said back.

He kept grinning then he dropped his head, kissed my neck, let me go and walked out of the bathroom.

Joe was quickly becoming accustomed to the fact that his ordering me to relax didn't mean I would, and apparently he was good with that.

I looked back at myself in the mirror and took a deep breath.

Then I washed my hands in preparation to go introduce my dead husband's parents to the man who replaced their son.

I couldn't say the last week with Joe in the house was uneventful.

It was eventful.

Very eventful.

First up was telling the girls.

They'd called the morning after Joe had moved in, waking us both up.

Joe, closer to the phone, rolled away from me and tagged it as I shook off sleep and rolled toward him.

"'Lo?" his deep, rumbling, *sleepy* voice growled.

I blinked sleep away.

"Yeah, girl. She's right here."

*Girl.*

Shit! He'd answered the phone, sounding asleep and told one of my daughters I was *right there.*

Joe calmly offered the phone to me. I got up on a hand and stared at it as if it had a mouth, that mouth was open, baring fangs and it was going to bite.

"Baby, it's Keira," Joe murmured his prompt, and I blinked again then got up to sitting and snatched the phone from his hand.

"Hi, honey," I said into it, trying not to sound sleepy and worrying that I failed.

"Hey, Mom," Keira answered, sounding awake and bouncy like always. Not traumatized in a way that meant, sometime in the future she'd enter a mall and mow down innocent bystanders with a machine gun because her mom's new boyfriend answered the phone first thing in the morning sounding sleepy and definitely being in bed with her mother. "We're packed up and just about to leave."

"Okay, baby," I said, curling my knees to my chest and wrapping an arm around them. "You want anything special when you get home?"

"A hot fudge sundae, your hot fudge, Fulsham's frozen custard," she replied instantly and that was my Keira—always knowing exactly what she wanted, how she wanted it and not afraid to say it.

"I can do that," I told her. "What about Kate and…um…Dane?"

"Hang on a minute," she said into my ear then I heard her shouting to Dane and Kate as I looked at Joe, who was lying on his back, watching me talk to my daughter.

His face was still gentled by sleep, his jaw shadowed with stubble, his big, powerful body relaxed, one arm cocked, hand behind his head, the other hand resting on his abs. His scars were on display along with his muscles. His skin had a beautiful olive tint to it, likely given to him by his mother. It and his hair were dark against my light green sheets and this, for some reason, I found unbelievably appealing. His blue eyes were on me. So clear, so blue, so startling, I remembered the first time I saw them and how they affected me and that effect had not diminished in all these months.

*I'm yours.*

The words he'd said to me two days before came into my head and they hit me like a thunderbolt. So simple, so Joe, two words, two short words, but put together and said by Joe their meaning packed a powerful punch.

It socked me right in the gut, so strong, I was sitting in my bed but I was winded.

Then I didn't know why, I unfolded my legs, twisted to him and bent down. I touched my lips to his throat then rested my cheek against his chest, settling into his warm, hard body, the phone still at my ear, my other ear hearing his heartbeat.

His hand behind his head came to me, sliding into my hair and staying there.

Keira spoke to me. "Kate says she doesn't want anything and Dane says he'd like some of your pork chops. Though, I'm thinkin' he's only sayin' that because he knows Kate likes your pork chops. I told them about the hot fudge sundaes and they're both in."

"All right, Keirry," I said into the phone. "Though, it being summer, I think we'll barbeque some pork chops."

Keira was silent. I was not queen of the barbeque. Tim always grilled the food. Since he died I'd tried on countless occasions and hadn't had much success.

"It'll be okay. I've got to get the hang of it eventually. Maybe tonight's our lucky night," I told her.

"Maybe Joe could man the grill," Keira suggested, and I laughed at the thought of sinister, rugged Joe Callahan doing something as domestic as manning a grill.

"I can do it," I replied.

"Great," she muttered.

I grinned. "Get home, be safe. See you in a couple hours."

"Yeah, Momalicious."

"Give Katy a cuddle for me."

"I will," she said, and I knew she'd do it. My girls were affectionate. They fought but the ill-will never lasted long.

"Love you, baby," I whispered into the phone and Joe's fingers tensed at my scalp.

"Love you too, Mom. 'Bye."

"'Bye."

I pressed the off button and Joe's hand at his abs came to the phone and slid it out of my fingers. I lifted up. He twisted and put it in its bed then twisted back to me, full-on, rolling me to my back.

Then his hands and mouth started moving on me, his hands on my ribs, his mouth at my neck.

"They're leaving," I told him.

"How much time we got?" he asked, and my stomach dipped.

"A couple of hours," I answered, and his hand came up and curled around my breast.

"Plenty of time," he muttered against the underside of my jaw.

"Joe, we need to let Mooch out."

"After."

"Joe—"

"After."

"Joe—" He pinched my nipple and that scored straight through me so I whispered, "Okay, after."

His head came up and he was smiling. Then it came down and he was kissing me.

Mooch, lucky for us, was patient.

We were in the kitchen when the kids arrived. Joe was standing by the sink drinking coffee, his hair wet from his shower. I was standing in the open fridge, a pad of paper in my hand, making a grocery list. My hair was dry and styled. I'd taken a shower first while Joe dealt with a phone call and I'd gotten ready while Joe showered and dressed.

I'd never seen Joe shower. I'd never seen his hair wet and it had been a long freaking time since I shared space with a man while getting ready.

I liked it, all of it.

But when the kids got home, his eyes went to the window then to me and he said, "They're home, buddy," I forgot how much I liked his wet hair, standing in the steaming bathroom while he showered and I wiped at the mirror and I panicked.

Joe saw it immediately and demanded, "Relax."

"Right," I whispered.

He shook his head and grinned.

I closed the fridge, put down the pad of paper and pen and we walked to the door.

Joe opened it and we walked out, Joe sliding an arm around my shoulders and tucking me into his side as we did.

Kate was out and standing in the door of the vehicle, but Keira burst from Dane's truck and ran, arms windmilling, hair flying behind her, *direct to Joe.*

"Joe!" she cried then skidded to a halt in front of him and kept shouting, "I got up on water skis!"

Then I watched, my body locked tight, as Joe's hand came up and out. He hooked it around Keira's head, pulled her to him as he bent low and he touched his mouth to her gleaming hair.

"Way to go," he muttered against her hair then finished, "Proud of you, honey."

He let her go and I saw her body was locked as tight as mine, her face frozen in wonder and she stayed that way as Joe moved around her, going toward Kate.

I forced my eyes from a still motionless Keira to Kate, who was standing by the truck staring at Keira. Joe walked right up to her, her body jolted when he arrived and she tipped her head back, peering up at him, giving him the perfect target when his head dipped down and he touched his lips to her forehead.

"Glad you're home safe, Katy." I heard him say. Kate's head turned, her eyes cutting to me, her face filled with the same wonder as Keira's had been.

*Honey.*

*Katy.*

Holy crap, but I didn't know anything more beautiful than Joe Callahan using those words with my daughters. The only thing more beautiful was their father doing it. But they'd never have that, not ever again. This wasn't the same, would never be, but it wasn't sloppy seconds either.

Joe took the bag Kate was holding from her hand.

"Where's Keira's bag?" Joe asked.

"Back," Kate said, her voice scratchy. "Truck," she finished, clearly unable to form sentences.

Joe moved to the truck.

It took some effort but I pulled myself together and said, "What? My girls are gone two days, they didn't let me say good-bye, they come home and no hugs?"

Keira came unstuck and jumped at me. I folded her in my arms as Kate ran to us and joined our huddle. I gave them squeezes, smelling their hair, feeling their bodies against mine and letting that settle in my soul. Then I kissed each of their temples in turn, Kate first, Keira last, and let them go.

"Right, let's get you unpacked." I looked to see Dane carrying a bag and hanging back. I smiled at him. "Hey, Dane, thanks for cutting your family time short and bringing them home safe."

"No probs, Miz Winters," Dane replied, grinning at me and coming forward.

Joe carried the girls' bags in. Dane carried his bag in. I held both my girls by the waist as we walked in.

An hour later, after the kids had unpacked, played with Mooch in the yard and we ate a lunch of sandwiches and chips, Joe took Dane to Fulsham's Custard stand to buy a tub of custard.

I sat the girls down at the stools by the bar, telling them we had to talk. They didn't say anything, just gave each other looks and went to their stools. They were on the dining area side. I stood in the kitchen at the counter opposite them trying not to hyperventilate.

For the last hour my head had gone over a million ways to open this conversation and decided all of them were lame.

Therefore I stood there looking between them not having that first clue what to say, and unfortunately, trying to think of what to say I stayed silent a long time.

Kate spoke first. "We get it, Mawdy. You're with Joe."

I stared at her.

"Yeah, no duh," Keira put in.

"So," I forced out, "you…this doesn't come as a surprise?"

Kate grinned and informed me, "Dane said a man doesn't fix a garage door opener unless he's fixin' to use that garage."

I felt my lips part. Even Dane had cottoned on to the situation way before me.

"And he came to the mall with us. Guys like Joe don't go to malls," Keira added, sounding wise beyond her years.

"You're not upset?" I asked, and Kate shook her head, still grinning.

So my eyes went to Keira and she was watching me.

"Who was the chick?" she asked.

"The chick?" I asked back.

"Yeah, that lady he was with before you went all…" she trailed off and then finished, "you know."

I knew. She was talking about Nadia.

Shit.

"She was…a friend of Joe's," I answered.

"She his friend now?" Keira asked.

"No," I replied instantly.

Keira kept watching me then went on. "So, we're his only friends now?"

I stared at my daughter and realized she thought we were a unit, which we were. Joe took us all or Joe didn't get us.

"Yeah, honey, we're Joe's only friends now," I said quietly.

"What about Mike?" Keira asked.

I drew in a breath and paused before letting it out and saying, "Mike and I—"

"You're better with Joe," Keira cut in before I could finish.

"What?" I asked.

"Mike's awesome, and he's hot, but I like the way you are around Joe," Keira told me.

"Me too," Kate put in.

"And I like the way Joe is around you," Keira went on.

"Me too," Kate repeated, and my eyes were going back and forth between my girls as they spoke.

"Mike was way cool and we liked him with you too, but he wasn't the same," Keira noted.

"He's a wonderful man," I said to her.

"Yeah, but he didn't fix our garage door opener," Kate remarked.

"And you don't look at him like you look at Joe," Keira stated.

"How do I…?" I paused to swallow, not sure I wanted to know not only how I looked at Joe but the way my girls noticed I'd looked at Joe. Then I asked, "Look at Joe?"

Keira shrugged.

Kate answered, her eyes on me were intense, "Like you looked at Dad."

I closed my eyes. Joe was right, the girls knew. They *so* knew. They knew even more than *I* knew or at least had admitted to myself.

With my eyes still closed, Kate went on. "And he looks at you like Dad used to."

Sock in the gut.

Winded.

I got my breath back, opened my eyes and told them, "Joe's stayin' a couple of months while his house is getting renovated."

"We know," Kate replied.

"No, baby, I mean…he's *staying*," I repeated, not sure how to explain it to my teenage girls. Worried I shouldn't. Worried, again, if I was doing the right thing. And hoping like hell it worked out with Joe because firstly, I wanted it to work out with Joe so badly I tasted it in my mouth and secondly, because I never wanted to have this conversation with my daughters again.

"Yeah, Mawdy, *we know*. Yeesh, it's the twenty-first century," Kate said to me.

"And it's been, like, *months*," Keira added, like I was slow off the mark and it was about time I speeded things up.

"Jenelle's mom moved her new boyfriend in in like, I don't know, a week," Kate went on and I knew this was true. But Jenelle's mom was definitely a slut. She made me look like a choirgirl. We'd lived there not a year and Kate's friend Jenelle's mom had moved *two* boyfriends in with her and her kids, moved both of them out and was working on the third.

But I didn't want them to think that this was like Jenelle's mom or *I* was like Jenelle's mom so I tried to explain.

"Joe and I…I don't want you to think…" Damn, this was hard. My voice got soft, I looked between them and I said, "He isn't just a guy. It isn't just because I'm lonely after losin' your dad. It's because he's…Joe and he… means a lot to me and you girls mean…" I paused then told them the truth as it hit me right then, settled in and made me smile a small smile. "You mean the world to him."

"He's lost everything so I figure he appreciates what he's found," Kate noted sagely, and I stared at her again.

"You know about…everything with Joe?" I asked.

"Oh yeah, kids at school talk about it all the time. About his wife and dad and son and how he's the lone wolf after all that, the *hot* lone wolf, the hot, *super cool* lone wolf. You nab him you'll be like…a *legend*," Keira informed me then grinned and finished. "And we'll be legends too."

"Yeah, 'cause we get to live with Joe too," Kate added.

"And we call him Joe and no one calls him Joe," Keira put in.

"Yeah. We're already kinda legends on that. Dane tells everyone we call him Joe. They think it's way cool," Kate said.

I didn't like everyone at their school talking about Joe, even though they obviously thought he was cool. There was something about it that rattled me.

But I let that go, took in a breath through my nose then I said, "You know, Joe's moving in, *our* Joe, not hot, super cool, lone wolf Joe that everyone talks about and him moving in makes you a legend. He's just a man. He might be a big and strong man but he's got feelings."

"Yeah, feelings for us," Keira replied.

"And feelings for you," Kate told me.

"And we have feelings for him," Keira went on.

"And you do too," Kate finished.

Yeah, I did, but it was good to know they did too.

"You like him?" I asked quietly.

"He's Joe," Kate answered simply.

That kind of said it all. He definitely was Joe.

I looked at Keira. "Before he came back, you seemed mad—"

"Mom, it's cool," she interrupted me. "I was mad but now we have him back and he came back when we needed him."

"When *you* needed him," Kate stuck with her theme.

"I—" I started, but Kate kept talking.

"When Uncle Sam…" She stopped speaking abruptly, looked away then swallowed and looked back at me. "When we came home, you were in Joe's lap then he carried you across the room and he…" She hesitated and her voice dropped to a whisper. "When we lost Dad, you didn't have that, someone to be there, someone to lean on, someone to hold you up because that was Dad's job and he was gone and that was why you…" She shrugged and finished, "I'm just glad that Joe's gonna be around."

I felt tears stinging the backs of my eyes and I pulled in another breath through my nose before I asked, "You're sure?" They both nodded so I continued. "It's only a couple of months then we'll talk again. This is *your* home. I want you to feel good in it and comfortable. If you ever feel funny, you need to talk to me."

"Mawdy, it's *no big deal.* Really. Yeesh. This is Joe," Kate sighed.

"Yeah," Keira agreed. "Yeesh."

God, they acted like this was no big deal and I should just…

Relax.

Thinking that, I smiled to myself and also defended myself. "I'm tryin' to be a good mom."

"You don't have to try," Kate told me.

Another sock to the gut.

Winded.

I'd never had a more beautiful compliment.

I took in my wonderful, gorgeous girls, leaned forward, my forearms on the counter and said, "I just want you girls to be happy."

And to that, Kate asked, "Yeah, you ever think that we want the same for you?"

That's when the tears hit my eyes.

"God, I love you guys," I whispered.

"Love you too, Mawdy," Kate whispered back, also leaning in, also with tears in her eyes.

"Yeah, me too," Keira whispered, leaning in as well with tears in her eyes.

I got off my forearms but reached out and grabbed both their hands, giving them a squeeze.

Then Keira asked, "Where are they with the frozen custard?"

Kate and I laughed, and finally I relaxed. They were good. They were even happy for me, for themselves and even for Joe. And Keira was right. Enough of the heavy stuff, we'd had more than our fair share of that. It was time to move onto hot fudge frozen custard sundaes.

I let them both go, grabbed my cell off the counter and called Joe.

It rang twice then, "Yo."

"Hi, talk's over, you have the Winters girls' seal of approval."

"Good to know, buddy," Joe said, sounding like he was smiling. Then again, our talk lasted about ten minutes so he knew he was golden.

"Though," I went on to warn, "you're gonna lose it if you don't get home soon with the custard."

"It'll be a while," Joe told me.

"Is it busy?" I asked.

"Don't know. We're at the garden center," Joe said.

I blinked at the counter then looked between Kate and Keira before asking, "Why are you at the garden center?"

"Buyin' you a new grill," he answered, and I blinked again.

My old grill out on the deck was covered by a tarp, an old tatty tarp which was good because the gas grill was older and tattier. It destroyed my whole deck vision with my wrought iron furniture and flowers, so it was hidden in a corner. Tim had meant to build me a built-in grill in our backyard. He had it all planned, even bought the bricks he was going to use, but he died before he could do it.

"You're buying a new grill?" I asked and Kate smiled at a smiling Keira.

"Buddy, don't even wanna look under that tarp," Joe answered.

"It's not pretty, but it works."

"A man's gotta have the grill he's gotta have," Joe told me.

"What?"

"I'm not grillin' chops on a shitty grill," Joe said instead of repeating himself, but I was stuck on the idea of Joe grilling anything.

"*You're* grillin' the chops?" I asked.

He sounded somewhat impatient when he replied, "Vi, I go to the grocery store, I grill chops. I'm a guy but I gotta eat and you get food at the store and guys grill meat, that's what we do."

"So you know how to grill?" I asked hesitantly.

"You know how Vinnie taught Benny how to make a pie?" Joe asked me.

"Yeah."

"Well, my dad could do one thing good. Grill. And he taught me how to do it. So, yeah, I can grill."

"Okay."

"We done talkin'?"

"Um...how long are you gonna be?"

"A lot longer, we're not done talkin'."

I smiled at the phone then told him, "The girls and me may be at the store when you get back."

"Be a fool's errand since I took your list with me."

"You're goin' to the store?" I breathed, thinking both of rugged alpha male Joe roaming the aisles of a grocery store (which was shocking in itself and I'd already faced this impossibility the day before, but it was such an impossibility it was worthy of further emotion) and of the fact *I* didn't have to go to the grocery store (which was a welcome change).

"Shit," he muttered into the phone, clearly not wanting to have the grocery store discussion again.

"Okay, buy a grill, go to the store, be domestic," I said quickly. "Just don't forget the custard."

"I won't forget."

"See you later."

"Yeah." Then he called, "Vi?"

"Yeah, honey?"

"It's all good."

"What?"

"Us," he said. I got that winded feeling again, liking the idea of "us," liking that he knew to get me, he got the girls and he wanted that and he wanted that to be good, and he went on. "Girls're home, we're together, it's all good. Now you gonna relax, baby?"

I tipped my head to the side and whispered, "Yeah."

"Be home soon."

Yes, he would and I liked that most of all.

"Yeah," I whispered. "Later, honey."

"Later, buddy."

I slid my phone closed and looked at my girls.

"We're getting a new grill," I announced, and they both smiled.

Joe and Dane didn't buy a grill.

They bought the grill to end all grills. It took them an hour to set it up on my deck. It was gleaming and huge and totally went with my deck vision.

Then they loaded up the old tatty grill and took it to the dump.

They came back and Joe grilled chops. We ate his chops with my homemade potato salad and blanched green beans tossed in sesame dressing. We finished this with my homemade hot fudge sundaes with huge squirts of whipped cream, chopped nuts and a cherry.

Joe was not wrong. His father must have been the master grill artist like Vinnie was a master pizza maker. Joe's grilled chops were the best, even better than Tim's and Tim could man a grill.

We ate on the deck.

All afternoon and evening, pretending to have stuff to do in her backyard but really being nosy, Tina came out every once in a while to watch this activity, the grill building, the chop cooking, the family eating on the deck.

Tina didn't look happy about Joe's sudden domestication.

Revenge was sweet.

"Buddy?" Joe called when we were in bed.

I was in his tee, my cheek to his chest, his heart beating in my ear and I was half asleep.

"Yeah?"

"That first time, shoulda made me a hot fudge sundae."

My head came up and I looked in the direction of his face, even though I couldn't really see him because it was dark.

"What?"

"Before I fucked you over the first time, you shoulda made me a hot fudge sundae."

"Why?" I asked.

"I wouldn't have fucked you over. I woulda taken you to Vegas."

"Vegas?"

"Married you, Vi," he said, sounding like he was close to laughing.

"What?" I breathed.

"They're that good."

"What are?"

His hand curled around the back of my head and he urged, definitely laughing now, "Stick with me here, honey. Your sundaes. They're that good."

My sundaes were good. I loved my sundaes. The hot fudge was Bea's recipe but I made it better simply by putting in a bit of cinnamon.

Still, I asked, "You wouldn't have told me you were done with me if I'd made you a sundae? Instead, you would have married me?"

"Yeah."

"Are you tryin' to piss me off when I'm half asleep?"

"Just givin' you a heads up on what'll keep me happy."

I pushed up higher. "You *are* tryin' to piss me off when I'm half asleep."

He curled up, his arms went around me, and suddenly I was on my back, Joe on me.

His mouth against mine, he muttered, "I'm teasin' you, baby."

"I don't like to be teased."

"Then whoever did it wasn't doin' it right," he whispered.

My breath caught, my body stilled and I stared at his shadowed head in the dark.

He *did* remember everything.

"Joe," I whispered back.

His mouth slid from mine to my ear and he murmured. "Don't say my name like that in this bed unless you want me to fuck you, Vi."

My arms went around him, my hands gliding across the skin of his back, my head turned slightly so my mouth was at his ear and I whispered, "Joe."

He laughed softly in my ear.

Then he fucked me.

In the middle of the night I jolted awake, breathing heavily, the dream still had hold of me.

"Buddy."

"I'm okay."

We were spooning, his arms tightened around me, and I pressed back into his body.

"Same dream?" he asked.

"Bits different. But mostly, yeah," I answered.

Joe rolled closer, giving me some of his weight, pressing me into the bed, his big body cocooning mine.

"You wanna tell me what it is?" he asked.

"No, no, I need to let it go."

"All right, buddy."

"Just, keep close," I whispered.

"Not goin' anywhere."

"Good."

I felt his face in my hair, his breath stirring it and he held me close, his body a protective shell, until I fell asleep.

Sunday, Joe (and Dane) learned what being a part of the Winters girls' clan meant when we all went to look at bathroom and kitchen fittings.

Kate and Keira's visions for Joe's house clashed significantly. They couldn't agree on anything and discussion got heated.

In store three when the salesperson was backing away, Dane was faking getting a text and I was about to intervene, Joe waded in.

"Right," he said in a commanding way, both Kate and Keira stopped arguing and their eyes cut to him. "Kate, you get the kitchen, Keira, the bathroom…" he turned to me, "Vi, you pick the paint and the carpet."

"I want the kitchen," Keira unwisely put in and Joe's eyes went to her so she snapped her mouth shut.

"That's cool because I'd prefer the bathroom," Kate said.

"Done," Joe decreed, and the girls smiled.

Simple, logical and doable.

Shit, he was like Superman.

Monday I went back to work, so did Kate. Dane went home to his folks and we managed our first day living life the way it was going to be without any real drama.

I was relieved to see that both girls acted like Joe was a natural fit in the house. But it became clear Joe didn't feel it was so natural. Joe had things on his mind.

This became clear at the end of the day when I was cleaning off my makeup in the bathroom, Joe was in my bed and I was thinking about our evening.

When I got home from work, Kate was already home and Keira arrived ten minutes after me. She'd been laying out by Heather's pool all day, dedicated to building her tan to the highest possible heights prior to school starting. When Keira got home, Joe told us he was taking us to eat at Shanghai Salon. I was thrilled at this idea, it meant I didn't have to cook. The girls were thrilled because they loved Chinese food.

When we came back, Joe got a phone call that lasted awhile and the girls and I put in a movie. Kate was in an armchair. Keira and I were stretched out on the couch, Keira in front of me, my arm around her, not unusual for us (or for Kate and me for that matter). Also not unusual for Tim and one of the girls when he was alive.

Joe was taking his call in the study. I heard it end and I felt him approach the back of the couch.

Then I felt the cushions behind me being pulled out and both Keira and I looked up as Joe put a hip to the couch and rolled over it, sliding in behind me. With his elbow in the couch, head in hand, his eyes went to the TV as his arm circled both Keira and me.

I laid still and breathless but looked at my daughter.

She was still and breathless, her neck twisted, looking at me.

Then her face went soft, her lips tipped up at the ends and she snuggled into me, forcing me to snuggle into Joe. His arm tightened, my body relaxed and we watched the movie. But before I looked back at the screen, I glanced at Kate to see her eyes on the television but her lips were tipped up like her sister's.

And, taking my makeup off, I realized this was Joe staking his claim in private and in public. We were his, he wanted us to know it and he wanted everyone else to know it too.

I stared at myself in the mirror, thinking that Mike told me Joe told him that he was going to give me everything. When Mike told me that, I didn't know what it meant. I just knew that the promise of it felt brilliant.

Now I knew what it meant.

I'd had everything once, and what was more, my daughters had it. In a way I didn't think it could begin again, the world had ended when that everything was ripped away, not just from me but from my daughters.

Joe was giving it back, to me and my girls.

Standing in the bathroom, I felt my side of the scale crash down, it was loaded so full by Joe.

I walked out of the bathroom into the bedroom and I didn't look at Joe as I walked to the door and locked it. Then I turned, my eyes went to Joe in our bed and I walked to the end of it. I stood there, and as Joe watched silently, I pulled off his tee, tugged down my panties and stepped out of them then crawled on all fours up his legs. I kissed his belly then slid the covers down.

"Buddy," he murmured.

I took him in my hand and slid him into my mouth.

"Christ, buddy," he groaned, both of his big hands sliding my hair back at the sides and holding on.

Not knowing how to give him everything, I gave him what I could, making him come with my mouth.

When I was done, he yanked me over his body, shoved my face in his neck, his hand went between my legs and he made me come with his fingers.

That was Joe, balancing out the scales.

"You good?" Joe murmured when my heart rate went back to normal, his fingers still sliding gently through the wetness between my legs.

Yes, I was good.

Except I found just then I wanted Joe's side of the scale to be heavier than mine.

For the rest of his life.

But I whispered into his neck, "Yeah."

His hand slid away and he moved me to his side.

"Sleep, buddy," he ordered softly.

"Okay, Joe," I replied.

His hand went to my hip to draw his random patterns and my mind filled with ways to unbalance our scale.

I fell asleep not coming up with much.

The nightmare came again that night. It woke me and Joe and he held me as my breathing steadied and the tremors slid out of my body.

He did this silently, but when I'd recovered Joe spoke.

"Don't like this shit, Vi."

"It'll pass."

"Don't like it," he repeated.

"I'll be okay."

"You have this when Tim died?" he asked.

"No," I answered.

"Shit," he muttered.

"I'll be okay."

His arms squeezed me then he said, "Yeah."

But he didn't sound convinced.

On Tuesday morning, while I was drinking coffee and the girls were still sleeping, Joe went out front, which was something he did first thing every morning since he'd moved in. I knew why and I chose to pretend it didn't happen.

That morning I couldn't because Joe came back in, stood in the door and looked to me.

"Come out here, buddy."

At first I panicked. Then I saw his lips twitching so I walked to the door and followed Joe outside and into my yard.

He looked to Tina's house so I looked to Tina's house and then stared.

The front yard, her trees, her fence, her bushes, everything was covered in toilet paper.

Once I got over the shock of seeing Tina's white, toilet-paper-strewn yard, I let out a strangled giggle.

"Know anything about that?" Joe asked, and I looked at him and shook my head.

"Nope," I lied.

Joe looked back at Tina's and noted, "Looks to me like Jessie Rourke's handiwork."

He was wrong. Toilet papering was Dee's idea.

I kept silent.

Joe looked at me again. "We got war here?"

"War?" I asked.

"She gonna retaliate?"

I thought it was highly unlikely Tina would retaliate with Joe's truck in my drive, but she was a bitch and I wasn't. What did I know what bitches did?

"Um…" I mumbled.

"She fucks with your yard, buddy, we got problems," Joe warned then suggested, "So maybe you two should have words, settle this."

"I'm sure it'll be all right," I assured him, *not* wanting to have words with Tina again.

"It isn't, I have to wade in, then it *really* won't be all right," Joe told me.

"Joe—"

"Talk to her."

"Joe—"

He got close, tipped his chin down and assumed his sinister look.

"Buddy, talk…to…her."

I tried to decide if I should mess with Joe when he was looking sinister.

This took half a second before I decided not to mess with Joe when he was looking sinister.

"All right," I muttered.

"Fuck," Joe muttered back, his eyes going to Tina's. "I finally find a woman and she's fuckin' friends with Jessie Rourke and enemies with Tina Blackstone."

Since he sounded aggravated, I suggested, "I'll make her cupcakes."

Joe looked at me and said not a word.

I bit my lip.

Joe looked at my mouth, shook his head then slung an arm around my shoulders and walked me back into my house.

When I got home after work that night, Joe wasn't home and neither were Kate and Keira.

I had three notes, two from Kate, one from Keira.

Note one:

*Heather's folks are taking us to Costa's. I get to wear my new dress, which looks awesome with my tan! Don't worry, using Joe's money to pay for mine. Will text you when I'm on my way home.*

*xxooxxoo-Keira*

I wondered if that was old Joe money or new Joe money he'd given her to go to Costa's. I decided to ask later when I wasn't tired after working all day. Or alternately, not to ask at all considering, being tired after working all day, my mood was unpredictable and I wasn't sure how I felt about Joe possibly giving Keira more money.

Note two:

*Joe said he's going to the office and he'll be home around the time you get home.*

*Xoxoxo -Kate*

Apparently Joe didn't write notes. Luckily Kate did.

Note three:

*Dane and I are going to a movie. We'll be back around nine.*

*Love you!*

*Xoxoxo -Kate*

I was alone in the house (again) so I went to the mailbox, got the mail, waved to Myrtle, went back in, let Mooch out of his box then let him outside taking my mail with me to open it while I kept an eye on Mooch. Once I sorted my mail, Mooch and I came back in. I dropped the post on the counter and went to fridge, trying to decide what to make for dinner.

While standing in the fridge, I heard Joe's truck in the drive. I closed the fridge, still not having decided what to make for dinner, and moved to open a cupboard and stare into that with the hopes of inspiration striking.

Joe walked in the side door. My eyes went to him, his eyes were already on me and he said, "Hey, buddy."

I smiled at him. "Hey, Joe."

He came right at me, hooked an arm around my waist, his head bent and his mouth hit mine for a short, hard, closed-mouthed kiss.

"Where are the girls?" he asked when he lifted his head and during the time I was thinking that my mood wasn't unpredictable anymore now that Joe was home and he'd given me a kiss (not to mention, him asking meant he didn't know Keira was at Costa's, which meant he hadn't given her money).

"Kate and Dane are at a movie. Keira is at Costa's with Heather's family," I informed him. He nodded but made no comment, so I went on to ask, "You hungry?"

"Could eat."

"Have a taste for anything?"

His eyes got intense and one side of his mouth went up in a grin, a new look, one that made my legs wobble.

I ignored my legs wobbling and prompted him to focus, "For food."

He let me go and muttered, "Steak."

"We don't have steak," I told him.

"I'll go out and get some," he replied, picking up my mail and beginning to sift through it.

"I'll make a quick list and go with you," I told him, and he again didn't speak as I went to the fridge. I got the pad of paper with the magnet on the back that was on the fridge door and opened the junk drawer to get a pen.

I was scratching down items to go with steak when Joe spoke.

"You need to call your bank and I'll give you Lindy's number so you can arrange to transfer your direct debits for the mortgage to my account."

My head came up and my surprised eyes went to him.

"What?" I asked.

He threw my mail down and turned to me, not answering my question but instead saying, "Utilities too. Lindy'll handle it."

"What?" I repeated.

"Mortgage and utilities to my accounts," Joe answered, and I changed my question.

"Why?"

"Why?" Joe repeated.

"Yes, um…why?"

"Live here, buddy," Joe answered.

"Yes, but, that's—"

Joe cut me off. "Pay my way."

I shook my head with confusion, then I got it and said, "Okay, I'm cool with that, but you can just give me a percentage, a quarter is fair."

"Pay your way too."

I blinked, back to confused. "I don't understand."

Joe leaned a hip to the counter and he studied me before asking, "What don't you understand?"

"Paying my way. I mean, that's generous but unnecessary. And it's really unnecessary to change the direct debits for the mortgage and utilities for just a couple of months."

Joe's eyebrows went up and his face darkened before he asked softly, "A couple of months?"

"Yes, if you want to contribute while you're stayin', I'm happy for you to do that. But you don't have to pay it all and we don't have to switch the direct debits because I'll only have to switch them back and that's a pain in the ass."

"While I'm stayin'?" Joe asked. He was studying me even closer and he was beginning to look a little scary.

"Yes, while you're stayin', until your house gets renovated."

"Sellin' the house once it's done, Vi, told you that."

"Yes, well…" I trailed off because it dawned on me rather belatedly that if he was selling his house that would mean he was moving, not living next door anymore. Then it hit me that he had a place in Florida and I wondered if that was where he was moving, which meant long distance relationship, or even worse, an end to "us."

And if it was Florida that would mean an end he already knew before he even moved in.

On that thought, my mood swung straight back to unpredictable and I asked somewhat sharply, "Where are you goin' after the house is renovated?"

"Not goin' anywhere."

"But if you're selling—"

"I'm staying here."

"Yes, but, then your house will be sold and fall is coming, winter's after that. Are you going to Florida?"

Joe put a hand to the counter and leaned slightly toward me. "Vi, stick with me, yeah? *I'm staying here.*"

He was getting impatient, but then again, so was I.

Not to mention I wasn't all that thrilled with him being patronizing.

"Yes, *I know that, Joe.* But what about after? You said you spent the winter in Florida. Is that where you're heading?"

"No, I'm staying here."

"For how long?" I asked.

"Jesus. For long enough to pay the fucking mortgage and utilities," he answered, losing patience. "How long's that say to you I'm stayin'?"

I stared at him, uncomprehending. Then I comprehended and my mouth dropped open.

Joe noticed and said with mild but undeniable sarcasm, "That's it, baby. I see it's penetrated."

I was moving from impatient to angry, as well as still confused with just a hint of afraid—a volatile combination.

"You're moving in?"

I watched as his eyebrows snapped together before he said, "I'm already in."

"Yes, for two months," I returned.

"No, for good," he shot back.

I shook my head, stunned at this news and said, "I didn't agree to that."

"I didn't exactly give you a choice, seein' as you were playin' games, fuckin' another guy and I needed to stake my claim. I did. I'm here. I'm stayin'."

The confused and afraid slid away, the angry snapped right into place.

"What did you just say?" I whispered.

"You heard me."

"I wasn't fucking Mike," I snapped.

"Right," he replied, the sarcasm less mild this time.

"I wasn't!" My voice was rising.

Joe's voice didn't rise. It got lower, which was even scarier. "He was caught on your hook. I've had a fair taste of you, Vi, man only gets that caught if he's had a taste."

I could not believe him.

I planted my hands on my hips and retorted, "Yes, Joe, he had *a taste.* That's all he had."

Joe's face went full-on scary when he returned, "I'll say it once, buddy, not a good idea to tell me about that shit."

"We were over!"

"We've never been over. We started when you begged me to fuck you and we've never been fucking over."

"You broke it off with me *twice*!" Yes, my voice was definitely rising.

"Not twice, it was you who tried to end it the second time."

"I *did* end it."

"Not even close."

"We were over!" I repeated.

"We weren't fuckin' over."

"We were!"

"Vi, since we started I been home twice when you weren't in my fuckin' bed. How the fuck is that over?"

I didn't know if this was true, though I reckoned it was, but it didn't matter. We were still over. However I knew I'd never convince Joe of that.

Therefore, I snapped, "It's ridiculous to fight about this."

"You're absolutely right," he bit out, making it sound like *I* was the one being ridiculous.

Not liking that one bit, I therefore declared, "You're not movin' in for good."

His face went from scary to sinister, he took two steps toward me, his legs being long meant this brought him into my space and he looked down at me.

"I'm in," he clipped.

"You can't be. This is too fast. The girls—"

"Yeah, the girls. Better for them I move in then move out for no fuckin' reason then move fuckin' in again?"

It pissed me off, but he had a point so I changed strategies.

"We haven't even been on a date!" I cried.

He stared at me like he didn't know who I was before he muttered irately, "Jesus Christ."

"Joe—" I started, but his hand came up, it did this fast, he hooked me at the back of my neck and pulled me in and up. I fell into his body, my hands going to his chest. He bent at the waist and neck and his face was an inch from mine.

"As fuckin' ridiculous and clueless as you're bein' right now, when you aren't bein' that, this is us. This is good. This is where we are and this is where we're stayin'. I'm not dickin' around with you anymore. I told you, I'm movin' in and I'm sellin' my house. Sellin' my house means I'd have no house, which means I'm *moving in*." Then he finished, now sounding not only angry but also frustrated at my stupidity. "Christ, Vi, what did you think?"

I didn't back down even knowing he was losing more of his temper, he was bigger than me, stronger than me and scarier than me. "Obviously, I thought you were staying until your house got renovated."

"Yeah, to get sold. Then what?"

"I didn't think about that!"

"No, you didn't, but that didn't mean I didn't fuckin' tell you."

"You didn't spell it out either!" I snapped.

"Maybe you might wanna learn to come to the obvious conclusion," he suggested.

"And maybe you might wanna learn that this is *me*. This is how *I am*. I've always got a million things on my mind. I don't need more, so you need to *spell it out*."

He didn't reply, just kept his mouth shut, but I saw a muscle flex in his jaw.

"We need to talk about you moving in," I went on, and his other arm went around me at the waist, pulling me into his body and he did this hard so my hands were caught between us.

"I'm in."

"Joe—"

He cut me off, saying, "Seventeen years…no, longer…I've been waitin' for you, waitin' for those girls. You're here and I'm lettin' go of my shit, finally fuckin' movin' on from all that. Movin' on to something good in my life, something to wake up and get outta bed for, and I'm not leavin' it because of some hang up you have. You and me, I haven't made it easy,

I'll admit that, but that's done. You gotta get over it or you're never gonna move on. I'm movin' on, Kate and Keira are movin' with me. It's only you who's gotta keep the fuck up."

I felt winded again, so I had to force out my, "Joe—"

"And I'm not livin' under the cloud of how it began, Vi. I fucked up. You know why, I explained it. You don't accept that, you keep handin' me this shit, we'll have problems we can't overcome and then I'll move on a different way and you'll be right back where you fuckin' started."

I felt my body get tight. "Are you threatening to leave?"

"I'm not livin' under that cloud," he repeated.

"How can you threaten to leave when you're arguing about staying?" I demanded to know (and I did this loudly).

"God fucking dammit," he bit out, his voice nearly a snarl. Then he let me go, turned away, ripped the sheet of paper off the top of the pad and stated, "I'm gettin' steaks. Sort your fuckin' head out while I'm gone."

And as I stood in the kitchen staring at him, he whistled for the dog and both Mooch and Joe walked out (well, Mooch kind of trotted). They went to his truck and they drove to the store.

Why he took Mooch, I had no idea and I was too angry to care.

The time he spent at the store I did not spend, as *ordered*, sorting my "fuckin'" head out. Instead, I spent it thinking Joe was a jerk and I should never have started it with him. I spent more time thinking this was never going to work, primarily because he was a jerk.

He arrived home with two bags of groceries in one hand, his phone at his ear in his other hand and Mooch, in doggie heaven after getting a ride in Joe's truck, at his heels.

He stayed on the phone while I started up the grill for the steaks and seasoned them (I also seasoned good steaks, salt and pepper, seasoning salt and Worcestershire sauce, brilliant), put some new potatoes on the boil and got the water ready for the peas when they needed to go in.

Then I took the steaks to the grill and was in the beginning processes of ruining them (with Tina sitting on her deck, reading a magazine and drinking a cocktail) when Joe came out and plucked the fork right out of my hand.

"I'm grilling steaks," I snapped, glaring up at him.

"Yeah, now I'm grilling steaks," Joe clipped back then fiddled with the knobs.

"What are you doing? I have it like I want it."

"It's too hot, Vi."

"So?"

"You're gonna burn 'em."

I crossed my arms on my chest, threw out a foot, tilted a hip and shot back, "I've been doing things just fine for nearly two years without your help. I think I can grill a couple fucking steaks."

He glowered at me. I glared right back. Then he said, "Right," handed me the fork and walked away.

I turned back to the grill and saw Tina smirking in my direction. I ignored her, readjusted the knobs and finished ruining the steaks.

Joe didn't get a chance to eat his ruined steak since he took off, not saying good-bye.

I added that to my list of reasons why he needed to move the fuck out right…fucking…away.

Keira and Kate were both home before Joe and they both asked where he was. Since he didn't tell me, I didn't have an answer. They decided, wisely, not to pursue it. They had, I didn't realize, been around when Tim and I fought and they knew, I didn't realize, that I could hold a mean grudge. So they steered clear.

In fact it was dark, the girls were asleep and I was in bed by the time Joe got home and I'd been in bed a really long time.

Long enough to cool down, get my head sorted out and remember three things.

One, Joe didn't have seventeen years with a partner to practice communication. Hell, I *did* have that time and Tim and I often got into tiffs, mainly because he was hot-headed and when my temper blew, it blew huge. I didn't know how long Joe and Bonnie were married but I didn't figure she was that good of a communicator and he certainly wasn't. I needed to cut him some slack.

Two, Jackie told me that the only way sure to fail was to give up and that was always the first thing on my mind, giving up on Joe. I needed to stop doing that.

And three, right in the middle of a fight he said he'd waited seventeen years (even longer) for me and my girls. I hadn't waited that long to find him but the time after losing Tim to finding Joe wasn't fun and I never wanted to repeat that again. So I couldn't imagine waiting seventeen years to find someone I gave a shit enough about to try out a life with them. After all that time, we'd given him something to wake up and get out of bed for, he told me that too, and that was huge. So I also needed to stop being a bitch.

I heard him enter the house then our room then I heard his clothes hit the floor and, seconds later, I felt it as he hit the bed.

I rolled into him instantly.

His body got tight.

"In no mood, buddy," he growled this warning, clearly not done being mad.

"I was a bitch," I replied. His body got tighter and I pressed closer and kept talking. "I didn't think it through. I have too much on my mind but you're important. I should have thought it through and I shouldn't have lost my temper when I was caught off guard." I kissed his neck and whispered in his ear, "I'm sorry, Joe."

He didn't reply, his body still taut, and he kept his silence for long enough for me to take a deep breath and a big risk and do everything I could not to give up on Joe.

So I slid to straddling him. His hands came to my hips and gripped them, probably to push me off. But I put my hands to either side of his head, dipped my face close to his, held on and peered at him through the dark.

"I'm gonna piss you off, honey, probably enough for you to want to leave. I've got a temper and so do you, we're gonna clash. It won't feel good, it'll feel not worth it sometimes but, you leave me, I'll wait for you to come back. And you'll come back because, something we've both learned, this, what we have is worth getting over it. Whatever it is that ticks us off or holds us back, we know it's worth fighting for. I won't give up on you, Joe, I promise. I just need you to promise the same thing."

He remained silent and I started getting scared, so I tilted my head so our foreheads were touching.

"Baby, don't give up on me," I whispered.

"Buddy, I came home," he replied, and it hit me that he did. It also hit me that his hands were still gripping my hips, not to push me away, he'd never tried to push me away. They were gripping my hips to hold me where I was. If he was giving up on me, he wouldn't have come home to my bed.

So my big speech was kind of unnecessary.

"Oh," I murmured. "Right."

"Jesus," he muttered then he rolled until I was on my back, his weight was on me, his hips between my legs and he said, "You're not real fast, are you?"

If he'd said this in an angry or sarcastic way, rather than a resigned and a tad bit amused way, I would have lost my mind.

Instead, I said honestly, "I'm not usually this clueless. But when my brother is murdered. I'm waiting for the next crazy gift to be delivered to my door which might cause my head to explode. I fall in love with a man and he moves in. And I have a future that includes another kid and I need to figure out how I'm gonna tell my daughters they might have a brother or sister sometime in the future, I get a little out of it. In my defense, most women would."

"What?" Joe asked when I stopped talking and I realized his body had gone tense again. So tense it felt like even his cells had stopped moving, he had that tight a rein.

I put a hand to his face and answered, "I thought you said you wanted a kid."

"Before that."

I thought for a second and asked, "My head exploding?"

His body moved but only to press mine deeper into the bed.

"After that, Vi," he growled, and I was getting confused again because he was sounding impatient again, very impatient, close to losing it impatient.

"I'm in love with you?" I asked quietly.

"Yeah, baby, that."

"What about it?"

"What about it?" he repeated.

"Yeah, um…do you…uh…" Shit! He wasn't ready for that. Now what did I say? "Is that too much for you? Should I have—?"

He cut me off by roaring with laughter. *Roaring.* So loud I was pretty sure he'd wake the girls (and Mooch).

"What's funny?" I asked him, and he shoved his face in my neck but his hands started roaming.

"You think maybe you might have wanted to tell me that?"

"Tell you what?"

His head came up. "Honey, keep up with me because this is pretty fuckin' important."

I felt my temperature increase as my anger elevated and I did my best to lock it down.

"I'm not following you, Joe. Maybe you could explain?"

His mouth came to mine and he whispered, "You're in love with me."

"Well, yeah."

"Didn't you think maybe you should share that with me?"

"Um…I thought I did."

He kissed me lightly then his mouth went away but not far away when he said, "Woulda remembered that, buddy."

"But, I gave up Mike and you're moved in."

"Yeah. So?"

"With me and the girls."

He didn't say, "Yeah. So?" again, he let his silence say it.

"Doesn't that say it all?" I asked. "I mean, I wouldn't let just any guy move in with me and the girls. I'm not like that. He'd have to mean something to me, like you do."

I felt his body relax into mine before he asked quietly, "When did you know?"

"What?"

"That you loved me. When did you know?"

I felt my temperature decrease and my hand slid up his back and into his hair. "I don't know. I just knew," I answered softly.

"Vi—" he said my name on a gentle warning.

Quickly, to get it out because, being Joe, he wasn't going to let it go and when I said it, it was going to make me sound stupid, I told him. "When you said, 'Baby, you aren't wearing any shoes' that second night we were together at your house."

Immediately he replied, "I knew you were the one when you were standin' in my living room, wearing those stupid-ass boots, your nightie and that ratty robe."

"That was the night we first met."

"Yep."

I was the one for Joe and he knew it the first night we met.

He knew I was the one. The one. *The one.*

And he knew it the first night we met.

I felt tears sting my eyes and my other arm wrapped tight around him.

"Joe," I whispered.

His mouth came to mine again as his hands lifted my legs to wrap them around his hips and he whispered back, "I love you, baby." I felt my breath hitch and the tears slid out the sides of my eyes, but he wasn't done. "And I'm not fuckin' movin' out."

"Okay," I replied instantly.

I felt him smile against my mouth then I felt his hand slide into my panties to cup my ass. He kissed me, and after that, he made love to me. He took his time, he let me take mine and it was better than any other time before.

So that was saying something.

After, Joe called, "Vi?"

"Yeah, baby?" I said into his chest.

"Move the mortgage and utilities, yeah?"

I sucked in breath then said, "Maybe we should—"

"Move 'em."

"Joe—"

His hand slid into my hair, fisted, and he tilted my head back as he lifted his and dipped his chin.

"Not gonna say it again, baby," he said softly.

"I've got more on my scales," I whispered in reply.

His fist unclenched and his hand cupped the back of my head as he asked, "What?"

"You keep unbalancing the scales, giving me more. It's not fair."

He was silent a second then he asked quietly, "You shittin' me?"

I shook my head.

His other arm went around me and he pulled me up his chest until I was face to face with him.

Then he spoke.

"Since I could remember, all I wanted was a family. My mom died, my dad lost it and I'd go to Aunt Theresa and Uncle Vinnie's house, bein' with their family. A family that was loud and in your business, which part of the time was annoying as hell but the rest of the time it just felt good because they were that way because they gave a shit. And I wanted that. My dad was so deep in his grief he lost his way and he forgot to give a shit. So I never had that, not at home. I got older and that changed and all I wanted was a good woman and a family. All my life, with a slight variation on theme, that's all I ever wanted. Buddy, you've given me both. You think, givin' me that, I could *ever* balance those scales?"

I didn't say anything, couldn't, because I was crying.

Joe wrapped his arms around me, rolled us to our sides and held me while I did it. Once I stopped crying, his hand came up, and he dried my tears with his thumb.

Then he whispered, "Move the mortgage and utilities, yeah?"

"Okay, Joe."

He tucked my face in his throat and he was still whispering when he said, "Love you, buddy."

"Love you too, Joe."

"Sleep."

"Okay. 'Night, honey."

"'Night, baby."

I lay in his arms and thought I'd been lucky, getting pregnant at seventeen by the love of my life. I'd even known I was lucky all those years I had Tim.

Until I lost the love of my life.

And here I was, with all the shit that had gone down, finding myself just that lucky again.

I cuddled closer to Joe Callahan then I fell asleep.

I didn't have a nightmare that night.

I slept the whole night through like a log, didn't wake up once.

Wednesday went by mostly without incident.

That was if you didn't count me coming home from work and Keira rushing out of her room, arms wheeling, Mooch following her yapping as she ran down the hall, shouting, "Joe bought us new computers!"

That day Kate had off from the Custard Stand, so I knew Joe and the girls were going out to make final decisions on kitchen appliances, faucets for both kitchen and bathroom and to select tile for Joe's house.

As far as I knew, computers weren't in the mix.

"New computers?" I asked my daughter as she skidded to a halt in front of me (though Mooch came right at me and jumped around my legs).

"Yeah!" she shouted, her face alight with glee.

"Computers. As in, plural?" I went on, bending down to pick up Mooch and give him a snuggle.

"Yeah, one for Kate, one for me and a new desktop to replace our old one and act as a server." Keira was watching my face, reading my expression and sensing my reaction. Therefore her enthusiasm faded and she quickly explained, "Joe says they're for homework. He says we need 'em for school. He says our old one is too old and one computer for four people is ridiculous in this day and age."

I let this information sink in, hearing Joe speaking these words in my head (and he probably used the f-word somewhere while saying them) as I juggled Mooch, dumped my purse on the counter and reminded myself that Joe had just got the family he always wanted. He was making up for lost time. It wouldn't be good for me to blow my stack at Joe's alarming tendency to spoil my daughters every chance he got. I had to be patient with him and find the right time to explain that new computers and the like were things family discussed. Or, more to the point, things *adults* discussed prior to them being purchased.

Then I heard what sounded like a drill.

"Is that a drill?" I asked Keira.

Keira turned her ankle to the side, bit her lip and stated, "Well, Joe decided we also needed desks to put our computers on while we're doin' our homework and..." She hesitated. "Um..." She hesitated again. "Shelves for our books."

"*Joe!*" I shouted, forgetting about patience.

Mooch yapped and Keira jumped.

Then Keira muttered, "Uh-oh."

The drill kept right on going as I dropped Mooch and stalked down the hall, repeating on a shout, "Joe!"

The drill stopped when I turned at the door to Keira's room and saw Kate holding up some shelves (that I had to admit, to myself only, looked really good in Keira's room). Joe was standing with her, his neck twisted to look at me standing in the door. I also saw there was a desk that matched the shelves. Both were painted white, both were immensely girlie, and the desk had a laptop on it, the cover looked like it was purple glitter.

I was screwed. Keira was never going to give up a laptop with a purple glitter cover.

My narrowed eyes went to Joe. Mooch, having come to sit by my feet, yapped, giving me puppy backup.

Kate's cautious eyes went beyond me to where I knew Keira was standing.

Joe put the drill on a shelf and moved toward me.

"In our room," I demanded. "We gotta talk."

He didn't let me turn and stomp to our room. Before I moved an inch, he hooked me with an arm at my waist, pulling my stiff frame into the room as well as into his body. I realized he was fighting a smile as I watched his face dip close to mine.

"Baby, you don't even have Wi-Fi," he said, and, being Joe, he started his explanation somewhere in the middle.

It was true. We didn't have Wi-Fi, because we didn't *need* Wi-Fi because we only had *one* computer.

"We gotta talk," I repeated.

"Girls can't get shit done, sharin' a computer," he went on.

"Bedroom. Talk," I bit out.

"Now they can work anywhere in the house where they're comfortable. They'll be more productive," Joe continued.

This made sense.

I didn't give him this point. Instead, I snapped, "Joe—"

His head dipped closer and he touched his mouth to mine, effectively quieting me before he continued. "Katy's gonna be a junior. She told me she's college prep, come second semester, she'll already be takin' college credit courses. Work's gonna get tougher. She'll need her own space to concentrate and she'll need a system to take with her when she goes away to school."

"Right," I replied sarcastically. "The rate your goin', you're not gonna buy her a new one before she goes off to college."

At my words, firm indication to Joe, as well as the girls, that Joe was going to be there in two years to get Kate a new computer, Joe's eyes went soft, his face grew tender and he grinned at me. Through this, I heard Keira stifle a giggle and Kate cough to hide her laugh.

Hearing my daughters' amusement, seeing Joe's face like that, I forgot why I was mad.

Joe saw it, or sensed it, and his arm around me tightened.

"If it makes you feel better, Kate bought the new beanbag for her room with her own money," Joe told me, and I rolled my eyes but I did this mostly for show.

When I rolled them back and looked at Joe, I stated, "No more shopping in your truck. You take my girls shopping, it has to be in the Mustang. Furniture and beanbags don't fit in a Mustang."

Joe was still grinning when he asked, "How'll you get to work?"

"We'll trade cars."

His arm gave me a squeeze and he said, "You don't drive my ride, honey. No one but me drives my ride."

"Why? You drive mine," I reminded him.

"Yeah, but I'm a guy," Joe answered.

"This is true, Joe's a guy," Keira put in, coming to stand at our sides.

I looked at Keira, now trying to fight my own smile then back at Joe before pointing out, "Yeah, you're a guy. Why're you shoppin' at all?"

"Rulebook says I can shop for furniture and shit with plugs. The beanbag was pushin' it. But since I didn't pay for it, I get a bye on that," Joe explained and I heard mirth burst forth from both girls again, this time they didn't smother it.

I put my hands on Joe's arms and, giving in, I asked, "Are those shelves gonna be done by dinner?"

Joe gave me another squeeze then he touched his lips to mine before letting me go, moving back to the shelves and saying, "Depends if dinner's gonna be ready in ten minutes or thirty."

I wanted to know what dinner took ten minutes to be ready. Then I wanted to know if it was any good and not nuked in a microwave.

I didn't ask, I answered, "Thirty, at least."

Joe picked up the drill and looked at me. "Then, yeah."

I looked at Kate, who was smiling a small smile and still holding up the shelves. Then I looked at Keira, who was standing at her new girlie desk, her fingertips on her new laptop, also smiling, but hers wasn't small. Then I looked at Mooch who was sniffing around on the floor, likely trying to find something to destroy with his puppy teeth. Then I looked at the girlie shelves that looked so good in Keira's room. Finally, I looked at Joe.

"We're eating at the table," I informed them, my eyes still on Joe.

"Works for me," Joe muttered, tilting his head and aiming the drill at the shelves.

"Me too," Kate put in.

"Me three!" Keira added.

The drill whirred. I shook my head and left the room, going to Kate's room to see she had black lacquered shelves and desk, a sleek, shiny black laptop, and a leopard print, furry beanbag. She'd already re-decorated, moving books and knickknacks she'd had piled on her dresser and nightstand to her new shelves and desk and rearranging posters.

This looked good too.

Though she'd need more books and knickknacks to fill it out.

I smiled as I walked to the kitchen. I made dinner with Mooch helping me (partly because I think he was afraid of the drill, partly because he knew I'd feed him scraps). We ate at the table. I did the dishes while the girls played with their laptops and did more redecorating.

When I was done with the dishes, Joe showed me around the new computer in the study that already had four users programmed in it, the names all in a column, starting with "Joe" on top, "Violet" under that then "Kate" then "Keira."

Something about our names all in a column on the family computer struck me. It was a good hit. So good, I wondered why anyone on earth would need drugs. You could get high just having a family.

Later, we climbed into the Mustang and went to Fulsham's Frozen Custard Stand. Joe and I got cones, the girls got turtle sundaes. While we ate them, Joe and Kate sat side by side on the top of a picnic table outside while Keira sat on the seat by Kate's feet and I sat on the seat by Joe's feet, my back leaning into his legs.

I listened to Kate and Keira talk to Joe, Joe not saying much, Keira talking most, but both Kate and Keira including him. Kate talking about her music and Keira talking about Joe's house.

While I listened, I noticed people looking at us. They didn't stare but their curiosity was obvious.

It was hot and muggy. We needed a storm to erase the humidity but hadn't had one in days. Because of this and summer coming to an end, school starting soon, the Stand was busy, tons of kids, some couples, more families.

Studying our onlookers, I noticed Joe was the focal point of their curiosity, the girls and I too, but not so much. It was clearly a sight to see, Lone Wolf Joe Callahan out with a woman and her two teenage daughters.

Again, this disturbed me. I couldn't put my finger on why and I told myself eventually it would go away, people would get used to us and that bad feeling I got would fade.

We went back home and the girls went to their rooms and back to their new toys. Joe went to the fridge, opened a bottle of white wine, poured a glass for me, got himself a beer and we went out to the deck. He pulled the chairs to the railing and we sat, side by side, our knees cocked, feet up on the railing, sipping wine and beer. At this point, I figured, since I loved him, since we'd had a good night and since this was us, it was good and this was going to be the way it was, I needed to know more about Joe.

So I asked Joe questions.

He didn't hesitate with any of his responses. Including the scary ones, such as him getting the scar on his belly a long time ago when he was a bouncer and some drunk guy slashed him with a knife.

At my indrawn breath, Joe murmured in a gentle voice, "It wasn't deep, baby, didn't cause any harm."

I didn't point out that it did, seeing as it left a scar. I just asked about the other one.

That one was scarier, seeing as it was a scar from a bullet wound Joe got while bodyguarding. He didn't say who he was guarding, apparently this was secret information and if he told me, he'd have to kill me (though Joe didn't explain it that way, he just said. "Can't tell you, Vi, so don't ask.").

What he did say was, "After that, focused on the systems. Dyin' young to protect assholes I didn't like fucked with my plan for retirement."

This was funny, Joe cracking another joke, and I laughed.

But I also leaned to the side, putting my head on Joe's shoulder and dropping my legs so they rested against his.

In return, Joe slid an arm along my shoulders and pulled me closer. The chair handle bit into my side but I didn't care. Bobbie had some lawn furniture that almost matched mine and there was a loveseat-style piece so I decided, since I didn't have to pay a mortgage anymore, and since I liked sitting outside with Joe, our knees cocked, feet to the railing, I was going to buy it.

While we did this, I thought that it was good Joe was wise and he had a plan for retirement. If he'd been gung ho macho, taking these jobs just for the money and the thrill and not thinking about his future, he might not be there, on my deck, drinking beer with me at his side and my girls in the house.

And I liked him there.

But I'd like it better once I bought that loveseat.

After the scary portion of the evening's conversation was over, Joe got up and got himself another beer, refilled my wine and he came back. We made plans to ask Lindy to come to dinner so the girls and I could meet her and we talked about the upcoming visit from my in-laws, something Joe didn't seem all that concerned about.

"They're people Vi, they got two choices. They like me or they don't. I deal either way. They're good people, even if they don't, they won't make it your problem or the girls'."

He was right. They had two choices and, knowing Bea and Gary, they wouldn't make it my problem or the girls' if they didn't like Joe.

The girls came out and said goodnight, first Keira who patted Joe on the arm but gave me her usual kiss. Then Kate, who gave me a kiss but didn't touch Joe. She just said, "'Night, Joe," to which he muttered, "Sweet dreams, girl," which made her look at me in that startled way the girls looked whenever Joe did something affectionate. But, startled or not, one day I figured they too would get used to being around an affectionate Joe.

Joe and I sat quiet for a while and this would have been nice if my mind didn't wander to Mike, wondering what he was doing, wondering if he was okay. I was also thinking how much it sucked that our situation wasn't one where we could shift to friends and I could call him, just to talk. I liked talking to him (amongst other things) and I didn't like that I no longer could do it. He didn't say that wasn't cool, but I knew in my heart it wasn't. I was happy with my decision and I knew I'd made the right one. But that didn't mean I didn't miss Mike.

However, I didn't share this with Joe.

Joe and I eventually went to bed and I figured, both of us being in a mellow mood, having a good night, he'd feel in the mood to make love and I was looking forward to it.

He wasn't. He was in the mood to fuck me, rough and hard, both of us on our knees, Joe behind me, his fingers between my legs, the fingers of his other hand working my nipple. I was mostly up, bent slightly, my hand holding onto the headboard, my other hand covering his at my breast and I was trying not to be too loud when he made me come. By some miracle, I managed this and luckily Joe had my neck to stifle his groan when he climaxed.

After, Joe kept me where I was and stayed buried inside me.

"You got the sweetest cunt I've ever had, buddy," he whispered in my ear, sliding out and gliding back in.

It wasn't the most flowery compliment in the history of man, but from Joe, who stayed planted and was filling me with his big cock, it worked really well.

"I like your cock too," I whispered back and felt him smile against my neck.

"Know that, Vi. Every time I fuck you, you act like it's been years since I've been inside you."

I twisted my neck to look at him and his head came up.

"You don't have to be conceited about it."

He pressed in deeper, heard my soft gasp and chuckled. "Baby, you don't want me to be conceited, maybe you should stop doin' shit like that."

I sighed, too mellow to have a tiff, even a lighthearted one.

Joe kissed my neck and pulled out. We settled in our usual position, the one with my head in his chest, and his fingertips roamed my ass and hip while I listened to his heartbeat and fell asleep.

I didn't have the nightmare that night either.

Thursday, I got home from work and barely got inside the door before Joe and the girls hustled me right back out.

Back to school shopping.

I didn't ask why Joe came with us, I was just glad he did.

We had dinner at a restaurant outside the mall then we went inside the mall and the girls bought some new outfits for school. They bought Joe his new shirt (which he didn't try on, but luckily it fit him). And I bought gifts for Bea and Gary, some new frames to replace the ones I broke and a few little nothings to send up to Mel in an effort to brighten her day.

Joe didn't pay for the shirt or the gifts for Bea, Gary and Mel, but he paid for some of the girls' clothes and the frames, even though I tried to pay. We had words right in front of the clerks in four different stores. Each time my fearless Keira waded in, twice taking my credit card and handing it to the clerk, twice taking Joe's. Neither Joe nor I could protest because this was Keira, what could we say?

While we were walking to the car, Joe used his arm around my shoulders to pull me close as he said in my ear. "Keirry's a natural diplomat."

He sounded proud. So proud I couldn't stop myself from turning my head and kissing his neck. He gave me a squeeze in return.

When we got home, inexplicably, Joe slowed as we drove in front of the house and he stopped on the street.

I looked at him and his head was turned toward the house.

"Joe, what—?"

I stopped when I looked at the house too, saw my yard and gasped in outrage. In now dead grass, the word "bitch" could clearly be seen. I hadn't driven in front of the house that day or the day before for that matter and obviously Joe nor the girls had seen it.

Joe exploded, "That fuckin' *cunt*!"

Both girls gasped, I jumped and Joe accelerated the Mustang off the street and into our drive so fast I knew he was beyond pissed, thus it probably wasn't the time to inform him that the c-word in front of the girls was an absolute forbidden.

Joe stopped the car, killed the ignition, opened his door and surged out of the car, stalking straight to Tina's.

I realized at this juncture that I should probably have taken her some cupcakes.

I turned to the girls and ordered, "Go into the house."

"Mom—" Keira started.

"House!" I demanded, opened my door, got out and ran to Tina's, hoping my girls would obey (Kate would; Keira, it was a crapshoot).

As I jumped the fence, Joe stopped pounding on the door, turned to look at Tina's sporty, red Corvette in the drive then he turned away and stalked down her steps.

As he got close to me, I assured him, "I'll talk to her."

Joe didn't look at me. He kept walking and I watched as he put a hand to the fence, threw his legs over it, landed on the other side, walked straight to his house, around it and then he disappeared, going to his garage.

I didn't know what Joe had in his garage, except his *Bullitt* car, the hood of which I knew intimately. But I didn't figure Joe going there was a good sign.

I also saw my girls didn't obey, not even Kate. They were standing in the yard. Kate was staring at the grass, looking pissed. Keira was staring after Joe, looking worried.

I jogged to Tina's door and knocked, shouting, "Tina, really, you need to open up. We need to talk before Joe gets back."

She didn't open the door. I knocked and called again. She still didn't open the door. I was knocking again when Joe was suddenly there.

He pushed me to the side and went into a squat. Then he did something with little tools at her lock, the door opened, he straightened and strode right in.

I stood in stupefied silence, not only because my boyfriend knew how to pick a lock but would and *did*, until I heard Tina screech, "What the fuck? You can't just walk into my house! I'm callin' the cops!"

"Call 'em, I'll wait," Joe replied, and I rushed in to see Tina at the mouth of her hall, Joe standing in the living room in his scary as shit, sinister, arms-crossed-on-chest, badass, alpha male stance.

"You broke in!" Tina shrieked.

"Yep," Joe agreed.

"What the fuck?" Tina repeated.

"Okay, everyone just—" I started.

Joe cut me off by ordering Tina, "Write a check. Five hundred dollars. Made out to Violet Winters and do it now."

"You're fuckin' *crazy*!" Tina screeched.

"You do it, this is done, no more," Joe stated. "You don't, I'm in this war and, trust me woman, you do not want me in this war. I'm done with you, you'll move to the next fuckin' county."

"Are you threatening me?" Tina snapped, leaning forward, clearly having a death wish.

"Yep," Joe replied, calm as could be.

"You can't break in my house and threaten me!" Tina yelled.

Joe looked around then back at Tina. "Pay attention, bitch, I just did."

Oh Lord.

I walked across the room and got close to Joe, wrapping my hands around his bicep, which was usually firm but now it was flexed and it felt like steel.

"Joe, honey, go home. I'll talk with Tina."

He twisted his neck and looked down at me. "Gave you that chance, buddy. I told you she fucks with your yard, we got problems."

"But, Joe—"

"She fucked with your yard, we got problems."

"*She* toilet papered *my* yard!" Tina shouted. "It took me hours to clean that shit up."

Joe looked back at Tina and I could only see his profile and it scared me. She got the full face and shrank back.

"She didn't do that to your yard, woman, she was in bed with me. You shit where you live, pissin' people off, you gotta expect retribution. And you make a habit of shittin' where you live. Who fuckin' knows who did that to your yard? All I know is, it wasn't Vi. You retaliated against the wrong person that person is my woman and your retaliation crossed a line. She can't clean that shit up without it costin' her and you're gonna fuckin' pay for it."

"Fuck you!" Tina shouted, and Joe shrugged, dropped his arms and turned away.

"So be it," he muttered, sliding a hand along my shoulders and moving me to the door where he stopped and turned back to Tina. "I was you, I'd think about it. You got until tomorrow mornin' to put a check in Vi's mailbox. You don't, it's on. You get me?"

"I'm callin' the cops," Tina returned.

"You think Mike Haines and Alec Colton and the boys who work with 'em are gonna be fired up to help you?" Joe asked, this finally penetrated, and Tina's face twisted. "Yeah," Joe murmured as he noticed Tina was realizing maybe she should have made some friends along with all the enemies she created along the way. "Five hundred dollars, Tina, in Vi's mailbox by nine o'clock tomorrow morning," he finished then he turned us again and walked us out the door.

When we hit the fence, he picked me up and lifted me over, setting me on my feet. He jumped it, took my hand and walked us to the dead grass in my yard where the girls were standing.

"It smells of bleach," Keira informed us. Joe's mouth got tight, Kate saw it and shoved Keira's arm.

"All right girls, take the shopping bags in the house," I ordered, wondering if I'd have time to do anything about my yard before Bea and Gary got there and thinking I wouldn't considering I only had one day and I'd be working that day.

"Should we—?" Kate started and I looked at her.

"House, baby," I said softly. "We'll worry about this tomorrow, yeah?"

She nodded, tagged Keira, they went to the Mustang, got the bags and went into the house. Joe stood staring at the word in my lawn.

"You okay?" I asked.

"Hope that check isn't in your box, buddy," Joe said to the yard then looked at me. "Be my pleasure to fuck with that bitch."

I looked at his face and hoped the check was in my box. Tina was indeed a bitch and her writing the same with bleach in my beautiful grass proved it. But I reckoned no one, not even Tina, deserved the fury Joe looked ready to unleash.

"You want a beer?" I asked and Joe stared at me.

Then he shook his head but answered, "Yeah."

We walked in the house, my arm around his waist, his around my shoulders.

"It's just grass," I told him softly.

He stopped us at the front door and curled me into his front. "Yeah, Vi, it's just grass. And your brother just died. I'd have a lot more patience with her shit if it was two months ago or six months from now. She's not gonna change but she should be human enough to pick her times. She wasn't so I hope that check is not in your box. She needs a lesson and I'm in the mood to give her one."

"Joe—"

His head dipped down and he touched his lips to mine before saying, "Don't worry, baby, whatever I do won't blow back on us."

"But, she's alone. Cory hasn't been back for ages and she's—"

He interrupted me. "A woman who needs a lesson."

"Joe—"

"Vi, beer."

I studied him and I knew enough to know Joe had made up his mind.

Therefore, I sighed, walked in my house and got my man a beer.

It was dark, the girls were asleep and I was cuddled into Joe's side.

"Joe?" I called.

"Yeah, baby," he answered.

"Scales are even," I told him on a whisper.

"What?" he asked.

I closed my eyes, pressed closer, opened my eyes and kept whispering. "Missed Tim, missed a lot of things about him. One of those things was knowin' there was someone who'd look out for me, the girls." I pressed my lips together and bit them both as I felt his body grow tight before I continued. "Remember that night we met? I had to get out of bed in the middle of the night to ask Kenzie to turn down the music?"

"Baby—"

"Tim would have done that. I wouldn't have had to put on those boots and go into the cold."

"Vi—"

"I wouldn't have had to leave our bed."

He rolled into me, murmuring again, "Vi—"

"I wouldn't have had to tromp through the snow, get cold or even get angry."

His hands started moving on me under his tee as he whispered, "Shut up, buddy."

"Tim always had our backs. He never let anything like that touch us. Never."

"Vi, shut it."

"You won't either."

"Shut it, Vi."

"We had everything. Everything. Tim gave it to us. Having Nicky, you had a lot, Joe, but you never had everything, so you can't know how much it hurts to lose it."

Joe was silent.

I kept talking. "Having it back, you giving it to us, the scales are balanced."

He didn't tell me to shut up again. He kissed me, not hard and greedy and demanding. No, it was long and tender and beautiful.

When he was done, he tucked my face into his throat and held me.

"Love you, Joe," I whispered to his throat.

"Love you too, buddy. Go to sleep."

"Okay. 'Night, honey."

"'Night, baby."

It took a while for me to sleep. It took longer for Joe. I knew this because I fell asleep before him.

It was strange I got to sleep because my mind was focused on wondering what was on his.

But I got to sleep.

And I again slept the night through without the nightmare.

The check was in the box the next morning well before nine.

Tina was a bitch but she was no fool.

Joe looked annoyed. I was relieved.

The girls were both up early. Kate had her last shift noon to four at the Custard Stand before quitting to go back to school on Monday. Keira had a full day of sunbathing and pool frolicking ahead of her at Heather's, her last hurrah before school started. I'd gotten them up because I needed to give them instructions before I left and they started their days.

"Keirry, baby, can you clean your bathroom before you go to Heather's?" I asked, though I didn't expect an answer. I just expected her to complain about it then do it. So to avoid the complaining I hurriedly turned to Kate and went on. "And can you vacuum and dust before you go to work? I'll mop the kitchen after dinner tonight, but I'll be late because I have to do the big shop for Gramma and Grandpap before I get home."

Before Kate could agree and Keira could bitch, Joe said, "Make a list, I'll swing by the store after I deal with the yard."

All three pairs of Winters girls' eyes went to Joe.

It was me who spoke.

"Deal with the yard?" I asked.

"Tim's folks'll be here tomorrow, buddy. Can't have that word bleached into the lawn," Joe answered.

This was true but a quick fix was virtually impossible unless you, say, killed all the grass around the letters. This was an option which held merit since I didn't want Bea and Gary to see the lawn like that and worry. But after the care I'd taken with my lawn, it wasn't one I liked overly much.

"How are you gonna deal with it?" I asked with curiosity.

"Dig it out. I'll be at the garden center sometime late mornin' to pick up some rolls of sod."

I hadn't thought of this option mainly because that was a lot of work, it would take a lot of time and it would cost some cake. The first one I could do. The second one, no way (making, for me, the task impossible, but not for Joe). The last one, since Joe was paying for everything, was also doable, but I wasn't used to having leftover money yet so it didn't spring to mind.

I had thought of watering the hell out of the yard to drain away the bleach and sprinkling grass seed then watering the hell out of the yard again. This would mean the word "bitch" would be in my yard for weeks, maybe months, which sucked.

Joe's solution was *so much better.*

Before I could tell him that, Keira piped up. "I'll help you!"

My mouth dropped open. So did Kate's.

Keira giving up sunbathing and pool frolicking to help Joe in the yard was a miracle. Such a miracle, if I was a Catholic, I'd notify the Vatican, no joke.

Again, before I could say anything, Joe, who was sitting on a stool next to Keira (Kate was behind the counter with me), reached out and wrapped a big hand around the back of her neck. Then he gently swayed her side to side.

"You're with me, honey, we'll have it done in no time."

Keira beamed at Joe. Kate turned startled eyes to me. I wished I had time to lead Joe to our room and rip his clothes off.

Since I had to go to work, instead I said to Joe, "Walk me to my car?"

Joe's eyes came to me. He nodded, gave Keira one last sway with his hand, let her go and walked me to my car.

I unlocked it, opened the door and stood in it as Joe came to stand in front of me.

Then I bunched his tee in my fist, pulled him closer, got up on tiptoe to get close to his face and whispered, "Anything you want."

His head jerked slightly and he asked, "What?"

"Tonight, payback for the yard, payback for makin' Keira smile like that, anything you want. You name it, I'll do it."

A slow smile spread on his face as his hands went to span my hips.

"That's quite an offer, buddy."

I got closer, both my body and my face to his, and I kept whispering. "Be creative, baby, don't know when I'll be feelin' this generous again."

"Oh, I'll be creative," he whispered back, and I felt my nipples get hard.

My hands slid up his chest and around his neck and I laid one on him, my brand of a hard and demanding kiss, and Joe liked it. I knew this because his arms wrapped around me and he growled in my mouth.

"Love you, baby," I whispered against his lips when I was done kissing him.

"Yeah, me too." He touched his mouth to mine then said, "You get a break, make a list for the grocery store. I'll pick it up when Keira and I come 'round to get the sod."

"Okay."

"I'll grill some brats tonight."

"Okay."

"We'll get store bought shit to go with the brats. Don't want you cookin', you'll need to conserve your energy."

I shivered at what his words meant and repeated, "Okay."

He grinned and it hit me he was grinning a lot lately. Smiling too. I liked this so I smiled back but I suspected my smile was a lot like Keira's beam. I suspected this because Joe's eyes dropped to my mouth, his face got intense and then he kissed me, hard and demanding.

He did it better.

When I got home that evening, the yard looked like a yard. No yellow-brown "bitch" in the middle of it. Joe and Keira did such a good job you could barely see the sod lines. And the rest of the yard had been mowed.

I walked into the house, seeing it clean and tidy. Even the kitchen was sparkling, including the floor.

I knew why when Keira came running from her bedroom, a boy band playing loud, so she shouted over it, "I cleaned the kitchen!"

I smiled at her. "I can see, baby."

"And the bathroom," she went on as I put my purse on the counter.

"Thanks, honey."

"Kate vacuumed and dusted and I put the pictures back in the frames," Keira continued, pointing to the pictures, which were in the frames and back on our shelves.

I looked but I didn't look closely. I wanted them back where they were but I wasn't ready to see pictures of Sam just yet.

Keira finished with, "Joe wanted you to put your feet up when you got home."

I bet he did.

At this, my smile widened and the back sliding glass door opened, Joe coming through it followed by a prancing Mooch. He looked sweaty and hot, seeing as he was sweating while wearing nothing but a pair of cutoff jeans and running shoes. He didn't even have on socks.

My mouth went dry.

"Joe mowed the yard." Keira kept the information flowing.

"Mm-hmm," was all I could get out seeing as my eyes were still glued to a sweaty, hot-looking, cutoff jeans wearing, bare-chested Joe.

Joe came to me, curled his hand around my head and pulled me up, giving my mouth a touch with his.

"Gotta shower," he muttered, then he turned away, nabbed Keira the same way as he walked by her but he kissed the side of her head.

Keira beamed up at him. Joe grinned down at her. Then he went to our room.

Keira looked back at me. "Joe says I'm the best assistant he's ever had. He's gonna teach me *security*!"

I was trying to listen to my daughter, but mostly I was thinking of Joe in the shower.

"That's great, honey," I muttered as I walked to the fridge and opened it in order to open a bottle of wine, thinking I should put my feet up and relax, starting now. Joe probably intended to be energetic, but even if he didn't, I did.

Then I stopped and stared in my fridge, which was so packed full of food, it was a wonder it didn't explode.

"What the…?"

"Oh, yeah, forgot to say, Joe and me, we went a little crazy at the grocery store," Keira told me, and I turned stiltedly to her to see she was walking back toward her room. "He said to put anything I wanted in the cart and anything you or Kate liked. So I did."

"Keira, honey, it'll take us a year to get through this much food," I called after her.

She stopped at the entry to the hall and turned back to me. "Yeah. So?"

Oh Lord, she was sounding like Joe and I had no idea if this was good or bad.

I also had no reply.

Fifteen minutes later, Joe was out of the shower, dressed in tee and jeans and in the kitchen getting a beer. I was sipping my wine, waiting for him to get a beer so I could sit out on the deck while he grilled. The boy band music was gone and Keira was on her back on the couch, marathon texting some boy (or, considering the number of beeps from her phone, half a dozen of them). And Mooch was gnawing a dog toy to shit when Dane's yellow pickup hit the drive.

Dane always took Kate to and picked her up from work. She'd been off work for over an hour and a half, but this wasn't unusual. They'd often dink around, doing their thing (what that was I did *not* want to know) or meeting with friends before he'd bring her home.

Therefore I wasn't paying much attention when I heard the pickup in the drive. I was watching Joe twist the top off a beer and then toss it in the bin.

The front door opened and it slammed, hard and *loud.*

Joe's head shot around to the door and I turned on my stool to see Kate stomp in, stop, take us all in, then shout, "*Never*! I'm *never* speaking to him again! If he calls or comes to the door, I do *not* want to talk to him and I do *not* want to see him. *Ever again*!"

She then burst into tears and ran to her room, slamming the door.

"Oh shit," I muttered, my eyes going to Joe who was looking at the hall. His head swung around to the window and he watched the pickup speeding away.

I put my wineglass down, slid off the stool and announced, "I'll go talk to her."

I went to Kate's room, knocked once and opened the door.

She whirled on me, face red, wet and heartbroken, and screeched, "*Get out!*"

I walked in, murmuring, "Honey—"

"Out! Get out! Out, out, *out*!" Kate shrieked.

Deciding my daughter needed some alone time, I started to back out, but hit solid Joe.

"Come here, girl," Joe ordered, his voice quiet.

Oh shit.

Kate didn't tell Joe to get out. She just glared at him, which was both smart and brave.

"Katy, come here," Joe called gently.

She took a shaky breath then walked woodenly to Joe.

He moved around me, put a hand to her neck then bent to get his face close to hers and I held my breath.

"First, don't talk to your mom that way. Ever. You're pissed at Dane, we'll talk about that in a while. But you're pissed, you be pissed at who you're pissed at. You don't take it out on your mom or Keira or me, yeah?"

I was still holding my breath. Joe was continuing to talk in that gentle voice but I wasn't sure he'd been around long enough to tell the girls what to do. Not that I minded, it would come to this eventually, might as well be sooner rather than later. However, now he had his hand on the neck of a teenage girl in the throes of her first big fight with her first real boyfriend (or, though I hoped not, her first breakup). I was thinking now wasn't the time to go all dad on her.

Nevertheless, at this juncture I had to keep my peace. Tim and I had a pact, even if we disagreed with what the other was saying, we never contradicted each other in front of the girls. That talk would come later.

Joe hadn't said anything I disagreed with, so that talk wouldn't come later. But I still needed to keep my peace. He'd waded in. I just had to hope he could handle it.

Kate took a big breath, it hitched half a dozen times while she took it, then she surprised me when she collapsed into Joe's body and cried, "He's a *jerk*. A total *asshole*! I *hate* him!"

I pressed my lips together and bit them as Joe's arms went around a now sobbing Kate and his eyes came to me.

"Let's go, honey," he said to Kate, his eyes not leaving me.

She jerked her head back and swiped at her face. "Go? Where?"

Joe tipped his head down to look at her. "Time for you to ride in the '68."

"I don't…Joe…" She took another stuttering breath and said, "I don't wanna take a ride, Joe."

"Let's go," Joe repeated.

"Joe—" Kate began.

"Honey, let's…go." He was still talking gentle but this was mingled with his "I'm not going to repeat myself" tone.

Kate looked at me then at Joe and, wisely, she nodded.

He slid an arm around her shoulders and led her to the door.

"We'll be back for me to cook the brats. Do *not* cook them yourself," Joe ordered as he walked by me.

I didn't know if he ordered this for me to conserve my energy or because he didn't want me to ruin them. It didn't matter either way since my mind was on the fact that I was obviously not invited on this ride in Joe's *Bullitt* car, and even though he seemed to be doing okay, I wasn't sure Joe had the skills to handle this volatile situation without me being mediator.

"Joe," I called as I followed them.

"We'll be back in a while," Joe said, but he didn't look back at me as he guided Kate down the hall.

"Joe, I think—"

He looked back then and he did it to say, "In a while, buddy."

I bit my lips again. Then I nodded.

I stopped in the living room, my eyes following them through the windows as they walked to Joe's house, and Keira got close to me.

"Where they goin'?" she asked.

"No idea," I answered.

"Is Katy okay?" she asked.

"Nope," I answered.

"I hope she doesn't break up with Dane. He's the hottest guy in school and he's nice. That means you both have the hottest, nicest guys in school and in town. This means good things for my future because I'm up next."

I stopped worrying because I started laughing.

Then I looked at my last born and kissed her cheek.

After I did that, I said, "They may be hot and they may be nice but they're also men. And men can be idiots. So it isn't smooth sailing, honey, and it never will be."

"I can handle it," Keira blithely assured me, so ready for her first boyfriend it wasn't funny.

I, on the other hand, was not ready for Keira's first boyfriend. If my sweet, quiet, mellow Kate could throw a scene like that, Keira's first drama would probably blow the roof off the house.

"I hope so," I muttered then said, "Let's sit on the deck. Summer'll be over soon, we need to get our deck time in."

"Yeah, let me get a pop," Keira replied.

She got her pop and her phone and I grabbed my wine. We sat on the deck and she told me about the possible boyfriends she had lined up for freshman year. She did this while she texted, lining up those possible boyfriends, multitasking.

While she did this, I sipped my wine and fretted about Joe and Kate.

Thirty minutes later, the sliding glass door opened. I twisted in my seat and saw Joe with Kate tucked close to his side walking through. Her face was still red but it was dry.

Kate disengaged from Joe and came to me. Bending down to give me a hug, she whispered, "Sorry, Mawdy. I was ticked."

"That's okay, baby," I told her, hugging her back.

She let me go, threw herself in a chair and I looked at Joe.

"It's cool," he said calmly and walked to the grill, ordering, "Keirry, babe, help me out, yeah? Go get the brats."

"Sure, Joe," Keira replied, jumping up, eyeing Kate but doing as Joe asked.

"Joe's car is the bomb," Kate told me when the door slid closed behind Keira.

I ignored the comment and asked, "Are you okay?"

She looked away then back at me before she said, "Yeah."

"Sure?"

She shrugged, looked at Joe who was standing by the grill, eyes on Kate, hands on hips. Then she looked at the yard.

"He messes things up with me, his loss," Kate told the yard, sighed and looked at me. "And he loses, he loses *huge*."

My eyes went to Joe, he shrugged and said, "They may be in high school, buddy, but not a lotta girls like Kate in this world. Dane doesn't get that, he's fucked. He'll spend the rest of his life thinkin' 'bout the one who got away."

For longer than was necessary, I stared at Joe after he finished speaking.

And I did it thinking, *Fuck, but I love this man.*

I sighed through that thought and looked back at my daughter.

"What'd he do?" I asked. Kate's breathing hitched again, my eyes slid to Joe and Joe shook his head. "Forget it, I don't wanna know," I finished quickly.

Kate nodded and looked at the yard.

Keira returned with the brats. Joe cooked them while Keira brought out plates, cutlery, buns, condiments and bowls of store bought macaroni salad and chips.

We ate on the deck.

Tina didn't attempt to spy, which I thought was an added bonus to having a man who could be threatening and in your face (could and *would*).

Kate stayed silent and thoughtful throughout dinner. Keira filled the silence with chatter and I helped her. Kate did the dishes on her own, the rest of us giving her space, and after, she disappeared in her room.

Keira put in a movie and she and Mooch camped out in the living room.

Joe and I sat on the deck with beer and wine.

"Tell me," I demanded.

Joe looked at me, back at the yard and he took a pull on his beer.

Finally, he spoke. "Stupid shit, Dane's bein' an ass. He's about to fuck up royally, he goes ahead with this gig."

"What gig?"

"Met a girl from Plainfield. She asked him out. Kate says she's pretty well-known, seein' as she puts out."

"Oh shit," I murmured.

Joe kept talking. "He wants a break from exclusive to test the waters, but he also wants to keep Kate on a string. Kate doesn't wanna be on a string."

"I don't like him anymore," I declared, and Joe looked at me.

"Won't be anyone to like, he does this to Kate. She won't take him back and he'll come back, buddy, believe me."

"She's hung up on him, you sure she won't take him back?"

"Yep."

"How're you sure?"

Joe took another pull of beer, looked at the yard and he spoke.

"Told her I been around, met my share of women, never met any like you, her or Keira. Not in thirty-nine years. Bein' like she is, she doesn't need to take shit. Her man doesn't hand her the world, she throws him back and finds one who will. No dickin' around. Told her she needs to look at her mom and learn. You had three men in your life, all of 'em willin' to hand you the world. She should accept nothin' less." He took another pull of beer then finished. "She got my point."

"Joe," I called.

"Yeah?" he answered, his eyes not leaving the yard.

"Baby, look at me," I whispered.

Joe looked at me.

I leaned into him and put a hand to his face.

"Sucks for you, you had to wait thirty-nine years," I told him.

"Yeah," he replied.

"But works for me," I went on, and he grinned.

"Yeah."

"I'll do what I can to be worth the wait," I whispered and his eyes got intense.

"You do that, buddy," he whispered back. "Startin' tonight."

I smiled, leaned further in and touched my mouth to his. I pulled back and whispered, "This is workin' great."

Joe smiled then promised, "Best is yet to come."

"Yeah?" I asked.

He leaned in this time and touched his mouth to mine.

"Always," he murmured.

That was good to know.

When the girls came out to the deck to say goodnight this time, they kissed me on the mouth like usual.

They kissed Joe on his scarred cheek.

Both of them.

The best came for Joe faster than it did for me.

We waited for the girls to be asleep before Joe showed me what being creative meant.

I thought he was already pretty creative.

I was wrong.

I decided if he ever earned payback like that again, we'd go to a hotel so I could make as much noise as I wanted.

Luckily, one time I came, my moan was muffled due to his cock being in my mouth.

The other three times, *I* had to get creative.

Therefore now, with my in-laws at the door about to meet my new man, you would think I'd be pretty relaxed, having had four orgasms before sleeping like a log.

And having had a good week, a topsy-turvy one, but if this was an indication of my girls and my future with Joe, I'd not only keep it, I'd take down anyone who tried to take it away from me.

Because of all that, you'd definitely think I was relaxed.

But I wasn't relaxed.

I wasn't relaxed at all.

# Eighteen

## Pie

I exited the bedroom to see Joe coming toward me, his manner was urgent and there was a strange light to his eyes and set to his mouth. I wasn't sure,.but I could swear he looked like he didn't know whether to laugh or shout.

He opened his mouth to speak, but before he made a noise, Keira shrieked, her voice chockfull of pure glee, "*Mom! You won't believe this! Uncle Vinnie and Aunt Theresa are here too!*"

I stopped walking and Joe stopped in front of me so close we were toe to toe. I tipped my head back to look at him and could actually feel my eyeballs bugging out of their sockets.

"Cool!" Kate yelled, and I heard her scrambling toward the door, following, I knew because I heard her shouts outside, Keira.

Then I heard the door close. Then I heard both the girls shouting outside.

The mingling of family wasn't supposed to happen, not now, not until Joe and I were having, say, our peony festooned engagement dinner somewhere fancy and close to water (I was thirty-five and this was the second time around but that didn't mean I didn't have fantasies). When Bea was comfortable with Joe, Theresa and Vinnie could be briefed about Bea's delicate disposition. And the situation could be contained.

"Joe—" I whispered and his hand came to my neck.

"Relax."

"Bea's shy."

"Buddy, relax."

"She spooks easy and Theresa and Vinnie are—"

He dipped his head and kissed me lightly.

When he was done, he asked, "Baby, what'd I say?"

I stared into his blue eyes.

Then I nodded.

His hand slid from my neck to around my shoulders and he walked me through the study, the living room and out the door.

The vision that assaulted us was Kate, Keira and Mooch jumping around Bea, Gary, Uncle Vinnie and Aunt Theresa, Mooch yapping, the girls giving exuberant hugs and kisses.

Kate stopped and grabbed Bea's hand, introducing, "Gram, Gramps, this is Uncle Vinnie and Aunt Theresa, Joe's folks. They're *awesome*!"

Bea started to take a step back, but Kate, knowing how her grandmother was, clutched her hand and she got close as Gary's arm went around Bea's waist.

"Yeah, they're *awesome*!" Keira concurred, her arm around Vinnie, her smile so big it had to hurt her face.

"This is great, isn't it Mawdy?" Kate called to me. "Like, most of the whole family together."

"Yeah," Keira agreed. "All we need is Mel, Benny and Manny and it'd be like a family reunion."

Theresa and Vinnie were beaming. Gary looked confused. Bea looked scared out of her brain.

One thing was good, the girls were thrilled and I liked it that they already thought of Joe's family as theirs. I thought it was a little weird, we'd only met them once, but I liked it.

The rest of it was bad.

I disengaged from Joe and walked forward as Kate announced to Theresa and Vinnie, "We *so* have to do that!"

Oh Lord.

I ignored the reunion planning and went to Bea first. "Hey, Bea."

Kate and Gary let her go and Bea walked into my arms. I gave her a hug and she gave me one back. When she did, I forgot the current drama and felt Tim's mom's arms around me. They'd been around me before, hundreds of times through laughter, through tears and just because. My eyes stung as the memories assailed me and I pulled her closer.

"Honey," she whispered.

"I'm okay," I whispered back, but my voice was hoarse.

I didn't let her go and shoved my face in her neck, smelling her perfume, the same scent she wore since forever, and the tears spilled over.

"Oh, my precious girl," Bea murmured.

"Missed you so much," I choked.

"Me too, sweetie."

I pulled my head away and looked at her to see tears in her eyes. I shook my head and laughed, not because it was funny, just because it was so *us*.

"We're the pair, aren't we?" I asked.

She smiled at me and I felt Gary get close.

"Lemme have a bit of that," Gary demanded.

Bea let me go and turned me into Gary's arms.

"Hey, Dad," I said into his ear.

"Hey there, my beautiful flower."

His words, words he meant, words I liked, words said so often to me, made me choke again and I shoved my face in his neck. He held tight until I pulled in a steady breath then he let me go and turned us to the rest of the gang. Kate, Keira, Bea and even Theresa had wet eyes. Vinnie was studying his shoes. Joe's eyes were on me.

Gary's gaze went to Joe.

"This your new fella?" Gary asked, his voice studiously friendly.

Before I could answer, Keira did. "Yeah, Gramps, that's Joe. He's *the bomb*."

Gary gave his granddaughter a small smile that I could see he didn't fully commit to, he let me go and offered his hand to Joe.

"Joe, I'm Gary."

Joe took his hand and said, "Pleasure."

They dropped hands and Gary looked Joe up and down. "Pam didn't lie, you're a big guy."

"Yep," Joe agreed and said nothing else for this was true, Joe was a big guy.

Gary turned and pulled Bea to his side. "My wife, Bea."

Joe pulled me to his side as he dipped his chin to Bea and murmured, "Bea."

"Am I gonna get a kiss or what?" Theresa demanded to know, getting impatient and butting in.

She bustled up and grabbed Joe's face, yanking it down to hers, kissing his cheek then his other cheek and back before letting him go and coming to me to do the same thing. When she jerked my head around I understood why Joe didn't protest. She was jerking my head around, sure, but the affectionate way she did it felt good.

"Cal, son." Vinnie shoved in, giving Joe a back pounding hug then he turned to me and whispered, "*Cara mia,*" and he gave me a tight hug and released me. He turned to Bea and Gary and asked, "So, momentous occasion, you meetin' your daughter's new man."

"Um…Vinnie," I said. "These aren't my parents. They're Tim's parents."

"Tim?" Vinnie asked me.

"My husband," I explained. Vinnie's eyes got big and I finished quickly, "He died just under two years ago."

I could swear Vinnie's face grew knowing and he looked at Joe.

Before I could assess what Vinnie's knowing look meant, Vinnie said, "Right," clapped his hands and finished in a booming voice, including Bea and Gary in his announcement, "Family's family, always is, always will be, thank God. Now, I need coffee. We been on the road since six and road coffee is shit." He leaned into Bea, who leaned back as he said, "Pardon my French."

Theresa slapped him on the arm and snapped, "Vinnie, the girls. They don't need to hear your foul mouth."

"That's okay, Aunt Theresa. Joe cusses all the time and he says much worse stuff, like the f-word and the c-word." Keira, doing her best to make Vinnie and Theresa feel better, threw Joe right under the bus.

I groaned because Bea, nor Gary, would shine their light on Joe cursing in front of the girls. The f-word, Gary would accept on occasion, but not in front of the girls. Never Bea. She went to church every Sunday and taught Sunday school for thirty years. The c-word for both, never, ever. Tim didn't shy away from swearing but he never did it in front of his mom or the girls. I wasn't certain I'd ever heard Tim use the c-word.

Joe slid his arm around my shoulders and pulled me to his side. I looked up at him and he definitely looked like he was fighting back laughter now.

I couldn't see what was funny.

Joe looked down at me, squeezed my shoulder and prompted, "Coffee, buddy."

"Right," I whispered, Joe turned me and we led the way to the house.

"Gram, this is my new dog, Mooch." I heard Keira announce and I heard Mooch yap his hello.

"He's cute, honey," Bea replied quietly.

We hit the house and the minute we did, Joe turned dad.

"Keira, babe, show Theresa and Vinnie around. Katy, help your mom with coffee. Yeah?" Joe ordered.

"Sure, Joe." Kate smiled at him and skipped to the kitchen.

"No probs, big man," Keira stated on a grin. She dropped Mooch and linked her arms with Vinnie and Theresa, tugging them through the living room into the hall.

I was staring at my youngest daughter, thinking, *big man*?

Then I looked at Gary and Bea whose heads were swinging back at forth between the girls.

"Why don't you guys sit?" I suggested. "Coffee's fresh. Joe brewed a pot not ten minutes ago."

Gary started then looked at me. "That'd be fine, Vi."

Bea looked up at Gary. "I need to get my pie out of the cooler, hon."

"Yeah," Gary muttered. "Right."

"Pie?" Kate asked from the kitchen where she was taking down mugs.

"I, uh…made, um…Joe here a chocolate cream pie," Bea answered shyly.

"*Killer!*" Kate shrieked then screamed, "*Keirry, Gramma made Joe a chocolate cream pie!*"

"No way!" Keira's voice shouted from down the hall.

"Way!" Kate shouted back.

"*Phenomenal!*" Keira yelled.

I looked at Joe and explained, "Bea's chocolate cream pie is really good."

Joe's mouth was twitching before he stated, "I'm gettin' that."

"I'll go get it," Gary muttered, his mouth also twitching, which I hoped was a good sign.

I went to the kitchen. Joe moved to Bea.

"Sorry, Bea, didn't know Vinnie and Theresa were comin'. You want, I'll take 'em somewhere, give you some time with Vi and the girls," he offered, my stomach melted and Kate leaned into me, bumping me with her shoulder.

"I'm fine, Joe. It'll be okay but…uh…thank you," Bea said softly.

Joe wasn't done. "They can get loud and in your business. It gets too much, just give me the sign, yeah?"

I was worried this was too honest. Being honest was, of course, Joe, and it was also sweet, but I didn't want Bea to think I was telling tales out of school.

I held my breath and she looked up at him, not quite meeting his eyes, then she lifted a hand. I thought she'd touch him but she dropped her hand and spoke.

"I'm sure it'll be okay."

"Right," Joe muttered and Keira, Vinnie and Theresa came into the room, Keira playing tour guide.

"So this is the living room, which comes complete with dining area and views of our sparkling kitchen, which *I* cleaned." She threw an arm out and sashayed around the room as if she was a paid model, showcasing a luxurious suite, before she went on. "And next, you'll see our *fabulous* study."

Joe grinned at Keira, hooked her around the chest as she sashayed past him and pulled her back to his front. Then he bent and kissed her hair. He let her go and she turned a radiant smile on him before sauntering into the study.

Bea watched him do this and her eyes came to me. I saw the sheen of tears but I also saw her smile.

I smiled back, thinking maybe it all would be okay and then I began to get down to the task of seeing to the coffee. But before I could, my eyes caught on Theresa.

She was staring at Joe, tears in her eyes too. She seemed locked in place. Even as Joe moved toward the kitchen, her eyes stayed glued to where he was when he kissed Keira.

"Aunt Theresa!" Keira called. "You're missing the *fabulous* study!"

Theresa's body jolted, her gaze moved swiftly to me then she looked away, swiping her fingers under her eyes before turning toward the study.

"Can't miss the *fabulous* study," she called back, forced cheerfulness in her voice.

Vinnie gave her a look before he gave me a look and finally he gave Joe a look. When Theresa got close, he pulled her into his side. Keira strolled around the study, bringing their attention to the "top-notch, state-of-the-art computer system that Mr. Joe Callahan recently installed" (her words). As Keira spoke, Theresa put her head on Vinnie's shoulder and I felt a lump of tears hit my throat.

My eyes moved to Bea, who was studying these goings-on closely, her face thoughtful.

Joe got close to me and whispered, "First shock of it, baby, they'll get used to it and it'll all be good."

I looked up at him and nodded. He touched his mouth to mine. Gary walked in with the pie.

"And now, Joe and Mom's phenomenal boudoir!" Keira announced.

"Fuck," I whispered.

Joe grinned.

Theresa, Vinnie, Bea and Gary all looked at Joe and me.

Joe remained silent.

I resisted the urge to kick him and announced, "Um…by the way, Joe moved in last week."

Kate came up beside Joe and me and unusually declared very publicly and with a drama that would make Keira proud, "Yeah, and thank God he did, seein' as my *ex*-boyfriend, Dane, the Jerk, was a *jerk*. Since Joe was here, he took me for a ride in his *Bullitt* car." She looked at Bea and explained like she knew everything about the history of Ford Mustangs (which she might, who knew what she and Joe talked about when I wasn't around). "That's a 1968 Mustang GT, Gram." She went on to everyone, "And Joe told me that we Winters girls were the best women he'd ever met and if Dane didn't get with the program he was gonna lose his chance because I shouldn't put up with anything less than my man handin' me *the world*."

This was okay, until she finished.

"And, he said if Dane ever hurt me again, he'd break his neck!"

"Oh shit," I muttered, but before I could intervene, Keira skipped toward the living room and carried on with the storytelling.

"Yeah, and when our mean, nasty, *loud* neighbor bleached Mom's yard with a dirty word, Joe and me fixed it and Joe said I was the best assistant he ever had and he's gonna teach me security so I can install systems like he does for people like Nicole Bolton and Jarrod Francis."

Kate looked at Joe and breathed, "You installed Nicole Bolton and Jarrod Francis's systems?"

"Not Bolton, babe, but Francis, yeah," Joe told her.

"Wow! Is he as hot as he is in the movies?" Kate asked.

Joe grinned. "Can't make that call, Katy."

Kate grinned back and suggested, "Maybe next time you do a job for him, you can take me along and I'll let you know."

Joe shook his head, still grinning then changed the subject. "You called Dane your ex."

Kate's grin faded and she said, "Yeah."

"You make that decision?" Joe asked as if he and Kate didn't have an audience of six.

"Yeah, last night," Kate answered, also not concerned about her audience of six.

"You tell him?" Joe asked.

"Texted him," Kate answered.

"He text back?" Joe went on.

"I turned my phone off," Kate told him.

Joe wrapped his hand around her neck and stated proudly, "Good play, babe."

"I can't wait to get a boyfriend," Keira sighed dreamily, and I heard Bea laugh.

This startled me and my eyes went to Bea to see she was looking at Keira.

"Don't grow up too fast, honey," Bea said softly. "It's not near as fun as it seems."

"Dane's hot, Joe's hotter. I wanna be just like Mom and Kate, lassoing all the good ones in and wrapping them around my finger," Keira replied ingenuously.

"Someone kill me," I muttered, and Joe burst out laughing, dropped his hand from Kate's neck, turned to me, wrapped it around mine and pulled me to him for a quick kiss.

Then he turned to Keira. "Finish the tour, Keirry." His eyes went to Kate. "Get the pie from your grandfather." Then he turned to the coffeepot and grabbed the handle.

The next ten minutes were spent with Keira finishing up her tour, Kate engaged in the impossible task of finding space in our fridge for the pie, Joe and me handing out coffees, me cutting up a coffee cake, putting it on a plate and setting it on the coffee table and everyone settling in the living room.

Vinnie and Theresa sat on the couch, Gary with them. Bea sat in an armchair. The girls sat on the floor. Joe sat in the other armchair and I perched on the arm.

Everyone stared at everyone else and sipped their coffee.

Vinnie had eaten two pieces of coffee cake before I said, "Bea, the girls need to go to get their school supplies. We waited for you to get here because we thought you'd like to come with."

"Yeah, we need notebooks and pens and rulers and stuff. You always came with us to get our school supplies," Keira reminded her, and Bea smiled at her granddaughter.

"That'd be just fine." She pulled in a visible breath, her smile turned timid and looked at Theresa. "Theresa, would you, uh…like to come with us?"

Theresa glowed. "I'd love to."

"Good," Vinnie declared. "Gives Cal and Gar and me a chance to do man stuff."

I bit my upper lip, wondering how Gary would take to being nicknamed "Gar," not to mention being sucked into "man stuff" with two men he didn't know when he'd come down to see the girls and me.

"Like what?" Kate asked.

"Anything that doesn't include shoppin'," Vinnie answered, and Kate giggled.

"You can look after Mooch," Keira suggested, Mooch in her lap squirming to get out in order to lay waste to something. "He doesn't like to be in his box much."

"What kind of dog is that?" Gary asked his granddaughter.

"American husky," Keira answered, and Gary's eyes came to me then back to Keira.

"What else?" Gary asked, and Keira tipped her head to the side.

"What else?"

"Yeah, he got anything else in him?"

"Nope, pure bred," Keira replied proudly, and Gary looked back at me.

"That's luck, Vi, finding a pure bred puppy at the pound," he commented, knowing I didn't have the money to buy a pedigree dog.

"We didn't get him at the pound. Keira's friend's dog had a litter. She fell in love with them so Joe bought him for her," I blurted, not thinking, too freaked out by the morning to watch my words.

"What?" Kate and Keira asked in unison.

"Shit," Joe muttered as my body tensed and I looked at my girls.

"Um…" I started.

"*Joe* bought him?" Keira asked and the look on her face was a look I'd never seen before on my daughter. She had a great number of expressions. Her face always spoke volumes, most of which I was fluent in. This one I was not.

"Um…" I repeated trying to read her expression and Keira looked at Joe.

"You bought him?" she whispered.

"Vi," Joe murmured on a prompt, clearly not wishing to wade in this time.

I made a split second decision and it was the same decision I almost always made with my girls. Complete honesty.

"I, honey…I didn't have the money. I knew you wanted him really badly but I couldn't afford him. I told Joe and he thought you should have a puppy so he gave me the money so you could get Mooch," I admitted, wishing this wasn't playing out there, in the living room with Tim's folks and Joe's folks looking on. In fact, wishing it wasn't playing out at all.

Keira and Kate were both staring at Joe.

Suddenly, Keira surged up and I jumped at her movement then froze, wondering what she was going to do. Mooch yapped and ran away and I watched in stunned silence as Keira threw herself full body at Joe. She ended with her knees to the floor, her body between his legs, her torso in Joe's lap, her face in his chest, her arms wrapped around him, and before I could open my mouth or even move, she burst into tears.

"I *knew* you were always lookin' out for us," she cried into his chest. "I *knew* it!"

That lump hit my throat again but it was so big this time, it choked me.

Joe's hand dropped to Keira's hair and he bent forward. "Baby, hey," he whispered.

"I *knew* it!" she sobbed into his stomach.

What I knew was this wasn't about Joe and the dog. This was about my sweet, crazy, strong, beautiful daughter losing her dad and losing her uncle and living in a world that was uncertain, being afraid of that world and needing something to hold onto. They'd been strong a long time, both my girls had. And I was proud of them. But even the strongest person in the world needed something to hold onto.

And the man who bought you the dog you always wanted was the perfect choice.

Further, my daughters' sudden connection with Aunt Theresa and Uncle Vinnie wasn't weird. It was them grasping onto any family they could get as the bedrock of their own kept shifting. It was just pure luck that Joe provided such excellent additions.

When Keira kept sobbing into Joe's chest, I blinked away my tears as Joe twisted and handed me his coffee mug. He put his hands in her pits and hauled her up into his lap.

"Keirry, honey, what's this?" Joe whispered into her ear when he had her in his arms and she'd burrowed in closer. He, too, knew it wasn't about the dog.

She yanked her head out of his neck, looked at him and demanded in a fierce tone, "Don't ever go away, Joe."

At my daughter's words, I felt my breath choke me so hard I heard it too and that choking sound wasn't just coming from me.

"I'm not goin' anywhere, honey," Joe replied gently.

"Promise!"

I hiccoughed with my effort to swallow back my tears and heard Kate's small whimper in an effort to do the same.

"I promise," Joe said, his tone just as fierce, then he put an arm behind her knees and he straightened from the chair, Keira held to his chest.

I straightened too, murmuring, "Joe."

"I got this, buddy."

"Joe—"

"Got it," Joe repeated and walked from the room down the hall.

I stood there, staring down the hall. Then I turned and stared at our group, seeing Bea and Theresa flat out crying. Gary and Vinnie were both looking at their laps. Vinnie had his arm around Theresa.

"I'm sorry," I whispered, my voice sounding suffocated. Kate's arm wrapped around my leg and she pressed in tight.

Bea got up and walked to me. Taking the mugs out of my hands, she said gently, "Nothing to be sorry for, Violet." She gestured to a chair. "Sit down, honey."

I didn't sit down. Instead, I bent down and pulled Kate up to her feet.

Then I told everyone, "Please, I'm sorry, we need a minute."

"Anything you need," Bea replied instantly.

I nodded, put my arm around Kate's waist and led her down the hall to Keira's room. Joe was in bed with a still crying Keira tucked into his side. His eyes came to us as we entered the room. Without hesitation, we all crawled into Keira's double bed and curled into Joe.

It would be much later when I wondered why my girls and I did this and why it seemed so comfortable. Me, maybe. My girls, no.

And when I thought about it later, I would come to the conclusion that it just came natural because it was us and it was Joe.

In other words, the new *us*.

So when a situation became emotional, what else would we do?

After a while, when the Winters girls got their shit together, I took my cheek from Joe's shoulder and looked at his face.

"That didn't go as planned," I told him.

"Far's I can see, buddy, it couldn't have gone better," Joe replied.

I looked at him and saw he believed what he was saying and his belief made me smile at him. Even so, my smile was shaky.

When Joe leaned into me, his kiss was firm.

When Joe was done kissing me and I was feeling a lot less shaky, Keira's head came up from Joe's other shoulder and she looked at him.

"Sorry I went all wussy on you," she whispered, her eyes not quite catching his, her voice trembling. I realized that she was worried she'd disappointed him and my stomach lurched.

Joe's arm went from around me and he turned toward Keira. Kate (who was tucked in front of me) and I came up on our elbows. We watched Joe put his hand to Keira's jaw to tip her face up further toward him.

"Never bury somethin' deep, baby," he murmured. "Takes twice as much courage to be who you are, say what you think, feel what you feel and let it show then it does to bury it. That shit you been holdin' onto will destroy you. You got a safe place to get rid of it, and you do, then you get rid of it like you just did. Yeah?"

"Yeah," Keira whispered, a shaky smile on her lips too.

I stared at Joe thinking maybe he *was* Superman.

There was the sound of a throat being cleared and we looked to the door to see Gary standing there.

"Um…sorry to interrupt, Joe, Vi, but…there's a young man at the door. Says his name is Dane. I tried to—"

My body jolted when Kate screeched, "*Aiyee!*" and leaped from the bed, ran past her grandfather and disappeared.

Keira sat frozen against Joe for half a second before she followed her sister with just as much energy. Joe was not far behind but he was hindered since he was dragging me with him.

"I thought I told you!" We heard Kate shout as Joe hustled us down the hall.

"Katy—" We heard Dane.

"No!" Kate interrupted him. Then she asked a very familiar question. "Do you have your head sorted out?"

Oh shit.

There it was. Proof that my daughters were soaking up all things Joe.

We hit the living room and Theresa was standing behind Kate like a sentry. Bea was close too, though not as close as Theresa. Vinnie was standing by the television, his eyes on the scene playing out in front of him. Keira was sitting on her knees in the couch, facing the door. I felt Gary come up behind Joe and I, but the minute we hit the room, Dane's eyes shot to Joe and his face paled.

I was thinking there were a lot of good reasons to have Joe around, but at that moment his putting the fear of God into pipsqueak boy-men (no matter how cute they were) who hurt my daughter was at the top of my list.

I crossed my arms on my chest and stared at Dane as he swallowed and his Adam's apple bobbed. Finally, Dane plucked up the courage and stepped forward.

"Mr. Callahan," his eyes came to me, "Miz Winters, I need to talk to Katy."

"You need to talk to Kate, why you talkin' to us?" Joe enquired, and I looked at him to see his arms crossed on his chest in a new sinister, scary pose. This one was both alpha-male and man-of-the-house-slash-father-figure-you-did-*not*-mess-with.

"Uh..." Dane muttered, struck dumb by Joe's sinister, scary pose.

"Your girl's standin' right in front of you, kid," Joe prompted when Dane seemed frozen to the spot and this lasted awhile and that while included a number of people as his audience, all eyes on him. "You came to make a move, make it."

Dane swallowed again, nodded, and looked at Kate. "Can we talk?"

"Only one thing I want to hear you say," Kate replied, and I was proud of my girl for sticking to her guns and not letting some boy-man (no matter how cute he was) treat her like dirt.

"Can I say it out on the back deck?" Dane asked.

Kate looked over her shoulder at Joe and Joe tipped his chin at her.

This was when I realized that I'd lost a little bit of both my daughters. They'd taken it from me and given it to Joe.

Other women might be jealous of this or they might be alarmed.

I wasn't.

Joe had given us everything. It was just our way of giving back. Not a lot of men would appreciate the gifts Keira and Kate were giving him and doing it so freely, but I reckoned Joe did.

"Back deck," Kate agreed and turned, leading a flush-faced Dane through the living room and study and out the back sliding glass door.

"That's Dane," Keira announced to the room unnecessarily when the sliding door closed. "He's Kate's boyfriend and he's in the doghouse."

Vinnie chuckled in the direction of Gary who was pressing his lips together.

"I need more coffee," Theresa declared. "Bea, do you need more coffee?"

"Yes, yes, I think I do," Bea said softly.

"I'll make another pot," I offered.

"No, *cara mia*, you sit, relax or better yet, find a place to eavesdrop." Theresa's eyes went to the back deck. "I'll make it."

"I'll help." Bea moved with Theresa to the kitchen.

"I can make it, that's okay. I don't eavesdrop on the girls," I told them, and Theresa *and* Bea stopped dead and turned to me.

"You don't?" Theresa asked, her voice horrified.

"I trust my girls," I said carefully, not wanting to be insulting by intimating she hadn't done the same with her children.

"Well," Theresa threw a hand out, "I guess I can see that, bein' girls and all. My Carmella was an angel but I also had three boys. Three hot-blooded Italian boys with more hormones than the Chicago metropolitan area could contain. If they weren't gettin' in trouble with girls, they were fightin' with boys. Bloody knuckles. Bras in their beds. Did my head in."

Bea just stared at me, knowing that hormones weren't exclusive to hot-blooded Italian boys. Hormones went both ways and they didn't discriminate by culture, they just ran rampant through teenagers as a whole.

"It'll be okay, Bea," I assured her. "I had a talk with Kate and Joe had a talk with Dane."

"Yeah," Keira put in, "and Joe scares the crap outta Dane."

I watched as Gary came forward and clapped Joe on the shoulder. "Saw that," he muttered. "Liked it," he went on, looking at his wife not at Joe, and my heart turned over with happiness. Joe had Gary's seal of approval, or at least it was heading that way. "Hon, could seriously use another cup," he said to Bea.

"Right, love," Bea whispered and moved to the kitchen, Theresa on her heels.

Joe was looking out the sliding glass doors, seemingly oblivious to everything going on around him, his mind on what was happening on the back deck. I walked to him, put my hands on his chest and pressed him down in the armchair. He resisted but not much, especially when I climbed into his lap once I got him seated. Maybe sitting in his lap was a bit too much but I figured since we'd already had a variety of dramas, the best way forward was just to be ourselves.

If Bea and Gary didn't like it, I couldn't help that.

Then again, with all the dramas, I reckoned they wouldn't have any problem with it.

"We don't eavesdrop," I told him as his arms came around me.

"Don't have to, buddy."

I cocked my head to the side. "We don't?"

"Dane isn't stupid. He'll do right by Kate. He doesn't, Kate isn't stupid. She'll dump his ass." He paused before finishing, "Again."

I got closer to his face and whispered, "You ready for at least four straight years of teenage girl boy drama?"

Joe's face shifted to tender, his eyes moved to Keira and I saw humor light them.

Then he looked at me. "Keira's up next so we might need to talk to Doc about Valium."

"You think you'll need Valium?" I asked, surprised.

"Was thinkin' for you."

"I'll be all right."

"Keirry's a bit wild, baby."

I got closer. "That's okay. I've got you to help me deal."

The humor left his eyes and they went intense. I held my breath because I was certain he was going to kiss me and do it hard. I was certain of this because he'd looked that way before, right when he kissed me and did it hard.

To stop Joe kissing me hard in front of Gary and Bea (and Theresa), something I figured they *might* have a problem with (especially the way Joe did it), I continued. "And to scare the bejeezus out of any boy who gets ideas."

Joe grinned at me right when we heard Gary ask, "What in *the hell*?"

I looked in his direction. He'd moved to stand at the back of the couch by Keira but he was looking out the window.

"Granddad!" Keira shouted and jumped off the couch as I stared through the window at my father walking along the front of the house.

"Oh my God," I whispered, my body solid, hoping my mother wasn't with him and also wondering what was next. The sky falling? The earth standing still? Perhaps a meteor would crash into the Atlantic Ocean and a tidal wave would wash half of the continental United States into the sea.

"What the fuck?" Joe muttered tersely, but his body was not solid. He was not thinking of meteors. His thoughts were something else entirely.

He surged up, his arms still around me taking me with him. He planted me on my feet, let me go and stalked to the door.

By the time he got there, me hot on his heels, Keira had it open and she was giving my father a big hug.

"It *is* a family reunion!" she cried with excitement, then asked, "Did you bring Mel with you?" and she looked beyond my father out the door. I noted she didn't ask if Dad brought my mom but instead she asked after Mel. My girls weren't big fans of my mother. No one was, of course, since my mom was a bitch. But Madeline Riley had been a cold, hard, disapproving mother and she was no less of any of those things as a grandmother—even not having been around very often.

Joe came to stand behind Keira and the second she cleared my father, his arm hooked around her chest and he stepped back, taking Keira with him and not letting go. His eyes were on my dad and they were far from welcoming.

I moved to stand by them. "Dad, what're you doin' here?"

Dad was looking at Joe. His eyes came to me and I noticed belatedly that something wasn't right about him as in *really* not right. He didn't seem to process that Joe was looking unwelcoming and pretty much no one but a blind person could ignore Joe's unwelcome look.

Therefore, I braced.

"Left your mom," Dad announced, straight out.

"What?" I whispered.

"Fuck," Joe muttered.

"What!" Keira shouted.

Dad yanked an agitated hand through his hair, shaking his head from side to side, not even aware he had a further audience than just Keira (who shouldn't be hearing this), Joe, (who he didn't even know) and me (who didn't *want* to hear this).

"I…I can't take it anymore, Vi. She…with Sam…and when Tim…" His eyes shot to Joe then came back to me and I watched as his face crumbled and he whispered, "Jesus, sweetie, I lost *my son*."

His hands covered his face and he dissolved into shoulder shaking sobs.

My heart right back in my throat threatening to choke me, I moved forward and wrapped my arms around my father.

"Dad," I whispered.

"I lost him. I lost Sam," Dad moaned into his hands, not taking them from his face. "And because of *her* I didn't have you. I didn't have the girls. My boy was gone and I didn't have *anything*." His head came up and his watery eyes caught mine. "You kids, both of you, living with that woman, you were my shining lights. The way she was when you…with Tim…" His breath hitched. "Then you were gone and my world dimmed, but I still had Sam. Now I don't have Sam and you come to the funeral and you don't even look at me and my grandchildren are nearly grown and *I barely know them*!"

He ended on a shout and ripped out of my arms.

"Dad," I muttered, trying to get close again, but he took two angry steps into the house and turned with a jerk to face me.

"This morning she found out about the money, that money I gave Sam to give to you and she went *berserk*!" Dad yelled. "Sam's dead not even a month and she finds out I gave you and the girls a little something and she acted like I sold state secrets!"

"Dad." I put a hand to his arm, but he shrugged it off and walked further into the house, starting to pace.

"Who does that?" he shouted. "Her son is dead and what? What's important to her? How obvious could it be that you'd made the right decision just at the wrong time? Tim was a good kid, he became a good man. He took care of you, the girls. How much proof did she need that she was wrong and you were right? How hard is it, when what lies in the balance is something you love, to admit you're wrong? How much more proof does she need that life's too damn short to be such a ridiculous, screaming *bitch*!"

"Pete," Joe said, coming close to me, but Dad stopped pacing and glared at him.

"*And you*! Who *are* you?" Dad bellowed, throwing an arm in Joe's direction.

I heard the sliding glass door open but couldn't tear my eyes away from what was happening in front of me.

Keira burrowed into Joe's side as she answered, "Granddad, he's Joe."

"I know he's *Joe*, sweetie," Dad yelled at Keira, and at my father's angry words aimed at her, Keira burrowed closer to Joe.

When she did, I watched with no small amount of concern as Joe's face went so hard it looked carved from stone.

But Dad was on a tear and he kept talking.

"My daughter has a new man in her life and all I know is that he's *Joe*." Dad looked at Joe and demanded to know. "Where do you come from? What do you do? How did you meet? Can you provide for my daughter? Can you take care of her? Protect her? Protect my grandchildren? The only ones *I'll ever have*!" He was shouting when he was done and Kate, in from outside, edged around him and pressed into my side as he did it.

I put my arm around my daughter and opened my mouth to speak but Joe got there before me.

"I appreciate this is an intense time for you, Pete, but you do not come into this house and shout, not in front of the girls and definitely not *at* the girls. Not during an intense time, not…*fucking*…*ever*." Joe still had Keira at his side, his arm was around her and he was holding her close but he was leaning threateningly toward my father. "You need to go somewhere and pull yourself together and you need to do it now or you'll find yourself not in this house. Do you get me?"

Dad stared at Joe, tardily realizing that he should have paid closer attention, and I opened my mouth to speak again but Vinnie was there.

"Pete?" he asked, his hand on my father's back. "I'm Vinnie, Cal's uncle. Let's you and me take a walk."

Dad looked at Vinnie in confusion as Vinnie pushed him toward the door, Dad resisted (but feebly), and Kate and I moved to the side to let them pass.

"Who's Cal?" Dad asked, looking around. His face having lost its anger, he was now full-on perplexed with a little hint of lost mixed in.

"I'll explain on the walk," Vinnie muttered, opened the front door and shoved my father through it before he could utter another sound. He shut the door and I watched him half-push, half-guide Dad down the walk.

I looked at Joe, who still had Keira tucked close to his side. "Can we call Doc now?" I asked, and in an effort to lighten the mood, went on to joke. "I could use that Valium and, maybe, a shot of tequila."

Joe's eyes sliced to mine. I noted that he didn't look amused. Kate giggled nervously and Joe's eyes moved to her.

"Dane's shit sorted?" he asked in an almost bark.

Kate didn't even flinch before she replied quietly, "He burned her phone number."

"He know he does that shit again I'll break his neck?" Joe went on.

"Joe!" I snapped, and this time Keira giggled, not nervously at all.

"I kinda alluded to that," Kate answered on a grin.

Now it was me who was not amused.

"Joe, I'm not gonna say it again. Stop threatening to break Dane's neck!" I snapped again.

Joe looked at me. "All right, buddy, there's a next time he acts like an ass, I'll threaten to rip his head off."

"Joe!" I cried angrily.

Joe ignored me and looked back at Kate. "Where is he?"

"He left. I asked him to go home so we could have our family drama and he wouldn't know we were all crazy, change his mind and want to break up with *me*," Kate replied.

Joe's arm curled Keira in an even closer sideways hug. "Thinkin', girl, he already gets that."

"Yeah, that cat's outta the bag," Keira agreed, her arm snaking around Joe's middle to hold on, and Kate laughed.

But I didn't.

Bea, Gary, Theresa and Vinnie were there, as was my father who had left my mother, at long last, but this was still a shock. My father had also shouted at Joe *and* Keira. Before that emotional scene we'd had another emotional scene which necessitated a timeout where we all cuddled in bed with Joe which was, frankly, a weird thing to do no matter how natural it felt. My eldest daughter was taking relationship advice from my boyfriend who wasn't all that great with relationships, or at least it took him a while to come around. And both my daughters were acting like my live-in boyfriend of one week had been around for the last year.

"I need to go to the liquor store," I announced.

"Buddy—" Joe started to say, his lips curving into a grin.

"No, we have wine and we have beer but we don't have tequila. I need tequila."

"Vi, baby, it's not even noon." Joe said.

"I need tequila."

"Relax."

"I need tequila."

"Honey, relax."

"I need tequila!"

Joe's hand whipped out, tagged me at the neck and I fell face forward into his chest. As I had my arm around Kate, she came with me so we ended in a four person huddle.

I pulled my face out of Joe's chest and looked up at him.

"Tequila," I muttered, and I heard Keira and Kate giggle.

"Baby," Joe muttered back and touched his mouth to mine before he finished, "Relax."

I was about to explain, again, that Joe telling me to relax didn't mean I'd do it when I felt a presence and I turned my head to see, shockingly, Bea had come close.

"Vi, sweetie, I'll make my sangria later. We can have it with dinner. How does that sound?" Bea asked.

Bea's sangria was brilliant. Way better than her chocolate cream pie.

And Bea getting close to our huddle even though she still looked timid, she nevertheless was close, was the best.

"We'll go to the grocery store when we get school supplies," I said to Bea.

"Perfect," Bea replied quietly and smiled at me.

Then I watched as she smiled at Joe.

It was then I relaxed.

Storms in the Midwest, bad ones, had a way of announcing their arrival well before they arrived. You could feel them and you could see them as the air went still and took on what I could swear was a tinge of yellow. You could even smell them.

Considering the emotional start to the day, the emotional months that had preceded it, and the fact that it looked and smelled like there was going to be a storm, a bad one, maybe even one that heralded a tornado (tornados being something that scared me shitless), it maybe wasn't so surprising when I lost it on the sidewalk outside the store.

See, making matters worse, I'd had nothing but a corn dog and a Slurpee for lunch and I was starving. Further, I saw the lightning and heard the far away thunder. The time between lightning flashes and thunder rolls was dwindling, the storm was fast approaching and I was getting antsy because I didn't want to be at a strip mall, a veritable magnet for tornado activity (in my storm fevered imagination). I wanted to be home.

What made matters even worse was Dad, Gary and Uncle Vinnie decided to come with us and Joe came along too, likely to play his self-appointed role of emotional bodyguard.

I was very aware of the facts that Dad and Gary weren't the best of friends. Bea was still stinging from had happened nearly two decades ago with Mom, and Dad was a stark reminder of that. Dad wasn't Joe's favorite person at that moment. The girls were with a bunch of people they loved, their favorite thing in the world *and* in full-on shopping mode, their second favorite thing in the world and something which nothing penetrated, even if they were only buying notebooks and pens. And I was a walking emotional zombie, barely holding it together. Therefore, Vinnie and Theresa were working triple time to keep our troop from descending into madness.

That said, Vinnie and Theresa, just being Vinnie and Theresa, weren't the best choices for this job considering they were naturally pretty bonkers.

Even so, we were somehow making it through the day. We'd been to the grocery store to pick up ingredients for sangria, it was closing in on Sangria Time and I'd started to count down the minutes.

After the grocery store, the girls got their stuff and they'd scored huge, what with Gary and Bea, Vinnie and Theresa, Dad, and lastly Joe vying to spoil them rotten, so they had enough school supplies to last them until they were eighty.

They also had new CDs by their favorite bands (Joe's contribution, though he flatly refused in a teasing way to buy Keira any boy band music to which Dad stepped in, thinking he was doing something good, and bought them which ticked Joe off for reasons only known to Joe, and Keira had to play peacemaker).

They also had new brushes, combs, shampoo, conditioner, moisturizer, makeup and enough hair accessories to service the entire freshman class (Theresa's contribution on a smile and a vague "All girls need a little…you know," when I tried to intervene).

Joe was loading their multitude of bags in the trunk of the Mustang while both girls were close, gabbing at Joe. Dad was trying to help at the same time looking like he was going to burst into tears. Vinnie was trying to distract Dad and failing, which meant Dad was getting in Joe's way. Gary, Theresa and Bea were down the sidewalk looking into the windows of the bakery, Theresa exclaiming loudly, "They have no cannoli!" to which Bea nervously giggled. And I was standing alone and slightly removed from the rest of them.

This made me the bizarre target for a beautiful blonde who walked right up to me and started speaking.

"Rumor's true. You broke him," she said, her eyes on Joe who was grinning down at Keira and ignoring Dad as he slammed the trunk of the Mustang.

I turned my head to look at her, seeing firstly that she was beautiful, and secondly that she had bitch written all over her.

"Sorry?" I asked.

"Cal," she tipped her head toward Joe but kept her eyes on me. "You broke him."

"What?" I asked.

"Tina told me," she went on, and I felt liquid steel injected into my spine at the mention of Tina's name. "I had a taste of him," she shared, smiled, and the way she did it I knew I was right. Total bitch. "Delicious," she finished.

I turned fully to her.

"Who are you?"

"Susie Shepherd," she answered. I vaguely knew her name from somewhere but I didn't have time to figure out where since I was focusing on her smile getting bitchier. This didn't give me a good feeling and I'd shortly find out why it was doing that. "You're done with Mike, you won't mind I have a go?"

That steel in my spine solidified.

"Are you kidding me?" I whispered.

"Or, my preference, you get done with Cal, I'd like another taste. More accurately, I'd like to give *him* another one."

"You're kidding me," I whispered hopefully.

She leaned in, dashing my hopes. "Best head I ever had. Cal works miracles with his tongue, sheer talent. He made me come so hard I thought for a second I died and I didn't mind one fucking bit."

I leaned in too and hissed, "My daughters are five feet away."

She leaned slightly back. "No worries. They get a bit older, he'll do them too. They got something to look forward to."

"*What?*" I shrieked, and she grinned a catty grin.

"Nails everything in town, don't you know?" she informed me. "We're all just wondering when he'll get done playin' with you."

"Susie—" I heard Joe say, his voice sounding supremely scary, even scarier than a very scary Joe could sound. But I'd had enough.

I was done.

There was a huge clap of thunder that rumbled through the air like a physical thing and this was accompanied by a streak of bright lightning.

The storm was there. The heavens opened and the rain poured down.

This all drowned out my scream as I took Susie Shepherd down right there on the sidewalk.

I found quickly that she'd grown up without brothers because she fought like a girl, which was why I was able to start beating the crap out of her.

That was until Joe pulled me off of her, set me on my feet, wrapped an arm around my chest, one around my ribs and backed us away several steps all the while I struggled in his hold.

"Get the girls in the car." Joe ground out.

"Cal—" Vinnie said.

"*Car! Now!*" Joe barked and this time it was an actual bark. "Get them outta here!"

"Mom, you okay?" Kate asked with worry in her tone.

I was so out of it, Kate's tone didn't register as I was still struggling to get at Susie Shepherd, a woman I did not know but I didn't care. I was going to rip all her now sodden golden tresses out by the roots.

"You *bitch*!" I shrieked.

She was pulling herself to her feet and wiping blood from her lip. She looked at the blood mixed with raindrops on her hand then she stared at me.

"*You busted my lip!*" she squealed.

"*I'm gonna bust more than that!*" I screamed then demanded, "Joe, let me go!"

"Come on, girls." I heard Dad say. "Get in Vinnie's car."

"Mom—" Keira called.

"Car, Keirry, sweetie. Please." Bea said.

"I'm gonna sue!" Susie shouted.

Joe was trying to move me toward the car but was having trouble since I was fighting like a she-cat to get at Susie. Fighting so hard even big Joe Callahan couldn't subdue me.

"If you're gonna sue then I best give you something good to sue me for!" I threatened.

"Cal, everything all right here?" a man asked, running up and holding a jacket over his very blond head and I saw it was Chip Judd, the man who put in my security system and screwed up the wiring so Joe had to fix it.

"You let *her* break you?" Susie asked Joe, ignoring Chip and pointing a finger at me. "*Her?*" she repeated, her voice filled with disgust, her mascara melting down her face and another rumble of thunder filled the air accompanied by a flash of lightning.

"Vi, quit fightin', get in the car," Joe muttered in my ear.

"You once were magnificent. You're nothin' now. The whole town's talkin' about it," Susie insanely taunted Joe.

"Shut your mouth, Susie Shepherd," a woman with long dark hair and a fabulous figure (and I knew this because her sundress was plastered to her body by the rain and the wind which had sprung up and was lashing all around us) rushed forward to stand by Chip. "No one's talkin' that trash but you and Tina." The brunette turned to Joe and me. "We're all real happy for you Cal."

There you go. Explanation of why everyone kept staring at us, and mostly Joe.

"Josie, do me favor, babe, don't get involved," Chip said to the woman.

"Like she'll listen to you." Susie's voice was dripping with derision. "You're so pussy whipped you're not even a man."

Acting on manly instinct at such a slur uttered at one of his brethren, Joe stopped moving. Chip pulled himself up to his full height, which was pretty tall. He dropped his arms and the jacket, but it was Josie who acted.

"You *bitch*!" she shrieked, lunged forward and shoved Susie in the chest, causing Susie to step back on her foot. "Don't you talk about my man that way."

"*Don't you touch me!*" Susie shrieked back.

"Susie, get gone," Joe warned.

"Fuck you, Joe Callahan!" Susie snapped.

"You wish!" Josie yelled. "Everyone knows you tried to get in there and nothin' goin'. Now everyone knows you and Tina are talkin' trash about Cal and Violet because you made your play and he didn't like what he got when he had his piece of you, so he threw it away. And Tina's been livin' by him yonks and couldn't catch his eye." She looked at me. "Can't deny, we're all real curious, the whole town is. But it don't take a psychiatrist to see you're hot, Cal's hot, hot attracts hot, so, you know, hot moves in next door, shit's gonna happen."

I'd stopped struggling because I was staring at Josie and now trying not to giggle as I got the rest of why everyone kept staring at Joe, me and the girls and I found it didn't annoy me anymore. It would hit me much later that Susie Shepherd was one of Joe's ex-lovers but when it did, it didn't hit me hard. She was gorgeous for one so that explained that. She was a bitch for another and that explained why Joe took what he wanted and didn't come back for more. Therefore it wasn't worth discussion, something which I decided Joe and I would never have and we never did.

"Um..." I started. "You know me but I don't..."

"Josie Judd," she said, coming forward, seemingly impervious to the rain, hand extended, "Chip's my husband."

I shook her hand and shoved wet hair out of my face while blinking against the fat drops of rain hitting my eyes as she stepped back and kept talking.

"Sorry Chip fucked up your wiring. He tried real hard to figure that shit out, spent all night goin' over Cal's plans. But Cal's a security genius. My Chip, he's good but he isn't a genius or I'd be livin' in LA gettin' a pedicure every week."

"Oh, please, this is gonna make me sick," Susie griped, and Josie whirled on her.

"Then go away and by the way," Josie said, "Chip likes my pussy but it's my mouth he loves and that's because *I* love his big, gorgeous *dick*. You stop bein' such a bitch, Susie, and use your mouth for good not bad, you might get a man with a beautiful dick who'll give you some on a regular basis instead of runnin' as fast as they can to get away from you. Only man you could hold onto was Colt and he was only fuckin' you 'cause you reminded him of Feb."

"Oh Jesus," Chip mumbled.

I was thinking this was a lot of information, most of which I didn't want to know, but I *really* didn't want my daughters to know it.

I twisted my neck slightly and whispered over the wind to Joe, "Please tell me my daughters are no longer here."

"Gone, buddy," Joe muttered, and he didn't sound pissed. He sounded like he wanted to laugh.

"Bea?" I asked.

"Gone," Joe answered.

"Thank God," I murmured.

"He likes your *trashy* mouth," Susie shot back.

My eyes turned to see she looked fit to be tied but she was also not stupid enough to go so far as to make it get physical again. She'd learned that lesson twice in the last five minutes. Now she was just trying to save face.

"Only one's got a trashy mouth is you, Susie Shepherd," Josie retorted, put a hand to her hitched hip and threw out a foot.

I tensed because this stance boded bad tidings in Catfight Land. Josie didn't seem at all fazed by the fact that it was pouring buckets and the wind was whipping her hair and dress all around, she was in the zone.

"I don't know what you said to Violet to make her take you down like that, but I do know you better watch your ass. You got enemies and we're not talkin' enemies like Denny Lowe. We're talkin' *women* who are up to *here*," she lifted a straightened out hand to her chin and continued, "with your and Tina's shit and we ain't takin' it anymore."

She'd mentioned Dennis Lowe, the serial killer that made Feb and Colt's life a living hell, and that was when I knew who Susie Shepherd was. I'd read about her in the articles about that whole mess. At the end, Dennis Lowe had held her hostage and shot her.

This shocked me. Something like that happened to me, I would likely not be wandering strip malls, randomly picking fights with my ex-lover's girlfriends. Hell, I'd never do that.

That was just me though. Maybe she was experiencing post-traumatic stress or something.

"Josie—" I started.

"You the one toilet papered Tina's yard?" Susie, eyes to Josie, asked over me.

"Nope, but I'll give you ten guesses as to who did it and I'll bet you *still* won't figure it out 'cause there's probably a hundred women in this town who'd do it," Josie answered. "Both of you tryin' to cozy up to our men, talkin' shit about what we do and wear, makin' trouble," Josie said. "You know, Susie, anyone shot me because I was a bitch, I'd learn my lesson. Maybe you should take some of your daddy's money, go somewhere quiet and reflect. For, I don't know, say," she paused then finished, "a hundred years?"

Susie paled and whispered over the wind, "I can't believe you'd say that to me."

"And *I* can't believe you'd get in Violet's face when her brother was murdered three weeks ago!" Josie snapped. "Let me set things straight for you, Susie. Your daddy's money didn't give you carte blanche to traipse around town bein' like you are and you can't trade on the tragedy of what happened with Denny Lowe to be like you are. We all know you sold Colt and Feb's story to that reporter. We didn't think much of you before, now we don't think anything at all."

"Josie—" Chip started.

Josie jerked her head to look at her husband and lifted a hand.

"I'm done," she stated, turned to me, switched topics and turned off her attitude so quickly I wasn't keeping up. "You two come over for dinner. Maybe I'll get Colt and Feb to come over too. I'll make my pot roast. That's a winter dish but my pot roast kicks ass. I'll call." She offered this invitation again like she wasn't standing in the pouring rain and like she hadn't just laid it out for Susie Shepherd in an extremely brutal way.

She came up to me and gave me a cheek kiss even though Joe still had me in his arms. I didn't resist and cheek-kissed her back mostly because I was a little scared of her. She moved away, smiled at Joe and trotted over to her husband while I could do nothing but stare.

"Sorry, Cal," Chip muttered.

"Nothin' to be sorry for," Joe replied and since his arms had loosened, I pulled a bit away and looked up at him to see he was looking at Susie.

"Later, Vi," Chip called.

"'Bye Chip," I said and Chip and Josie moved away.

"You done or is Vi gonna have to put up with your shit every time she sees you?" Joe asked, and I looked to see he was speaking to Susie.

"You gonna threaten me like you did Tina?" Susie sneered, and I stared again since I couldn't believe after that scene that she still had a sneer left in her.

"Nope, just not gonna pull her off you next time," Joe replied.

"Whatever," Susie muttered and started to turn away.

"Why?" Joe asked, and Susie stopped.

"What?" she asked back.

"Why are you such a fuckin' bitch? Honest to God, I don't get it. You have everything and you always had."

Susie's face twisted briefly, a flash of pain then gone.

Then she snapped, "Not everything, Cal. Didn't have a mom."

I almost felt sorry for her before Cal replied, "No excuse, woman, I didn't either."

They locked eyes and I was acutely aware that I was enduring their staring contest while standing in the wind and rain with a possible tornado approaching.

"Joe," I whispered and Joe's arms tensed around me.

"Learn from today, Susie," Joe advised.

She rolled her eyes, flicked out a hand and repeated, "Whatever."

"She won't learn from today," Joe muttered, let me go, took my hand and turned us toward the Mustang.

I noticed Vinnie and Gary's cars were gone. We'd had to take three to fit everyone in, what with Dad coming along, we were one over. This turned into a good thing as they had plenty of room to get everyone in and they'd all disappeared.

Joe moved me to the passenger side, bleeping the locks as he went.

He had the door open and I was about to fold in when we heard Susie call.

"Cal!"

We both looked at her.

"Don't piss me off, Susie," Joe warned.

She pulled her wet hair from her face and held it at the back of her head. Her eyes moved to me then back to Joe.

"I can make a man happy," she announced.

"Seriously?" I whispered, my body getting tense and Joe put pressure on my back to push me in the car.

"I don't mean you!" she shouted and her head jerked to the side and back to the front swiftly, reflexively, making her look like she'd suffered an invisible blow. Something about that made me get even tenser, but not with anger, with surprising compassion.

She was struggling with something and whatever it was, it was big.

"Why can't I—" she started, but Joe interrupted her.

"Jesus Christ, it's rainin', Susie. What the fuck?" Joe asked.

"Joe, listen to her," I whispered urgently, my eyes glued to Susie.

But at Joe's impatience she'd lost it. Her face closed down and she turned away.

"Forget it," she shouted over the wind. Lifting a hand and dropping it in a weirdly defeated way, she jogged away, her ruined-sandaled feet making splashes in the puddles as she ran until she was under the awning that came out over most of the sidewalk in front of the strip mall. She kept running until I lost sight of her because Joe pressed me into the car.

He slammed the door behind me, jogged around the hood as I wiped wet off my face ineffectually since my hands were just as wet, and he folded in beside me.

"We're goin' to Florida, buddy, first fuckin' chance we get," Joe declared the minute he slammed his door. He hadn't even put the key in the ignition and we were both dripping rainwater into the seats and carpet.

"Joe—"

He turned to me and cut me off. "Fair warnin', there's nothin' there. Just the house and the beach, a coupla houses either side. Nothin' to do but fish, cook, sleep, eat, fuck and read."

"Can the girls come?" I asked and watched his face darken to a scowl.

"You ask shit like that again, I'll turn you over my knee."

I felt my stomach flutter. He'd turned me over his knee the night before, part of him being creative, and I'd liked it.

I smiled, leaned into him and whispered, "Joe, not sure that's a deterrent."

His eyes dropped to my mouth and he didn't answer, though his lips twitched.

"Still think the day couldn't go any better?" I asked and his eyes came back to mine.

"Your mother-in-law make good sangria?" he asked back.

"The best," I whispered.

"Then let's get the fuck home," he growled.

I laughed so hard, I had to close my eyes.

This meant I missed the first part of Joe coming in to kiss me.

But I didn't miss the rest.

"Therefore," I finished as the girls sat at their stools in front of me, "getting physical is never the way to go."

I was giving them the hardest lecture in a parent's arsenal. The lecture where you try to teach them not to do something you yourself had done.

These lectures, by the way, never worked.

Kate and Keira's eyes went over my shoulder. Then they both fought smiles.

I was standing at the kitchen counter in front of them and I turned around to see Joe behind me, his hips leaned against the back counter, his arms crossed on his chest, his feet crossed at the ankles, his head bent and he was looking at his boots.

"Joe?" I called. His head came up and I saw he was biting his lip and he was doing this in a clear effort not to laugh. "Joe!" I snapped.

It was relatively late. We'd come home, changed clothes, dried off and I'd done needed repair work on my hair and makeup. We'd had sangria. We'd had steaks Joe braved the storm to cook on the grill and loaded baked potatoes. And we'd had chocolate cream pie (Joe had two slices, partly because he was being nice, mostly because it was the bomb).

The tornado warning turned to a tornado watch and then the storm became rain.

Everyone was gone. All of them, even Dad, were staying at the hotel by the highway overnight and were coming over for pancakes tomorrow morning. Everyone had avoided discussion of me jumping a blonde woman on the sidewalk for no apparent reason for all they knew. Everyone that was except Uncle Vinnie, who every once in a while when he looked at me would snicker, and twice he out-and-out laughed.

Now it was just us. I needed to address the issue with my girls and I didn't need Joe mucking up the works.

"This isn't funny," I hissed at Joe.

"Baby—"

"It isn't!"

"Vi—"

"Stop laughing!" I demanded because he wasn't laughing but he was smiling big and I knew, inside, he was laughing. "This is serious!"

"Buddy," Joe's voice sounded strangled. "Fuck me, baby, but you took her down." He uncrossed his arms, lifted a palm ceiling up and smacked his other hand down on it, making a huge clapping noise before the heels of his hands went to the counter and he burst out laughing.

So did my girls.

"Joe—"

"In the rain," Joe choked out.

"Joe!"

"Both of you wet," Joe continued.

"Joe!"

"You coulda sold tickets to that shit," Joe went on.

"*Joe!*" I shouted.

"Word gets around, honey, gonna have to beat the men back," Joe finished.

I glared at him and then I swung my glare to the girls who were both giggling their asses off. Keira had her elbows to the counter, her face in her hands. Kate had collapsed onto her bent arm on the counter.

"I'm glad you all think this is *so funny*!" I snapped and moved to flounce out but I was caught at the waist and pulled into Joe's arms. My head jerked back and I demanded, "Let me go, Joe."

"Baby—"

"Let…me…go!"

One of Joe's hands curled around the side of my neck and his grinning face got in mine.

"Vi, honey, shit happens, you gotta laugh. You can't laugh, you're fucked."

"You don't know what she said," I whispered, hoping the girls were still giggling so hard they couldn't hear.

"I heard enough to know she deserved a busted lip and then some and any woman talks to Kate or Keira like that, I hope they got enough attitude to do the same fuckin' thing."

My body got tight and I informed him, "Girls don't do that."

"Maybe they should. Tina and Susie had that lesson taught to them a long time ago, maybe they wouldn't be such bitches," Joe replied.

This, I had to admit, was a point to ponder.

"Okay, I don't want *my* girls doin' that," I amended my statement.

"You're tellin' me, some woman comes up to them and treats them to what Susie did to you, you want them to walk away?"

"Yes," I kind of lied.

"What'd Susie do to you?" Keira asked from behind me, and I turned in Joe's arm but didn't move away because his arm was now around my belly and it tightened, pulling my back into his front.

"It doesn't matter. I was hungry and emotional but I still shouldn't have acted that way," I told Keira. "The better woman turns the other cheek."

"Then she gets the upper hand," Joe put in. I got tense and twisted my neck to look up at him as he kept talking. "Maybe wrestling with them on the sidewalk in the rain isn't the way to go, but don't let anyone treat you like shit. No woman and especially no man. Anyone talks trash to you, you walk away. It follows you, you deal with it. You wanna know how, no matter where you are, you call me and I'll tell you how."

"Okay, lecture over," I announced before Joe got on a roll.

"Thanks, Joe," Keira said, and I sighed because I had a feeling everything I'd said to her during my ten minute lecture about how physical violence was never the way was totally forgotten, but Joe's last words about getting the upper hand were etched into her brain.

"Yeah, Joe, thanks," Kate said and added, "And thanks Mawdy. We'll start with turnin' the other cheek."

"Great, *start* with that. Makes me feel better," I muttered.

Kate smiled at me then said, "I'm gonna listen to music and put my new CDs on my MP3. Is that cool?"

"Sure, baby," I answered.

"I'm goin' to my room to get on Messenger and tell all my friends my mom got in a catfight at the strip mall today. Is that cool?" Keira asked, Joe chuckled, Kate giggled and I looked at the ceiling.

Then I looked back at my daughter. "Laptop confiscated, you do that."

"Right," she muttered and grinned. "Then I'll put my new CDs on my MP3 player."

"Good call," I told her.

They moved off to their rooms and Joe's mouth moved to my neck where he kissed me then said in my ear, "You know, even if Keira doesn't share, that shit's gonna get around. Josie Judd's got a big mouth."

I sighed again then turned back to face him. I put my hands on his chest and leaned in deep.

"I know."

He grinned. "You're gonna be a local hero, buddy. Susie isn't real popular."

I bit my lip, lifted a hand to fiddle with the collar of his tee and watched my fingers doing this.

"Joe," I called and stopped speaking.

"Vi, you're pressed up against me, baby."

I looked up at him. "What happened to Susie's mom? Do you know?"

Joe's head tilted slightly to the side and he answered, "More 'burg lore. Drunk driving accident."

"Oh," I whispered, thinking that was awful.

"The person drivin' drunk was her dad."

I felt my eyes get huge and I repeated, "Oh."

"He walked away without a scratch. She broke her neck."

"My God," I breathed.

"Spent the rest of his life makin' it up to Susie by spoilin' her rotten," Joe continued.

This explained a lot. It also made me feel extremely guilty for busting her lip.

"Get that shit outta your head, buddy. It sucks that happened. But it doesn't excuse bein' a bitch," he said.

He was right, it didn't. Or at least not *that* much of a bitch.

"Life's pretty fucked up for everyone, isn't it?" I asked.

"Pretty much," Joe answered.

"You think," I pressed my lips together then went on, "The girls... Sam, Tim, what happened today?"

Joe's brows went up. "You think they'll turn into bitches?"

I shook my head. "I just worry that all of this—"

Joe cut me off. "Look at you."

I blinked and asked, "What?"

He didn't repeat himself. He gave me a squeeze and said, "Look at me."

"Joe, I'm not following."

"You lost your husband and your brother and you got some asshole fuckin' with your head and you keep on keepin' on. My wife killed my kid and my dad died and the last thing he knew in this life was that shit went down. It took me a while but now I'm here. You think Katy and Keirry won't make it through?"

"But—"

"Susie's weak because her daddy was weak. That's what he demonstrated when he got behind the wheel of a car smashed. That's what he taught her then and kept teachin' her. With what I've seen of your dad and mom, got no idea where you learned yours from, but I got mine from Vinnie and Theresa. Bonnie didn't have a moral compass and didn't pay attention when I tried to give her one. When Nicky came into this world, she should have automatically found one and she still didn't. Weak." His arms gave me a squeeze and his face dipped to mine. "Your girls have one, buddy. One they'll never lose. They aren't weak, never will be. You got nothin' to worry about."

"What doesn't kill us makes us stronger," I whispered the words Feb said to me days ago.

"Yeah," Joe whispered back. "At least for some of us."

Suddenly I smiled and I felt something light and golden bubble up in me. Something I used to feel a lot, almost every day. Something I hadn't felt in nearly two years.

"Shit, Joe," I was still whispering, "I got in a catfight today on the sidewalk at a strip mall."

Joe smiled back. "Yeah, honey, you did." I felt my body start shaking and Joe's smile got bigger. "In the rain," he reminded me.

"In the rain," I repeated on a suppressed giggle.

"In a skirt," he went on and my giggle erupted. "That might be my favorite part, outside you bein' wet," he continued and my giggles took control. I collapsed into him, my cheek to his chest, my arms tight around his waist and I laughed out loud.

When I got control of my mirth and was back to quiet giggles, I moved my head so my forehead was pressed against Joe's chest but I didn't release my arms.

"Worth the wait," Joe muttered and my head tipped back.

"What?"

"Every bit of it. Every day, every week, every year, every fuckin' second, buddy." He kept muttering, his eyes intense, his face serious and my breath caught. "This. All of it. Worth the wait."

"Joe," I whispered.

His hand moved to my jaw and his thumb stroked my cheekbone. "Love you, Violet. Even when you're bustin' some bitch's lip open."

I smiled, pressed even deeper into him and whispered, "I love you too, Joe."

His head dipped, his mouth captured mine, and he started to kiss me hard. But our lips broke when Keira called, "Yeesh! Get a room!"

Joe's arms didn't move from around me but he looked over my shoulder and I did too to see Keira walk into the kitchen and direct to the fridge.

"I'm havin' more pie. You guys want pie?" she asked.

"No," I answered.

"Yeah," Joe said.

"Katy!" Keira shouted, "Joe and me are havin' pie! You want pie?"

"Yeah!" Kate shouted back.

Keira got out the pie. Joe's arms gave me a squeeze. I put my cheek to his chest and squeezed him back. Music hit the house then Kate opened the door to her bedroom and it got louder. Keira got the pie cutter. Kate came in and got plates.

I held onto Joe, Joe held onto me, the girls dished out pie and I concentrated on really listening to Kate's music for the first time ever.

It was great.

# Nineteen

## At Peace

Vinnie preceded Cal out to the back deck, and as Cal slid the door closed behind him, he looked through the window at Vi, Theresa and Bea in the kitchen vying for maternal supremacy, thus control over the pancakes.

Three months ago, even knowing Vi was a strong woman and a great mother but not knowing Bea at all, Cal would have put money down on Theresa.

But after yesterday and the shit he heard coming out of Susie's mouth when he'd walked up to them way too late, and Vi's reaction, he knew she was no pushover and she was on her home turf.

And Bea might be shy, but the gentle, loving way she was with all his girls and the soft looks Vi, Kate and Keira aimed at her, he figured she had her ways and she wasn't exactly a dark horse. Not to mention, the woman made one hell of a chocolate cream pie.

Now he wouldn't even place a bet, just sit back and wait for the results.

His eyes moved to Vi's dad, who was bustling around the girls, desperate to make up for lost time. Cal found this annoying and he'd have to have a word with the man. Best way to make up for lost time was to let his granddaughters get to know who he was by acting natural around them, not shoving his nose up their asses.

Finally, his eyes moved to Gary, who was sitting at the table comfortably sipping coffee. Gary had sat at that table a lot over the years. He was always welcome there and he knew it. Gary learned yesterday from watching Pete that he could let go past bad blood. He saw that he'd been reaping the rewards of being a good dad for seventeen years and Pete had been living the nightmare of being a coward for that same time, if not longer.

"Cal, son, we gotta talk about Hart," Vinnie called from behind him and Cal turned from the door feeling his mouth get tight.

His eyes hit his uncle and he moved away from the door, so even if someone looked out they couldn't see him.

He rested a hip against the railing and crossed his arms on his chest while he watched his uncle reach a hand out to one of Vi's pots of flowers that was sitting on the railing. Vinnie dropped his hand before he touched the bright, healthy flowers spilling up, out and down the sides of the pot, and his eyes went to Cal.

"Vi's good with flowers," Vinnie remarked as his gaze took in the rest of the deck.

"Yeah," Cal replied and watched Vinnie give him a look before Vinnie turned his head to look into the house.

"Keeps a nice house," Vinnie went on.

"Uncle Vinnie—" Cal started to cut him off, knowing where this was going but Vinnie's eyes came to his.

"Great girls she's raised. Sweet kids. Funny. Smart," Vinnie continued, not to be stopped.

Cal sighed and said nothing. He knew Vinnie needed to get this out so he let him.

"Care about you," Vinnie noted.

"Yeah," Cal repeated.

"The three of 'em do," Vinnie said.

"Yeah," Cal repeated again.

"Theresa called Carm the minute we hit the hotel last night. She talked about Vi and those girls for two hours. Thought I'd never get to sleep," Vinnie told him, and this surprised Cal considering he hadn't had a follow-up call from Carm in order for her to bitch him out about never calling, not telling her about Vi and the girls, and to arrange her own trip where she could nose into his life and give Vi her personal seal of approval.

"Instead of sellin' my place, should build a bridge considerin' the Bianchis are gonna be spendin' some time down here," Cal quipped.

Vinnie's eyes narrowed. "You think you can walk those girls into my Pizzeria wearin' the suit you wore to take her to her brother's funeral and lookin' at her like she flies out the window on fairy wings and hangs the stars every night and *not* be right back in the Bianchi fold, you got another think comin'."

Jesus. Fairy wings?

"Uncle Vinnie—" Cal started.

Vinnie cut him off. "Don't think I'm stupid, boy. You walked them in for a reason, to give them some family back after they lost theirs."

"Vinnie—"

"Been waitin' seventeen years for this, Cal."

"Uncle—"

"Longer," Vinnie bit out. "You know, Theresa lights a candle for you every week. Every fuckin' week. Been doin' it for over thirty years. You know how many candles she's lit for you?" Vinnie asked.

Cal didn't respond.

"Too many," Vinnie answered his own question.

"She doesn't have to light them anymore," Cal pointed out.

"You got Hart ridin' your ass, she finds out, she'll be at the church every day," Vinnie returned.

Finally they were where he wanted their conversation to be.

"You talk to Sal?" Cal asked.

"First, I'll say this once and that's it. I'm happy for you. I'm happy for her. I'm happy for those girls. Never seen you like this. Not before, not with that other one. Not unless you were with Nicky, and even then you weren't like you were yesterday. You were always watchin' her, guardin', bracin' for what that bitch would do next."

Cal's mouth got tight again as did the rest of his body. "That's done and we're done talkin' about it."

"Waited a long time to say this Cal, gonna say it only once and you're gonna give me that," Vinnie told him.

Cal sighed again, forced his body to relax and leaned deeper into the railing, his eyes on his uncle.

"She's smilin', son," Vinnie said softly and Cal closed his eyes and turned his head toward Vi's yard. He opened his eyes when Vinnie continued. "Lookin' down on you and Vi and those girls and Angie's finally at peace."

Cal clenched his teeth, pulled breath into his nose and looked back at his uncle on the exhale.

"Now you done?" Cal asked.

Vinnie stared at him. Then he grinned.

"Yeah," he said.

"Good," Cal replied then repeated. "You talk to Sal?"

"Yep," Vinnie leaned against the railing too and said no more.

"And?" Cal prompted.

"He's not big on avenging a cop," Vinnie replied. Cal pulled in another breath in order to speak but Vinnie continued. "I haven't told him your involvement, just said I had a friend in Vi and felt the waters 'cause I been thinkin' about this and I'm not big on you owin' Sal a favor."

"Not your choice to make," Cal noted. "Thought I made myself clear on that. And it isn't a favor. It's callin' a marker."

"Somethin' this big, it's a favor, Cal, and favors to men like Sal have a way of lastin' a long time. Lived that with Vinnie Junior. Now got a lifetime of livin' the consequences."

Cal looked back at the yard and crossed one foot at the ankle in an effort to call up patience.

"You got skills, don't think Sal don't remember that shit. You tried to leverage it to pull Vinnie Junior out," Vinnie reminded him, and Cal's eyes cut to his uncle.

"Took a bullet for Sal, Uncle Vinnie," Cal had his own memories to share.

"He hasn't forgotten," Vinnie muttered.

"He owes me, he owes you. You remind him of that?" Cal asked.

"He don't need reminding," Vinnie answered.

"Then what the fuck?" Cal asked.

Vinnie took two steps toward Cal, stopped and whispered, "You're talkin' a hit, son."

"Yeah, I am. I took a hit and Vinnie took the ultimate hit. Your nephew, your son. He owes you, he owes me," Cal repeated.

"He'll want a return," Vinnie said.

"He's already fuckin' *had* it," Cal replied, uncrossing his arms and thumping his fist on his chest under his shoulder where his bullet scar was and then thumping his uncle over the heart.

"You're talkin' a hit," Vinnie repeated.

"You already said that," Cal told him.

Vinnie's brows went up. "You can live with that?"

"Yep," Cal returned. "Absolutely."

"The cops are closin' in," Vinnie explained.

"They been closin' in on Hart for the last decade," Cal clipped.

"You'll carry that mark on your soul—" Vinnie started, but stopped when Cal leaned forward and threw an arm out toward the house.

"He put a bullet it Katy and Keirry's father's *brain*," Cal ground out. "Blew his fuckin' *head off.* I was here when Vi found out he did the same to her brother and she fuckin' *unraveled.* I watched it, Vinnie. I held her in my arms and fucking *watched it.* That's all I could do. No control. No power. He took that from her and he fuckin' took it from me. I stood next to her when she told her girls their uncle was gone and Keira couldn't even keep her fuckin' feet, man. It took about thirty seconds longer before Kate collapsed and she did it in my arms too. I was fuckin' *there*, Vinnie. Hart wants her enough to take them both out. You think that asshole isn't gonna be aimin' at *me*?"

"You can take care of yourself. I been askin' around. The brother didn't know what the fuck he was doin'," Vinnie pointed out. "He should never—"

Cal cut him off. "Tim was a cop, Colt says a good one. You gonna tell me he didn't know what he was doin'?"

"I—"

"You don't talk to Sal, I will," Cal interrupted his uncle.

"Cal, you don't want to owe that man," Vinnie warned.

"He owes me. He got my blood and he got my cousin. He knows that," Cal shot back.

"Cal—"

Cal leaned back an inch. "What the fuck is this? Why are you—?"

Vinnie's torso moved forward two inches. "I lost one boy to him. You think I'm fired up to lose *two*?"

Cal shook his head angrily. "Jesus, Uncle Vinnie. I'm not gonna fuckin' work for him."

"He's persuasive," Vinnie returned.

Cal pointed to the house again. "Nothin' would persuade me to jeopardize that."

"Yeah, and Vinnie Junior had Francesca and he looked at her like she hung the stars and he wanted to give her everything. So he went out to find a way to do that. Easy way is Sal."

"He was twenty-five," Cal reminded him.

"He was in love," Vinnie retorted, jerking his head to the house to make his point.

"Don't pin that shit on Frankie," Cal clipped. "You been singin' that song way too long and you know that shit's not right." Vinnie pressed his lips together and looked away but looked back when Cal kept talking. "I got a business. I got money. I don't need that shit."

"For fuck's sake, Cal, you nearly took her dad down for buyin' Keirry a CD!" Vinnie's voice was rising. "Vi hangs the stars for you and I know you. You're a Callahan. You're a Bianchi. You'll wanna hand her the moon."

"I've already handed her the moon, Vinnie," Cal told him and Vinnie jerked back.

"What?"

Cal didn't repeat himself and he wasn't about to explain. "And I was pissed at Pete because he's up in the girls' faces and he bought Keira a fuckin' boy band CD and I live in this house. I gotta listen to that shit."

Vinnie stared at him a second before he burst out laughing.

Cal didn't laugh.

"I'm not twenty-five anymore, Uncle Vinnie and I'm not Vinnie Junior," Cal stated.

Vinnie stopped laughing because he knew what Cal was saying. Vinnie Junior and Cal had a lot in common with everything. They both thought they found what they wanted at a young age and they both gave up everything for it. Cal wanted Bonnie and he wanted a family and he did everything to make that real. Vinnie wanted it all, but most of all he wanted Frankie and he wanted to prove to her that he was worth her love.

But that was then. This was now.

Cal had learned the hard way that if you found something good, you didn't have to give up anything. If it was good, you got everything you needed without giving up shit. Vinnie Junior hadn't lived to learn that lesson because that lesson killed him. He hadn't lived long enough to learn that Frankie loved him if he could hand her the moon or if he was making pizzas.

Vinnie Junior never got that and Vinnie Senior never admitted out loud that his son made mistakes with the choices he made in his life and the way he'd fucked up everything for himself and for Frankie.

"You unleash Sal or I do it. One of us calls the marker," Cal ordered. "And we do it for Vi, and I'm tellin' you in case you haven't figured it out yet bein' around her and those girls, there's no better fuckin' reason to do it. Daniel Hart took away her man, her kids' father and her brother. They were tight. All of them. He could have destroyed her. He could have brought her low. He could have changed those girls. He could have made her Bonnie. He keeps goin'—"

Vinnie cut him off. "I'll call the marker."

Cal crossed his arms back on his chest, demanding, "Do it now."

"Now?" Vinnie asked.

"Right now," Cal said.

"But…" Vinnie looked toward the house then back at Cal, "pancakes."

"Now," Cal repeated.

Vinnie stared at him and Cal held his stare.

Then Vinnie pulled his phone out of his shirt pocket.

"Christ, son," he muttered on a sigh.

"He needs to have a word with me, I'm standin' right here," Cal offered.

Vinnie looked to the heavens. Then he flipped open his phone and called Sal.

The door slid open and both men's heads jerked that way to see Kate walking out, Cal's phone in her hand.

"Hey, Joe," she said as Vinnie smiled at her as he wandered down the deck steps and out into the wet grass. "Colt's on your phone."

Cal took his phone from her when she got close. Then he lifted his other hand and tugged gently at her hair.

"Thanks, girl," he muttered.

"Yeah," she grinned, glanced at Vinnie who was now several feet into the yard, his back to the deck, his head bent, his hand to his hip and his other hand to his ear. Kate turned and skipped back to the door, went inside and closed it behind her.

Cal put the phone to his ear.

"Yo."

"Need you at the station, man," Colt said without greeting and Cal's back went straight as a bad feeling hit his gut.

"Why?" he asked.

"How soon can you get here?" Colt asked.

"Why?" Cal repeated, losing patience.

"You need a brief," Colt explained.

"About?" Cal prompted.

"Some things you need to know. Some new things have happened," Colt told him.

"Hart?" Cal asked.

"Yep," Colt answered.

"Fuck," Cal bit off.

"You had a bunch of cars in your drive yesterday. You guys still have company or do I have to send out a squad?" Colt asked casually but this question wasn't casual. This question set that bad feeling in his gut to toxic.

"We got company," Cal said and looked at Vinnie. "But send a squad."

"Right," Colt muttered. "He'll be unobtrusive," Colt assured him.

"Don't care if he sits in the fuckin' driveway," Cal replied as he walked to the sliding glass doors. "Just want him here before I go."

"Copy that," Colt said, and Cal flipped his phone closed.

He whistled and Vinnie jerked around to look at him. Cal lifted his hand and flicked his finger in the air. Vinnie nodded. Cal turned, slid open the door and walked through, wracking his brain as to what he'd say to Vi to explain his needing to go to the station.

Then he slid the door closed behind him.

Dad, Gary and Uncle Vinnie were outside in the front yard inspecting the sod Joe and Keira had laid. I was sitting in the living room with Bea and Aunt Theresa. We were sipping coffee with the girls on the floor playing with Mooch. I was thinking about Joe's hasty exit, which he vaguely explained. I was also thinking about the squad car that was parked across the street, the fact that it slid up and stopped before Joe kissed me and walked out the door, and the fact that it didn't move an inch in the ten minutes Joe had been gone.

These thoughts exited my head when Aunt Theresa picked up her big, mailbag sized purse and plopped it on her lap.

"Who knows how long Cal'll be gone, gotta get this done," Aunt Theresa muttered, sounding distracted, but in a businesslike way.

I looked at her then at Bea then at the girls.

"What done?" Keira asked, but Aunt Theresa didn't look up from rummaging around in her small-piece-of-luggage-sized purse.

"You find the time but you find it to give him this," she ordered oddly. "It's time Cal had Nicky back."

I sucked in breath at her words and my eyes flew to Kate, but Kate and Keira were both staring at Aunt Theresa's bag.

"Who's Nicky?" Bea whispered.

"Cal's son," Aunt Theresa answered without even a little ado then went on still without any, "Died when he was a baby. Stupid skank of a wife left him in the bath. Drowned…" Bea gasped and her eyes came to me, but Aunt Theresa pulled out a big square thing wrapped in a black scarf and turned to me. Whipping off the scarf, she announced, "Nicky."

Then she handed me a photo frame.

Automatically my hand reached out and I took it. I brought it toward me and stared.

In it was Joe sitting on one of the benches just inside Vinnie's Pizzeria. There was no one sitting with him. He was alone and in profile, the scarred side of his much younger face to the camera.

It was a black and white, but the sun was shining through the windows of the door and it gleamed against the highly polished wood all around Joe. His shoulders were to the high back of the bench, his legs were stretched straight in front of him, his feet crossed at the ankles.

Smack in the center of his big chest was a little baby, Joe's arm curved around his baby bottom, the baby tucked in that baby ball only babies could make. His baby knees under him, his baby booty in the air.

The baby was asleep, his face turned toward the camera, his cheek on Joe's chest, his little baby fist also resting on Joe's chest close to his beautiful little baby face.

Joe's head was leaning back against the bench, his eyes closed. He looked asleep too. Even if he was asleep, the way he had his son nestled against his chest, safe in the protection of his powerful arm, his bicep stretching the material of his ever-present t-shirt tight, screamed the fact that Joe would allow nothing to hurt his boy, asleep, awake, *ever.*

Unless he wasn't there.

Which, when something hurt his son, he wasn't.

I stared at Joe's profile. He didn't look happy. He looked at peace and that peace had nothing to do with sleep.

Father and son taking a catnap at the family Pizzeria.

God, but they were beautiful.

Silent tears slid down my cheeks.

"I don't know if he has photos," Aunt Theresa said. "He wasn't around much after, so we didn't come down much and then we stopped because he was never around at all."

Kate and Keira had scooted to me and they surrounded me. Both put a hand to the photo and I felt Bea lean in.

"I got tons of pictures of him. Some with the skank in and Manny says he can scan them and do somethin' called Photoshop her out. But I figure Cal'll know she was there and I don't want him to have that reminder of her with him and Nicky," Aunt Theresa said, still businesslike, even brusque, and I knew she had to be because if she wasn't, at that moment she'd be a mess just like me.

"No," I choked, my eyes still riveted to the picture. "No, you're right. Bonnie doesn't get that."

"But enough time has passed. Nicky needs to come home," Aunt Theresa declared. "So we'll start with that one, and later, I'll give you the rest."

"Yes," I whispered, the tears still sliding down my cheeks. "Nicky needs to come home."

And I knew where Nicky would live. By Tim and Sam on our shelves. Tim and Sam would take care of him. They'd always be together and they'd always be with us.

"That Joe's boy?" Kate whispered from beside me. I nodded then turned my head to my daughter, and as hers was so close, I leaned in and kissed her hair. Then I inhaled its scent and I memorized it even though I already had it memorized.

"Yeesh," Keira breathed. "Joe's even hot holdin' a baby."

"Keira!" Kate snapped.

But a short giggle came out of me and I turned to my youngest and kissed her hair too.

"Can I see?" Bea asked softly, and me and my girls turned to her.

"Yeah," I said softly back, handed her the frame and wiped the tears from my cheeks.

She took it and bent her head to study it.

Then, her eyes not leaving the photo, she whispered, "He lost his son."

It hit me belatedly that this was something they shared and it hit hard and sharp, piercing my heart.

"Bea," I murmured, my hand moving to curl around her leg and Keira shifted to sit on the floor at her feet where she leaned in and put her cheek to her Gramma's knee.

Bea settled a hand on Keira's hair as Kate moved around the back of the couch to sit on the armrest by Bea and she leaned in to put her cheek to the top of her Gramma's head.

Bea's eyes moved to me.

"I know how that feels," she said quietly.

"I know you do," I said on a throaty whisper as fresh tears hit my cheeks.

"I had mine longer, though," she went on and her gaze went to Theresa. "He had time to give me my babies."

"Yes, *cara*, count your blessings even through your loss," Aunt Theresa advised gently, knowing, too, what it felt like to lose a son.

Bea looked at me and handed back the picture.

"I like him, hon," she said quietly. "But…"

"What, Bea?" I prompted when she stopped talking.

"You think he liked my pie?" she asked.

I felt my brows inch together at her strange question. Kate's head came up but her arm slid around her Gramma and she gave her a squeeze.

"He *loved* your pie, Gram."

"Yeah," Keira affirmed, looking up at Bea. "He had another piece after you left."

"He did?" Bea asked, her voice weirdly hopeful.

"Yeah," Keira answered, smiling. "He did."

Bea looked at me again. "You think…?" she started then stopped.

"Think what, Bea?" I asked.

Bea looked down at Keira and touched her face.

"Nothin'."

"Family's family," Aunt Theresa piped up, and everyone looked at her but Theresa was looking at Bea. "Family's family," Theresa repeated.

"Does Joe think that?" Bea asked Theresa.

I looked back at her and finally got it.

I squeezed Bea's leg and leaned toward her. "You're a part of our lives." I whispered.

"But he won't want to be reminded—" she started, and I laughed.

"Bea." I leaned in further. "Katy and Keirry look exactly like Tim." I lifted my hand and gestured to the pictures of Tim all over our shelves. "He's everywhere. He'll be everywhere." I touched Keira's hair and finished, "*Forever.*"

"Family's family," Theresa repeated firmly, but Bea still looked unsure.

"I'll never forget Tim, Bea," I promised. "I don't want to. I couldn't lose that, couldn't lose him, everything we were, everything he gave me, us. I'll never lose Tim and Joe wouldn't want me to. He'd never ask that. And he'd never want me to lose you. He knows what you mean to me, the girls. He'd never ask that either."

"You tell him, he likes my pie, I'll make it every time we come visit," Bea promised back.

"Come with your pie, without your pie, he won't care. Only thing that would piss him off is if you didn't come thinkin' you couldn't because of him."

Bea licked her bottom lip. Then she whispered, "Tim would like him."

This was freaky weird, uncomfortable and heartbreakingly sad.

It was also true.

"Yeah," I whispered back.

"You can make your pie for me," Keira put in, trying to lighten the mood.

"And me," Kate said. "But I vote strawberry next time."

"Sugar cream," Keira placed her own vote.

"I'm thinking butterscotch," Bea stated.

"Next time I'll bring my cannoli," Aunt Theresa declared.

"Shit, I'm gonna get fat," I muttered, and Bea laughed.

"From what I can see, hon, fat, skinny, your hair can fall out and Joe won't care," she said.

This was true too.

"Yeah," I smiled at her.

She smiled back then it wobbled. "Just like Tim," she whispered.

My smile wobbled too. "Just like Tim."

Kate put her cheek to her Gramma's hair. Keira put hers to her Gramma's knee. I curled Joe and Nicky tight to my chest and looked at Theresa.

"I'll give him Nicky, soon's I can," I promised.

Aunt Theresa's eyes slid through Bea, Kate and Keira then back to me.

"*Grazie, cara mia,*" she whispered.

"You're welcome," I whispered back, got up, bent in, kissed Aunt Theresa's cheek and then took Nicky and Joe to our bedroom and tucked them safe in my lingerie drawer.

When Cal hit the top of the steps at the station he saw Colt, Sully and Mike Haines in the bullpen, all of them standing around a desk he knew was Colt's.

He knew this because he'd been there before, but even if he hadn't, he'd know it because it had three framed pictures on it.

One was of Colt and Feb at J&J's, Colt seated on his usual stool, Feb standing between his legs, they were pressed close, both of them laughing.

One was like a picture Vi had on her shelves. Feb was laying in a hospital bed, newborn baby Jack in her arms, her face pale and tired, Colt was lying on the covers in the bed with her, his arm around her shoulders, his other hand on Jack's diapered bottom. The last was recent, taken at the barbeque. Colt and Feb standing, Colt had Jack in one arm, his other around Feb. Feb had a gray cat in one arm, her other around Colt and their puppy was sitting on Colt's foot, his tongue lolling out. They were all smiling, even baby Jack and the puppy looked like they were smiling. Although the cat looked like he wanted to be anywhere else but there.

Happy family and about fucking time.

"Yo," he said as Colt unfolded from his chair and Sully and Haines locked eyes on him.

Cal tipped his chin to Haines and watched Haines's jaw get hard. That toxic feeling in his gut churned because he didn't figure Haines was a man to hold a grudge, but if he was Cal didn't figure he was stupid enough to give away his power by letting on that he did.

No. His jaw was hard because of something else.

"Yo, Cal," Colt said quietly and that toxic feeling churned deeper. Cal knew Colt was gentle with women. Otherwise he wasn't loud but he also wasn't quiet.

Cal stopped at their huddle.

"You gave me nothin' on the phone, Colt. Don't make me wait," Cal stated.

"Gotta explain somethin' first." Colt was still being quiet, his eyes watchful and Cal noted that he was more than his usual alert and so were Sully and Haines.

"Do it fast," Cal demanded low.

"First, you gotta know Mike's here for a reason and it's a good one," Colt said, and Cal nodded. He didn't like this at all and it wasn't getting any better.

"Second, you and me had a conversation on your deck a while back, you remember?" Colt asked.

"I remember," Cal answered, his eyes locked on Colt.

"That's between you and me," Colt said still talking quiet.

"It is then why we talkin' about it now?" Cal asked and jerked his head to Sully and Haines.

"Because of that conversation, I made a decision that night that you aren't gonna like," Colt replied, and Cal felt Sully and Haines both close in. They only moved slightly, it was their increased vigilance that filled their huddle like a physical presence.

That poison agitated even deeper in his gut. "Colt—"

"I didn't know things would change. I didn't know they'd do it as fast as they did. And, sorry, man, but once they did, I couldn't be sure it'd take," Colt went on.

"What the fuck?" Cal asked.

"Vi's been getting gifts," Sully said quickly, and Cal's eyes sliced to him.

"I know," Cal told him.

"Every day for nearly three months," Haines put in, and Cal took a step back in order to put distance between him and his friends so he could get control.

This took some doing, but when he accomplished it, he whispered, "What?"

"I didn't know either, Cal," Haines bit off. His eyes cut to Colt and Cal knew that Colt had been having an uncomfortable morning.

Cal's eyes cut to Colt too and he ground out, "Explain."

"You two were focused on Vi and I needed focus on the problem," Colt said.

"So you kept this shit from me?" Cal asked, now his voice was quiet but it was a different kind of quiet from Colt's.

"I made a call," Colt stated.

"It was the wrong one," Cal clipped.

"You disappeared for over two months, man, remember?" Colt shot back.

"I wouldn't have, I knew she was gettin' gifts," Cal returned.

"Bullshit," Colt muttered.

Cal moved and Sully moved too, coming between Colt and Cal.

"Not gonna help things, Cal, you know that. Stand down and listen," Sully said softly.

Cal's eyes were over Sully's shoulder and on Colt.

"Haines was here, why'd you keep it from him?" Cal asked.

"Focus," Colt answered.

"You are so full of shit," Cal bit off.

"Fuck it, Cal, you're talkin' to a man who knows what losin' focus means!" Colt snapped. "I let Feb talk me out of protective custody the day we shoulda gone into custody, the day *before* my woman, fuck, my *women* got kidnapped and taken hostage. One of them was shot. Another one spent months in counseling. That day one man got dead, another man shot, another man shot and hacked to shit. It coulda been worse. I know the importance of keepin' fuckin' *focus*." It sucked but Cal had to give him that and Colt went on. "Neither of you had it. Sully and I do."

Cal stared at Colt then stepped back. Sully stepped away. Haines pulled in a breath and let it out.

"Keep goin'," Cal growled.

"Things have changed," Colt explained.

"Yeah? How?" Cal demanded to know.

"Gifts stopped," Sully said.

"When?" Cal asked.

"Day the brother was murdered," Colt told him.

"But he's still active?" Cal pushed, and they all looked at him.

Then Haines moved. Leaning into Colt's desk, he slid a manila envelope off it and handed it to Cal. Cal took it and Haines started talking.

"Got that in my mail at home yesterday," Haines said.

Cal looked from Haines to the envelope.

"It been printed?" Cal asked.

"Yeah," Haines replied.

"Get anything?" Cal went on, knowing the answer.

"Nope," Haines gave him the answer he knew.

Cal opened the envelope, pulled out a picture, looked at it and felt his mouth get tight.

It was black and white. Taken with a telephoto no doubt, Haines and Vi standing by Vi's Mustang. Haines had his hands at her jaws, his head bent forward, Vi's head was bent back and they were kissing.

Scrawled on the bottom of the photo in black marker was, "Make sure this was good-bye."

Colt twisted and took another envelope from his desk and handed it to Cal.

"I got that in my mail yesterday too," he said. "It's been printed."

Cal opened the envelope and slid out another picture. It was black and white and it was of Vi and him two days ago standing in the drive in the door of her Mustang. It was when she told him she'd do anything he wanted. They were in a tight clinch, mouths locked, going at it.

Scrawled across the bottom of that photo was, "Tell him he's gone or he's next."

Cal closed his eyes and muttered, "Fuck."

"Open threats," Sully said. "New."

"Barry Pryor know about these?" Cal asked, leaning around Colt and tossing the photos on his desk.

"Yep," Colt said.

"What's he think?"

"Thinks you and Vi and the girls should consider protective custody," Colt replied.

Cal's brows went up. "You offerin' that?"

Colt bit his lower lip, something he did when he was pissed. Sully shuffled his feet. Haines made a noise like a growl.

"Talked to the chief. Don't have the resources," Colt told him.

"So it's vigilance," Cal deduced.

"Squads on the street, escorts for you, Vi and the girls," Sully said.

"You got the resources for that?" Cal asked.

"Nope, just talked to the crew. They're in. It won't be constant but they'll do what they can," Colt's eyes caught Cal's. "Chief doesn't need to know," Colt shared.

"You got a gun?" Haines asked.

"Yeah, but it's not sittin' out in the open with Vi and her girls," Cal answered.

"Her girls are old enough to know better," Sully put in.

"Still not doin' it," Cal stated.

"Man, their dad was a cop. They gotta be used to it," Haines noted.

"Yeah, maybe with Tim they were used to it. With me they aren't and I make my gun visible, they'll know somethin's up," Cal returned.

"You aren't gonna tell them?" Colt asked, his voice surprised.

"Fuck no," Cal answered.

"You're shittin' me," Haines muttered.

"You'd tell them?" Cal asked, and Haines held his gaze then a muscle jumped in his jaw. "That's what I thought," Cal said quietly.

"Gonna be hard to give them escorts if you don't tell them," Sully pointed out.

"They won't have escorts, they'll have tails and it'll be up to you and your crew to keep themselves invisible," Cal replied.

"Cal, I can see you wanna keep Kate and Keira in the dark, feelin' safe. But Vi—" Colt started, and Cal looked at him.

"Her brother was murdered three weeks ago, Colt. You think I should go home, tell her someone's taking photos and makin' threats? Against Mike? Against me? After Sam was killed she had nightmares. Bad ones. They're gone now. Now you want her to try to sleep knowin' that? To let her girls go to school? Me go to the store? Mike's a father, it didn't end bad between them, it just ended. She cares about him. You think she'll be okay with thinkin' she brought this shit into *his* life?"

Colt lifted a hand. "All right, Cal, I get it."

No one said a word for a while until Sully ended the silence.

"So now what do we do?" Sully muttered.

"Cal backs off," Haines said, and Cal's eyes sliced to him.

"Come again?" he asked dangerously.

"You'll explain things to her after the Chicago PD takes him down," Haines went on.

"You think he should move out?" Colt asked incredulously.

"I think we make Hart think his threats worked," Mike explained. "Keep Cal safe. Keep an eye on Vi. Pryor says he's close."

"Close with what?" Cal growled.

Mike's eyes caught Cal's. "Tax evasion."

"Jesus Christ," Cal bit out. "That's a fuckin' joke."

"They got a lock on a second set of books," Mike returned.

"A lock?" Cal asked. "They don't even fuckin' have the books?"

"The Feds are involved now," Colt explained. "They're makin' deals."

Cal shook his head. "You want me to leave Vi and the girls for tax evasion?" Cal returned, knowing Mike's game. He didn't want Cal safe. He wanted Cal to leave Vi. "They get him, he's bonded out in hours."

"Odds are, they'll hold him without bail," Colt noted.

"He's got money. He's got lawyers. In his business he knows this shit could happen any time. He'll be prepared," Cal told Colt.

"They set bail, it'll be set high," Sully noted.

"He'll be out," Cal shot back.

"Like I said, Cal, you explain it to her after it's done," Haines repeated.

Cal turned fully to Haines. "Last night she stood in the kitchen in my arms giggling herself stupid. You think after she's walked through two years of hell, I get her to the point of giggling herself stupid, I'm gonna rip that away for tax evasion, you're fuckin' *whacked*," Cal returned, and now Haines's jaw was hard for another reason, his hands were clenched and his body was solid.

Haines glared at Cal. Cal scowled back.

"Boys," Sully mumbled.

Cal looked away from Haines and saw Colt and Sully both were on alert.

"Security, vigilance, tails," Cal declared. "I'll keep my gun where I can get it and carry when I'm not with Vi and the girls."

"You got a permit to carry concealed?" Sully asked.

"Man, do you know what my job is? I got a concealed permit in forty-seven states," Cal answered.

"Right," Sully muttered, his eyes slid to Colt and his lips twitched.

Cal did not find anything funny and his eyes hit Colt.

"He's gettin' impatient and he's gonna fuck up. Every man standin' here knows that. Your job is to make sure he doesn't fuck up with Vi, Kate or Keira in his crosshairs."

"You need to stick to town, not go out on a job," Mike put in. Losing his bid to get Cal out of Vi's house, he was changing his tune and Cal's eyes cut to him.

"Yeah, Mike. Thanks for that heads up," Cal's sarcasm was obvious and Mike straightened.

"We're all on the same side here," Sully noted as the air around Cal and Haines again grew heavy.

Cal speared Sully with a glance and looked at Colt.

"You got the gifts or you send them to Pryor?" he asked.

"Sent an inventory and photos to Pryor. Gifts were delivered here, they've stayed here. They're in evidence," Colt answered.

"I want to see them all. Chronological," Cal demanded.

"Why?" Sully asked and Cal looked at him.

"*Do* you know what I do for a living?"

"Security," Sully answered.

"Stalker sub-specialty," Colt muttered, and Sully looked at his partner.

"No joke?" Sully whispered.

"No joke," Colt repeated.

"Wow," Sully was still whispering. "I didn't know that. We should have brought you in sooner."

Colt looked at the ceiling. Haines pressed his lips together. Cal growled.

"You feed the Feds this shit?" Cal asked Barry. He was sitting in the seat beside Colt's desk after having gone through a fuckload of expensive gifts that got chronologically more expensive, more desperate to make an impression and more demanding to get a reaction.

"Feds aren't interested." Cal heard Barry's answer through the phone.

"Not interested?" Cal asked.

"You're interested. I'm interested. Any Chicago police officer is interested, they knew Tim or not. The Feds…no," Barry answered.

"Nothin' ties him to this shit," Cal surmised.

"I looked into it, Colt looked into it and nothin' ties him to that shit. She was still in Chicago, gettin' visits, maybe they'd care. Harassment isn't a big deal but they'd be happy to pin anything on him, it keeps him locked away even a day longer. But she's in Indiana gettin' gifts we can't pin on him, they don't care," Barry replied. "They want him shut down. They think they got a lock on that and so they're focused."

Cal clenched his teeth. If he heard the fucking word "focused" one more fucking time he was going to do bodily harm.

"You suggested protection, Colt's people can't offer it. You got the resources up there to give Vi and the girls that?" Cal asked.

"She's out of our jurisdiction," Pryor answered.

"What about the Feds?"

"Sorry, man, like I said. They're not interested."

*Fuck!* The word exploded in his brain then Cal took a deep breath and laid it out for Barry.

"You need to keep him busy, Pryor, his mind on other things," Cal advised. "Shake up his operation. Give him headaches. Even if you can't follow through with what you're doin', just be a nuisance."

"How's that gonna help?" Barry asked.

It wasn't, Cal knew from the gifts it wasn't going to stop Hart doing what he was doing.

Daniel Hart was like Kenzie Elise. He was used to getting what he wanted just wanting it. The gifts he'd been sending, the shakeup in the schedule since Vi moved, the escalation of attention were not good signs. Colt knew it and was doing what he could do.

It wasn't right he didn't share with Cal, not only considering what Vi was to Cal but what Cal did for a living, but he was doing all the right things. Including making it so Vi could live her life and only worry about all the shit that was in it, not adding anything extra.

The fact that she was protected, not even receiving the gifts, and Cal had no doubt Hart knew she wasn't, was probably driving Hart up the wall. He couldn't get close, not with a restraining order and a cop living on Vi's street. He wasn't stupid and wouldn't take that chance. Colt would take him down in a second. Hart could only hope Colt would mess up, miss a delivery, she'd get her diamonds and he'd get his reaction. Something Hart needed to function and something Colt had kept from him.

What Cal had to find was Hart's Marco. Marco held Kenzie's strings and yanked them when she got out of line. No man was an island. Not even the top of the heap in a crime syndicate. Hart had buyers, sellers, suppliers, employees—people he had to keep happy. Focusing on the mother of two daughters in Indiana when his focus should be on business, business that was all of a sudden getting a shakedown from the cops, would not make any of those people happy.

And then Sal could do his work which would make all those people really not happy and hopefully end in Daniel Hart being dead.

That was Cal's plan. It was shit but at least it was a plan.

"Feds makin' deals, cops on his ass, his attention is scattered, his operation goes into disarray, someone's gonna notice and he's gonna have to make a choice. He chooses Vi, his operation falls apart, people get pissed, he's fucked. He doesn't choose Vi, shifts his attention away, gets with the program, she's free. Either way, she wins," Cal explained.

"You're askin' me to put a shitload of boys in danger. This guy does not like to be messed with," Barry replied.

"I'm askin' you to serve and protect. Tim did it and died doin' it," Cal reminded him.

Barry was silent and when he spoke his voice low and pissed.

"I met you, I liked you, but don't fuckin' use the Tim card on me," he warned. "You didn't know him, you don't get that card."

"His daughters go to bed under the same roof as me. I know him, Barry," Cal said quietly. "You've seen the waste Hart laid to those girls' lives but I'm cleanin' it up and you think I won't use that card for them, you're fuckin' crazy."

Barry was silent again, it lasted longer this time then he bit out, "We'll do what we can."

Cal didn't respond.

Barry spoke again, "You tellin' me you're livin' with Vi and the girls?"

"Yeah," Cal answered.

Cal heard movement on the phone and he knew it was Barry seeking privacy when he said, "I checked you out."

Cal pulled in breath and closed his eyes.

"Your line clean?" Barry asked.

Cal opened his eyes. "I'm on Colt's phone at the station."

"You talk to him, you do it on a clean line," Barry advised, and Cal was surprised.

"He's family," Cal replied.

"You talk to him, you do it on a clean line," Barry repeated.

"Barry—"

"I don't wanna know," Barry cut him off.

"You know," Cal said again quietly, and heard Barry sigh.

"Yeah, I know."

"That shit doesn't blow back on me," Cal warned.

"We didn't have this conversation," Barry stated.

"Good," Cal replied.

"Jesus. All the luck, Vi moves away from that fuckface and moves next door to a security specialist with mafia ties. Fuck me," Barry muttered.

"She doesn't seem real lucky to me," Cal remarked.

"Maybe her luck has changed," Barry returned. "I gotta go. I got a captain to try to convince to commence operation shakedown on a guy who's whacked one of his detectives and put two others in the hospital, one's still a vegetable three years down the line. Lucky for you, Vi and those girls, he misses Tim's shortstop on our softball team."

"Tim good?" Cal asked.

"The best," Barry answered.

"I'll bet," Cal murmured.

Barry was silent again. Then he whispered, "Keep her safe."

"You got it," Cal promised.

Barry disconnected and Cal put down the phone.

Colt rounded Cal's chair and sat in his own.

"Pryor in line with your plan?" Colt asked, and Cal looked at him.

"Yeah," Cal answered.

Colt studied Cal then asked, "We good?"

Cal studied Colt then asked back, "I tried to take on Denny Lowe without keepin' you in the loop, would you be good with me?"

Colt's face went hard. "Not the same thing and you know it, Cal."

"Explain to me how."

"You were there when we had our conversation."

Cal leaned into his friend. "Fuck, Colt, just you roundin' my fuckin' house to *have* that conversation meant you knew."

Colt held Cal's stare and then his jaw clenched.

"I stepped out for two and half months, leavin' her alone," Cal reminded him.

"You're in that line of work, Cal. You knew what was goin' down and where it was gonna go. You stepped out for a reason. You can't tell me you weren't workin' through some shit," Colt returned.

"I didn't have the intel, Colt, you kept it from me. I was workin' through some shit but I woulda worked through it next door to her fuckin' house and in the know about the escalation of attention," Cal shot back.

"We had our eye on her and the girls," Colt informed him.

"That be good enough for you, someone was takin' pictures of Feb and Jack?" Cal asked.

"Like I said, I made a call. You didn't like it but nothin' I can do to change it. We knew what was goin' on, we kept our shit sharp and she's good. Pryor knew all about it and her brother did too and they still did what they thought they had to do so that isn't on me. You're welcome to stay pissed at me, man, but it's a waste of energy. It's done."

This was all true and it pissed him off.

Cal stood and looked down at Colt. "Now are you assured of my *focus*?"

Colt visibly bit back a smile. "Yeah."

"Thrilled, man," Cal growled and turned to the stairs.

"This is over, I'll get Feb to make you one of her frittatas," Colt called after him.

"Can't wait," Cal called back but didn't turn as he took the stairs.

This was true too but he wasn't giving Colt that. He'd heard about Feb's frittatas. According to her brother Morrie, they were heaven in the form of eggs.

They might be good but Cal would bet a thousand bucks that Vi's seafood shit was better.

Cal was nearly home when his cell rang. He looked at the display and it said "unknown caller."

He flipped it open and put it to his ear.

"Yo."

"You're gettin' a call in ten minutes at your office," a man's voice said then disconnected.

Fucking Sal. Always the drama.

He turned away from home and toward his office. By the time he unlocked the door, the phone on Lindy's desk was ringing. He picked it up and put it to his ear.

"Yo."

"Cal, *figlio*," Sal said in his ear and Cal could hear the smile in his voice.

"Sal," Cal greeted, not smiling.

"I hear you were in Chicago. Saw Vinnie, Theresa. No visit for me?"

"It wasn't a social call," Cal told him, and Sal was quiet.

Then he said, "Yeah, bad business. Vinnie told me."

Cal was impatient. "Listen, I got a woman at home, she's got daughters and someone's takin' snapshots and sendin' them to cops. I don't wanna be in the office. I wanna be home. You have a good talk with Vinnie?"

"We talked but I think you need to come up to Chicago. We'll have a sit down," Sal said.

There it was. Sal was in the mood to be persuasive.

"Sal, respect, goes without saying," Cal told him. "But I got a woman at home whose got daughters and someone's takin' snapshots, sendin' gifts and puttin' bullets in the brains of the men in her life. The man who's ordering that shit is in Chicago. I don't wanna be in Chicago, I don't wanna be away from her and I don't want *her* to be in Chicago. If you talked to Vinnie then we don't need a sit down."

"I can see why this would make you impatient but there are things to discuss," Sal countered.

"You want to discuss, I go this alone," Cal returned, and Sal let out a very loud sigh.

"We're talkin' a cop's wife here, *figlio*," Sal noted.

"We're talkin' my woman here, Sal. Hart sent a picture. I'm next," Cal told him.

"How 'bout this? I send a message to Hart, explain you're family and that he should move on," Sal suggested.

"How 'bout this?" Cal returned. "This guy isn't family. This guy is a mean motherfucker who clawed his way to the top and took down everything that got in his way. He doesn't get family. He doesn't get respect. He doesn't get anything but what he takes. He took from you. He took from me. He took from my family and your family and he took from my woman, who, Sal, cop's widow or not, she's mine now and that means she's family and you can't deny that, and he's *still* takin' from her. Are you tellin' me, he did all that, you're gonna send this fucker a note?"

"I gotta get organized, Cal."

"You gotta ask a soldier to put a bullet in a gun," Cal replied.

"We're talkin' war," Sal pointed out. "War requires organization."

"That's not what we're talkin' and you know it. The big man is out, you move in, you get back what you lost seven years ago and then some."

"Takeover like that, like I said, needs organization."

"You're up for that challenge."

"This is big what you're askin' me."

"It was bigger what I gave to you."

Sal was quiet again then he sighed loudly again. "The Bianchis. Always a pain in my ass."

"The pain was in my shoulder, Sal. You had a situation, Frankie called me and I stood up for you. I put myself in its path and took that bullet *for you.* You're breathin'. I'm askin' you to make sure I keep doin' it and Vi lives the rest of her life doin' it easy."

Cal listened to silence and this lasted awhile.

Finally Sal stated, "All right, *figlio.* I do this, we're square."

"You got it."

"*Fin,*" Sal pressed.

"*Fin,*" Cal repeated.

"You come to Chicago, you sit at my table, we're nothin' but family."

"Yeah Sal, me and Vinnie, we learned that lesson a long time ago."

Another sigh. "Vinnie Junior was a good man."

"He's on Hart too."

"I remember," Sal said softly.

"And I'll never forget."

"You Bianchis. Your loyalty is rabid."

Cal shook his head and reminded him, "Bianchi blood is in your veins."

"Luckily Giglia blood is dominant. Bianchis think with their hearts. Giglias think with their balls."

Cal smiled. "Giglias think with their dicks, and you see Vi, you'll think I got Giglia blood."

Cal listened as Sal laughed then he listened to that laughter die.

"Vinnie said she's a good woman," Sal said quietly.

Cal didn't respond. Sal was family and now Vi was family. Their paths would cross. Sal would find out for himself one day.

"You held this marker a long time," Sal noted. "You're pullin' it for her, she must be."

"Make my woman safe, Sal," Cal ordered softly.

"*Fatto, figlio.* Done," Sal replied just as softly. "But when it's done, I want her at my table. Gina will make cannelloni. You like Gina's cannelloni."

"I figure Vi, the girls and me will be in Chicago a lot, Sal. We'll be at your table."

"It'll be good to see you, Cal," Sal said and he meant it, the crazy fuck.

Cal didn't reply. He liked Sal just as much as he didn't. But Gina's cannelloni would be worth dinner at his table.

"I'll make contact when it's done," Sal went on.

"I'll expect one of your boys to call, tell me what to do and hang up and I'll expect it soon," Cal said, and Sal laughed.

"You can't be too careful," Sal remarked.

"No, you can't," Cal replied with zero humor.

"Right," Sal whispered. "So you be careful."

"You too," Cal replied.

"You're a good man, *figlio.*"

Cal didn't know what to do with that, coming from Sal, so he just said, "Thanks, Sal, later."

"*Ciao.*"

Cal heard the disconnect, put the receiver in its cradle and shook his head at the phone. Then he left his office, locked it and walked to his truck so he could get home.

I sat in bed wearing one of Joe's tees and rubbing moisturizer in my face as Joe walked out of the bathroom wearing nothing but his jeans.

All the family was gone, which was a relief. Not that I didn't like them being there, and the girls loved it, just that I was glad to have this first meeting done and be back to just us.

Joe had been busy that day, having a conversation with Uncle Vinnie, taking off for a couple of hours then having a conversation with Dad. The good part was, after his conversation with Dad, Dad seemed to settle down. The bad part was, Joe seemed tense all day, after the conversation with Vinnie, after getting home, and even after Dad seemed to settle in.

I watched Joe pull off his jeans, toss them on the floor, throw back the covers and slide into bed. I put my moisturizer aside as he yanked the covers to his waist then I moved to sit astride him. His big hands went to my hips, spanning them. My hands went to his shoulders and I leaned down so our faces were close.

"You okay?" I asked, searching his eyes.

"Yep," he lied.

"You sure?"

"Yep," he lied again.

"What was with the squad car that was outside the whole time you were gone?" I asked.

"Colt was at the station, he needed to talk to me, he wanted you covered," Joe answered casually.

I didn't know if this was a lie or not, but what I did know was that Joe wanted me to let it slide. The problem with that was I couldn't.

"Okay, breaking that down, he's been gone before, and you've been gone too, and no squad car was sitting outside," I pointed out.

"Colt was in the mood to be cautious."

I bit my lip then let that go. "Okay then, why did Colt need you at the station?"

Joe's fingers flexed at my hips and he spoke gently. "Baby, your brother was murdered and then things got intense for you and for me. After that happened to Sam, he and I needed a brief. We needed one a while ago but Colt gave us some time to get our shit sorted. Our shit is sorted, he called me for a brief."

This made sense but I still didn't trust it.

"You wouldn't lie to me, would you?" I whispered.

His reply was a little scary and he did it on another flex of his fingers at my hips which made it scarier. "I'd do anything for you, buddy."

My head tipped to the side. "Was that an answer?"

His eyes never left mine. "Only one you're gonna get."

We stared at each other several moments before I whispered, "You want me to let it go."

"How many times do I have to tell you to relax?" he asked.

"A billion a day," I answered.

He grinned then said, "Relax."

I looked at the pillow by his head and muttered, "Right."

"Baby," he called, and I looked back into his eyes. When our eyes caught, he lifted his head and touched his mouth to mine. After he settled back down, he murmured, "Trust me."

"Okay," I whispered instantly because he needed me to and because I did.

His hands started to slide up my sides, taking my tee with it when I asked, "What did you talk to Dad about?"

His hands went from the outside of the tee to the inside so I felt the heat of them against my skin. "Told him to cool it with the girls. Told him he did the right thing, leavin' your mom. Told him she wasn't with him, he was always welcome here. Told him the best way he could work his way in was not to work so fuckin' hard. And finally told him his granddaughters already loved him so he could relax."

One of my hands slid to his neck. "Lucky you, considering he actually seemed to listen when you told him to relax."

Joe grinned again. "Yeah. You could learn from that."

I laughed as I felt Joe's hands divide, one went up my back and pressed me down, one went into my panties and curved around my ass.

I dropped my mouth to his and said softly, "Joe."

"Yeah, honey," he said back.

"Aunt Theresa gave me something to give to you," I blurted.

Now wasn't the right time, I knew that. I should have done it after we had sex when he was mellow and hadn't had a day that made him tense. But that picture in my lingerie drawer felt like a smoldering ember ready to burst into flames. Not only it being there and me knowing it was there but the girls knowing it was there and wondering when it would come out for air. Who knew? One of them (probably Keira) might let our scene in the living room that day slip.

He was keeping something from me, I knew it and I was going to let him. For whatever reason, he'd made the decision to make that play and I was going to let him have that too.

We were in a relationship. I had to trust him and I did. If I needed to know, he'd tell me. Tim had been a badass macho man too and he'd had times where he clammed up about shit at work or shit he had to do, stuff that would make us worry. I knew when my man was erecting a shield around me and I knew he had to do what he had to do. If I fought that, it wouldn't be pretty. No matter what it was, I had to let Joe do what he had to do and trust that he could protect me and my girls. And I did.

For my part, the conversation with Theresa, the picture of Joe and Nicky, I couldn't sit on that and I couldn't keep it from him.

For me, it had to be out in the open.

"Vi," Joe called, and I focused on him to see he was very focused on me and this time his fingers flexed into the flesh of my ass. "Jesus. What'd she give you?"

"Something to give to you."

Joe closed his eyes and muttered, "Oh fuck."

I lifted a hand from his shoulder to rest it against his cheek and guessed, "You know what it is, don't you?"

He opened his eyes and started, "Vi—"

I dropped my head to rest my forehead against his. "I want him on the shelves." I watched Joe close his eyes again and pressed on, "With Sam." Joe's hand clenched my ass as I finished on a whisper, "And Tim."

Suddenly, he knifed up to sitting, taking me with him, both arms wrapped tight around me and I knew it was in order to set me aside, so I held on.

"Joe—" I said to his profile, his head was turned away.

"Not ready for that, Vi."

"Joe—"

He turned to me and repeated, "Baby, I said I'm not ready."

If he wasn't ready after seventeen years, it was time for him to be ready.

"He's part of you, Joe, which means he's part of this family. Let me bring Nicky home."

I watched his face get hard and his hands moved to grasp my waist, definitely ready to set me aside. But I clenched my thighs on his hips and held on harder with my arms.

"You said you'd help me with Sam and you are. And you said I could help you let what happened with Nicky go and you have to start letting me do that."

His face stayed hard and his voice was tight when he said, "I've let it go."

I risked moving my hands to his jaws and whispered, "Joe, you won't even look at his picture." Joe glared at me, his fingers gripping my waist hard, and I risked more. "He was beautiful, honey."

He closed his eyes again, pain slicing through his face and my fingers tensed at his jaws.

"Christ, Vi—" he started.

"And you've always been beautiful."

His eyes opened and the pain was there too.

"Baby—" I whispered when I saw it.

Joe cut me off. "I got rid of 'em."

"What?" I asked.

"The photos, his clothes, his crib. Everything."

I felt the sting of tears in my eyes when I asked, "Why?"

"Breadbox," he answered, and I blinked, feeling a tear slide down my cheek.

"What?"

"His casket. The size of a breadbox."

At his words, what they conjured and knowing that memory was burned on his brain, the sob tore from my throat. I couldn't stop it and it was so strong it seared a path of fire.

"Joe—"

"She'd been straight since before she got pregnant. The longest she'd gone. I thought we had it beat."

"You don't have to explain this to me."

He went on like I didn't speak. "The Bonnie she was, I'd never leave her with him, not with Dad that fuckin' sick. I'd never even have a kid with her. But I didn't think she was that Bonnie anymore."

"Joe—"

"So I left her with him."

"You didn't have a choice, baby. You had to keep your family fed."

"I thought we had it beat," he murmured.

"Stop it, honey. You weren't responsible for that."

He pulled in breath, closed his eyes and kept them closed a long time before he opened them. Then his fingers wrapped around my wrist and he pulled my hand down to his chest so I could feel the strength of his heartbeat.

"He's here, buddy, that's all I could take, that's all I need. I had to let go the rest. The rest is too much," he told me.

I was a mother and I was a widow. I knew better than that.

"You need all you can get," I whispered.

"Can't take anymore," he replied.

I pressed my hand into his chest. "That just isn't true."

"Vi—"

"Bring him home."

"Violet—"

"Let me bring him home."

"Buddy—"

I pulled my hand from his and put it back to his face. "He's a part of you and I want you, *all* of you. I want my girls to have all of you. Joe, honey, please let me bring him home."

We stared at each other again for a long time before Joe whispered a tortured, "Fuck…get it."

I didn't delay. I let him go, jumped from the bed and went to the dresser. I pulled the picture frame from the drawer and hustled back to our bed. Then I climbed into Joe's lap, snuggled close and kept my eyes glued to his face when I turned the picture to him.

Joe's eyes locked on the picture and the pain came back, stronger, contorting his features as I felt his body turn solid against mine.

When he didn't say anything, I whispered, "You looked at peace." My tears could be heard in my words but Joe's eyes didn't move from the picture.

"I had the world sleepin' on my chest," he replied, his voice low, thick.

I looked at the photo. "Funny how the world can fit in your arm."

"Funny," Joe repeated quietly, and I looked at him to see that now he was looking at me and then his arm slid around me.

"Joe—" I started, new tears gliding down my face.

"Put him on your shelves, buddy."

I hugged the photo to my chest and wiped the wetness from my cheeks. The only words there were to say were the words I said.

"Thank you."

Before I could move he asked, "Girls there when Theresa gave you that?"

I nodded. "Keira said you looked hot, even holding a baby."

A short laugh came from him. It sounded startled, like he didn't think he'd ever laugh again.

Then he looked down at my chest and muttered, "Fuck."

"What?" I whispered and his eyes came to mine.

"He'd be old enough to date Kate," he answered.

I didn't know what to do with this or what Joe was doing with it, so I stayed still and silent and waited.

"Fuck," Joe repeated.

I braved the uncertain vibe and informed him, "He got even a little of you, Dane wouldn't stand a chance." Joe looked at me and I continued, "Or Keira would make him her mission and they'd likely be fightin' over him."

His hand slid up my back until his fingers sifted into my hair.

"It sucks, sayin' this, I hate to say it but I'm going to," he said.

"What?"

"He lived, I might still be with her and you'd be next door and I wouldn't be right here."

Quickly, I reminded him, "For good or for bad, that didn't happen, Joe."

"You'd be here, alone, or…fuck, you'd be with Haines," he went on like I didn't speak.

I was seeing that this was heading down the way, way, *way* wrong path.

"Joe, don't. Life is life, baby. That's all it is."

His eyes locked with mine.

"It'd never be good with her. She wasn't gonna change and she didn't. But, if he lived, I'd never leave her and that's all I'd have. Except for Nicky, I'd never have somethin' sweet."

I set the picture on the nightstand and moved to straddle him, pushing him to his back.

"Yes you would." I pressed my face into his neck and my lips to his skin. "I saw you, I'd go all Tina and do everything to catch your eye. Watering my flowers in a bikini and all sorts of shit. We wouldn't be able to fight the attraction and we'd have a torrid affair," I told him. "It would suck and I'd feel shit, but you'd leave her for me and I'd pay you back by givin' you all sorts of sweet things."

As I spoke, my lips traveled his neck and throat and his hands started roaming my body.

"You're full of shit, buddy. I'd see you waterin' your flowers in a bikini, I'd come onto you and you'd go prude and freeze me out."

I lifted my head and looked down on him just as his fingers curled around my breast.

"Joe, you fucked me on the hood of your car even when I was seriously pissed at you," I reminded him. "I think we can take it as read I wouldn't go prude."

His thumb swiped my nipple, my lips parted and my hips jerked. At this, his eyes grew dark in a seriously sexy way and his lips tipped up at the ends.

"Yeah," he muttered. "Forgot about that."

I blinked then felt my body get tight. "You forgot?"

His lips curled into a full-on smile. "Thanks for reminding me."

Even though I knew he didn't forget and was just fucking with me, I still heard an angry noise escape my throat. I started to pull away but Joe rolled so he was on top and his face disappeared in my neck as his thumb circled my nipple.

"We had an affair, buddy, we'd probably have to do it on the GT more than once," he noted against my neck.

"We'd have to do it so you'd remember we did it before," I snapped back, but this wasn't as effective as it should have been since my breathing was getting heavy and my legs were moving to tangle with his.

I felt his chuckle against my skin then his lips moved to my jaw. "We'd probably have to do it in the car too."

"Would you remember that?"

He ignored my semi-irate question. "And be creative about other places we did it."

"Joe—"

"In your car."

"Joe—"

"In your garage."

"Joe—"

"In my truck."

"Joe!"

His mouth went to mine and I stopped breathing at what I saw in his eyes.

"You're right, though. We would have found each other."

My body relaxed under his and I whispered, "Joe."

His head came up and he grinned slow. "You realize, buddy, that we're discussing the ways I'd cheat on Bonnie."

It struck me that we actually were and that was kind of funny, therefore I giggled.

Then I said through a smile and while running my fingers along his scar, up his cheekbone and into his hair. "I met her once, honey, and I didn't like her much so I'm not too broken up about that."

His head came down and he kissed me through his gentle laughter.

Then he fucked me, but nothing about that was gentle.

It would be later, when I was almost asleep, that I realized we'd both laughed about Bonnie, but more importantly, Joe had done it.

And I fell asleep thinking that, even though it was funny, what we said was also probably true.

And that was even funnier.

The next morning while Kate and Keira were running around like they'd never gotten ready for school in their lives, Keira working herself into a frenzy because it was her first day in high school, and Joe was making them oatmeal and being calm, which had no effect on them being in a tizzy, I walked out with the photo frame filled with Joe and Nicky and I put it on the shelves.

Kate saw, smiled at me but she didn't say a word.

Keira didn't see me because she was arguing with Joe. "But Joe, I can't eat oatmeal. My stomach feels funny."

"Nerves, baby, eat," Joe replied.

"I'll get sick," Keira returned.

"No you won't," Joe said.

Keira looked at me and cried, "Mom!"

"Eat your oatmeal, honey," I told her.

She stomped a foot on a repeated, annoyed, "Mom!"

"Keirry, the last time you vomited you were in second grade and had the flu. The last time you threatened to vomit was two days ago," I said. "You need food or you'll get cranky before second period. Eat your oatmeal."

"Argh!" she shouted and then snatched up her oatmeal.

Keira ate her oatmeal and we had seven more dramas before she and Kate climbed into Kate's Fiesta and they headed out while Joe and I waved them good-bye (well, Joe stood by me while I waved good-bye, he didn't wave).

When they were out of sight, I turned and moved into Joe, wrapping my arms around him. I looked up at him and he looked down at me.

"Shit, my baby's in high school," I muttered.

"Yeah," was his reply.

"Shit," I repeated, pressed my face into his chest and his fingers wrapped around the back of my neck.

"Let's just hope she doesn't snag a boyfriend on day one," Joe told the top of my head.

I tipped my head back. "She's on a mission so don't hope too hard. You do, you're cruisin' for disappointment."

Joe grinned, dipped his face to mine, kissed me and then guided me into the house.

He knew the picture was there, I knew he did. He didn't say anything and neither did I.

I got ready and went to work and Joe got ready with me and went to his office.

Life goes on.

And life went on, safe and sweet in most ways, insane and crazed because two teenage girls lived in our house.

But that shield Joe put up was strong and held true for two beautiful weeks.

Then Daniel Hart blew it to smithereens.

# Twenty

## Collapse

Benny heard the knock on his door, his eyes opened and the woman in his bed moved. When she reminded him of her presence, he struggled to remember her name. He could remember her lips, could even call up a vision of them. Full, soft, a nice red-pink even without lipstick. Heaven wrapped around his cock, especially with all her long, dark hair all around, soft against his skin. He usually liked to watch and would pull their hair back. Her hair was so soft he left it where it was.

It came to him. Carla.

She lifted her head. "Whas that?"

"Go back to sleep. I'll take care of it," Benny told her, throwing the covers back and grabbing his jeans from the floor.

Carla collapsed back into bed and he heard her soft snore.

He yanked up his jeans, left the room and hit the stairs, surprised her snores began immediately. He knew then that was it, she was out.

Not that she'd made an impression on him, only her lips had, but even if he woke up beside her and she rallied, he knew she was out. He hated snoring and he also couldn't call up much emotion for some bitch who could hear a knock on the door in the early hours of morning and leave him to it.

He wouldn't let her do anything, but he figured Violet would not go back to sleep and leave Cal to deal. She'd wait to go back to sleep when she knew he was back in bed with her, safe. And he knew she'd do this with her dead husband too. She'd do this before she learned knocks in the moments before dawn could mean bad shit had come calling. She'd do this because it was the right thing to do if you were a good person or you gave a shit about someone.

Not many good ones out there, he was thinking as he walked down the stairs. He was just glad Cal finally found himself one of them.

He stopped at the foot of the stairs and felt a clutch in his chest when he heard the knocks coming from the back door, not the front.

"Fuck me," he muttered, went to the hall closet, grabbed his gun and headed back toward the kitchen.

Standing to the side of the door, he shoved the curtain partially aside and saw Frankie standing on his back stoop.

His first instinct was to open the door, shove the bitch down the stairs, close the door, walk upstairs and kick Carla out. Just seeing Francesca put him in no mood to be around any woman. But his mother would have a conniption if he put his hand on a woman in anger, even if that woman was Francesca, who his ma detested, so he didn't do this. His mother in a conniption wasn't worth the trouble, even for the satisfaction of laying his hands on his dead brother's bitch.

Therefore he switched on the outside light, turned the lock and opened the door, keeping his gun in his hand.

The life she led with Vinnie, Francesca had learned and she clocked the gun first.

"Benny," she whispered.

"Say what you gotta say, bitch, and get the fuck outta my space," Benny replied.

Her eyes lifted and the second thing she clocked was his chest. Stopping there, her face got pale, he could see it even in the dark. Stupid, greedy slut.

"Two seconds," Benny warned, and Frankie's eyes shot to his.

"It's Cal," she said quickly and that feeling in his chest got tighter.

Benny opened the door further, stepped back and Frankie moved in. Benny shut the door, locked it, flipped off the light switch and grabbed her arm, yanking her into the hall.

"Benny—" she started when he stopped them in the hall.

"I got company," he told her, his voice quiet and he saw her head tip back to look up the stairs.

"Figures," she whispered and her voice was tight.

"You got somethin' to say about Cal?" Benny prompted.

"Who is she?" Frankie asked, and Benny pressed his lips together. Then she went on and her voice was lower but lighter. Apologetic. "Benny—"

"When'd it become your business who I fuck?" Benny asked.

"Ben," she whispered.

"That sign went up on the restaurant, Frankie, but when it did I didn't become a millionaire. Got no more than Pop which wasn't good enough for you. Not gonna give you the chance to wrap your golden cunt around my cock and get me to sell into a franchise like you tried to talk Vinnie into talkin' Pop into doin'."

In a flash he felt her attitude hit the hall.

"You're talkin' that trash to me and I used to be a member of your family," she hissed.

"You came to my house in the middle of the night with info about Cal and you're leadin' with this shit, so brace, babe, 'cause you brought it on yourself. You gave up your position in this family when you led Vinnie by his dick straight to Sal. I'll remind you, this isn't the first time after we lost him you tried to get it from me and I told you before, that shit is *not* fuckin' happening. You came here to say something, say it."

"I needed to be with someone who loved him like I did," she snapped in her defense.

"Yeah, bet he was smilin' down from heaven when he saw you tryin' to shove your hand down my pants," Benny fired back.

"We were both emotional. Things got outta hand."

"No, nothin' got *in* your hand."

"*You* kissed *me*," she returned.

Benny leaned in and got in her face. "Bullshit, you pressed up against me, laid it on me and I was wasted."

"I was wasted too."

"Woman, your boyfriend had been whacked."

"And your brother had been whacked."

Benny wanted to relive this like he wanted to be kicked in the gonads. Therefore he went silent and started counting to ten.

He got to three when Frankie kept at him. "You still kissed me."

"Babe, tits like yours, I'm blotto, doesn't matter who you are. They're pressed against me and they got a mouth attached to the same body, it's on mine, I'm gonna stick my tongue in it."

She reared back. "God, Ben, I forgot how much of a fuckin' dick you are. Always were. I shouldn't have even come here."

"Now we're talkin' about what I wanna talk about. Why did you?"

"'Cause Cal never treated me like shit and Sal ordered a hit on Hart and it went bad. Word's spreadin' fast that Hart's gonna be aimin' for Cal. Someone's gotta warn him. I don't have his number and I couldn't go to your dad so, stupid me, I came to you."

Benny went solid for half a second. Then he moved. Leaving Francesca where she stood, he hit the stairs and took them three at a time.

He turned on the light and Carla moaned, turned then got up on a forearm. By the time she did this Benny had laid his gun on the dresser and was pulling on a t-shirt.

"Whas goin' on?" she asked, pulling hair from her face and Benny looked at her.

Knockout. Fantastic lips, just like he remembered. Great tits. Frankie's were better, he knew that even if he hadn't seen them or touched them, only had them pressed against him once, but Carla's were sweet.

Still, he'd had his fill of Carla.

"Darlin', you need to go on home," he said, going to the dresser and grabbing some socks.

"What?" she asked, blinking.

"You need to go home, Carla," Benny repeated and walked to the bed, sitting on the edge of it. "Now."

He had his socks on and was reaching for his boots when he noticed she hadn't moved, so he looked at her. She was looking at the door so Benny's head swung that way to see Frankie standing in it.

"Pretty, honey," Frankie muttered. "You always had good taste."

Benny's mouth got tight and he pulled on a boot.

"Who's she?" Carla asked.

Benny didn't answer. Instead he ordered, "Out of bed, babe. Go home."

Carla was up on her ass with the sheet to her chest and her narrowed eyes were glued to the door. "Who's she?" she repeated.

Benny pulled on his second boot, saw Frankie hadn't moved but was smiling her smile that made his dick start to get hard.

There was a reason Vinnie gave it all for her. The bitch was beyond a knockout. Only a quarter Italian, the rest of her was mutt and she got the best of it all. Almond-shaped eyes with light brown irises and naturally long, curling lashes. A thick head of rich, dark brown hair she always wore long. Flawless light skin that made your mouth water just to taste it and made you wonder if that creamy skin was the same everywhere. Fantastic tits, great ass and a tiny waist, which were the only things that made her long legs not look like they went straight to her throat.

And the way she smiled that smile, like she had a secret, a really fucking good one you had to know and the only way she'd tell you was when you were close, deep inside and she'd whisper it in your ear. The perfect package from top to toe.

He straightened from the bed and looked down at Carla. "Not gonna say it again, babe."

Carla looked at him. "Are you tellin' me that you just let me suck your cock and then I let you fuck me and you wake me up in the middle of the night to shift me out for round two? You're good, Benny Bianchi, fuckin' great, like they all said, but nothin's good enough to put up with *that.*"

Benny put his hands to his hips. "See this failed to sink in, woman, but I just got dressed and put my boots on. I'm gonna fuck someone else, she's standin' in line at the fuckin' bedroom door, would I put my clothes on?" She opened her mouth to speak, but he didn't wait for her to answer. "I got somethin' to do, somethin' before the crack of dawn, somethin' fuckin' important. I asked nice, now I'll say it straight. Get your ass outta my bed, get dressed and get the fuck outta my house."

She glared at him and then asked sarcastically, "You think maybe she can leave while I get dressed?"

Benny walked to the dresser and grabbed his gun. Carla's eyes rounded on it, the situation of a wakeup call at that hour dawned on her and her body went still. But Frankie spoke.

"Sure," she said, turned and walked from the door.

Benny waited while Carla dressed and she hurried out the door not sparing him a glance and not getting close. This was either because he'd been a dick or because he was still carrying his gun. He didn't much care which. She was gone.

He went to his nightstand and tagged his phone. Scrolling down, he called Cal while he shoved his gun in the waistband of his jeans. He waited for a pick up but there was none. It went to voicemail.

Benny figured, he had Vi in his bed, he would likely not pick up the phone at that hour either because he was busy with something not worth disturbing to answer the phone or sleeping after being exhausted by doing something that wasn't worth disturbing to answer the phone. Benny disconnected the call and tried again. Voicemail. On the third try, when he got voicemail, he left a message.

"*Cugino*. Benny. It's urgent. Call me."

He left the room and Frankie was waiting at the bottom of the stairs.

He stopped in her space. "Did I ask you to stay?"

"Will you call me when you find out everything's all right?"

Benny clenched his teeth. She was worried. He heard it. She didn't even try to hide it.

He knew her life since losing Vinnie had been totally fucked. He thought she'd move on but she didn't. He didn't want to know but he had to admit he'd gone out of his way to keep tabs. Alone, she didn't date, didn't even look as far as he knew. She went to work. She came home. She'd go to Rico's by herself once in a while and she'd go home by herself. She went on vacation by herself. All in all, she just kept herself to herself.

She was close to Sal, had made friends with some of his boys when Vinnie was working for Sal and she stayed that way because they were the only family she had left. Everyone else had turned their backs on her because they blamed her for Vinnie.

The Bianchis were clean and always were. The Giglias were dirty and always were. They met at reunions, weddings, funerals and when they had to because they were family. The mingling of blood two generations ago was not a happy occasion for the Bianchis. But family was family.

His path crossed with Frankie's because Sal considered Frankie family. Her man had been whacked under his watch and Sal might be a piece of shit but he took care of family. After Vinnie died and Benny made it clear he didn't want her company and she stopped coming around all the time, Benny saw her, but rarely. He knew she'd got tight with Cal because of Vinnie and stayed that way for reasons known only to her and Cal. That was to say she stayed that way as much as Cal would let anyone stay close—which was to say that she probably hadn't seen him in years.

But she was worried and, fuck him, he fucking hated hearing that in her voice.

"I'll call," he gritted out.

"Thanks, Ben," she whispered and turned toward the kitchen at the back which brought something to Benny's mind.

"Frankie," he called, she stopped in the dark hallway and turned to him.

"Yeah?"

"Why'd you come to the back door?"

She hesitated then he saw her shoulders shrug. "Old lady Zambino lives across the street."

"So?"

"So, she's Bella's grandma."

Benny was getting impatient. Therefore, he asked again, "So?"

"So, Bella works for you."

"Frankie—"

In a rush, she explained, "She's old and she's nosy. If old lady Zambino sees me and tells Bella, Bella tells Theresa, Theresa doesn't care why I'm here she just doesn't want me near any of you, 'specially you. So Theresa gets pissed but she'd get pissed at you. I was tryin'…"

She stopped speaking but he knew what she was trying to do. Save him from the wrath of his ma because she was right. Frankie saw him from two blocks away and his mother knew it, Ma would lose her fucking mind. Since Benny's ma lost her fucking mind on a regular basis, Benny could handle it, but it'd be a pain in the ass like it always was and it was cool Frankie tried to shield him from that shit.

He didn't say thanks, he didn't speak at all, and she turned again and walked away.

She stopped at the doorway to the kitchen and turned back.

"Benny," she called.

"Got things to do, Frankie," he reminded her.

She didn't listen or didn't care.

Instead, she said, "It's a sin to speak ill of the dead."

Benny felt his body get tight.

"Don't—" he whispered.

She did. "I never told anyone this before."

"Frankie—"

"Everyone thought it was me. The franchise idea. That sandwich shop that went bust. Sal."

Benny started toward her but she didn't stop talking and she didn't move.

"It was all Vinnie."

He grabbed her arm and pulled her through the kitchen.

"Ask Sal. He knows," she told him as he reached for the door, but he never made it. She dug her heels in and yanked her arm out of his hold. "I didn't say shit because I loved him. I didn't want anyone to think he was weak. I didn't want anyone to think he'd failed. I didn't want anyone to think he was anything but what they thought he was. That he was great because he was. He just wasn't perfect."

"Save this shit, Frankie, I don't wanna hear it."

"But I don't want you to think that, not about me," she kept on. "I don't know why but I don't want you to think it."

"Too bad. I know this is bullshit."

She got close. She didn't touch him, but she got close enough he could smell her perfume and her hair.

"You know it isn't," she whispered. "Vinnie Senior, Theresa, Manny. They were blind, but you know. Cal knows. Carm knows. You *know.* Cal, Carm, they won't say it but they know it. You got them away from Vinnie, from Theresa, you asked, they'd tell it to you straight. But you…you just won't admit it."

"Babe, I got shit *to do*," he reminded her.

She stared at him and then shook her head. "I don't know why I…" She stopped speaking and reached for the doorknob, "Don't bother tellin' me about Cal. I'll get it from Sal."

The tone of her voice had gone hard, dead. Benny didn't like. It didn't suit her. These days she was all about attitude but it wasn't hard. Back in the day, she laughed a lot. Even if someone told a joke that wasn't funny, she'd laugh and it'd sound real, even though she was only doing it to make them feel good. And she was all energy. She seemed electric even sitting curled up to Vinnie and watching TV.

He hadn't seen that in years, hadn't heard her laughter, but he'd never heard her voice sound hard and dead.

He put his hand to her arm. "Frankie—"

She yanked her arm free and pulled open the door.

"Be well, Ben," she said in that same voice and she did it without looking at him. Then she moved down his back stoop.

For some fucking reason he followed her, grabbed her arm and swung her around. When her head tipped back to look at him, he had no goddamned clue what to say.

"What?" she asked.

"I'll call about Cal."

"Like I said, don't bother."

"I'll call."

"Ben, you don't wanna talk to me, fine. I get it. It's cool, been livin' with that for years. I'll get the news from Sal or one of the boys."

His hand tightened on her arm and he brought her closer to his body, close enough to smell that perfume again, and in a moment of lunatic honesty, he had to admit he liked it.

"I'll fucking call."

She went still for a moment that seemed to stretch for a long time and she stared up at him. As she did, all he could see were her eyes, her hair and all he could smell was her perfume and his hand automatically tightened further on her arm.

When it did, she whispered, "Suit yourself."

She yanked her arm from his hand and he watched her walk two paces then for some reason she started running. He stood still as he listened to his back gate open and close and he stayed still as he heard her start her car and drive away.

The current situation hit him, his body jolted, he cleared his mind of Frankie, turned and jogged into the house.

I felt Joe's hand on the small of my back and his hip pressed to mine in bed.

"Buddy, girls need to get to school," he said into my ear.

He was sitting on my side of the bed. I was lying on my stomach in it. He'd been up for a while. I had not.

"Mm," I replied and didn't open my eyes because my eyelids weighed three tons.

"They've had breakfast and they're ready to go," Joe went on.

I continued to ignore him and made no reply.

Joe sounded like he was trying not to laugh when he finished. "Don't you want to say good-bye?"

"Go away," I mumbled into my pillow.

"Baby—"

"Away," I partially repeated myself.

I heard Joe's laughter and if I had it in me I'd glare at him. Lucky for him, I didn't have it in me.

His lips were back at my ear. "Best part about last night was you comin' home."

At this point, if I had it in me, I would have rolled my eyes.

"And then you makin' me come," he continued, his voice lower. "That is, after you made me watch you makin' yourself come."

"Leave me alone," I muttered not wanting to remember even as good as it was. I'd been out of control. No inhibitions, none. It had been wild, and considering our sex life, that was practically unbelievable. Even Joe had been surprised, I could tell. He didn't complain nor did he resist, but he'd been surprised.

"Gotta get you drunk more often, buddy," Joe decided.

"Alone," I begged.

"Every night," Joe kept at me.

I forced my eyes open, shifted only my eyeballs to him and declared, "No more drink. No more sex. Ever."

He burst out laughing which shook the bed and made me hold onto the pillow tighter and close my eyes against my stomach roiling.

"Colt's bachelor party tonight means I'll be home drunk," he told me, and I groaned. It was Feb's bachelorette party last night that set the scene for my drunken sex attack on my boyfriend. When he spoke again, his mouth was again at my ear. "So you better rest up, honey."

I wasn't hungover enough not to get a little thrill at what Joe might dream up drunk. I liked what he could do sober and I liked what he let me do when I was drunk. Joe drunk was probably going to be *awesome*.

Nevertheless, I asked the pillow, "Didn't I say go away?"

"Yeah," he answered, and I could hear the smile in his voice.

"Then go," I demanded.

I felt his lips on my shoulder then I felt his fingers tuck my hair behind my ear.

"I'll tell the girls you said good-bye," he offered.

"Thanks," I muttered.

"I'm goin' into the office."

"Great," I said.

"You feel up to it, we'll go to Frank's for lunch."

I groaned again and burrowed into the pillows.

"Don't talk about food," I whispered, he chuckled and his hand slid from the small of my back over my ass.

"Get rest and then get fluids in you," he advised.

"Mm," I mumbled.

"Only you could be cute hungover," he muttered as I felt his weight leave the bed.

"Don't be nice when I'm hungover," I demanded.

"Why?" Joe sounded surprised and amused.

"I like to be nice back when you're nice and I can't move," I explained.

I felt his lips hit my neck and then they went back to my ear. "You can be nice tonight when I come home drunk. We'll start with that thing you did when you climbed astride my stomach and move on from there."

I closed my eyes tighter as memories invaded of me drunk and naked, climbing on top of a just awake Joe and then giving him a one-woman show. A show he liked so much he turned the light on to watch.

My body trembled with embarrassment.

"Ugh," I grunted.

"Fuck, baby, never forget that. That beats you wrestlin' wet and in a skirt with Susie Shepherd."

I lifted and turned my head, opening my eyes to glare up at him. His head moved back with my movements and I saw he was smiling huge which meant he was laughing inside.

"Go away, Joe!" I snapped and winced but his hand wrapped around the back of my head, he lifted me up further, kissed me hard and closed-mouthed and then he let me go.

"Rest," he ordered.

"I would if you'd leave me alone," I informed him and he just grinned.

Then he smacked my ass lightly over the covers and walked out of the room.

I collapsed into the bed and listened to Joe talk quietly to the girls. Then I heard them leave. After that, I fell into blissful sleep having no idea that shield Joe had built around me was about to collapse.

Colt climbed the stairs of the station and saw Sully's head come up when he hit the top. Then he watched Sully smile.

"Was Feb as shitfaced as Raine when she got home?" he asked before Colt even made it to his desk.

Colt smiled. Feb was beyond shitfaced. Feb was so wasted she could barely move. However, she wasn't so wasted she couldn't use her mouth, which she did to spectacular results after which she kissed his chest, grinned up at him like she'd just succeeded in climbing Mount Everest instead of sucking him off and then promptly passed out.

"Too bad Feb only gets one bachelorette party," Colt muttered as he shrugged off his blazer and hooked it around the back of his chair.

"Yeah." Sully grinned. "Bachelorette parties are my favorite part of my friends gettin' hitched."

Considering Sully's wife Lorraine got smashed after a daiquiri and a half, Colt figured Sully had a pretty good night.

"I'm doin' a Meems run," Sully told him, straightening from his chair as Colt sat in his. "You want a coffee?"

Mimi's Café was two blocks away and her coffee was so good, you never said no when someone offered it.

"Yeah. Cappuccino," Colt replied as his phone rang.

He reached for it and Sully reached for his blazer.

"Colton," he said into the receiver after he put it to his ear.

"Colt? Pryor. We got a situation," he heard Barry Pryor say. He sounded far from happy and Colt's eyes cut to Sully. Sully saw the look in them and stopped moving.

"What?" Colt asked.

"Last night was a bloody one for Chicago," Pryor answered.

"What?" Colt asked again.

"Someone tried to whack Daniel Hart. This whack failed to take down Hart but it took down two of his top boys. Hart didn't hesitate with retribution and a drive-by at Sal Giglia's favorite haunt saw four of his soldiers buy it, not to mention a waitress and the bartender is critical."

Colt closed his eyes and sat back in his chair muttering, "Fuck."

"You know about our friend?" Pryor asked, and Colt opened his eyes to see Sully sit in the chair by Colt's desk.

Colt knew. He knew that Cal's grandfather's sister married a Giglia. He knew the Giglias were big time mob, not low level, upper echelon and they had been for a long time. He knew Cal had briefly worked security for Giglia during the last war Giglia had with Hart. He knew Cal had lost his cousin to that war and took a bullet protecting Giglia during it. And lastly, he knew that Cal was impatient enough to act reckless and activate the family.

"Yeah," he answered Pryor.

"Well, my guess is, Hart does too. My guess is Hart knows that our friend is losin' patience. My guess is Hart's gonna know what our friend's up to," Pryor stated.

"What have your boys been doin'?" Colt asked.

"As you know, captain agreed and Fed's approved so we been gettin' in his business. He hasn't been likin' this much," Pryor replied.

"He put that two with the other two and get four?"

"He's a psychopath but he isn't stupid."

"Was Sal Giglia at that restaurant last night?" Colt asked.

"Yeah. He's fine but I'm guessin' he's also pissed which means the earth under Chicago shifted last night and we all gotta hold on," Pryor answered.

Colt suspected he wasn't wrong. He just hoped that quake wouldn't hit his town.

"Any more to report?" Colt asked.

"Last night was busy. Feds got the books," Pryor told him.

Finally, good news.

He looked at Sully and said, "They got the books."

Sully's brows went up but Pryor kept talking.

"They got forensic accountants combin' 'em and a judge on hold for a warrant."

"How long's that gonna take?"

"They're fast-tracked."

"That isn't an answer," Colt told him.

"My gut?" Pryor asked.

"Lay it out," Colt answered.

"Make some calls. They're workin' fast but Hart'll work faster. This isn't about Vi anymore. This is about retaliation."

"Right," Colt said.

"I'll keep you briefed. You do the same," Pryor ordered.

"Yeah. Later."

"Later."

Colt put the receiver in the cradle and then twisted to his blazer to get his cell asking Sully, "Someone on Vi this mornin'?"

"Chris," Sully answered. "What's up?"

"Call him. A hit on Hart went bad last night. Two down, Hart survived. He retaliated against Sal Giglia and five were killed and the kills were sloppy, they took out a waitress and the bartender's critical. Giglia's gonna move back. They got the books. It's goin' down."

"This gonna blow down here?" Sully asked, moving quickly back to his desk.

"My guess, Pryor's gut? Yeah. You call Chris. Tell him she needs to be home behind Cal's security fortress and Chris is glued to her. Then you call who's on the girls. They're taken out of school and they're home. We got someone on Cal?"

"Adam," Sully answered, his phone to his ear.

Colt scrolled down to Cal and hit go. He put the phone to his ear and waited, getting voicemail. He disconnected and called again and again got voicemail.

"Fuck," he hissed as he waited for the message to clear and heard the beep. "Cal, Colt. Minute you get this, call me. Shit went down in Chicago last night. You, Vi and the girls need to be home. Sully's talkin' to Chris who's got Vi and we're movin' to get the girls."

He disconnected and scrolled up to Adam.

"Chris isn't answering," Sully said, and Colt looked at him.

"What?"

"Called twice. No answer," Sully said. The receiver still at his ear he spoke into it. "Connie," he said to the woman who was working dispatch. "Get a callout to Chris. You connect, you tell him to move on Vi, take her home, batten down the hatches and call me in that order. He can brief her after he gets briefed."

Colt stood and grabbed his blazer, hitting go on Adam on his phone. He started to move to the back stairs and saw Mike alighting them, so he stopped and lifted a palm to Mike who took one look at his face and halted.

Colt got voicemail.

"Fuck!" he clipped, flipped his phone shut and turned to Sully. "I'm goin' to the high school. You get a callout to whoever's on the girls. I'll meet them there." He turned to Mike. "Shit's blowin' down from Chicago. You need to go to the garden center."

"Fuck!" Mike hissed, turned without a word and sprinted down the stairs.

Colt looked back at Sully. "Find Cal."

Then he ran after Mike.

"You get Cal?" Sal asked his boy.

"Voicemail," was the answer.

Sal stared at him and then quietly said, "Take a hike. Keep at him. Tell me when you've connected. 'Til then, my eyes don't see you."

Sal took in the nod from his boy who missed his hit. That boy disappeared and then he was alone.

Sal picked up his phone, scrolled down and hit go.

"Yeah?" he heard a groggy Vinnie answer.

"You're comin' to me or I'm comin' to you but we gotta meet and we gotta do it ten minutes ago."

There was silence.

Then Vinnie said, "I'm comin' to you."

Sal flipped his phone shut.

Kate disarmed the alarm and opened the door. She walked in, Keira followed and Colt followed Keira.

"Stand there," Colt ordered gently.

The girls were just inside the door. He looked over his shoulder at Eric who had tailed the girls to school and stayed for a while to make sure things were okay. Eric was in plainclothes, standing on the front porch, and Colt gave him a nod.

Eric nodded back, stood sentry at the front door and Colt did a walk-through of the house.

Vi and Joe's bed was unmade, something that nagged him considering both the girls' beds were made, there were no dishes in the sink, no crumbs on the counter and only a glitter purple laptop was sitting on the coffee table and a pair of flip-flops were in the corner. Other than that everything seemed in order. Vi kept a tidy house. No signs of struggle.

"Mom here?" Kate asked when he hit the living room.

"She'll be here soon," Colt said, even though he'd learned from the girls she wasn't at the garden center. She had the day off preparing for the possible aftermath of the bachelorette party. She wasn't at home but her Mustang was in the drive.

Colt looked at Eric again and Eric moved out of the door.

"Settle in, I'll be back," Colt said to Kate and Keira and followed Eric. Once he got the door closed and walked Eric into the yard, he turned his back to the house and got close. "Call it in. She's gone. Bed's unmade, car's in the drive. All eyes peeled for her. I want officers here. Plainclothes in case the girls see them canvassing. Door to door. Did they see Vi leave the house? What was she wearing? What was she driving? Was she with someone? Did they see anyone suspicious? Every house. They're not home, you get to Feb, get their phone numbers and call them at work. Copy that?"

Eric nodded and headed to his car. Colt jogged to his house. Feb had the door open before he was halfway across the street. She looked tired and not well, wearing her hangover on her face, which to Colt made her no less gorgeous and at any other time he would find this hilarious. Now, he did not.

When he made it to her he didn't say hello.

"Call Jackie. She comes to get Jack. You go over and wait with the girls."

Feb's face got even paler and Colt watched the line of her body turn static.

"Wait for what?" she asked.

"Feb—" he started but didn't finish. Her eyes sliced to Vi's house before she nodded and without a word hustled back into the house.

Colt started to jog back across his yard when his phone rang. He slowed to a walk, pulled it out of his blazer, looked at the display, flipped it open and put it to his ear.

"What you got for me, Sul?"

"Chris and Adam down." The words sounded like they'd been dragged out of his partner's throat and they made Colt stop dead right in the middle of the street.

"Down how?"

"Don't know. They're both breathin' but they're also both in ambulances."

"Vi isn't at her house," Colt informed him.

"Mike called. She isn't at the garden center either."

"She didn't have a shift today."

"Yeah, Mike talked to Bobbie," Sully said then hissed, "Fuck, why did we not know this?"

"Where was Chris found?"

"Car on the side of the road outside town found by a Good Samaritan. Door open. Radio smashed. Chris unconscious in a ditch."

"Any idea why he was there?" Colt asked.

"No clue, but it looks like he didn't make his shift," Sully answered.

"Adam?"

"Mike found him."

"Where?"

"Mike left the garden center, went to Cal's offices. He found Adam in his car outside."

"Cal?"

"No sign and his girl isn't there either."

"Struggle?"

Silence and Colt started walking again, his eyes on Vi's house, both girls looking out the window at him.

"Sully, were there signs of a struggle?"

"Colt…" Sully stopped speaking and Colt stopped on the sidewalk, turned with his side to the girls but faced away, across the street, so the girls couldn't see him when he reacted to what he was about to hear.

"Sully, tell me."

"You're friends with Cal."

"Sul—"

Sully sighed then spoke fast. "Mike says it's bad. Boys are goin' to the scene. Two men at the scene shot dead. Mike doesn't know either of them but says there was no muss no fuss with the gunshot wounds. Mike says prelim looks like warning shots fired meant to incapacitate, not meant to take them out, kill shots fired when they didn't stop. But he says there's lots of blood, place is a mess, looks like it was bad and there's no Cal."

"Cal said he'd keep his gun on him, he wasn't with the girls," Colt muttered.

"Any chance he'd have Vi with him?"

"Girls say they left together this morning. Them for school, Cal headed for the office. Kate said Vi was hungover. He left her in bed. Somethin' got her out of that bed but she didn't make it and she also didn't make a mess gettin' ready. Nothin' that looks like she even left in a hurry."

"Cal wouldn't—?"

"Grab her and go? Not without the girls."

"I'll get a man at the school, just in case they turn up," Sully said.

"I'm doin' another sweep of the house," Colt told him then asked, "Where's Mike?"

"Climbin' the bloody walls at Cal's office," Sully answered, not being funny, being almost literal.

"He may need to be locked down," Colt advised.

"Boys headin' his way know, everyone knows. Sean's off today, but he's been called and he's headed to Mike."

Colt looked back at the house to see the girls hadn't moved.

"I gotta get into that house," he told Sully.

"Yeah. I'm command central as of now. You get anything, you feed it to me."

"Got it and what you get, you feed to Pryor."

Sully didn't have to agree, he'd do it. Instead he said, "While you're lookin' around, pray."

Colt didn't normally have time for that. He was of a mind that God didn't need to be informed of His own business. But with what was going down and those two girls looking out the window, he'd make time.

"Out," he said to Sully.

"Later," Sully replied and disconnected.

Colt forced himself to walk calmly to the house. He opened the door and both girls were no longer at the window. They were at the door waiting for him.

"Mom?" Kate asked, and Colt shook his head.

"We're lookin'. Feb's comin' over. Can you make coffee?"

Kate nodded but Keira spoke and what she asked meant Kate didn't move.

"Where's Joe? Has anyone called Joe?"

Jesus. How did he answer that?

Shit.

"We can't find Joe," he answered, and Keira turned to Kate, her movement jerky, panicked.

Dammit, where the fuck was Feb?

Kate's arms slid around her sister but her eyes stayed on Colt.

"Keirry, let's make Colt coffee."

"But—" Keira started, and Kate looked at her sister.

"Coffee," she whispered.

Keira's lip quivered and then she nodded.

Both girls moved to the kitchen and Colt went to the bedroom.

He stood in the center of the floor space and looked around. Unmade bed. Cal's jeans on the floor. All of Vi's clothes, including bra, tossed to the floor around Cal's jeans. The top of the dresser was tidy, the drawers all closed, no clothes hanging out as if hastily pulled out and the drawers shoved closed. Some jewelry sitting on top but there was more on Cal's nightstand.

She'd taken off her clothes before she hit the bed and she hit the bed on Cal's side but he'd taken off her jewelry last night, put it on his nightstand. Her nightstand had a lamp, a book and a jar of moisturizer. Nothing else. If she took off her jewelry in bed, it'd be on her nightstand. Cal took it off her.

"Talk to me," he muttered as he walked to the bed and he saw it.

The covers weren't thrown back like you do when you get out of bed. It was like she slid out from under them. Colt walked to them, carefully lifted an edge of the covers and saw a phone in the bed.

"Fuck me," he murmured and picked up the phone. He flipped it open and went to received calls. The last one was from Cal. Colt looked to the bedside clock. She got the call just over thirty minutes ago.

He looked back to the clothes on the floor.

Cal's jeans, socks, Vi's skirt, top, bra. Colt's eyes scanned—a pair of sandals that looked like they were kicked off, sitting by the side of the dresser.

Cal wore tees and Colt reckoned Vi wore underwear.

He went to the clothes and toed them.

No tee and no underwear.

She'd put on Cal's tee and her underwear from last night.

"Fuck me," he repeated.

She *had* been in a hurry. In such a hurry that she hadn't even dressed. Just pulled on Cal's tee, her underwear and took off. She got the call while in bed, dropped the phone, slid out without even moving the covers off her, got dressed and went.

Whatever Cal said to her made her move. Or whatever someone said to her on Cal's phone made her move.

Colt opened his phone, hit Sully's number and put it to his ear.

"Talk to me," Sully said.

"My guess, she's in Cal's tee, black, not wearin' shoes. She left her phone in the bed."

"How you guess that?"

"Yesterday's clothes are still on the floor, her underwear missin', Cal's tee missin' and her phone was in the bed. I don't picture Cal as a man who picks his clothes up off the floor. Vi does it like Feb does for me, in the morning when she gets up. He stripped off before goin' to bed like he probably always does. She stripped off because she was drunk. This morning she got a call from Cal's phone thirty minutes ago. She grabbed what was handy and she moved."

"But moved where? Eric reports her car in the drive."

"No clue."

"We need to see if we can track the GPS in his phone, got his number?"

"I'll text it to you."

"Do it fast."

"You got it. I'll keep lookin'."

"Not much, just knowin' Vi moved out quick and she's wearin' a black tee." It sounded like a complaint but Sully was just bitching because he was worried.

"Get Pryor on the line. I want Daniel Hart's MO. And get him to call Sal Giglia. This is family and Giglia could use some brownie points with the cops."

"Giglia's got issues, he needs to focus."

"Giglia's issues are with Daniel Hart. He cooperates, his war gets a lot less bloody."

"You ever hear of a big man in the mob sittin' down with cops, family or not?"

"Nope, but I've heard about Giglia and I know he's unpredictable, he's got brass balls and he does shit just because it amuses him. Maybe we'll get lucky and this'll amuse him."

"Yeah," Sully muttered. "Maybe we'll get lucky." Then Colt heard the disconnect.

Colt scrolled to Cal's number, memorized it and then texted it to Sully.

He moved into the bathroom as he heard Feb call her hellos to the girls, thank Christ.

"I don't wanna hear this shit," Vinnie said, sitting out on Sal's back porch, Sal's breakfast and coffee dishes on the table, most of the food untouched, the coffee, though, was gone.

"Vincent," Sal muttered.

"Somethin' happens to Cal—" Vinnie started.

"Got my boys on it," Sal stated, his face closed.

He was locked tight. This was because he was worried.

Sal was an asshole and Vinnie hated him. Vinnie grew up with him and never much liked him, but when Sal took his son, the hate began. But Sal was a family man, you worked for him or not. He felt what happened to Vinnie Junior and he felt it deep. It wasn't just one of his boys who he also thought of as family. It was just plain family and that went deeper. Cal, the same. Vinnie Junior was family, he was one of Sal's boys. But Cal was also family and he was smart, sharp, honest and didn't take shit. And Cal had taken a bullet for Sal. Cal was not only family to Sal, Sal respected him. That went even deeper.

This shit cut to the bone beyond Sal surviving last night's bloodbath. It wasn't Sal who screwed the pooch but it was his responsibility that his man missed. This was on him and he felt it.

"What I hear, Hart doesn't fuck around. He finds his mark, the bullet goes into the brain," Vinnie noted. He hated saying it, hated even thinking it, but that was what he knew.

"He won't get Cal," Sal remarked.

"He does—"

"He won't."

The two men stared at each other and then Sal's eyes went over Vinnie's shoulder.

"You get Cal?" Sal asked, and Vinnie turned to see one of Sal's soldiers standing just outside the house.

"No, but the cops are on the phone," his boy answered.

"Talked to the cops last night. Today, got things to do. You call Indianapolis like I asked? Get someone down there to move in?" Sal pressed, and the boy's face stayed solid. He was locked tight too.

Vinnie knew why when he spoke. "They're steerin' clear. It's all over the radio. Joe Callahan and his woman are both missin'. Cops in some 'burg fifteen miles west of Indy are on the hunt. Two boys shot at Callahan's offices. Chicago PD preliminary identification from pictures puts them in Hart's army."

Vinnie's ass came off the chair. He didn't stand but he also wasn't sitting.

"Vi's girls?" he asked, and the soldier's eyes came to him.

"What?"

"Cal's woman's daughters. They safe?" Vinnie explained.

"Haven't heard anything about them," the man answered.

"Find out and tell the cops to go fuck themselves," Sal ordered, and the man looked at his boss.

"They want a meet. They want cooperation. Feds are in town and they got news for you. They say they think this meet could be mutually beneficial," the soldier said to Sal.

This was news, such news it was shocking. The Chicago PD and Feds sitting down with family to make mutually beneficial deals? In this mess, that was a ray of light. Theresa, if she knew about it, which she fucking didn't, would call it a miracle.

Vinnie forced himself to sit down and he forced his voice to a whisper when he demanded, "Take the meet."

Sal didn't take his eyes from his boy and his face betrayed nothing.

"Sal, take the fuckin' meet." Vinnie kept whispering. "This is about Cal."

"Tell them we meet here," Sal ordered his man.

"Tina reports she saw Vi get into a black Cadillac sometime after eight o'clock. She said Vi was wearin' nothing but a t-shirt. No shoes. She just ran out of the house, caddy was on the street. The door was thrown open, she got in and the car took off," Eric told Colt.

Colt studiously kept his eyes from going to Tina's house. If they went to Tina's house, he might feel the need to walk over there and shake her until her fucking teeth rattled.

"That bitch knows Vi has a situation. Fuck, the whole town knows, and Vi's jumpin' into cars wearin' nothin' but a tee and she didn't say shit until I knocked on her goddamned door over an hour after Vi was taken," Eric continued, his voice vibrating and Colt knew Eric had similar thoughts in his head about Tina.

Colt bit his lip then he asked, "She see Cal?"

"Nope, but she reports a black truck was behind the caddy."

"Cal's truck is in his office lot," Colt informed Eric.

"She says it wasn't his truck. An SUV. Escalade."

"She get plates?"

"Said she wasn't payin' that much attention."

Colt knew that was a lie. She was paying attention, just not to the license plates.

"Highway Patrol been notified?" Colt asked.

"Yeah," Eric replied.

"What about Lindy?"

"She's not home. Her man says she works seven to four."

"She was at the office," Colt whispered.

"She was at the office," Eric repeated.

"Pryor says Hart's MO is not to mess around. Go for the kill," Colt noted.

"He may have done him in the SUV but he didn't do him at the offices. Blood's from the boys Cal took out," Eric remarked.

Colt called it down. "Been to Cal's offices. Lindy sits out front. Cal has an office in the back, doesn't use it much, but he's got it. They went in, Cal put up a fight but they got to her and somehow managed to use Lindy as leverage. This meant they've probably got Lindy and Cal. They got his phone, called Vi from it while sittin' in front of her house. She knew, the call comin' from his phone, bad shit had gone down and she didn't think—husband dead, brother dead—she just acted and she did it hungover and fast, doin' exactly what she was told."

Eric rocked back on his heels and said quietly, "Yep, reckon so."

Colt looked over his shoulder at Vi's house. Feb was in there and now so was Cheryl. He looked to the street, saw Jessie's car pull up to the curb in front of Vi's house. Then he looked down the street to see Josie Judd's Jeep heading toward the house.

"Let's hope he goes off script," Colt muttered as Jessie exited her car, threw the door too and half-walked, half-ran to the house.

"I'm already hopin'," Eric muttered back.

"God dammit," Benny muttered when the cars he was following separated. The black caddy Benny knew was carrying Violet went one way. The black SUV Benny guessed was carrying Cal went the opposite way.

Benny made a decision and followed Cal. If his cousin was still alive, they got him to where they wanted him to be, he wouldn't stay that way much longer. Violet had a better chance.

Benny made the turn and his eyes went to his rearview mirror.

Frankie was shit at a tail. He'd clocked her outside Chicago when he'd left at four that morning.

Benny had made the decision to drive down to Cal's 'burg when repeated calls went unanswered. He had no choice. It was a hell of a drive but Cal needed to be warned.

Frankie had been following at his high speed for the last seven fucking hours, all the way down through Indiana and, once there, seeing what he saw, then all the way back up. He had to spend half of his time keeping himself invisible and half of his time making sure she was the same way.

He watched her leave him and follow the caddy.

"*Fuck!*" he exploded, tagged his phone on the seat beside him, scrolled down to her number, which he'd meant to erase about seven dozen times in the last seven years but he'd not only not done it. He'd programmed her new numbers in the three times she got them.

He was okay with her on his ass and he left her to it. She went it alone, that he was not okay with.

He hit go and she answered, "Hello?"

"Stand down, Frankie," he growled.

"He's got the woman. You're on Cal, I'm on her," she said, her voice calm.

Jesus, he forgot this about her. Francesca was a fucking nut. Nothing scared her, not before life got scary. Attitude mixed with idiot fearlessness and a whole lot of not knowing what the hell she's doing. Not a good combination. Christ.

"Stand…*the fuck*…down," he repeated.

"Benny, I won't do anything. I'll call Sal. He'll send—"

He cut her off. "You get the location, you call Sal, you get the fuck outta there."

"I'll just stay, keep an eye out," she replied.

"You'll get the fuck outta there." He was again fucking repeating himself.

"I'll hang tight and they won't see me," she said.

"Woman, you have no idea what you're doin'. I know you've been on my ass since the turnpike."

She was quiet before she said, "Oh well," then she stopped speaking.

"Oh well?" Benny asked, wondering if it was possible for his head actually to explode and thinking if it was, he was close.

"Ben—"

"They're stupid enough to let you know their location, you feed it to Sal and you get the fuck outta there."

"Ben—"

"I got things on my mind, babe, and I don't need you bein' one of them."

She was quiet again then she said, "He's not gettin' another one of us."

Fuck. Now he knew where her head was at. This was about Vinnie. This was about Cal. This was about Frankie being family even though that family turned their back on her.

"Frankie—"

"He's taken enough from us."

Benny's voice went soft. "Francesca, honey—"

"You don't do anything stupid. You call backup too."

"Babe—" he said to no one. She'd disconnected.

Fucking *hell*.

He scrolled down to Sal's number in his phone and he hit go.

"You think you mighta wanted to tell me this shit when you saw the woman climb into that car?" Sal asked Benny who was on his phone.

"You made this mess. Do *you* think I was fired up to call you in to clean it up?" Benny asked back.

Fuck, but only Benito Bianchi would speak to him that way. Even Cal had respect. Benny played the game before his brother bought it, since then he didn't give a fuck.

The fucking Bianchis. Always a pain in his fucking ass.

"I was in Indiana, Sal, what were you gonna do?" Benny went on.

"Get fuckin' *organized*," Sal snapped into the phone then ordered, "Stand down."

"He's been in there the length of this call and they've also got some girl. Blood on both of them, Sal. She didn't look too good. I'm goin' in," Benny told him.

"The cops and Feds just left my house. They want this. Bad. Let me call them so they can get boys on it," Sal demanded.

"They need to hurry. I'm goin' in," Benny returned.

"Benny," Sal said to a dead phone.

He flipped it shut and had trouble catching Vinnie's eyes. He didn't need to look at his cousin to know that he was barely keeping his cool and his seat.

He was saved having to say anything when his phone rang and he saw on the display it was Frankie.

He flipped it open. "*Amata*, now's not the time."

"Cal's woman is at Hart's house," she informed him, and Sal went still.

"How do you know that?" Sal asked.

"Because I'm—"

She didn't finish.

Instead she let out a small scream and the line went dead.

# Twenty-One

## Bare Feet

Cal watched the goon toss Lindy aside. She hit the floor and went skidding, leaving a trail of blood.

He stood, silent and still, his eyes moving from Lindy to lock on both the boys who had them. They were in good shape, lean and fit. Neither as big as Cal nor nearly as tall, and one was so lean he was almost slight. Could mean he was wily. Could mean Cal had lucked out.

His hands were behind his back in plastic restraints that they put on too fucking tight and they'd done it because they were pissed after the gunfight and pissed he'd taken down two of their boys. But they were clearly following orders so they hadn't taken him out with a bullet to the brain at the scene. During the ride the restraints had dug in deep, rubbed raw, breaking the skin.

He had bullet grazes to his right hip and just below his left shoulder. They both had bled a lot, but the bleeding had stopped and the nagging pain was easy to ignore.

This was because his mind was focused on three things. He needed to get out of this alive. He needed to get Lindy out of this alive. And he needed to find Vi and take her home to her girls.

How he was going to do all of that weaponless and with his hands tied behind his back, he had no fucking clue.

Why he was still alive, again, he had no fucking clue. The only thing he could figure was that Hart wanted to play with him.

Not good.

"On your knees," one of them ordered. Cal stared at him and didn't speak nor did he move. "Knees!" the man shouted, his eyes narrowing, jaw tight, lips puckering, giving it away.

He had the gun and Cal was in restraints but Cal intimidated him. He wasn't wily. He'd survived a gunfight where Cal took down two of his comrades. He was pissed and he was scared. He knew Cal wasn't going to make it easy and he wanted to get this done.

Cal's eyes went to Lindy. They'd shot her in the thigh, which was the reason they both were there.

No, that wasn't the reason they were there. He'd shot two men dead, clearing a path for her to get away and he'd ordered her out the back door while he was providing cover.

She instead went to the safe, grabbed a gun and tried to join the fight, not about to leave Cal behind with four armed men in the office, all of them firing, two men already down and Cal having suffered two graze wounds that looked a lot worse than they really were. Though she didn't know that.

They got her before they got Cal and put a bullet in her thigh then lifted the gun to her temple.

Then they got Cal.

The woman was a glorified receptionist and a bookkeeper but she was also the daughter of a decorated marine who had three sons, one daughter. It was made clear that day that Lindy's dad didn't sexually discriminate when it came to life lessons.

*Semper* fuckin' *fi.*

After he assured she was going to leave this building breathing, he paid the co-pay for her hospital visit and he knew she'd walk again, he was going to fire her ass.

"Knees!" the man shouted again. He came at Cal and it was now or fucking never. If he got to his knees, he'd get a bullet to the brain.

He hoped to God that Lindy was conscious because someone was going to have to find a way to cut the restraints off after he somehow took them both down with his hands tied behind his back.

The man got close and Cal was fucking thrilled beyond belief that he did it stupidly, moving in front of the other one. Cal let him get close, and at the last minute, he dipped a shoulder and hauled ass.

He took the man in the gut with his shoulder. The man let out a surprised, winded, "oof," and went back into the other one. When they hit the second man, Cal kept right on moving. Both men hit the wall, Cal pulled back then moved again, catching the one in front with a sharp knee to the balls.

He dropped his gun, made that winded noise again, and this time it even hurt Cal to hear it considering why he made it. His hands went between his legs and he instantly went down to his knees.

The other one recovered and started to lift his gun, but Cal was faster. Moving in, he head butted him. The man took the blow to the head twice, front from Cal and then against the wall at the back.

He let out a yowl even as he blinked, but Cal moved again. Whirling, he planted a foot and lifted the other leg. Connecting with his boot, Cal roundhouse kicked him away from the wall.

Going fast, Cal recovered, got close then twisted his lower body. He clipped the man with a calf around his knees and the man went down. Then Cal kicked him, boot straight to the face and watched his head and neck jerk back, as did his torso. The gun went flying, but Cal stayed focused and aimed a boot to his crotch. This connected, also sharp but this time vicious, and the man groaned as he curled forward immediately, knees up, forming a man-sized ball.

Cal's attention turned to the other one who had yet to recover but Cal didn't hesitate. He needed them incapacitated. Cal landed another kick then another, the force of the blows sending the man rolling. Arms, face, spine, gut, ribs, any target he could get, again and again, Cal following him as he rolled.

He heard a gunshot, his body jolted and he whirled around.

Lindy was up, balancing on one foot and holding a smoking gun in two bloody hands.

"Don't *fucking move*!" she shrieked, her eyes were wild and they were on the other man who was up on a forearm, the other hand still cupping his crotch, but his eyes were glued to the gun that she had right in his face.

They'd been stupid to sexually discriminate. They should have restrained her too. Then again, captured, she'd gone docile and acted scared. She'd even managed a few terrified whimpers on the long drive to Chicago.

Clearly these were bullshit.

Christ, he had GI Jane as his receptionist.

"Jesus, Cal, you didn't leave me anything to do." Cal heard Benny's voice, and he, Lindy and the man down but not whining all looked at Benny who was strolling casually into the room like he was walking through his pizzeria, except he had a gun in his hand and a crazy motherfucking grin on his face.

"What the fuck?" Cal whispered, but Benny lifted his gun and pointed it at the roller.

"Think you should stay still," Benny suggested to him and came to a stop close to Cal, his eyes not leaving the man on the ground.

"Like I said, what the fuck?" Cal ignored the man and stared at Benny.

"Frankie came callin' early with info. Couldn't get you on your phone so I moved out. I been on your tail since Indiana," Benny answered, his hand went into his front pocket and he came out with a small army knife. "You," he said to Lindy. "Limp over here and cut Cal loose."

Cal watched Lindy do as she was told and limp toward Cal and Benny, keeping her eyes on her target and her gun up as she dragged her leg with her. She took the knife, opened it and cut Cal loose. The minute he was freed, he pulled the gun out of her hand and trained it on her man.

"Next time bullets are flyin' and I say the words, 'leave out the back door,' you *leave* out the *fucking back door*," Cal ground out.

"If there's a next time, Joe Callahan, I quit," Lindy snapped back.

"Can't quit, seein' as your fuckin' fired," Cal returned.

"Kids, can we have this domestic somewhere on the way to Violet?" Benny asked, and Cal's head swung to him.

Then he walked to man one who took one look at his face and started crab walking backwards on all fours. Without hesitation, Cal drilled a round in each of his thighs, which made him stop crab walking and start screaming in pain.

Cal ignored this and turned to man two who was scrambling in the direction of the loose gun. But Cal got to him, kicked him in the chest so he flew to his back and he drilled a round in each of his thighs.

Then he walked to the gun, picked it up and handed it to Lindy on his way out the door. He heard Benny helping Lindy and following. He walked straight to the Escalade and shot out all four tires. Then he walked to Benny's Ford Explorer.

When they were all in and Benny was on the road, Cal in the passenger side, Lindy rifling through a first aid kit in the back, Cal asked, "You know where she is?"

"No, but I know where Hart lives," Benny answered.

"Good." Cal looked out the windshield. "We'll start there."

"Don't you think we should start by droppin' her off at the hospital?" Benny suggested.

"It's just a flesh wound," Lindy put in.

Fuck him. A flesh wound.

On his next job application there was going to be the question "What did your father do for a living?" and if an applicant filled in "Marine," "Police Officer" or "Commando," he was shredding it.

Benny glanced at Cal and Cal saw his lips twitching.

Then Benny muttered, "I think I'm in love. Where do you find them?"

"Just drive," Cal growled.

In the distance, three squad cars going in hot could be seen, sirens wailing, lights flashing, an early invitation for Cal and Lindy's captors to get down to business if they already hadn't done it.

Cal scratched having a word with Pryor on his mental to do list.

The squads flew past them and Benny kept driving.

"Not to give you bad news on top of what hasn't been such a good day for you, *cugino*," Benny said. "But Sal made a deal with the cops and when I called him ten minutes ago, he told me he was sendin' them in for the rescue."

"I didn't have time for that rescue," Cal remarked. "They wanted me on my knees."

Cal watched Benny nod and then Benny spoke. "Let's hope, they see the mess you left them, they'll feel lenient seein' as they wanted you on your knees. I'm a man, most cops are men, we all understand why you wouldn't wanna be on your knees."

Cal stared at his cousin. "Benny, they wanted me on my knees so they could drill a round in my skull."

"Why would they take you all the way up to Chicago to do that?"

"How do I fuckin' know?"

Benny drove silent for a while then muttered, "Thank Christ they did."

"After we rescue your girlfriend," Lindy piped up from the back, "can I get a coffee? By the time those assholes barged into the office, I was only halfway through coffee numero uno. By this time, I'm usually on coffee numero doce and I need a fuckin' fix."

Cal was in no mood to laugh but that didn't mean he didn't smile. "Sure, Lindy, we'll get you a coffee on the way to the hospital after we rescue my girlfriend."

"No, got my belt on it even though the bullet went clean through and I don't think it's bleedin' anymore. You can just take me home. Dad'll stitch me up," she said and Cal closed his eyes and wondered what Lindy's boyfriend was like.

Cal had trouble enough fucking Vi on her back. Even though he knew she liked it like that, she also felt compelled to climb on and Vi was like Keira, a woman but still all girl. What he learned about Lindy that day, she was probably prepared to fight to the death to take the dominate position and ride her man. Cal figured her man had learned to just lay back and enjoy the ride.

He heard Benny chuckling before he heard, "Again, *cugino*, where do you find them?"

Cal opened his eyes and answered, "Her father's a marine."

"Ah," Benny replied.

Cal was done playing.

"They sent six men after me. I took down two at my offices. Two came with us. Two in another car where I suspect they took Vi."

"I saw 'em," Benny said quietly. "There were two."

"While you were tailin', you see anything else?" Cal asked.

"Like what?"

Cal didn't want to know but he had to know.

"Kate and Keira."

"I hit your house first, all was quiet, Vi's car in your drive, Vi behind your security system. I left her there thinkin' she was safe. But there was no car for you so I went to your office to give you the lowdown. When I hit it, they were movin' you and her out," Benny jerked his head to the backseat.

"Name's Lindy," Lindy introduced herself.

"Hey, Lindy. Benny," Benny introduced back.

"Nice ta meetcha," Lindy muttered, and Cal heard the sudden tiredness in her tone mixed with a bit of pain she couldn't quite hide. Adrenaline crash. They needed to keep an eye on her.

Cal twisted in his seat to glance at a pale but hanging in there Lindy as Benny kept talking. "I tailed them from your office back to your house. They were there maybe three minutes before Vi ran from the house and got in the car and then your convoy hit the road. No girls."

That didn't mean someone else didn't have them.

"We had protection," Cal told Benny as he turned to face forward. "It wasn't steady but there's a possibility there are more of Hart's men because, if Colt had men on us, someone had to take those boys out."

"Saw a man in a car outside your offices. He didn't look too good. Boys who took you probably took him out. Nothin' I could see at Vi's."

"They still could have the girls," Cal muttered then stated, "But that means Vi's got at least two on her. What do you know about his house?"

Benny's phone vibrated, he leaned forward and reached to his back pocket as he finished, "Tell you about the house in a second. Right now you need to know that Frankie followed me. When the cars separated, I took you. Crazy Frankie took Vi."

Cal stared at his cousin's profile and whispered, "You are shittin' me."

"Nope," he answered, and Cal knew even with that one word Benny was pissed and he was worried. Then Benny flipped his phone open and put it to his ear. "Sal, I got 'im. He's good. Did Frankie call you?"

Benny listened to Sal for approximately three seconds before he put his foot to the floor, the SUV shot forward, he flipped his phone shut and threw it on the dash.

Then he whispered, "Vi's at Hart's house and Hart's got Frankie too."

"Sal call the cops?" Cal asked.

"Don't know, don't care, didn't ask, wasn't gonna wait for an answer."

Cal studied Benny and saw with clarity that his cousin was now on a mission.

In normal circumstances, Cal would question this response considering Benny hated Francesca. All the Bianchis did except Carm, who lived in LA, and Cal, who hadn't really lived anywhere for seventeen years.

He didn't question this response however, because he was just happy Benny finally got the lead out.

He leaned forward and nabbed Benny's phone, sat back and dialed the house phone.

Feb answered with a cautious, "Hello?"

"Feb, Cal. You got the girls?"

"Cal," she whispered, relief so stark in her tone it was a physical thing coming over the airwaves. Then he heard commotion behind her.

"Feb, the girls," Cal prompted on an impatient growl.

No answer, then Colt.

"Cal?"

"Colt, are the fuckin' girls there?"

"They're here. Safe. Scared. Though things perked up the minute Feb said your name. Where are you?"

"Chicago. On my way to pick up Vi."

"She okay?"

"She will be."

A pause then, "Talk to me."

"Hart has her at his place. We're headed there."

"You know this for certain?"

"Intel from Sal."

"Sal made a deal with Pryor. This mean Sal told the cops where Vi is?"

"Don't know. We didn't ask and don't got a line to Pryor. They're there, they're not, they don't have her, I'm goin' in."

"Cal, let me call Pryor."

"She's not out, I'm goin' in."

"Cal—"

"Make your calls," Cal ordered and then shut the phone.

I stared out the window at Daniel Hart's beautiful lawn and garden. He had a swimming pool that Keira would love.

"Violet." I heard him say and I turned.

He was walking toward me, smiling and holding a glass of water and what looked like a pale green silk robe was slung over his forearm.

"I brought you aspirin and water for your hangover," he told me when he made it to me.

"Thanks," I whispered and took the glass and pills from him.

"A robe," he offered the green silk to me. "You can get out of that shirt."

My choice? I would wear Joe's shirt until it fell off me.

But I didn't have choices anymore.

Joe was dead and I was here. That was it. That was my life.

Joe was dead and I was here.

Joe was dead.

Joe was dead.

I turned back to the window and looked out.

"Violet," he called.

"Yes?" I said to the window but he didn't speak further for long moments.

Then he said, "I can see you need some time."

*Yes, you fucking lunatic! I need some fucking time!* My mind screamed.

"That'd be good," I whispered not looking at him. I knew what he looked like. Brown hair, not light, not dark. Hazel eyes. Fit and slim. Nice trousers, sharp crease pressed in. Khaki. A long-sleeved polo neck shirt. Burgundy. Also nice. Totally fucking crazy.

I'd have him, in that outfit, telling me calmly and with no emotion that he was sorry, Joe was dead burned on my brain for the rest of my life.

They'd told me on the phone, if I went with them, they'd let Joe go.

They'd lied.

"Change. I'll be back in a while and we'll share a late lunch," he murmured, but I felt him there. He didn't move and neither did I before he went on. "I'm glad you made this decision Violet."

It was then I turned and met his eyes.

"You killed my husband, my brother and Joe. Did I have a choice?"

"Violet—"

I turned away, tossed the pills to the floor and took a long drink of the water.

"You should take the aspirin, Violet. It'll help—"

I turned to him again. "Do you honestly think I'm going to consume pills *you* handed me?"

He looked shocked before he stated, "I'd never hurt you."

At those stunning, crazy, unbelievable words, not thinking, losing it, I leaned into his face and screamed, "*You killed Joe!*"

I watched his face start to go hard but I stopped watching when we both turned to the door after we heard, "Danny."

A man was standing there, one of the two who'd been in the car with me during the longest, most uncomfortable, most terrifying ride of my life. The whole time I felt like I was going to get sick not only because of my hangover but because of my fucking *life* and the fact that I knew they could never have Joe's phone without having Joe. I didn't know what they had to do to get to a man like Joe. I just knew it wasn't good.

"I'm in the middle of something," Hart said to his minion.

"We got a situation," his minion replied, and Hart stared at him looking unhappy.

He turned to me.

"Change," he ordered.

"You gonna kill me if I don't?" I snapped.

He leaned forward and barked, "*Change!*"

I leaned forward too, too far gone to read the warning behind his quick shift in mood from Mr. Charm to Mr. Mean and shouted, "Fuck you!"

"Danny! For Christ's sake, we got a situation," the minion repeated.

Hart didn't turn to him. Instead he said to me, "I recommend you get smart pretty fuckin' soon."

"And I recommend you go fuck yourself," I shot back, and then suddenly I was on my hands and knees. This was because he backhanded me hard.

I'd never been hit, not in my life, and it hurt. I stayed still, blinking away the pain and felt him lean over me.

"Change," he whispered then I felt his presence move away.

I didn't move while I waited for the pain to clear and then I decided I wasn't going to change. Fuck him. Fuck him. Fuck *him*!

I got to my feet and sucked in a long breath. Then I looked at the pool and I looked at it for a long time.

Doing that, I decided that my beautiful daughter Keira was never going to stick even her toe in that pool.

I didn't know how I was going to get out of this but I knew I was going to have to get out of this. Then get to Barry. They might not take someone hanging out on your street and sending you gifts very seriously but they sure as fuck better take kidnapping seriously.

That asshole was going down.

And I was going to get on with my life. Again.

Without Joe.

I should have been like Theresa and taken pictures, loads of pictures. Pictures of him sleeping. Pictures of him with the girls. Pictures of him drinking coffee. Pictures of him mowing the lawn. Pictures of him watching TV. Pictures of him breathing.

Joe was so wrong to get rid of his pictures of Nicky. I needed pictures. I needed the memories. Lots of them.

I only had one picture of him. The one with him and Nicky already on my Dead People I Love Shelf.

Well at least that was a timesaver. I wouldn't have to move it.

I laughed, the sound was harsh and the feel of it bit at my throat.

Then I felt a tear slide down my face.

My mind moved to my daughters. I didn't know what time it was but they'd know when they got home something was wrong. Then they'd have to find out Joe was never coming home. Then I'd have to find a way to put the pieces of us together again.

I felt another tear slide down my face but this time it coincided with a sob sliding up my throat.

I choked it down and put a hand to the glass as my legs started trembling because I knew I was clean out of emotional glue. This one had broken me. I knew it. I felt it. I was broken. There were no strong arms to hold me together. No big, hard body to climb into bed with and hold onto. Not this time. Never again. Not…ever…again.

"Let's move," I heard an impatient voice saying, and I whirled around to see one of Hart's henchmen moving closer to me.

"What?" I asked.

He didn't answer. He grabbed my arm and dragged me out of the room. I dropped the robe on my way out.

"I'm Frankie," she whispered.

"I'm Violet," I whispered back.

"Cal's woman," she said, and I swallowed.

"Yeah," I replied and that one word broke because I was for a short, glorious period of time where me and my girls were able to make him smile, make him laugh, give him what he always wanted.

Hell, just that morning he was teasing me.

And I'd told him to go away.

And he did, to tell my girls good-bye for me after seeing to it that they got ready for school.

I closed my eyes tight as the memory assaulted my brain.

She was silent a moment then she said, "He'll be okay."

"They killed him," I told her.

"What?" she asked, her voice getting louder, tighter, pissed.

"Quiet!" the henchman barked.

Sitting in the back of the car, Frankie and I got quiet.

She reached out and took my hand.

Then she squeezed.

"House's clear. They hauled ass," Pryor told Cal and Benny.

They were standing on the sidewalk outside Hart's house. There were cop cars everywhere, Chicago PD and Feds crawling all over the place.

"Any clue where they'd go?" Benny asked.

"Got men out everywhere," Pryor answered, his eyes on Cal. "They musta got a tipoff that we were comin'."

"Frankie," Benny muttered.

"Boss," a uniform called as he walked to their huddle. "We got film," he said when he stopped and all the men's' eyes turned to him, but he was eyeing up Cal.

"Film?" Pryor prompted.

"Civilians," the uniform murmured, using his chin to indicate Benny and Cal.

"Spill it, Krakowski," Pryor bit out.

The uniform looked at Pryor and nodded. "They took him," his head jerked to Cal, "to a warehouse with cameras. Feed went to the house. Boys figure they hauled ass when he," another jerk of the head to Cal, "took down Hart's two boys then drilled rounds in their legs."

"Self-defense," Benny stated instantly.

"Right," the uniform replied, his gaze shifting to Benny, his mouth hard. "By the way, did I mention *we got film*?"

"We'll sort that out later," Pryor cut in then went on, muttering to himself, "So he saw Joe got loose and took off where?"

"More film," the uniform said and Pryor's eyes focused on him.

"Jesus, Krako, spit it out," Pryor snapped.

"Security of the house. They got a brunette too. She was sittin' in her car outside," he pointed at a sweet, old model, red Nissan Z car at the curb. "They nabbed her, took her into the house, five minutes later both women were in a car with a coupla Hart's boys and headin' out. Hart followed in another car. Got the cars and plates. They're already out on the line."

Pryor looked at Cal. "It's somethin'."

Cal stared at Pryor and didn't reply.

It was something, this was true, it just wasn't fucking much. And after Benny and Pryor briefed him, now Cal knew that Hart knew Cal had called Sal for the hit which meant his motivation had shifted. He also knew that Cal was loose and he likely knew the Feds were on his ass.

The man was whacked, which meant him knowing all that he wasn't going to follow script. He was going to be unpredictable. This was evidenced by the fact that he drove Cal all the way to Chicago to finish him off. Outside his MO. Hart normally didn't fuck around. Hart wanted Cal in Chicago because Hart wanted it filmed because Hart wanted to watch him die.

Cal wasn't a chore, a mess to clean up. This was retribution.

And he had Frankie and Vi.

"Fuck," Cal muttered.

They all turned when a paramedic jogged up to them.

"Gotta get the girl to the hospital," the paramedic said and all eyes shifted to the ambulance where Lindy was sitting on the back and another paramedic was squatting by her leg. "You comin'?" the paramedic asked Cal.

"Nope," Cal replied, and the paramedic's gaze moved through both of Cal's graze wounds before they went back to his eyes. "I'm good," Cal finished.

"You need those seen to," the paramedic advised.

"I'm good," Cal repeated.

"But—" he started. Cal's body shifted slightly and he stopped speaking then muttered, "Right." He nodded to Cal, Pryor then hoofed it back to the ambulance.

Cal started to move away, saying, "We'll be at Sal's."

Benny moved with him when Pryor called, sounding surprised, "You waitin' this out?"

"Not much else to do," Cal responded and headed to Benny's SUV.

"Um…" the uniform mumbled loudly. "We might have some ques—"

"Later." Cal heard Pryor cut him off.

"But—"

"Later."

Cal swung into the passenger side of Benny's SUV as Benny climbed behind the wheel.

Benny turned to him. "We goin' to Sal's to wait it out?"

"Fuck no," Cal replied. "We're gonna find Ricky."

"Cal," Benny said low, and Cal turned to him.

"Ricky, Benny."

Benny stared at him, got that crazy motherfucking grin on his face again, started the car and then shot from the curb.

"What the fuck, Danny!" Frankie and I heard the minion's angry shout from the other room.

"Don't," Daniel Hart returned.

"This shit is fucked," the minion shot back. "We don't got a situation. We got fuckin' *four*."

"I'm handling it," Hart retorted.

"Yeah, right," the henchman snapped. "You're not handlin' shit. You're *still* chasin' twat. Fuck! We shoulda took him out in Indiana. Crazy ass shit, bringin' that fuckin' guy to Chicago."

"I wanted to watch," Hart replied, and I closed my eyes and pulled in breath.

Frankie grabbed my hand.

"Like I said, fucked!" the other man was still shouting. "Two boys down there, Danny. Took out *two* of *ours* down there. Cops in our business everywhere for weeks. And I got sources tellin' me the Feds got the books. Giglia's boys are on the hunt and our men are scramblin'. And that guy's stone cold. You saw what he fuckin'—"

"Quiet." Hart's voice was low but sharp.

"Hands behind his back, Danny."

My eyes opened and I looked at Frankie who for some reason was smiling.

"*Quiet!*" Hart shouted and there was quiet.

I felt Frankie's body get tense then she released my hand. I tore my eyes from the closed door we were behind and watched her move.

"Frankie!" I hissed, but she just lifted a hand and waved it at me as she moved on silent feet across the room.

"I'm your man, Danny," the minion said, his voice quieter. "Been your man a long time but I'm not goin' down for some dead cop's cunt."

"What did you say?" Hart asked as I watched Frankie at a window. She was taking her time, trying to be quiet and slowly working it up.

I left the couch we were sitting on and ran on bare, thus luckily silent feet toward her.

"You heard me," the henchman stated.

Frankie pushed the window up and it made a noise which was drowned out by a gunshot. Frankie and I jumped and looked over our shoulders at the closed door.

"Danny!" the other henchman in Hart's posse shouted. "Jesus Christ, you just shot Brady. *What the fuck*!"

"Go," Frankie whispered and I looked at her. Then I threw myself through the window, landing on soft turf. I rolled away from the window and got to my feet. She followed me out.

I grabbed her hand, yanked her up and we ran.

We heard the second gunshot as we went.

Benny led and Cal followed as Benny opened the door to a sleazy bar that had the name of Slim Jim's.

Ricky was sitting at the end of the bar looking the same as ever. Thinning non-descript hair. Thin non-descript face. Thin non-descript body. Weasel eyes, and even though Cal couldn't see him or hear him, he knew Ricky had bad teeth and was a mouth breather.

Ricky's head came up when Benny came in. He clocked Benny and then he was on the move.

Benny and Cal sprinted after him.

They caught him out the back alley. Benny grabbing him by the back of his shirt, he yanked him to a halt then turned him and shoved him face first against the wall.

Benny grabbed his wrist, twisted his arm around and up, got close to his back and asked in his ear, "Why you runnin', Ricky?"

Ricky turned his head, saw Cal and his face got white.

"Jesus," he whispered then rallied, "Hey, Cal."

"Talk," Cal replied.

"About what?" Ricky asked. Benny pushed in closer and Ricky's eyeballs slid way to the side in an effort to take in Benny. "Yeesh, Benny, man, what the fuck?"

"Talk," Benny repeated Cal's word.

"Like I said, about what?" Ricky asked.

"About where Hart would take Cal's woman," Benny answered, and Ricky's eyes went to Cal.

"You got a woman?" he asked, openly surprised, or acting that way.

"Ricky, we don't got a lotta time," Cal said instead of answering.

Benny pushed off and moved a foot away so Ricky could turn to face them, back still to the brick wall of the alley.

Ricky's eyebrows went up. "You two workin' for Sal?"

"Cal asked you a question, Ricky. We don't got a lotta time." Benny reminded him.

Ricky's eyes went to Benny. "Don't know nothin' 'bout Hart."

Benny looked at Cal. Cal caught his eye and looked at Ricky. Then he moved, dipping low, he caught Ricky with an upper cut to his kidneys. Ricky's arms went around his belly, he bent forward and coughed.

After doing this for thirty seconds, his head shot back and he wheezed, "What the fuck?"

"Where would Hart go on the run?" Cal asked.

"Hart's a crazy motherfucker. Don't know nothin' 'bout him, don't *wanna* know nothin' 'bout him," Ricky answered, and Benny moved in, hand wrapping around Ricky's throat, pinning him to the brick wall.

"It's your business," Benny reminded him. "Mr. Information. You know everything about everyone."

"Don't know about Hart," Ricky rasped, his fingers curling around Benny's forearm.

"We don't got time to deal. You sell information. Today, you're buyin' it with your health," Benny informed him.

"Ben," Ricky choked. "You know Hart. I got in his business, he'd get in mine. Don't need that shit. I steer clear."

"You got to have heard somethin'," Cal told him, and Ricky's eyes came to Cal.

"I hear it. I forget it. I stay breathin'," Ricky's voice sounded strangled and he was tearing at Benny's forearm with his fingernails.

"What'd you forget?" Benny asked, leaning in close and Ricky gagged. "What'd you forget?" Benny shouted in his face.

"Ben, boy can't talk if you choke him to death," Cal said quietly.

Benny looked over his shoulder at Cal and stepped back.

Benny's phone rang and since it was in Cal's back pocket, Cal pulled it out, looked at the display and his brows snapped together. He flipped it open and put it to his ear.

"Yo," he said.

"Collect call from Francesca Concetti. Will you accept the charges?" an operator asked.

"Yes," Cal clipped, his eyes sliced to Benny and he mouthed, "Frankie."

Benny's back went straight.

"Ben?" Francesca whispered.

"Frankie?"

"Oh Jesus." She was still whispering, "Cal?"

"Frankie where the fuck are you?"

"Boathouse—" she started then he heard Vi, her voice tight, high, something weird in it.

"Is that Joe?"

"Yeah," Frankie whispered.

"Give it to me." Cal heard Vi demand and then he heard a tussle. Finally, Vi came on the phone. "Joe?"

"Baby, where are you?"

"*Joe!*" she squealed.

"Jesus, Violet, keep it down." He heard Frankie hiss.

"Oh Joe, Jesus, honey, oh God," Vi whispered then he heard a tortured sob.

"Buddy, hold it together and tell me where you—" He stopped talking when he heard the phone moving around and then he was back to Frankie.

"Hart told her you were dead," Frankie explained, and Cal clenched his teeth because this was a cruel thing to do to anyone, especially Vi, because he could still hear Violet's sobs, because he was getting no information, and lastly because they were on the phone but it sounded like they were unsafe.

"I'm alive. Where are you?"

"He took us to a boathouse. North. We're on the lake. We climbed out the window, went through the trees and broke into another house," Frankie answered.

"Hart's not there?"

"No, he's—" She was cut off by Vi.

"Let me talk to him."

"Girl, we gotta—"

"Frankie," Cal cut in. "Stay on the line."

"Let me talk to him!" Vi demanded.

"Shit," Frankie muttered then he heard a faraway, "Here."

Cal's teeth were still clenched and he was glaring at Benny, who still had Ricky against the wall with a loose hold at his throat. But his eyes were locked on Cal.

"Joe—" Vi began.

"Honey, I know you're freaked but you gotta give the phone back to Frankie," Cal told her.

"Why?" Violet asked.

"Because she's got her shit together and she can lead me to you."

"But I know exactly where we are. Dad had a boat up here. We're—"

He heard Frankie cut in. "Violet, I hear somethin'."

"Where are you?" Cal asked urgently.

"Oh God, they're here," Violet whispered.

"Violet, God dammit, *where are you*?" Cal shouted, but the line was dead. "*Jesus fucking Christ!*" Cal roared, snapped the phone shut, got into Benny's space to shove him aside and wrapped his hand around Ricky's throat. "Where's Hart's boathouse?"

Ricky's eyes were bugging out and his hand came up to claw at Cal's arm but he managed to gag, "Boathouse?"

"*Boathouse!*" Cal barked in face.

"Don't know. Swear to God…don't—" He stopped speaking and started full-on gagging, Cal released him and stepped back.

He flipped the phone back open and dialed home. Colt answered on the first ring.

"Colton."

"Colt, ask Kate what her grandfather's phone number is." Cal ordered.

"Sorry?" Colt asked.

"I don't have a lotta time. Ask Kate what Vi's father's phone number is."

"Hang on," Colt said and then Cal heard him calling Kate and the phone was jostled.

"Joe?" It was Kate saying his name, his second favorite way of hearing it.

"Hey, Katy," he said softly.

"You okay?"

"Yeah, baby."

"Mom?" she asked, her voice tense.

"Gettin' there," he replied vaguely. "Now listen to me. I need your grandfather's phone number."

"I'll go get my phone," she said quickly.

So Kate. She didn't ask questions. She wasn't messing around. She knew he needed something and she was getting down to business.

"That's my girl," he whispered.

"Everyone here is really freaked out," she told him and he knew she was walking and talking.

"Tell them they can relax," Joe said and he heard her short, surprised giggle.

"Jeez, Joe, that's what you always say."

God he loved that kid.

"I know you're in a hurry but can you hang on? Keira wants to talk to you," Kate asked.

He couldn't but he would.

"Yeah, tell her it has to be fast."

"Right," she said into his ear and then the phone was away from her mouth when he heard her say, "It has to be fast, Keirry."

"I'll be fast." He heard Keira promise, then in the phone, "Joe?"

Tied for second.

"Hey, honey."

"Joe," her voice broke on his name then the tears were audible.

"Come here, darlin'." Cal heard who he guessed was Cheryl whisper and the phone moving.

"It's me. I'm back," Kate said. "I got the number."

"Give it to me," Joe replied and listened to it as she gave it and repeated it. When she was done, he said, "We'll be home soon, yeah?"

"Yeah," she whispered.

"Love you, baby."

"Love you too, Joe."

He flipped the phone shut and looked at Benny and Ricky who were both staring at him. Benny with a grin on his face. Ricky with his mouth hanging open.

Cal ignored their reactions and said to Benny, "They're in a boathouse, north, on the lake. Vi said her dad had a boat there before we were disconnected. I have his number. We'll call on the way."

Benny was already on the move when he said, "Gotcha."

We stopped in the trees, both of us breathing heavy, but we listened for footfalls in the leaves.

We'd been running willy-nilly for what seemed like hours. At first because we were panicked and didn't know what the fuck we were doing. Then because we were lost and couldn't get our bearings. Finally, we came to a spot that was familiar to me and I knew we were close to safety.

Now we just needed to catch our breath.

"You think we lost them?" Frankie whispered.

I knew Daniel Hart never gave up. We didn't lose them.

I looked at her and shook my head.

She looked through the trees then at me. "We should separate."

I snatched up her hand. "What? No!"

"They won't know who they're followin'."

"So? They could catch either one of us, but—"

"You stay here, I'll go. They'll hear me, follow me, you know the lay of the land. You wait awhile then go to that shop you were talkin' about and I'll lead them away."

This was a crazy plan and no way I was doing it.

"What if they find you?" I asked.

"I'll think of something," she answered.

"That's crazy!" I snapped.

She got close. "Violet, honey, you got no shoes on. You're in a t-shirt. You can't be out here, running on this—"

I cut her off. "I'm fine."

She got closer. "Listen to me—"

I shook her hand at the same time I squeezed it. "We're not separating."

"Vi—"

I lifted my other hand and wrapped it around the side of her neck. I did this because Joe did it to me more than once, and when he did I shut up and listened to him (sometimes).

"We're…not…separating."

Frankie stared me in the eyes then she nodded.

There you go. The hand to the neck business worked even if you weren't a huge badass rugged alpha male.

I filed that away for future reference and we both took off running.

Cal and Benny stood in the empty boathouse with the broken window. There weren't many but this was the third one they'd been in. The second one had two dead men in it that Cal recognized because they'd shot at him this morning. The boathouse he and Benny were in was the closest to Hart's and it was the one where the women had used the phone. Cal knew this because the place was dusty, but the dust was disturbed and most of the disturbance was around the phone.

Cal had Benny's phone to his ear and Pete was on the line.

"Where would she head?" Cal clipped into the phone.

"People. Civilization," Pete muttered.

That would be difficult. They weren't far out of Chicago but there weren't a lot of either of those where they were, which was fifteen minutes out of Chicago but still right in the middle of fucking nowhere.

Then Pete said on a near shout, "The shop!"

"What shop?" Cal asked.

"Main road, half a mile up from the house we used to have. Only thing on that road except the lake houses. We used to drive out of our way to go up there so I could get the kids ice cream. I didn't want the ice cream to melt—"

Cal interrupted him, "So it's half a mile up from your old place, you mean north?"

"Yes," Pete answered, and Cal looked at Benny and did the mental calculation from what Pete had told him.

"So maybe five, six miles from here," he said to Benny.

"Long way for her to go if she's barefoot," Benny replied quietly, and Cal was glad Vi's fucking foot had time to heal so both of them could be torn to shreds running through a goddamned forest because fucking Daniel fucking Hart was right now literally stalking his goddamned woman.

"Gotta go," Cal said into the phone as they headed toward the door.

"You'll call?" Pete asked.

"I'll call," Cal answered and flipped the phone shut.

Then he jogged behind Benny but followed him to the driver's side.

Benny turned to him. "I'm drivin'."

"I'm runnin'," Cal returned.

Benny's brows shot up. "What?"

"I'm on foot. You drive to the shop. I'm takin' the woods."

Benny moved closer. "Cal, you haven't had food, you—"

"Time's wastin', Ben."

"You been shot twice," Benny reminded him.

"Grazed."

"Cal, God dammit—"

"They might catch them before they reach the shop. They could be anywhere in those woods and they're scared, not covering their tracks and therefore leavin' footprints," Cal pointed out and finished. "I'm trackin' through the woods."

"Yeah, you get caught up in somethin', we only have one phone."

"Go to the shop. They're not there, brief the people who work there, tell them to call the cops, tell the cops to call Pryor and you drive the road. I find them, that's where I'll lead them."

"Cal, I haven't been shot today, or shot *at*. Let me run."

"Get in the truck, Benny."

"Cal—" Benny didn't finish.

Cal turned and ran into the woods.

---

He was gaining. He wasn't hungover and he had shoes on and he'd had something to eat that day.

I should have let Frankie separate. I was slowing her down.

"Go!" I shouted. "Go to the shop!"

"We're not separating!" she shouted back, her hair flying behind her, running in front of me. She had my hand in hers and she was holding on tight.

"Frankie!"

The gunshot rang out. It was so close I could hear the hiss of the bullet through the air and we both reflexively dove for cover.

By the time we rolled to our backs and looked up, Daniel Hart was standing over us, pointing his gun at Frankie.

"Liability," he muttered then fired.

Cal heard the shot, it wasn't close but it wasn't far away.

He stopped running and started sprinting.

Seconds later, he heard the second shot.

Benny had the windows open to the SUV. He heard the shot, it wasn't close but it wasn't far away.

He pulled the Explorer to the side of the road, shut off the ignition, tagged his gun and threw open the door.

His boots hit the ground and he heard the second shot.

He sprinted into the woods.

"*Shoot me!*" I shrieked.

He was pointing the gun at me but I was staring into his eyes.

"You took everything from me," he stated calmly.

"I took everything from you? You took everything *from me*!" I screeched.

"I handed you the world gift by gift. You didn't even bother to open the boxes."

"You're a lunatic. You think the world fits in a box?" I snapped.

He leaned forward and his face twisted in a way that I did not like.

"You would know if you bothered to *open the fucking boxes*!"

I leaned forward too, keeping his focus as I heard Frankie dragging herself away.

"I *do* know what it feels like to be handed the world, you asshole!" I shouted, "Tim did it when he got me pregnant at seventeen and then gave me a beautiful life until you took his. Then Joe gave it to me again and he did it just by giving a shit that I'd walked across a goddamned yard in bare feet! And here I stand in front of you, and you think you gave me the world when you don't even care that I'm running through a forest *in bare feet*!"

Cal stood ten feet to the side of Hart, raised his gun and took aim.

He did this listening to Vi and smiling.

Frankie's head came up, her eyes hit Benny and she quit dragging herself through the leaves.

Benny squatted low and put his finger to his lips.

Frankie squished her lips into her nose and mouthed, "Bare feet?"

Benny hoped to all hell that this meant the blood coming from her middle wasn't oozing the life out of her.

Benny grinned at Frankie, shook his head, straightened, raised his gun and took aim.

Hart wasn't listening to me, firstly because he was focused on his own shit and secondly because he was a maniac.

"I built an empire and I put it at risk for you."

"I didn't ask for that, didn't want it, *still* don't want it," I snapped back.

"And now it's gone," he whispered. "Because of you."

"Let me enlighten you, Mr. Hart. After they put you away for a thousand years, by some miracle you get out and you find a woman who catches your fancy, she doesn't want an empire. She wants you to give a shit. That's it. She just wants you to give a shit."

He still wasn't listening.

"I gave it all for you," he whispered, his voice quiet in a scary way.

"You didn't give anything." My voice was quiet too. "You just took." My eyes moved to his gun and I made an invitation that I hoped he didn't accept but instead would finally fucking listen to me. "So take now. Take my daughters' mother away. Take again from Joe, someone who life hasn't allowed to keep hold of many good things. Take me."

He raised his gun to point at my head.

I kept staring at the gun and I wondered if Tim and Sam felt like this in their last moments. If they felt their heart racing. If their throat had closed. If they felt every inch of their skin tingling. If their mind moved to me, the girls, Mel. If they sent out a prayer that someone would make us all right when they were gone. If they hoped to all that was holy that we'd never forget that they loved us.

I raised my eyes to his.

"I hate you," I whispered.

He smiled.

Then I heard the gunshots.

# Twenty-Two

## Heartbeat

Frankie opened her eyes. She felt supremely weird, confused and definitely not at her best. She looked around, saw she was in a hospital bed and she remembered.

She was about to mutter something unladylike when she saw Benny standing at the window looking out. His dark hair was wet and had been slicked back, but because it was drying, part of the front had fallen onto his forehead and the back had begun to curl around in that sexy way it did. He had on a white t-shirt and jeans, boots, the usual, mostly. He could dress up and look good. It wasn't better when he dressed up. It was just his usual too…fucking…good.

She knew she was going to hell. She'd been shot and she still was perving on her dead boyfriend's brother. Granted, he was hot, there was a lot to perv on. Still, she was going to hell.

He turned, looked at her and she saw the worry in his face. When his warm brown eyes caught hers and he saw she was awake, he hid the worry and his face went soft.

Her mouth watered.

Yeah, definitely perv-worthy.

He walked to her bed, yanking a chair with him so it was close. He sat in it and leaned even closer.

"Hey, Frankie," he whispered.

"Hey," she rasped.

"How you doin'?" he asked.

"How you think I'm doin'?" she asked back, and he grinned when she hit him with her attitude.

"Never been shot, babe, but I 'spect you ain't doin' great," he remarked.

"You'd be right," she returned.

Benny looked to her belly then back to her eyes. "Bullet didn't hit anything major," he informed her.

"Finally, good news."

He grinned again. "You lost a lot of blood," he went on but she already knew that. She'd felt it.

She didn't know if it was the right thing for Benny to do when he picked her up and ran through the forest with her in his arms, straight to his SUV, but she guessed it wasn't. Still, there was no stopping him, even when she laid the attitude on him telling him to put her the fuck down and call an ambulance. He didn't listen. He was on a mission.

"They want you in here a while," he finished.

"Call the Pope, tell him I'm gonna miss our meeting," Frankie muttered and she heard his soft chuckle.

Damn, but she liked to make him laugh. She'd sell her soul to make him laugh. Even before, when she was with Vinnie, she liked to make Benny laugh. He had a great laugh, a great smile, a great face. Expressive.

But he'd been like a brother then, a good one, a sweet one and she'd loved him. She'd loved Vinnie's whole family. Hers wasn't great and she knew great when she felt it. That had been the best gift Vinnie gave her. She sometimes wondered if she loved Vinnie's family more than Vinnie. Then Vinnie would be Vinnie and she'd quit wondering.

How Benny went from sweet, funny brother to perv-worthy, Frankie didn't know. She spent seven years trying to figure it out. She'd never thought of him that way instead of in a detached way when she'd hear other girls talking about him. Any woman could see it; Frankie just had Vinnie so she didn't much think about it. Then she didn't have Vinnie and she found herself thinking about it.

Definitely going to hell.

"Cops wanna ask you questions." Benny broke into her thoughts and she focused on him.

"Okay," she replied, and he shifted closer.

"Ma and Pop are here," he hesitated. "They wanna see you."

Frankie stared into his eyes for half a second then looked away. "No."

"Frankie, babe…" Benny whispered.

She got it. She knew Theresa, Vinnie Senior, Manny and even Benny had to blame someone. They loved Vinnie. He was a great guy, a great son, a great brother. They needed to shift the blame for all of Vinnie's fuck ups to someone. And she loved Vinnie enough to accept it.

But she'd paid enough of Vinnie's penance. She loved him and you do that kind of thing for someone you love. But enough was enough.

She looked back at Benny and whispered, "No."

He reached out and took her hand in both of his. His were big and warm. Strong. He leaned in even deeper and lifted her hand so he could rest his chin against her fingers and his elbows in the bed.

"Francesca," he said quietly. "What you did today was crazy stupid."

"Thanks." She was quiet too, but it was quiet sarcasm not quiet gentleness.

"Babe, listen to me," Benny ordered. "It was also crazy brave."

She didn't reply. She just stared into his dark brown eyes.

"What you did, for family, they're gonna wanna heal the breach."

"Too late," Frankie whispered, and Benny's hands tightened on hers.

"Honey—"

"I got a job in Indianapolis," she announced.

"What?" he whispered, sounding surprised and maybe a little pissed, like he knew everything about her and wasn't expecting a surprise.

"Finally leavin' this shit behind."

"Frankie—"

"Not sayin' I'm not glad maybe they don't hate me anymore. You're here, bein' nice, maybe you don't. That's all good. But I'm gone."

"You're not movin' to Indy," he declared.

"Waited too long. It's time to start over. Clean slate," Frankie said.

"Babe—" he started, but Frankie looked away and closed her eyes.

"I'm tired," she whispered and his hands tightened again on hers.

"Frankie—"

"Go away, Ben. I need to rest."

His hands tightened even further. "Look at me."

She tried to pull her hand away.

"Francesca, fuckin' look at me."

She opened her eyes and looked at him.

"You're not movin' to Indy," he repeated.

"Go away."

"We gotta talk."

"Nothin' to say."

"Frankie—"

It took a lot of effort and the rest of the energy she had, but she yanked her hand from his.

Then she whispered, "I took my hit for your family today. I atoned. It's done. All I did was fall in love with Vinnie but you took your penance from me like I did wrong and I loved you all once, so I gave it. I bled for you today. This is good this happened. It gave me my chance to do what you needed me to do. But you aren't gettin' anything more."

Benny left his seat but he did it in a bent over squat, his face getting in hers.

"You've had a bad day," he stated. "So I'll give you this shit right now. Then I'm comin' back and we're gonna talk."

"No, we aren't," she replied then sucked in a painful breath when both his hands came up and framed her face and his got so close all she had to do was tilt her chin and his lips would be on hers.

"Yes, we fuckin' are."

His eyes dropped from hers to her mouth where his thumb traced the lower edge of her lip while he watched it move and she held her breath. Then he released her and she watched him saunter out of the room.

Sal avoided Theresa and Vinnie's eyes and looked to the couch.

Cal was sitting there, hair nearly dry after his shower, wearing new jeans and a t-shirt that Theresa had run out and bought him. The bandage on his arm could be seen under the sleeve of his tee.

His woman was curled on her side on the couch beside him, her head resting on his thigh, her hand curled there in front of her face. She was wearing new jeans and a long sleeved t-shirt that Theresa also bought. Her hair was wet too, but it was drying fast since Cal was sifting his fingers through it. Her knees were curled up to her chest and she didn't have shoes on. The bottom of her feet were clean and glistening with antibiotic goo. Being clean, you could see the redness and scrapes.

She'd stayed at the hospital wearing nothing but Cal's t-shirt which was spattered with Daniel Hart's blood, getting her feet seen to, talking to the cops, eating the cannelloni Gina brought, speaking to her daughters on the phone and waiting for word to come out about Frankie. Once they knew Frankie was all right, Cal carried her to Benny's car, he climbed in with Benny and they all went to his house to shower. Just over an hour later, they all came back.

Sal studied her sleeping face. He was a younger man, he'd want in there. He could see Cal going all out for that. He could see something like her healing a bad break in a strong man. He could even almost see Hart being willing to lose it all for his shot. But only almost.

Benny walked into the waiting room and Sal noticed he looked pissed. He didn't have to guess why. Francesca Concetti could throw some attitude and Sal figured she was so good at it she could even do it after being shot. She had a lot of different blood in her but Italian always won out.

Sal wondered when Benny would get his head out of his ass about Frankie. Seven years the boy had been dicking around. Sure, it'd be strange, Frankie moving onto Benny after she'd been with Vinnie. But heart was heart, gut was gut and balls were balls. You want something and that something was worth you wanting like Frankie was, who gave a shit?

"We gotta get on the road." Sal heard Cal say and his eyes went to Cal.

Violet was awake, eyes blinking. She'd lifted herself partially up but she still had her fingers curved around Cal's thigh.

Benny stopped in front of them. "Right. Let's go."

She looked at Benny then twisted to look at Cal. "Can I see her before we go?" she asked.

Sal watched as Cal didn't even hesitate. He just shifted her so she was in his arms and he carried her out of the room and down the hall toward Frankie's room, giving her what she wanted without argument.

Sal grinned to himself and then his eyes scanned the room. He saw Benny, Theresa, Manny and Vinnie Senior all looking after Cal and Violet. Benny still looked pissed. The rest of them were smiling.

Sal's phone rang and all their eyes came to him and none of them were smiling.

He pulled out his phone, looked at the display, flipped it open and put it to his ear.

"You got me," he said into it.

"Weird," he heard one of his boys say in his ear, "cops are scratching their heads seein' as that footage of Callahan has been in evidence less than a day but the hard drive has been wiped."

Salvatore Giglia grinned.

"Christ, they havin' a party?" Benny muttered as he drove up Vi and Cal's street, which was lined with cars around Vi's house.

It was late, dark, and Vi was out in the backseat.

"People like Vi," Cal muttered this truth and he was glad the girls had that support. But he was so fucking tired he didn't want to put up with this shit. He wanted to see Kate and Keira and he wanted to go to bed and sleep for a year.

Benny pulled into Vi's drive, parking behind her Mustang. He didn't even shut down the ignition before the side door to the house opened and both girls flew out.

Cal opened his door and jumped down. His feet hadn't hit the cement before he went back into the SUV when the power of two teenage girls slammed into him. Their arms wrapped around him in a fierce way and both of their faces burrowed into his chest.

How they both got in there, he had no clue, but they did and they were glued to him.

They were also both crying, relieved tears, but totally uncontrolled.

Listening to their emotion, experiencing that kind of relief after what he knew they endured that day, he had a chance at a life rewind, he'd take it and put another bullet in Daniel Hart.

He gave them a minute, his arms moving around both of them and then he said, "Katy, Keirry, I gotta see to your mom."

They didn't let go at first. Then Kate moved away, pulling Keira from him. They both wiped their faces as they looked up at him.

"Okay, Joe," Kate whispered.

"Got some of that for me?" Benny asked, and they turned and treated Benny to much the same. It wasn't as intense but he knew it felt good when he saw Benny's face get soft.

He moved to the back passenger door and opened it. Vi had missed all this. She was still out. She didn't rouse until Cal undid her seatbelt and shifted her out of the car.

She lifted her head, looked around and then asked, "My babies?"

"Here Mom," Keira called.

She was craning her neck and looking around. Then she demanded, "Cal, put me down."

"When we're inside."

"I wanna—"

"Buddy, they slammed into me and nearly took me off my feet. They can say welcome home when you're sittin' down."

He made his order, but he didn't fuck around so she didn't complain. He got her inside and set her down in the couch and then both girls jumped her. He stepped back, looked around and saw it looked like a party. Feb, Colt, Cheryl, Jessie, Mimi, Dee, Morrie, Josie, Sully and Mike.

He moved away and Benny, Colt, Sully, Morrie and Mike moved with him as the women moved in on Vi.

He hit the kitchen and the men huddled.

"Any word?" he asked Colt.

Colt knew what he was asking. While Vi was showering, Cal was on the phone with Colt getting briefed.

"Chris is stable. Adam's critical."

"How's it lookin'?" Cal asked.

"He survives the night, they'll feel better. Now, touch and go," Colt answered.

"You get word on Lindy?" Cal asked.

"She discharged herself when her father and brother showed. She got home a coupla hours ago," Sully answered.

"Just a heads up, you need to flag her. She goes for a gun permit, it needs to be refused," Cal noted.

"What's that mean?" Sully asked.

Cal ignored this question and went on. "She's already got one, you need to revoke it."

Mike chuckled and remarked, "Hoyt Atkins, gung ho. Guessin' he passed that shit down."

Cal turned his eyes to Mike. "Let's just say Lindy doesn't shy away during a firefight."

"And let's just hope she doesn't get a shot at another one," Colt muttered.

Cal didn't reply as it went without saying he agreed.

Instead he said, "I appreciate the support but I gotta get my girls in bed."

"I'll start the clear out," Morrie murmured and peeled off.

Colt's eyes moved with Morrie and then went to the back of Vi's head that could be seen on the couch, one of her girls tucked close on either side.

Colt turned back to Cal. "She okay?"

"Uncertain," Cal replied and he looked at Vi. "Could be she feels relief even seein' Daniel Hart's head explode while he was holding a gun to her face. Could be she doesn't. You need to text me the number to victims' assistance."

"Gotcha," Colt replied.

"You okay?" Sully asked Cal.

He was. He was beyond okay. He already knew he felt relief that it was over. He also knew he would lose no sleep from his decision to fire a kill shot. Vi might relive that as a nightmare but he sure as fuck wouldn't.

"Yep," he answered.

Sully nodded. Colt studied him. Benny leaned against the counter and crossed his arms on his chest.

"We're off," Colt said.

Cal nodded then said to Colt and Sully, "I'll get Vi to make her seafood risotto."

"Feb's comin' over in the morning with shit for her frittata," Cal replied.

"Maybe I should spend the night," Benny murmured.

"You're not?" Cal asked.

"Gotta get back," Benny answered.

"For what?" Cal went on, and Benny just looked at him.

Francesca.

Cal grinned but advised, "You've driven down here twice today. Put a bullet in a man. Rest. Eat frittata. Go home tomorrow."

"Gotta get back," Benny repeated, and Cal turned fully to him.

Then he said quietly, "Ben, she's in a hospital bed. She isn't goin' anywhere."

Benny's jaw got tight before he repeated, "Cal, I gotta get back."

Cal studied his cousin. Then he nodded.

Everyone left with Benny the last to go. He gave Vi a hug and then he turned it on the girls. Cal walked him out to his SUV.

They were standing by the driver's side door when Cal said, "You get tired, you pull over."

"Right," Benny muttered.

Cal was silent. So was Benny. Neither of them moved.

Then Cal said softly, "Wouldn't be here right now, wasn't for you."

"I remember it right, by the time I got there, you had the situation under control."

"I didn't mean me, I meant Vi," Cal replied.

Benny held his gaze.

Then he repeated, "Right."

"Huge," Cal said.

"What?" Benny asked.

"Owe you huge."

Benny shook his head. "Nope. This was family."

Cal sighed. Then he said, "Still owe you huge, but even so, you get back and you fuck that up with Frankie, you answer to me."

He watched Benny's body tense. "Your day was worse than mine, but mine wasn't so fuckin' great either. Don't piss me off."

"You all been swimmin' in muddy waters where it comes to Frankie and doin' it for years. Don't fuck it up."

"Okay, now, gotta tell you, you're pissin' me off."

"Just layin' it out."

"You think you might've wanted to lay it out seven years ago? Even before?" Benny suggested.

"Would you have listened?" Cal asked a pertinent question. He knew this because Benny's face grew hard. "Don't fuck it up," Cal repeated.

"I'll be sure to call, case I need advice," Benny replied sarcastically.

"Don't know if you noticed," Cal jerked his head toward the house, "but I got it goin' on."

Benny stared at him three seconds. Then he burst out laughing.

"Yeah, kinda noticed," Benny stated when he'd stopped laughing. "Though, I could do without runnin' through the woods and shooting at bad guys and carrying damsels in distress, who bleed all over my clothes and give me attitude, back through those fuckin' woods."

"So maybe you best get in there while things are quiet," Cal advised.

"I would, you shut up and let me get in my fuckin' truck," Benny returned, and Cal chuckled and stepped back.

Benny opened the door, got in but Cal put his hand to the door when Benny moved to close it.

He leaned in and whispered, "Owe you huge."

Then he let the door go and walked into his house.

Joe threw the covers back and settled on his back in the bed. The minute he did, I curled in.

"They asleep?" I asked.

"Keira is," he replied, snaking an arm around me and pulling me closer, "Kate's restless."

"She okay?"

"She says she will be. Listenin' to music."

"Maybe I'll go check."

"Buddy, you move, I do too and that would be to tie you to this bed. Sleep. She'll be okay."

I lifted my head and looked at his face in the dark.

"I should check."

"She'll be okay."

"She might need her mom."

"Vi, this is Kate. She's got her mom. She knows that. We're all home. We're all safe. Safer than we were yesterday. And we'll be safe tomorrow. Just fuckin' safe. Let her be. She doesn't need you fussin' because she's got enough in her head. She doesn't need to worry about *why* you're fussin'. She needs to think you're safe and sleepin'."

He was right, which was annoying.

"It's annoying when you're right," I muttered.

"Better learn to get over that, you'll need to get used to it."

I rolled my eyes and settled in, head to his chest, ear to his heartbeat.

We were silent for a while, me listening to the pounding of Joe's heart. I didn't know what Joe was doing.

"Today, I thought for a coupla hours you were dead," I whispered.

"Vi—"

"Tomorrow, I glue a camera to my hand."

"Violet—"

"I won't need them. This is over and it's just us now. But I want memories. Millions of them."

He was silent.

Then he said, "Whatever you want, buddy."

I would have lifted my head but I didn't want to lose his heartbeat.

"Whatever I want?" I asked.

"Whatever you want."

"Careful what you promise me, baby, even in your state."

His body shook gently with his chuckle and his hand at my hip gave me a squeeze.

We were silent again then I called, "Joe?"

"Yeah, buddy."

"I never said thank you."

"Honey, for what?"

"For handin' me the world."

"Yeah you did," he replied.

"I did?"

"You do it all the time," he said. "Fuck, baby, you're doin' it now."

God I loved him. I more than loved him.

"What's beyond love?" I asked and felt Joe's body give a slight jolt.

"What?"

"What's beyond love?" I repeated.

"Don't understand the question, Vi."

I didn't explain. Instead I said, "Whatever it is, that's what I feel for you."

He was silent and still for a second. Then he rolled into me.

"Joe—" I whispered when his hands went into my tee.

"Shut it, buddy."

"Joe—"

"Shut it."

I shut it.

# Twenty-Three

## Crash

"Momalicious!" Keira shouted. "I'm gonna go to the beach and lay out."

"Big surprise," Joe muttered and pressed deeper into me as I looked at the nightstand and saw it was barely nine o'clock.

I lifted up from the pillow as far as I could go with Joe's weight against my back holding me down and shouted, "You had breakfast, baby?"

"Toast!" Keira shouted back.

"Where's Kate?" I yelled. "She still sleepin'?"

"Um…" Keira muttered loud enough for me to hear, and at her hesitation I felt Joe's head come up and his body move. I twisted my neck to look at him. "That boy from next door is out on the beach. She's out there talkin' to him."

I wondered when Taylor had become "that boy next door" since I was under the impression, considering the amount of time Keira spent talking about him, that she had a crush on him. Not to mention the amount of time Taylor spent out on the beach, which I reckoned meant he had a crush on Keira. Perhaps I was wrong and he had a crush on Kate.

This was not good.

"Bummer for Dane," Joe murmured and even with my misgivings about the Kate/Keira/Taylor teenage triangle, I grinned.

It had been months but Dane had not fully made it back into my good books yet, nor Joe's. Kate had forgiven him and they were as tight as ever, so Joe and I should give it up. It was just that we couldn't. If you hurt someone's child that forgiveness takes a while. But Dane was determined and I figured he'd get there one day. As long as he didn't act like an ass.

"All right, honey," I yelled.

"See you on the beach," Keira called then we heard the door close.

Joe settled back in and I did too.

It was Christmas break and we were at his beach house in Florida for two weeks. The house was up on stilts and painted a faded blue with white woodwork. It had a deep deck all around and a big locked garage which held Joe's Land Rover, a beach buggy and a huge barbeque grill which was the first thing Joe (with Keira's help) rolled out onto the deck.

The house had wood floors all through, even the kitchen. It was rustic, but cute with two bedrooms, open plan living room and kitchen, a small utility with a deep sink, a washer and dryer and a bunch of hooks for beach towels, and one bath. But the bedrooms and living room were huge and airy and all the furniture was way comfy. There were so many windows that there was barely any wall space and all you could see was ocean or trees. It was fantastic.

Even as fantastic as it was, my first order of business was to make Joe take us to town where we bought a Christmas tree and all the decorations. We also bought bright, braided throw rugs, new linens and bathroom and kitchen towels to perk up the place.

Further, I bought a huge windsock which Joe installed on a flagpole out on the corner of the deck.

Lastly, I bought some wind chimes because nothing said "Florida" (or "beach" for that matter) better than wind chimes. Joe put those up on the overhang of the deck.

We'd been there three days and the girls were already golden tan from playing Frisbee, laying out and traveling the beach in the buggy Joe taught us all how to drive.

He was mostly right. There wasn't much to do but fish, cook, eat, sleep, read and, for Joe and I, have sex.

He was only mostly right for there was a beach, which meant the girls could lay out, Joe had the buggy in which the girls could tool around and the girls bought a Frisbee that provided them with hours of entertainment.

The kitchen had been updated with top-of-the line appliances so I was in throes of ecstasy. I'd already finished two books while sitting out on the deck or in the sand, and the beach house next door had the aforementioned cute boy-man in it named Taylor. Therefore, the Winters girls were not at any loss for things to do and were nowhere near bored.

I, particularly, was not bored. I was a lot of things but bored was definitely not one of them.

It was the best vacation I'd ever had, bar none. Even the ones I had with Tim and that was saying something. And we were only on day four.

There was a reason for this and I lifted my hand to my face and stared at that reason. On my hand was the princess-cut diamond ring Joe slid on my finger last night over shrimp at a shrimp shack in town. He did this without saying a word, just like Joe, letting his face and his actions speak for him. He also did it with the girls looking on, Kate crying silently, Keira giggling excitedly.

Only Joe Callahan would propose in front of his woman's daughters.

Many would find this unromantic, such an act being a couple's thing.

I thought it was perfect.

Therefore I'd cried too, all the while giving Joe a kiss that communicated my "*Yes!*" and tasted of tears.

A tearful kiss might not have been the thing, but Joe didn't seem to mind.

In our Florida bed, Joe's hand went from my belly to slide up my forearm then his thumb tweaked the ring.

"How much time you think we got?" Joe whispered into the back of my hair.

"Kate's just havin' fun. She won't step out on Dane, especially when I think Keirry's got a thing for Taylor. She could be back anytime," I told Joe.

"Mm," Joe murmured.

"Keira's out for the long haul," I went on because I knew she was and I also knew she looked cute in her bikini and I reckoned Taylor felt the same. Or at least I hoped so, for Keira's sake.

Joe chuckled and his hand left mine and went back to my belly where he pressed in. He moved slightly away and I fell to my back and looked up at him. His hand started to move from my belly but my hand went there to hold it where it was.

"Joe?" I called even though he was up on an elbow, not but a foot away and looking down at me.

"Yeah, buddy?"

"I like that you proposed in front of the girls," I whispered and his face got that tender look and started to dip closer, but I kept talking. "It was sweet you included them." His face kept coming at me so I said quickly, "Joe."

His head stopped its descent and he said, "Right here, Vi."

"I liked that but what I have to say right now needs to be between us."

That tender look left his face and his eyes locked with mine.

"What?"

"Not that the girls can't know…"

"What?"

"Soon…*ish*," I went on.

"Buddy, *what*?"

"We just gotta figure out…um—"

"Vi…" he was getting impatient, I could tell. He always was when he had to repeat himself, which, unfortunately for Joe who lived in a house with three women, was often.

"I'm pregnant." I blurted and Joe's entire frame went solid.

Then he whispered, "What?"

"I know it's soon. It seems my body's incapable of waiting to get pregnant until *after* I've said any marriage vows. But I missed a couple of pills and I thought I caught up but—"

"Vi—"

"I guess I didn't."

"Buddy—"

"And this is a lot. I know. The whole mess and then the next mess and then more mess and now this vacation and then you asking me to marry you and now this. The girls, I don't know—"

"Baby—"

"I'm worried. Only so much they can take. Keira's been the baby since—"

"Vi. Shut it."

I shut it and stared at him.

"How pregnant are you?" Joe asked.

"How pregnant can you be?" I answered nervously, not certain about his question and I saw his mouth get tight.

"How many months, Vi?" he continued.

"Eleven weeks," I answered, and his sky blue eyes went unfocused.

"Nearly past it," he muttered and I stared.

"Past what?" I whispered as there was a certain mark you couldn't cross for an abortion and I thought he might be thinking about that.

If he was, I would be shocked and it would hurt a lot, too much and furthermore, I couldn't do that. I thought he wanted a baby and I thought he'd be happy and I wanted a baby if it was our baby and it was. I figured maybe he wouldn't want it this soon, but I thought he'd still be happy.

Though it was too soon. We still hadn't settled. He'd just proposed the night before.

Well, thinking about it, he seemed pretty settled and the girls seemed okay with everything. But it was all still relatively new, living life as us without the cloud of Daniel Hart and the heaviness of mourning shrouding our lives.

"Past the three month mark," Joe answered. I thought his answer followed my train of thought and bit my lip.

"Yeah," I said and his hand pressed gently into my belly as his eyes went there.

"We'll wait." His voice was soft and his eyes were still at my stomach.

"For what?" I asked and his gaze came back to my face.

"You two. To get past the three month mark. We'll wait until we know it's all good with you and the baby then we'll tell the girls."

I felt a shimmer of electricity against my skin and I whispered, "Joe."

If I meant to say more, I couldn't have. Something shifted into his eyes and stayed there. Something peaceful and warm and so beautiful, looking at it, I couldn't breathe.

"Crash," Joe whispered back, and I blinked.

"What?"

"That's the sound of my side of the scales, buddy," Joe said, and my hand left his at my stomach and went to his scarred cheek.

"Joe," I whispered again.

"Kid'll be beautiful," Joe whispered back.

"Joe," I repeated.

His hand pressed in at my belly again, a slight movement, a sweet one. "Gorgeous," he murmured.

"Aren't you gonna kiss me?" I asked.

"Yep," Joe answered, but didn't move.

"Well?" I prompted, and Joe grinned.

Then he moved but he didn't move toward my mouth. His hand slid up the tee I was wearing and his head moved to my belly. His arm wrapped around my hip and I watched his dark head bend, felt his nose slide along my skin and then his lips rested there.

That's when I felt the tears slide out the sides of my eyes.

"You happy, baby?" I whispered my question, and his arm at my hip convulsed but his head came up and he looked at me.

"Yeah," he replied, the word was heavy and it was thick.

Both my hands went to his face and I smiled through my tears.

"Good."

His head bent again and with my hands still at his cheeks he kissed my belly once more. Then he moved up and rolled, his arm at my hip taking me with him so I was on top. One of his hands slid into my hair and the other one slid into my panties and over my ass.

"Mawdy! Joe!" Kate shouted. Joe's hands stilled and my head came up, but Joe's eyes went over my shoulder to point in the direction of the door he couldn't see. "Taylor's got boogie boards but the water's cold and he says we need wetsuits. He says there's a surf place in town where we can get them. He's gonna take us there. Is that cool?"

"How much do wetsuits cost?" I shouted back.

Joe's hand tensed on my ass and I knew he didn't care how much wetsuits cost, firstly because he tended to get the girls anything they wanted even after we'd had several conversations about him *not* doing this (conversations he totally ignored). And secondly because them going to town, which was a twenty minute drive away, meant we'd have some serious alone time.

"Don't know!" Kate shouted back.

"Ask Taylor," Joe ordered. "My wallet's on the kitchen counter. Grab the cash you'll need."

"Cool!" Kate shouted.

"Joe!" I hissed, looking down at him.

"Baby." Joe grinned, smiling up at me.

"Oh!" Kate kept shouting. "I sussed it this morning! Taylor's got the hots for Keirry. Just so you know. I'm Little Miss Matchmaker!" she declared proudly.

At these words, Joe got tense and then he knifed to sitting, me astride him. His eyes were pointed at the door and they were narrowed.

One look at him and I knew that he hadn't quite cottoned on to the beach frolicking and teenage flirting, likely because Keira was Joe's little helper. Even though logically he knew she was a teenage girl with a gorgeous face, fantastic hair and a body built for a bikini, illogically he couldn't conceive of these same things and couldn't abide a boy-man named Taylor who lived next door acting on liking them.

"Joe," I murmured as we heard the door slam.

Suddenly Joe shouted, "Kate!"

I jumped at his shout, but he set me aside and knifed out of bed at the same time he grabbed his jeans from the floor.

"Joe, Keira's fifteen," I reminded him as he pulled up his jeans.

Joe ignored me, stalked to the door buttoning his jeans and repeated, "Kate!"

"Joe!" I yelled, but he was gone.

That's when I realized, even with a new baby, Keira wouldn't stop being one, fifteen years old, thirty or a hundred and five.

And that's when I fell to my side, curled my knees into my belly and burst out laughing.

I stopped laughing and smelled Joe's hair on the pillow, his scent all around me, and the bright sun shone down on our bed through the many windows. Then I heard Joe's indistinct deep voice and Kate and Keira's not indistinct giggles.

I put my hand to my belly and tilted my chin down to look at it.

"Crash," I whispered to Joe and my unborn child.

Our baby didn't reply but that was okay. I figured, in our family, she'd one day learn the way to make her opinion known.

Five minutes later Joe came back and he told me the girls were gone with his cash, his ATM card and his PIN number.

Before I could protest this, he also told me that Taylor had been given the Joe Talk and knew if he fucked around in his Jeep or did anything else to piss Joe off, there would be badass-alpha-male-father-figure retribution (this was not Joe's description, it was mine).

Before I could protest *this*, he took off his jeans and rejoined me in bed.

Then I found that being pregnant had the added bonus of me getting the top with my favorite part of Joe underneath me between my legs. Then I found that being pregnant had the further bonus of inspiring Joe to break his record of giving me as many orgasms in as many positions as he could perform.

Which was to say a lot.

A lot later, after I had a nap and the girls had come back. After they boogie boarded while Joe alternately walked into the kitchen to feel me up and walked onto the deck to scowl at Taylor and I putzed around in the kitchen making Christmas cookies that felt weird to make with the sun shining and me wearing shorts (but I didn't mind). After all of us eating Joe's delicious grilled halibut while sitting out on the somewhat windy deck. After Kate retired to her and Keira's room to text Dane and listen to her music and Keira retired to a moonlit stroll on the beach with her Christmas Vacation new boyfriend, I walked out on the deck in a cardigan and jeans and stared at the dark sea.

Joe walked up behind me and one of his arms closed around my chest, the other one around my belly and I felt his lips touch my neck.

"Baby," I whispered.

"Yeah?" he said in my ear.

"Are we lucky?" I asked and his arms tightened.

"Nope," he answered.

"Nope?" I asked, surprised.

"We earned this, Vi."

"Yeah," I whispered and settled back into my man.

Like always, Joe was right.

It was morning, the restaurant quiet, Theresa Bianchi the only one there.

She roamed the floor, moving through the hostess station, by the bar, then winding her way through the tables, passing the booths, all the while her eyes on the walls.

Even though she scanned the walls just in case a different inspiration struck, she knew before she even got there where it was going to go.

She went to the booth Cal, Vi and the girls sat at that first night they came to the Pizzeria.

Theresa slid in and set down on the table the hammer and nail she was holding as well as the tape measure, level, pencil and frame.

Carefully, she lifted the photo of thirteen year old Vinnie Junior and Cal off the wall and then pulled out its nail. She measured. She deduced. She used the level. She used the pencil. She hammered in the nails. Finally, she hung the frames.

Vinnie Junior and Cal back over the booth they always sat at when Vinnie was alive, their favorite since forever.

And the booth that Bella always led Cal and Vi to when they were up with the girls—if it was free.

Next to the old picture was the new.

Another eight by ten. Another black and white. Katy and Keirry standing front and center by the bar, both wearing tomato sauce stained white aprons, both holding forth a big pizza pie that Benny had taught them to make.

To their back right Benny and Vinnie Senior stood. Vinnie's eyes were on Keira and his mouth was open, saying something that made both girls laugh. Benny was looking to his right where Cal and Vi stood.

Vi had her head to Cal's shoulder and her arm around his waist, but she was laughing into the camera, or more accurately, at Theresa behind the camera. Cal had one arm around her shoulders and the other arm was curled around Angie, holding his baby daughter to his chest.

But his eyes were pointed at Benny.

Benny and Cal were smiling at each other, men's smiles, secret smiles.

Theresa stared at the picture thinking her boys looked handsome.

And everyone looked happy.

She picked up the hammer, level and tape measure, and grinning, she walked away.

**The 'Burg Series continues with *Golden Trail.***